A Soul to Revive

Duskwalker Brides

Book Five

Opal Reyne

Cover art: Sam Griffin
Internal Illustrations: Opal Reyne
Editing and proofreading: Kelly Messenger

<u>Author's note on language</u>

I'm from AUSTRALIA.

My English is not the same as American English.
I love my American English spoken readers to bits. You're
cute, you all make me giggle, and I just wanna give you a big
ol' hug. However, there are many of you who don't seem to
realise that your English was born from British English, which
is what I use (although a bastardised version since Australians
like to take all language and strangle it until it's a ruined
carcass of slang, missing letters, and randomly added o's).

We don't seem to like the letter z.

We write colour instead of color. Recognise instead of
recognize. Travelling instead of traveling. Skilful instead of
skillfull. Mum instead of mom. Smelt is a past participle of
smell. We omit the full-stop in Mr. Name, so it's Mr Name.
Aussies cradle the word cunt like it's a sweet little puppy,
rather than an insult to be launched at your face.

Anyway, happy reading!

**Trigger Warning**
Major spoiler below

**Important:** this is not a skippable book within the series. Despite the triggers listed, skipping this book will leave a massive hole in the overall series arc, and you will miss out on important information and interactions with other characters. Skipping A Soul to Revive will make the next book, which is directly tied to this one, difficult to read.(There is no cliffhanger, so don't worry.) I promise that I give a HEA at the end, and everyone will find a bride.

Trust in me.

If you need a place to scream about your emotions during the book, or need a vent space for some of these triggers, consider joining my discord server. There are plenty of readers who will be more than happy to guide you, support you, and be there for you during any part of this book. We have a spoiler section, and I am often around. You can find the link to it in my linktree across any of my social media platforms, or at the end of this book.

Please only read further if you have triggers, otherwise you will seriously spoil the book for yourself.

Firstly, I will list what triggers **AREN'T** in the book so you can stop reading before the upcoming spoilers.
_NO:_ rape, non-con, purposeful harm done to the FMC by the MMC, self-harm, ow/om drama, mental/emotion abuse, fat phobia, incest, abortion, drug/alcohol abuse, breeding, or animal abuse. There is also no pregnancy with the FMC.

Please consider stopping here if your trigger has been detailed above as the rest are major spoilers.

Triggers are: Infertility, and dealing with this while being around a pregnant mother. The FMC does not get pregnant herself. She is fully accepted and supported during this emotional time. However, if that isn't something you can handle reading due to trauma, I am so sorry you have faced hardship.

Healed scarring, vivid memories of being burned, and the insecurities this brings. Self-sacrifice. Toxic past relationships. Anal. There is a scene with slight dub-con done to the MMC, mainly because he doesn't know what his peepee is and the FMC is panicked, confused, and just trying to help the poor guy. She does get verbal consent to continue once he understands, and there is a lot of comedic relief from the FMCs chaotic thoughts.

Intense loss, family loss, intense grief, and hopelessness. Lack of direction and self-worth due to not only one vital death, but later a second. Depression and PTSD, resulting from trauma. Torture, medical/surgery torture, mostly off-page, but is being witnessed by a main character. Blood, wounds, and gore. A minor, but quickly resolved, attempt at suicide.

To all the MonsterFuckers out there that love a horny himbo,

this book is for you.

Will he know what his cock is? Absolutely not. Will he give it to you good once he does? Absolutely. We sincerely love a terrifying, skull-headed monster who is also tender, cute, and ready to rail us into blissful oblivion until our eyes cross.

Enjoy our bird brain — I made him just for us!

ONE

Run, we have to run, Ingram thought, as he leapt over his kindred to duck around a dense cluster of trees. Mist cloaked the surrounding area, so still and peaceful, unlike their frantic panting and fogged breaths.

It was unusual for them to run from any fight. Together, they were an unstoppable force of snapping fangs, slicing claws, and frightening roars.

He glanced at Aleron, whose bat skull turned – as though they shared a desire to look upon each other.

They both knew the truth. *There are too many of them.*

It had started with only two or three Demons, but over the hours the fight ensued, more had come. They'd killed a number of the shadowy creatures in the hours they had been hunted, and had long ago succumbed to their darkest and most erratic thoughts.

It became too much.

Rivulets of dried blood stuck to the scales of Ingram's neck and chest from when he'd been severely wounded. Although he was perfectly fine now, despite the deep wound still gaping, it'd been what shocked him out of his enraged mind frame.

When he'd cowered in fear, with a wall of Demons in front of him, his kindred had mirrored his behaviour. Like they were sharing their fear, pain, and a conscience, they both ran.

Ingram was slower. He'd lost blood, and he was more injured than his kindred. His strength wasn't at its normal capacity.

Aleron never left his side.

His panic-stricken heart gave a warm pang for his kindred whenever he dropped back to keep pace with him. Even though Ingram was limping, and the deep impact of his hand hitting the firm ground caused him to whine, he was never left behind.

The middle of the night had long passed, and dawn was beginning to colour the sky. He couldn't see the change through the dense canopy of thick brush, but dew was evaporating all around him and the familiar tang of it infiltrated the nose holes of his raven beak.

It smelt like morning.

Ingram knew where they were heading, even though neither had spoken of it.

Merikh's cave is not much further.

Out of all the Mavka they'd met, Merikh was their least favourite. Fortunately though, his home was close, since they were in the southeast of the Veil – whereas the other Mavka were all northwest. His glowing red protective ward would still be in place, even though he'd disappeared.

He always disappears.

We will be safe there.

They could recuperate. Could heal. Could figure out where they wanted to go once the chaos had died down.

Ingram looked up when white swooped into his sight.

The Witch Owl.

Currently, she flew over them in her human-sized, white owl form. Though their sprint through the forest was sporadic and unpredictable, she continued to fly above them.

All throughout the night, she'd been there.

Neither knew why she was following them, nor why she had eventually fought alongside them in her human form.

Both had been surprised when a woman with brown skin and long, curly dark hair had pulled a dagger from somewhere on her person. They'd attempted to destroy her. The invisible hands massaging the goo of their brains had rendered their thoughts violent, telling them she was a threat.

Everything had been foe, had been *meat*. Only they were safe from each other in their monstrous, enraged states. Not even other Mavka were spared.

Only them; one bonded unit.

"Keep going," Aleron barked, nudging Ingram forward when his injured arm caused him to trip in a ditch.

Usually, Aleron would have snickered at him for almost falling on his face, but there was no time for laughter now.

"Not much further." Ingram nudged him back so he could quicken his kindred's pace. *"Do not slow down."*

"I am with you."

Ingram's purple sight flashed bright pink in answer, mimicking his kindred's normal orb colouring. *"I know."*

Warmth flared in his chest, knowing his kindred was with him always, but it was suffocated by the snarls and gurgles that drew closer.

They were faster than their foes, but they were growing in number by the hour. They came from everywhere, calling to each other – as though it had been planned.

A snarl reverberated off the wall of trees they sped past. *The Demon King.*

They couldn't see the castle, but Ingram still sensed the foreboding structure that loomed in the back of his mind.

The Demon King was nowhere to be seen. He had not come to attack them, but they knew without a doubt this was his doing. The Demons had never banded together like this. It was like an *army* had been called to destroy them.

This had only begun after they were offered a chance to join the Demon King's army, and they both had laughed their way through the forest. Laughed and laughed, as they heard his threat in the distance behind them.

A misguided thought from many, many full moons ago.

"Do you think Merikh has anything to do with this?" Ingram asked.

His kindred shook his bat-skulled head. *"I do not know."*

Annoyance lifted the spikes going down his back. Why didn't Aleron know? Why did he never have any of the answers to his questions?

It never registered that Ingram couldn't answer Aleron's either – or that they experienced everything at the same time, growing knowledge and humanity simultaneously.

"The Demons began attacking us more forcefully since his disappearance," Ingram pushed.

Merikh and the pretty Elven creature they'd met had disappeared from his cave almost five full moons ago. They had liked her; she was nice to them. They'd never had anyone outside of Mavka be kind to them.

Ingram had liked the stars in her eyes, and Aleron had liked the smell of her coily white hair.

"Do you think he joined Jabez?"

"I do not know. Would he want us destroyed?"

"Maybe?" Then Aleron thought better of it and answered, *"No."*

"No," Ingram repeated. *"He would let us rest in his home."*

"He named us. He always leaves."

This is true.

Merikh always left his home, unknowing that they would rest there regularly whenever he was gone. It was their safe place – even when he was there and would try to half-heartedly shoo them away.

"Then why is this– Above!" Aleron roared, a moment too late.

A serpent Demon, who had been using the cover of leaves, fell on top of Ingram. Sap was smeared over her, as though the serpent had covered herself in it to hide her scent.

She coiled around him and reared back to sink her fangs into the back of his shoulder. Aleron darted forward and took her venom instead.

She didn't get the chance to give much, as Ingram twisted his neck one hundred and eighty degrees and launched his maw forward. In just one peck of his raven beak, he took out her throat, and Aleron pried her upper jaw backwards.

Her coiling tail loosened, giving him room to crawl out from underneath her. Aleron dug his claws into the wound Ingram had made, likely ensuring she was dead, but that didn't stop Ingram from darting forward so he could rip his claws into her spine.

They both pulled, and his claws tore down her body until he found a pair of hip bones. He crushed them as he tore them from her dying body, and part of her spine with it – just as Aleron twisted and removed her head.

She didn't even have a chance to scream in agony.

Just as they discarded her body, both huffing wildly as they turned their bony faces towards each other, their orbs shifted to white at the same time.

Aleron was barrelled into by two medium-sized Demons, while three little but speedy ones attached themselves to Ingram.

It was too difficult to see past their swiping claws, chomping fangs, and a barrage of black, void-like limbs to distinguish their features. All he knew was his yelps and cries twisted and tangled with his kindred's in the air.

Alone and separated, they fought to remove their attackers.

Crimson flared in his sight, only to be snuffed out by a flash of white as agony crawled across his bleeding flesh.

The Witch Owl cleared a spot above him so he could see the trees. Her shriek was an infuriated war cry as she slammed a glinting silver dagger into the back of a Demon's neck.

The first beast she'd managed to rid him of turned from where she'd dragged it back. She slashed her dagger sideways, slicing open its neck, just as Ingram dug his claws into the shoulders of the last one remaining, so he could hold it still. He slammed his short, upward-jutting goat horns forward until he had perforated its skull, then caved it in.

Silver reflected a random and rare beam of sunlight touching the ground in the Veil, as the Witch Owl's dagger sailed through the air.

With a distinct thud, one of the medium-sized Demons shrieked as they reared back above Aleron. They clawed at the side of their neck to remove the dagger. It gave him the space and time to twist and then kick his second opponent to the ground.

Ingram ran forward to assist with a menacing, bubbling snarl, only to halt when two winged Demons landed in front of him. Their wings flared, as though they wanted to shield his sight from his kindred. Saliva flicked off their fangs when they hissed, but they didn't approach.

The Witch Owl ducked behind them to assist Aleron in his

place, her white feather cloak easy to distinguish in the darkness and mist surrounding them. For the most part, she was silent. That, or she just couldn't be heard over Aleron's struggles as more Demons came upon them.

One of the large, winged Demons gave Ingram their back so they could keep an eye on Aleron. The winged ones did nothing to assist the battle. They only assured that he and his kindred remained separated, both physically and from view.

At every turn in his fight, as he battled Demon after Demon, his whitened sight desperately sought Aleron.

His friend. His companion. The only person he'd truly known from the moment he'd taken his first breath in the world – and perhaps someone who had been with him even before that.

He didn't doubt that his kindred was doing the same.

It was the longest they'd ever been separated.

Usually, they would take any chance they possibly could to create a link. Whether it be by sight, as their skulls and orbs connected over a distance, or by one brushing their elbow over some part of the other's body. Often, they overlapped their fingers when they stood next to each other.

They shared a bond, a devotion to each other no one in this world could truly understand – at least not to the obsessive level they did.

So, to not even be able to glance at him now, had Ingram's panic setting in. He feared; not for himself, but for his kindred.

Hearing his cries echo over the small distance made his insides crawl. Not even when a Demon bit into the side of his neck did his mind stray from the thought of seeing his kindred. To make sure he was okay.

"Aleron," he whimpered.

He tore the shadowy beast from his throat as he bucked another off and over his skull.

There were so many claws and fangs that he was becoming numb to them. All he could feel was pain, no matter the tool inflicting the damage.

Throughout the entire time he fought, only one thought remained. *I must get to Aleron.*

Together they were strong. Together they were one. Together

they could make it through this.

As if sensing the deep desire to return to each other, the Witch Owl took down one of the winged Demons while Ingram's back was turned. She did not make it through the second. When she spun around, she was pinned down on her front with a three-toed claw against her backside.

Black tentacles that appeared to be made of powdered chalk and glitter shot up around the winged beast. Winding around all of its limbs in a constricting hold, the magical bindings yanked the Demon back. The sounds of bones crunching and snapping were drowned out by wet, frothing maws around him.

Its death squeal pierced the air.

The Witch Owl weakly rose to her feet but staggered to the side as her form flickered in and out of incorporeal and physical. She was severely wounded, her own blood staining her until the white of her dress ran red.

It was obvious she couldn't properly hold her incorporeal form, becoming physical for long enough to morph into a human-sized owl. She took flight, fleeing. Even her feathers in her owl form were soaked in crimson.

Ingram and Aleron were left to defend themselves alone, but at least Ingram could see him now.

Despite how much the sight before him shuddered his insides with revulsion, there was a comfort in seeing his kindred. Aleron's black wings were both twisted and lay the wrong way as they dragged upon the ground.

Every time Aleron managed to rid himself of the parasites upon him, he was dragged backwards by a Demon grabbing his feathery tail to yank him back into chaos.

His kindred gave a long cry, one that had a purple, blood-filled mist puffing from his maw.

"Aleron!" Ingram roared, managing to crawl out from his own attackers to leap forward.

He crashed into his kindred's back, ridding him completely of his attackers, before knocking them both to their sides. Aleron whimpered as he rose on three limbs.

His kindred was desperately trying to flee.

"Run!" Ingram roared, nudging his behind so he could move

quicker.

There was a gap, a way out. They just needed to dart for it.

Aleron shook his skull, as though he didn't have the capacity to sprint. Just as Ingram noted that one of his legs had been clawed to bone, he ran forward to cover Aleron's body with his own.

He didn't get the chance to protect Aleron. The stump of his tail was pulled back and a blanket of shadowy beasts was upon him.

His orbs flared red, rage took hold, and he called for the remaining strength in his body. He stood, spun in a circle, and with claws tensed and threatening, he bellowed out one of the most ferocious roars he'd ever conjured.

The beasts warily stepped back, fear startling them – only to remember that he and Aleron were cornered.

He readied himself to leap to his kindred's side. He couldn't see Aleron underneath the pile of beasts upon him, but his panicked and distressed cry echoed through them.

Just as he leapt, a weight slamming into him from above shoved him to the ground so hard spittle burst from his mouth as his beak separated.

Then, the pressure was gone, and he faced his opponent.

The Witch Owl? Once more, she was in her human form.

On one knee, covering her midsection and leaning against the ground with a hand, she looked up at him. Her features were twisted into a mix of sympathy, pity, and... something else. Something that had his hackles rising.

Her face had been split apart by multiple claws. The bones of her forehead and cheek were visible, with one eyelid gaping open. The arm across her stomach was broken.

There were too many wounds for him to figure out how else she had been harmed. A sickly sweet aroma was cascading from her skin, hiding the scent of her blood.

Her singular brown eye met his orbs. It crinkled in anguish that looked as though it had nothing to do with the physical pain she was in.

"I'm sorry," she whispered.

"Help us!" he snarled, turning to Aleron when he heard a

harrowing yelp. *"Merikh's ward is nearby."*

It was so close he could smell Merikh's lake. He could even hear the waterfall that streamed over the Veil's cliff wall right next to his cave entrance.

It was there, not far past the trees. Just there, but out of reach or sight.

"It's too far," the Witch Owl wheezed out.

Ingram head butted an invisible wall. He slammed his fist upon it, unsure of it what it was. Actually, it wasn't invisible – at least, not completely. It was black and dusty, but a protective dome had formed over him and the Witch Owl. It was thin, but no less effective in keeping him from the fight.

He clawed at it, slammed into it with his shoulders, and even roared at it. He tried everything in his might to get past the wretched dome, confused as to where it came from.

Demons attacked it from the outside, but they couldn't get through.

"Let me out!" Ingram wailed, staring at Aleron, who continued to try to crawl away despite his attackers.

I have to go to him! Nothing he did allowed him to pass through, and every second longer inside it constricted his chest, his lungs, his very heart.

"Let me out! Aleron!"

Aleron spared him a glance and then tried to crawl in his direction.

Ingram's claws snapped, bending at the nail beds. He broke multiple fingers trying to get through. He would have cracked his own skull just to get to his kindred's side, to bring him into this temporary safety he'd found.

"I'm sorry," the Witch Owl cried out, before a shuddering sob broke from her.

He didn't understand why. He didn't care. He just attempted to get free.

Panic lodged in every muscle and bone in his body, every fibre of his being. His heart was beating so erratically in his large chest that it felt moments from giving out.

Aleron's yelp cut short, followed by a loud, sharp, and harrowing *crack!*

The Demons who were crawling on top of the protective dome disappeared. The forest disappeared. The dirt and the sky, gone.

The only thing that remained was the dark, clawed hand that lifted a large fragment of a bat skull, and the second that held a lower jaw.

Ingram's heart stopped.

A piece of it shattered and lodged deep within his soul, piercing it so profoundly he knew nothing could remove it.

The Demons' cheer was drowned out when his orbs turned so crimson it was blinding, and he let loose a feral, frothing roar. He noted the red droplets of liquid that floated and hovered around his empty eye sockets, as though he was crying ethereal tears. They looked like droplets of human blood as he let loose.

They'd killed his kindred, destroyed his friend... his *home*. They had broken the only thing that had ever mattered to him, *would* ever matter to him.

He didn't truly understand its meaning, but the love he held for Aleron was of its purest form in all the world, and any other. They were each other's shadow, each other's warmth, and the shared voice that nursed any tender aches that tried to form within their hearts and minds.

They were one being split into two forms.

Losing all will to care for his own wellbeing, Ingram's determination to escape doubled.

He attacked the dome keeping him away. The dome that had kept him from protecting Aleron, that had forced Ingram to be nothing but a spectator while he died.

It finally cracked under his rabid and uncontrolled twisting, squirming barrage. Yet, it never let him through, not even as he started bashing his skull and horns against it, uncaring if he broke his own head in the process.

Nothing else was able to take his attention except for the multiple Demons fighting for a fragment of skull – for a shared piece of the reward.

Every action, every word from them, sunk him further and further into hopelessness.

"I'm so sorry," the Witch Owl whispered behind him. "Please

forgive me."

Her voice reminded him of her presence.

Between the moment she'd spoken, and when he spun around, she had just enough time to turn incorporeal before he descended upon her. It was barely a second, but she'd escaped him.

He didn't know where she'd gone as he darted his raven skull one way and then the other, having to twist his head to properly see around his white beak for anything close by. Occasionally, he thought he saw intangible white moving within his form, like she'd hidden inside his massive body, but he couldn't be sure.

Before long, his chaotic mind drew back to the circle of Demons surrounding him and this wretched dome. The shadowy beasts with void-like skin were either sitting or standing there, waiting for the dome to be released or for him to break his way through it.

They snickered, called out, and teased.

Those that held his kindred's skull taunted him with the pieces, often inciting more fighting between each other. Every time he saw a white skull fragment, his single-minded desire to escape his containment grew more ferocious.

He wanted to collect each piece.

They were his. His to keep, to heal, to touch, to guide, and hopefully *revive*. Because he refused... he refused to believe this was the end for Aleron.

The cold burning sensation that festered within his chest refused to believe there was no way to bring him back.

Kitty, Faunus, whatever his new name was, had come back – by evidence of the gold-filled crack in his skull. There must be a way.

"They aren't going to leave," the Witch Owl stated, her voice quiet and distant.

Ingram only answered her with a scratchy snarl. His lungs wheezed on every painful intake, and he was unsure if their shuddering was caused by his internal pain or his external wounds.

"I need you to calm down. Please. I cannot lose you too."

He turned and spun, searching for her so he could end her

infuriating pestering. He'd rend her in two, so long as she gave him the peace of her silence. He chased her within the dome and even clawed at his own body when she tried to hide within him.

Ever since she appeared at his side, this dome had existed around him. Was she the reason he remained separated from Aleron? He would have preferred to go to the afterworld with his kindred, rather than be left as a writhing mass of agony that didn't have enough humanity to understand just how deeply he felt loss – or how to navigate it.

He felt alone; it was not something he'd ever experienced before. So completely and utterly *alone*.

"Ingram, please settle!"

Standing on his hind legs, he lifted his raven skull to the sky as he opened his maw and let loose a bellowing roar. It was silenced abruptly when a warm hand grabbed his horn to keep his head still... Then the Witch Owl removed it from his neck.

Blissful nothingness greeted him.

TWO

When Ingram came to, he was completely healed and within Merikh's protective ward. It glittered red around the area, one third of it hidden within the Veil's cliff wall.

The waterfall brought fresh, wet scents. The grass was bright as it danced in the soft wind, waving past the two trees and boulders situated next to the lake. Sunlight showered him with warmth, and a dragonfly buzzed around his skull before returning to skate along the water's surface.

His wake was sudden, and it was missing something vital.

A wing that would normally be draped over the top of him. Limbs that would normally be threaded around his own. A feathery tail his own lizard one would be coiled around.

His waking was absent of the heaviness of another body threatening to crush him, or the gentle pulsating movement of lungs working beneath him as he attempted to crush them instead. It lacked a familiar and comforting scent, a heartbeat he'd learned to distinguish – a pattern that often beat in unison with his own.

Aleron...

As usual, waking from a decapitation was disorientating for the first few seconds, but he attempted to stand anyway.

Ingram whined and searched for his kindred.

His usually purple orbs turned crimson at the memories that slammed their way to the forefront of his mind. Even more so when he saw the Witch Owl kneeling on the ground right next to where he'd been laying.

He cared little for her wounds, which were still unhealed, unlike his own. Her injuries were insignificant compared to the soul-crushing agony he was experiencing at the very core of his being.

"You," he snarled, stepping towards her in his monstrous form, all four of his limbs moving in perfect unison.

He didn't give himself time to wallow in his loss, not as rage swept through him and threatened to break him apart from within.

Swiftly rising to her feet, she put her hands out to warn him back. A translucent, dusty black barrier formed between them, like a small shield.

It was similar to the dome that had trapped him.

"It was you, wasn't it?"

"You don't understand," she beseeched.

He didn't care for her reasons. He lifted up on to his hind legs so he could smash his forearm sideways across her barrier.

She winced, as though it strained her to hold it, and he ended up knocking it to the side with her following it. She kept it above her as she crawled backwards with her backside slipping across the dirt.

"It is all your fault!" he roared, shoving his entire weight onto her shield. She let out a cry when her barrier slammed into her and crushed her into the dirt. ***"I could have gone to him! I could have saved him!"***

The Witch Owl let out a bellowing yell as she attempted to fight back against being pulverised. Cold coils wrapped around his neck and armpits, yanking him back.

He bashed against the ground and tore at the dirt and grass as he slid back.

"If I had let you go to him, you would have died alongside him!"

Getting to all four limbs, he shook his head to clear his dizzy mind, and turned his crimson sight to her. *"Then I should have died with him!"*

"I had to make a choice! I could not save both of you, and Aleron was too overrun with Demons for me to get to him." He didn't understand why her good eye, since the other was still swollen and shut, filled with liquid before a tear fell down her battered cheek, moistening the blood caking her face. "It was either you or him – you have no idea how hard it was for me to make that choice."

"I was brought into this world with him. We always lived it by each other's side, and we should have left it together!" When he sprinted for her, intending to bash his skull and horns against her shield, she turned incorporeal and made him go through her. *"You should not have interfered. You should not have saved either of us!"*

He knew Aleron would have felt the same way. If neither could be saved, then neither would have wanted to be without the other – or watch the other perish.

They would have happily crossed over to the afterworld together, laughing and teasing each other on the way. They were one being, a unit, a kindred bond that was supposed to reach over time and space.

A piece of him was missing: his other half.

It felt wrong to be here without him. The space next to him was too empty. The world was suddenly twice its size. He felt betrayed by Aleron's loss, and he also felt like the betrayer.

He was cold, when usually he was warmed by another.

Aleron would have experienced the same loss. He didn't need to ask him; he just instinctually knew.

Who would be there to *not* answer the questions he had? Who would blanket them in the middle of sleep if it were not his wing? Who would make him laugh, or huff with irritation, or sit with him when he gained new humanity and was struggling to adjust to it?

Who was Ingram... without Aleron?

He was nothing.

He sat on his hind legs so he could claw at his back, trying to get to his heart from behind and rip it out. Flesh and muscle flared as he gouged, and yet he didn't cry against the pain when the turmoil within was far more excruciating.

"You should have let me die with him," Ingram whimpered.

"You cannot say that to me," the Witch Owl whispered, her

bottom lip trembling. "I know you're upset, but why must I bear this every time? A mother is not meant to lose her children! No one cares how I feel, having watched two of them die." She covered her face with both hands, her loose corkscrew curls bouncing as she shook her head. "It's not fair... and you all blame me for it when it's not my fault. I'm not the one hurting you, and I'm not the one who has sent an army out for you. I'm trying everything I can to protect you, to save you."

Ingram huffed, having no idea what she was talking about. He didn't know what this 'mother' title was that she had apparently given herself.

She was the Witch Owl.

A strange woman that played with and protected them. He figured it was because she wanted to, since Aleron was wonderful. And if Aleron was wonderful, then so was he.

Why should she care for them beyond her own entertainment? Just as they hadn't cared much for her.

"You, your brothers... There is only so much I can do as one person. I could not bear to watch you perish alongside Aleron, to lose another one of you."

He stopped clawing at his back, pausing the need to dig into his broken, bleeding heart, so he could answer her. *"Whatever this brothers thing are, I would have gladly traded them for Aleron."*

She pulled her hands away from her face to glare at him, her dark eyes narrowed. In just one expression, she looked both angered and exasperated.

"Aleron was your brother! All the Mavka are your brothers! You all came from me, and yet, when you grow your skulls, you forget who I am to you."

Once more, he snorted a huff.

Aleron was his only bond and kindred. The rest of the Mavka were of his species, but there was nothing special there. Sure, he had no desire to harm them, but he would have gladly destroyed all their skulls if it meant Aleron did not... leave him alone like this.

"Merikh is your older brother, as are Orpheus, Magnar, and Faunus. Even Aleron was brought into this world before you." She pushed her cloak to the side as though she wanted to reveal something. "And there are more of you, that is why I could not–"

Ingram turned before she could finish.

Faunus, he thought, heading in the direction of the feline-skulled Mavka. *Faunus' skull was cracked, and now it is solid with a gold scar. He escaped death, so maybe I can do the same for Aleron.*

Because Ingram refused to believe there was no way to bring Aleron back. He wouldn't be without him for long – he knew this for certain.

However, first, he would change this world. He would make it safer for Aleron's return. He would make it better. He would not see him perish *twice*.

Ignoring the Witch Owl, as she was of no significance to his constant and often erratic bouncing thoughts and attention span, he headed towards the forest. His sight drifted in the direction of the Demon King's castle, and his orbs flared an even darker crimson.

Whether it was with Ingram's last breath or the returning of Aleron's, Jabez, the Demon King, would *pay* for this. He would learn what it felt like to have his skull crushed.

He had ordered for the death of all Mavka, and his actions had taken away the most precious creature to Ingram, who was not beneath vengeance. He would make sure it was painful, even if it had to be *swift*.

"Where are you going?!" The Witch Owl shouted as she ran to be in his way once more.

He gave her a warning snarl before stepping to the side.

"To the other Mavka, to bring back Aleron."

He needed a direction, a task, something to give him hope, or he'd sit here digging for his heart for the rest of his life.

"He is gone, Ingram," she answered with a sob. "The other Mavka cannot bring him back."

He roared barely an inch from her nose.

"Then if he cannot come back, I will destroy everything that took him away from me!" He swiped his front paw at her, stabbing his claws into her side and dragging her to the ground. He was above her within a second. *"I will start with you if I*

must!"

Just as he snapped his skull forward to shove her head into his maw, she turned intangible. She floated through him and backed up as he slowly gave chase, saliva flooding his mouth cavity.

He didn't like that she could so easily escape him, but it also meant he was disinterested in fighting her. He had desires, and currently they wanted bloodshed – to hunt, maim, and eradicate the one creature he could truly blame.

"I want to help," she stated, her voice echoey. "But if I could bring Aleron back, I would. I would have brought back the serpent-skulled Mavka years ago." Then she turned physical and assumed a brave stance, facing him. "I am not your enemy, Ingram."

"Then help me destroy the Demon King."

"I will. I promise I will, but I still don't know how to defeat him. At least, not in a way that won't cost more of your lives. You need to be patient. Please, I promise."

Her answer and following plea were insufficient.

"If you will not help me now, then I will go by myself."

Her colour turned ashen. "You cannot go after him by yourself, Ingram. He will kill you."

"Then I will make the other Mavka help me."

He was sure they had just as much of a desire to kill the Demon King.

Just as he redirected his path to go to the northeast of the Veil, where the three Mavka he knew resided, she stepped in front of him again, arms open.

"You cannot go through the forest! You must leave the Veil, Ingram. You are without a ward or a home, and the Demons are waiting for you to leave this protection. It's no longer safe for you here."

"Then I will go around the forest!" he yelled, turning to the Veil's canyon walls.

There was a path there that often got sunlight. He would walk along it.

She ran to intercept him once more, ducking when he tried to head-butt her with his small, sharp horns. He snapped his beak forward, but she only turned incorporeal to evade him and then back to physical to speak with him clearly.

"The other Mavka cannot help you either. They have brides, Ingram. Some of them have younglings. They either cannot or will not go with you."

"I WILL destroy the Demon King. With or without your help, their help. I will *bring Aleron back."*

"Unless we have an army to fight against Jabez's, nothing you do will make a difference. You will not win. You will only die, and I cannot bear to see another one of my children perish!"

His head tilted at just one word of her entire rambling spiel. His skull made a rattling sound, as though it was empty of a brain and instead filled with bones.

He was aware there were many blank spaces within his thoughts, and that he was not wise nor knowledgeable. He could only retain so much information, and he could then only decipher so much of it as well.

A lot of what was said to him fell on uncomprehending ears.

"An army?" He paused so he could tap an index claw against his bone-white raven beak. *"An army to fight an army?"*

That made sense to him.

The biggest issue with getting to Jabez was the number of shadowy beasts in the way. He was sure, if it were just him and the Demon King, he would be able to remove his head.

Ingram only struggled with a fight when there were many foes, but he'd always won any that were more evenly matched.

The Witch Owl tilted her head, but it was her unsure expression that grabbed his attention. Why did she look so worried?

"What are you thinking?" Her tone sounded like a warning, one full of suspicion.

"You said I needed an army."

"I said an army would be needed, but there is no army that would fight alongside us."

"This is not true. There are others who want the Demons gone just as much as me."

She was right. Ingram needed numbers if he wanted to get to the Demon King.

He turned away from the Veil completely, fickle with his decisions in his agitated state. He could scale the cliff wall with his claws, so he didn't try to find an easier path to the surface world.

The Witch Owl grabbed his tail to yank him back with all her might, letting out a tooth-gritting yell as she did. "No! If you seek to ask the humans, you will not find any friends there."

He flicked his tail to the side, ridding himself of her, and he began to climb.

The only thing that was keeping the loss at bay was his determination for vengeance. He would find an army, otherwise he feared he would quickly succumb to the nagging anguish that was festering within his chest, right below the surface of his flesh.

Had she not removed his head to bring him to the safety of Merikh's ward, resetting his thoughts, Ingram may never have gained consciousness throughout his agony-filled rampage.

"Ingram, please! Stop!"

His sight shifted to a hopeless blue.

Aleron...

THREE

Staring up at the rocky ceiling of her tiny bedroom, Emerie noted the patterned lines of where the person wielding a pickaxe had carved out her room generations ago. Her nose twitched in irritation at the poorly done job.

With her head bobbing against her scratchy, hard, and uncomfortable bed, it was an odd detail to note... considering the action she was in the middle of.

I wonder what they'll be serving for dinner tonight.

The food here at this impenetrable fortress was pretty bland, but at least it was hearty. She needed something right now to make her full, since she felt rather empty.

Something warm and wet slid over the arch of her neck, and she twisted her head to offer more surface to play with. Once she patted his head in reassurance, she resumed her thinking.

I'm glad I'm not part of the watch tonight.

Her gaze roamed over to the two dim candles sitting on her oak bedside table. They were just enough to illuminate the scarcely furnished room. A brown scratchy blanket lay beneath her on a bed made of hay, a layer of wool added for warmth and 'comfort.' A chest at the end of her bed stored her few personal items, and a plain wardrobe to her right held her clothing.

The only other piece of furniture was a small writing desk that had just enough room to fit her elbows on it, with a piece of parchment between them.

Her sleeping chamber was hollow of life, overly small, and

almost identical to the many others housing her fellow guildmembers.

But it was hers, which was all that mattered.

Bryce groaned above her, and she looked over his sweat-slicked forehead.

At least he's enjoying himself.

How long had she been dating him now? Eight months, maybe more?

Honestly, when he'd asked her out, she'd been surprised someone had taken an interest in her. She'd liked him enough. He was decent looking, seemed to have a kind heart, and was dedicated in his work.

At first, she'd enjoyed being with him, especially when their relationship had quickly formed into something physical, then sexual. She'd missed being touched, had missed feeling like... a woman worth getting hard for.

Her heart had ached for the intimacy, as much as her pussy had pulsated with the need she'd often tried to take care of on her own.

But... it'd been a while since Bryce's touch had ignited anything within her. Now, she worried she was just placating him, allowing her body to be used so she didn't have to face the ugly truth.

When liquid warmth filled her inner walls, each spurt nipped at her chest like a horrible parasite. Not once had he asked if he could, just doing as he pleased because they both knew there were no repercussions.

She was starting to feel like a cum dump.

It didn't help that the moment the last of his twitches receded and he was done rudely crushing her underneath *all* of his heavy weight, he was quick to pull himself out and tie up his pants.

She leant up on her elbow when he searched for his shirt.

"Where are you going?" Emerie asked, her brows furrowing. He was already dressing to leave – without saying a word. "I haven't come."

"So?" He glanced at her and must have noticed her jaw muscle twitching. "You're better at it than me anyway."

"So?" she mimicked. "Pleasure is supposed to be equal. If I

didn't come, you should help."

Bryce rolled his brown eyes as he combed his fingers through his wavy blond hair, the length of it barely even two inches. He smoothed it back, as if she had gripped and tugged it out of place in the wild throes – which she hadn't.

"I have the third round on the watch, which you already know, *Co-ordinator*."

Emerie stood so she could find her pants, then stabbed her foot through one of the legs, followed by the other. "Yeah, but that's not for a few more hours."

"Hey," he said, his voice pitched higher as his eyebrows rose suggestively. "I thought you were going to finish?"

Brushing her hands over the skintight shirt of her uniform, she sulked to herself. *I'm not in the mood anymore.* Out loud she retorted, "Everyone has to do the shitty watches, Bryce."

His upper lip twitched in annoyance. "You don't."

This time, Emerie was the one to roll her eyes. "There are other, more gruelling tasks I must complete that keep me up until that time."

Yeah... like a mountain of freaking paperwork and recordings that needed transcribing. Then again, the watch on the wall was just as boring, although colder.

"I still can't believe you're ranking up before me," he grumbled, side-eyeing her. "They said there weren't any positions opening up in the guild."

A sigh deflated Emerie.

Considering Emerie had been a Demonslayer two years longer than Bryce, there were many other reasons why he'd been told this.

One being that he was aloof and didn't like taking direction from others. A Master had to be obedient in their prior training, had to take orders and follow the instructions given to them, and execute them perfectly. Every failure, no matter how small or minor, was added to a tally. A mark against their name would see them taking longer to rank up, if at all.

Emerie had been told she only had one mark against her name, but it had also aided in her favour. Her sacrifices had made her worthy of ranking up – although the Elders had taken their sweet time about it.

The other reason was because, although he was strong, he had very little else going for him. He could be cunning, but he wasn't particularly smart.

Emerie, on the other hand, wasn't overly strong, but she had always been a formidable opponent. She was smart, well-read, swift, and... lost. Lost to be nothing but a slave to the Elders and their wants. She was hollow, Bryce wasn't.

Many of the other Demonslayers weren't. They still had hopes, dreams, desires.

Emerie had one need, and it was the death of Demons.

Which aligned perfectly with the guild's goals.

She was also acutely aware that the reason the position had been offered to her was because the Head Elder had her sights set on Emerie. She was a little too interested in her training, as they were two of the very few who shared certain similarities: a lack of proper identity, and a steely heart – one of which... was a lie on Emerie's part.

"Look, if you're still awake when I finish my watch, I'll finish you off," Bryce offered, tossing her a grin. "Even if you're not, I can come wake you with this." He gripped his junk through his pants, before leaning forward to kiss the right side of her face. "Just leave your door unlocked."

Bryce had just guaranteed that she'd not only be locking her door, but she also wouldn't be around to hear him bashing at it. For all she cared, he could release into his own hand.

I might go sleep in the library tonight. The Elders had never cared that she often found peaceful rest there.

Peaceful because she was so fucking exhausted from studying, that she passed out with her head on a table and her nose in the spine of her book.

When he straightened, her eyes flicked side to side as she looked over his attractive face. He was clean shaven, his brows high and masculine, with one sporting a scar through it. He wasn't the sexiest man she'd ever laid her eyes upon, but he was pleasant.

Why do all my relationships end up like this?

It didn't help that they all involved guild members.

She clenched her fist. *No. I can't just throw in the towel. I haven't even sat down with him and told him how I feel.* That he made her feel like shit, even if he didn't mean to – or maybe he did! Who freaking knew? She was making up assumptions, because she hadn't sat him down and had a proper talk with him.

Then again, chatting between them was limited to while he was either undoing or redoing his fucking pants.

Her insecurities nagged at the nape of her neck. She rubbed it with her palm.

"Hey. Tomorrow, could we sit down and tal–"

An alarm bell echoed down the halls, booming and reverberating against the stone.

Emerie and Bryce shared a look between each other, one where he appeared paler and her own expression was filled with surprise. Rooted to the spot, his mouth opened and closed.

"Move!" she yelled, shoving him through the doorway. She grabbed her sword next to it as she shot through it. "Get to the wall."

Bryce's footsteps echoed behind her as they hurried through the fortress before their sounds were drowned out by many others joining them in the halls. Although there was a minor stampede, it wasn't of panicked civilians.

Instead, they were all heading to the armoury where they would be issued their weapons. They would be free to take a bow or a spear, depending on their preference or availability, and then they would head to those weapons' allocated starting points.

Archers on top of the wall, and footmen wielding swords or spears at the three gates available.

Most already held a personal sword at their hip, one they either made by hand or hired someone more experienced to make.

They had to fight through a sea of people to reach the armoury doors. Just as she and Bryce reached out for a spear, both likely coming to the decision to fight alongside each other, her shoulder was grabbed.

Emerie halted and faced the Elder, who had been standing nearby.

"Not you," he said firmly, the outline of his features barely visible through his uniform's face coverings. "Head Elder Wren wants to see you."

Moving out of the way so other guildmembers could obtain their weapons, Emerie nodded her head just as Bryce came up beside her.

"What about me?"

Only the Elder's dark eyes could be seen through the open slit of his mask, and he narrowed them at Bryce. "What about you? Go to the wall with everyone else."

"The fuck?" Bryce spat as he darted his head towards her. "Why does she get special treatment these days? Everyone is to go to the wall when we're under attack."

She squinted at his expression, as well as his tone. She wasn't particularly fond of jealousy, especially when it came to guild activities. "I'm following my orders, as you should. The reason doesn't matter."

"Exactly," the Elder bit out, his voice cold and unfeeling. "What Wren wants is her business, and as the Head of the eastern sector, her wants are final. Any arguments regarding it will be noted for future reference." Then, with a hint of humour crinkling the corners of his eyes, he added, "That's if you don't die this night."

A knot of muscle ticked in Bryce's jaw, his lips firming into a hard line. However, he nodded and stepped back.

Emerie stopped him from retreating by clasping his wrist, ignoring the rush of people moving around them. Despite the negative energy of their night so far, she held his eyes with sincerity.

"Don't get killed, okay?" she quietly pleaded. "Stay safe."

His annoyance deflated out of him, and his gaze softened. "Of course, Em. Don't worry about me. I promise I'll be okay."

There was no kiss, hug, or further affection shared between them as they split up – not that they would have done something so public. Their relationship was a secret, by his request, mainly.

Bryce made his way out of the armoury to head to his station, while Emerie climbed a spiralling staircase that led to a higher section of the fortress. The Elder didn't follow her, likely picking out other guildmembers among the crowd that Wren had given additional orders to.

Zagros Fortress was the Demonslayer stronghold of the eastern part of Austrális. Both the east and the west had the largest area of the Veil cutting through their land, making them far more dangerous than the north or south lands.

From its topmost tower, anyone could see the burnt ruins of Rivenspire. It'd long been destroyed by Demons and panicked people creating fires.

To the south, they traded with the farmlands for food by offering additional protection. The same offer of protection had been given to the mining town who shared their mountain, although much further north.

East was nothing but treacherous sea.

Zagros Fortress was cold, foreboding, and loomed over the lands below. The fortress itself had been carved into the very stone of the mountain, and what stone had been taken from it built the rest.

It was composed of six towers.

Two for the lower areas right where the wall touched the base of the mountain.

The middle two were watch towers for the north and south, situated at its furthest lengths and jutting from the mountain's body. They also sheltered the centre of the fortress – which housed their living and training areas – from the northerly cool winds.

The topmost two towers allowed them to see the east and west simultaneously. The areas between them housed the library, the records chamber, and then a higher section that only a certain few were permitted to enter.

First, she had to go deeper inside the mass of the mountain before she would be closer to the summit, where Wren was likely situated on her viewing and planning platform.

Pushing down on the pommel of her sword to stop the tip from smacking against the stairs, she began the long and gruelling climb. Sweat trickled down her back, causing her black Demonslayer uniform to cling to her heated skin, but she never slowed or wiped her brow.

It still amazes me that Wren climbs these daily. No wonder their Head Elder was so damn fit.

Her own lungs were moments from seizing, and her side already burned with a stitch.

As she reached the last steps, her tired and wobbling knees threatened to give out, but she used the last of her energy in a burst to the top of them.

She was greeted by two Master rank guildmembers. The blue insignia pressed into the upper chest of their uniform in the centre of their sternum matched her own. A circle that tapered off at the end before it could finish completing, with a sword stabbing all the way through.

It was impossible to tell who was who, since their uniforms matched so completely with their face coverings and hoods. She couldn't even assume the eyes of the person staring back at her belonged to who she thought. Everyone had to be treated the same for their station.

It gave their positions autonomy.

Emerie hadn't put her own hood up yet, as that was something they usually did only when at their stations. Emerie only had to take orders from any of those who had a silver emblem – an Elder.

But all had to obey the command of their medallion wearer.

Both Master rank guildmembers standing guard nodded. They stepped to the side, allowing her freedom to enter. Emerie rapped the back of her knuckles against the door.

"Head Elder, you called fo–"

"Enter, Emerie." The weight of Wren's voice boomed past the thick, distressed timber of the door.

Once she was inside, she closed the door behind her. Then she promptly knocked her ankles together, clasped her hands behind her back, rolled back her shoulders, and lifted her chin. She stood at the ready, waiting for Wren to start the conversation.

The room was bleak, made completely of stone and the rare marble that had been found when they'd carved into the mountainside. It was dimly lit. Wren rarely used more than a handful of candles – just enough to allow her to see their plans on the table, but not enough for others to steer their footing around the furniture.

Wren was under the belief that they should all be able to see in the dark, just like their formidable enemy.

The Head Elder stood at a rectangular, glassless, waist-high window that spanned the entire left-to-right curved section of that wall. Standing similarly to Emerie, she looked out over the entirety of the fortress like she was a hawk searching for its next prey.

Her hands were loosely clasped behind her back. Emerie's were stiff, as though having just a muscle out of place could be taken disrespectfully.

There was no one else in the room with them, and the silence Wren forced upon them was long and uncomfortable. Especially with the waning, near-full moon highlighting her silhouette and casting a dark shadow over her.

"You are among the few who are an expert with a whip," Wren factually stated without turning. "It's not an easy tool to master."

Emerie's gaze darted down to the whip coiled neatly at the woman's hip. It was different than the generic version that other guildmembers were given, as it had a singular thread of blue within its plait.

When Wren dipped her head ever so slightly to peer at Emerie from the corner of her eye, she stiffened further.

"That is correct," she answered, despite having not been asked a question.

"You are to join the team of Elders who are currently readying themselves on the floor below. You will join them outside of the gates."

Her brows twitched to knot, but she quickly managed to stop her confusion from fully forming. *I don't understand.* She nodded, before stepping back to do as she was told.

"Halt."

Emerie stood straight once more.

Shit. Wren had noticed her facial twitch, and her hawk-like gaze pierced all the way to Emerie's centre as she examined her.

Her feet were silent as she drew away from the window to

fully face Emerie, and a mirror threatened to stare back at her. They had no blood relation, as made apparent by the fact that Wren was much paler than her and lacked that scattering of freckles. She also had dark chestnut hair in comparison to Emerie's usual orange nest of knots, but much about them was the same.

Their blue eyes were similar, their busty statures were the same, and even the scarring on their faces mirrored each other's.

It'd always been difficult for Emerie to look at the impression of her own appearance on Wren. From her forehead, down the right side of her face, all the way down to the visible part of her neck, Wren had the webbing evidence of a burn scar. Emerie's was on the left and was almost identical; both of their scarring showing signs of going lower down their bodies.

Even the singular claw mark splitting their bottom lip was the same, just on opposing sides.

For the longest time, Emerie had wondered if that was the reason the Head Elder had taken an interest in her. Given that they were also both excellent whip bearers, obedient, and outwardly cold – although that was a farce on Emerie's part – it was like she was looking at an older version of herself.

Did Wren feel the same way, just in reverse?

There had been whispers that Wren was looking into her replacement, who would train under her until her death or when she stepped down. She was egotistical and political; it wouldn't be an unjustified assumption that Wren would replace herself with a potential younger version.

"I give you the freedom to speak." There was a calculating glint to her icy-blue eyes.

"I don't mean to be disobedient, Head Elder, but whip bearers are rarely needed on invasions. The best tool to use at the fortress is a spear, and we have the advantage of having a large number of soldiers and a wall. Whereas a sword is for ease of movement on assignments, and whips are usually a last resort against Demons."

"Usually you would be correct," the woman answered, before drifting back to the gaping window. Rain began to pitter-patter against the ledge softly, but loud enough to echo. As if to punctuate her next words, a beastly roar faintly thundered in the distance. "However, our foe is not a Demon."

If it's not a Demon... And since *that* sound definitely couldn't belong to a human bandit, that meant...

Her lips tightened, not in fear but in realisation.

Lightning struck within the grey clouds.

A Duskwalker.

"The fight has begun." Wren's face hardened. "Someone made a foolish mistake." When Emerie made no comment, choosing not to interrupt the woman's musings, Wren eventually chuckled. "I hope you don't mind, but I've sent your companion to be fodder."

Emerie's body language made absolutely no change, and Wren's humour brightened.

"Good. Your attachments aren't deep."

"Whatever you order is for the best of the guild. I would never question your decisions." The lie fell easily from Emerie's lips.

Bryce meant a lot to her, even if he unwittingly made her feel like a cheap hole to be fucked every once in a while. They'd shared other pleasant memories and had saved each other's lives numerous times. They had problems, but not enough to truly deter her... she didn't think. Or was she just being stupidly hopeful?

Even if she didn't outwardly show it, Emerie was exceptionally self-conscious of her damaged appearance. The scars on her face and neck weren't the only ones she bore, and there were many others that went soul deep.

She was also missing a chunk out of her. Although she'd willingly done it, had made that choice, it still lingered in the back of her mind that she was incomplete – and therefore unlovable in the long term.

Bryce was a chance for her to find some form of companionship along the hard road she'd taken. The fact that Wren had purposefully put him in harm's way just to test Emerie didn't sit well with her, although she had no other choice but to accept it.

With an unfeeling expression, Emerie waited to be

dismissed, hoping their conversation would end. There was much she wanted to say, but couldn't, *wouldn't*.

"How's your fear these days?"

Wren was aware she was going through a recent bout of trauma and mental recovery.

"It's managed. Once my wounds healed up, I remembered why I stopped being afraid in the first place."

Wren nodded, appearing satisfied with her answer. "The Elder's team you have been assigned to will have your whip ready. Be careful in the rain, Emerie. The creature will have the advantage." Then she inclined her head towards the door. "You may l–"

Just as she was about to thankfully be dismissed, hurried footsteps pounded up the staircase. The person didn't wait for permission to enter, and knocked into Emerie as he passed her.

"Wren." He stood in the same position as her. "The Duskwalker has begun its attack."

"What happened?" she asked with a lack of ire. "I told everyone to hold off on the attack until our whip bearers were ready."

"One of our bowmen accidentally unleashed an arrow into its chest. It grew enraged and tried to scale the wall."

"Idiots," she bit in return. "What Duskwalker is it?"

"It has a beak, that's all I know."

"The raven." She spared a glance at Emerie, before shaking her head. "The winged one won't be far away. They never travel without each other. It's likely lurking in the shadows, waiting for an opportunity to push through the gates. Double the foot soldiers, don't allow them through."

"Understood, Head Elder."

The man left.

"You." Emerie didn't think it was possible, but her back straightened further. "Tell the leader of your unit that I no longer care if it's alive. Two will be difficult for you to battle against, but I want one of them. I don't care which one, and I no longer care if it's dead so long as I have one."

"Understood."

When she was given a nod to leave, Emerie finally escaped.

Now that she was alone, her eyes narrowed. Her lips pulled tight to one side as worry twinged.

Shit. A Duskwalker?

She'd signed up to slaughter Demons, not face an omen of death.

FOUR

Rope? Check. Whip? Emerie tapped the whip loop on her weapons belt to make sure it hadn't somehow unbuckled. *Check.*

Sword? Check. She didn't need to feel for it, since it was smacking against the side of her thigh.

Four Elders in front of me? Check, check, and double check.

It was an odd experience being assigned to their unit. She was the only Master rank present, and she thought of herself as a toddler.

She knew all of their names, not that she could currently tell them apart from behind. It was an even split of genders between them, with Emerie making it outnumbered.

Why am I the fifth person? She didn't understand why Wren was assigning her to such an important task.

Capture a Duskwalker? What a pitiful, laughable feat. *I'm going to die tonight.*

There was no doubt about it. Death awaited her, and she wasn't as prepared for it as she thought she'd be.

She eyed the backs of the Elders in front of her once more. *Are they scared?* She wouldn't say she was petrified, but never in her wildest nightmares did she think she'd have to fight one of those monsters face-to-skull.

Demons were predictable, even if they were pesky to battle. Duskwalkers? Nothing could take them down. Nothing could weaken them. And... it was rare someone came back alive.

Cool air blasted over her as their troop shoved open a wooden side door to the fortress wall. It was well hidden behind shrubs and trees, and not even Emerie had known of its existence.

Figured we wouldn't be waltzing out the front gate. Which was where the army could be heard fighting.

Her gaze lifted to the waning moon shedding a streak of light through the trees, allowing a curtain of moonbeam to touch the ground. The stars were bright, distant, and sparkling, and slowly fading as rain clouds continued to thicken. Any moment now, and the last remaining gap would shut, shoving them all into foreboding darkness.

A beastly roar vibrated her bones. She swallowed thickly, before taking in a calming breath through her nose – not that it helped much against her panting.

She tried to switch off her heart and emotions, putting her training to use.

There are plenty of foot soldiers. She'd been informed that they were a distraction for her team. *Their fear will mask mine.* Her own wasn't strong, but it was present, radiating a tightness in her chest.

A handful of screams pierced the air.

Demon or Duskwalker, I have to do my duty.

The leading member of her team clenched their gloved fist near their head to halt them, before signalling to approach the edge of the tree line slowly. When the area opened up before her very eyes, mainly an expanse of dirt leading to the fortress gates, bile rose in her throat.

A line of Demonslayer foot soldiers were frozen, except for the odd one or two that ran to their very quick deaths.

The Duskwalker stood on the other side of the clearing. The moonlight coming off the grey clouds and the discarded torches that lay about was just enough to highlight its horrifying features to her.

Standing on all fours like an animal, black, oil-slick scales almost covered its entire body from neck to the tip of its long and tapered tail. She shuddered at the sharp, protruding spine bones that trailed all the way down that length – the shape of its vertebrae inhuman. More bones covered its body, almost all of them visible, including its hands, forearms, rib bones, and legs.

A small amount of fur ran down the back of its neck and shoulders, but the lizard spikes that jutted out from its body, down its back, legs, and arms, looked hard and frightful. One stray knock of a limb could see a human be severely injured on those spikes.

Even compared to Demons, she'd never seen anything more monstrous. Its raven skull and short, upward-jutting goat horns made it appear like a corvid devil set to feast on death.

Raindrops fell faster, splashing into blood puddles and creating little ominous ripples. Mangled, broken bodies with missing limbs lay discarded all across the area. There were at least a dozen of them, if not more. Many were headless, as though the monster had decided the quickest course of action was to decapitate.

Currently, it fought while hunkered over a corpse it was almost finished eating. Anytime a guildmember ran forward with either a spear or sword raised, they wouldn't last more than a few breaths. With a swipe of black claws, or a downward smashing fist, it obliterated the attacking human.

Then the Duskwalker would go back to its meal.

She was about to throw up her entire stomach, not just the contents, when it parted its beak and simply swallowed the limbless torso it had already picked apart. It was quick to start consuming the next closest kill.

It started by tearing off what remained of its victim's loose arm. Then the Duskwalker swallowed it whole with its bony face pointing upwards, letting gravity do most of the work.

It didn't chew – she imagined that would be impossible with its beak – but it did use it to help crush up bones for easier swallowing. And it kept eating, like its stomach was a bottomless pit that was incapable of being full.

How many people has it already eaten? she thought, her hands trembling. *Fuck.*

It ignored the arrows sailing through the air and impaling its monstrous body all over. With the number already imbedded into its back, like it was an echidna of arrows, she imagined it was accustomed to the pain by now. It would roar and then continue to devour. It looked insatiable as it ate comrade after comrade.

Emerie's face paled as she looked over the dead bodies, hoping none of them were Bryce. She darted her gaze to the line of foot soldiers who were too wary of rushing closer with the sea of bodies between them and it. *Please be there. Please be safe.*

There was a list of other people she hoped hadn't found salvation within its stomach.

It had been nearly an hour since the first bell rang, and the carnage just this one monster had produced in that short amount of time was terrifying.

A stick breaking in the trees behind her had all the hairs on her body rising. *Wren said it usually travels in a pair.* Where was the winged one she'd spoken of? Surely this one Duskwalker hadn't produced this much death on its own.

Gloved fingers snapped directly in Emerie's face, and she flinched. Her frantic gaze darted to her team.

She noted all of them had irritated squinted eyes.

"Sorry," she whispered, ducking down to be at their level. "What's your orders?"

"You're not going to fuck this up for us, are you?" Lily, the finger snapper, quietly bit at her. "I'm not interested in dying because Wren paired us with a coward."

"No," she said as she shook her head. "I was just shocked. I hadn't expected to see so many dead yet. It's barely been forty minutes since the fighting started."

"Never seen a Duskwalker before?" Connor said behind his mask, his voice easy to pick out.

"Have you?" Sahira snapped back. "Look, I was freaked out too, but as long as we all keep our resolve, there's no point in judging the newbie yet."

Newbie? She was a Master rank Demonslayer!

"At least she didn't piss her pants," Daemon said, nodding his material-covered nose to the line of foot soldiers. "I'm betting half of them are aiding us with the stench of fear and piss right now."

"This would be a good time to start," Emerie chimed in, wanting to steer the conversation back to why they were here.

"Wren said this one doesn't travel alone. We may only have a small window to catch this one before its friend shows up."

"She's right." Connor roamed his grey eyes over the trees behind her.

Lily's hard, dagger-like stare softened at Emerie, likely in appreciation of the reminder and the confirmation she wasn't planning on backing out.

"It has a tail," Lily noted, and they all turned their attention to the Duskwalker eating a new person. "We can use that against it."

"If one of us can get an enchanted rope around its beak, we might be able to rule its face out as a danger," Daemon added in.

"That won't work," Emerie said. "It'll be able to slide the rope off its beak, since it's tapered. It will also still be able to peck at us."

"We still have to shut it," Lily argued.

"Yeah, but" – Emerie pointed to its skull – "if we can thread the rope around its beak and horns together, that will at least keep it closed. Then we just have to avoid any quick strikes from its skull, horns, and beak."

"Obviously, we have to go for its legs too," Lily added.

All five of them nodded.

"Okay. We've noted the areas we need to attack. From now on, it's just whoever can get to that limb first." Sahira pulled a dagger from her hip and uncoiled her whip. "Let's get this over with. Give the signal."

Connor lowered his mask just long enough to place his thumb and middle finger to his mouth. He let out a whistle.

For a few breaths, nothing happened as they watched and waited. *They aren't attacking,* she thought with her lips flattening in worry.

After too long, Elders shoved foot soldiers forward, forcing them to attack. They skewered the cowards who wouldn't with their swords. Some continued to refuse, and the Elders killed just enough people to frighten the mass of soldiers into charging.

The moment the first brave soldier came upon the creature, Emerie and her team were moving. She didn't have time to think, only react – and she was thankful for the quiet of her thoughts amongst the chaos.

She sidestepped around soldiers and spears, occasionally ducking when a person was thrown through the air by either a strong arm or the long, thick lizard tail. She noted the vertebrae going down the flexible limb were white and protruding from its flesh.

The closer she got, the more she was able to take in its features.

Wren was right; it had a raven skull for a head, with a long, almost straight bone-coloured beak. Two short, upward-jutting goat horns were small and a dark, sandy brown. Now that she was close enough, she took note that it would be difficult to get a rope around its horns and beak, since all were tapered. And it no doubt wouldn't hold for long.

There was a small amount of short fur situated around its shoulders and back of its neck, as well as its groin and upper thighs, but it appeared to be... slowly disappearing the more it ate. The rest of it was covered in smooth black lizard scales that matched the dangerous and obviously strong length of its tail. There were small spikes going down its spine, forearms, calves, and tail.

Most of its scales had a blue, oil-slick glint to them.

Almost its entire body had been covered in protruding bones, but as the fight progressed, she *swore* she saw some of them sinking beneath its dark-grey flesh. She put that up as a trick of the eye and lack of light. There was no possible way it was... changing, right?

The foot soldiers were a perfect cover for her to dart closer, closing in on her target. There were no trees here to shield her. As much as she was against the idea of using a *person* to escape the sight of the Duskwalker, that's why they were there.

That's why Wren had sent these people to their death. They were to aid the five whip bearers, her team, into capturing this mindless, rabid beast.

However, they were also a detriment, as many were obviously afraid and had no idea what they were supposed to do.

One of her teammates used his whip to hold the

Duskwalker's tail still as he threaded the end of a rope around the thick centre of it, lodging it between a set of spikes and its vertebrae. His scream cut through the racket of the battle as he was flicked to the side by said limb and flew through the air with flailing arms.

She winced when he landed belly-first on a jutting spear. The woman holding it shrieked. She fell back with him dying on top of her and weighing her down, and her continuous scream caused the Duskwalker to silence her with a quick death.

Emerie didn't let her focus slip.

A few of the soldiers grabbed the rope around the tail to keep it in place.

Just as it raised its claws with a snarl, Emerie flung the end of her whip forward, expertly fastening the length around its wrist. A tooth-gritting groan exploded from her as she tried everything in her might not to be dragged across the ground.

It turned its crimson-coloured orbs on her.

Horrified terror struck through her.

It yanked forward, almost throwing her off her feet, but she flicked her whip to let it go. It bolted for her. Her heart threatened to explode in fright when it leapt, but another person shoved her to the side just in time.

A soldier was above her, weighing her down.

While her chest huffed wildly, their eyes remained on the Duskwalker. It had lost interest in her when someone else shoved a spear through its midsection.

The soldier above her turned their gaze down, and she almost sighed in relief. The yells, snarls, and clangs of weapons accidentally hitting each other were drowned out as she looked up into rich-brown eyes staring back at her.

She would know them anywhere. It helped he had a scar slitting his right eyebrow.

"You okay, Em?"

She nodded, thankful Bryce had come to her rescue. He got off and offered his hand out to help her to her feet.

The rain was pelting them in full force now, turning the blood-soaked ground even more slippery. Her clothing clung to her, making it difficult to twist and turn how she needed.

"How'd you know it was me?"

He shook his head, his bulging eyes frantic as they darted around the chaotic battlefield. "I didn't. I could just tell what your team is trying to do." His spear was lost somewhere, so he picked up a stray one. "I'm guessing your orders are to capture it?"

"Yeah. I need to get a rope around its face."

He nodded. "Follow me then. Let's get you in the air."

Together, they moved through the storm of people to get closer to the Duskwalker. Just as they came upon it, the monster closed its beak around the head of a soldier. They screamed inside its mouth before it closed shut and then twisted and pulled to remove their head.

"Now, Em!" Bryce yelled, holding both ends of his spear while crouching right next to its side.

She only had a few short metres to get a run up. Then she jumped onto the length of his spear and jumped again as he pulled upwards.

Emerie flipped in the air and landed on the Duskwalker's back. She ignored the shooting pain that assaulted the bottoms of her feet, her boot soles thin, as she broke multiple arrow shafts.

She didn't wait for it to notice her; she only had a small window.

Unhooking her rope from her belt, she heard Bryce's call as he threw her lost whip to her. She managed to catch it by the handle with one hand. Then she flicked it forward, and it spun around the Duskwalker's neck, giving her a makeshift rein to hold onto if he tried to buck her off.

She also threw the looped end of her rope. She wanted to get on her knees and thank the gods when it wrapped and then tightened around its closed beak. She used both the whip and the rope to keep herself to it, balancing herself on its back, as she spider-crawled her way forward.

"Pass, Em!" Bryce shouted, with his hands out.

She threw the rope to him. She doubted he wanted her whip – he wasn't very adept at using one.

The moment he had it, he slid underneath the Duskwalker,

threw the rope over its neck again, caught it once more, and threw the line back to her. All she had to do now was attach it to something.

It spun its head around a hundred and eighty degrees until it was looking down its back. She didn't know why she paused, but she couldn't help it. Its red orbs floating in its empty bony eye sockets struck her as soulless.

She'd never seen anything more terrifying.

She was snapped out of her trance when it snarled and darted its head towards her to peck. She stepped back and almost lost her footing on its spikes.

Using Emerie as a distraction, another whip bearer threaded a rope between its forelegs. The beast had too many foes to fight, and its attention kept bouncing between them all. It threw its head forward so it could untangle its legs, only to give a muffled roar, when a spear was slammed into its side.

Pulse racing, heart threatening to give out, and skin drenched in rain and sweat, she ran to its shoulders. She looped the rope around its neck to itself, knowing it wouldn't last forever but should hold it for now.

Shit! The Duskwalker managed to pry its arms free. She was nearly out of time!

"Give me the rope!" she demanded with her hand out to those trying to hold its tail in place.

They threw it, and she tied both pieces together, stopping it from being able to properly use its tail to attack.

Then she jumped off, landing on a knee and hand, before diving for the end of her whip still attached to its throat. After a few failed attempts at shaking it to get the thong to release, she called soldiers to help her pull to distract it, while the whip bearer who had tangled its front paws earlier tried to recapture them.

Realising what was happening, the Duskwalker attempted to peck the Demonslayer between its legs. It couldn't when it pulled on the rope Emerie had fixed to its tail. It shook its tail, but only the tip was free enough to swipe in short strikes.

Emerie had threaded its two most dangerous features to each other and rendered them useless. It bucked, trying to free itself, only to take away its own weight from its arms.

The person attempting to bind those limbs together finally won.

With the help of multiple people, they managed to get the Duskwalker to its belly by tripping it forward. It wriggled like a snake upon the ground to get free, but everyone pulled in opposite directions so it wouldn't get any purchase.

The third and only other remaining member of her team worked on tying its lizard-shaped legs to its own tail, trapping it completely. It snarled and growled, uselessly lunging the sharp point of its beak and flicking the free part of its tail at anyone who tried to get close.

For the most part, the Duskwalker was immobile, but they'd work on completely entrapping it so it couldn't move a muscle. She'd never been more thankful that the masked, magic-wielding humans from the temples had given them enchanted rope.

If only they were able to give them weapons that could easily kill.

Her part done, she stood off to the side, huffing wildly and watching everyone work.

She looked down at her shaking hands, her knees about to give out. *How the fuck am I not dead?*

The heavens hadn't been especially kind to her in the past. Why were they so generous as to keep her breathing after riding this creature's back like she was trying to tame a wild horse?

She was gobsmacked, but obviously relieved. She wasn't ready to die, didn't feel like she'd spilt enough Demon blood to make up for what they'd done to her, for what they'd... taken from her.

Then again, the night's still young. She blinked through the rain, water fluttering from her eyelashes, as she looked up to the looming grey clouds. She noted the muted light of the moon behind them.

Her ears tingled with alertness, overloaded by the feral noises coming from the struggling monster, who was still wriggling like a worm.

In the background of her frazzled mind, she kept waiting for the second Duskwalker to show up, to defend and rescue its kind. Any minute now, and it would burst from the trees and slice her in half with a violent set of claws.

It never did.

FIVE

Ingram knew how he found himself in his current predicament.

Well... at least why, since he didn't quite remember the rest of his battle against the Demonslayers, nor when they'd managed to bind him. His rage had been so blinding that all he remembered was he felt pain, the smell of blood, and the sounds of people fighting... and dying.

I should not have come here.

When he'd approached the closest Demonslayer stronghold to Merikh's cave, he'd done so cautiously. With his head lowered, showing a submissive stance, he'd come upon the gate.

There had been many eyes peering down at him from the wall of their stronghold. The shining moon behind the hazy clouds had highlighted the sharp glints of metal attached to wooden shafts – he didn't know the name of the tools, but they appeared to require the use of string to propel them forward.

A bell had rung loudly and annoyingly from within the keep.

I just wanted to speak with them.

Was it him bashing on the gate that incited their rage, or was it fear? He just wanted to be invited inside, like he and Aleron had watched other humans do for each other at their human huts. *Knocking,* he thought it might be called.

It mattered naught. A pointy stick had launched straight into his chest.

Startled by the suddenness of it, the pain of it, and the betrayal of it, he'd let loose a bellow. Then more rained down upon him.

He'd never gotten the chance to speak, and he remembered very little after that.

One thing he was acutely aware of was... he'd eaten a lot. And the more he'd eaten, the dizzier he got, the more energetic he became, and the harder he ruthlessly fought. The more they hurt him, the more he sought to replenish himself with their meat.

He'd been battling his fury, his confusion, his body changes, and random straying thoughts *bludgeoning* their way into his expanding mind as much as the attacking humans.

Their identical uniforms ensured he remembered no faces, and at one point, he'd begun to see them as Demons.

The Witch Owl was right. There are no friends here.

Bound and alone in a windowless stone room, he let out a whine with his sight a morose shade of blue. *Aleron...*

He wished he could move. He couldn't even turn his head to fully take in what captured him so totally in place.

Currently, he was trapped on his knees, part of his back flush against some sort of board and mechanism, with his arms stretched backwards. It was obvious he was too tall for this contraption, and his legs had been tucked underneath the board to accommodate his large frame. Chains had been threaded around the length of his biceps and forearms, and his shoulders were turned so far back that he worried any tension would dislocate one.

His legs were chained to his tail. Any attempt to move them brought pain up his spine. Even his neck and horns weren't spared, linked to each other. He hoped they hadn't damaged his horns; he was rather proud of their stout lengths.

Every attempt to get free was in vain. Although he was large and daunting in this small room, he felt undeniably helpless.

All he'd wanted was help. He'd intended no harm to the Demonslayers, and yet they hadn't even given him a chance.

Why?

Strange thoughts pressed into his mind, jumbled and heavy. He wasn't accustomed to so much internal chatter. He wasn't used to this level of humanity.

He groaned, wishing he could lay his aching head down so he could remove some of the weight. His brain felt hot and swollen within his skull.

Any time he'd gained humanity in the past, it'd been slowly. One stray and random human at a time – occasionally a second. Those humans had been shared between him and his kindred, slowing their progression.

How many humans had he eaten this night? *Why does my stomach continue to grumble?* Why wouldn't the hunger cease? Even now, he could smell the blood of the humans he'd killed beyond the walls.

The coppery, tangy scent threatened to pull him back under the swallowing waves of his bloodlust and hunger. This windowless room was just enough to keep it at bay, the smell not so strong where he was being held deep underground.

His throat was parched, despite the well of liquid trapped within his beak. He swallowed.

The wooden door in front of him creaked open, and four Demon-looking uniformed humans piled into the circular room with him.

They also brought firelit torches, which they placed in metal rings bolted to the dirt-stained grey walls. Ingram hadn't needed the light, perfectly capable of seeing without it, but he was sure it was easier for them to see his battered and helpless form.

His injuries screamed against his unusual position when he lunged – and barely achieved a centimetre of movement.

Only three of the four humans in front of him wore their black masks. Every single one of them had a silver emblem etched into the sternum of their uniform, but only the maskless one wore a blue-jewelled silver medallion.

Her unfeeling gaze inspected him like he was hate-invoking. She clasped her hands behind her back, stood tall, and flicked her long dark hair back over her shoulders with a twitch of her head.

"I know your kind can project your voices past your skulls. Will you speak?" she asked, looking down her nose at him.

His blue saddened sight flared crimson.

He snarled in answer. *If they know we Mavka can speak, then they chose to attack me on purpose.* They hadn't wanted to communicate with him, so why should he do so now?

He no longer desired their help. Actually, he wanted them all to crawl inside his maw so he could swallow them whole and take their humanity. He would steal their cunning and use that to destroy the Demon King.

They could have made a friend, but they instead made an enemy of him.

"Has it tried to talk?" she asked one of the other people in the room.

"No. Not even as we brought it to the dungeon."

Was that the name of this room?

Ingram might have tried to bargain with them as he was dragged into this dungeon, but he'd still been enraged. Much time had passed, and he'd been taken away from the scent of blood. He was calm now, although rightfully furious.

"Where is your bat-skulled companion?" the woman asked, her expression unchanging as though she felt nothing looking upon him.

He couldn't help the whimper that exploded from his chest at the reminder of his loss. To hide it, he growled and tried to snap his head forward threateningly, but was met with the tightness of his constraints.

"Why did you come here? Was your intention to destroy our fortress?"

He didn't answer.

She stepped forward and bravely cupped the underside of his beak to ensure he was looking upon her. The bridge of her nose crinkled.

"Listen here, you bird-brained fuck." He wished he could crack her head open with a single slam of his bony forehead, or perhaps even with one of his horns. Especially when she grabbed the shaft of a stick jutting from him with her free hand. "You will answer my questions."

She yanked it from him, and a yelp exploded.

The pain of it almost threw him back into mindlessness.

"Did the Demon King send you?"

His snarl was so fierce that even he thought it sounded

twisted as it bounced off the stone walls.

The Demon King is my enemy, he darkly thought. *And had your people not harmed me, I would have asked for aid to destroy him.*

"What is he planning? Why are there more Demons on the surface? Just a month ago, we lost many to a small army of them. Tell me why."

When he gave no answer, she yanked another stick from him.

"Start talking, Duskwalker. Otherwise I'll gain other answers I seek."

There was a phrase he'd overheard humans say to each other, as well as Merikh had uttered it to him and his kindred. He'd never truly understood what it meant, why someone would say it, until this very moment.

It felt perfect.

"Fuck... off," he rumbled.

Her screwed nose, like it had been broken, twitched and crinkled tighter. Then, a glint brightened her features as snide, cruel humour, when she leaned back.

"Have it your way then." She gave him her back, her hands once more behind her. "Bring me the doctor, as well as Emerie. Make sure she's aware that after her actions tonight, she's been promoted to Elder and my replacement underling."

"Are you sure you wish to bring her in for this, Wren?" a male asked.

"If she is to one day take my position, she needs to experience firsthand the extent of her duties."

"As you wish, Head Elder."

The man left, and the other two people came forward to crank two wheels he hadn't realised were behind him – the door guard eventually helping when they couldn't do it alone. The board his back was firmly against began to lift and tilt, his knees and then feet eventually coming off the ground. He was forced to lie upon it with his legs dangling off the edge from the knee down.

Wren, as the male had called her, came close enough to loom directly over his skull and peer into his red orbs. Her crooked grin caused his blood to boil; he didn't like it, didn't trust it. The scarring on her face made it appear evil.

"Let's see how one of you *ticks*, shall we?"

Emerie stared at Bryce as he lay huffing next to her.

This bout of sex wasn't particularly his fault, considering she'd been the one to instigate it. Could anyone blame her? They both could have died tonight.

She didn't know if she'd just been celebrating not fucking dying, or just the emotional high from the fight, but one thing had led to another...

So why did she still feel so frantic and hollow?

Since she was lying over the bed on her front, with her pants around her thighs, she wriggled them back up and turned to sit on the edge. She placed her face in her hands as she leant her elbows on her knees.

She needed a proper moment to digest the night. She needed a moment to breathe. There had been many other times she'd been close to death, but nothing could compare to the frightening visage of a faceless monster roaring, snapping, and eating her companions.

So many people died tonight. By just one creature. *Fuck.* What if one of her friends had died, and instead of finding out who, she'd been busy getting dicked down because she was freaking the hell out?

Guilt nipped at her chest.

No wonder the guild forbids alcohol from being consumed within their strongholds. Everyone would likely have been useless drunks by now.

Images of the battle played behind her closed eyelids, and she cringed at multiple scenes. New nightmares to be had.

"Hey, Em," Bryce groggily groaned.

"Yeah?" she asked, her voice breaking an octave.

She wasn't going to cry. She *swore* she didn't feel the tingle of tears tickling her nose and cheeks. Yet, why did water begin to fill her eyes?

He patted the bed next to her without looking. "Can you hurry up and leave already?"

She peeked at him. "Can I stay the night? I'm not sure if I want to be alone right now."

The last thing she wanted was to be by herself. She'd probably start pathetically crying in a damn ball on the floor of her room, seconds from having a panic attack. Already she could feel the constriction in her chest, like she was one rushed breath away from freaking the hell out.

With lazy lids, he lifted his head and leaned it on his bent elbow.

"You know why you can't do that." He walked the index and middle fingers of his free hand up her biceps. "You know what the other guildmembers are like. They pick on and try to break up guild couples for entertainment."

She knew that was partly true, but that was usually for new couples. Eventually they all came out of secrecy, and Emerie had been waiting for Bryce to approve it so she could tell her friends.

Gosh, she wanted to tell her friends so badly. Maybe they could help her piece her muddled thoughts together about this confusing, and sometimes one-sided relationship.

"Can I just stay a little longer then?"

He shook his head and turned to lie face down. "I'm about to pass out. Coming took the last bit of energy I had out of me."

She couldn't believe this! He was seriously kicking her out when it was obvious she wasn't okay!

"Are you seriously not concerned about the events that happened tonight?"

Bryce shrugged in answer. "Who cares? We're alive. Just another day in the guild."

"You know what..." she snapped as she stood and spun to him. "Sometimes I'm this fucking close with you."

She pinched her fingers together, leaving a sliver of a gap to show how short her patience with him was getting.

"Close to what?" He tilted his head to the side, inspecting her stance, before he chuckled. "Leaving me? *Pfft*, as if. You and I both know you won't do that since you're in love with me. So why don't we just stop this fight before you say something you regret? I can only put up with so much womanly shit, Emerie."

Her face turned cold.

He was dead wrong about her loving him. Could she have loved him if he wasn't a dick to her at times? Absolutely. She *wanted* to love him, she wanted him to give her a chance to let that feeling grow, but he kept metaphorically punching her in the heart.

If he kept going, he'd lose her.

Actually, considering he made it out to sound like she was some love-sick puppy, who was too scared to leave him, and he didn't even have the decency to console her after tonight... she was done.

She wasn't a doormat, and she sure as shit wasn't the kind of woman to be beaten down by a guy like him.

"You know what, Bryce? We're over. I can't do this anymore with you."

That made him sit right up, his eyes flinging open wide. "The fuck? Are you seriously trying to break up with me?"

"Trying implies I was unsuccessful."

Bryce stood after Emerie picked up her sword, attached it to her hips, and walked towards the door. "Wait. Stop. Let's talk about this, Em."

Oh? So now he wanted to talk with her? As a last effort?

"Okay fine, stay the damn night." He pulled her into a forced hug, and her skin immediately crawled.

"Don't touch me," she bit out, shoving him off. "If you can't even give me comfort when I need you the most, then you're a real piece of shit as a partner."

He scratched at the side of his unruly hair, that never seemed to stay in place no matter how much he tried to stroke it back. "It's not like you tried to comfort me either," he grumbled, just as she placed her hand on the doorknob to leave.

Her eyes grew so wide she thought they'd fall from her face. She spun around and gripped the collar of his shirt so fast that he stumbled in shock.

"Don't you dare try to manipulate me into feeling like shit. I have been there for you every time you have asked me to, and it was only ever to get your fucking dick wet." Then she laughed as she let him go as cold realisation settled in. "That's it. That's all you've ever wanted, isn't it? You don't care about me at all, so why should I continue to care for a selfish little boy? No wonder you can't get promoted."

His bottom lip pouted slightly under the tension of his mouth flattening in anger. "I'm not a fucking boy – I'm a man. One that's treated you better than anyone else."

"You're actually a little bitch. I was just trying to be nice."

His mouth dropped open, and Emerie took that as her chance to leave.

"I saved your life tonight, you ungrateful bitch!" She rolled her eyes as she shut the door behind her. While she was walking away, he opened the door to yell, "You better fucking tell Wren I helped you bring that monster down like you promised."

Emerie gave him the middle finger as she stormed down the hallway. A few people cracked open the doors to their dorm rooms, but she just raised her chin. She hoped her blush wasn't showing; she hated it when it made the white scarring on her face redden.

At least her anger was keeping all the hurt of this, and her earlier panic, at bay.

Can this night get any worse?

Emerie was about to, in fact, learn that this night could get worse... *much* worse.

She didn't even make it to her own dorm before she was ushered by an Elder to Wren. Along the way, she was given a new uniform top, one with a silver insignia on it, as they informed her she had just ranked up.

There was no fanfare, no celebration.

She barely had a moment to register it before she was told to go down an empty hallway and change her shirt right there and then. Out in the open. She did it, but she would have preferred complete privacy, hating it when anyone looked at the scars marring her torso.

Her escort had given her his back, but a wandering guildmember could have stumbled upon her. All she could think was, *I just wanted to go to bed.*

Emerie was exhausted. Her head, heart, and body ached, and she wanted nothing more than to collapse onto her bed and pass out.

Once she was fully dressed, including her face coverings, she was escorted down the mountain fortress. Her brows deeply furrowed in uncertainty when she was taken to the dungeon just below ground level.

She wasn't told why she was being brought here, only that Wren had ordered it.

When she saw the Duskwalker strapped to the table, surrounded by Wren, two other Elders, and one of the guild doctors, she hesitated to enter. She was gently pushed inside, despite her frozen feet.

She hadn't trusted the device he currently lay upon. Although it appeared like a table, it was actually a device that could be pivoted so it could turn upright. She'd seen it before, although only in passing when they'd first given her a tour of Zagros Fortress.

Attached to a metal board was a triangular frame that was anchored to a rotating gear. Those gears locked into place to hold the table position, but could be released so the imprisoned subject could be pivoted into a standing position, or in the case of the gigantic Duskwalker, a kneeling one. That secondary gear was then attached to another triangular frame that had been bolted to the ground by pins for security.

A wheel crank on both sides controlled the positions, and required the strength of multiple people to turn it, depending on the weight of the subject strapped to it.

It had been designed for medium-sized Demons. The reason for its creation had been unknown to Emerie – until now.

Horror befell her features, hidden behind her mask, when they began to cut the Duskwalker open... while it was *alive*. While it screamed, roared, and jangled its chains to escape.

The doctor was eventually able to examine inside its cracked-open chest cavity after using bolt cutters, hammers, and other heavy tools to get into it. It was bloody, disgusting, and felt so wrong, so immoral, that bile rose in her throat.

Even her eyes watered in sympathy for the Duskwalker,

threatening to spill every time he yelped, and even more so when he whimpered.

"Why are you doing this while it's alive?" Emerie finally blurted in outrage. "The least you could have done was give it the mercy of death before you began playing with its damn insides!"

Wren cast her a knowing look, one that said she'd predicted Emerie would react this way. "Because they don't die. I thought that would have been made obvious to you after tonight's events."

"This..." Her hand fisted at her side. "This is wrong. We shouldn't be doing this."

She wished she had known this was why Wren brought her here. It would have given her the opportunity to deny the order. And she would have. Down to the pit of her soul, she would have denied it – no matter the repercussions.

"I must admit, it is easier to watch this when it's the corpse of a Demon." Then Wren faced her, giving Emerie all her attention. "However, this is something that needs to be done. Just like the Demons we've been forced to cut open, we need to know how they are made, why they are so much stronger than us. We need to learn how to kill them. I refuse to not seek answers when they lie before me."

Emerie's eyes tightly clenched shut at a particularly hollowing sound that came from the Duskwalker being tortured. The squelching of blood and muscle between fingers made her vision split in two from disgust.

Her voice was weakening, growing croaked and hoarse. "I still can't get past how cruel this is."

"Do you know how many Demons have wanted inside our keeps, using tricks, asking for false mercy, only to turn on the very humans that let them inside? None of these monsters deserve a shred of your pity." Wren then stepped closer with a commanding gait, and lifted her chin superiorly when she was barely a foot away. "I have decided that I will begin training you to take over my position when I die, or when I am too old to be of use anymore. This is the start of that training."

"Why me?" Emerie asked. "There are other members who

would be far better at it. Those that have perfected all weaponry and trades."

"Because it's not a sword that leads, but a mind. You are smart and have saved members of your teams time and time again by using unorthodox methods. This choice wasn't made lightly."

With her eyes drifting over to the poor creature, Emerie confidently stated, "If this is the cost of obtaining your position, then I sincerely don't want it."

Wren sighed and shook her head. "You will learn to be desensitized to it, as I was. I'll forgive any transgressions for now."

Emerie wished she hadn't been looking at the Duskwalker when they pulled its still beating and attached purple heart from his chest. It looked mushy and weird, with black veins.

She pulled down her mask, spun to the furthest wall right next to the door, and proceeded to violently vomit. *I can't.* Emerie didn't have a weak stomach. She wasn't usually squeamish or queasy from staring at the insides of another creature.

If she could have crawled out of her skin and disintegrated, it would have happened the moment the Duskwalker let out a harrowing squeal.

"Well, it's definitely a male."

Emerie heaved again, harder than before, having to place her hand against the wall to steady herself. Acidic liquid splattered against the ground between her boots.

This is disgusting. Nothing deserves this torture. I don't care what it is... it – he – doesn't deserve this. It doesn't matter what he's done, who he's eaten. It's wrong.

"Stop," Emerie whispered, her legs wobbling like she was going to pass out. "Stop torturing him."

When they didn't, a blaze lit up within her. She bolted forward to grab the arm of the doctor to stop him. She never made it there.

Two Elders grabbed her and forced her back. She attempted to claw and kick forward, her feet scraping and sliding against the ground as she fought.

"I said fucking stop!"

"Hold her there," Wren commanded, before she came over to grasp Emerie's jaw and keep her gaze steady on her older reflection. "You are just like me. From your face, to your abilities, to you wanting to save this horrible creature." She yanked Emerie's face forward with her nose crinkled in determination. "And just like me, you will be better for witnessing this – just as I was once forced to."

For the first time since she'd joined the guild, Emerie no longer cared to follow the rules. She didn't want to do as she was told, to stand there quietly and turn a blind eye to what was happening around her.

"I hope to the gods that a Demon eats me if I turn out like you."

Wren chuckled and released her face so she could playfully tap her cheek. "Atta girl. That resolve will be the reason people will blindly follow you."

"Why don't you choose someone who actually wants to take over your position?" Emerie bit through gritted teeth, her eyes dark and narrowed.

"Because those that don't crave a seat of power are often the ones most suited for it." Then Wren turned back to witnessing the doctor pull out other... inhuman parts of the Duskwalker. "Keep her awake. It's going to be a long night."

It had already been far too long.

SIX

Against her will, Emerie was shoved back into the Duskwalker's holding cell the following night.

She'd barely slept a wink.

The sun had been breaking through the clouds when she was finally pulled from this dungeon the first time and locked inside a bedroom. It wasn't her own, and it wasn't even near the normal sleeping dorms. She was being kept separated from the rest of the guild.

Sleep had eluded her.

Then she had been taken to Wren, who explained her new tasks, what was to be expected of her, and how things were going to operate for Emerie from now on.

Anytime she spoke out against it, Wren silenced her – or just outright ignored her outrage.

Apparently, she'd been put in Emerie's exact same position once, but with a Demon they wanted to dissect while it was alive. That was many years ago, and her Head Elder at the time had seen potential in her, just like Wren did in Emeric.

Honestly, it was like the crazy bitch wanted someone to suffer the pain she had. Just because they wore the same facial scar, just because they were similar people, didn't mean they were the *same* person. People in the same environment with the same life experiences often became very different.

Emerie knew she could never become someone like Wren. It just wasn't in her to order something so despicable as torture.

She hated Demons, despised them, but not even she would do something so horrible to one of them. No matter how much she tried to explain this, Wren refused to listen.

The Head Elder was adamant about her choice, and that she would break Emerie of her fears and disgust. Being forced into this dungeon again as a cleaning maid was apparently just the beginning.

What God did I piss off to be subjected to this nightmare?

Her grip tightened on the mop and bucket that had been shoved into her hands. She shuddered as she took in the Duskwalker.

His scales, covered in dried purple blood, glistened in the low firelight. His tail was trapped to his ankles, but the base of it was visible through his parted knees. He looked helpless with the rope and chains binding almost every moving part of his body, but the lizard spikes that covered him allowed him to keep his fierceness.

The protruding white bones that covered most of his body were stark against his black, oil-slick scales and dark-grey skin. His raven skull, with empty eye sockets filled with white orbs, was hard to look upon.

She wished his natural features were the most harrowing part of him, but they weren't what caused her to grip her mop and bucket handles harder.

They hadn't even bothered to close his chest cavity, not that she thought it would have been possible. His wound looked gnarly, and she had to immediately turn her gaze away in shame.

It was too painful to look at him. She wished she couldn't hear him wheezing in agony. He didn't even have the strength to growl at her, instead kneeling limply with his arms chained behind him.

Wren probably thought it would help to desensitize her to all the blood, gore, and his whimpers, but it only made her stomach twist and her heart ache for him.

Tears welled in her eyes for him, for herself, but she made sure his white orbs couldn't see them. *What right do I have to cry? I'm not the one suffering.*

Since they'd informed her she wouldn't be permitted to leave until every inch of this room was spotless, she began cleaning. She desperately wanted out.

She avoided getting close to him for as long as possible, starting with the edges of the room. However, the bulk of blood and questionable lumps were most present around his knees.

He weakly growled when she came too close. *How is he still alive, let alone... conscious?*

When something caught on the fibres of her mop, and she knew she had to fish it out to clean properly, she threatened to make a new bile puddle. She'd already cleaned the first. She backed up while shaking her head, dropping the mop to the stone ground with a clatter.

Falling against the wall, she pulled her mask down and her hood back, needing unfiltered air. The coppery stench twisted her stomach with nausea, but she couldn't take the way her clothing was suffocating her.

Considering he wasn't reacting to her, she knew it must not be fear she was feeling. How could she fear him when he looked so pitiful?

"Shit," she whispered, choosing to look up at the ceiling. "Shit, shit, *shit.* I can't do this." Over the course of the last day, those four words were becoming her mantra. She couldn't recount how many times she'd either thought or said them, or how many times she persevered through them. "I signed up to kill Demons, not be a spectator to a Duskwalker's torture. It's not fair."

He let out a bubbling huff. She bet he was thinking she didn't have the right to say that, considering his state.

She wanted to apologise to him, but the weight of anything she said would be pointless. Nothing she did – no apology – would ever make up for this.

Instead, the silence between them was heavy, and after what could only be an hour of her sitting there, her eyes grew unfocussed. Her face turned cold in lethargy, her mind fuzzy with exhaustion. She needed to get up. Any second longer and she would...

"Hey! Get back to work," someone shouted as they bashed on the door.

Emerie jolted from her sleep, finding herself partially bent over on her side. Her eyes squinted with grogginess, even more tired than before.

The peephole thudded shut.

She straightened up in her seated position and rubbed at her face. *How long was I asleep for?* Her gaze found the Duskwalker. His orbs were still a stark white, and she was unsure if they were staring upon her or not.

It was a little creepy to think he'd been watching her sleep. Had he been kneeling there, planning every way to torture her in return for what he'd suffered?

The little hairs on her body stood on end at the idea of someone wishing that upon her while she vulnerably slept before them. She wanted out of this dungeon even more. She didn't want this Duskwalker to remember her face, her scent, her voice.

If only she could turn invisible and disappear.

She crawled over to her discarded mop and bucket and stood.

"Listen," she croaked out, holding the mop handle with both hands. His skull rattled as he jerked it. "I don't want to be here, just as much as I'm sure you don't want me here." His orbs flared red before quickly dulling and returning to white. "But I have to clean this room. I-I have to approach you, but I'll try not to hurt you, okay?"

His orbs didn't change, nor did he move to indicate that he heard or even understood her.

Emerie cautiously stepped closer. When he didn't do anything, she grew bolder as she swiped the mop against the ground to clean up his blood. To keep to her promise, she moved slowly to avoid knocking into his gaping torso.

She tried not to take in his raven skull, or the fact that purple blood had tracked from his nose and ear holes, and through the seam of his beak.

He's a statue. I'm just going to pretend he's a really delicate statue. He wasn't alive, or letting out shallow, shuddering breaths. No, not at all.

The worst of the gory puddle was between his knees, and it brought her far too close for comfort. He jerked his entire body forward as hard as he could.

Emerie let out a squeal of surprise, before quickly covering her mouth. Startled, she backed up in case she was producing a strong fear scent, assuming he reacted to it like Demons did.

Like he'd been waiting for her to be just beyond his beak, despite his wounds and how much he would have known it would hurt, he'd purposefully tried to scare her.

The chuckle behind the door was joined by the Duskwalker's wheezy snicker.

"You are lucky I am chained to this room," he grated, causing her eyes to widen. He spoke! With his beak tied shut, he fucking talked! *"And that my nose is too blocked to fully take in your delectable scent of fear."*

Great, he was going out of his way to be a *dick*.

She put space between them, her hand still covering her mouth. She shoved the mop head into the bucket and slid it back with her.

She tapped her knuckles against the door. "I need to change the water."

The guard opened the door and took both her cleaning tools. She'd been hoping he would let her out so she could have a moment to collect herself. *Damn!*

Many minutes later, the guard returned with a fresh bucket and a clean-ish mop. It was still stained with the Duskwalker's blood, but it at least looked wrung out.

Her eyes darted to the blood between his knees and around them, since she hadn't cleaned there yet either. Her eyes crinkled in emotional anguish. She didn't want to approach him again.

Should she just cry insanity to get out of this? The fact she was wearing a Demonslayer outfit was a disgrace, but she'd been dealing with far too much shit over the last twenty-four hours that she was just waiting to break.

However... as weird as it was, the fact he'd tried to freak her out had put her back up. She didn't like it, not when she may be the only person in this whole fortress that felt sympathy for him. Call it petty, but it eased some of her distress.

He's bound, Emerie. Get your shit together. What's he going to do? Jump out of his chains and go 'boo'?

With a renewed resolve to escape this room, she stormed forward. She tried to quickly clean around him so she could leave. His knees were mostly unscathed, which she was thankful for as she shoved the mop head at them.

She ignored his threatening sounds, drowning them out with her panted breaths.

Then her eyes grew wide once more when black, glittering dust started to flutter around him. She didn't know what was going on, but when she tried to clean it away, nothing happened. The flurry of it grew up his limbs.

She flinched as arrows clattered to the ground, as though they were being pushed out of his body. The process was slow, but he shuddered and groaned at the loss of each one.

"H-hey!" she called out while backing up, her startled eyes glued to him as she twisted her face towards the door. When her back slammed against it, she bashed at it with the bottom of her fist. "Something weird is happening."

Yeah, something weird, and she didn't know if it was dangerous or not! Could the Duskwalker use magic? If so, what if he blew her up or something?!

Then again, he would have done something like that by now to escape if he could.

The guard opened the peephole long enough to observe, rasping, "holy *shit*," before shutting it.

Just before the last of the sharp, pointy sticks with feathers attached to their ends popped out of him, that female strutted in with two others following.

Like his current unwanted companion in his holding space, she was the only other person not wearing a mask and hood over her face. The guard from earlier, as well as the other two newcomers, wore their uniforms from head to toe.

He could only make out their eyes.

He noted the two females looked similar, besides a few

differences like their skin tone and hair, and the newcomer had more wrinkles on her face. She also had a cold, unfeeling gaze, whereas the other female had eclipses of many emotions – many of which she'd turned to him, as well as others she'd tried to hide.

Wren, as he'd learned their leader was called, raised a brow when another stick clattered against the ground. He breathed a small sigh of relief.

"He's shedding the arrows," she commented, before her gaze drifted over his bound form. "So, this is how they heal. It was roughly this time last night that he approached the fortress. Considering he's remained wounded the entire time, I was wondering how they could survive an attack and emerge unscathed weeks later."

"What of his chest?" one of the faceless males asked.

Ingram wondered if they knew their uniforms made them appear like Demons. He wondered if it was on purpose.

Wren cast the male a bored glance. "That came later." Then she brought her blue eyes back to him. "Didn't it, Duskwalker?"

He gave her a light growl, unable to muster a proper one.

Had he not been missing his entire heart, he might have attempted a better threat. He hadn't expected them to remove it, or for it to disintegrate like black sand in the doctor's palm right before his very orbs. They hadn't been able to keep it, which he was pleased with – despite the pain that had brought.

He did vaguely remember them saying that the *arteries* and *veins* it had been attached to had moved and reattached somewhere else. He figured that's why blood was still coursing through his body, flowing like a river; just not pumping. He'd lost every ounce of energy, and instead was pushing blood around like a continuous stream to keep him alive.

Once the last *arrow* slipped from him, Wren's interest in him died. She turned to his unwanted companion.

"Looks as though you have more to clean." Then she sighed, while shaking her head. "You look like shit. The fact you haven't finished cleaning just a few small puddles of blood and haven't gone to bed is beyond disappointing."

Just... a few *small* puddles of blood?

His nose holes may be clogged, but even he had been able to smell the stench of his own fur, scales, and blood that had been around his knees. It had not been small, by any means.

Somehow, his unwanted companion suddenly looked even more drained, the scarring on her face paling further. He was surprised she'd fallen asleep earlier, considering he'd been right there, but somehow... watching her jugular pulsating had been a soothing distraction for him.

He'd watched it, imagining all the ways he could escape his confines so he could pull it from her. She wouldn't have even woken up to realise she'd died.

"Hurry up," Wren bit at the tired female. "You have a big day tomorrow, and I expect you at my station just after sunrise." She turned to someone who had been scribbling on parchment. "You. Stay here as well and note all his changes."

After that, his unwanted companion and the scribbler were left alone with him.

The scribbler did nothing except move to lean against the wall, waiting and watching.

The female without a face covering was quick to pick up the arrows and place them near the door, probably to remove later. She'd braved coming close to him, and him jerking forward hadn't frightened her this time.

She was quick to adjust to his antics.

He didn't like her near him.

Her proximity meant he was able to somewhat smell her, and he knew her scent had been in this room when they'd cracked him open. She'd watched, had been a part of the agony he'd undergone.

There was also the smell of... something else on her.

It repulsed him, despite not knowing what it was. It obviously didn't belong to her feminine scent, was far too masculine, and gave him the impression of *mine* that belonged to another. She was under someone's gaze, under someone's protection, and they'd made that known by marking her.

Any time she accidentally touched him, that scent and his recent experiences caused his skin to flare with revulsion.

She wasn't to be trusted.

Her gaze drifted to his raven skull as she swished her mop near his right knee. She nudged against it in an attempt to clean where he'd been kneeling.

Despite the obvious difference in their height, currently they were almost face to face. He watched her, his sharp and hyper-clear sight picking up on her tiny pores, the translucent drop of sweat on her brow, and the softness of her small lips as she tightened and relaxed them.

He'd thought her eyes were the same as Wren's, but they actually appeared icier in their blue, like the top of a frozen lake.

They were an odd contrast to her wavy hair, which appeared as though it was warm like the sun, streaked with bright orange and dark red. He was sure he'd seen many dusks and dawns cast such colours across the sky and clouds.

Her face was dirty though, since she had dark spots all over it. She needed a bath more than he did, and that was saying a lot coming from a Mavka whose own blood was clumping against his body.

His sight followed her as she picked up her bucket and shoved the arrows into it. Then she bashed on the door to be freed, stating she was done.

"The Duskwalker is still dirty." The guard chuckled.

"If Wren thinks I'm going to wash him while his chest is open like that, tell her I'll take a knife to my throat. She also didn't tell me to. Now move."

The male tsked behind his mask. "Fine."

Then she was gone, leaving him alone with the scribbler.

She never got to see his chest closing up an hour later, nor how he writhed to free himself now that his strength had fully returned.

Ingram did wonder if she heard his bellowing and restrengthened roars reverberating through this wretched stronghold.

He hoped it gave them all nightmares for the rest of their days, which he intended to make short once he was freed from his bonds.

SEVEN

Ingram watched his unwanted companion as she used her mop to clean the edges of the room, only daring to come closer when she had to.

More of his blood had puddled around his knees from when they'd rotated him from lying on his back to kneeling once more.

The day after her last visit, they'd brought the doctor back, along with the teasing scents of dawn and fresh air clinging to their clothing. Since they couldn't remove his organs without them disappearing, they'd decided the best course of action was to play with them while they were still attached.

He'd cursed them more the second time. He'd spent the entire course of their hands-on exploration telling them how he was going to kill them, eat them, take out their insides, and let them watch as he played with them instead.

He'd been left alone after that.

Ingram had been annoyed they hadn't sent this female to him, so he could distract himself while he sat in suffering.

Only after his torso had healed the next day, was she brought inside – once more wielding a mop and bucket. He only knew what they were called, as she'd asked for them to be cleaned before she continued.

He was learning much from them: new words and tools, as well as what parts of his body were called.

Her name was Emerie. He had no idea if it meant anything,

like his name did.

She is no longer wary about looking at me, he thought, despite knowing she still chose not to for whatever reason.

At least her gaze wasn't filled with... sympathy this time. *Wait, that may not be true.* He still noted crinkles of it in her eyes, but it wasn't as intense as the first time she was put in this room to clean it.

Perhaps it was because he was no longer visibly wounded.

He was healed, he was strong, and he fought to free himself as he did every moment he was trapped. If it weren't for the coiling rope over every limb, including his waist and shoulders, he was sure he could have ripped a limb from himself so he could escape.

Ingram would have removed his own head if given the chance, so that he could heal his complete body later. He would have been free then, instead of... this.

Emerie looked more rested than the last time he'd seen her, but her features often tightened and grew exhausted before she regained some kind of will. Like when she slapped the mop head right at the puddle around his knees.

He let out a deep, rumbling growl.

"Oh, quiet you," she bit out, her blue eyes darting from her task to his skull. "Growl and snarl, and have a tantrum all you like, but I *have* to do this."

Ingram did, in fact, quieten. He tried to tilt his head, his sight threatening to shift dark yellow. Instead, it remained crimson, and he was beginning to forget what the purple colour of his usual sight looked like.

He hadn't seen it in days, instead only seeing the red of his anger, the blue of his sadness, and the white of his fear and pain.

"Why even bother cleaning the ground when I will only dirty it later?" he asked with a snarl, his voice holding a treble bass like usual. *"It is pointless."*

She flinched, likely unsure as to why he'd even spoken to her. Other than his incoherent rage gargles from when they cut him open, the only person he'd willingly spoken to was her.

This was only the second time.

But Ingram wanted to know what the point of all of this was.

Why bother cleaning at all? Let there be a sea of his blood on the floor. He wanted it to stick to the bottom of their shoes, so they could remember him wherever they went, remember what they'd done to him. And, when he finally came for them, *why* he was rending them in two.

Her pale-pink lips hardened into a thin line before she released them. She eventually sighed. "It's not like I want to do this," she whispered. "I don't want any part of this."

"And yet here you are, aiding it," he answered, aiming to unnerve her. He jerked forward so he could jostle his chains – wishing they would break so he could fall upon her. Other than a twitch on her cheek, she made no other reaction. *"You watch, just as the others watch."*

She had been present the day before, standing there while they pressed their fingers into him the second time. He had not seen her face, but her scent had been there. At least, that was before his nose had clogged with his own blood that had poured from every orifice in his skull!

"I don't want to," she grumbled, turning her face away from him as she cleaned her mop in the bucket so she could continue. "You probably won't believe me, but I'm against what they're doing to you. It's wrong. No creature deserves this."

She is lying. She had to be lying.

She had a choice to be in this room with him, to follow their orders, to be a part of this terrible human army. She had chosen to be here, and therefore, had chosen to allow this to happen to him.

All these humans had chosen to be despicable, vile creatures.

They have no right to call me a monster. And he was tired of them calling him that.

"If that were true," he started quietly, his tone as dark as possible, *"then you would have freed me. You would not have allowed it to happen again."*

Her head dipped, and her shoulders slumped.

"I would have tried to, if I knew it would be successful." She looked upon him once more, this time with a hardness in her icy eyes. "But it won't be. Removing your chains and rope would be easy enough, but you would only find yourself right back where you are. The hallways are small, and you don't know the way out. They'll find a new way to trap you."

"Do you think I would let myself be caught a second time?" He asked this, but he understood the reality more than she did.

She was likely right.

If they harmed him, they could incite him into a mindless rage once more. Then he would hunt these hallways until he slaughtered everyone in search of their meat. That, or he would hurt someone as he fled, and the delicious scent of blood would churn his gut into a thoughtless, ravaging hunger.

Still, he would have preferred the opportunity to *try*. He would have liked to kill as many as he could before they chained him to this room a second time. Maybe his claws would find that other female with the blue eyes and scarring – he'd be undeniably pleased about that.

Wren's eyes were cold. Not in the way Emerie's were. They were a dark blue, like the ocean he'd seen from afar. However, it was the way they looked upon him: like he was small, insignificant, and disgusting.

Emerie's eyes were a cold colour, but even he noted the warmth in her gaze – even when she turned them towards him.

Perhaps that was the only reason he was choosing to speak with her.

With a whisper, she added, "You'll probably kill the only person who actually cares for your pain if I let you go. Then you'd find someone else mopping up your blood, someone who may go out of their way to deepen your suffering."

Once more, he wished he could tilt his head.

Deepen my suffering? His sight found the length of her cleaning tool before he raked it over her tightly clothed form.

It is true that she has never tried to hurt me.

Unlike some of the guards who had come in here, chuckling as they poked and prodded his injured form. They'd uttered dares to each other, seeing who would spook first.

This female had never gone out of her way to callously harm him.

He pondered this as she cleaned to the best of her ability. He still didn't trust her, but a strange part of him grew anxious when she went to the door to leave.

She was entertainment. She was a hope he could convince her to let him free.

I don't want to be alone.

When she was here, he didn't have to remember what they'd done to him, *were* doing to him. He didn't have to wallow in his own self-pity or grieve in the loss of his kindred.

Ingram thought of Aleron every second he was alone in this room, wishing he had not abandoned him in this world. That he had not died and made Ingram decide on this foolish, idiotic mistake.

Had Aleron still been alive, they would have been wandering the forest together. He would have been... undeniably happy.

Instead, his mind was a constant swirl of emotional anguish – and he was starting to enjoy the physical pain because it distracted him from his grief.

No, I hate it. I do not like the pain, he reminded himself. He just liked that it emptied his mind because he couldn't focus his thoughts. Instead of his heart hurting for Aleron, it hurt because they'd taken a blade to it.

It was wrong. He knew it was wrong.

He feared the longer he remained here, the more he'd grow attached to such a morbid desire. *I want out.*

He looked at the back of the female as she knocked on the door. The urge to ask her to stay gnawed at him, but it was his own pride and his dislike of her that silenced him.

The tension that had tightened every muscle in his body eased when she only asked for the water to be changed. She also asked for a new tool – a rag.

Once she had them, she discarded the mop and instead ducked her cloth into the bucket of clean water. She hesitantly approached him with both.

She lifted the cloth towards his abdomen. "Can... can I wash you? I'm sure it'll feel better to be clean."

Ingram tried to duck away but was held firm. ***"Don't touch me,"*** he snapped.

Human hands of late had not been kind to him; he didn't want another set on him. She also still smelt of that masculine, possessive scent, and although it had lessened in its intensity over the past day, it was still present. The idea of her touching him when she wore it made his skin itch.

She flinched, the loudness of his voice, and the depth of it giving her pause. "I promise I won't hurt you."

Like she thought that was all that bothered him, she tentatively wiped down his bare chest with a soft stroke. She kept the rest of her body away, and it allowed him to view her past his beak, although not very well.

Ingram tensed with a threat bubbling in his throat.

Her next words, spoken so quietly and sincerely, silenced him. "I'm sorry."

His red orbs finally gave in and turned dark yellow in curiosity. *She is apologising?* He didn't know why a human, a Demonslayer, would want to.

Her strokes were gentle against him as she continued. "I know it probably means very little, but I am sorry this is happening to you. Had I known they would do this to you, I wouldn't have..."

Her long orange eyelashes moistened, as the spike of salt teased his nose holes. She cleared her throat and leant forward – past his beak, where he could no longer see her.

"I'm sorry they're dissecting you while you're alive. I can't even begin to imagine how it feels, but my torso burns for you, like I'm experiencing a small thread of it with you."

I do not understand her.

She was cleaning him with care – even he could tell this. Her words sounded sincere, her voice soft. He couldn't see her face, but the cold, wet cloth dabbing at him was oddly pleasant. Water trickled down his torso, cleansing him further.

He wished she wasn't showing him this kindness; he found it confusing. It ached his heart, while soothing his muscles so they'd loosen. He'd rather she be like everyone else, hateful and humour-filled at his pain.

It would be easier to bear.

"Why are you doing this?" he asked quietly, his orbs morphing to blue – before the bottoms of them broke. Floating blue liquid hovered around his skull, glittering as it disappeared.

"Someone has to clean you eventually. I doubt you'd be susceptible to infection since you heal, but I always feel better when I'm clean." Her singular snorting laugh lacked any humour. "Isn't this nicer than someone else tossing water on you?"

A saddened breath shuddered out of him.

"No. I mean, why are you saying this?" When she leaned back to face him, he could only just see her past the edge of his beak. *"You humans call me a monster, and yet your kind have been vile to me. Why would you show any kindness towards me?"*

Her hair shone in the dim firelight as she wrung her cloth out over the ground – it seemed she was trying not to dirty the water she was going to wash him with – before wetting it once more.

"What's happening here... I didn't sign up for this. I didn't join the Demonslayer guild to torture Duskwalkers. I came here because I wanted to kill Demons, to get back at them for taking everything I cared about away from me. But even then..." Once more, she was gone from view as she wiped the scales covering his pelvis and thighs. "I wouldn't even wish this upon a Demon."

Funny that. Ingram, despite everything he'd suffered, would gladly do this to a Demon if it would bring back Aleron. He just didn't want it done to him, especially when, in his mind, he hadn't done anything to deserve it.

What were a few human meals when he knew they killed each other? He and Aleron had been drawn to such battles between humans when their blood called them closer. How could they justify doing something like this to him for whatever vengeance they believed, when they were no better to each other?

"How..." he softly muttered, feeling his anger and hatred towards her lessening. *"How do I make them stop? How do I make them free me?"*

As much as he had gained a substantial amount of humanity, it was nowhere near enough. Half his mind and thoughts were still grainy and empty. Although he could understand some things, he didn't have the intelligence to think his way out of this.

His body and instincts had always been his tool; he'd never truly needed his mind before.

"They won't," she answered definitively. "They won't let you go, and they won't stop doing this until they know everything about your kind and how to kill you. No guild sector has ever captured a Duskwalker before, so you're currently the most valued asset we've ever had."

*"I will **never** reveal how to kill my kind, and they will not find that answer inside me."* His tone held the deep underline of a threat.

"So, your kind *can* die..." she mumbled, slowly standing so she could wipe his shoulders and neck.

His head twitched, causing a rattle to come from him. Then, his orbs flared dark crimson. *"If you think your kindness will be enough for me to give you the answer of how to kill me, you are wrong."*

He'd never considered such a tactic before, but was this a new way to get information out of him? Wren had asked him many questions, of which he'd given her silence in return. Were they using this female as a way to lure his secrets out of him?

"I wasn't asking you," she stated firmly. "But... wouldn't you prefer death over this?"

"No." He clenched his clawed hands into tight fists. *"I will not accept death. There is something I must do first."*

"I would," she quickly interjected, ringing out her cloth before wiping his arms. "I know it's not the same as what you've felt, but I have experienced pain." His reddened sight grew focused on the scarring on her face. "I have spent many weeks in agony, wishing someone would put me out of my misery. If I were in your position, I would have pleaded for death the moment they put the blade to my flesh."

"I am not so weak as to allow my enemy to kill me as I sit so helplessly."

And yet, the idea of joining Aleron in the afterworld sounded peaceful. If Ingram wasn't so determined to somehow kill the Demon King and find a way to bring his beloved kindred back, he may have allowed them to kill him.

But he wouldn't.

He wouldn't give them the satisfaction. He wouldn't be the reason they were able to destroy another of his kind. He'd rather suffer this for the rest of his life than betray the other Mavka.

"You're braver than me, then." She dared coming closer to gingerly dab her damp cloth on his face. Surprised that she would even willingly touch it, he remained still. "Are-are your eyes, or orbs, or whatever, solid? Will it hurt if I try to clean your, uh, eye holes?"

Her asking meant much, even if it was useless to do so.

"No. I cannot feel them."

She nodded, then proceeded to clean them.

I wish she did not have that marking on her. Her arms were close to his nose holes, and the scent cascading off them was pleasant. It was a mixture of flowers, sweet fruit, and dew. She almost smelt like the aftermath of rain as it wet the earth and cast a flurry of scents into the air when it dried.

It was fresh, clean, and inviting.

Breathing it in, it was the first time since he'd been captured and restrained that he grew drowsy. He was too wary of his current surroundings to actually sleep, but it at least quietened his thoughts long enough to give him a few moments of peace.

Even her wiping his skull was easing the hostility in him.

"You shouldn't have come here," she whispered, as she cleaned his forehead and horns – despite them not being caked in dried blood. "I tried to stop them, you know. I told them to stop hurting you."

His head jerked at that. *Was she the one I heard screaming?* Someone had shouted he be released from his tortures. It had been so crackly and shriek-like, that it was completely different to the current sweet voice she spoke with now.

"I... wanted help," he admitted without truly meaning to, focusing on the way she smelled and foolishly allowing it to lull him.

"Help?" she softly gasped out. "You came here for help and we..."

She backed up, robbing him of the tranquillity he'd found, so she could stare at him properly. He choked out a breath, suddenly feeling like he was suffocating as his mind grew alert once more.

"What do you want help with?"

"To kill the Demon King." When her lips tightened, but she didn't look surprised, he figured she already knew of him. *"I cannot get through his army by myself. He is hunting my kind, and I wish to stop him."*

He was giving her an answer to the question the other humans had asked him, when he had, not many moments ago, told Emerie he wouldn't.

He didn't know if it was her actual scent, the fact she'd cleaned him, their conversation, or maybe even the hope that if he revealed the truth, it would aid in his potential release. Perhaps it was even the strange emotion in her icy eyes. Something had urged him to speak, even though he didn't trust her.

Maybe he wanted to trust Emerie, to trust... someone, *anyone*.

Ingram was desperate to find a friend here.

"He came here for help," Emerie stated firmly, while watching Wren write a detailed letter with an ink quill pen.

By the special ink stamp in the top right corner, it was intended for the other head guild sectors. There were two identical ones she'd already written.

"Help with what?" Wren asked, never waving for Emerie to take a seat or do anything but stand on the other side of her desk.

Emerie had requested a meeting with her, upon which she had promptly been escorted to her office. With features tight, Emerie detailed what she'd learned from the Duskwalker in the short time she was with him.

The second time had been more bearable to look upon him, despite the evidence they'd done more unspeakable things to him. At least he hadn't still been wounded, nor had he been letting out little whines she knew... just *knew*, he'd been trying to hide from her.

She still couldn't believe she'd washed him.

She hadn't been ordered to, but she couldn't help pitying him. At some point, they would have tossed water on him to remove the coppery, heavy stink of his own blood. Emerie had pre-empted it, wanting him to feel something pleasant in the mess of everything else.

She wanted to show him the depth of her sorrow, and that not all humans here were terrible.

Emerie knew the other Demonslayers would have no issues with doing her task or witnessing what they were doing to him. There would be few, if any, that didn't see him as wholly offensive.

Actually... once she'd wiped him clean, she hadn't found him distasteful.

Plus, he'd kind of smelt nice, like burnt sugar and hickory bark. Her nose had tingled the entire time. It even became more prominent when he'd accidentally huffed directly against her face while she'd been wiping his horns.

He was odd, weird, different, and definitely a monster, but she didn't find him ugly – unlike most of the Demons she'd faced. Funnily enough, his skull head helped.

It made him different from them, which was easier for her eyes to digest.

Perhaps it was because he was covered in lizard scales and obviously had a tail like one, but she'd expected him to be cold. Instead, his body was so hot that he'd begun to warm her wet cloth as she'd been wiping him.

She didn't like his voice, though.

There was something about it. Something that vibrated bass through her flesh and sunk all the way down to her bones. It sounded monstrous, inhuman, and had made the little hairs on her body stand on end. It was as though it was split between three deep tones, one that always had an underline of threat and became frightful when he somehow made it *boom*.

It hadn't been enough to stop her from trying to help him in some small way.

It was probably pointless. He likely thought she was a heartless cow like the woman in front of her, but that couldn't be any further from the truth.

She cared. Even more so when Wren looked up from her letter and rolled her eyes once Emerie was done telling her of what she'd learned.

Wren slid back her chair with a grating, skin-crawling scrape and stood, acquiring a book from a shelf behind her. She threw it on the table in front of Emerie.

"Open it to June twenty-third, two thousand and eighteen," she demanded as she sat back down to continue her letter.

Doing as she was told, Emerie opened the journal to the date, and silently read it. There were careless ink blots on the page, and the writing was messy, as though the person had been shaky or intoxicated when writing.

I lost a quarter of my members today. Good men and women. All because I allowed a Demon to enter my stronghold.

Emerie quickly flicked back to the beginning of the book to note that it was a copy of the diary belonging to the Head Elder from the western sector.

It was living among us for a year. Apprentice Charles looked like a human. His fucking face looked human, but we'd never seen him without his uniform on. It was only once we killed him and removed his clothing to clean him for the funeral pyre that we noticed the Demon void patches of skin. It must have been him. Charles was the one who opened the gates to allow through a team of Demons.

I can't believe I sat and ate with him in the hall. That I didn't question why most of his teams would die, but not him. I just thought he was an excellent soldier, ready to move through the ranks.

They're beginning to look and act so much like us that we can't even trust our fellow members.

They're growing intelligent.

They're learning.

Soon enough, humanity will be dead.

From this day forward, we'll be doing a physical examination of all applicants, and a yearly one, to ensure they haven't tricked us.

So many died because of my carelessness. Never again.

Emerie turned her eyes away from the diary to find Wren watching her. Her elbows were pressed against the table, while her clasped hands hid her lips.

"They can't be trusted," Wren stated, her dark-blue eyes flicking between Emerie's. "Whatever that Duskwalker told you, it's probably a lie."

Emerie placed the book on the table. "We've always known that Demons and Duskwalkers are different."

"And yet they both eat and hunt humans," Wren countered. "They could be working on the same side. He could be lying so he can be freed."

"What if he's not?"

"Say we do decide to aid him," Wren started, leaning back in her chair and placing her clasped hands on the table. "Can you wear the burden if we call the entire eastern sector army into the Veil, only to find out that it's an ambush? The Demons outnumber us. When there are a few of them, we can handle it, but if this is nothing more than a trick, the entire eastern side of Austrális could face being overrun because you have decided to trust a monster."

It was hard to deny how valid Wren's point of view was.

Emerie scratched at the back of her head through her Demonslayer hood in annoyance.

"I'm not saying we should follow him to the Veil." Emerie sighed, shaking her head. "But what if he's telling the truth? We would be torturing a creature that sought aid. Does that not feel wrong to you?"

"No," Wren retorted. "I don't care what his reasons for coming here were, whether they were noble or despicable. We are the first sector to ever capture a Duskwalker. This may be humankind's only chance to learn about them, and how to kill them."

"So, you're justifying this because of morbid curiosity and justice?" Emerie gave a dark laugh, as spite and hatred boiled in her chest. Before too long, those emotions would bubble over and spill.

"I'm justifying this for the greater good of humankind. The Duskwalkers are just as much our enemy as the Demons, and even though there are far fewer of them, they are ten times stronger. They can, and have, decimated entire towns on their own. If we learn how they work, how to kill them, it might be the key to unlocking a way to save hundreds, if not thousands, of people."

"You've already opened him up!" Emerie shouted, slamming her fist against the table. "What more can you possibly learn beyond that? Keeping him locked up in that dungeon–"

Wren's cheeks twitched with dark humour at Emerie's outrage, while a fierce glint sparked in her eyes. "It's exactly what we'd do to bandits, murderers, rapists, and thieves."

"We wouldn't hurt them in the process," Emerie argued back, turning her head to the side.

"No, instead they either succumb to madness in their cells, or we hang them. The only thing stopping the Duskwalker from achieving freedom is his desire to live. I had hoped to question him, but he won't give answers. I'd rather him dead, to be honest. It brings me no joy to watch his suffering."

Emerie's jaw muscles ticked.

Even if she understood Wren's point of view, even if it made sense, even if it was the right thing to do for humankind, she couldn't accept it. It went against something deep down inside her.

She was, by no means, a saint, but even she thought there should be limitations to achieving answers. If they couldn't be done... humanely, then they shouldn't be done at all.

"If you know how I feel about it, then why are you forcing me to wash his cell?"

It was a question that had been nagging at her since the first moment they'd placed the mop and bucket in her hands.

"Because it'll make you used to it. He'll eventually show you his true colours." Her lips twitched as she leant forward. "I wouldn't be surprised if he's already tried to scare you. The guard did mention you squealed at one point."

"The floor was so slippery I almost fell arse over head," Emerie said, unsure why she was lying for the Duskwalker.

Wren's lips curling downwards revealed she didn't believe her. She tsked.

"Your goal was to kill Demons, was it not?" Wren tilted her head, making her long hair wave to the side. "What if us doing this is the reason you finally find the Demon you've been searching for?"

Emerie's right hand enclosed into a fist. There was a face that haunted her nightmares. Until she was the one to destroy it herself, she knew she'd never sleep peacefully.

"The Demon King is making more moves as of late," Wren stated, eyeing her closely.

Her back straightened.

Emerie had only learned of him the previous day when she'd been forced to go through text after text relating to all the information they'd obtained. Under Wren's watchful eye and eagerness to answer any and all questions Emerie had, she'd read about him.

A tall dark-skinned man, who had red eyes that sometimes appeared brown. Long white hair, black backwards spiralling horns, pointed ears, claws and fangs. The sketches of him had all been different, some depicting him as handsome, others gnarly.

It's why Emerie hadn't batted an eye when the Duskwalker mentioned him.

New information was being forced down her throat with the aim of widening her perspective. There was a mountain of books she still needed to read, but she'd been given the permission to read such sensitive information because she was Wren's underling.

"We don't fully know what he is, as the Demons give us different answers. All we know is that he is at the centre of the Demon scourge, and that he is intelligent. That he has magic, power, and strength. Why would the Duskwalker ask for our aid, rather than pledge allegiance to him? It just sounds too suspicious to me. And why now? It's been hundreds of years – why only seek our aid now? These are the questions you need to ask yourself, Emerie, before you come into my office, demanding I stop what I'm doing."

She remained silent, unable to find a suitable response. Instead, she just inspected Wren's face, her lips tight and her right hand refusing to unclench.

"You're starting to understand, aren't you? You can see why I'm doing this." There was humour in Wren's eyes, even if it didn't reach the rest of her face. "If I free you from solitary, I trust you will keep what you learn to yourself. Yes?"

"I would never be so stupid as to leak information," Emerie bit out. "That's how I find my head on a spike above the main gates."

"Exactly," Wren confirmed, that humour finally touching her features to give her an ugly sneer. "Now, let's continue your training."

She was ushered to sit at a different table within Wren's office, where there was already a pile of leather-bound books waiting for her.

Emerie usually enjoyed reading, but she couldn't think of anything worse right now.

Her workload was so daunting, the stack felt bigger than mount Zagros itself.

EIGHT

Beneath her Demonslayer face coverings, Emerie paled.

She watched as they dragged out the corpse of the doctor who had been the one wielding the scalpel against the Duskwalker for the last few days. The beast was rattling his chains as he fought against them, having just enough freedom to thrust his head one way and then the next.

He snapped his long beak, and even attempted to peck at one of the Elders trying to wrangle rope around it in order to secure it.

Honestly, the death of the doctor could have been prevented had they not wanted to go poking around inside his mouth.

One of the Elders also wouldn't have lost their fingers in the process. They'd tried to help fight off the creature as he pecked and bit at the doctor's neck, chest, and face, and accidentally put their hand in danger's way.

Part of Emerie believed the doctor deserved it, the other half of her rebelled against the death of a human. And just how many had this one Duskwalker killed?

"Release me!" the Duskwalker roared, wriggling with all his might for freedom. *"Release me!"*

Within seconds, his beak was tied shut again, and she doubted they'd risk releasing it again.

He's just defending himself, she thought, eyeing the human blood that streaked right next to her and out the door. *If he'd been telling the truth about why he came here... then he was just defending himself outside the gates too.*

She didn't know if it was true.

Every second of every day, Wren's voice whispered in the back of her mind. Emerie couldn't help agreeing with much of it; a lot of it was reasonable, even if it *was* undeniably sick and twisted.

"See?" Wren snorted as she glanced back at Emerie, who was hiding her inner panic with a casual expression. "When given the chance, he'll kill."

The forceps the doctor had been using to hold his tongue lay on the ground and reflected the flickering firelight, as did the scalpel he'd been intending to use. Where, Emerie wasn't sure.

She couldn't deny the truth of it, not when it had happened right before her. She squinted. *But I've bitten the fingers of a bandit when he tried to remove my tongue.*

Then she'd managed to get to freedom and slice her attacker's throat.

How was it any different? It fucking wasn't.

They cranked the wheels on either side of the Duskwalker to angle the table forward and force him to kneel again.

"I'm guessing I'm on cleanup duty?" Emerie sneered, causing humour to light up in Wren's usually cold expression.

"I was going to give you a break, but with that tone? Absolutely."

Emerie didn't even move out of the way as they exited, forcing them to barge into her shoulder. Then she waited for them to give her cleaning tools as the Duskwalker continued to roar.

He was uninjured – they hadn't managed to hurt him yet – but he wasn't calming.

He seems enraged. She eyed the ground. *Is it because of the blood?*

Funnily enough, she found it easier to clean up the blood of the guildmembers. Perhaps it was because they'd gotten what they deserved.

She didn't know what it was, but she was becoming desensitized to their deaths, and more vulnerable to him. Yet Wren's constant barrage of opinions just spun her mind into a confused ache.

What was right and wrong? Good and bad? Evil and righteous? Emerie was tired of being in limbo.

She was heart-sick from it. Unable to eat, unable to sleep. It festered within, causing her skin to itch until she threatened to break it apart. She was covered in small rashes underneath her uniform.

She would eventually need to pick a side and wholly accept what they did.

It barely took any time at all for her to clean up the blood from the room, and she was stupid enough to approach him to wipe the worst of it from his thrashing face – the tip of his beak. She spooked quickly and backed up. Not long after she asked for a new bucket of water – an excuse to remain with the Duskwalker – he eventually calmed, albeit very gradually.

Or, rather, when the remaining bits of blood on him dried.

He gave wild huffs through his nose holes, his chest rising and falling in rapid succession. She knew his red orbs were upon her, and she didn't find them as hollow and soulless as she once did.

"You–"

"Leave me alone!" he yelled, jerking and causing the sound of bones to rattle from him, as well as the *chink* of his chains.

"They will just use a different doctor," she told him.

"Then I will destroy that one too," he rumbled, his words unnerving.

Her skin rose in goosebumps.

"Did it feel good to kill him?"

She didn't know why she asked him. Maybe she wanted a reason to hate him, to make her okay with all this happening.

"Yes," he snarled.

A humourless, singular snort of laughter escaped her. *I felt that way about the bandit.*

Since she'd also asked for a cloth, she approached the Duskwalker again now that he wasn't mindlessly thrashing.

"I'm going to clean you," she informed him.

She needed to do something in this room before they took her from it.

"Don't touch me."

Emerie ignored him and wrung her cloth of water before she faced him. He jerked, but his bounds kept him in place.

"Were you lying when you said you came here for our aid?" she asked, dabbing at his chest to rid him of a few crimson droplets.

This time, she thought it best to start with the place they weren't just fucking with.

"You look like a Demon," he snapped, the swirling vortex of his orbs reddening.

Emerie paused with her eyes narrowed. Then she hooked her index finger into the side of her hood to unclip her mask and pushed both away.

"Is that better?" she asked, already noting the colour of his angry orbs softening.

"Yes."

He wasn't lying. Considering his reaction to her uniform, it was obvious he felt hatred towards them.

Emerie held her breath as she gently gripped the underside of his beak, expecting him to jerk. He didn't, his orb redness fading even more, and she was able to comfortably wipe the seam of it.

She noted the tension in his shoulders eased, and she thought he may have even rested a bit of the weight of his head in her palm.

Then her eyelids flickered when his orbs changed to a colour she'd never seen before. An orchid hue of purple.

She'd already summarised that red meant anger and hunger, and white was fear. She could only guess that blue was sadness.

She didn't know what orchid meant.

His skull twitched in her palm, and she was surprised the bone was so warm.

"That scent is gone from you," he stated, quick huffs escaping him. He was sniffing her. *"The one that smelt possessive."*

Her head darted back. She had no idea what he was talking about.

"If..." she started, lowering her voice to make sure the guard couldn't overhear. "If I were to release you, would you promise not to harm anyone?"

She thought he would leap at the potential opportunity to escape. He didn't, and his silence was crushing.

"Duskwalker?"

"Ingram. My name is Ingram. Do not take away my name when I only just obtained it."

Emerie, done cleaning him and merely wiping at a now-white skull, stepped back. *He has a name?* Why did that gouge at her chest? A real monster... wouldn't have a name. *Does that mean someone cares about him?*

Gosh. Was there someone out there who *missed* him?

"You did not answer me, Ingram," she whispered, hoping he would follow her lead.

"Promises are things that should not be broken, yes?" She nodded. *"Then I cannot promise this."*

Her lips parted at his honesty. He was a fool! He'd almost had her in the palm of his hands, and he'd chosen to reveal he'd gladly kill her fellow Demonslayers.

"Okay, fine," she grumbled, turning her back to him so she could collect her supplies.

"You are angry?" his high-pitched tone of surprise was unmistakable.

"I'm not going to free someone who will go out of their way to hurt my people."

"I would not be able to help it if they harm me, or I them."

Her lips tightened. She halted from leaving to toss her head to the side and look at him from her peripheral. "How so?"

"Mavka cannot help letting their rage take over. We... do not always mean to hurt, especially if we have been harmed."

Mavka? Is that what they call themselves rather than Duskwalker?

She slowly turned around to warily face him. "Sometimes it's an accident?"

"Yes. Like when your people struck me with arrows as I knocked *on your gate. I could not calm down once they started to attack me."*

The word 'knocked' lingered in her mind.

Emerie cupped her chin in thought. *I see. So Duskwalkers turn mindless? Like an instinct to destroy?* At least when she killed, it was completely on purpose. *Animals act out when cornered for self-preservation.*

And if Wren and the other Elders had been doing this to a wolf or a bear – that was immortal and couldn't die – she would have long ago tried to free it.

Hell, even humans behaved differently when cornered and afraid.

"I also hunger. The scent of blood calls to me. It is never-ending, never goes away."

Emerie chewed at the right corner of her lips. She muttered, "If you smell blood, you'll go bat-shit crazy like when we captured you?"

Great! The likelihood of that was high. He wouldn't even make it out of the hallway just beyond his dungeon door before he lost his shit.

She couldn't think of a solution right now. She wasn't even sure if she would actually let him go. Emerie was just trying to figure out what she wanted to do, how she would handle this.

Emerie needed to pick a side, but first she would determine what was actually possible – and wouldn't get her killed for no reason.

Maybe I'm selfish, but I kinda, you know, want to live?

She was so deep within her musings that she wasn't sure if he'd actually answered her or not. It didn't matter. It was bedtime, and she doubted her mind would shut the fuck up from thinking to let her sleep. She needed as much rest as she could, even if it was just to close her eyes and let them relax before they were forced to read more boring diaries and texts.

She headed to the door, and her heart shrivelled in her chest when he let out the tiniest whimper.

"Please don't leave me alone."

She halted as his plea instantly squeezed at her heart. A Duskwalker was begging for her to stay, and she didn't think she'd ever heard something so depressing.

She bit her bottom lip so hard she feared she'd draw blood. "I'm sorry, but I have to," she whispered back, glancing at him and his blue orbs.

She knocked on the door to be let out.

Ingram's pulse raced with anxiety as he watched the female leave.

Her hair streaked with orange and red, and those light-blue eyes, had brought colour to the four grey walls that constantly surrounded him. Her pretty scent, finally free of that wretched underlying note, had been lung achingly sweet. Her voice had battled with his thoughts, gentling and calming him when he doubted anything else could.

And her touch underneath his jaw had been warm, soft, and pleasant. Under the strength of her holding his weighty head when he'd been lulled by her scent, her voice, and the sight of her, she had managed to bring back his normal purple hue.

Now it was a suffocating blue, highlighting just how anxious he was about being alone in the room – waiting for them to do more unpleasant things to him. His sight darted to every crack in the wall, like he was searching for a way out.

The walls were slowly closing in on him.

He closed his sight to escape it, wishing his mind would cease being so alert so he could finally sleep.

I am so tired.

"You are not alone," came a feminine voice, echoey but warm.

His sight flashed open to blue, and he looked around as best as he could in his confinements.

The Witch Owl stood before him in her ghostly form.

His entire essence tried to leap forward so he could hug her. She was safe. She had protected him in the past, even if she was part of the reason Aleron was gone.

"Free me," he whimpered. *"I should have listened to you. I am sorry. Please free me."*

Her hovering, intangible form turned solid, and her bare feet slapped against the ground as she darted forward. She began pulling on the rope around his beak and head, and her scratching nails made his ear holes itch.

"I'm sorry," she muttered quietly. "I tried to come sooner, but I lost one of your siblings. I had to chase down the Demon who stole them before I could come to you."

He didn't care that she hadn't come sooner. She was here now, and that's all that mattered. She was here to save him.

"Curses," she spat as she stepped back. "The knot is too tight."

She pulled out a dagger from somewhere underneath her feathery cloak and tried to jimmy him free. When that didn't work, she attempted to just cut the rope free. She couldn't.

"Curses," she bit out again. "The enchantment those Anzuli put on these makes them impossible to cut without the right blade."

She even used shadowy magic, tendrils of it forming around his kneeling form – to no avail.

"Cut off my head," he pleaded.

The Witch Owl shook her head, eyeing the length of one of his binds. "The chains have locks, and they are enchanted as well. Currently, they are attached around your horns, and I could break you trying to get you free."

"Fuck," he snarled.

Her full lips pulled tight. "Why do all my children have naughty mouths?" She went to say more, then snapped her mouth closed when approaching footsteps and chatter could be heard.

The moment he shifted his sight to the door, the Witch Owl was gone.

Wren and two other Demonslayers entered.

"This is your subject, doctor," she said, gesturing to him.

"I will try to find the key to your chains," the Witch Owl whispered from somewhere within him. He realised she'd turned incorporeal to hide. "Please, just wait a little longer."

The lightly tanned female doctor turned a set of brown eyes on him, and her stare was hard – and perhaps just as unfeeling as their leader.

"I see, the Duskwalker. No wonder you've been secretive about your actions as of late. What has already been done in terms of research?"

"Johnathan dissected him – twice," Wren answered, and the doctor cracked her neck.

"I'll need those notes before I begin. Was it just an autopsy?" The doctor came over to Ingram like she held not an ounce of fear or anxiety towards him. The other doctor had been frightened upon first seeing him, but she didn't even bat an eyelid when he threatened her with a snarl. "Have you done a proper physical examination?"

"Not yet, no," Wren confirmed.

The doctor tsked. "Of course Johnathan just opened him up. He was always so... crude." She circled Ingram and touched the spikes on his back and the vertebrae of his spine with deep strokes. "I must admit, Wren. I'm disappointed you didn't call for me first."

"Johnathan was a higher-ranking member," Wren answered in a bored tone.

"Yes, but not a better doctor. All I lack are years with the guild, not experience." He jerked, pain flaring, when she scratched a scale from him. "Interesting. It seems to be made up of different animal parts. I'll do a physical examination today while I wait for Johnathan's notes. Once I read them over, I'll see if they're adequate or if I need to redo his work. Did he examine its brain?"

"No, not yet," Wren admitted.

"Okay. I'll do that last. I've heard a Duskwalker's skull is near impossible to break. Let's find out if that's true, and maybe I can see what kind of intelligence it's truly capable of in the process."

Ingram's sight morphed into a stark white. He was thankful none of them realised the depth of his fear, since his orbs often turned this colour.

Wren left after the doctor shooed her off, then she began looking him over. At least it wasn't truly painful, as she only poked and prodded at different parts of his body.

But every moment with her revealed that she was far more

thorough than the other doctor. Her hands were cold wherever she touched him, inspecting him from horns to tail tip.

Her eyes peered at him like he was an insect – which was odd, considering he would have towered over her tiny stature.

Sometimes the smallest Demons were the nastiest.

NINE

Okay. Okay... shit, Emerie thought as she navigated Zagros Fortress, trying her hardest to hide her frantic body language.

Since it was late afternoon, the sun shining through the hallway windows was bright. It would soon begin its descent over the horizon, but she wished it would hurry.

There weren't many people loitering in the hallways, as most were in the eating hall. The odd few were those either leaving or switching their shifts.

There were hundreds of positions within the guild, from stable workers for their few messenger horses, to cooks, cleaners, and even watchers. Organising the rosters had, up until recently, been one of her more permanent duties, despite most usually rotating their tasks.

They all had to do the watch shift at some point – and be on different hours for it – to share the load.

There are too many people in the hallways. It would have been better if it was past curfew for those who didn't have duties to perform, but Emerie couldn't wait any longer.

Her last visit to the Duskwalker's dungeon revealed the new doctor wanted to have her own peek inside him. The poor guy just couldn't catch a break.

That wasn't what had lit a fire underneath her arse.

Even though he'd already healed his wounds – she hated that cleanup duty was the only reason she was permitted to visit him – his breathing had been short and shallow. Stark white orbs had flashed blue at her, before being once more engulfed by his fear, and he'd tensed up upon seeing Emerie.

She clenched her eyes shut tightly at the memory.

"Please," he'd whined. *"Keep her away from me. Don't let her break my skull."*

Emerie had already been informed of Sabrina's intentions earlier from Wren. She'd also already made her decision.

She'd already been actioning her plans.

But his words... how urgent and panicked they were... *His skull is significant.* She didn't know how, she didn't know why – all she knew was that she couldn't wait.

I should have just figured my shit out sooner.

But it was hard to break years of brainwashing, training, fear, and hatred. It was hard to go against everything she'd ever known, everything she'd ever learned, to do the right thing. Especially with a pest like Wren in her ear.

Tonight, she was going to free the Duskwalker.

Would she die? Probably!

Either the Duskwalker would take his anger out on her, or Wren would hang her for being a traitor while shoving him back in that dungeon. But she just couldn't do this anymore.

She couldn't sit idly by and allow this to keep happening.

Her life wasn't precious. She wasn't special.

Emerie didn't deserve to cling to life so selfishly, not when she was the only person who could or *would* help.

Other than rope, I should have everything I need in my room. Really, the only thing she was taking with her was a water sack, her travel bag that held all her tools, a keystone obsidian blade to free him, and a bow she'd recently made out of boredom.

She had a sword and whip on her already, upgraded and given to her by Wren. *I shouldn't need much more than that.*

However, she'd been fashioning something else last night after she made her decision. She thought she'd stolen enough rope to finish making it, but she'd fallen short by one long length.

If she wanted any hope of living past this day, she needed more.

Someone bumped into her in the hallway, but she didn't pay

them any notice. That was until they grabbed her wrist and tugged her back, forcing her scheming mind to the present.

"Emerie?" he asked, and she would know that voice anywhere.

Even though she was in her full uniform, she wasn't wearing her face mask. It was obvious he'd been following her for quite some time, probably yelling at her, and she'd been too lost in thought to notice.

She ripped her arm from Bryce, but he held strong. "Let go of me," she grated out.

He yanked her closer to allow room for those passing around them in the narrow hallway.

"You've been gone for six days," he snapped through clenched teeth. "Where the fuck have you been?"

"Busy," she answered.

It was funny, though. If it wasn't for the Duskwalker, Emerie may have had a different reaction.

In the past six days, Bryce had barely been in her thoughts. Wren, the Duskwalker, all her sorrow and regret... she hadn't had a single moment to spare over her breakup with him.

Had so much not been going on for her, had more important things not been weighing on her, Emerie probably would have bawled her eyes out for the last few nights. She would have wept, wondering if she'd made a mistake.

Other than when it happened, not a tear had formed for him.

But it had for the Duskwalker.

In the privacy of her room, whether it was her usual one or the one she'd been hidden away in, Emerie had cried for that creature. Cried for his pain, and the heavy burden of guilt that she had the biggest hand in capturing him.

It was her fault.

If she could go back in time, she would have stopped herself. *I helped put him in that stupid dungeon.*

"I tried to order a meeting with Wren about the Duskwalker's capture, but they said she was unavailable. You didn't tell her I helped you, did you?"

"It slipped my mind," she muttered honestly, grunting when she attempted to yank her arm away multiple times.

Then she winced at the tight pressure around her forearm, like he was trying to snap it in half.

"If you didn't want to continue being a useful fucking hole anymore, that's fine, but the least you could have done was not be a bitch and hog all the glory to yourself." He shoved her until her back met the wall, and the back of her head thudded against it. "You will tell her, or I'll start telling everyone what a whore you are. How easy it was for me to get you to lower–"

He didn't even get the chance to finish. Bryce went cross-eyed with fury as she kneed him so hard in the balls she *swore* she felt something pop. Maybe she was imagining it, but it was oddly satisfying.

He let her go as he silently screamed, tears welling in his eyes. While clutching his junk, he sagged to his knees.

"I don't have time for your shit," she snapped down at him. "Feel free to tell everyone what you want. I'm a whore, a bitch. I really, *really* don't care."

She was utterly sincere about that.

"Ugly... bitch," he wheezed, unable to stand.

Okay, so that one hurt a whole lot, but Emerie tried to ignore it as she stormed off.

Why do guys always call you ugly when you don't give them what they want? And of course, Bryce would know. She was particularly sensitive to that insult.

Then again, she couldn't remember if he'd ever complimented her.

I can't. I can't think about this right now.

She could dwell on it later... if she was still alive.

Emerie went down a few levels so she could enter the armoury. The guard wrote down that she was obtaining supplies, but didn't stop her. Why would they? It was normal for guild members to come here for training purposes.

She headed back to her room, navigating the long and windy hallways slowly emptying of people. Zagros Fortress had always felt cold and foreboding, but it sent a chill through her more than usual.

She looked out the window, noting dusk was barely casting enough light to see the red and orange autumn leaves. *I need to pack my jacket.*

Every time she added a new item to her list, her chest hollowed out. How pathetic would her full bag look next to her corpse? She was being foolishly hopeful.

Rushing to get this over and done with before she changed her mind, she finished packing her bag, storing the rope inside it. Then she clipped her whip and sword to her waist, knowing no one would bat an eye at them.

Her bow and quiver, on the other hand, might cause eyebrows to raise.

Her jacket was made from the animals she'd hunted for food on her travels and was made up of mismatched patches. She threw it over the top of her bow to hide it, even though the ends stuck out past her shoulder and behind her leg. Her quiver made a noticeable impression behind her, but she shrugged.

It was the best she could do.

With her mask and hood firmly in place, she exited her room, not even sparing a moment to glance back at it. The four grey walls carved from stone, her timber-framed single bed, her tiny writing desk that had carvings in it from other dead guildmembers... Nothing belonged to her. It was just a place to sleep, and it had never really felt like home.

Emerie made sure to avoid other guildmembers as much as possible, going the long way to the ground level. People were sparse down here, and it wasn't difficult to sneak her way to the cleaning house.

She acquired a mop and bucket, using the mop head to hide the top of her bow, and calmly made her way to the doors that would take her down to the dungeon level.

The Master rank member guarding the doorway to the top of the stairs let her pass freely, used to seeing her go down to clean the Duskwalker's cell. She wasn't sure if it was complacency or stupidity on their part that they didn't notice she wasn't being escorted.

Considering no orders had been sent to clean it, the Elder rank member guarding his cell barred her from entering.

Emerie dropped her bucket, quickly pouncing on him before he could even register what she was doing, and placed the mop handle around the front of his neck from behind. He let out a choke, scratching at the handle as it cut off his airways and circulation.

He swiped backwards at her face and dug his nails into it through her mask.

She held strong, her front flush against his back as she pulled with all her might.

When he eventually sagged, she released him and checked his pulse. *Good. Still alive.* With some of the spare rope she'd acquired, she bound his hands and feet together before using a rag to cover his mouth.

Fishing the key from his weapons belt, she moved quickly to unlock the dungeon door.

Emerie's gaze met the Duskwalker's white orbs.

Knowing it wouldn't lock, Emerie closed the door once she'd dragged the guard inside. Then she spun to the Duskwalker while removing her face coverings, remembering he didn't like them.

Now, his orbs were a dark yellow.

"What are you–" he started before she leapt into action.

"Let's get you out of here," she rushed out around quick breaths. She stormed to one of the crank wheels beside him and shoved against it with all her might until the board forcing him into a kneeling position came away just enough for her to get her arms behind him. "However – please don't take this the wrong way because I'm sure you feel the same about me – I don't trust you."

While he was still trapped and unable to stop her, Emerie wrapped enchanted rope around his waist. Then she twisted the free lengths together to make an anchor point and pushed each end of the rope through the loops already wrapped around his wrists. Threading back to the centre point and giving him plenty of room, she then did the same with the rope at his ankles, as well as his tail.

It almost looked like his back had a knotted harness.

Luck favours the prepared. And she was going to need the universe to give her a lot of luck tonight; it was better to aid it along the way.

"Are you freeing me? Why?"

She wrapped a cloth over his nose holes and secured it, making sure the herb bag attached to it was firmly against those concave notches in his skull. *This better work. Hopefully he can't smell blood through this.*

"Because I don't agree with any of this, and I don't deserve to live if I allow it." Emerie then yanked her obsidian blade from the holster on her thigh. She pointed the tip of it at his beak. "But hear me now. Without me, you won't escape this place. You'll get lost down here. I'm going to ride your back and give you directions, and you're going to promise me that you won't hurt anyone on purpose."

"I told you. I cannot make this promise," he whined, his orbs flashing blue. Once more, his honesty on the matter touched her.

She was glad he wasn't a liar.

Regardless of what he said, she still cut the connecting part of the rope around his neck, leaving the loop of it so she had something to hold onto while she rode him.

"I know," she muttered. "I know you said you won't be able to help it for a few reasons, but I'm asking you to *try*. That's all I ask in return for freeing you. To not kill my people if you don't have to." She cut away the loop around his chest, then the one around his waist she hadn't placed on him. "I know you probably want retribution for the higher-ups hurting you, but you'd be an idiot for trying. They might capture you again, and they will kill me for freeing you. You won't get another chance. Please, promise me."

"I... promise to try."

For the first time in days, he was able to move his hips back and forth. He was also able to move his head slightly, despite the chains still clamped around his horns.

Just as she went to bend down to cut away the looping section that was threaded around his thighs and calves, someone fisted her hair.

Emerie gasped as she was yanked back and tossed to the ground. Landing on her side, all she could think was, *What the fuck?! I didn't hear the door opening!*

However, the woman straddling her torso while raising a

knife above her to spear her chest wasn't wearing a Demonslayer uniform.

Instead, a white feather from her cloak fluttered between them. A woman with brown skin and dark hair glared down at her with an expression so fierce it was *harrowing*.

"Wait, stop!" Ingram yelled, just as that blade came down. Emerie shoved her obsidian dagger up to block it.

She punched the woman in the side of the face with enough force to knock her to the left. Emerie pushed her off and bounced to her feet.

"Who the hell are you?" Emerie snapped through gritted teeth, her dagger at the ready as they circled the room.

Both poised to strike, both ready to defend themselves.

"I am life, and I am death," she muttered before she lunged. "And I will free this Mavka from your tortures!"

Emerie's eyes widened. She crouched low enough so she could bash the woman's hand upward to evade it before rolling to the side.

The woman wearing a white cloak of feathers, a dirt-stained white dress, and no shoes, swiftly turned to her. There was a dangerous, calculating glint in her eyes.

"Wait! Just hold up a second." She put her hands up, one still holding her dagger, in a surrendering position. "I'm also trying to free him."

That dangerous edge to her dark-brown eyes softened. She didn't look away from Emerie, untrusting and still ready to attack.

"It's why I'm here." She pointed to the currently bound guard who had awoken at some point and was screaming against his mouth gag.

The woman looked Emerie up and down. "Why are you helping him?"

"No reason." She shook her head. "There's no ulterior motive. Just his release."

"It is true," Ingram agreed, who had enough room to shake his chains more.

The keen gaze of the mystery woman flicked to the already cut bits of rope around his knees before coming back to Emerie.

"Fine." Then she nodded in the direction of the door. "I can do the rest."

This was her opportunity to back out of this, knowing someone was on his side – even if it wasn't her. But with a guard who had witnessed everything, the many others who had seen her walking this way, plus those at the armoury... she'd be the first suspect.

There was also one other problem.

"I know the best way out of here," Emerie stated. "Zagros Fortress is like a labyrinth to those that don't know it, and he'll never make it through the front doors. I know a side door that leads to the yard and then another door that leads to the forest."

Had they not shown her the night she'd captured this very Duskwalker, she wouldn't have known about them.

"We will be fine," the woman answered. "Those we come across will not get in our way."

"He promised me he wouldn't hurt anyone on purpose," Emerie pleaded.

"Their deaths are deserved after what they've been doing to him."

"I know." Emerie's features twisted with a wince. "But I'm offering a better chance of his escape. One that may not have to end in bloodshed. You're human, you should understand."

"Human?" the woman mused. "That I am not." Then she turned to the Duskwalker. "What do you want?"

Ingram's head tilted just enough to show he was looking between them. He seemed just as surprised as she was that the woman had asked him.

"I made a promise..." he hedged, then his orbs shifted to a bright orange. *"I don't wish to break it. She is also the only one who has been kind to me here."*

With a sigh, eyeing Emerie from the corner of her eye, she nodded. "If that's what you want."

She pulled out an iron key from inside her cloak. It was only now that Emerie realised the woman had been wielding an obsidian dagger as well.

She gasped and took a step forward. "Where did you get that key? That should have been impossible to steal."

The woman knelt down to unlock the metal shackles around his ankles. An additional defence in case he managed to get free of his rope bindings.

"Your leader may have hidden this away in a safe, but she wore the keys for it on her person. Once I figured out where both the keys and safe were, it was effortless." Then she grumbled to herself as she said, "But it took me far too long to find the safe. Did they hurt you further?"

"Yes."

Her eyes narrowed and her lips flattened at that, as did Emerie's.

Emerie cut away the rest of the rope binding him, thankful she wouldn't have to use her hammer and the tip of her blade to remove the locking pins of his chains. She actually hadn't known if it would work, but she'd also been hoping he could just yank them free from the wall.

At least this was better.

Emerie's heart quickened when he was finally unbound. She held her breath, unsure if he would suddenly leap on her with claws at the ready.

"Everything hurts," he groaned, darting his head between them. He stretched his arms and legs out on all fours.

She let out her pent-up breath.

"Why did you leave these on him?" the woman asked, moving her stolen dagger to the ropes crossing over his back and down his limbs.

"Don't," Emerie cut in before gently grabbing her wrist. "Don't remove them. I need them to stay on."

The woman's gaze was suspicious, her brows lowering as she glared. Thankfully, after a moment, she nodded.

Emerie walked over to the Duskwalker and clenched her jaw when his raven skull freely turned to look over his shoulder at her. Even on all fours, his skull was close to her own head height.

"C-can I climb onto your back?"

His head darted to the woman, who nodded, and he lowered himself for her. Once she was firmly on his back, she cringed. *Crap. I forgot to put my jacket back on.* It would have been perfect to sit on to protect her pubic bone from being annihilated by his lizard spikes.

She placed her bag there instead, hoping it was enough.

She gripped the rope around his neck. "Okay. Now don't forget I'm up here and cut my head off going through a doorway."

She let out the tiniest squeal when she jolted side to side as he stood properly. He absolutely did *not* feel like riding a horse.

"I'll take the lead and clear the way," the woman said, moving to open the dungeon door. "Let's go."

Emerie laid down the moment Ingram was in motion but kept her face firmly up to guide them. She struggled to keep her bearings on their location with how fast he sprinted, her hair whipping behind her from the chilly air streaking past them.

His paws and hands slapped and thudded against the stone ground, echoing in the hallways.

"Left," she shouted. They turned down a short hallway that came to an intersection. "Left again. Then straight."

At the end of the hall was the stairway to the ground level.

The woman opened the door, frightening the shit out of the guard before Emerie and Ingram emerged right behind her. Emerie glanced at them, and their bewildered eyes met her own determined ones.

"Go right!"

She yanked on the rope around his neck when a handful of guildmembers passing through the wide and tall hallway noticed them. Hard not to notice a giant Duskwalker, if she was being honest!

Ingram turned in that direction, and they were immediately followed.

"The door on the right," she instructed, trying to keep her voice low.

A small staircase took them to the entrance of the lower south tower. She didn't know if Ingram was panicked, but his breaths snorted from his nose holes, and his motions were more jolted. His body was hot against her knees and torso, and his muscles working beneath her brought attention to how... unbelievably strong he felt.

The alarm rang, and Emerie's pulse thundered in her ears.

Shit! I was hoping we'd have more time.

They sped down the hallway that would lead them to the northern lower tower, and as they were coming up to a staircase that lead to the top, a guildmember appeared in the entryway.

They took one step in their direction, started some outraged shout, then the woman running in front of them pounced. With one swift motion, acting so fast that Emerie barely had time to register it, she sliced their throat open.

Ingram leapt over the Demonslayer, who cupped their wound in a futile attempt to stop the bleeding, and Emerie's eyes crinkled in guilt.

"I said not to kill anyone!"

"*He* made that promise," she callously answered. "I did not."

Gripping the rope around Ingram's neck tighter in vexation, she glared at the back of the woman for a moment before admitting, *There's nothing I can do to change it.* Only one person dying tonight was better than dozens. Besides, there was no time to lose focus.

"The door at the end leads to outside," Emerie stated. "It's locked. He'll have to break it down."

"You heard her, Ingram."

With a snorting huff and a nod of his head, his pace quickened until he was swiftly gaining on the woman who had been dictating their pace.

The gasp that tore out of Emerie was so sharp and loud, it punched her lungs on its way out. Her eyes nearly bulged out of her skull when the Duskwalker sprinted through the woman!

She looked back to find her following them closely. *She turned into a Ghost!* Her entire body had turned colourless and transparent.

Then, before her very eyes, she turned corporeal. Brown skin formed from the tips of her toes and fingers, before quickly spreading up her limbs. Her hair, which had been white, nearly transparent, and floating, slowly dropped around her face and shoulders.

She couldn't have been a Ghost for longer than a second, but Emerie knew what she'd seen. Knew it wasn't a trick of the light or her mind.

Emerie's gaze connected with the woman, who had a stern expression.

Too busy gaping behind her, she almost missed something critical. She only had enough time to lay flat against Ingram's back after he roared, and he shoulder barged his way through the thick timber door. It broke in half and flung off its hinges, destroyed like it was nothing but paper.

It would have taken at least ten humans with a ram to knock it down over the course of minutes.

Wood splinters flew in all directions, forcing her eyelids shut when they rained over her face. She knew a few would be caught in her long, wavy hair as it fluttered wildly behind her.

She pulled back on the rope around Ingram's neck while also yanking it to the right. "Watch out!"

He skidded across the ground as he tried to halt before jumping against the mountain wall directly in front of them. He darted to the right, but immediately paused when two rows of Demonslayers stood at the ready with spears.

"Shit," Emerie muttered under her breath. "They beat us here."

Then again, the route she'd taken them wasn't as direct as going through the front doors.

At the back of the two rows of Demonslayers was Wren.

Her glare was as sharp and steely as a sword, and her uncovered face revealed just how pissed off she was. Their leader obviously expected Emerie to give up on Ingram and become used to it, and this turn of events was not something she foresaw.

There was betrayal in her eyes, and regret.

"I'll take care of them," the woman shouted as she sprinted forwards. "Get him out of here before he succumbs to bloodlust."

The woman – who she still didn't know the name of, or why she was here – leapt. Her cloak fluttered, seeming to make her glide through the air. Then she spun, knocking into spears with her feet to shove them away, as she landed in the middle of the soldiers.

Two barely had a chance to react before she'd slit their

throats.

Emerie unthreaded her bow from around her torso, obtained an arrow from her quiver, then held onto Ingram's neck reins. She kicked her heels into his side for some stupid reason, treating him like a horse.

"Go, Ingram! Go!"

The door was just past these soldiers. They just needed to get to it.

He, on the other hand, had a different idea.

He turned to the left and made Emerie scream as he jumped and vaulted off the fortress stone gate, so he could reach a jutting ledge in the keep. She nocked her arrow on her string, pulled back, and unleashed it at a bowman aiming at them from below.

She quickly nocked a second, releasing it and grabbing another. There was no time to be hesitant about killing her fellow guildmembers, no space within her racing heart to feel guilt. She couldn't; they were too close to freeing Ingram.

The woman had most of the attention of the foot soldiers, besides the odd few that tried to toss their spears at Ingram as he scaled the side wall. He was finding his own way out, and she wondered if he had chosen this path because it had the least potential of death on his hands.

Why did the idea of him keeping his promise to this degree touch her so deeply?

Ingram let out a little growl as he backed up over a roof section of the fortress, his sight obviously fixed on the large expanse of space between it and the stone gate. More bow wielders were at the top and already shooting at them.

She didn't know why her gaze darted down towards the ground. Wren was gone, and her panicked gaze flickered everywhere to find her.

Fuck! Where did she go?!

Ingram bolted, and the closer he got to the ledge, the more her heart tried to detach so it could crawl out her mouth to safety. *We won't make it.* It was too far. Nothing could make that distance.

Instead of expressing her fear and sheer panic, she just held onto the rope around his neck and prepared herself for anything.

With dust and loose rocks being kicked off the edge, Ingram leapt. They sailed through the air.

They started to fall.

They crashed against the side of the walls, just short of the top, and his claws ate away at stone like they were made of diamond – strong and unbreakable.

Emerie gasped when she started to slip away and held onto the rope in one hand with all her might. Her inner turmoil urged her to let go of her bow and use both hands, but she stubbornly didn't want to. What if she needed it? It was the only long-range weapon she had.

She sighed in relief when he didn't even need to climb. He just launched himself forward with all his strength and they were ascending metres higher than the gate's wall.

It was in this moment that she fully understood how Duskwalkers destroyed towns. A wall of wooden spikes? What a useless attempt of a barricade.

For a few short seconds, she was floating, then her heart dipped to her stomach. They fell on top of the wall, and a rasp tore through her when she landed hard on him.

Something broke when her entire torso landed against the spikes on his back. Only her pubic bone, saved by her bag that had come between them, was spared. Instead of a scream tearing its way through her at the pain, a pitiful sob did.

Ingram fought against someone who had threaded a whip around his head, tangling it in his horns to stay secure.

Through her watering eyes, she noted people were coming.

Emerie didn't even think about it. She nocked her arrow and blindly shot while he freed himself.

He took those few steps needed to get to the edge of the wall's pathway so he could... she didn't know, maybe leap to freedom?

She blinked the worst of her tears away, and it took her a moment to see Wren there. Even longer to notice the arrow sticking out from her forehead. Her Head Elder sagged to her knees and toppled to the ground on her side.

Shock slapped her into alertness and rendered her immobile. She didn't even hold onto Ingram for a few brief seconds.

I killed her, Emerie thought, utterly flummoxed, eyes wide and disbelieving. *I killed Wren.*

She truly hadn't meant to.

Emerie didn't take her eyes away from Wren's corpse, yet her arms moved instinctively, her hands grabbing the rope around Ingram's neck.

"Emerie!" someone shouted to her left, and her head spun that way.

With her mouth agape in shock at herself, she found the guildmember who'd spoken to her. It was a woman's voice, likely one of her friends, but she couldn't make out who. Now she understood *why* Ingram thought they all looked like a bunch of faceless Demons.

Whether her friend spoke again or not, she was no longer listening. Ingram finally jumped, and she barely realised she was falling.

All she knew was... she'd just given up her life as a Demonslayer for this Duskwalker.

TEN

Wheezing, Emerie twisted her torso so she could cup her lower ribs. *Okay, I've definitely broken something.* Or at least fractured something, considering she was breathing fine except for the sharp pain every time she inhaled.

It also didn't help that Ingram was still sprinting. Each time she bounced, it was like she was being punched. He was putting as much distance between them and the fortress as he possibly could.

The woman who had helped them was nowhere to be seen, and Emerie hoped she was okay.

Her adrenaline was still high, aided by the fact she was going so fucking fast she thought they were two seconds away from flying. The air was cold as it hit her nose, then split around her head and through her hair, causing it to whip wildly behind her. Thankfully he was warm, but she barely registered it through her pain and distress.

So much had happened.

There was too much to consider.

She couldn't believe she had made it out of there alive.

I killed Wren.

And, in doing so, she had just ensured she would be hunted as a traitor for the rest of her life. Imprisonment was for those who abandoned the guild, but killing the Head Elder? Death awaited her, and her features were easily distinguishable.

She looked behind her, no longer able to see the fortress – or any other remnants of the life she'd just left. Although she had a few friendships, they weren't particularly deep. It was hard to be attached to people who could easily die the next time they went out for a mission.

"Please," Emerie pleaded, pulling on the rope around the Duskwalker's neck. She needed to rest, to figure out what her next plan was. "Please stop. I need a–"

Ingram halted so abruptly that Emerie squealed and kicked her legs as she was tossed forward. A scream burst from her at the pain in her side when she landed, while sticks jabbed into her body when she slid.

Her waning adrenaline restrengthened as she crawled to her knees.

Even more so when the Duskwalker pounced. She only had a split second to roll to the side before she was impaled by his claws or crushed to death.

"Wait," Emerie huffed out. She put her hand up to ward him off as he turned his raven skull and red orbs to her. "Wait. I don't understand. I saved you."

The way his next snarl rumbled from him, like a quiet, unnerving storm, had her hackles rising. It was beastly, terrifying, and the arrow sticking out of his jugular gave her just enough insight to understand that the lights may be on, but no one was home.

"Ingram?" she asked, hoping his name might break through to him.

It didn't. His orbs were dark crimson, his spikes were raised, and even his scales looked lethal as they flared. The base of his tail was straight, the rest of it kinked.

She knew enough about predators to know when one was about to attack.

He's angry, afraid, and in pain. He'd managed to get himself out, but not without being harmed. Had he forgotten she was on his back as he bolted? Was she really that light in comparison to his strength? *Right now, I am dressed like the people who hurt him.*

Fuck.

Emerie eyed her bag caught around the spikes of his back, as well as the harness she'd put around him. Twigs snapped under her thinly soled boots as she stepped to the left. When he roared and jumped that way, she sprung to the right and ducked behind a tree.

She didn't stay there.

Pulling her whip from her weapons belt, Emerie ran for her life. She wasn't fast, not compared to a Duskwalker, but she used the density of the forest to shield herself.

Will this nightmare ever end?! She mentally squealed as he dived out from a bush she had been inside of not even seconds before.

For almost six days, Emerie hadn't known a moment of peace! She was exhausted on so many levels that she worried her soul would give up and leave her living body just to escape this torment.

This is the worst week of my life. Okay, that wasn't entirely true, but it was on the tippy top of shit weeks.

Thank goodness she hadn't removed his beak binding, otherwise she was sure he would have nipped her when he got too close. She had to lurch her body into an arch by going to her toes to avoid being pecked, before purposefully falling to her back and somersaulting to get away.

I just need to get behind him. That wasn't going to be an easy feat, not when she constantly had to move.

"Ugh!" she screeched. "Fuck this!"

Emerie ducked between two trees he couldn't fit through, came back around, and sprinted for him. There was no surprise for him, like he was so focused on killing her that he didn't care.

Right as he jumped to catch her in both clawed hands, Emerie flung her whip forward around a branch. She went over the top of him, let the handle of her whip go, and landed on his back to ride him reverse cowgirl.

Within the span of a breath, she unlatched the hook between his shoulder blades that was connected to the harness she'd placed on him. She'd secured it to him for just this kind of situation.

Luck favours the prepared.

Just because she was expecting to die didn't mean she hadn't come up with a backup plan to prevent it!

He bucked her off as she was leaping away, and her arms cartwheeled as she flew through the air. Her stomach impacted against a tree branch strong enough to hold her, and she grabbed ahold of it before climbing up onto it.

The Duskwalker turned one way and then the next, searching for her. He finally scratched off the scent-cloaking package she'd tied over his nose hole.

This is my chance. He didn't know where she was right now, and she needed time to secure her end of the rope leading to him. She fisted it tightly, envisioning her plan.

He was going to have to unknowingly help her with some of it.

Dropping to the ground, she sprinted around the tree and noticed she'd caught his attention by the time she was coming back around. She secured the hook around the rope's length after she looped it around the trunk and then ran in the opposite direction.

Please work. He chased after her, almost at her back, almost within swiping distance. *Please work!*

Ingram let out a choking noise before his heavy, massive body thudded against the ground. Underneath the animalistic, enraged roars, she heard shuffling like he was wriggling to get free. Leaves scattered, sticks snapped and sprung away, and dirt puffed around him.

She turned around swiftly.

Emerie panted until she thought she'd hack up a lung, barely able to feel the pain in her fractured rib. Right now, she just felt like she had a massive stitch, but that was sure to worsen over time.

Trapped on his side, with his wrists, feet, and the base of his tail bound behind his back, he thrashed.

The long piece of rope she'd threaded loosely all over his body had pulled all his limbs in tight when he'd reached the end of it in his pursuit of her. She'd turned him into a living parachute.

Probably the most ingenious idea she'd ever had, to be honest.

She did feel bad for him, though.

He'd just escaped being trapped, and now he was hog-tied in the forest. His body was unnaturally bowed, especially since his tail was so curled back it threatened to wrap around his own throat. That didn't look comfortable at all, and she thought it would have slipped off by now, considering the appendage's tapered length, but the rope was caught on his tail spikes and vertebrae.

Despite his aggression, Emerie approached him.

His head was free, so she steered clear of it and its pecking ability. She knelt beside him and patted his abdomen, hoping to calm him.

"Shh. Hey, it's okay. I'll let you go once you calm down and we have a chat."

Of course, it was like talking to a brick wall, but she continued to do it, hoping it would help. She could be patient, they just needed to wait this out... she hoped.

The beastly, feral noises he made were unsettling.

Emerie sighed with relief when his orbs finally flickered white for a moment, guessing it was a better colour than red. He thrashed even harder for a few seconds before white came back to linger longer.

Continuing her soothing strokes of his abdomen and sternum, he finally settled enough that his sight remained that hollow colour. *He must be so confused. Do Duskwalkers remember what's happened when they turn mindless?*

Ingram let out a whine.

"Hey, it's okay," she reassured again. "I'm right here. I'll–"

"It stings," he whimpered out. His scales stiffened and became even more jagged, as he let out a violent shudder. *"It stings! Why does it sting?"*

She gasped and retracted her hands, incidentally slapping herself on the cheek.

Shit. Did I hurt him? She turned from looking at his skull to lean over his side. She checked his hands and feet touching each other behind his back but nothing looked broken or injured.

Emerie let out a shriek when something wiggled in her peripheral vision. *What the hell?!* There was a freaky *dick* at his groin!

She fell to her arse and crawled backwards like it was a terrifying spider hunting her. It wasn't hard to mistake it for one when it had four tentacle limbs writhing in the air! However, the centre was unmistakably phallic shaped, with what she figured was his version of a nutsack embedded in the base of it.

Bright purple at the base, it darkened in colour until it was almost a purplish black at the very tip.

She had no idea what was going up three sides of him, but they almost looked like large, downward pointing scales.

Regardless of its oddity, it was huge and... there... when she'd never seen any genitalia on him. Where the fuck had it come from?! And more importantly, why?

It didn't even look hard, since it was kind of flopping to the side.

"Make it stop," he pleaded, and Emerie acted without thinking.

She grabbed it. Right in the centre, with a tight, panicked grip, she grabbed his giant cock with two hands.

She let go the moment her palms touched something thick and slimy. "Oh my god, it's wet," she cried, her eyes bowing in distress. "Eww! Why is it wet?!"

It thickened.

"Please. It hurts."

She had two choices right now.

Release the Duskwalker and... she didn't know. Fucking die as he chased her? Or try to use this *thing* against her – which sounded worse than death.

Or...

With her shaking lips pulling to one side in trepidation and a small amount of self-disgust, she grabbed his dick again, this time with both hands.

She stroked it. It was probably unpleasant since she was going too fast, didn't know if it was too hard, and was just generally crazed in her movements. Still, it grew thicker, and each stroke made lubricant seep onto her hands and moisten him.

Once it was fully engorged, she peeked back at Ingram's

raven skull when she noted he'd settled. He was no longer whimpering, and that was all she cared about right then.

This big Duskwalker had suffered enough torture.

If a little hand job would stop his pain, then Emerie would help. Hopefully he calmed right the fuck down after this.

She turned back to the... cock slipping between her quickly moving hands. The tentacles surrounding the base of it kept slapping around, trying to grip her wrists and forearms to the point she could only really stroke the first quarter.

Oh my god. What the fuck am I actually doing right now?

The laugh that bubbled past her lips was completely unhinged and utterly panicked, as she wondered how she'd gotten herself into this position. *"So, what did you do today, Emerie?" "Oh, nothing unusual. Just jerked off a Duskwalker. You?"*

Everything was made more unpleasant by the squelching she not only felt but heard from his grossly oversaturated cock. At least it didn't smell bad – it was kind of sweet scented – but she couldn't stop staring at how freakish it was.

The whole thing just felt wrong in her hands. Those soft, pliable, spikey scale things tickled her palms, and it made her want to let go. It was too hot to belong to a human, too big, too *everything*.

She stroked harder when Ingram released a shuddering, pleasure-filled groan. He was moving again, but this time to buck into her hands rather than to escape.

Like staring it in the eye had been the safest thing to do, as though it was a monster that would leap if she wasn't watching it, she finally braved looking away. Emerie took note of where it'd come from; a seam or a slit had parted right at his groin where the scales lined up perfectly to hide it.

She could tell it was under a lot of pressure from his unnaturally curled up, bound position. *It must have fallen out because of his arch.* Great, had she'd known that, she may not have added his tail to her harness trap.

She considered letting go to free it, but decided against it.

Right now, he was hard, which meant he was horny. She'd gotten him to this point, and it would be safer to finish him off if she didn't want him thinking he could use it on her.

Her lips tightened and turned downwards. Yet, they relaxed at Ingram's quick huffs of pleasure, and the low groan he gave when a bubble of precum welled at the very tip.

His cock now felt hot, slick, and swollen. It was beginning to repeatedly thicken in her hands before going down, like his pulsating was much stronger than a human's.

Gods, she just wanted this over with. She felt as though she was milking him like a cow.

Emerie stroked faster, frantically. Anything to get this Duskwalker to finish so she could stop fondling his weird, freaky privates. *I've totally lost it.*

Ingram let out an acute whine, and she slowed.

"Fuck. Did I hurt you?"

"Don't stop." He tried to buck into her hands but was barely able to move an inch. His chest pumped in and out with quick, excited huffs. *"Feels good."*

"Okay. Feels good is good." What was she even saying right now?

However, she should have taken that whine as the warning it was. Especially when he tensed up, released another one, and then completely froze.

She had just enough time to stand up to avoid being drenched in the first rope of semen that spurted from him, just as he let out a mangled yell. She continued to stroke him, letting him spill against the ground between her feet, while she tried not to gawk at just how much came out of him.

She even had to spread her legs to avoid the growing puddle threatening to touch her boots.

Her hands were so wet now that they squelched even louder, and she only stopped working his cock when it had been a few seconds of nothing else coming out of him.

I milked him dry. Oh god, I milked a Duskwalker's balls dry. I'm insane. This is insane.

She finally let go and threw her hands up in the air. Backing up like *it* was a rabid beast, she wasn't sure what she was supposed to do now. *Do I try to shove it back inside?* She doubted that would work; it'd likely just flop back out.

She glanced at his face and took in the fact his orbs were a deep purple. He looked like a lump as he panted, little twitches visibly dancing across his body, like he was assaulted with aftershocks from his release.

"Are-are you calm now?"

"Y...es," he rasped out, his voice laden with satisfaction.

"If I let you go, will you promise not to hurt me?"

She liked that he didn't seem to lie about promises and was pretty sincere in keeping them.

"Promise."

Emerie bounced forward and quickly cut him free so that his body would no longer be arched. She checked back to make sure his dick went back inside and was relieved when it did – although messily and slowly.

Emerie removed every bit of rope from him, including the one around his beak. Then she put space between them and placed her hands upon her face.

Eww! She smeared weird lubricant on her cheek and lips. It was what finally sent her over the edge into full-blown panic.

I'm trembling, she thought as she pulled them away to look at her palms shaking before her. *I never tremble.*

Tears welled in her eyes as her breathing sawed in and out of her. When she tried to steady herself with a deep inhale, she let out a pain-filled cry and cupped her aching ribs.

She turned around to lean against a tree. She was moments from hyperventilating from stress and anxiety when Ingram began rising to all fours.

A white fluttering form landing in front of her spooked the crap out of her, making her jump, but her vision was splitting into two. *I'm getting dizzy.* She needed to breathe. She needed to not feel like her heart was about to give out.

Every breath felt like razors in her lungs, and yet it burned her side. Her fingers were numb, her chest warm, her head fuzzy.

"You ran far. Sorry it took me so long to find you," the woman who had aided them earlier stated.

Where she had come from, and how she'd fallen from the sky, Emerie didn't know. Nor did she care right then.

Please, she inwardly cried. *Please tell me she didn't see me jerk him off.*

She stumbled to the side to get away from her, from the monster she'd freed. To get away from the insanity of what she'd just done to the Duskwalker, and from the many, many moments – days – leading up to all of this.

"Are you okay?" the woman asked as she approached Emerie. "If you're injured–"

Emerie smacked her hand away when she placed a caring touch on the back of her shoulder. "I can't breathe." She choked as her throat threatened to close. She clutched it, and the wetness of the Duskwalker's cock lubricant smeared across it, which made everything worse. "I can't breathe."

The woman ran in front of her and gripped her shoulders tightly, forcing her to look at her.

"What colour are my eyes?" the woman asked, and Emerie took them in, her blue ones darting back and forth between them.

Somehow, Emerie found their sparkling depths comforting.

"B-brown," she gasped out.

"The sky?"

She looked up. "B-black."

"What time of day is it?"

"Night."

"What is your name?"

"It's..." She sighed when she was able to take a proper breath. "It's Emerie."

With every question and answer, Emerie's chest loosened a little more.

She chased her breaths, focusing on the woman's face and how her brown skin was smooth, and clean – when she thought it'd be stained in blood. Her brows were high, but gentle in their arches, and her cheeks were strong but feminine. Emerie took in the way the wind made her dark, loose-corkscrew curls dance around her dainty yet commanding features.

Her full lips, with a small amount of pink lightness at the seam, took her attention when the woman tried to breathe with her, *for* her – to give her a rhythm to match. Emerie appreciated that so much, for someone to just help her exist when she thought she was about to truly give out.

Even the smell of her was calming, heady, and delicate.

She would have blushed, but the woman's gaze held not an ounce of judgement. It wasn't often Emerie was clutched by a panic attack, but her mind hadn't been able to handle how she'd just batted off a monster.

She couldn't even look at him, shame prickling at her nape.

"Are you hurt?" she asked Emerie when her shoulders relaxed.

"Yes. I think I fractured a rib."

With a nod, the woman closed her eyes. Black sand and mist glittered between them, but she wouldn't let Emerie escape when she tried to back up in surprise.

"There," the woman said once the flutter of magic disappeared. "Is that better?"

Emerie finally took in a breath that didn't radiate agony around her side. Even the weakness in her arms from holding onto Ingram faded, and she looked her over with a puzzled expression.

She healed me?

"My name is Lindiwe. Thank you for helping us." Then Lindiwe turned to Ingram. "I'm glad to see you are okay."

It was only then that Emerie realised the woman's clothing was covered in splatters of blood, and yet the Duskwalker wasn't reacting to it. Then again, the weird smell cascading off her was undeniably strong – and inhuman.

Lindiwe's brows drew together as she frowned deeply, and when Emerie followed her gaze, her own brows crinkled.

Ingram's orbs were a bright reddish pink, and he was obviously staring at Emerie with the way his raven skull was pointed. Crouching, with one of his hands upon the ground for balance, the other was clutching at his lower stomach.

An absurd amount of heat flared in her face to the point she thought her hair might spontaneously combust. Averting her gaze, she winced when she realised Lindiwe had been barely an inch from stepping, bare-footed, into his dirt-soaked puddle of freaking jizz.

Hopefully that meant she hadn't seen Emerie give him a quick handshake with his dick. *Greetings, Duskwalker. It's a pleasure to release you.*

She snorted a laugh at herself, needing to use humour as a coping mechanism right now or she'd flip back into hyperventilating.

They both gave her their attention, heads tilted.

Her back stiffened. *Oops.*

With his sight still a reddish pink, unsure if it was embarrassment at not understanding what she'd just done to him, or shame due to her reaction afterwards, Ingram couldn't pull away from staring at her.

Did I do something wrong?

He'd never experienced anything like what she'd done with her hands. He'd never been gifted with something so... astoundingly pleasurable that his entire body tingled from the crown of his skull all the way to the very tip of his long tail.

He, at the time, thought his entire being was about to jet out of the purple jutting part of him she'd been stroking. It had felt so good right before he released that it bordered on pain, and he thought he was about to pass out. He had mindlessly ground into her hands to achieve whatever crescendo he was climbing.

He'd spilled – and his spirit had soared.

Then, as she'd promised, she'd freed him.

He'd been a lump laying in the dirt and sticks of the forest, huffing wildly to release his strained lungs. That was until she'd gotten up, faced away from him, and began... breathing erratically.

She hadn't smelled of fear, but even he, who wasn't used to being around humans, could tell something was wrong.

Was I not supposed to release that white liquid? His sight flickered to the puddle on the ground. *What came from me?* She avoided it like it was a dangerous fire. *But she was the one who brought it forth.*

Ingram clutched his stomach tighter, just above where the

jutting rod had come from.

She wouldn't look upon his skull now, although she'd had no issue doing so within the dungeon. He didn't like that she was averting her gaze. It only deepened his worries that he'd truly done something wrong.

He was so distracted with his thoughts he hadn't noticed the Witch Owl come up to him. So, when she gently cupped the top and bottom of his beak to force his skull to her, he flinched.

Then she pressed her hand near his neck and he flinched again, this time from the pain.

"Do you want me to take the arrows out, or leave them?" she asked, and he couldn't help noticing the warmth and care in her dark eyes.

"Leave them," he grated. *"I will heal them away later."*

She nodded as she stepped back, but not before giving the top of his beak a caring stroke. She'd never touched him so openly and affectionately before.

No one other than Aleron had.

"I'm sorry you had to endure so much." Her voice held such genuine remorse that his sight inadvertently shifted to a dark, gloomy blue. "I wish I could have come sooner."

"I should not have come here."

"It's okay," she cooed. "We all make mistakes."

Her reassurance soothed the worst of his self-loathing. *Has she made mistakes?* She often appeared infallible.

Emerie, with her fist over her mouth, cleared her throat. His skull lifted, as the Witch Owl's head turned.

"Sorry, I don't mean to interrupt," she said, lifting her arms, "but what now?"

"For you, nothing," the Witch Owl answered sternly. "For now, I will return to the Veil, and Ingram will find his home somewhere here on the surface."

Dark yellow filled his vision as he stepped away from her. *"No. I must find a way to destroy the Demon King."*

He hadn't given up on his vengeance for his kindred. No matter what happened to him, he would bear it if he could bring Aleron back into a world that was safe and peaceful for them.

A world where he wouldn't... lose him again.

"I told you, Ingram. Unless we have an army, which we don't, there's nothing we can do right now but try to find a way to be safe."

"You want to kill the Demon King?" Emerie asked, her orange brows furrowing tightly. "So you *truly* came here for aid?"

He didn't know why she was asking him again when he'd already answered this back at the stronghold.

Her icy-blue eyes darted to the ground and flicked side to side in obvious thought. Then, her twisted and tight expression fell away, and she lifted her head up while rolling her shoulders back. "What if I help?"

"He needs an army," the Witch Owl bit out. "What can a single human do? You're likely to abandon him the moment your fear becomes too much, or he'll eat you because of it."

Emerie's features stiffened, and her gaze shadowed, became... unfeeling, even. He had the urge to growl when it reminded him of the Wren creature.

"I just threw my life away for this Duskwalker, and you're saying my help is not good enough?"

The Witch Owl gave a mocking snort. "You chose that. Were you expecting some kind of reward?"

"That's not what I'm saying," she stated with a sigh, brushing some of her dishevelled hair out of her face with the back of her hand. "I joined the guild for a reason. What I did today... I just signed my own death warrant. If I'm going to die, I'd rather it be doing something I originally set out to do, instead of being killed for deserting my own people."

Ingram tilted his head in curiosity, the dark yellow of it flaring in his sight. *She seeks revenge too?*

"You understand death awaits you if you follow him?" The Witch Owl had a high tone to her voice, like unmasked surprise.

"Death awaited me the moment I signed up with the guild." She lifted her chin defiantly. "The only fear regarding it is the failure of not achieving what I set out to do."

Ingram's head tilted the other way, his orbs deepening in their hue. *In this, our hearts are the same.*

"I... would like her help," Ingram stated as he stepped

forward while crouching, using both hands to steady himself. *"She trapped me so I could not harm her. She gave me freedom."*

She also smelt nice, and he liked the colour of her hair and eyes. She'd also touched him until bliss shot from him, and he was very, very curious about that.

Would she do it again?

The Witch Owl looked between them, but when she finally fixed her gaze on Emerie, something glinted in her features. Something dark, and yet somehow warm. Was it possible to express guilt and pride at the same time?

Then again... what would he know when it came to the complexities of humans and their emotions?

"Then I'll entrust him to you," the Witch Owl said, letting a smile fill her face for the first time during their conversation. "I think I would feel better knowing he had someone around that would guide him."

"Me? Guide him?" Emerie's little brows drew together once more. "Wouldn't it be the other way around?"

The Witch Owl let out a deep laugh. "No, not at all. If left to his own devices, Ingram would wander into the Veil in search of the Demon King."

She patted his side, absolutely unbothered by his presence, which only confused him. She'd never been this close with him, but... he didn't mind it.

At least someone cared for him.

The space next to him didn't feel so empty... or lonely.

"The wisest thing to do would be to go west," the Witch Owl continued, turning her face to Ingram. "To your brothers. They will have answers for you, and they will assist you in achieving our collective goal."

Once more, that word – brothers – was spoken. He'd like to know what this meant, and why it seemed so important to this female.

"So, avoid the Veil and go west?" Emerie asked, cupping her chin while crossing one arm across her chest. "How far west? We're right near the eastern sea. If you want us to go to the western sea, that'll take us almost a month."

"Not with a Duskwalker," Lindiwe answered with a smile.

Her expression morphed into a grumbly one. "What about you?"

"I will fly back to the Veil. I am needed there more than here if Ingram has you."

Emerie nodded like she understood until she shook her head and gaped. "*Fly* back?" She lifted her hands to her shoulders so she could flap them. "Like a bird?"

The Witch Owl let out a cackle. "Yes, dear child. Fly like a bird."

After a short conversation, it didn't take long for her to demonstrate what she meant. She morphed into a human-sized barn owl and eventually took flight, leaving behind a white feather speckled with brown.

After a long moment where Emerie stared in the direction the Witch Owl had gone, her eyes so wide twin rings of white were visible, she turned to Ingram. Her gaze softened.

Then, the white scarring on her face darkened with pale red, as did her cheeks. She averted her gaze to the forest.

"I guess I should just get it over with and say sorry about my reaction before." Blue instantly lifted into his sight at the cold reminder. Emerie rubbed at the sleeve of her black uniform. "It's been a really tough few days and my emotions just kind of boiled over. Sorry if I alarmed you. It had nothing to do with you, nor was it your fault. I just want you to know that, considering you might be embarrassed because of how I just started having a panic attack right after you came."

Came? Is that what he'd done?

The blue lifted away from his orbs to be replaced by their usual purple, and he was relieved to see that colour naturally after so many days.

He hesitantly stepped forward. He dipped his head almost submissively. *"I did not do something wrong?"*

"Do something wrong?" she answered with a flinching laugh. "No, not at all."

Relief sailed through him like a warm gust of wind. She looked southward from their location in the forest, and a breeze fluttered her colourful hair over her shoulder.

"We better get moving before the guild catches up to us.

They'll be disorientated for a while since Wren is dead, but that'll only be for so long." Then, once more, she turned to him, this time gifting him with a smile – one that closed both eyes and appeared more like a cringe. "Guess it's just you and me now."

Just you and me. The way she'd said those four words hadn't been with disdain, but perhaps hinting at something pleasant.

Warmth tickled his chest as a bright yellow lifted into his sight this time. His long tail shifted the dirt as it slid side to side in response.

I am not alone now.

ELEVEN

Ingram followed next to the female as she took the lead, tilting his head one way and then the other while ducking around trees to stay with her.

"Should we not be going west?" he asked, unsure of why she was taking them this way. *"We are north of the Veil's canyon."*

The crack of earth that spanned across the entire world from west to east was relatively narrow in comparison. They were currently north of it, so it made sense to go west from their current location.

Holding onto the strap of her bag directly between the two generous mounds on her chest, Emerie blew a stray strand of waving red hair from her face. "Yes, it would probably be faster to go straight from here, but then we'll be entering a dangerous territory."

His head rattled like dry bones were trapped inside his skull. *"But I will protect us."*

Does she not think I am strong? His sight wandered to the side as annoyance spiked in his chest, bruising his ego. *Does she think I am weak because I was bound so helplessly?*

That wasn't fair. His trappings had been tight within that dungeon. His captors had also made sure to anchor all of his moveable joints, ensuring he couldn't rip his own limbs off to escape.

Shouldn't that show how formidable he was?

"It'll only add a few extra days if we go south first. The north has more shade because of the trees and is closer to many mountain ranges. Whereas there's a large expanse of fields south of the Veil. That means less Demons, and..." She peeked over to him. "The northern Demonslayer sector is larger. Zagros Fortress has probably already sent messenger birds to all the guild sectors with my description and crimes. Sometimes a human hiding in the shadows with a bow and arrow is more dangerous than a Demon. You don't hear your death coming."

"But I cannot die," he answered. At least... not so easily.

"But I can." She smiled as she spoke the words, yet it didn't reach her eyes. "Plus, say they missed and only cut me instead. My blood would send you into a frenzy, correct? Accidents happen, but it's best to do everything in our power to prevent them."

Ingram decided to let it go and just follow her, having to slow his pace to a snail's crawl to stay by her side. Her breaths were sharp, like she was exerting herself, but she never changed the pace of her determined march. The entire time, her shoulders were firmly rolled back, her spine straight, and her head high.

Ingram eventually dropped back slightly so he could inspect her freely without her knowledge. He made sure his foot and hand steps were quiet as he came inches from her back and sniffed.

That possessive scent is no longer on her, he thought as he took in her sweet smell, nearly shuddering at it. *When she touched me, what came from me smelt similar.*

Was that why she hadn't wanted it to be on her, so he couldn't leave his own possessive marking on her? Why not? Ingram didn't think he was too bad.

He had a pretty skull in comparison to the other Mavka. He didn't have snapping sharp fangs, and his horns weren't tall and daunting; instead, they were rather stout. He was the only one he knew of with a beak. He figured these differences made him better.

He came around the other side of Emerie and snuck another sniff of her. He wouldn't mind shielding her mouthwatering smell with his own, ensuring no one else could take it in. Instead, they would only be reminded of his presence.

I do not know how to do that, or why I even want to.

His sight shifted over the mounds on her chest, the plumpness of her backside, and back up to her narrow waist. He deemed all of them insignificant, instead checking over her thighs and biceps to assess whether or not she was a strong human who could survive this travel with him.

His sight lifted to her face, taking in her light skin, the white scarring on the left side of her face, and the dirt sprinkled on her. Even though she still, apparently, needed a bath, he couldn't help finding her attractive.

Perhaps, even... the prettiest human he'd ever seen.

That might solely be based on the fact that she'd been kind to him, saved him, had touched him with profound pleasure, and had a goal that resonated with his own. Plus, her eyes were like cold water, yet they held such warmth that even the sun was cooler in their presence. They were framed by long, curling orange lashes, reminding him of a winter sunrise streaking over a frozen lake. He could remember sitting next to Aleron one dawn, watching it under the blanket of his big and heavy wing.

The flaming edges of his vision shifted blue as the weight of his grief struck him like a falling ice shard, embedding straight into his chest.

Emerie flinched as she raised her hand to shield her features when the sun broke through the trees. "It's morning already?" she groaned out while squinting. "Just how long were you running before we stopped? No wonder Lindiwe didn't find us easily."

Lindiwe? Was that the Witch Owl's true name? He hadn't heard it before... or it was possible he'd been too distracted and wasn't listening.

Emerie's silvery voice broke him from the sudden trappings of his thoughts, bringing his mind back to the examination of his new companion.

The trees opened up, revealing the cliff edge of a ravine. Water sloshing, frothing, and rushing below bombarded his sensitive hearing. The sun shone down on them as she led them along it, likely to find a way to cross – even though he could have easily leapt it.

Ingram was assessing her shadow and the way it danced behind her when something glittered in his peripheral. Mild yellow lifted into his sight, a melding of joy and curiosity as he brought his gaze up.

Unable to help himself, tantalised by what he saw, he reached out and grabbed it. Emerie hissed and jerked back when he'd grabbed a fistful of her hair, his orbs brightening at the mesmerising lure of it.

His head twisted one way and then the other to better see past his beak, as he watched her hair glitter with an array of wild, autumn colours. Yellow like the sun, gold like the earth, orange like a sunset, and red like fire.

I've never seen such colouring on a creature. At least... not while they were alive, in the sun, and within reaching distance for him to play with.

"Ow!" she cried when he brought the long, wavy, but tangled strands closer to his skull so he could look in close detail. She twisted, looping it around his fist, to face him. She grabbed the length of it at the base of her head and tried to yank it away. "Why'd you pull my hair?"

"It looked pretty in the sun," he answered, not seeing the problem. *"I wanted a closer look."*

"That really hurt," she rasped, tugging again.

Oh. He loosened his fist and allowed her to untangle the clump from his claws. *"I did not mean to hurt you."*

Yet, a second later, he cupped her face when he noted the sun reflecting in her eyes and making them shine like crystal. The orange lashes framing them glittered just like her hair, and he couldn't help being mesmerised by them both.

Currently, she was glowing. So bright and full of life.

He'd never seen anything as wonderful.

However, her eyes shut as she pulled back, cupping her cheek. The moment he spotted the bead of blood welling on the scarring over her cheek, he halted his breathing so he couldn't smell it.

"You cut me," she whined, her brows drawing inward.

Shying back, he cradled the hand that had harmed her in his other, his sight shifting to an orange. Guilt swirled around his heart, especially since he hadn't *meant* to hurt her further.

"I am sorry," he offered, clasping his hand to his chest as his tail curled around his feet nervously.

"You have to be gentle with me, Ingram," she stated firmly, shaking her head at him. "I'm not a Duskwalker. My skin is soft, and your claws are so sharp I've seen them nearly split a person in half with just one swipe."

"But I was being gentle," he argued, turning his gaze down to the claws glinting at the tips of his fingers. They were so sharp that the ends were nearly invisible to even his eye.

"Gentler, then." She brought her hand away from her face, and already the bleeding had stopped. The scratch wasn't deep. "You can't just pull my hair or reach out to me so carelessly. You can't just grab me and throw me around. I can be hurt very easily."

His shoulders slumped in defeat as he continued to cup the back of his hand. *But I liked touching her hair and face.*

The meagre contact he had with her skin had greeted his fingertips with undeniable softness. It had been smooth like silk on one part of his hand, and textured in a way that tingled his finger pads on the other. Her hair, pretty as it was, had been so hot from the sun in his palm that it threatened to singe him – and he'd been hoping it would score him to the bone.

Ingram stepped back from her to put space between them.

Something is wrong with me. He'd never had these desires to touch or look at a human before. Their hair had never dazzled him like a shiny rock, nor had their eyes.

So why now? Why her?

Yet, he couldn't deny that he wasn't completely opposed to it. It was a new thing forming within him.

"I will be more careful."

His gaze drifted around until he found what he wanted. Then, to demonstrate that he would do better, he dragged his claws down a large boulder.

He did internally wince when he gouged into it and created ten deep grooves. He did it a second time, just to make sure, before assessing his claws.

He came over hesitantly and presented them to her.

"Is this better?"

Emerie's full pink lips pulled to the side as she held the back of one of his hands in her left palm and tapped his index finger claw with her right. Her lips curled upward, and she turned a smile to him.

"That is much safer, thank you." She closed his hand for him, and the softness of her flesh brushed over the backs of his knuckles. "But still be gentle. Okay? No more sudden grabbing."

Her smile and touch, as well as the acceptance of his idea, made his tail swish back and forth across the ground. *I am smart. That was a smart idea.* His tail swished faster when she didn't immediately pull away from him, instead patting the hand she was holding. *She is pleased with me.*

However, Ingram didn't promise that he wouldn't grab her again, unsure if he could stick to it.

His resolve weakened further when he looked down to their touching hands and remembered, vividly, hers stroking him into bliss. His scales and small amount of fur lifted at the memory, as a strange stirring sensation tingled his groin.

He wanted her to do it again, already obsessed with the idea.

Especially since he'd never experienced anything like it in his life, and he was growing more curious about it the longer it was since he'd experienced it. He wanted to know what it was, and why the strange thing had sprung from him.

Emerie stared at the raven-skulled Duskwalker before her, unsure of what to do with him.

Already her short amount of time with him was... odd.

His sniffing of her had not gone unnoticed, although she'd chosen to ignore it. If he wanted to be curious for his own sense of security, she would accept it.

She wasn't the one who had been captured, tortured, and afraid as she ran away. He wasn't the one who had purposefully put her in harm's way or betrayed her without knowing what that would mean later.

It was hard to deny that he might have a sweet side, which, considering what he was, was hard to accept. She'd always heard of Duskwalkers being monsters. Cruel and frightening. A nightmare that could walk in the day and night, and sometimes a child's worst fear, even in the bright sun.

An omen of death.

So, to have one pet her hair, or even try to brush her face was hard to take in. He'd also steadied her once on their walk when a loose rock had slipped underfoot, forcing his shoulder up to catch her from falling flat on her face.

All this, from a creature she was supposed to hate, only twisted the knife of guilt in her gut. Deeper and deeper it cut, until she thought it would make a permanent hole.

Even more so when she took in his bright-yellow orbs, and they came across as warm, and almost... joyful in response to her touch and reassurance.

I don't know how to make up for how much I've wronged him. Was freeing him from the confines she herself had put on him enough?

It couldn't be, not with everything he endured afterwards.

She tried to smile for him but knew it didn't go past her lips. Emerie let him go and turned so she could continue to lead the way – and, more importantly, give him her back to hide her pained expression.

She hadn't offered to travel with him just to make it up to him, although that had been a big factor in her decision. Her reasons for being here were self-serving.

I joined the guild with a purpose... She rubbed her nape as uncertainty laced with her determined resolve. *But his cause seems even more important.*

Kill the Demon King – the centre of power for all the Demons – in the hopes that it could put an end to the worst of their chaos? She wondered if it would be the equivalent of killing a bee queen and watching her workers buzz around without rhyme or reason. Or would the Demons quickly establish a new leader before they perished?

Regardless of her musings, it was a thread of hope for her people, for herself.

Lifting her face towards the rising sun, she closed her eyes as she basked in its light and heat. *I know I'm doing the right thing, even if no one else will see it.*

"Emerie," he called, breaking her from her musing as the dark, bass rumble of his voice reverberated through her. The tiny hairs on her body stood on end as it tingled her brain in the most disconcerting way.

She couldn't even remember telling him her name. She guessed he must have overheard it within Zagros Fortress.

"Yes?" she croaked out, unable to look at him due to her weird reaction. Even her cheeks had heated a little in embarrassment, likely making her facial scarring more noticeable – and she hated it when that happened.

Smoothness rubbed down the back of her forearm until it slid into her relaxed palm. The movement in her peripheral told her it was his beak.

"Will you do what you did to me before?" He seemed to almost groan out his question, each word slow and hoarse.

Her eyelids snapped open, and she jerked away. She crossed her arms as she faced him, shaking her head since she knew *exactly* what he was talking about.

His purple orbs appeared a little darker than the orchid hue she'd seen them turn, but she put it down to a trick of the sunlight hitting them for the first time.

"N-no," she squeaked. "That... uh, was only one time."

He stepped closer to crowd her. *"Why? Your touch felt good."*

Emerie put a hand out to ward him back.

"B-because I only did that to calm you and because you said you were in pain. That's, um, that's something you're only supposed to do with someone special."

The Duskwalker confidently placed the curve of his beak right against her outward reaching hand. It tilted to the right under her fingertips and palm.

"I can be special." That's not what she meant! She retracted her hand from the air. *"What was it? I have never seen it come*

from me before, but you touched it so... willingly."

Emerie wanted to squirm in embarrassment, her cheeks heating with it to the point even her chest flushed.

Touched it so willingly?! He was making her feel like a sexual deviant!

"You don't know what came out of you?" she squeaked out, her voice so high pitched it threatened to give out.

When he shook his head, Emerie wanted to expire.

Oh gods. I feel like I took advantage of him.

She'd just wanted to help him! He'd suffered enough pain that she didn't want him to experience another second more of it, even if it meant she had to give him a quick hand job and forget it ever happened.

But she should have known he wouldn't make it a one-time thing. She'd given him release. She'd had an inclination he would try to seek more from her, but she'd also just been hoping he... wouldn't.

Do... Do I tell him what it was?

Part of her wanted to change the subject, and another part told her the right thing to do was to explain it to him. It wasn't fair to withhold knowledge from him just because she wanted to die of shame and embarrassment.

Pull up a chair, class. It's time to learn sex education. She groaned in dismay before her shoulders slumped.

She'd been retreating from him as he stalked her, but her feet eventually settled. Emerie let out a haunted sigh.

"A cock, or dick. That's what came out of you." Then Emerie's brows drew together. "Wait. How have you not seen it before? Wouldn't you have needed to... you know?" When he tilted his head like he obviously had no idea about what she was talking about, something dawned on her. "Oh shit! You don't pee!"

She'd never had to clean that up in the dungeon, thank goodness.

His orbs morphed to dark yellow, and he sat back on his haunches. *"Pee? What is pee?"*

Emerie rubbed her cheek in tiredness. She hadn't slept last night, and the mental strain of everything, plus this conversation, weighed heavily on her.

"Look," she started as her hand moved to her nape, "what came out of you means you are a boy, or urm, male, I guess?" She explained her theory, unsure if it was true or not. "Since you don't pee but produce seed or, um, cum? I'm guessing it's purely a pleasure and reproduction function for you."

"This is what it means to be a male?" He lifted a hand and wrapped it around the end of his beak in what she figured was deep thought. *"What does your dick or cock look like then if you are female? Is yours also purple?"*

Her face paled, and her eye twitched.

I'm in over my head here. It was obvious Ingram was intelligent enough to understand certain things, but he lacked knowledge. The question was, how much?

"No. I-I don't have a cock. I have, um, something else. Something different."

"Like what?" He tilted his head. *"How is it different?"*

She opened her mouth to answer, then promptly shut it before she said something very stupid, and potentially dangerous. As much as she wanted to explain to him the female anatomy, she wasn't going to put herself in a position where a curious and horny Duskwalker went searching for a warm and wet place to shelter himself.

It was probably better if he didn't know there was one.

"A pussy, or cunt," she answered with a grim smile, giving him a name in case he ever needed it. "But let's get back to the main point. What I did, we won't be doing again, okay?"

"Why not? I liked it, and you said I did not do anything wrong."

"Because you should do that with someone you care very deeply about," she answered, trying not to feel pity for him. "You *can* do it with someone you just feel desire or arousal towards, but it's nicer when it's someone who makes you feel good in here." Emerie pointed to her heart, hoping to convey that it should be done with someone who made him feel warm and fuzzy inside.

It only reminded Emerie that's what she'd been hoping for with Bryce, and she couldn't remember the last time she felt that way. As much as she had insecurities about her body, she'd been desperately seeking intimacy.

In her own way, she knew she let Bryce sexually use her so she could pretend she had that with him. Was it wrong to pretend she felt loved and adored?

Maybe that's why Emerie had stroked Ingram... because intimacy no longer felt like anything but a *chore*.

Ingram touched an index claw to the sternum bone protruding from his chest, twisting his head downwards as though to look there past his beak.

She observed the Duskwalker sitting before her while he was in the light of the sun, getting the chance to really take him in.

Most of his bones appeared to be sitting on the outside of his flesh. All of his ribs, his sternum, his collar bones, his hip bones, his knees and elbows, and even his legs and forearms. The white bones seemed to come from where the flesh was the thinnest on a human, including his feet, ankles, wrists, and hands.

The vertebrae of his spine were visible from the back of his skull all the way to his tail tip, although they protruded a little more than a human. They almost looked like spikes themselves. She thought that was the freakiest part of him.

Most of his body was covered in black lizard-like scales that glinted with a blue sheen in the sun. That same blue was present in the short, barely noticeable fur that covered the back of his neck and shoulders. Soft places, like his stomach, the inner crook of his elbows, and the backs of his knees, were dark-grey skin.

His feet were... odd. They were thinner than a human's, once more following a lizard likeness, yet his hands were like hers. Just far bigger, fatter, and tipped with deadly claws.

His tail was quite long, and the tapered end of it curled where it rested against the dirt.

He was covered in spikes that ran down the backs of his arms, legs, and down the sides of his visible vertebrae.

Gosh, she'd never seen anything more otherworldly than Ingram.

Everything about him – from the tips of his short, upward-jutting goat horns on his raven skull, all the way to the long claws of his toes – was inhuman. He looked like a frightening monster standing in the sun, and yet his naivety about his own body made him come across as sweet... and kind of adorable.

Even the way he was touching at his chest was cute, obviously trying to understand what his heart was supposed to feel.

Before Ingram could jump back into his uncomfortable questioning, Emerie stepped to the side.

"We should keep moving, Ingram." His skull darted up to her, as though she'd taken him by surprise. "We have a long journey ahead of us, and I want to put more space between us and the guild."

He fell to the side smoothly to drop his hands to the ground and walk on all four limbs.

She was thankful he let the conversation go.

TWELVE

Ingram watched his travelling companion brush her hands together to rid them of dust as she came out from the human dwelling she'd led them to. Grime had streaked across her cheek, and a small clump of spider webbing had caught in her hair.

Ingram rubbed at his nose holes. The dust clinging to her made him want to sneeze.

"Okay, I've moved the nest to another room to make space in the middle of the house," she answered as she bounded down the five steps.

When they'd first emerged here, she'd explained the Demonslayers knew of a few empty homes.

Most humans had gone to live behind the walls or died in the forest. Demonslayers used them on *missions* so they had a safe place to stay for a night or two, or Demons would inhabit them with semi-permanent nests.

By the evidence of the Demon carcass with an arrow sticking out from the back of its head, this one had been occupied. There was little blood from the medium-sized creature, and he doubted it would be enough to draw in more of its kind.

He considered eating it, not that it smelt appetising, but he didn't know if that would make him hunger further and turn that craving upon her. It was best to just leave it, thankful it was towards the back of the house and where they mostly couldn't see it.

They were both prepared for the creature, as Ingram had been able to hear it scuttling around inside from a distance. Emerie told him to let her take care of it. Less blood, she'd explained.

As for now, Emerie sat down against a log that appeared to have been purposefully cut and placed. She pulled out a package wrapped in cloth from her bag.

"We'll stay here for the night."

"Would it not be best to keep moving?" Ingram asked, sitting down across from her in the tiny, moss-covered clearing.

"Yeah, probably," she answered as she nibbled on... food. He couldn't even begin to decipher what humans consumed, but it looked dry, which made it hard to distinguish if it was meat or not. "However, I haven't slept in nearly two days. I need rest, otherwise I'm going to make myself sick."

She shivered in her uniform. It didn't appear to be thick or warm since it clung to her so tightly.

When he tilted his head, she paused and furrowed her brows.

"Is... it okay if I eat in front of you?" She pushed the hand holding her package of food forward and gestured at it. "I don't have a lot, but I can share if I need to."

Ingram inched his head forward, not really closing much of the distance between them, to sniff at the air. He shook his head. What she had did not smell appetising.

"I do not consume things such as this."

"Figures." She let out a snort of laughter before retracting her hand. "You have a pretty good nose. If it wouldn't trouble you, if you could sniff out things like berries and mushrooms on our travels, it'll really help me. I could only bring so much between my tools, water, and food. I can ration for a few days, but I'll eventually starve." Once more, she let out a half-hearted laugh as she looked down at her food. "Guess it's a good thing, in a way. I started getting pudgy lately with all my new tasks and studying, since they'd stopped sending me out on missions."

Ingram understood about half of what she said, but his tail still shifted slightly behind him. He was happy that the little human was speaking with him – like it didn't matter they were different or that he didn't completely understand everything.

He asked her a lot of questions, mostly out of habit from

when Aleron had been by his side. However, unlike his kindred, Emerie would have an answer. If she didn't, she would try to explain it as best she could.

He pointed to where there was a disturbed pile of rocks and loose charcoal. *"Are you not going to light a fire? I have seen many humans do this when they rest."*

He'd also like to see how one was made.

"It's not smart to have a trail of smoke leading to us. It can attract all manner of creatures, as well as inform the guild of where we are."

As a Duskwalker who had followed the scent of fire, he thought this was wise.

When silence and night fell upon them, and he only inspected the female before him because he had little else to do, he noticed her eyes drooping. They closed, and a few minutes later, she jerked up.

She rapidly blinked and then groaned as she rubbed at her face.

"I need to sleep," she said, and yet didn't get up. Now that she'd stopped to rest, she seemed incapable of moving again.

"Do you need me to carry you inside?" he asked, since she'd laid down a *sleeping bag* that had been hidden away in the shelter.

"What? No," she quickly uttered, springing to her feet suddenly. "I'm okay. Thanks though, I guess."

Why did she seem alarmed by that prospect? He must admit, she was awkward with him. Constantly, he sensed she was wary and unsure.

Ingram stood on all fours to follow her. *"It will be faster if I carry you on our journey. You are slow, and I can move throughout the night."*

As she was climbing up the stairs, she glanced back with her lips tightly pulled to one side. She opened her mouth to say something, only to shut it.

"I'll think about it," she stated, confusing him on the matter.

At the pace they'd walked today, they wouldn't make it to the westernmost point of the Veil for over an entire moon cycle. If he were to carry her on his back, he'd likely halve it – and even more so if he were to sprint on all fours.

He'd find out later why she was hesitant and attempt to change her mind.

Ingram wanted this journey over sooner rather than later, hoping to bring back Aleron as quickly as possible. That was his goal, and every day without his kindred left a crumbling hole in his chest. He wanted to fill it again.

The female said nothing about the fact he'd followed her inside, and she simply laid down with her back towards him. After a few moments, she rolled to check on his whereabouts.

"You should sleep too."

He nodded and obediently laid down where he was, thumping to the ground in a curled heap. Even though it was early night, Ingram drifted off due to the consistent lack of sleep over the course of the past week.

His dreams were unpleasant.

The images that haunted him flickered between hazy memories of his pain: the sharpness of evil human faces inflicting them, and the Demons who had hunted him. And, in each of his darted gazes around the stone room or the gloomy forest, Ingram searched for his kindred – only to find himself alone.

Even in sleep, he could tell his heart had accelerated and his breaths had sharpened. The whines and yelps of his memories mixed in with the present ones that quietly burst from him.

Unable to cope with the intensity of his nightmares, kicking and clawing to be free of them, he jerked to his feet to escape. He paused, his orbs opening from blackness to a pale blue of combined fear and sorrow as he reorientated himself in the human dwelling.

On shaking limbs, his skull turned to the closest noise and scent.

Despite the darkness, her orange mass of hair was vivid as it lay sprawled around her on the distressed wooden flooring. *It looks... warm,* he thought, remembering how it had almost singed his palms in the sunshine.

He took a singular step towards her.

She smells nice. Almost sweet... and comforting. He wished

142 OPAL REYNE

he knew the names of the plants she reminded him of as he took another step closer.

I can hear her heart. It was tiny in comparison to Aleron's. It sounded fragile, like *she* was fragile, as he took that last step.

Standing right next to her, he watched her sleep for a little while. Some of the anxieties in his chest faded at her lulling breaths, the way her chest waved in and out, and at her... peacefulness.

He was envious of it. He wanted her to share it.

Ingram hesitantly and carefully lowered himself into a curl with his back touching hers. He was ready to leap away and pretend he hadn't been seeking the comfort of her unwitting touch if she woke.

He waited, then eventually eased when she didn't.

It was such a tiny spot touching him, perhaps just the small of her lower back pressing against his ribs – his spikes jutting over her sleeping form – but the warmth of her spread into him. It soothed the rapidness of his heart and lungs, heating him as it travelled throughout his body and down his limbs.

His pale-blue orbs first lifted to just blue, realising simply this was enough to quell some of the loneliness that had been weighing on him. The longer he stayed there and listened to her heart, focussed on the rhythm of her breathing, and took in the scent of her, the more his sight gradually shifted to its normal purple.

She may not be Aleron, but for now, for tonight, she would provide him the tranquillity of sleeping next to someone.

It might have been the contact between them that allowed him to finally have peaceful dreams.

The only thing was... when he woke, he realised he'd changed positions. So had she. He was lying on his stomach with his arms and legs folded and tucked underneath him, whereas she was on her side. It brought more warmth, more touch, and comfort.

I am too restless to sleep. He was still exhausted, but his dreams – although pleasant – had been of Aleron. Somehow, behind the veil of those dreams, his loss lingered, tainting those precious moments he'd experienced with his kindred.

Ingram searched for a window in this unfamiliar room. The waning half-moon was high, and he thought it may be the middle of the night.

He slowly lifted his head as to not disturb the female who had curled into a ball with her forehead resting against the side of his biceps. Her knees were also jabbing into him, but he didn't mind.

Since his head was above hers, he twisted it so he could see her past his beak.

Her hands were tucked up near her chest, with her face buried against her fists and his shoulder.

She looks paler than normal.

Was it the stream of moonbeam crossing over her, or because she was so deeply asleep due to her fatigue? With the end of his beak, he managed to nudge some fallen hair away from her face so he could better see it, revealing more of the scarring that marred her forehead, cheek, jaw, and neck. She shivered when he revealed her ear, which was also scarred and missing sections of hair around it.

Although he didn't know what the marks were from, only that they looked like webbing, he didn't mind them. They were Emerie – part of what made up her face, as much as a raven skull made up his.

What did bother him was the dirt sprinkles on her nose, cheeks, forehead, and chin. *When I find a lake, I will have to toss her in it.* She mostly smelt clean, other than the residual sweat from all their walking over the last day. He was disappointed she didn't know how to clean her face properly.

It never registered with him that those spots had never changed.

Ingram took in her light breathing as it waved over him, the warmth of her next to him with more contact than before, and her pretty scent. Unwilling to move, he watched her, curious about the little human.

I have never truly spoken to a human before. He didn't count the evil ones back in the place she called Zagros Fortress.

Then again, that might not be true.

There was... Raewyn. He mused on the female with coily-curled white hair he'd met around five full moons ago. *But she said she was not human.*

She'd called herself an Elf, and he must admit, her long, pointed ears were far different from Emerie's.

Yellow lifted into his sight as he watched Emerie's closed eyelids flicker side to side while she twitched. *Raewyn had been kind as well.*

He thought of Emerie as kind. She had been nice to him in the Demonslayer stronghold, had gently washed him, and freed him.

She also touched my cock... *and made it...* come.

Ingram deeply shuddered at the memory, his sight closing and turning black momentarily. He gave a singular pant and opened his orbs to a slightly darker purple than usual.

He tried not to think about it, instead focusing on the female laying vulnerable next to him. However, his sight eventually drifted to her fists. He'd gotten a glimpse of them stroking him when he'd been bound in the forest, and they had been stark against the purple of his cock and... tentacle-like limbs. Then his view shifted when he'd arched from an undeniable urge to *grind* into her beautiful hands.

The seam at his groin twitched as something moved and began to throb behind it. Each deepening thrum, as heat built and built, had his mind drifting back to that one moment. Her hands, the wetness that coated him, even every breath she'd unwittingly blown on him to give him additional warmth, had aided in his very first mind-numbing release of seed.

Ingram shuddered as hardness built from deep within, poking at his insides, and he lifted his hips to ease the pressure – unknowing that it would allow it to escape. The moment his cock broke from his seam and the exposed head slipped across the ground, he thrust forward with a quiet groan.

He didn't appreciate the rough wooden texture that greeted him, so he stood and looked down at his own body. His tentacles weren't shielding him, instead wriggling in the air like they were unsure of what to do.

Ingram's chest tightened as his groin clenched, and he turned his gaze back to the little sleeping female... and more importantly, her blissful hands.

I want her to touch it again.

His sight darkened in its purple, something that had never happened to him before he met her. He realised that every draw in of her sweet scent was deepening it. Looking at her was deepening it.

He craved her in ways he didn't comprehend.

Ingram lowered his head, ready to stir her with the curve of his beak so she could ease him. The air was getting to it, and there was a spot that stung, although it wasn't too uncomfortable yet.

However, he stopped just before he could nudge her cheek, recalling what she'd said last time he'd asked her to touch him – although his dick had not been freed at the time.

He didn't like that she'd said no. He didn't understand her reasonings, why it wasn't okay or why he should be seeking something in his chest before he did it. He wanted someone to touch. He wanted *her* to ease the ache that had come from him – especially since she was the one to teach him about it.

"Emerie," he gently called, pushing at her cheek when the stinging in his cock became more noticeable. He winced, and his skin crawled and puffed in repulsion.

She cringed, groaned at him without opening her eyes, covered her face with her forearm, and hid from him by burrowing down.

Ingram let out an annoyed huff before giving a deeper wince.

He gripped his dick, desperate to stop the stinging ache that began to pierce it. Every second longer was making it dry.

"Hmm?" His own grab didn't feel... terrible. It also stopped the worst of his pain.

He curiously looked down, gave himself a stroke, and let out a deep, pleasurable huff. *That feels good. I can also do this?*

Yellow flickered in his dark purple sight.

He almost sat to explore this further, but Emerie's light snore caught his attention. His sight morphed to a reddish pink, unsure if this was something he should be doing.

He backed away from her to hide and explore by himself – free from the possibility of her judgement.

It took a few seconds of fumbling with the tiny doorknob to open it, but he let himself outside while holding his dick with one hand to shield it. He went a little to the left, still out the front in the small clearing, but away from immediate view.

Ingram knelt and twisted his head so he could see what he was doing. Since he was gripping around the centre, his entire hand encompassing the girth, he drew it downward until he came to the two ovals embedded into the base of his dick. The liquid covering him was thick, but as he stroked all the way to the tip, it thinned and became slippery.

A small shudder jostled him when the ring of his fingers massaged over the rim of his cock head, and a second one followed as he went back down over it. He was more sensitive here, so he explored it further with his own touch.

With just a few strokes, his head lifted back.

Dark purple stained his vision as he noticed the stars seemed brighter than normal. And the more he stroked the first half of his cock, the darker the world turned and the brighter those lights glittered.

His first deep, shaken groan parted his beak. His scales and spikes lifted as his flesh rippled in waves against the new and enrapturing pleasure. Lubricant bubbled between his fingers to drip over the backs of them, and down the ovals embedded into the base of him.

Nhnn. Why does this feel so good?

Gripping himself harder, his groin tightened and his hips twitched in reaction when he squeezed all the way to the core. He even rocked a little.

Yet, despite how pleasurable it was, it was different from when Emerie had touched him. Her hand had been soft, small, and gifted him with surprises, whereas his was rough. It didn't matter she couldn't hold him as powerfully; she'd still made his entire brain fog and his body heat until he thought he was moments from evaporating.

He wanted the same feeling. The craving to be so filled with pleasure that he was moments from crawling out of his own skin. *I want her touch again...*

He closed his sight so he could focus on the memory of her

doing this to him.

Another deep groan had his lungs feeling tighter.

An undeniable urge to thrust nagged at him, and the faster he stroked, the harder it became to deny.

He tilted his head forward so he could place his free hand against the dirt. His huffs grew louder now that they were directed towards the ground, and only became breathier when he tentatively and slowly pumped his hips into his tight fist as he stroked.

A pant fell from him, and his straightened arm gave out. *More,* he pleaded to himself. He clawed at the dirt as he thrust harder, squeezing his cock until he thought he'd mangle it – and yet it felt... wonderful.

A small growl slipped out, just as a flash of red burst in his sight.

Something spooked in the distance, and he tried his hardest to remain quiet as he picked up the pace, clamping his beak shut. *More. I need more.* His tail kinked before it flicked wildly when he gave a violent shudder that started from the back of his skull all the way to his very tail tip.

Drool pooled in his maw, dripping from the edges. *I want to spill. I want to come.*

His tentacles squirmed, aching in a way he couldn't ignore, couldn't understand. He shot his free hand down to touch them and they gripped his fingers, twining around them. He gripped the base of his cock to let them clutch however they pleased.

Ingram shoved himself against both fists as he rested his chest against the ground. Then, he moved his hips as hard and as fast as he could, and all sounds ceased from him except for his bliss-filled pants. His sight blackened, his hearing became muffled, and all scents around him diluted as his senses switched over to just the feel of his own touch.

His cock was moving swiftly, but it was unbearably hard and thick in his palms. The little scale-like spikes going down three sides of him tickled and gave him additional texture and tingles. He already knew the groove underneath was sensitive, but he couldn't get his fingertips inside them with his claws.

Not like how *she* did.

He didn't know if he was hurting himself, not when bliss engulfed him as he tried to rid himself of this jutting, needy ache.

A whine finally burst from his lungs just as those embedded ovals at the base of him clenched inwards so tightly that agony radiated all throughout his groin. He'd experienced this before, and just like then, he thought his very soul was about to shoot through his cock.

His toe claws gouged at the ground in tension.

Too much. It's too much! And yet, he didn't stop moving.

His lower hand let go so he could cover his beak to hide the worst of the agonised sounds that escaped him.

He feared he'd cracked his own skull when his lungs seized, just at the pinnacle point. He gripped both his beak and cock harder and harder as he froze, trying to steady himself through this.

The pleasure was so intense it felt as though something had shoved its claws into his groin while also tickling the centre point of his spine – where it was attached to his tail.

Then he released, and his roaring groan was suppressed by the overwhelming tightness in his chest. Liquid rapture burst from him. He couldn't stop his hips, needing to work every drop out to remove the pressure. His pulsating, throbbing dick swelled over and over again in his drenched fist, as the splatters of copious amounts of seed painted the dewy moss and grass.

His heart pounded so rapidly and heavily that he grew light-headed when the last string of white liquid shot from him.

Ingram was unable to move a muscle, twitches and jerks assaulting every part of his body like his bones were trying to dance out of his skin.

It took him a while to open his sight to dark purple and look around to check he was still alone. He was.

He loosened his grip on his drained cock but didn't let it go. Instead, with wet fingers, he gently tickled it as he explored it in more depth. Each movement caused it to jerk in excitement, despite it softening.

Now that he could understand where all the liquid had come from, he slipped his drenched fingers to his embedded seed sacs. Tickling them as he explored, they were too sensitive. His back arched against the strange, wonderful torture.

It almost bordered on pain, so he quickly moved away.

Rubbing over the head with just his fingertips had muscles leaping and his sight turning fuzzy. That felt really nice, so he kept doing it. He even just circled the flared rim, since it made his thighs twitch and his knees turn inwards.

I did not know I had something like this on my own body. Had he known he could make himself nearly pass out in pleasure, he would have played with it earlier.

He didn't think he would've stopped, just like now, as it started to harden under his light touches. He gripped it more firmly again.

More sensitive than before, he stroked softer but fast, moaning at himself. He was trying to replay the way the little female had touched him, since he didn't particularly like how forceful he'd needed to be with himself.

I need more. Of this, of releasing until he could find out if he couldn't spill another drop. Of the little female who was withholding her light, gentle, and barely fast strokes – that had been far superior to his own fist.

Emerie, he mentally groaned, then he was forced to tighten his grip.

THIRTEEN

Emerie's stomps down the steps weren't as light as she'd hoped, and she ended up startling the Duskwalker awake. He'd been off to the side, lying in a ball... or something. She wasn't quite sure, since he was on his knees, his butt in the air, but his face was down.

That's a weird way to sleep. She didn't dwell on it. *Whatever makes him comfortable, I guess.* She didn't know enough about his kind to judge his habits.

At least he was still around and hadn't wandered off.

With her bag strapped across her torso, the thin sleeping bag she was intending to steal inside it, she raised her arms above her head. With her hands interlocked, she stretched as she went to the tips of her toes and let out the most unladylike groan.

"Alright," she announced. "Let's go. I feel a lot better now that I've slept properly for the first time in a week."

Turning to the Duskwalker, she took in his odd position. He was seated on the ground with his feet flat and his hands on his bent knees. His orbs were a reddish pink.

He didn't say anything, seeming to wait for her.

"Did you sleep well?" she asked, taking a step towards him. He bounced forward and met her halfway, as though he didn't want her coming closer. "Hopefully my snoring didn't force you to come outside for some peace."

"Snoring. No, that is not..." He paused what he was going to say, his orbs deepening in their hue. *"You did snore."*

Her brows furrowed deeply.

She'd actually been joking, and he hadn't confirmed nor denied if that was why he was outside. She hoped not. She was usually pretty quiet, but when she was exhausted, people told her she sounded like a freaking thunderstorm.

She would have blushed, but it didn't matter. The sun had risen. They'd slept much longer than she intended, and they needed to go.

We're just asking for trouble remaining in one spot for too long. She didn't know if the guild would catch up to them, but she'd rather not find out.

They likely wouldn't rest until they punished her for her crimes: releasing a prisoner, desertion of the guild, and for the many murders she'd committed, like Wren's. She'd also be charged as an accomplice to Lindiwe's murders.

If Emerie was caught, she'd be up shit creek without a paddle.

She eyed the Duskwalker and knew the truth. *Even if I'm caught, it was still worth it.* So long as they didn't try to use her as bait to recapture him.

She clapped her hands together. "Ready to go?"

Just as she stepped forward, he darted in her path, pointing behind her. *"Let's go this way."*

Examining the house and the clearing they were in, she really didn't see the difference between the way she'd been intending to go around it and the way he pointed. She tried to look over his shoulder to see what he was hiding but couldn't spot anything amiss.

Emerie shrugged. *Maybe he just wants to feel in charge? It's probably best if I don't upset him.*

If Duskwalkers had tantrums, she didn't really want to see it.

"Aye aye, captain," she said, saluting while spinning and then going the way he pointed. He immediately followed and came up beside her on all fours. "Yesterday I asked if you could find me some berries and mushrooms. Could you? I don't have a lot of rations."

She peeked at him, and he tilted his head. His orbs were back to purple – she was beginning to wonder if this was his normal colouring.

"I don't know what they are."

"Well... shit," she grumbled, pushing back a few locks of hair from her face. "Then I'll find some along the way and show you."

A strong gust of wind pushed behind them from the right. *I really wish I'd grabbed my jacket.* It was the beginning of autumn, and she hoped this trip was over before the first snow fell. Otherwise, she'd need warmer clothing.

I should probably try to visit a town and buy new clothes. Considering what she'd done, she didn't deserve to wear her Demonslayer uniform anymore.

Ingram paused while grabbing the back of her hood to still her, and she made a choking noise as she was forced to a halt. He quickly explained, *"Emerie, I smell humans."*

Trailing her gaze across the clearing, she followed the direction his skull was turned, off to the right. She waited for movement in the trees, or voices, but saw and heard nothing.

"I cannot hear them," he said, tilting his head one way and then the other, as though he was listening out. *"I did not notice until now, but their scents are strange."*

Well, that sounds ominous. Her lips tightened as she scanned the forest again.

"Strange, how?"

"It smells like they are one with the forest. I cannot even be sure which direction they are, or how many."

He finally turned his raven skull to her, only to swing further to the left and growl at whatever presence he sensed in the distance. His legs widened, and he lowered his chest to the ground as though he was readying to pounce.

She saw nothing and heard nothing in that direction either.

"Fuck," she cursed, grabbing one of his small horns to tug at him. "Come on, we need to go."

He didn't budge. Instead, his spikes and scales lifted into sharp points.

"I cannot see them, but I know they are there."

"Come on!" she shouted, groaning as she tugged.

She gave up when it seemed like he'd turned to stone, and

she just ran away. The big, bad monster could deal with it and catch up later!

She pumped her arms, keeping them close to her torso, so she could gain the best speed. *It's either bandits or the guild and I'm not waiting around to find out!*

Emerie's squeal was loud when a few seconds later she was tossed over Ingram's shoulder.

"Do not run from me, female," he rumbled, as he darted through the forest. *"I considered playing chase with you had you gotten any further."*

She would have worried about what that meant if he didn't suddenly pick up speed. Bouncing on his shoulder and back, she gasped when she started slipping to the side. She had to grab hold of his spikes to stop herself from falling. Then she worked on hooking her left leg over his shoulders so his neck could keep her centred.

Shit! Emerie ducked when a stray arrow whistled through the air, right in her direction. She didn't need to. Ingram had already passed its landing zone long before it could reach them.

It'd been low to the ground by the time it neared her. *That was a long-range shot.*

Bouncing against his shoulders and holding on for dear life as he bounded through the trees, she sighed with relief.

She knew, without a doubt, it belonged to the guild, but they'd been nowhere near Ingram and Emerie's location. Perhaps close enough to see them from a distance, but they'd likely only just been found.

Had I been alone, they would have caught me. They would have slowly and quietly surrounded her while she'd been walking. She looked behind her at the back of the Duskwalker's skull her arse was currently sitting on top of. *He was able to sense them even with such a great distance between us.*

"I think you can slow down now," she shouted once she thought it was safe.

Honestly, she just didn't like their position. Her legs were dangling down the front of his torso, and her knees occasionally hit his chest. She was the wrong way for riding him, and she must be heavy.

"No. We run."

Ingram forced her to lie down on his back when he leapt off a small hill, and she nearly screamed when she started floating. Her torso smacked against his spikes when she landed back on top of him, her features contorting in pain.

Screw this. She worked on spinning around so she was facing forward and in a better riding position.

She brought her knees up and under her so she could lift off his spikes, worried about destroying her clit and pussy if she sat on them. She removed her bag so she could sit on it like a saddle. Then she threw the strap over his head so it would catch around his neck; firstly, so she didn't lose it, and secondly so she could hold onto it like a set of reins.

Only having to watch for the occasional branch that threatened to swipe her off him, since he didn't think to avoid them for her safety, she stared at the back of his white skull.

She'd thought Ingram was freaked out, but when he revealed the side of his face by darting his skull one way to search for his path, his orbs were purple.

They weren't red like he was angry, or white as though he was afraid.

Why is he sprinting for his life?

Emerie pulled on her makeshift reins, trying to halt him.

"Ingram, slow down." She cringed when she was slapped in the face by a leafy branch, unable to avoid it. When he didn't slow, she attempted to soothe him by patting his neck. "Hey, it's okay. Calm down."

"You said you are easily harmed. I am taking you away from the danger."

Oh. Her lips parted in surprise, then she almost laughed. She didn't have the heart to tell him he was putting her in potential danger by going this fast.

The wind was cutting through her clothing and whipping her hair over her shoulders. She held on tight to prevent him from accidentally tossing her off.

When she almost got bitch slapped by another branch, this one intending to cut her head right off, she ducked to get to his level. Shuffling back and laying flush against him, she gripped his horns and kept her head down to stay below their tips, since he avoided everything that was low enough to be near his horn height.

He'll settle when he's ready. When he knew for certain they were safe. *Hopefully he's going west.*

Emerie didn't know how long Ingram ran for. An hour, maybe two? All she knew was that he'd travelled a great distance, and it was unlikely the guild would be able to catch up to them again.

However, something pink in the corner of her eye caught her attention. She sat up and pulled on his horns at the same time, jerking him into a weird stumble.

"Wait, stop! I see berries!" she yelled.

Whether it was in reaction to her shout after hours of silence, or her sudden yank, Ingram finally halted. He stopped so suddenly he threw her forward and Emerie flailed helplessly as she flew through the air.

"Oh SHIIIT!" she squealed, as she crossed her arms protectively over her head.

An arm caught her around the waist, right before she went headfirst into a fucking tree. With her heart nearly in her throat, she looked back and found orange orbs glowing down at her.

"Sorry, Emerie. I did not mean to throw you."

She laughed, not because she found it funny, but in mild panic. That could have been bad, like *really* bad. Either she would have split her face open, or she would have broken her nose or skull. Either way, she would have bled and then become his lunch.

With her back flush against his chest and her legs dangling half a metre in the air, she held onto his forearm tightly. "It's fine."

Ingram carefully placed her on her feet when he was forced to lower back onto his hands. She immediately bounced into action. Going back the way they came, shoving branches and shrubs, as she searched for the pink berries she'd seen.

The grin she produced was wide and toothy when she found them.

"Fuck yeah!" she cheered, curling her hand into a fist and

pumping it into the air in joy. "This lilly pilly bush is huge."

No wonder it'd caught her attention – it was nearly triple her height! It was also full of ripe pink berries. She waited for Ingram to come over so she could unthread her bag from him and start shoving as much as she could inside.

She didn't even care that she was about to give up her saddle. She'd just use the thin sleeping bag that she removed and tied around one side of the strap. Food and water were a priority. She'd figure out his back spikes and how to not impale her pussy on them later.

"These are the berries you seek?" Emerie nodded, eating them as she picked. Following her lead, he easily reached up to take the ones higher up since she wouldn't be able to reach. *"I will search for more in the future then."*

When her bag and stomach were full to capacity, she pulled her strap over her shoulder and tucked her nearly bursting bag behind her. It was heavy, and that pleased her immensely.

"Thank you for helping me," she said, tying her water sack where the bag and strap were connected, since it wouldn't fit inside. "Also, if you happen to sniff out a stream or lake, let me know. I'll need water soon."

"You cannot hear the water nearby?" Ingram asked, pointing a claw in a random direction. When she followed his thick dark-grey finger with her lips tightening, she figured he understood that she couldn't. *"You humans are not very formidable creatures. No wonder Demons and Mavka easily hunt you."*

Her eyes narrowed into a slitted glare, unsure if she appreciated that. "Humans are smart, that's what keeps us alive."

"Not smart enough to not be eaten," he argued, walking on all fours in the direction he'd pointed. She wasn't the kind of woman to pout and cross her arms in annoyance, but she considered it. *"Come. I will take you to water."*

Emerie cracked her neck to relieve some of her tension at his rudeness. She just put it up to him being a Duskwalker and not knowing better.

Especially since he'd already tried to eat her, and there was a high chance he'd probably try to do it again.

Ingram tilted his head to the right and almost made it go upside down in confusion. Perplexed, his sight turned yellow because of it. He didn't understand why the little female was cranky with him.

Is it because I said she is dirty?

When they'd reached the shallow river, Ingram had demanded she wash. Her lips had parted wide before she promptly shut them.

Or is it because I will not leave?

She'd agreed to his demand but asked that he leave. When he wouldn't, she pushed and shoved at him to no avail.

"I'm not going to wash in front of you, Ingram!" she shouted, grunting and groaning. She even spun around so she could shove at him with her back, the heel of her boots slipping against the dirt and grass.

"No. I want to make sure you do it properly."

"I know how to wash myself," she argued back. "Pretty sure humans came up with good hygiene, not Duskwalkers."

He straightened his head and then sighed. *"And yet, your face is always dirty."* When she directed it at him with her cute orange brows drawn in tight, he wished he could look upon her with clarity. *"Even now there is much on you."*

Emerie stepped back and wiped at her face before checking her hands. He noted they were mostly clean, and yet the dots remained. "There's nothing on me."

His orbs shifted to a dark yellow in curiosity, wondering why she couldn't remove what he could clearly see. *"But it is all over you."*

Her icy-blue eyes shot open wide, as did her mouth. Then, the corners of her eyelids crinkled as she made this strange noise – one he'd only learned recently was a laugh.

His orbs threatened to turn bright yellow. *I like this sound from her.* It tickled his chest, like he wanted to return it.

"Are... are you talking about my freckles, Ingram?" She pulled back the tight sleeve of her uniform, revealing the back of her right arm. A multicoloured beaded bracelet tied around her wrist sparkled in the sun. "I have them everywhere. It's not dirt."

He reached out to grab her and halted when she flinched at his sudden movement. She paled with wariness, but eventually placed her tiny arm in his palm for him. She remained still as she allowed him to inspect it in close detail.

He tried to gently scratch one off with the side of his claw. *It stays!*

"Why do you have dots such as these?" he asked in wonder.

He didn't realise humans were so strange. Being around her was making him realise he knew little about them. He was growing infatuated with the idea of learning more.

Ingram was also beginning to experience a deep desire to learn about *her*. He knew her name, knew she was a Demonslayer, but other than that, everything else was unknown.

He didn't know what questions he should ask her to unravel her mysteries. Not because he was nervous or there were too many, but because... he'd never gotten to know a human before.

They were different. He doubted what he'd ask a Mavka would be the right things to ask her.

"Freckles form on some humans who are more susceptible to the sun. My body has a few of them, but not many because I'm usually in my uniform. What I have is mainly from my childhood." She took her arm away, even though he wasn't done looking at it yet. "I've been sunburnt on my face many times though, which is why they're really noticeable there."

"I see," he said, cupping his beak as he pondered on this. *"I did not know humans could be spotty like animals."*

Her smile was odd, especially since she'd bit her lips shut and her gaze was alight with... humour, perhaps?

"Okay. So now that you know I'm not dirty, and we can agree I do, in fact, know how to wash properly, it's time for you to go." She flicked both hands forward in his direction while giving him a 'shoo.'

He didn't rise from his seated position.

"Why must I leave? It is safer if I am with you."

Ingram had decided Emerie was the most delicate thing in the entire world. Therefore, he must protect her always. From creatures, humans, and even the water that could suffocate her.

He would dive into the river and ferociously maim it if it tried to swallow her alive.

Her neck kinked as her head fell back, and she released a sound of frustration. "Because I need to get naked to have a bath and I'm not doing that in front of you!"

"I do not understand the problem." He really didn't. He even leaned closer and tried to pull her shirt up so he could remove it himself. *"I do not wear clothing."*

He was, and always had been, utterly naked.

She fought him when he wrapped his other hand around her to keep her steady, wriggling and squirming to get free. When he got her shirt halfway up on one side, she shoved the other side down, and he noted her face turned pink, whereas some of the webbed scarring flared red.

He tried to yank her pants down instead.

"No!" she screamed in a high-pitched and frantic tone.

Ingram recoiled.

His orbs switched to white, and he backed up when he realised he'd been doing something wrong. Emerie stumbled and almost tripped over, her features twisted into an expression he'd never seen before.

There was even a tiny amount of fear coming from her – just enough to stir hunger and alarm him.

"I am sorry," he uttered quietly, lowering his head and body in submissiveness. *"I did not mean to upset you."*

Why do I always upset her? He didn't mean to keep doing the wrong thing, and it often made his insides radiate with an ugly sensation.

Staring at him as she continued to shove her shirt down, her blue eyes flickered side to side, seeming to take in his skull and white orbs. After a few seconds, she eventually sighed, her shoulders loosening until they slumped.

She rubbed at her neck while looking off to the side. "Hey,

it's okay."

When he didn't ease, his spikes still raised and his tail curled in apprehension, she ran her hand over her hair. Her eyes crinkled as one side of her face twisted into a cringe.

"Look, I don't like people seeing my skin. It's a thing I have." Then she lowered her hand, staring down at her palm as she opened and closed it, until a snort of laughter came from her. She flashed a small smile in his direction. "Plus, it's pretty normal for a person to want some privacy while they bathe, especially women."

"It... is?" he asked, her reassuring smile soothing him. She wouldn't do that if she was angry or frightened of him... right? *"Why is this so important for females to have privacy? I thought clothing was for warmth, since humans do not have fur or scales."*

Ingram was interested in discovering more about this. All he'd known was that males and females produced their own distinct scents – it didn't matter their species.

She'd told him that she didn't have a dick and instead a... pussy. The question was: did it look the same as what he had, and what was its purpose?

Her smile flattened but didn't disappear. It was a warning for the giggle she produced next.

"Clothing for humans is more than that. I can't believe I'm about to say this..." she grumbled, averting her gaze as pinkness flared in her cheeks again. "We, uh, aren't like you. Our privates aren't hidden within like you were, so they're constantly exposed. We don't show them to people unless we are about to be... intimate with them."

Their privates are on the outside?

She wouldn't have noticed since his orbs never revealed where he was truly looking, but he darted his gaze to the vee area between her thighs. He couldn't even begin to imagine what she had, but he was growing more curious from everything she taught him.

Emerie crossed her arms over her torso to shield it, sticking her hands under her armpits.

"Women also have breasts on our chests, and we like to keep

them hidden too, same with our arses."

Ah, so that's what the lumps on her chest were called. He'd seen them on females, and he noted hers weren't the largest he'd seen, but they definitely weren't small.

"These are places that can only be touched and seen by those who are special to you?"

When she nodded, it only made him wonder, once again, why he couldn't be special to her.

Her touch felt nice. Could I not make her feel good in return?

If these were secret places, did it mean they were sensitive like his dick? Could he touch and stroke them to make her produce seed as well? Could... she produce cum?

Ingram liked Emerie. She'd been kind and understanding towards him, and the more he discovered about humans, the more he found her... pretty. He'd never had the time to assess a human, let alone a female one, that wasn't screaming in fear and about to be eaten by him.

Until now.

Every second he spent with her, more and more things began to click into place for him.

Her pleasant scent he couldn't name. The sound of her voice and how it eased him. And her orange hair kept stealing his attention, especially when it was glowing in the bright sunshine like it did now. He liked that her eyelashes had the same glow, and they warmed the ice of her blue eyes.

Now that he knew her *freckles* were a part of her, he found them cute.

Her expressions confused him, but he wanted to unravel the simple mysteries of them. Even more so since she never looked at him with fear or disdain – although often with wariness.

And what she'd just taught him about her body, that what lay underneath her clothing was naughty to reveal, only made him want to see it more. The features he'd first thought were insignificant – like her breasts, her arse, and that vee between her thighs – were suddenly very, *very* intriguing.

Ingram had a new appreciation for them.

His purple sight darkened a little when movement shifted behind his seam as he stared down at her breasts. *I want to see the naughty places on her.*

He wanted to know what they looked like. Would they be soft or firm in his hands? Were they boring or fun to play with?

He'd thoroughly enjoyed the pleasure she'd given him with her hands, and he was starting to crave the idea of doing it in return so she could experience it.

I want to touch, he thought with a groan, just as his seam started to part.

"Ingram?" she called, breaking him from his predatory gaze on her. He looked up, tilted his head, and flicked his long and flat tongue out so he could lick over the top of his beak in interest. "Can you please give me some privacy so I can bathe? The sun will go down soon, and the water will already be cold."

There was something about her expression that nagged at him. It was a little pale, and it was obvious she was attempting to look anywhere but in his direction.

When cool air brushed over the exposed flesh of his cock, he looked down and inspected the partially jutting shaft. His sitting position was mostly hiding it.

"But I want to stay," he grumbled.

"Away, Duskwalker!" Emerie shouted, shooing him once more with her hands. "Or I won't bathe at all."

With an annoyed growl, he stood. Then he huffed as he turned, upset she wouldn't show him what she looked like underneath her clothing when he was so curious.

On all fours, he stomped into the forest with his tail swishing angrily behind him.

"Good! And you better not watch me from the bushes like a freaking creep or I promise I'll be really, really upset with you."

Ingram winced, since he'd been planning to do exactly that.

I take it back. Emerie is mean.

By the time he was far enough away that she was out of sight but not out of earshot, his cock had already gone soft and retreated.

With an annoyed plop, he dropped his backside to the grass with his back to her. He folded his arms across his chest, mimicking her from the few times she'd done it at him when she'd been upset.

She will not let me see. Will not touch me. He tapped his tail tip against the ground as he thought. *Why not? I am pretty, and my horns are small and not imposing.* He grumbled to himself. *How do I make her do these things?*

Then something struck him. Something that had his orbs shifting to blue as he scratched at the side of his beak in apprehension.

Is... is it because I am Mavka?

FOURTEEN

Emerie sighed when the Duskwalker asked yet *another* question, wondering when they would end.

With her head craned to look at the sky for mercy, the backs of her hands against his back, and her eyes rolling, she wanted to perish. *Someone put me out of my misery.* Not even the strangeness of riding him to make this journey faster was enough to distract her.

At least he wasn't sprinting and threatening to behead her with a branch.

The questioning wasn't actually too bad, if she were being honest. It was just that it had been a constant barrage.

Ingram would ask why the leaves were green, or why water fell from the sky, or how birds flew whenever he saw one in the distance. He asked how the Veil came to be, not that she knew, or how humans came into being.

He wanted to learn anything and everything, questioning names, meanings, and origins.

The first one hundred questions had been easy, but the longer they travelled, two days having passed already, the more complex and harder some were to explain. He was lucky Emerie was privy to a lot of knowledge due to her constant studies back in Zagros Fortress.

"Ingram, please," she whined when he started to ask about yet another thing. "Just a few moments. That's all I need."

"But I desire to know the name of that plant," he stated as he

pointed his beak towards a weed flower. *"The yellow one. I have seen it many times."*

"It's a dandelion," she answered on a sigh. "In spring, it'll turn into a white puff so that it can spread its seeds."

"Oh!" he rasped, twisting his head over his neck in the most disturbing way to look at her where she sat on him. His glowing orbs morphed to a bright yellow. *"Yes! I know that one. If you shake it, it breaks apart and floats away. I did not realise they were the same plant."*

Picturing Ingram shaking a dandelion in delighted curiosity, Emerie's eyes crinkled and her lips curled with mirth.

His joy at learning even the simplest things was the only reason Emerie didn't hate this. She was just tired, and riding a Duskwalker's spikey back with a makeshift saddle was a lot harder than she thought. Her thighs ached from constantly pushing her body away from the protrusions, and most of the time she had to sit on her hands to protect herself.

At least he's not asking me sexual questions.

Oh, but he'd tried.

When his dick had been just sitting there, casually erect when she'd tried to make him leave so she could bathe, she was acutely aware she had told him something she probably shouldn't have.

Had he'd been staring at her tits? Whether it was her own prickling awareness of them or him trying to burn a hole through her shirt, they'd tingled. The urge to cover them like a virgin had crossed her mind.

After she'd bathed and they started back on their travels, Ingram had been a little... too close. He kept sniffing her hair or walking directly behind her. If he'd been trying to be sly, he did a horrible job of it.

He also asked her questions regarding her breasts and her pussy as he came up beside her. Emerie, unwilling to make this problem worse, found ways to redirect the conversation.

The more he learned, the more worried she became that he would start... trying things with her. A sexually curious Duskwalker sounded like a dangerous combination.

Even if she were to consider letting him discover all this with her, which she wasn't, Emerie was worried about the size of him. Not just his massive dick that she'd needed to hold with both hands just to contain, but also his body.

What if he got too carried away and accidentally clawed her? Or crushed her as he laid down on top of her?

If he tries to shove his dick in me, he'll split me in two. She rubbed her closed eyes with one hand, digging her thumb and fingers in. Frustration bubbled. *He's a virgin. Virgins don't have any idea what they're doing and barely understand their partner's limitations.*

Because if he did manage to fit in her much tinier and delicate hole, he'd probably pump her to death – and not in the fun way.

He's really sweet, though.

Whenever she needed to rest, he would find a really soft section of grass for her. That, or he would make a nest of branches that had thick leaves to comfort her. He even offered to curl into a ball so she could lie on him when they stopped in a rather rocky area. She'd declined that option, of course, but it had made her heart burn with a tenderness.

He was also protective of her.

Whether it be a fox, a rodent, or even a bird, he'd warn it away with a snarl. It was unnecessary, and somewhat foolish, but the more harmless the creature, the more it made her smile warmly.

It was like he didn't realise he was the most hazardous thing to her. Every moment with him meant the threat of death lingered over her head.

She stared at the back of his white raven skull. *At least my grim reaper has a pretty face.*

She'd found it a little off-putting at first, but that had diminished over time. His glowing, colour-changing orbs helped. She'd once thought of them as soulless and hollow, but now saw them for what they were.

Life. Emotions. The essence of a creature who couldn't smile, but could show his joy with a simple bright-yellow glow, or instead express curiosity with a darker tone.

Once she figured out what each colour meant, he became

easy to read.

The pinkish red means he's either embarrassed or ashamed. He didn't show this colour very often, but when combined with his inward-turned body language, he easily gave its meaning away.

Ingram could be shy, and each time he was, something stirred in her and made her belly flitter. A big, scary, towering monster acting bashful and nervous? How could anyone's heart not warm to that?

White means he's either scared, wary, or... in pain. She felt terrible when his orbs turned white when he'd been trying to undress her near the lake. She'd given him a fright. Him! A Duskwalker!

She didn't plan to reveal the truth as to why.

I just didn't want him to see my scars.

Emerie couldn't remember if she'd ever shown anyone. She hated them. She hated that they were a part of her. They were a stark reminder of her past, her pain, everything she'd endured, and everything she'd lost.

She wondered if she would have shown Bryce, but he'd never, not even once, been inclined to have her remove her shirt. He'd just fondled underneath it, and mainly on her... right, which was where she didn't have many scars.

A sinking feeling in her heart had her eyes stinging, and she quickly blinked the forming tears away.

Nope. Don't want to think about it.

She didn't want to think about Bryce and how she'd been an idiot to not see the obvious signs. She'd been used because she'd allowed herself to be an easy lay in her desperation for intimacy. She'd just wanted to feel... beautiful.

She hadn't felt that way in a long time. *I feel like such a loser.*

A howl in the distance, thankfully, broke her from her spiralling thoughts. Two more followed, and both she and Ingram pointed their faces in the direction the sound was coming from.

"What is the name of those creatures?" Ingram asked, huffing in their direction before wisely veering away. He climbed down a rocky hill to land in a lower part of the forest.

"They're wolves."

"A Mavka has one of their skulls as his face."

"He has a wolf skull for a head?" she asked, bouncing forward in interest.

"Yes, and spirally horns on his head. I have only seen him from afar, but he lives in a human dwelling."

"Where does he live?"

"In the Veil, like all Mavka. He did not like it when we trampled over his... I don't know what it is called, but it was filled with human food plants, like your berries."

"A vegetable garden?" Emerie hummed, tapping at her lips. "Why would a Duskwalker need a garden, or a house?"

Ingram's big shoulders shrugged beneath her knees. *"I don't know. He has always lived there. I think that is where the Witch Owl wants us to go."*

Emerie didn't need to ask who that was, not when she'd seen Lindiwe turn into a giant owl in front of her.

Still tapping her lips with her fingers, she eventually pursed them in thought. "Lindiwe said we should go to your brothers. I'm guessing this wolf-headed Duskwalker is one of them?"

Once more, he shrugged. *"I am unsure. He is Mavka, as we all are."*

That... didn't really answer her question.

"Well, where did you come from then?"

"I... do not remember, Emerie," he answered honestly, rotating his head to look upon her with his usual purple orbs. She'd figured out over the course of the last three days that they were his normal colouring, since no emotion seemed to be attached to them from what she could tell. *"The first thing I remember is my kindred."*

Since his bony face was eerily staring at her, she was forced to watch his orbs be swallowed up by deep blue. Her lips flattened, knowing that meant something akin to sadness, and the darker the colour, the deeper his sorrow.

Her heart ached for him, even though she didn't know why he was sad.

Before she could question him on it, his head snapped forward, and he said, *"The Witch– Lindiwe... said she is my mother. She said I came from her, that all Mavka came from her."* He halted his steps to scratch at the side of his neck in obvious irritation. *"What does this mean? Did she grow us like a tree? Or did she bleed us from her veins?"*

Emerie's jaw dropped, then threatened to unhinge and fall off.

"Excuse me... what?!" she shouted in shock, causing him to flinch. "What do you mean you came from her and that she's your mother? She's a..." Emerie was about to call her a human, but then remembered what she'd done.

She'd turned into an owl and a Ghost.

Oh my god, she's not human! What is she then? Emerie was willing to bend the rules of reality to accept this, only because she'd seen what the woman was capable of.

Lindiwe had also gone out of her way to save Ingram. Now that she was thinking back, she'd also bravely grabbed his beak affectionately in the forest. It'd been with care, like a motherly, concerned touch.

"Okay, so she's your mother." She rubbed down her right cheek, then jaw, to stroke her chin. "That would mean she gave birth to you."

Ingram's silence was telling, and she sighed as she craned her neck back. *I'm about to have the birds and the bees chat with a Duskwalker.* She pursed her lips. *And I have to do it without explaining what sex is.*

Snapping her head forward, she glared with determination at the back of his white raven skull and little sandy goat horns.

"When a mummy and a daddy love each other very much, they–" She knew she'd immediately lost him by his skull twisting one way and then the other.

"What is a mummy and a daddy?" He spun his head around to look at her with yellow orbs. *"I also do not know what love is."*

Fuuuuuuuck, she internally groaned. *I'm out here doing a saint's work. The gods better smile upon me.* Maybe not human gods, but Duskwalker ones – if they had them.

"When two people care about each other very deeply, they come together and make a baby." When his damn head tilted again, she quickly spoke before he could interrupt her with another freaking question. "A baby is a small human. They are made within a woman's... belly. But they didn't eat them! Just to clarify. There's a special place inside us that can grow life, and that's what she did. She grew you inside her and then gave birth to you. She gave you blood and breath, and she is the reason you are here."

His beak opened, and then clipped shut. He faced forward so he could watch where he was going.

Emerie cringed. "Does any of that make sense?"

"I think so... She is a creator of life. I did not know other creatures could do that."

Okay, so that's a good start.

"Yes, and it requires both a male and female – most of the time. They come together, and once they make a baby, that child will call them mother and father, or mum and dad." She shrugged with one arm. "Really depends on the kid. So, if she is the mother of all Duskwalkers, that means she grew all of you, and you all share her blood. You are related and have a special bond unique to all of you. Brothers are usually your male siblings, and sisters are females."

"I don't think there are any females of my kind." He paused momentarily, his beak lifting up. *"Brothers... then why is my kindred so special to me?"*

Absolutely stumped, her brows furrowed. "Kindred?"

He was quiet for a long while, unusually so. Why was that worrying?

"Aleron," he uttered quietly. *"It is what we called each other. He is all I have ever known. He is the first thing I remember. His scent, his warmth, his presence. I cannot think of a time he was not by my side... until now."*

Until now... she was afraid of what that meant.

"He sounds like he is your brother. Do you know if he was born before or after you?"

"Lindiwe said before, but... another Mavka, Kitty, said we were created at the same time. Is that possible?"

"Oh, Ingram," Emerie rasped, her voice laden with sympathy as understanding dawned. Her eyes crinkled in sadness for him.

"If you were born into this world at the same time, that means he was your twin. That's probably why your bond with him was so special. Many twins are inseparable and often feel like halves of each other."

Emerie bit her lips together, clamping them shut when his torso shuddered. He kept walking, but his steps seemed heavier, like he was weighed down.

Just as bubbles of glowing blue floated around his skull, right where his empty eye sockets were, a tiny, agonised whine escaped him.

"I do not like this conversation. I do not like learning we were... more."

Leaning forward, she rubbed the side of his thick neck, hoping it felt soothing. He tilted his head to watch her hand, and it revealed that she'd been right. The floating bubbles around his face had been ethereal tears.

I didn't think Duskwalkers could... cry. How heartbreaking.

"You must have loved him very deeply." She clenched her jaw, swallowing the thick lump of emotion in her throat. "And you must miss him terribly."

Because, if he was not by Ingram's side when they'd been inseparable, then... he was likely dead.

His whimper hollowed out her heart and replaced it with a big chunk of himself.

She gave him a small, sad smile as she continued to pet him. "If it makes you feel any better, I know how it feels. I lost someone really dear to me as well. It hurts when I think about them, and I think about them every single day."

"It does not," he rudely answered. *"Aleron was special. We were... are the same being. There is no me without him."*

And yet here Ingram was, bravely facing the world on his own. Well, not completely, since she was here, but she also knew she probably meant little to him.

She was just a human who had decided to tag along.

I guess I don't know how it feels to lose a twin, she thought, lifting her face to the dusk-stained sky throwing orange and purple across the horizon.

But I did lose my adopted brother, and that hurts too. She bit her lip at the clouds, remembering his face as clear as she saw those puffs of white. *And he's the reason I started all this... He's the reason I'm here now, with you.*

Emerie opened her mouth to explain this to him. She'd suffered loss, not just with her adopted brother, but also her parents. She'd lived in pain – physically, mentally, and emotionally – for weeks, perhaps even months, afterwards.

The world had chewed her right up and then spit out a woman who was lost.

Ingram was not alone in his pain, and she wanted him to know just how much she could relate to him. She hoped it might comfort him in some small way.

However, she promptly shut her lips. *Not everyone understands that trauma sharing is bonding.*

Not everyone understood that when someone shared their pain with another who had just spoken of their own, the person was just trying to relate. To show them they cared and were someone they could truly lean on who didn't *need* to imagine how they'd felt, but rather remember it on a deeply ingrained level.

Unfortunately, it could often be misconstrued as a competition. Or sometimes people took offense to it, thinking they were belittling their pain, or trying to make it feel insignificant.

Emerie quietly sighed through her nose as the floating bubbles glittered faster around his skull. He was still crying his mournful, ethereal tears.

He isn't very smart. I don't want to accidentally make him feel bad if he takes it the wrong way.

She also didn't want to prolong a conversation he already mentioned he didn't like. *He must still be grieving. Loss for humans is difficult to accept, so I can't imagine how difficult it must be for a Duskwalker.*

And, coupled with the fact he'd recently gone through a terrible ordeal back in Zagros Fortress, Emerie could only guess how messed up his mind was.

The fact he was gentle with her at all was a miracle.

She chewed her bottom lip and her eyes crinkled in sympathy

for his anguish.

I want to make him feel better, though.

Ingram wished his chest would stop hurting. Why did it have to feel physical? Like a part of him was missing just as much as his kindred, his... *twin.*

There was a wound just below the surface, right where his heart was. It was cold, like a ball of ice had grown there to replace it so he didn't bleed out.

If it wasn't for the little female on his back, he would have attempted to claw at his flesh and dug until he removed it.

He tried to focus on her, on the warmth of her, the weight of her, how she stroked his neck. He tried to take in her pretty scent, or her little fluttering heart, the comfort of her breath.

When that didn't help, he looked for something around them to take his mind off the unbearable ball of ice. The smell of the grass and dirt, the sap of trees. There were a few small skittering animals, and even a squawk of a bird.

Nothing was strong enough to distract him, or to settle the liquid floating in front of his sight that constantly blocked his vision.

A whimper rattled out of him, seizing at his lungs.

"Ingram," Emerie softly called, but he refused to answer.

He didn't want to talk about this... about Aleron... anymore. *It hurts too much.*

So, he searched for something he could question her about. Anything.

"Hey, can you let me down for a moment?" she asked, and he shook his head in response.

He worried if he put her down, the loss of her warmth would freeze him entirely.

It didn't matter. She found a way to safely slide off him, and he halted so he could face her. Just as he was about to grab her and throw her back on top of him, she reached her arms out to him.

His head reared back when her hands came up near his skull, unsure of what she was doing. Then she slipped her palms over his shoulders, around the nape of his neck and into the small amount of fur there, before her arms crossed behind the base of his skull. She pulled herself up until her chin was resting on his shoulder, while his beak sat on top of hers.

"What are you doing?" He wondered if she might be trying to choke him.

"It's called a hug. Doesn't it feel nice?" she whispered in return, soft-spoken and *kind*.

It... did.

Ingram placed a hand on her waist, unsure of what he was supposed to do in return. The moment he made contact with her, she leaned forward until her chest was pressing against the top of his own bowed forward one.

A desire to bring her closer nipped at his entire being, from the encompassing way her essence brushed over him. It ate at him, called to him.

He didn't care if he wasn't supposed to wrap his entire arm around her and shove her against him, but he couldn't stop himself. When she started to dip underneath his body while he stood on three limbs, he leaned back and sat with his knees bent, his feet pressed firmly flat, and his tail curled to the side to balance him.

Ingram took her with him, and the changing of positions made her body lay flush with his torso. Her heat radiating through him burned at the frozen ball in his chest, like she was trying to melt it away herself.

With one arm curled around her until he was threatening to claw at her stomach, he wrapped the other across her back until he was gripping her hip.

He squished her against him until she was completely between his knees and huddled himself around her entire form.

And, when she turned her head and buried her face against the side of his neck while tightening her arms around him, something inside him slithered into place. His sight closed and blackened as he took her in completely, allowing all of Emerie to thaw him.

For a few peaceful moments, all he sensed was her.

Her lips were soft against his scales, as was her body. Her breaths were wet but warm, gently puffing over him and causing his fur and scales to lift and ripple from the pleasantness. Her scent was embracing, stealing the world to drown him in her.

Her heart is so... little.

He'd always been able to hear it, but this was the first time it'd fluttered against him. It felt delicate, and its rhythm was so utterly soothing that it was impossible to not be mollified by it.

She is so soft.

He didn't think he'd ever held something this soft, and squishy, and breakable in his arms before. She was so tiny against his much larger body, not just in height, but also in width. He'd already thought her fragile, but this only deepened it.

And yet, Ingram couldn't stop himself from tightening his arms around her. He wanted her to turn into liquid and seep beneath his flesh, so she could comfort him from the inside permanently.

Some of her hair pushed over his beak from the light wind, and he sightlessly buried his skull into those magnificent strands until they shielded him. He also brought his tail tip forward so he could wind it around her calves, trying anything to make their contact more intimate.

Even when she sagged against him, like she couldn't hold her own weight any longer, Ingram made sure to support her with his arms and tail.

He refused to let go, and Emerie never tried to pull away.

It was like she was letting him take his time with it, waiting for him to stop this *hug* when he was done with it. He didn't know if he'd ever be.

Although Aleron had held him similarly many times, as they often slept like this, he'd never had another outside of his kindred embrace him. But with Emerie... it was different.

There was no reason for her to do this, no bond like he'd shared with Aleron. Yet, she'd instigated this, and had gifted him the first moment of peace he'd felt in weeks by doing so.

There was also another emotion taking shape within him. It was small, barely a flowering blossom, yet it reminded him of the affection he felt for his kindred.

After a long passage of time, something rumbled between them. It wasn't the first time her stomach had informed them she was hungry, but it was definitely the loudest.

"Quiet, Emerie's stomach," he grumbled, demanding it leave them be.

Her burst of laughter was so strong it shook his arms. It was the most enchanting sound he'd ever heard, even more so since he'd been able to experience it by touch as well.

"Sorry, I can't help it," she answered with a dying giggle. "Are you feeling better yet?"

Ingram gave her an unrelenting squeeze, and it forced a small choke from her. *"No. I wish to stay like this."*

Perhaps until the end of time, he would have liked to hug Emerie's yielding and lush form.

"Not so hard," she said with a wince. He loosened his hold a little. "I'm really sorry, but I need to eat... among other things."

Then she repeatedly petted the back of his hard skull and a shiver tore through him. He almost crushed her again in reaction.

The fact she was being kind and gentle to a place on his body he knew to be fatal if destroyed... caused a tender ache to swirl behind his exposed sternum. Demons and humans alike had tried to destroy him, and here was this little female petting him.

"A little longer?" he pleaded, unwilling to part from her just yet.

"Fine," came her muffled whisper. "Just a little longer."

FIFTEEN

Emerie was aware she'd sleep-drooled on the Duskwalker's back when she woke up. It was hard not to when she was face down with her cheek squished against his scales. Her arms and legs dangled down on each side of him, and her empty satchel and thin sleeping bag were doing a poor job of truly making this comfortable.

Her breasts and stomach were soft enough protection against his spikes. It was mainly her bones she needed to shield.

Sleeping on the back of Ingram was horrible, but he was adamant he didn't want to stop moving throughout the night. Honestly, it was her exhaustion and the rhythmic sway of their bodies that eventually pulled her under for a few short hours here and there.

Rubbing her face against him with a groggy moan, she peeked open her eyes. It was still night, but the sky was grey as though the sun was beginning its creep over the horizon.

Emerie pushed up to sit on him, and lazily blinked.

It's been four nights since he's slept.

Ingram had not stopped walking since that first night, ferrying Emerie almost the entire way. She asked to be let down a few times to stretch and shake out her aching legs. It was tiring work doing absolutely fuck-all.

She wouldn't have been so worried about his state of rest if he wasn't slowing down little by little. The big guy, for some reason, didn't want to stop. Even now, when she could tell his steps were languid, and a little wobbly.

After their long cuddle the previous day, one that had been just as therapeutic for her as it seemed to be for him, she'd decided she would make him rest once she'd done so herself. One of them needed to keep watch. Since he'd been able to hold out a little longer, she'd made him wait so she could be fully alert.

When he was walking through a decently sized gap in the trees, she patted his neck. "Hey, can you let me down?"

Without saying a word, he lowered himself so she could safely slip off.

"We should stop here and let you rest for a few hours," she told him, hoping her firm tone would make it definitive.

"I do not wish to stop," he argued.

Why did I have a feeling he'd say something like that? It was like he wanted to walk himself to death.

Rolling her eyes, she made her way over to a log that had conveniently fallen most of the way through the clearing. She sat down with her legs crossed, leaned her back against it, and folded her arms.

"You will sleep, Ingram. I'm not getting up until you do."

With an annoyed huff, he stomped over to her. Just as he reached out to pick her up himself, likely so he could toss her over his shoulder, she lightly backhanded his hand away. She sternly pointed at him with her index finger.

His orbs flashed white momentarily as he darted his arm back. Then he gave her a light growl with red flaring.

"No growling or grabbing. Lay down, close your... eyes? And go, the fuck, to sleep."

"Why must I? I am not tired," he grumbled, turning his raven beak away.

"Do not lie to me, Duskwalker! I can see your arms shaking as we speak." She pointed to her left to gesture to the clearing. "Lie down!"

With a snarl, he spun away and plopped down two metres away from her. Giving her his back, he curled into a ball on his side.

However, after a few moments, his tail tip tapped against the ground. She squinted her eyes into a glare at it.

"You better be sleeping, Ingram."

A huff snorted out of him before he got up and crossed to the other side of the clearing. He was a little further away now, giving her his back once more. The second his tail started tapping, he was back on all fours. He spun in a circle and kneaded the ground with his hands, like he was trying to make himself comfortable, then plopped down again.

This time, he faced her, and she had a funny feeling his purple orbs were focused on her. She stared back and raised one of her brows, so he knew she was watching him.

Minutes passed, and she thought he'd finally given in. It was odd to watch the glow in his orbs grow smaller, like that was a Duskwalker's version of their eyelids becoming heavy.

Just before the glow disappeared completely, they flashed brightly like a spark of white fire, and he was on his damn feet again!

Why is he so restless? If she'd been walking for four days straight, she would have fallen asleep as soon as her head clonked on a pillow.

As he crossed the clearing once more, it was obvious now that he was sulking. He did lay down, much closer to her than before.

His orbs were quicker to grow smaller before they eventually disappeared. When his head tipped to the side to reveal the underside of his beak, she knew he'd passed out.

Fucking hell, finally.

Listening to her surroundings, she inspected the forest.

All was quiet, although that didn't necessarily mean it was safe. *I'll likely hear a Demon coming.* That she knew for certain. *But if a snake or a predator comes along, they'll be harder to spot.*

Then again, she was with a Duskwalker. Hopefully just his presence kept everything dangerous from approaching.

Emerie had been on watch for many missions for the Demonslayer guild. They all knew rest was important to stay alert and strong, and she had no qualms about taking the latest shift – which was one most tended to hate.

Those few hours before the sun rose seemed to be the hardest for most. For her, it was her favourite time of day.

It was the coldest, but she often thought it was bewitching. A new day would rise like a ray of hope that could be witnessed at only this time. Dusk brought fear, but dawn chased away the shadows and everything that lurked within them.

Her gaze fell on the Duskwalker.

Well, it chases most things away.

She brought her knees up so she could lean her elbow on it and shove her cheek against the back of her knuckles. *It's scary that your kind can walk in the light. It means we're never truly safe.*

Then again... if all Duskwalkers were like Ingram, would humankind be safe from them if they just stopped being afraid? The skull face made them off-putting because it was a clear reminder of death, but if humans removed their prejudices, would they have been safe from them?

A small whine breaking from him had her drawing her face away from her knuckles. Yet it was his sudden twitching, all his muscles leaping and his tail twisting, that had her brows furrowing deeply.

"Ingram," she softly called when he gave another whine, hoping not to disturb him fully, but to startle whatever nightmare gripped him.

She wasn't dumb. She knew approaching him mid-dream could end up with her on the wrong side of his claws.

Just as she opened her mouth once more, intending to be a little louder, he sprung to his feet within the span of a breath. Orbs white, stance wide like he was ready to fight, and breaths sawing in and out of him, he stared into the forest – at least, she thought he did with the direction his skull was facing.

"Hey there," she cooed to grab his attention. His skull darted to her as his body flinched back a step. "Bad dreams, huh?" Her question had been spoken casually, letting him know she understood why he'd woken and that it was *okay* to be afraid.

His tone was gravelly, his words spoken with a sense of urgency. *"There, I have rested."*

"A few minutes is not rest, Ingram." However, she was

starting to realise the root of the problem. She chewed on the inside of her cheek, wondering how she could help him. "I used to have a lot of nightmares too. Bad ones, where I'd wake up in a layer of sweat, barely able to breathe."

Ingram did not respond, and his orbs bore into her.

Emerie sighed, rubbing at her cheek. "I don't know how to help you. I'll be honest with you, Ingram... I have my own internal scars that haven't truly healed, and I doubt what worked for me will work for you. I don't know if sharing my own stories will help you or burden you, but I want you to know that I do care ab–"

"I do not like being alone," he quietly stated, cutting her anxious rambling short.

Her head jerked, and a frown creased her forehead. "But you're not alone. I'm here with you."

His orbs morphed into blue. *"But I... feel alone."*

"I don't know how to fix that for you," she answered honestly, turning her gaze downward.

Emerie had experienced her fair share of loneliness while in a crowded room. It was a terrible emotion to wallow in, and an even harder one to crawl her way out of.

She'd been trying for years, yet it was always present. It clung like a parasite, a leech, unwilling to let go until it was finished feasting.

"If I did, I would try," she continued. "Like when I gave you that hug, remember?"

Like he was cautious, Ingram took a hesitant step. Then he came closer, and closer, until he was towering over her and she was forced to crane her neck.

Emerie didn't move, unsure of what he was doing.

He placed his palm against the fallen tree, paused, then *shoved* it to the side. She almost fell over when her back support was gone, but quickly righted herself. Then he walked behind her and slowly laid down until he became her wall instead. She looked over her shoulder at him and noticed he was tense.

The silence that lingered between them as they stared at each other was heavy with an unspoken question on his end. He was waiting to see if she would reject him.

For some reason, despite everything she'd witnessed pertaining to him, she thought this might be the most vulnerable she'd seen of Ingram. His tears had been harrowing but uncontrolled. This was him openly revealing his anxieties.

Was this the wisest position for her to be in? Probably not. If he had another nightmare, he would unwittingly hurt her.

Still, the sadness and loneliness in his yawning blue orbs niggled away at her trepidation. The big Duskwalker wanted to cuddle her like a freaking living teddy bear, and she was unwilling to deny him.

Emerie pet his tail since it was the easiest to reach, showing him it was okay, and all the tension eased out of him. Slowly, like he wanted to be sly about it, he curled around her until she was shielded from the elements on three sides.

Ingram tucked the tip of his tail between her arse and her feet until it was wrapping around her. After a few moments, he grew a little braver, a little more confident.

Using the very tip of his beak, he nudged it against her legs until she was forced to put them into a crossed position. He placed his head on her lap, and once more grew stiff. She eventually lowered her arms until one was resting over his neck with her hand between his short goat horns.

"Is this okay?" she asked, lightly patting the downward crease on his forehead to reference what she meant.

He became completely lax. *"Yes. It feels nice."*

"Good. Now go the hell to sleep, or do you need me to sing you a lullaby too?" she tried to tease, in case he had any remaining worries.

When he snorted out a contented huff, Emerie gave him a small smile as tenderness bloomed within her.

Ingram passed out within seconds.

How can a monster... A Duskwalker, who has a skull for a face, be this sweet? She almost pictured him as a gigantic puppy demanding cuddles from their master, wanting to be as close as possible.

After hugging him earlier, and now this, she understood that he meant physically when he said he felt alone.

She kept brushing her fingertips from side to side, hoping the action would help prevent any nightmares. She looked up at the brightening sky with a small smile.

At least this is much warmer.

Ingram quietly grumbled as he paced back and forth in the forest by himself.

Water splashing a small distance away caused his skull to face that direction. The urge to follow the noise niggled at him. Instead, his scales lifted in annoyance, and he continued to pace.

Why will she not let me see?

Emerie was bathing, since the stream had opened up again and allowed her space to dip inside. He'd wanted to stay and protect her, watch her, and just be in her general vicinity.

Although a large part of his reasoning was because he was curious about what lay beneath her clothing, he also just... liked looking at her. Her presence was soothing, and being alone in the forest bothered him.

If she wasn't constantly on his back while they travelled, he would have stared at her pretty, dot-covered face, or her shiny orange hair, or her light-blue eyes. But she was touching him when she was on top of his back, and that often satisfied him.

Yet, whenever he let her down to walk, he'd found himself examining the mounds on her chest that were so tightly contained by her shirt they barely bounced. Her waist was narrow, and he wondered if he could wrap his hands around it completely until his fingers overlapped.

Her arse was round and pliable from what he felt against him. Her thighs even gained his attention.

Anything that had a barrier between them – from her long-sleeved uniform – was making him more curious by the day.

He was beginning to see her feet, always in shoe coverings, and her elbows as naughty as well. Naughty because she said he couldn't look or touch when he wanted to. She said only special people could see her without her garments.

She allowed me to sleep next to her last night... His tail swiped to the side as he snorted out a huff. *Gave me that hug...*

And since both, he had a craving to do them again. To hold her, feel her against him.

He wanted more. He wanted her to touch him again until she brought forth liquid pleasure, and he was beginning to wonder if he could return it.

I would like to make her feel good. She made him feel good, both physically, with her hugs, pats, and sleep cuddles, as well as... deep inside.

In his loss-and-grief-filled heart. In his mind, where he hadn't known peace was possible again, until she gave him strange affection that calmed him.

Emerie was kind to him.

She listened to him, she answered his constant questions, and she even played with him – he hadn't known her sarcasm was a form of playful teasing until she explained it. If something was bothering him, like his memories, she would find a way to distract him until he forgot.

Not once had she made him feel terrible about his lack of knowledge, nor had she made him feel like a monster to be feared and hated. She never looked at him with spite, but rather with a warmness he was realising he'd always craved from others – he just hadn't known.

The more she did this, the more he felt himself falling into some kind of spell.

Yet, there was an obvious barrier between them.

Not only would she not let him see and touch her unless he was seeking a comforting embrace – which she seemed happy to supply – she also revealed little about herself.

He didn't know what he was supposed to ask her, and she wasn't forthcoming with it.

As he'd asked himself many times, he thought, *Is it because I am Mavka?*

Just because she didn't treat him like a monster, didn't mean she... liked him. Or trusted him with her secrets.

Would it have been easier had he been a human?

Ingram paused his pacing so he could reach up to his skull

and drift his claws down his raven beak. *I am different to her.*

His face was different, his body was different. There was nothing about them that was similar. He even had a tail and walked on all fours, whereas she didn't.

It hadn't escaped his notice that other Mavka sometimes walked on just two feet.

"Okay! I'm done. You can come back now," Emerie called out.

He immediately headed back over to her, thankful to escape being alone.

Her hair was darker than normal and appeared heavily weighed down by the water. She was just twisting it and wringing it when he came upon her.

"It's a really nice afternoon and my body is a little sore from sitting still all the time," she said, dipping her blue eyes over to him. "I'd like to walk for a while before night falls."

Ingram nodded, having no issue with this, even though she was incredibly slow.

Leading the way, she opened her bag and scooped out a handful of berries, popping them into her mouth as she walked. *She always eats. She is a hungry thing.* Ingram tried to find as many of them as he could, since she often looked cute when she was delighted to see them.

He liked that she'd turn that delight towards him.

She popped another berry in her mouth and gave a hum as she chewed. He watched her, as he often did when they were side by side.

Her arms weren't elongated like his were, and they swayed at her sides in rhythm, yet she was able to utilise them whenever she wanted. Ingram inspected her feet and the way they moved against the ground. His sight drew up her legs, noticing they weren't bowed like his were.

If he walked like this, similar to her and other humans, would she be more inclined to like him in return?

He could rear back if he wished to, but he'd never tried to walk. Ingram fell behind and pushed up so he was on two legs.

His torso was curled too far forward, unbalancing him, and he fell to his hands. He quickly caught up to her when she'd gained a small distance.

With his second attempt, he dug his claws into the bark of a tree, using it to hold him steady. One side of him dipped forward, unable to maintain it with the way his back was permanently bent.

Were the other Mavka born differently? He and Aleron had never stood tall. Neither had tried to do this. Ingram sat and looked down at his palms. *I wish there was a way I could change my form.*

The strangest sensation rippled inside him.

He twisted his head to inspect his own body, attempting to see past his beak. Dark yellow swirled into his sight.

It was slow to start, but his arms shrank in length and became thicker. His legs, on the other hand, grew thinner and longer, shaping into something else. His toes shortened as his feet widened.

He winced when his back cracked, but that was only because it was straightening. His shoulders pushed back, and even the arch of his neck changed, along with the way his skull sat above it.

The fur over his body shortened even further until it almost disappeared completely, leaving him only covered in scales.

His hands stayed the same, still large and calloused. His skull never changed, but it was weightier on his neck and began to dip to the side. He straightened it, and it almost went the other way.

"What are you doing?" Emerie asked.

Shifting carefully into a crouch, he brought his gaze up to find there was a decent distance between them. She had turned to him and was waiting.

"I... do not know," he answered honestly. He wasn't sure what was happening.

Even his voice was different, not as growly and deep. He touched at his beak like that was the answer to figuring out why the rough bass of his voice had softened.

She waved for him to come over. "Well, it's weird you're the one slowing us down. That's my job."

When he reached forward with his arm to resume walking on all fours like he normally would, she turned to continue walking.

However, he noticed his shoulders moved in a way that was less comfortable, and he was pretty sure his backside was tipping towards the sky.

It no longer felt natural.

He caught up to her and mentally assessed the changes within himself. She peeked over her shoulder to make sure he was with her and then looked at their path.

My body changed... Reaching to the side, he dug his claws into a tree, and lifted up.

The moment he was upright, he knew he could maintain it. His back was straight, his skull fell into a natural down position, and there was no longer a strain on his legs.

Bright yellow filled his sight in joy.

Yet, when he took a step forward and let go of the tree, his legs shook, unused to walking like this. He quickly had to steady himself again or he'd fall.

Emerie didn't get far before she sighed, noticing the space next to her was empty.

"What are you doing back ther–" Her eyes widened, her face darted upwards at his towering skull, and she fell onto her backside like her knees had instantly given out. "Oh my god!"

Concerned, he reached out to her while stepping forward. "Emerie?"

She clenched her eyes shut and threw her hands over her face to protect her head... when he started to fall. He groaned and winced when he had to stop himself from crushing her with his elbows and knees.

I almost landed on top of her. The reddish pink flared into his sight.

He pushed up onto his straighter arms to give her space, and she drew her hands down, peeking over them at him.

"What are you doing, Ingram? You gave me a fright, towering over me like that."

The embarrassed hue of his sight brightened. "I am trying to walk like you," he admitted with a small grumble.

He backed up and was able to stand without assistance this time, but he did have to use a tree to balance himself when he swayed.

Partially laying on the ground, she gawked up at him. Even when she rushed to her feet, she still had to crane her neck to stare at him with her lips parted and her eyes wide.

Something became startlingly obvious as he gazed down at her, and he twisted his head at her.

"I did not realise you were so... small," he said, since she barely came to the bottom of his sternum.

He'd always known she was thinner than him, and little in height, but she looked... tiny.

"Small?" she rasped. "I'm five foot seven! I'm just not a massive Duskwalker like you." Her wide eyes trailed down his body until she was looking at his feet, before slowly coming back up. "Holy shit. What are you? Seven foot? Seven foot five? You didn't look so big before."

Ingram's head tilted the other way as he noticed her expression appeared... guarded and mistrustful. His sight shifted to blue and an unpleasant emotion crept across his chest.

"You don't like it?" She didn't smell afraid, but her features appeared like she might be. *Should I have not done this?*

The leaves above shook with a small gust of wind, causing dappled light to sprinkle over her face. Even with the noises of the trees shifting, he could hear her heart racing, and her breaths were sharper.

However, the longer she stared, his orbs turning a darker blue with each second of silence passing between them, the more she relaxed. Her posture softened, and she averted her gaze into the forest as she rubbed at her cheek.

"No, it's fine," she grumbled. "I just wasn't expecting it."

"I can change back if it will ease you."

He hoped he *could* change back.

His legs were stronger than they were moments before, and they ceased shaking. He did wobble when he cautiously drew his hand away from the tree trunk, but he was able to stand on his own with minor swaying.

"Sorry, I didn't mean to freak out." Emerie closed some of the distance between them, forcing her neck back even further. "If you want to walk like this, then you can."

"You don't like it," he stated, turning his head away as he

internally pouted.

"Sure, I do! I just didn't know you could do this." Then, she laughed as she said, "I just don't like surprises. I like to know what's happening."

Is she lying?

It was hard to tell for a creature who understood little about humans. Her expressions often confused him.

One thing he did know about Emerie... was that she was *accepting*.

"I also did not know I could do this." He had to admit, it was harder to see her like this. He needed to lean to the side just to look at her feet. "But I have seen other Mavka do it. I thought if I walked like you, you would be more at ease with me."

Her little brows drew together as her pale-pink lips tightened. "But I have been at ease with you."

His sight shifted to a reddish pink once more, unsure if he should be truthful or not. Ingram wanted to be closer with her, and he worried that revealing the depth of what he wanted, and still didn't fully comprehend, would make her unsettled.

To test her, Ingram hesitantly reached forward.

Her eyes warily darted to the side at his claws nearing, but she didn't flinch or try to evade him. When he was able to touch his careful fingertips to her marred cheek and then brush his claws into her hair so he could hold the side of her face, his heart tightened with tenderness.

He decided to just brave it, already frustrated with his obsessive thoughts of her.

"I don't know how to learn about you. I know your name, and that you are a Demon hunter, but I do not know where you came from. I do not... know why you are here with me."

Why had Emerie chosen to come on this journey with him?

Part of him hoped it was because she wanted to be by his side after helping him in the mountain stronghold. Did she save him because she had been able to see he didn't want to be a terrifying monster? He'd been seeking for some way to escape the loneliness that had bitten its fangs into him after Aleron was taken from him, and he thought maybe she recognized that.

I want her to share with me. In the same way he wanted to

share with her, but found it difficult to do so whenever it pained him.

He wanted her to take that pain away somehow.

He wanted her to fix it.

She was smart and kind, she must know of a way.

If she had her own pain, Ingram wanted to frighten it away. To be a source of comfort, as she had already been for him – without him needing to ask her to.

But he didn't know if she held fears or sadness within her.

Since she hadn't answered him, her lips opening and closing like she was unsure of what she wanted to say, he braved stroking her cheek with his thumb. He was careful of his claw near her eye.

"There are times where you look into the forest with a sad expression on your face. I do not know if that is because of me, or if something else is saddening you."

Her eyes lowered to avoid his stare. "I'm fine, Ingram. You have enough on your mind."

A low growl rumbled in his chest. He pushed her face back up to meet his own, not liking that she wouldn't look upon him. "You smile, but it is only ever at me."

"Isn't that a good thing?" she laughed, fidgeting and rubbing her elbow.

As much as he liked her smiles, and that they mostly appeared genuine, he shook his head. "Sometimes they are lies. When you think I am not looking, that is the only time I am truly seeing you. Yet, you do not show me this side willingly."

Day had brightened the world six times since she freed him, and he knew nothing more about this creature than he did that first night.

"It's not like you've asked me anything."

When her hair lifted and waved due to a light gust, Ingram stared raptly at the long strands. He brushed his claws and fingers down them, touching them, and found they were even softer than he'd imagined. They were silky, even as they caught on the rough callouses of his hands.

"I do not know how to start this with you," Ingram admitted. Yellow brightened his orbs at being allowed to play freely with her pretty hair; especially after so many days from when he'd first callously yanked it. "I have never had a human companion before."

She let out a deep, long breath, and her shoulders became less rigid. "Well... what do you want to know then? I'll try my best to answer you."

That sounded like she was intending to hide things from him.

The desire to trap her to him gripped him like a set of claws around his throat. Ingram fisted the long strands and leaned forward to tower over her. His growl was a warning for her not to hide things, but also in anticipation of discovering all about Emerie.

"Everything," he rumbled. "I want to know everything."

Ingram would start by learning *all* of this little female. Like him and Aleron, he wanted them to share everything. Their thoughts, their touch, their hearts. In doing so, maybe she could fill the yawning hole in his chest he was desperate to be rid of.

At least... until Aleron was returned and made him whole once more.

SIXTEEN

"M-maybe you should change back," Emerie suggested through clenched teeth.

Pushing up on Ingram's chest, her hands cupping hard exposed bone, she used all her might to keep him upright so he didn't fall. At least, until he was able to support himself again. She kept her hands out, ready to catch him – which was probably a stupid idea.

This is how I turn myself into a Duskwalker-flattened Emerie pancake.

"No. I want to do this, to walk like you and the other humans," Ingram argued.

Why does he always argue with me?! She mentally threw her hands up.

He made it a few steps before he stumbled, but it was at least further than the last attempt. It was like his knees wanted to give out after too long, or his equilibrium was off.

Fucking hell. It's like walking with a drunk.

A drunk that was seven and a half feet tall and would probably kill her if he landed on top of her. A drunk that didn't want to listen, who she was forced to chase after.

Then again, he was getting better the longer he tried.

At least he's not pestering me with questions. Or, more importantly, trying to get her to talk about herself.

She wasn't against revealing her past because he was a Duskwalker. She didn't mind what he was, and she'd grown to trust him and his big claws a long time ago.

I just don't want to burden him, she thought, steadying him for only a second before he strode forward.

Emerie doubted any human had pleasant stories. Almost everyone she'd ever spoken to at the guild had some dark past, some worse than hers, many not. It's why most people joined in the first place.

It was hard to hide how terrible her life had been when it was so easily seen on her face. The fact that Ingram hadn't asked her about it, when most humans liked to ask her what had caused her scarring, was a relief.

She didn't want to talk about that night.

A night that had left her not only disfigured, but also startlingly alone in this big world filled with sharp teeth.

Sharing any part of her life would, undoubtably, force her to talk about her worst memories. It was impossible to skirt around them.

Just as it was impossible to forget them.

She wished she could. She wished she could bury them deep within the recesses of her mind and pretend they didn't exist. She couldn't, not when they painted a story on her face she was forced to read every time she saw her own reflection in a mirror, or the bottom of a cup.

They haunted her wherever she went, and not even sleep could give her peace since they lingered in her dreams.

It didn't help that whenever she told most people, their expressions would turn sympathetic.

Then they would spout nonsense. *"I'm sorry for your loss, Emerie."* Or, *"I'm so sorry you had to suffer through that."*

Their apologies were pointless. They didn't change anything. They didn't do anything to lessen her burdens, instead only worsening them.

Their pity made her feel weak, small, feeble.

She didn't need the Duskwalker making her feel that way. Not when he had his own wounds to heal.

What if sharing her story only made his harder to swallow?

As Ingram finally walked on his own, yellow lifting into his orbs like a beacon of joy, she gave him a commiserating smile.

We are so alike. Our pasts are filled with loss and pain. The difference was: she'd had plenty of time to deal with it. She'd bandaged her wounds and just treated her infection when the symptoms of it flared.

Ingram was still bleeding.

On the battlefield, she wouldn't check her infection when her comrades were bleeding out. She wouldn't show them her older wound when they had a fresh one in their stomach.

Yet... it was obvious her lack of sharing was bothering him.

Maybe I could give him a watered-down version of it?

And, since he was managing to walk on his own, flaring a small amount of pride in her, she might as well spill it now.

"Okay. Since you wanted to know about me," Emerie started, staring at the darkening horizon with the sun dropping behind them, "maybe I should start with when I was a child?"

When he tilted his head at her, she worried he wouldn't comprehend a lot of it.

"I grew up in the southlands. There's a town right near the border on the eastern side called Fishket. It's not too far from the sea."

"Is the southlands where that wall of tree trunks is?"

"Yep, exactly right. There's a big wall of log spikes humans have built to keep most of the Demons out, but towns and villages still have their own for additional protection." Emerie placed her hands behind her to clasp them, trying to appear as carefree as possible. "I lived there for most of my life. My parents were really good people who lived well in comparison to most. Because of this, they tried to share what they could with those who weren't well off. They were highly respected within the town, so a lot of people flocked to them. I had a lot of friends when I was younger, since there were many children my own age."

"Friends?" he asked.

"Like a companion, but many of them."

He perked up. "Like my kindred?"

"No." She smiled warmly with humour. "Not like your kindred. They were not related to me, but other humans that would spend time with me even though they didn't have to."

"I... see." Then he cupped his beak, like he was deep in thought. He placed his hand on a tree trunk to steady himself. "Does that mean we are friends?"

"Sure. We're friends," she answered, and his orbs brightened in their yellow hue. "However, I had a special friend when I was really little. His name was Gideon. Our parents were really close, so I played with him a lot even though he was from the poorer side of town. When I was older and allowed to go out by myself, I was always with him." She covered her mouth with a fist as she let out a small laugh. "He always got me into trouble because he was a rascal."

"If he was special, does that mean he saw beneath your clothes?"

Emerie, taken aback by what he said, almost tripped and fell on her face.

"What? No!" She couldn't believe he'd asked her that! However, she nervously rubbed her arm and averted her eyes to the forest. "Then again, I thought he would. Our parents were discussing an arranged marriage when we were young, but that never happened." Just because she knew he'd ask about it, she quickly added, "Marriage is where two humans get together and form a family. A bond, if you will."

For a few moments, he was silent. She peeked to find his orbs were dark yellow, rather than red with anger. It was a relief he wasn't jealous.

"Why did you not form a family with this... Gideon male?"

Her features tightened. "A sickness tore through our town and his, uh, parents fell ill. My parents took him in while they tried to recover, but they eventually passed away. He was adopted into our family."

"A... dopted?"

"It means to take someone else's child and make them your own. It happens when either the parents die, can't take care of them properly, or just don't want them. He became my brother, although... that isn't really the reason we never married. We still could have, since we weren't related."

"Then why not? If he was special to you, would you not want to form a bond with him?"

"I did." Emerie awkwardly laughed. "I grew up thinking we would, especially since my parents pushed for it because he was such a sweet boy who had always been respectable towards me. But he, uh, he liked men, not women."

Ingram's head jerked to the side, causing the sound of dried bones to rattle from him. "He liked males? I do not understand why this would matter."

Why do I keep having to have the birds and the bees chat with him?! Emerie almost rolled her eyes. *Then again... this was more like the bees and the bees chat,* she thought with humour.

"So, remember how I explained that men and women would get together to make a baby? Well, that's not always the case. Sometimes women and women, or men and men will form a bond and be together. They prefer to be with their own sex."

"Then it does not matter the gender of your partner?"

"No, only that they are the one who makes you happy."

His orbs brightened in their yellow hue once more. "I see. So you could not make him happy because you are female?"

"That's a weird way to put it, but yes." Emerie scratched the side of her head in annoyance. "It was really hard for me to accept it, to be honest."

"You were not approving of this... pairing?" Why did his voice hold a hint of disappointment?

"It was more that I'd had this big plan in my head for my future, all of it involving him, and I felt like that had been ripped away from me. I guess I was also really angry that he'd hidden something so important from me, and I found out by accident when I was seventeen and found him and his boyfriend at the time doing... *things* when I came home early from working the farmlands. It'd been really hurtful to accidentally find who I thought would be my future husband in bed with someone else, no matter their gender."

"What was he doing that was so bad it hurt you?"

Emerie's eyes widened, and she looked at the ground.

She couldn't say it was hugging, since she'd hugged Ingram and didn't want him to make his own weird thoughts about that. However, she didn't want to explain sex to him in general, not just pertaining to men on men.

"Annnnyway," she said slyly. "I eventually realised it had nothing to do with me, and I just wanted him to be happy, even if it wasn't with me." She turned a bright smile at Ingram to show just how sincere she was about that. "The reason he'd never told me is because he knew how I felt and didn't want to hurt me. He didn't trust me, and discovering it made me realise there had always been a barrier between us. Once I accepted we weren't the right fit for each other, I truly began to see him as my older brother and our relationship grew really strong. He was my best friend, and he meant the world to me."

"If this is true, then where is he? Or is it like how Mavka are *brothers*? We often venture near each other, but we don't remain in each other's presence for long."

"He is... in heaven," she answered sadly.

Tilting his head, Ingram leaned forward a little. "Why do you look saddened by this? Can you not just visit him, or is heaven far away?"

Emerie didn't know why she found his words funny. Perhaps it was because it allowed her to say Gideon was gone, without having to say just how permanently.

"Yes, Ingram. Heaven is far, but I'll visit him one day."

"Once we destroy the Demon King, I can come with you, so you are safe. We can find Aleron along the way."

Tears dotted her eyelashes, and she blinked them away as best she could. The fact he wanted to keep her safe was sweet, but that wasn't a journey he could come with her on. She didn't want to tell him that, in case he took it the wrong way – like she didn't want him by her side.

However... something he said allowed her to avoid it altogether. Something that had her gaze darting to him and her features crinkling into a deep frown.

"What do you mean, find Aleron along the way? Where is he?"

She'd assumed he was dead. *Was I wrong?*

Lifting his skull towards the sky to gaze at the stars beginning to sparkle, his orbs turned blue. "He is in the afterworld. But I will find a way to go there and bring him here, so I can see him again like you will see your Gideon person."

Her eyes bowed with deep sympathy.

She didn't know if telling the truth would be wrong, but she did know false hope was a bitter curse. One that was better lifted before it was too late.

"Heaven is the afterworld, Ingram."

"It is?" he asked with a high note of curiosity. He darted his raven skull to her. "Then we can find them at the same time. We can do this together."

Emerie reached out and grabbed his arm, stopping him and making him turn to her. This conversation was too important to have while walking.

"People don't come back from the afterworld, Ingram. It's not a place you and I can go while we're still alive."

"You don't know this," he argued defensively.

"I do," she answered, making her words stern. "I know you want him back, just like I want Gideon back, but that's not how life works. Death is permanent."

He dismissively wagged his head from side to side. "For a human, perhaps."

"For everything. It doesn't matter what creature, whether they be human, animal, Demon, or even a Duskwalker."

"The Witch Owl said that Mavka are life and death. That we are limbo." When she opened her mouth to refute him, his blue orbs turned bright crimson, and he jerked forward to growl. *"You are wrong, Emerie,"* he snarled, his voice changing into the monstrous one she'd always heard, but it was startling with him more humanoid like this.

She flinched and threw her hands up like she was warding him back and surrendering. "Okay. I'm wrong," she conceded, unwilling to further upset him.

If that was what he wanted to believe, then she would let him. Who was she to say otherwise? He was a Duskwalker, and humans knew very little about them.

Maybe he was right. She was even hoping that was the case, and if not... well, that was *his* battle to face. If she was still alive for it, she would just try to comfort him through it.

It was said there were five stages to grief: anger, denial, depression, bargaining, and acceptance – although not necessarily in that order.

She knew, for certain, Ingram was stuck in the denial phase. She wondered if his level of humanity was capable enough to transcend into acceptance, or if he would be stuck in this state forever.

Hope could be a cruel master. It could make people do reckless and stupid things... like a Duskwalker asking Demonslayers for aid.

Or trying to kill the Demon King.

At least if I stay with him, I might be able to convince him not to do anything... foolish.

Sitting on the ground with his tail curled around his crossed legs, Ingram kept his arms folded across his chest. Although his body was facing Emerie, his head was purposefully directed away from her.

"If you keep sulking, I'll treat you like a kid," she playfully bit out.

Orbs red and his tail tip tapping against the ground in irritation, he huffed in answer.

"Awww, come on. Don't be like that." When he didn't settle, she walked in front of his face and put her hands on her ample hips. "I already said I was sorry."

Ingram rotated his head until it was behind him and threatening to come back around the other side. In his peripheral, he noticed she stuck her tongue out at him.

He'd never seen her do this before, but her scrunched-up features informed him he was upsetting her. Then it was even more obvious when she threw up her hands, rolled her eyes, and stormed out of sight.

It was done at him in retaliation.

So Ingram spun his head around and did it back at her, sticking his purple tongue out past the tip of his beak.

"Rude!" she exclaimed, plopping her arse upon the grass.

"How dare you do that back to me! You're lucky you're cute, otherwise I wouldn't offer for you to come sit next to me while I sleep."

"I do not want to be near you," he grumbled, hating how his tail coiled in delight that she'd called him cute.

She'd never called him that before, but he remembered Raewyn, his Elf friend, had done so and explained what it meant. Cute, adorable – he liked these things.

She had better not be pacifying him, though. She'd been doing that all evening.

I can return Aleron to this world. He didn't know how, he didn't know when, but he refused to believe anything else regarding it.

He didn't like that she'd tried to convince him otherwise.

In his mind, he could not exist without his kindred. So, if he was still here, then a part of Aleron was as well. They were one, and that would cross time and space. It was the only reason why the ball of ice in his chest hadn't frozen his heart and stopped it from beating.

It was the only reason he was still moving, and wasn't a crying heap in the forest, waiting to be eaten by Demons.

"Come on, bird brain," Emerie cooed, patting the spot next to her. "You know you want to."

"Bird brain?" he rasped, rearing his head back. "You insult me and expect me to come closer?"

Her lips curled in humour. "It wasn't an insult, Ingram."

He unfolded his arms and pointed a claw at her. "Only Merikh calls me this. I did not understand it before, but I think he meant I was stupid."

Now that he looked back on those times, Merikh, the red-orbed Mavka, only said this to him when he did something silly. Actually, he said it to both him and his kindred.

She propped her elbow on her bent knee and rested her cheek against her enclosed fist. Her humour brightened, making her blue eyes glow.

"Did you know that birds are a highly intelligent species?"

"No? They do nothing but peck at the ground and squawk."

"That's not true. They can scavenge and puzzle food from

humans even if we have preventative measures in place. They set up traps to lure prey like small rodents. They even remember faces, and tell each other who to avoid and who to befriend. We teach them to carry messages for us. Ravens, in particular, are very wise creatures."

Ingram reached up to stroke down his beak. "I have that bird's skull."

"I know," she answered warmly, her eyes glinting mischievously.

Wise? This is the word she thinks of when she looks upon my face? Once more, his tail curled in delight.

She was trying to please him, and to his dismay, it was working.

When he took too long to move, she gave him a sigh and laid back. Turning on her side, she brought her knees up and tucked her hands under her marred cheek. She curled up on top of her sleep bag, as if she preferred it to cushion her rather than warm her.

He'd noted a while ago that she always began her sleep by lying with her scarred side face down.

Ingram shifted his position until he was on his hands and feet, and crouch-walked until he was near her. With an oomph, he laid down behind her with his back touching hers, unwilling to face her when he was still upset.

Emerie turned, causing him to stiffen. She stroked his side.

"I really am sorry for upsetting you." He huffed in response, selfishly refusing to answer in hopes she would keep stroking him. "Fine, I'll leave it be. Just don't fall asleep, okay? I'll take the early watch so you can get a few hours in before we set off again."

Ingram didn't see the point in her watching over him while he slept. Her protection felt very mediocre, considering she was such a little human who wouldn't be able to fend off anything dangerous. If Ingram wanted to, he could easily pick her up by the back of her shirt and toss her.

After a little while, her hand languidly slipped down his back and her breaths evened out into light huffs. He rotated his head so he could look over his shoulder, inspecting whether she was truly unconscious.

Slowly, as to not disturb her, Ingram rolled over.

He gingerly slipped his arm underneath her head to cushion it before wrapping both around her torso. He drew Emerie closer until she was firmly pressed against him.

I like this new body.

Having a similar shape to a human allowed him to lay flush with her, rather than having to curl his much larger body around her smaller one.

Staring down at her, all his earlier irritation bled out of him – assisted by the fact she'd insinuated he was wise and called him something pleasant.

He'd also learned what the word beautiful meant today, and he was pleased he already found something that appeared this way to him. Starting from the centre of her throat, he carefully drew his blunted claw tips up and down behind her ear with the arm she was leaning on. *Beautiful, shiny, little female.*

He let her heat spread over him while experiencing her softness all along the front of him. He took in her sweet scent and the sounds of her life.

He didn't know if Emerie had experienced terrible dreams in his presence, but there were times where she appeared tired when she woke. There were often dark smudges underneath her eyes that faded as the day went on. He drew his free hand down her body in the hopes of soothing her so she could sleep well – like she'd once done for him.

He noticed there was a small pocket of space between them, and dissatisfied with this, he grabbed her plump arse and thigh to pull her closer. Her hips pressed against his, and just the mere warmth and touch of her against his seam had movement shifting behind it.

Something distracted him enough to still his cock, and he let out a thoughtful *'hmm?'*

What had only been to pull her closer turned into him grabbing her arse to feel it within his palm. *It is squishier than I thought it was.* His orbs shifted to yellow as he enjoyed the way it jiggled and moulded between his thick fingers. *I did not know it was so much fun to play with.*

Emerie groaned, swatted at his hand in her sleep, and buried her face against his chest. Ingram's sight shifted to orange. He hadn't meant to disturb her; he'd merely gotten distracted.

That didn't mean he let go, too content with grasping it.

At least she hadn't woken and realised what he'd been doing.

Once she had fallen back into a deep sleep, he just petted her throat, jaw, and the side of her face with his claws. She released a little breathy rasp when he tickled right over her pulsing jugular. When he did it a second time, she gave another rasp and even tilted her chin up like she wanted more.

I like this sound and reaction, he realised.

It sent the strangest thrill through him, starting from his ear holes until it lanced straight to the centre of his groin. His seam clenched as his dick jerked. Even his sight shifted to a different shade of bright purple.

How and where else could he evoke this reaction from her?

He skated his claw down her ear, across her brow and down her cheek, but gained nothing. It was only when he tickled the back of her neck that a hitch of breath broke from her.

It was so quiet, such a small reaction in the grand scheme of things. Yet, it had been loud to him... distinct.

A weird but new tang lifted into her usual scent. One that had every scale, every fibre of fur, every bit of his skin prickling in awareness – of her.

It was also something that had his mouth drooling and his cock stiffening within seconds. It didn't matter that it was a light, barely noticeable change, it still struck him like a thunderbolt.

With a groan, Ingram gripped her arse tighter and shoved her hips against his own, trying to use her body to stop himself from extruding. He hadn't meant to grow aroused; he'd just wanted to pet this female.

His powerful reaction was startling.

Something is wrong. Why does she create this reaction from me? He was beginning to understand what emotion this colour of purple signified in his orbs, but not why Emerie called it forth so violently.

He craved something, but he didn't know what. It had something to do with the now throbbing and hot thing putting an uncomfortable amount of pressure inside him. It desired something, hungered for something, but there was a piece missing in his mind.

Without that knowledge, he was unsure of what he needed to ease it, other than obtaining release.

Now that he'd stopped touching her affectionately, that tang in her scent became almost non-existent. That did not quell the arousal within him, nor did it settle his suddenly erratically beating heart.

No, it grew peskier, nagged louder.

Ingram winced and flinched as his cock thickened and hardened more, and not even her shoved against him could help contain it. His beak parted on a deep exhale as it slipped from him, as well as his tentacles that did not shield him like they did when they drew him back inside.

Despite the overwhelming craving to thrust against her abdomen after the initial blissful stroke of it slipping against it, he didn't. He just stayed tense, hoping it would eventually go away and that their bodies huddling it would help to keep the air from making it sting.

How do I make it go away?

"Ingram," Emerie called in a groggy voice, all broken and croaking. Even that had his dick swelling. "You're hurting me. It's too tight, I can't breathe."

She weakly pushed against him.

White sparked in his orbs for just a second, cutting through the purple. He loosened his hold on her, not realising he'd been desperately gripping her.

Her chest no longer pressed against his own so tightly, and her breaths settled. He wanted her to fall back asleep, to not register what was currently nestled between them.

Oh, but he knew the moment she did. His tentacles were twitching and moving, and were hard to ignore. When she slipped her hand down to inspect the movement, one curled around her fingertip and tugged.

Emerie gasped and attempted to roll away and escape, but Ingram held strong. He placed his hand on the back of her head and pressed her face against his chest.

"Sleep, Emerie," he grated, and even he could tell the demand was strained.

"I can't go to sleep with... with *that* against me!" she squealed.

He didn't know why guilt and shame prickled the back of his neck, or why he felt like he was doing something wrong. "I am... sorry."

He let her go when her squirming caused two reactions from him: one was a blissful thrust since she was stroking him with her contorting movements, the other was a hunger stirring in his gut.

She immediately stood and stared at him with wide, stark eyes. "Why... why are you hard?" Her eyes darted down to his groin when he sat up, but quickly averted away. Her cheeks grew pink. "I wasn't even doing anything. Oh god, please tell me I wasn't grinding against you in my sleep."

"Grinding?" She could do that and receive this kind of reaction from him? He suddenly wanted to find out, which only made him pulsate, and fresh lubricant seeped to the surface. "No. Your scent changed, and you felt nice in my arms. Soft and warm."

He wished he could better explain it, or what he felt. If he did, would it make her want to touch him, or let him touch her in return?

Gripping his cock to shield it from the air and lessen the sting, he attempted to make her understand. "You said that I should feel this way with someone special, and that they should make here feel good." He pointed to his chest with his tail curling in apprehension. "You do this."

"Nooo," she argued, pointing down at his dick. "I made you feel good there and you want more. It's just your dick brain telling you it's your heart because I'm the only female here."

Sadness washed over him as his sight flickered blue. He didn't like what she was insinuating.

"I have been around another female before, and she did not make me feel this way." Then again... he hadn't known he had a cock when he met Raewyn, but he didn't tell Emerie that. "You are... beautiful. I like your face, your scent, and how you are kind to me."

He tilted his head when her cheeks grew bright red. "B-beautiful?" she stuttered out, her lips opening and closing like she was speechless.

His chest radiated with pride when he realised she liked being called this.

"Your hair is pretty, and I like how it glows bright orange in the sun like a sunrise. Your eyes look like a frozen lake, yet you look at me with warmth. And when you smile at me... your entire face hurts my chest. I find these things beautiful."

Even with the small distance between them, he could hear her heart picking up. Her cheeks reddened further, and she lifted her hand to cover the left one, where some of the webbed scarring of her features darkened from its usual paleness.

He wanted to keep explaining what other features he found attractive, but they were all reminders of what he was currently gripping. It made him want to blissfully stroke while he thought about them.

He was tempted to.

"We... we can talk about this after you go take care of *that,* okay?" she whispered, glancing at him before looking off once more. "You know, while your dick isn't hard, and you might be thinking more clearly?"

She wanted to talk about it more. He hoped that was a good thing.

"Will you touch me?" He wanted her hands upon him more than anything right now. Just the idea had a hot and heavy pant falling from his parted beak.

"Go take care of your erection, Ingram," she demanded, pointing into the forest. When he didn't move, she squirmed on the spot. "Go jerk off. Go come."

She curled her hand until she made a ring with an empty space in the middle. She moved it up and down in the air like a demonstration.

He mimicked her while gripping his *erection* and a small shudder wracked him, lubricant coming to the surface to moisten and protect him.

"Not here! In the forest." He wasn't sure if he was correct or not, but two little beads had pebbled on her chest through her tight shirt in reaction to him. He'd never seen that from her before. "*Please*, before I lose my mind."

He almost denied her request when that delicious tanginess tangled into her scent again. However, her bright red, yet pleading expression made him stand and walk away... in disappointment.

Once he was as far from her as he could handle, he knelt, doubting he'd be able to stand for this.

Did he mind that she was nearby and knew he was doing this? No, not when his first stroke tightened his flesh over his bones and muscles from pleasure. Actually, the thought of her there, aware, deepened the throbbing of his cock.

Since she wouldn't touch him, he would have liked to do this while he stared at her and have her watch him. He would have been thrilled to let her see the need and desire she brought forth within him.

Emerie, he internally groaned, having to squeeze his cock and stroke it harder, wishing it was her soft hand instead.

I want her to stroke me. He craved her touch, craved taking in the sight of her right now, the scent of her – especially with the new tang to it.

He tried to imagine every part of her essence so it could help him achieve release. His strokes grew swifter as he slipped his fist around his slippery, wet cock.

Yet, the longer he tried, the more forceful he had to be.

He didn't mind that she was nearby, but he didn't like... being on his own. It felt cold and wrong while he did this, like he should be ashamed of this part of himself.

When he realised this, the needy ache started to annoy him. He tried to go faster to get it over with, strengthening his grip to squeeze the core of him. He focused on the tip, and small groans fell from him.

Yet, no matter how good it felt, his release didn't near. Instead, it pestered at the base of him, making his tentacles wriggle unhappily and with annoyance.

The tiniest whine escaped his chest.

He didn't want to be stuck like this, or with it, by himself.

SEVENTEEN

Emerie pressed the backs of her fingers to her heated cheeks, wishing her roaring flush would fade. It didn't, at least not for long. Every time her shaking breaths calmed her, she would remember there was currently a Duskwalker off beating one out in the forest.

Oh, my gods, she internally whined, covering her face to hide the evidence of it from the world.

The problem with closing her eyes was that it allowed her to vividly remember him stroking his cock right in front of her. It also gave her the same startling, alarming, *insane* reaction.

Her pussy clenched, and her nipples gave a throb.

Why did the most disturbing, bewildering thing she'd ever witnessed – a Duskwalker pleasuring himself – have to also be the hottest and most erotic thing she'd ever seen?

In his own large, claw-tipped fist, his giant cock had looked normal in size. But it was a violet purple with a darker head, and four long tentacles that wriggled at least halfway up its length.

Get ahold of yourself, Emerie, she demanded, patting her cheeks to wake herself from this reality. *He's a Duskwalker. You can't be imagining touching his cock.*

Oh, but she was.

It's wrong, you dickhead. Wrong!

So why was she biting her lip, and half-heartedly considering going to him? Why was she kind of regretting telling him to leave and take care of it by himself? If she had allowed him to stay, would Ingram have masturbated over her standing before him?

He called me beautiful. The moan that escaped her was of utter turmoil.

Emerie couldn't remember the last time someone complimented her appearance. No one had ever said her hair looked like a sunset, or that her eyes were like a frozen lake. No one had willingly cupped the scarred side of her face like Ingram had days ago, nor had they ever been this... innocently sweet with her.

Over the course of the last week with this Duskwalker, a scary monster had turned into the most adorable creature she'd ever met. It was hard to deny him affection when he so readily welcomed it and, in his own way, tried to return it.

No, I shouldn't.

Hugging and cuddling was different to sexually touching him.

She was glad she couldn't hear any noises of pleasure coming from within the forest. Emerie was certain she would have lost her marbles and waltzed over to him.

It was salacious and mind-tingling to know he was just beyond the trees, masturbating. It was even more lewd knowing he was probably thinking of and picturing her, the centre of his carnal desires.

Holy crap... I'm a Duskwalker's jerk-off material. A giddy squirm made her press her thighs together, knowing she was probably broken in the head to think that was hot. *I don't think any guy has jerked off to the idea of me.*

Maybe they had, but Emerie was secretly super insecure. She tried not to show people that, but it was hard to hide in the bedroom. She didn't like fully undressing for sex. She preferred to keep her shirt on like it was glued to her skin, and insisted on doing it mainly in the dark or dim light.

Even after what Ingram said to her, it didn't magically make that go away. Part of her knew if Ingram saw what lay beneath her clothing and he got turned off by it... she didn't think her bruised ego could handle it.

If a monster thought her body was ugly, what hope in the

world did she have?

Pressing down on her nipples, she tried to get them to soften and stop being erect. They kept scraping against the inside of her shirt, reminding her of their awareness of the situation.

Ingram had been gone a little while, and she wished he would hurry up and return so they could discuss what he'd said before. She'd like to help him understand what was going on in his mind, and maybe his heart, so she could fix it.

He shouldn't want her. He should want his own species – if they have females that aren't related to him – or a human that was perhaps prettier and kinder than Emerie.

Someone who hadn't done wrong by him in the past; something she was too afraid to apologise for in case it made him hate her.

Just as her mind eased its frantic reeling, sticks snapping under heavy and approaching footsteps made her flinch. She turned in the direction she heard movement, and her blush deepened at being caught red-faced with her strange and abnormal lustful thoughts.

"A-are you all done?" she quietly asked.

Ingram emerged from the tree line, gripping his still-hard dick, and Emerie's gaze averted so hard she almost spun around. Her heart doubled its beats and wanted to give out. *Nope! Definitely not done!*

She worried he was going to approach her and *force* her to take care of it, but the thwack of his body hitting the ground made it obvious he wasn't. Peeking from the corner of her eyelids, she noticed that he'd sat down in the clearing with her, but with his side facing her.

His knees were up, shielding his crotch from her.

A frown marred her features, especially since his arm wasn't moving like he was playing with himself. Honestly, Ingram was just sitting there. The only things moving were his panting chest and his tail tip tapping at the ground like it did when he was annoyed.

Her voice sounded weak to her own ears as she said, "What are you doing? I-I told you to go take care of it."

Ingram snapped his head away from her.

"I do not like being on my own." Then, his shoulders slumped and turned inward, just as his orbs glowed a reddish pink bright enough to illuminate the side of his bony cheek. His voice was softer when he said, "It will go away. But I must... I must hold it so it does not sting. The air hurts."

Emerie bit her lip as a gut-churning emotion surged behind her sternum. She knew the colour of his orbs meant he felt either shame or embarrassment.

I didn't mean to make him feel like that. She didn't want him to be ashamed of his own body, or embarrassed about something that was completely natural.

Shit. I feel like a hypocrite.

She'd let plenty of men use her body for sexual release just to ease her own loneliness. Couldn't she do that for someone who, in just a few short words tonight, made her feel prettier than anyone else ever had?

For someone who had made her heart squeeze in the strangest, most tender of aches, when it had been a long time since she'd felt that for another person. Just moments before, she'd had palm-sized butterflies in her stomach because of him, and smaller ones fluttering beneath the flesh of her nipples and clit.

The thing was... Emerie didn't step closer because he needed her, needed *someone* to ease his ache. She approached Ingram simply because she wanted to derive pleasure in a disjointed embrace. One that she could tell... he wanted but was denying for her sake.

Unlike many cruel human beings, he wasn't going to force her or assault her just for his own pleasure. He was doing the bare fucking *minimum* to be a good person, and it made her want to touch him even more.

The fact he was also sitting there, just to be near her, meant that he didn't simply want release. There was something else beneath his desires, and its vulnerability called to her.

Ingram's muscles visibly bunched when she neared, so she approached more cautiously. She nibbled at her lips as she did, and each crack of a twig beneath her shoes made her more nervous... and *giddy*.

"Do you still want me to touch you, Ingram?" she softly asked, tentatively reaching out to his biceps.

"No," he sneered, darting his head away once more, but not before his orbs brightened in their reddish pink. "I don't want you to touch me when you don't want to."

Once more, shame stung behind her sternum.

Just as she was about to put her hand on his biceps, a quiet but menacing growl rumbled from him. She hesitated for a long moment, then pressed her fingertips against his scales. His skull turned to her with orbs flaring bright red, and his rumbling worsened.

Oh god, please don't bite me, she thought with a plea, coming around to stand between his feet. *Don't bite me. Don't bite me.*

"It's okay," she tried to reassure, bending so she could reach out with her other hand towards his cock. "Let me touch you. I want to."

The moment her fingertips made contact with his exposed head, he let out a groaning expire. His orbs instantly shifted to bright purple – although a different tone of it in comparison to its usual orchid.

When she palmed the bulbous tip and gently grabbed the head, she'd expected him to release the centre of his length and draw her in. Instead, he gripped himself so tight the tip swelled against her palm.

"Why?" he rasped.

Emerie slid her other hand up his biceps and cupped the very corner of his jaw. "Because I do want to touch you. I'm just... nervous. I can be shy at times."

That wasn't the whole truth, but it was at least part of it.

Ingram's size, from height, to mass, to penis, was massive. In some ways, he was frightening. She was scared of being pinned beneath a big virgin who didn't know his own strength and how much that could damage someone small like her. His claws were sharp, and they'd already cut her, although he had somewhat blunted them since then.

Then there were her own feelings. They were as surprising as they were terrifying. Emerie didn't know why she was growing attracted to this Duskwalker, but her earlier arousal hadn't gone unnoticed.

Ingram was not virtuous – what he was made that impossible – but he was pure in thought and heart. Somewhere in the core of her soul, she craved the utter honesty that was Ingram.

Because he wasn't trying to use her like human men had, Emerie was going to give him what he wanted, and already knew she would *enjoy* every second of it.

Her reassurance and explanation had him loosening his grip, and it allowed her to glide her hand down and push his own away. His reaction was immediate.

"Emerie," he faintly groaned, shoving one clawed hand into the back of her hair while the other slid around her waist, both drawing her closer.

She lowered from her standing position and used her knees to push his legs down until he was forced to cross them. She knelt on his thighs to stay at head level with him, and he let her lean back in his arms so she could look at him.

The slick of his shaft had been thick and sticky at first, but as she stroked him fully from head to base, fresh lubricant swelled to the surface. Now thinner and more slippery, when she brought her hand away for a second, the liquid webbed between her fingers and his cock. Unlike last time, she decided it felt nice coating her skin, and she even played with it a little.

"You poor thing," she whispered as she explored him *properly*, for the first time. She was going to go slow, to really let herself savour what she was doing and touching, and let him experience every wicked twist and stroke she planned to give. "Your cock feels so hot and hard. It must ache terribly."

His answering whine was abruptly cut short by a sharp hitch of breath. Every time his chest expanded, his back arched more and more as his head tilted upwards slowly. He wasn't gripping her tightly at all, but rather like he'd lost his strength under the power of her small hand, just lightly gliding over him.

He realllly likes this.

Dragging her teeth over her bottom lip and leaving behind wetness, she thought about how she had only just started touching him, and yet he was already reacting so fiercely.

With her entire hand wrapping barely halfway around his

girth, she squeezed him a little tighter. His cock jerked beneath her palm, and his tentacles tried to latch when she went halfway down. She made sure not to stroke into their depths, worried she wouldn't be able to draw back.

The perfect blend of burnt sugar and hickory bark infiltrated her senses, and Emerie leaned forward so she could take in his heady scent straight from his flesh. Her cheek, nose, and lips rubbed against the soft scales that covered the front of his throat, and she felt the corded, straining muscles beneath them.

It took her a while to notice the sound coming from him, yet her pussy spasmed powerfully in reaction to it. She'd never heard something so erotic from a man before, not when they usually groaned or grunted with aggressive need.

It instantly made her nipples ache and her pussy spasm.

Oh my gosh… his moans are so cute, so soft. They were free, passionate, and gentle. Her eyelids flickered, becoming drowsy with growing desire. *I want him to make more.*

Just the sounds on their own were profoundly erotic; she would have continued to do this just for those quiet little bliss-filled rasps. He sounded so *needy*, like he was a twisted-up ache inside and the only salvation was her hand.

But there was so much more, and everything about this was tingling her senses.

His decadent and masculine scent wrapping around her head rendered her brain useless. The way his higher-than-normal body temperature had all her muscles relaxed and pliant. Even his claws digging into the back of her skull and hip were sharp little dots of pleasure.

"Does this feel good, Ingram?" she purred, stroking just the flared rim of his cock head to see if it was sensitive there like a human. His quaking shudder was the perfect answer. "You feel really nice in my hand."

Last time she'd done this, she hadn't appreciated it. Now she took her greedy fill.

"Emerie," he groaned, so deeply that her name came out broken, hoarse, and scratchy. His cock swelled and thickened in girth momentarily.

He tilted his head forward until it bumped against her

forehead, and then he stroked her with the side of his jaw. He desperately nuzzled her as soft little pants came from his beak. His hand on her hip came down so he could grab her arse and the crook of her thigh.

She bit her lip to stifle a small noise, then had to loosen her bite before she tore through her skin. *He seemed to really like me complimenting him.*

Leaning to the side slightly, she looked down so she could observe what she was doing. In the darkness, with barely a strip of moonlight, her hand was just visible enough to see she was stroking a very inhuman, violet cock.

The soft, pliable scale spikes on the top and sides of him scraped against her sensitive palm, and she stroked them playfully with her thumb. Her fingertips dug into the deep groove underneath his shaft, hoping he could feel her touch all the way to his centre.

He didn't seem to have any foreskin, which made it easier to feel the protruding and deeply throbbing veins. He was swollen, and she imagined him jerking off by himself earlier had only made it much worse.

"I like how wet you are. It makes it easier to stroke you." It didn't feel like she was dry rubbing him and about to start a fire. Instead, she was able to play with his lubricant, letting it squelch in her palm and between her fingers. "And you're so hot and stiff that it's like you're made of warm stone."

"Nhnn. She likes this," he quietly uttered, as though he'd accidentally let a thought slip out. His cock twitched like crazy, and the first thick well of precum lifted from the eye of his dick. He let out a strained sigh, like that small release of pressure had been relieving. "Smells so good. Why does she smell so good right now?"

Her hand stilled as her lips parted. *Can... can he smell that I'm turned on?* That meant he could smell her pussy, which was currently warm and drenched, from all the way up there!

Ingram groaned, shoved her against him until she was forced to bury her head into the crook of his neck again, and rocked his hips back and forth.

"Don't stop, Emerie."

She matched his pace as she returned to stroking him. However, the moment of rest made her realise she'd been doing this for a while and her arm was tiring. She wanted to bring the other one forward, but it was trapped to his side.

"What can I do to help you come, Ingram?" she softly purred, pushing his cock around in a circle.

"This is perfect." Then he fisted her hair so he could make her lean back. He poked his flat tongue past the tip of his beak, revealing it was much longer than she thought it was, and messily licked across her cheek. "I want to stay like this."

Stay like this? To be honest, she thought he'd blow after a few strokes, like an inexperienced man.

Emerie was enjoying this. Her pussy was pulsing with quivers, so wet she didn't think it would be much longer until she soaked through her underwear and then her pants. Her nipples were enjoying his rough chest rubbing over them every time he breathed.

But, at the end of this, she knew there would be no relief for her. This was about Ingram and *his* release.

The longer she did this, her body telling her she was craving the monster dick she was currently petting, the more she wanted to peel off her pants and mount it. Or his fingers, or maybe even that big beak of his; it kind of looked good to grind on right now with its long and wide curve.

I really want to watch him come.

Last time he came quicker than this. She'd gone faster, harder, and had wrapped both hands around him.

She tried to emulate what she did the first time, but only with the one hand. Her change of tempo and strength caused a loud and rumbling groan to expire from him.

His hips jerked, his cock thrusting into her welcoming palm, and a delighted grin curled her lips.

With great effort, Emerie managed to wriggle her free hand between them until she was able to push off and wrap it around his meaty cock. She did have to slide back a little, almost falling off his thighs to the ground, but she kept herself there by her toes.

Using both hands, she moved them up and down the first

quarter of him with hard, jarring, and swift strokes. She also twisted them, going in different directions, so he wouldn't know what part of his shaft would receive her palms, thumbs, or fingers.

His head shot back as precum leaked and started to drip onto her hands. He gripped her shoulder like he needed something to hold onto, while his hips rocked faster.

"Gentle, Emerie," he pleaded, and yet it had a titillating, growling undertone. "It feels too good."

"Don't you want to come for me?" she purred.

"Emerie." Was it another plea? A warning? A curse? Right now, she didn't care. Her name being called, like she was torturing him with the sweetest rapture, was a wicked sin.

She needed him to keep saying it until he roared to the world like he wanted every living thing in it to know she was the one who gave him release.

With wild, heated pants falling from her lips, she squeezed and massaged his jutting erection with every bit of her might.

A gasp tore from her when she was shoved to her back by him lunging forward with a snarl. Her legs slipped between his thighs as he knelt above her, folded his arms above her head, and began to thrust into her hands.

She didn't let go, but her eyes widened in worry. However, she'd gotten what she wanted.

Between his lost, lust-hazed moans, he called her name. Over and over, 'Emerie' panted from him.

He also lowered, little by little, until he was almost lying on her. It forced her arms down until she was gripping the bottom half of him instead of the top, and his tentacles wrapped around her forearms to keep her to him.

Her arousal outshone her fear, but it nagged at the back of her mind. Even more so when the tip of his cock slid back and forth over her abdomen, riding her shirt up bit by bit.

With her arms trapped, she couldn't yank it down.

Just when the bottom of the fabric caught over the tip and she thought he was about to rip it in two, he popped underneath.

"I-Ingram," she called, hoping to settle the Duskwalker currently grinding his cock into her hands and burrowing into her stomach.

His arm tightened against the top of her head like he wanted to pull her against him, but instead, he pushed her down. Emerie squealed when his cock thrust up over her sternum.

Her head tilted back and her chest arched at the feeling of the hard, hot, and drenched girth slipping between her breasts. With how tight her shirt was around her sizeable tits, he had utilised a decent amount of force to get what would fit between them. He was pillowed, snugly cushioned, and his thrusts gentled at the enveloping softness he found.

Her arms were also bent at her sides because she was attached to him by swirling limbs, and it meant her hands were deeply inside their cavity. Two ovals embedded into the base of his cock were massaged by her palms, and her touching them slowed him even further.

Moans came from his throat, yet with her head so close to his chest, she could hear the tiniest rattling whines seizing his lungs.

"Oh shit," Emerie moaned in return, looking down to see half his cock hidden underneath her shirt and moving back and forth. "Why does that feel so nice?"

Her breasts were sensitive, and the texture of his cock, the little pliable scales, the obvious flare of the head, the wetness and massaging hardness... all of it was sending her body into a lather. The mounds were moving around, and her right nipple was often grazed by him.

Her clit throbbed each time he drew back, only to make the inner walls of her pussy clench.

"Oh fuck," she rasped out, her eyelids flickering when she thought she might actually come just from him fucking her tits. If her pussy didn't stop spasming, she might find release after all.

"Oh fuck," Ingram repeated, and she realised she just taught him a new way to use this curse.

Licking at the seam of her lips as she panted, she kind of liked him swearing like this. She wanted him to do it again. And whatever fight she had left in her was rubbed away by it, and from him playing with her breasts.

Instead of letting what she assumed were his seed sacs just

move back and forth over her palms, she pressed her fingers in slightly to deepen the pressure.

His needy little whimper was the sweetest song, and his violent, full-body shudder was beautiful.

"Fuck," he snapped out when she lessened the pressure. His chest shook as he fought to release the breath he'd been tensely holding. Since his hips hadn't stopped moving, she figured he liked it. She did it again, and he yelped, "Fuck!"

His thrusts quickened and the sound of his claws gouging into the dirt crunched in her ears.

"Haaa. No more. I cannot take it."

"You're about to come, aren't you?"

He had to be with how hot his sacs were and how they sunk momentarily inward like he'd clenched.

"Yes," he rasped.

His kneeling stance widened as he curled around her below him, and his thrusts slowed. His whines were cute, even if his tentacles – tightly wrapping her arms until she thought they might bruise – weren't.

His sacs tightened and almost disappeared, right as his cock swelled and stayed engorged. His roar was loud and strained, drowning out all sounds except for his pleasure.

Even her own stifled moan was lost when he started coming and liquid heat squirted over, between, and around both her breasts. He was making an absolute mess inside her shirt, but it was so warm and nice that she pressed her chest up for more.

Her tongue fell forward to help ease her pants out, as she thought, *Come on me. Don't stop.* It was so messy and vulgar, but she wanted her shirt to be soppy and sticky.

He even came directly over her nipple, and she tried to rub it against his shaft with how much it was tingling.

He came so much it pooled in the crevices of her collarbones and dripped into the creases under her breasts.

When he was done, she was thankful he didn't fall in an exhausted heap on top of her. He was utterly still for a few moments, but his relaxing tentacles gave her up as they grew languid. The bottom two gently tickled her abdomen.

"Emerie," he grated, lifting so he could back up.

The first thing she did was shove her seed-drenched shirt down until she was fully covered. Whether he noticed or cared, he didn't show it.

He scooped her up so her shoulder blades were lying on his forearm, and buried his skull into the crook of her neck. He rubbed it against her.

Ignoring the throbbing ache in her pussy, she patted his heaving chest soothingly. "Feel better?" she asked, her voice croaky and sultry with desire.

He groaned as a delayed aftershock tore through him. "You smell like me."

A giggle bounced her in his arms. "I bet I do."

He pulled one of his arms out from under her so he could glide his fingertips and claws down her side.

"You smelt like this back in the stronghold, but of someone else's." Emerie stiffened, and her flush of desire brightened with embarrassment. "I like that it is mine now marking you."

How could something so... weirdly territorial and possessive come across as so tender?

"Oh, Ingram," she sighed, rubbing her cheek against the top of his skull. Currently her heart felt lighter than it had in ages, and she wanted to share that by returning his nuzzles.

"However," he croaked, his claws finishing their draw down until they reached one of her thighs. "There is a delectable scent coming from you."

Emerie let out a surprised squeal when he grabbed her leg, and incidentally spread her thighs when he yanked her up. On his knees and straightened arms above her, his skull twisted and tilted, showing her his orbs were trying to find the source.

Her eyes darted down to find that, although his tentacles were languid, his cum-covered cock was still hard.

Uh oh! She rolled onto her stomach so she could crawl out from under him.

Ingram grabbed her leg, turned her back over, and shoved the front of his skull against her stomach. She didn't even have a chance to stop him before he went lower and was burying his head between her thighs. Her back curled and her legs shot into the air when he lifted just her hips off the ground. Then he sat her right where his beak met the rest of his skull – which just so happened to be where his nose holes were.

He squished her delicate folds and pushed her wetness around with his beak, forcing her to feel just how aroused she was.

Her face heated in a blush that was so intense she wanted to expire when he took in a deep inhale. Oh god, he was sniffing her! She'd never had anyone do that before. She covered her face in mortification, unsure of how to react to such a primal, carnal action.

With a deep groan, he shuddered so hard that his tail made leaves rustle as it curled, twisted, and pounded the ground behind him with hard thumps.

Emerie didn't get the chance to wonder if it was in delight, not when, at the same time, she let out a pain-filled scream.

Ingram flinched.

She only had enough time to wrap her legs around his skull before he pulled away. She even grabbed his horns to further trap him.

"Emerie?" he asked, his voice higher pitched than normal due to the sound she'd made. His orbs had flickered white in alarm, then dark yellow, before settling back to purple.

"S-stay, Ingram," she begged, as tears welled in her eyes.

Her gaze darted to the four, inch-long claws currently *fingertip* deep in her thigh. He must have followed her gaze because he started to pull them out, until she reached over and held them down. "Don't. Don't pull them out."

Currently, they were plugging the wound and stopping the worst of her bleeding.

"I hurt you, Emerie," he whimpered.

Her lips trembled as she said, "It's okay."

It absolutely was *not* fucking okay! But she knew it was an accident from when he'd tensed up while smelling her.

She wasn't upset about his claws. Once the initial pain happened, her adrenaline had taken over to ease the worst of it. What she wasn't okay with, was the fact that the only thing stopping him from likely eating her was her pussy acting as a barrier of scent.

In Emerie fashion, she laughed when she found humour in that. She was probably the first and only human that would find herself in this predicament.

"Will you go crazy if you see blood?" Already it was beading around his claws.

"No. Only if I smell or taste it."

I knew it. I knew something like this would happen eventually. Of course, with her rotten luck, it had to ruin something that had been enjoyable for both of them.

Her worries were proven right.

Since his orbs were white, she tried to muster up a reassuring smile – it probably came across as a grimace.

"H-how long can you hold your breath for?"

"A while."

"A while is good." She dipped her head back to search for her bag and found it a metre or two away. *Too far.* "You're going to hold your breath for me, and then slowly put me down and take out your claws. Okay?"

After a tiny nod in confirmation, he did exactly as instructed, like an obedient boy.

"Don't breathe until I tell you to," she said, getting up so she could limp to her bag.

Blood trickled down her leg, and she kept her eyes on the forest in case a Demon picked up on the scent of it. Picking up her bag, she opened it and limped back over to him.

Although his orbs were bright orange as he knelt there, staying still, she didn't have the time to ease his guilt over it.

"You understand this is really bad, don't you?" she asked as she pulled a long length of enchanted rope from her bag – thankful she'd remembered to take it from when he'd been hogtied.

When he nodded in answer, she returned it.

"I need to tie you up, okay? Otherwise, you'll kill me."

Right now, she didn't have a chance in hell of running away. Her leg would slow her down, and there was nothing she could do to stop him from mauling her to death, regardless.

She went behind him, and he rotated his head to keep his sight on her. When she went to kneel and tie his wrists together, he jerked them away from her.

"Not there. Not my arms."

The fact he could project his voice from his skull was so useful right now.

"Ingram," she warned.

"I cannot break this rope, yes?"

"Well, yeah. It's the same one from the guild."

"I will do anything to get to you, including harm myself." Emerie paled, hoping he didn't mean that he would break or rip off his own arm or something. He turned his skull forward, before pointing it downward towards the dirt. "Tie it around my neck."

She hesitated as her heart clenched. "What if you choke yourself?"

"I cannot die this way. If I remove my own head, you will be safe from me, and I will come back tomorrow. I will heal."

Gripping the rope tightly, she bit her lip. She didn't want to do that. It sounded painful and unpleasant.

"Hurry, Emerie. My chest is beginning to hurt."

With tears dotting her lashes, she coiled the rope around his neck as he lifted his head to expose it for her. When he told her to tighten it until it was digging into his flesh, she did.

She led him to the thickest tree in their vicinity and secured him to it, then he knelt while she dug through her bag again. Although the herbs were dried and probably useless now, she tied the same scent-barrier satchel across his nose holes that she'd put on him a week ago.

Then she backed up, putting space between them while facing him.

His orbs weren't white in fear or apprehension like she thought they'd be; instead, they were still bright orange.

"Aren't you scared?" she asked. If their roles were reversed, she probably would have been terrified.

"Scared? No, but I am worried for you."

Just that simple statement made her stomach clench in a painfully tender ache. "I'll be fine. I brought some medicine and bandages."

Hopefully everything's okay and he settles down quickly.

Hell, surely the barrier cloth over his face would be enough to prevent him from going too crazy.

"Emerie..." he whined in a near whisper. "I am sorry."

EIGHTEEN

The big Duskwalker sulked as Emerie bounced in his arms every time he took a step. With his pace, he walked swiftly through the brightly lit forest, yet the warmth of his chest against her side kept out any chill.

After he realised he could switch between forms, he'd offered to carry her on his back in his more monstrous one. The sweet side of Ingram had regained full control of his mind while in that form, just after the sky was starting to splash its light across the world.

Emerie had denied his offer, explaining that she'd be in too much pain to kneel on his back with the current state of her leg. She also couldn't walk beside him without slowing them down.

Instead, she was safely within the cradle of his strong arms.

She didn't mind this. It was comforting, and she kind of liked being walked around like a princess. A *badass* princess who had a dagger and sword strapped to her waist and wasn't afraid to use them.

Did her leg hurt? Abso-fucking-lutely.

But it would be okay. His claws hadn't hit any major arteries or veins, just muscle. They were semi-moon-shaped puncture wounds, so they should heal up relatively quickly – as long as she didn't get an infection.

Hopefully the healing salve she'd taken from her personal belongings at Zagros Fortress would aid the process. Since there had been no point in stitching herself, she'd just bandaged her leg to stem the bleeding.

Honestly, the worst part about this morning was watching him lose his fucking shit.

Right after he'd apologised to her, he'd finally taken a breath. About three seconds passed before his orbs flared crimson and he leapt for her like a frenzied animal – only to be yanked back by the rope with a choke.

For hours, this Duskwalker had tried with all his might to get to her.

He'd lunged to the end of the rope repeatedly, clawing at the dirt and grass, then turned so he could back up from the rope to break free while wildly shaking his head around. He'd even started scratching at his own neck.

The entire time, he snarled and snapped at her, his skull rarely facing away from where she sat.

If this had been a week ago, she may have just rolled her eyes as she waited him out. But after what had transpired between them last night, and all the little adorable sides of him he'd revealed on their travels, it had made it hard to bear.

Watching someone who was usually so protective, sweet, and tender turn into a horrible monster that wanted nothing more than to maul her to pieces and eat those pieces whole... had been unnerving. It didn't help she still had semen coating her chest and his lubricant drying on her hands.

Once her blood dried and she washed the worst of it away with her drinking water, he'd eventually come to.

With gouge marks and churned earth all around him, his orbs had finally flickered to yellow, and he'd sighed her name out in relief. Which, of course, only lasted until the heaviness of guilt overtook him, bowing his shoulders.

She looked up at him now to find his orbs were still orange with it.

"You don't have to feel bad anymore, Ingram," Emerie said with a sigh, wishing the colour would change. "Why can't you just let it go?"

His hands clasped her tighter. "There is a burning sensation in my chest, and I don't know how to make it go away," he admitted.

Aww. His chest hurts? She rubbed at his sternum to ease it. There was little else she could do to help. He said he didn't know healing magic like the Witch Owl, or much magic at all.

"You didn't eat me, so I'd say that's a giant win," she tried to joke, adding a thumbs up, only to gain a whimper in response. "Oh, for heaven's sake, Ingram! I'm covered in scars, so what's a few more? I'm alive – that's all that matters to me."

She was also clean, since she'd demanded he take her to the river so she could wash her clothes of both blood and seed. She'd eaten, slept. Other than her wounds, she was peachy.

"Here, I'll show you a few." She pointed to the slice scar on the right side of her bottom lip. "I got this one during sword training one day." Then she dipped her head forward and showed him the back of her head, where she knew there to be a large scar. "This one happened when I was playing with Gideon, and I fell off a veranda and hit my head on the back of a garden rock." She cupped her right knee. "You should see this one. It kind of looks like a dagger from far away, which I think is super badass."

She paused when his orbs shifted to bright yellow. Her brows twitched, not expecting such a positive emotional change. Most people tended to be weirded out when she spoke about them so much.

He took her silence as an opportunity to gently nudge the cheek closest to him – the left side. "How did you get this one?"

Anxiety forked through her gut like lightning striking across dreary clouds.

Emerie averted her gaze in the direction they were travelling. "That one... It's a long story."

"Will it take you our entire journey?" She knew he meant literally and wasn't being sarcastic.

It'd taken her a while to realise that sarcasm went over her head, completely misunderstood. He was a literal kind of guy.

"That's not what I mean," she grumbled. "It's something humans say when we don't want to talk about something."

"Why do you not want to talk about it?"

"Because it's not a nice story," she bit out.

It wasn't often she got frustrated with Ingram because he

didn't understand social etiquette, but this was one of the times it grated on her nerves. Most humans would have let it go by now.

His steps slowed before he stopped walking completely, his arms tightening. Since her legs were resting on top of one forearm, and her back against the other, it made her knees almost rise to her chest.

"Do you not want to share with me anymore?" he asked, the deep, solemn tone of misery quietening his voice.

Damnit, Emerie mentally sighed. She peeked at him to find his orbs had turned a swallowing blue. "It's not because of what happened last night."

"I said I was sorry for hurting you and trying to attack you. I do not know how else to please you."

"It's not you, Ingram," she tried to explain, rubbing at her unmarred cheek in annoyance at herself, more than him. "It's just... when this happened, it was a really bad time in my life. It hurts to talk about it."

"I am here, though," he argued. "I will try to soothe you as you do for me."

Emerie rubbed at her closed eyes, wishing she'd never started the topic of her scars.

I'm going to have to tell him, aren't I? If I don't, he'll think it's his fault. He'll think I don't want to share with him because I don't like or trust him. She wished she could turn her emotions off for it, but what bothered her was that she was probably going to fucking cry. And she hated when she cried.

It had been eight years.

People thought she'd be over it by now. *She* thought she'd be over it by now, but every time she talked about it, it was like a scab was torn off and she was stuck with an open wound.

No one knew she was black and blue inside. If it were possible to see her soul, she wondered if it would be bruised.

Emerie thought she'd rather sit through physical torture. *I'm damned if I do, damned if I don't.*

She glanced up at the Duskwalker again, and her heart made up her mind for her. Screw her own sadness, she couldn't handle the way his made her feel.

This big, silly goofball would get what he wanted.

"You're lucky you're cute when you sulk," Emerie grumbled with a pout, causing his head to perk up. "Can you at least promise not to look at me while I tell you?"

"No. I cannot promise this. I like looking at you." Then he loosened his hold and held her out from him – like she weighed nothing. "Especially when you are in the sun. Your hair and skin glow bright and shiny."

Uggghhh! Fine! See me ugly cry then. She wriggled in his arms and folded hers across her chest. *Probably won't find me pretty after that.*

For a moment, she considered giving him the most watered-down, flavourless version she could, but knew that wouldn't be fair. This story was a big part of who she was, and it explained much about her.

So, where to start? From the beginning, she guessed.

"Like I said a few days ago, Fishket is east of the southlands. It's a pretty isolated town closer to the sea, and we had more Demons coming from the water than the Veil. Water Demons aren't really adept at climbing, so we were mostly safe from them so long as we didn't leave our protective walls."

Emerie paused and unfolded her arms so she could clasp her hands in her lap and fidget with her fingers. Since Ingram started walking again, she gazed out at the bright forest, glad she had something other than him to look at.

"I... did something really silly. I was young, though, which I don't think excuses me, but it at least explains *why* I acted like a hormonal idiot." She gave a humourless laugh, doubting he understood all of that, but she wasn't going to explain it. "I was nineteen, had a boyfriend, and thought I was invincible. I'd never seen a Demon before, so I just did whatever I wanted. Well... one night, I decided to sneak out in the middle of the night, knowing my parents wouldn't approve of me going out in the dark. It seems so foolish now, but I wanted to go to my boyfriend's house and then come back. Maybe he was stupid for letting me leave, or didn't truly care enough about my wellbeing to convince me otherwise. It wasn't the first time I'd done it."

"What is a boyfriend?" Ingram asked.

"It's a boy you're dating to see if you have a future together. Someone you hope you will form a bond with, and maybe marry and have a family with."

"Have you had... many of these *boyfriends?*"

Emerie blushed a little, especially since his tone was somewhat... darker than usual. She peeked at his face before staring completely.

His orbs are green. I've never seen that colour before.

"I've had a few," she grumbled honestly.

"Are these like those special people you said were allowed to see and touch you?" His tone was even darker than before, with an obvious growl radiating from his chest. It even vibrated him, as his orbs brightened in their green hue.

"Yeah, I guess you can say that." When his growl worsened, she narrowed her eyes into a glare. "Do you want me to tell you my secrets, or would you rather continue a conversation that is upsetting you? Because pick one, and I'll never speak of the other willingly again."

His beak opened, just so he could clack it in annoyance. He turned his skull partially away from her.

"Continue," he bit out.

Good boy, she thought with mirth.

"Like I said, I was nineteen and had never seen a Demon before. I had it in my mind that we couldn't be infiltrated." She lowered her gaze to her fidgeting hands. "I was walking home with an oil lamp, and when I got there, Gideon was waiting for me. Since he often went outside the walls to cut down timber with the other workers, he was more aware of the dangers. He started arguing with me right out front of the house, but I didn't want to listen to him. I wanted him to be quiet because our parents were sleeping and I didn't want them to know what I was doing."

She could still vividly remember her and Gideon whisper-arguing out front of their home.

She'd been too stupid to realise he was just trying to protect her as her older brother. She'd thrown it in his face that he had his own partner, and it wasn't fair to intervene in her relationships. She'd just wanted to hurt him because he was overprotective and annoying her.

"One minute I was telling him to 'get fucked,' and the next I was being lifted off the ground." She cringed when the sound of her oil lamp shattering against the dirt still rung in her ears after all these years. "When we both realised a flying Demon was trying to take me, Gideon grabbed my legs to keep me on the ground and was instead carried off with me."

How her scream hadn't been heard by her parents, she would never know; especially since others came out to investigate before hiding back inside their homes.

Sudden flickering images flashed every time she blinked, and she fluttered her eyelids in a desperate attempt to fast-forward through them...

There was darkness all around her. A small blaze ignited below her feet as she looked down at Gideon's scrunched-up face of determination while he climbed her body. His tanned features were fixed on the winged Demon who was slowly taking them higher and higher. With Gideon, their combined weight was too heavy for it to fly off properly.

It released one of its three-toed, clawed feet from her shoulders to kick at him, so Gideon jumped to its leg. The silver glint of his dagger was a cold white in the moonlight, and yet reflected the growing flames below.

She never forgot the way terror had set its fangs in her gut, or how her frantic heart thought it would give out. Nor could she forget Gideon's grunts, or the Demon's disgusting snarls, let alone the hair-raising sound of its voice as it demanded Gideon let go.

And when she looked up, the image of its feathery, flapping wings was seared into her mind's eye to further haunt her every dream. Its red eyes glowed in her nightmares, filled with blood – her blood, as it hungered for every drop. Its white fangs were like a wolf's, yet somehow bigger, sharper, and more frightening.

Then Gideon had pulled his dagger out, but it didn't have enough time to stop him from stabbing it in the leg that gripped her.

Her scream rung out like a hollow echo even now, and she

cringed and twisted as if that would help rid her of it.

Her breaths turned shallow and sharp, whereas Ingram's chest had stilled completely, likely to avoid the scent of her fear.

"The Demon dropped me to grab ahold of Gideon, and I fell." Emerie's bottom lip trembled. The images, her memories, didn't stop, and the longer she tried to remove them, the more liquid spilled from her eyes, saturating her long lashes. "When I landed, it was right near where I had dropped my oil lamp."

Fuck, she gasped with a flinch, her eyes clenching shut.

She still remembered the snap she'd heard from how she landed on her arm when she threw it over her head to protect it. She'd felt the heat of bright flames coming closer until she landed in them on her left side.

After recovering from being momentarily stunned by the fall, the first thing she tried to do was escape it as liquid fire clung to her skin, her clothing, her hair. Her scream was ear-piercing, even to her own eardrums, and the disgusting, charred smell of her own skin singed the inside of her nostrils.

She barely heard the yell from above, but a copious amount of liquid falling on her head snuffed out the worst of the flames covering it before someone threw a blanket over her.

Stop, drop, and roll didn't register past her agony. No logical thought was able to surface other than her panic and pain. She tried to put out the flames by patting her body erratically, all the while staring at them on her arm, unable to think about *how* to do that.

In that moment, she'd known nothing but her skin bubbling and boiling. The smell of oil, skin, hair, and clothing burning. All she'd heard was crackling, punctuated by her own cries.

"I didn't even have time to register that I'd broken my arm when all I felt was fiery agony," she whispered, her voice quivering.

She needed to finish her story; she'd told it before. She could do this.

Emerie sucked in a large, cooling breath.

"I didn't even know until later that my home was in flames and that my parents were trapped inside." She lowered her voice until it was barely comprehensible, as she said, "It wasn't until later that I was told what saved the worst of my face from being melted away was Gideon's blood and insides landing on my head."

Emerie dug her nails into her shirt when her heart ached beyond recognition. She wanted to pull it out, to tell it to stop hurting. She wished her breaths hadn't turned so shallow and short, or that her skin hadn't suddenly flared with heat everywhere she was scarred from that night.

With just a small amount of fuel, she feared she'd combust and have to relive those burns.

"In one night, my whole family, my identity, my life, was taken from me. Because of a Demon, because of my own stupidity. I spent months in an infirmary with burns on twenty-five percent of my body. Those first weeks... I remember nothing. Then, when I finally came to, I had to learn that everyone I cared about in this entire world, people I didn't think I could live without, were gone, and that it was all my fault. It bothers me every day that the last thing I said to Gideon was an insult."

Learning that half of the left side of her face and neck had third-degree burns had been horrifying to see when she'd first looked in the mirror. She also had them from her thigh all the way to her chest, with the worst being on her shoulder and biceps.

They had been even harder to accept.

She'd lost strength in her arm, and she still sometimes struggled to move it without her scars pulling. They were tight, sunken, and some days itchy if she didn't air them.

Emerie had to learn to live with all this, plus the insecurity it brought, and didn't have the people she needed the most there to soothe her through it.

Gideon was gone, and his green eyes would never again shine at her the way they used to, full of brotherly love. She'd never see his light, near-caramel-coloured hair play in the wind, or feel his arms wrap around her, bringing her in for a tight hug.

The world would never hear him mangle a guitar or sing while pissed drunk, tone-deaf and completely unaware of it.

He would have been there for her every single day had he

been alive. He would have petted her uninjured hand, spoon fed her soup, and tried everything in his might to make her laugh at his stupid puns and jokes.

And her parents... although they were getting old, they'd been robbed of the last few years of their lives together. They would have done everything in their power to make her comfortable, and never would have tried to make her feel bad for doing this to herself.

These three people would have unconditionally loved her, accepted her, and still thought she was beautiful.

Instead, the world had turned cold, lonely, and unbearable. It had grown dark, even on the brightest of days.

It had become empty.

When she opened her eyes to look at the forest, her expression cold and stark, tears immediately fell. Everything went murky, only clearing for a split second when she blinked, before more tears clouded her vision.

"I pushed away everyone. My boyfriend eventually stopped visiting me in the hospital, saying it was too difficult to look at me." Gosh, that had set into motion the insecurities that only worsened over the years. "Some of my friends stuck around until I was released, but most didn't. Maybe it was because they couldn't help my pain and they couldn't handle not being able to out of shame, or maybe it was because I was really... volatile. No one had the answer to fixing me or my pain, so I took it out on them. One friend let me stay with her because I had no home, but once I was capable on my own, she eventually asked me to leave because I was upsetting her children."

Unable to handle the way her swollen lips stung with salty tears on them, she wiped them with the back of her hand. That's what reminded her to wipe the rest of her face, knowing it was blotchy and tear-stained. Her knees knocked inwards when she had to remove snot too.

Emerie was a gross, ugly crier, made more noticeable due to her skin being delicate and light.

"I lost a bunch of weight though, since I was pretty chubby before all this, so I guess that's a good thing."

With her eyes closed to avoid actually looking at Ingram, she gave him a false smile and a thumbs up. Her joke was in poor taste, and it just made her cry harder because she knew she was only doing it to cope with how she was feeling.

"Even though I'd just lost everything, I still didn't want to die. It's weird, but it made me more desperate to live. Maybe for the wrong reasons, but my memories and nightmares ate at me, and I thought if I found that Demon again, and killed it, it would let me forget. So, I joined the Demonslayer guild in the eastern sector, away from the sea and my hometown. I wanted them to help me stop being afraid, and if I knew how to fight, it would make me feel safer."

There, she'd told her story.

Ingram's silence allowed her the chance to collect herself.

Yet, it only made her linger on her history. All the bad that had happened.

She'd been through so much more since then. She nearly died multiple times because of the guild, and was kidnapped by bandits when her team had been called to stop raids at a nearby town. She'd seen more death, more blood, and had lost many friends.

Her life had truly been unpleasant.

But it's mine.

No one could take it away from her. No one could change it. And, if living it meant someone else didn't have to, she would do it.

Her mistakes were her burdens to bear, and her life was the penance for them. She was all that remained of her parents and Gideon, and until she took her last breath, she would fight for her life and avenge them by killing Demons in their honour.

In the last eight years, she stopped being a foolish little girl who snuck out in the middle of the night where Demons lingered, and she wised up. She sought knowledge, drowned herself in books, and made sure she used her brain and common sense in everything she did.

At least, she tried to.

So, why was she here with the Duskwalker?

Had she made the right decision, or had she made another mistake? *I don't know what I'm doing anymore.*

Knowing Ingram was likely staring at her made her feel as if she was being inspected while at her worst. He'd even stopped walking, and she didn't know how long he'd just been standing there, holding her, watching her.

A sob broke from her, and when she tried to wipe her face, she abraded her facial scars with the sleeve of her uniform.

"W-why did you s-stop?" she asked, her voice weak and hoarse.

Instead of continuing their journey, Ingram lowered until he knelt upon the ground. At the same time, he gently moved her, being careful of her wounds, until he forced her legs around his narrow waist. With her arms squished between them, he placed her chin on his shoulder, as he did the same to her, but with his beak.

He wrapped his arms snugly around her.

"I do not know what to say to take this pain away from you," he stated with a dark tenderness. "But I can hold you, as you did for me."

In the past, many people had brought Emerie in for a comforting hug, and it had done little to help. They'd told her they understood, or that it was okay, and she hadn't been able to swallow their lies.

Yet, this Duskwalker did understand. He had loved, and he had lost. He had suffered torment and had come out the other side different and broken – just like her. He didn't need to tell her, he didn't need words.

That's why, when she pushed her arms out from between them and wrapped them around his skull, a shuddering, hollowing cry broke from her. Gripping the small amount of fur at his nape, she heaved against him.

She buried her face into the soft scales on the sides of his corded neck, tightened all her limbs around him, and clung to the first being that truly gave her comfort from their sympathetic embrace. As much as it was soothing, it was painful in a way that was cathartic.

She sobbed against him, wetted his scales with her salty tears, and dug her nails into the backs of his rigid, spikey shoulders when she drew him closer. He squeezed her, and it wasn't enough to still her heaving chest, but the pressure felt remarkable.

I want him to squeeze me until he pushes out all my pain.

Despite her unbecoming behaviour, she sensed there was no judgement. It allowed her to share this side she had never shown another. To share these cruel and unfair emotions with someone who was a monster, and yet was purer than anyone she'd ever known.

He was huge, and strong, and scary. His body was too hot to be human, too hard and scaley, and yet it created a blanket of security she hadn't worn since she was a naïve teenager.

Even his scent of burnt sugar and hickory bark smelt inhuman, like he was a part of the forest. Yet its pleasantness cut through the salty tang of her tears and gave her something nice to focus on.

"Even though you have a raven skull, I'm really glad you don't have wings, Ingram," she admitted on a muffled whisper, digging her nails harder into his scales. "They would have frightened me."

"Aleron had wings," he responded.

"W-were they made of feathers?"

"Yes. They were black ones."

Emerie shuddered in repulsion at the thought; he would have reminded her of the Demon that tore everything away from her. In some of her nightmares, those soft, fluffy feathers turned into millions of sharp, tiny daggers.

"They were big and comforting," he continued. "When I was inside them, they blocked out everything but him. The world disappeared except for us."

Gosh. How can he make that sound nice?

Still, she couldn't think of anything worse. Suffocating and *wrong*.

She'd take Ingram's lizard butt and tail over a big set of frightening dark wings any day.

NINETEEN

Ingram rotated his neck to look over his shoulder momentarily, noting he was making a very obvious trail through the tall grass. Occasionally, bits of fluffy greenery, like animal tails on thin bits of grass, swayed just slightly taller. Most of it came to the bottom of his lowest ribs, and he knew he would have lost Emerie in it had she been wading through it.

She wasn't.

She was securely in his arms. From the moment he'd scooped her up in them, he'd enjoyed carrying her.

Her weight was light, and her soft body easily moulded to him. Her breasts and thighs jiggled a little at the impact of each of his heavy footfalls, and her feet bounced along with them. Her hair danced as it swayed in the air, and her eyelashes flittered like the fuzziest wings.

On his back, he hadn't been able to view these things freely. In his arms, he could leisurely stare at her as much as his heart desired, and it craved for him to do so.

The only thing that diminished it was *why* he was carrying her. The blood-spotted white wrappings around her right thigh were obvious and unavoidable to look upon. They were always there, tarnishing his tantalising view of her.

I hope she will let me carry her like this in the future.

He would even like for her to request it, rather than him ask for it. For her to reveal she wanted to be held by him in this kind of embrace.

"I've been to that town," Emerie stated, pointing off into the distance. "It's called Greenshire."

He drifted his gaze to the town situated in the middle of the valley they were passing. Since they were so high up, human dwellings were easily recognisable from their grey stones or their straw huts, even with the circle of log stakes protecting them from Demons.

It was a wise location, considering there were barely any trees except for a few small clusters of them here and there.

"The town is really well set up, and they actually farm land outside of it because it's pretty safe to go outside the wall in the daytime." Emerie pointed to a thick, lush area of greenery next to it. "Except for there. Those are the cornfields, and only a few are brave enough to pick corn since Demons can hide in there. During harvests, they send out soldiers first to kill them, but at least two people die every year while they pick the corn."

"Then why would they?" Ingram asked, staring at the green stalks.

"It doesn't look like it from here, but it's a lot of food. To not pick it would mean most of the town would starve." In his peripheral, her lips tightened into a flat line of disapproval. "However, they always send the poorest people by offering them the most amount of free food for doing it. I've always hated how humans exploit each other like that."

"Should we go there to obtain food for you then?"

Surely he would be able to protect her while she picked this *corn*.

Emerie shook her head, causing her wavy orange hair to play across his forearm. "No. They'll see us coming. I'd rather avoid human towns that can spot us approaching in case the guild manages to catch up, even if it's unlikely. I also didn't think to bring any money, and it's rare for towns to have their farms outside of them like that one."

He didn't argue with her, figuring she knew what was best.

Before long, the town was gone from view once they went over the hill he'd been ascending, so he could go down it on the other side.

What lay before them were more fields, more meadows of

grass – varying in length – and more hills. There was no forest in sight, not even the speck of one on the horizon. There were odd scatterings of trees, but nothing dense enough to hide a Demon, not if it didn't want to get burned at some point throughout the day.

Ingram found it as peaceful as the first time he'd seen it all those years ago with Aleron.

At the thought of his kindred, his sight turned blue. That was quickly overshadowed by Emerie when she patted and rubbed at his sternum, seeming to do it absent-mindedly as she stared out at the horizon.

She must have seen his orb change in the corner of her eye.

He lifted his gaze in the direction hers was in.

Thick grasses moved like waves as wind dipped through their stalks, rustling quietly. Brown birds glided above them, before darting high in the sky in twos or threes, only to drop back down and fly above them. Their chirping didn't sound panicked or aggressive, as if they were only playing with each other.

Ingram changed direction slightly, making sure to avoid that area so he didn't disturb it with his imposing presence. Instead, he created a path to where he could see the grass was much shorter, and from there they climbed another hill. As they reached the highest point, he followed along it towards the tops of trees that appeared in the distance.

He was a little disappointed to see them.

Although she hadn't said it, Emerie was enjoying the unimpeded sunshine. She often closed her eyes, stealing his ability to admire them, so she could bask in it with her face turned upwards.

At one point, he'd thought her hair reminded him of fire as much as it had the sun. Now, he no longer wished to associate it with her, not after how she had cried against him. Currently, it glowed and sparkled, like streaks of malleable crystal.

His gaze dipped to her freckled cheeks, nose, and forehead, noting a few new spots and none of the redness from days ago. Even after she'd rested the night she told him of her story, her cheeks and nose had been swollen, pink, and kind of cute. He knew it was terrible he felt that way about her teary face, but he thought he found it appealing because she'd been vulnerable with him.

She had willingly let him comfort her, and he was rewarded with a cuddle that had ached his chest while making it swell with tenderness.

Her tears had alarmed him, of course. They reminded him of the floating drops that hovered around his face whenever he deeply missed Aleron.

She shared with me. She also shares... my pain. Although their stories weren't the same, the emotions that came from them were.

He hadn't realised Emerie had faced a tragedy so horrid.

I always knew she had sadness inside her. Now I understand why.

Like he once told her, when she wasn't focussed on him, her gaze was sombre as she looked off into the world. It'd taken him a while to realise what she was secretly expressing.

She looked... lost. It was the same hopelessness that had grown inside him from the moment his kindred was taken from him.

She even wore it now as she eyed those trees, then a disdainful expression flickered over her features.

She didn't want to go into the forest, either.

"Hey," she said, looking up at him. "Could you put me down? I'd like to stretch my legs for a few hours, and I think it would be better if you rest here in the daytime. It'll be safer."

I do not want to put her down, Ingram mentally grumbled, as he carefully lowered her to her feet. He knew she'd argue with him if he didn't.

The grass only came to her knees, and he was glad he didn't lose her.

Her pretty face grimaced as she took a step, but she made no noise of discomfort. She did, however, lift her arms above her head, go to the tips of her toes, and let out an awful, grating groan as she stretched.

His sight shifted to yellow at her doing this, at her.

She is a funny human.

"Alright, big bird. Time for you to have a nap."

Ingram, glad to rest his legs, sat with his clawed feet inwards, his legs bent and falling slightly open. He didn't want to straighten them, since he'd been walking on them, but he also didn't wish to cross them.

"I will sleep soon."

He would like to... *decompress* first, as she often said before she actually laid down.

Shrugging, she turned and limped over to the other side of the hilltop. With her hands on her flared hips, she stood, surveying the landscape before her, and he took the opportunity to look his fill.

There was barely a breeze, but it still played with the ends of her hair, making them sway just above her tightly clad arse. When she turned her head to the side to look somewhere else, his sight ran down the profile of her nose, noticing the slightest bump near the middle. Her lips were currently thinned in thought, but they were usually pink and plump.

He wasn't sure if she realised, but she'd turned the scarred side of her face to him.

He had a new appreciation for it.

Despite her struggles, despite the pain she must have endured – as he himself had been burned many times by humans waving sticks of fire at him – her scars were the evidence of strength. Strength she shouldn't have needed to wield, but had done so anyway and was alive, here with him now.

He touched a claw to his chest, remembering when it had been cracked open so someone could show him his own beating purple heart.

He did not bear scars like she did. His suffering had only lasted a day before it disappeared.

As his gaze dropped down to her still-injured leg after days of it happening, he wondered how his mind would have twisted had he been forced to live with his wounds. For days, weeks, months.

Ingram knew he wouldn't have been able to bear it; not like she had. He didn't like pain, and even when it lasted only a day, it still took too long for his wounds to heal.

Emerie was stronger than him – not in body, but in mind.

Perhaps that realisation should have made his sight turn blue in sorrow or self-pity, but it turned yellow with pride for her.

A moment later, his orbs darkened in their hue when something flittered past his skull. Easily distracted, Ingram followed what was flapping around his face. Colourful and tiny, it flew away erratically.

When he returned his gaze to her, she'd already turned back to him. His tail tip curled against the grass in delight at knowing her blue eyes were upon him. The light beaming down on her made her appear to glow, and he didn't know if the warmth he saw was her expression or a result of the sun's rays.

Then her eyes crinkled and bowed, and her lips curled up in his direction.

Just as Ingram tilted his head, unsure of what he'd done to be rewarded with a smile, something fluttered in front of his skull again. Like before, it was colourful, small, and stole his attention.

Since it lingered near him, he darted his hand forward to grab it so he could inspect its colouring in closer detail. He missed, but as he was trying again, a set of hands lightly ran up his forearm to his wrist.

"Don't try to grab them," Emerie whispered, her face inches from his own. "You'll only damage their wings."

"What are they?" he asked, watching as a brown one, lacking in rich colours, flapped around her hair. "I have seen these before, but never in the Veil. Only on the surface."

And since he and Aleron were often distracted in their play with one another, they often didn't notice the tiny fluttering creatures until they were fleeing.

He'd seen many of them today, but that was because he'd disturbed the grass they were hiding in. They were always trying to escape, never stopping to play around them.

"They're called butterflies." She lifted her hand out to one that flew just above them, like she wanted it to land on her reaching fingertips. "You have to be gentle and patient with them. Let them come to you."

I do not want to wait for them to come to me. It would be

easier if he were to capture one when it was least expecting it.

Yet, when Emerie placed one of her delicate and small hands into his calloused dark-grey palm, he decided to follow her lead. She was touching him, and he was at peace with this because of it.

She backed up to give his hand space, and he held it out with his claws pointing upward. When a butterfly flew near it, he went to follow it until she told him to stay still.

It landed on his face instead.

Ingram stared as it slowly opened and closed its wings on his beak. It was bright blue, with black around the edges. Now that he was looking at it properly, it did look rather small and fragile. Its wings were thin, with its body thinner than his claw tip.

"They say it's good luck if a butterfly lands on you," she said with a quiet giggle, drawing his attention to her.

His sight shifted to bright yellow at the many butterflies that were choosing to rest in her hair or on her shoulder. She didn't seem to notice them there, and he wondered if they were attracted to the brightness of her.

Pretty female. His chest was tight with a strange emotion akin to adoration at the sight of her with multicoloured insects on her.

Like them, she appeared colourful, small, and fragile.

When another butterfly landed on him, this time on the shiny claw of his pointer finger, its orange colouring blended with her hair just behind it.

In all his life, Ingram didn't think he'd ever experienced such a serene, tranquil moment. He'd never just existed quietly and still with the world, letting it come to him rather than him violently reaching out to inspect it.

Had it not been for Emerie here, he would have squished and killed every butterfly he could just to look at it. His patience had been rewarded.

He attempted to bring his new friend closer, and it fluttered off.

Ingram didn't mind. Not when he had his own bigger, brighter, and better colourful butterfly. One who had lost all her own new friends as she crawled over to sit between his legs with her back pressing against the inside of his left knee.

It was like she'd known he preferred the comfort of touch, even if it was something as minor as this.

"Emerie, the butterfly has landed on me. Does this mean I shall forever have good luck?" He let out a chuckle, allowing her radiance and his enjoyment of it to seep through him.

Since he'd been hoping for a smile, or maybe for her cheeks to do that reddening thing they did, his head jerked when her brows twitched like she wanted to frown.

"Why do you appear... unsure? Is it bad to be compared to them?"

"Huh, what?" She gave a little laugh as she rubbed at the side of her neck. "No, it's actually really sweet. It's just... I've never heard you laugh before. I was beginning to think you didn't know how."

His sight returned to its normal purple, and he lifted his skull slightly so he could look up at the light-blue sky.

"I have laughed many times." After watching a fluffy white cloud for a few seconds, trying to remember the last time he'd made such a sound, he eventually sighed. "But no. I have not done so for a long while."

He darted his skull down when she moved, bringing her knees up so she could wrap her arms around them. She placed her cheek against her knees and, while facing him, asked, "Since your Aleron?"

Although sadness washed over him, his sight didn't change when a rather big blue butterfly landed on the back of her head. Once more, she didn't seem to know it was there.

"Yes, since him."

"Did you guys have a home?"

"A place that I go to rest and be comfortable?" he asked, tilting his head in thought. She nodded, making her friend flap its wings, but it didn't fly off. "He was my home."

"No cave or house in a tree?"

"We had no need for this. We slept in whatever place we found ourselves at the beginning of dawn, no matter where it was."

"Where did you go and visit?"

Ingram tilted his head. "Wherever Aleron wanted to go."

Emerie rolled her eyes, and yet a smile twitched the corners of her lips. "Okay. Well, where did he want to go?"

He didn't know why this conversation wasn't hurting him. Perhaps it was this hill, or her, or their colourful friends. Maybe it was even the warmth on his back from the sun, or the crisp scent of the grass mingling with her pretty aroma.

Either it was something, or everything about this moment, but he felt... tranquil within, despite the cold lingering sadness.

"Wherever I wanted to go," he answered. When she groaned and rolled her eyes again, he let out another chuckle. "I don't know what you want me to say, little butterfly."

"I'm trying to get to know you, dummy," she grumbled with a pout. "Where you went, what you were doing before I met you, what your hopes and dreams were."

"Where I went was anywhere that had Aleron. What I was doing was being with him while we played in this world. My dreams were of him, and my hopes were that we would continue to explore."

She sighed, before burying her face against her knees.

"It's like you're saying your entire existence revolved around him. I can't imagine what it's like to lose someone that is so completely and utterly the centre of your world." For a moment, his sight morphed to dark blue, but it only lasted until she turned her face towards him and shone those bright eyes, glinting with sunlight, at him. "What about your other brothers then? The other Duskwalkers?"

"We don't know them well," he admitted, his orbs their usual purple. "We always thought Merikh was... mean, but he also named us and let us rest at his home. Kitty was our favourite, as he often played with us. There are two other Mavka, but one did not like us in his territory." Ingram scratched a claw at the side of his beak, suddenly feeling remarkably... guilty. "It may be because we destroyed part of his home."

He could remember, very vividly, the day he and Aleron trampled over the impala-horned Mavka's garden because they were curious about it. He had been lucky the charms around his human dwelling didn't allow them inside it. So, they'd gone exploring through his garden and tore up plants to sniff and discover their scents, and plucked entire bushes from the ground.

The Mavka had become quite enraged at them, causing a fight involving all three of them – that saw the other one losing to him and his kindred. Then again, it had been an unfair fight. Not that they'd cared, though, since they'd been upset that they had to lick at their wounds.

They threw his skull between them for fun before losing interest in playing catch and walking off.

Any time they went near that particular Mavka again, it had not gone pleasantly. He hated them.

Should I be concerned that the Witch Owl wishes for us to go to his home? he thought, realising it was in the west – his current direction.

He shrugged, hoping it would be fine.

"Aleron and I did not know we shared a bond with other Mavka," Ingram continued. "So we did not spend much time with them, only when it entertained us. All we did was be each other's kindred, which was all we knew and wished to do. Nothing else mattered."

"A life so shared it was like you were one being," Emerie stated, and his orbs turned bright yellow as his tail tip curled in utter delight.

"Yes, exactly. We were one, and we shared everything." Then he put his arm around her and curled his hand around her side, swallowing it up completely within his palm. "And when he is returned, you will then become *our* companion."

His head jerked, sharply tilting, when her face paled and her eyes widened. Her mouth opened and closed as though she'd lost the ability to speak. She swallowed what sounded like a thick lump in her throat.

"I am only helping you on this journey, Ingram," she answered, crossing her legs and folding her hands in her lap.

"I do not understand."

He really didn't. Emerie was now his companion. She was his friend, and he wanted to keep his new friend and show her to Aleron. His kindred was kind and warm, and he was sure to like her as much as he did.

"I don't think I could handle two of you, to be honest."

"Why not? We can protect you better together. Once we kill the Demon King and make the world safer, the Demons will no longer attack us like they have been. We can keep you safe in the Veil, and you can play with us."

Her eyes opened even further, just as her cheeks darkened with a cute redness.

"Y-you said that you gained a lot of humanity when you came to the guild." Her words came out with a squeak. "Aleron will not be as... smart as you. H-he may not understand that I am easily broken and hurt."

Hmm, he thought, lifting his head and curling his hand around his beak in thought. She was right. Even Ingram had hurt her, and he had much more humanity than Aleron currently.

"Then... we will find him humans to eat, and I will let him grow until he matches me."

Ingram's tail tapped against the ground at his ingenious idea. He turned to her with his sight yellow in pride at himself, only for it to quickly snuff out to purple, then orange when she looked horrified at the idea of him feeding his kindred her kind.

He reached out and patted her head, and she was so frozen she barely reacted to it.

"But not you. I will make sure you are safe."

Emerie reached up and grabbed his wrist to stop him. She pulled it down and looked like she was about to say something, only to cringe.

"Look, let's get to that later. This... is a lot to unpack, and I really don't know where to start. I cannot live in the Veil, Ingram, and I cannot be shared between you. I don't see me living through that." Then she placed his hand on her thigh to fiddle with his thick fingers. "If you had a fight with each other, and I was caught in the middle of it, one stray claw strike could see me dead."

His immediate reaction was to deny her, to say he and Aleron did not fight, but that wasn't true.

Although they shared everything, they also playfully fought over everything. Food, things that took their attention, an Elf they originally asked to name them until they almost tore her in half because they fought over who wanted to be named first.

The more he thought about it, the more he realised that if Emerie took both their attention at the same time, they could end up playing tug-of-war with her.

"But you can teach us things," Ingram argued. "Show us how to be careful around you, as you have done with me. You are smart. You even stopped me from eating you – twice."

Emerie slapped her face into her palm. She drew her hand down, and he noted her cheeks were red again as she stared up at his skull with nervous eyes.

"I guess I have to be more direct?" He nodded, hoping whatever explanation she gave would better help him figure out a way to convince her otherwise. "You liked it when I touched your, uh, dick, yeah?"

The thrill that tore through him was instant. It sent a shudder all the way down to his tail that smacked against the ground.

"Yes," he grated.

"If you want me to do that, and Aleron sees, he may want it too." Ingram's sight turned a dark shade of purple at just the thought of her touch, and he absolutely knew his kindred would want to experience it once he learned of how... wonderful it felt. "Do you understand what I'm trying to say?"

His first thought was joy in letting his kindred experience someone touching his cock. If Ingram now craved it, Aleron would be the same.

However, the longer he wished this for Aleron, the more he began to picture it. When that image turned into Emerie touching Aleron, something strange spiked in his chest; it was a nasty emotion he didn't particularly like.

He wrapped his hand around his beak once more as he looked out at the horizon. *Emerie touching Aleron...* How did he feel about this? He wanted his kindred to know what he did, to experience pleasure, but with this little female he'd found?

His mind turned to the last time she'd stroked him.

There had been something deeply satisfying about having his own seed scent marking her skin. Even just the memory of it had his cock twitching behind his seam.

But I did not like that other male's scent on her. The one that had smelt very human and possessive.

His orbs turned green – a dark green – at just the thought of any kind of seed scent on her that wasn't his own. Although he and Aleron were one being, they were two separate creatures. He liked having his kindred's scent on his body, but it had been comforting and brought security in its familiarity. He would like that on Emerie, but he could already tell he wouldn't like a sexual marking on her.

"What is it called when you want something that someone else has?" he asked, still holding his beak and keeping his gaze on the grass instead of her.

"Jealousy."

Ah. So the emotion he'd been feeling since the first time she touched him, and he remembered her having another's sexual marking on her... was jealousy.

He hadn't liked how that felt, how it hurt and made him feel lonely at the same time. His orbs had turned *bright* green because of it.

"What about when something is yours and someone tries to take it from you?"

"Possessive."

No wonder the marking felt possessive then, and he now understood that they were the two emotions warring inside him. He would be jealous if Aleron was to lay that claim on her, which meant the idea of Emerie touching him and bringing him release brought on a deeper, enraging pit of it in his gut.

His hand curled around her side tighter, as the word *"mine"* rumbled in his thoughts – towards Aleron.

"Ow!" Emerie winced, jumping forward to escape, only to be brought back to exactly where she'd been. He wouldn't let her go.

"Stay," he warned, wanting to keep her near as aggression flared within. He did, however, loosen his grip so it wasn't hurting her. "We will find Aleron his own Emerie," he decided. Then he nodded, agreeing with himself wholeheartedly. "We will not share you. Not like this."

"Ingram," she huffed out in exasperation, like what he said

didn't appease whatever objections she had.

Now that he'd placated his own concerns, joy filled him once more at Aleron learning all about pleasure, but with someone else. Yes, that would please him, and then there would be... four of them.

More companions, more people sharing their bond.

His tail tip tapped against the ground as he pictured it. One of his fondest memories with Aleron was sitting on a hill just like this one and staring up at the night sky, wondering what those twinkling dots were. Doing so again, but with this little female and his kindred, sounded like bliss.

It would be even better if there were more butterflies in her hair, like the many that had latched on now.

He lifted his skull to the sky as tenderness bloomed at the picture he conjured. His tail curled so hard it turned into multiple rings halfway down to the base. A fluffy, pleasant feeling sprouted in his torso.

When the image was gone, but not the lingering emotions, he looked upon her. With a chuckle, feeling lighter than he had since his kindred left him, he fully wrapped his arm around Emerie. Then he laid back against the grass and pulled her to his side until she was lying against him as well.

A swarm of butterflies lifted off and fled from him and the surrounding area.

She tried to sit up, but he tugged her back down.

"What are you doing?" Her body tensed in his grasp.

"I am supposed to be sleeping. I wish to rest now."

He'd like to relax with this warmth in his chest, something he'd only ever experienced within Aleron's feathery wings.

"Yeah, but I need to stay awake and watch out for danger."

He lifted his hand to gesture to the sky. "The sun is bright, Emerie. No Demons will come while it shields us. Sleep, enjoy its heat."

She lifted onto her elbows, since he wouldn't let her go any higher. She pursed her lips at him. "If I have a nap, I won't sleep properly tonight."

"Then don't sleep," he stated, lifting his skull so he could tilt it at her. "I prefer carrying you while you are awake."

She nibbled at her bottom lip, catching his attention. He remembered them being soft against his neck, and how they'd whispered little brushes against his scales.

"Okay, fine," she grumbled, lying back down and turning to her side with her forehead pressing against him. She stroked his side, petting him like she often did. "This area really is lovely, and the sun does feel cosy."

Lovely... cosy... I like these words. He added them to the list of the many, many others she'd taught him in their short time together. As well as the few he associated with her.

He watched a cloud float past, wondering why he wasn't ready to drift off yet. Then, he realised the problem and grabbed her plump backside so he could slide her up until her head was cushioned on his biceps. He wrapped his hand around her knee to keep her to him, his body surrounding her from all sides.

With his other arm, both legs, and tail straight and spread out from his centre, Ingram closed his sight. *Perfect.*

TWENTY

Emerie held the sides of her thigh to brace it, while mentally preparing to wince. She never did, even when the Duskwalker carefully dabbed at her wounds with a hot, damp cloth.

There was a gaping hole in her pants, purposefully made so she could tend to her wound freely without having to take them off during their travels. Emerie was *not* willing to forgo pants with this guy around.

With her straightened leg on top of his thigh, he was being very cautious of his claws. His purple tongue even slipped out the side of his beak in deep concentration.

She had to bite her lips shut to stop herself from laughing.

I still can't believe I'm letting him do this, she thought, just as Ingram dunked the cloth back into the metal cup filled with boiled water.

He'd pestered her about it. Pushing and pleading to let him take care of her wound ever since the moment it happened. She'd said no the first few days, especially since cleaning it had caused droplets of blood to well. Now that it'd been quite a few days and the four punctures were well and truly scabbed over and mending, she didn't see the point in denying him.

He wanted to make up for them, to aid her in any way possible.

Other than the pain each step gave her, and the way the fucking thing itched, the worst part about this was caring for it.

It'd taken her a long time to get used to fire after her incident when she was nineteen.

She wasn't comfortable, less in fear of it and more at the triggering of the memories and anxiety it brought. However, fire was essential to life for a human, so she was forced to suck it up and make it whenever it was required. For instance, for boiling purposes so she didn't use unsanitary water on her injuries and cause infections – or give herself parasites.

Opening a jar for him, Emerie gave Ingram her medicinal salve.

She remembered the first time he'd tried digging into the yellowy ointment and took out far too much. Now, he used the back of his claw to obtain only a small amount. He wiped it next to the wound and then lightly used the back of his knuckle to apply it to the four scabs.

Once he was done, he handed back the jar so she could put it away.

"Alright, Doc. What do I owe you?" His head jerked to the side, making the sound of dry bones rattling. "All I've got on me is a berry and some string. Will that be enough?"

His head tilted the other way, orbs morphing to a dark yellow. "I don't want anything for helping you, Emerie. I want to make up for hurting you."

Her lips flattened as she tried to stifle her grin.

"It's a joke. You know... like ha ha?"

"You are not very funny, Emerie," he stated bluntly.

"I'm just trying to make you laugh again," she answered, before pouting her bottom lip forward.

Ever since the day on the hill, she had made it her mission to get this Duskwalker to laugh again. It wasn't going well. He was absolutely right in the fact that Emerie wasn't very funny, and even if she was, most of the time her jokes didn't register in that brain of his.

Ingram reached out and cupped the left side of her face. She was growing used to it, since he'd been doing it more frequently. She no longer flinched. He rubbed his thumb against her protruding bottom lip, dragging it down further, then letting it flick back into place.

"I like it when you do this."

And I like it when you do that, her thoughts answered, resisting the urge to lean into his massive, rough palm.

She thought Ingram may have been the first person to ever hold or touch the scarred side of her face. He only deepened the tingling sensation within her heart when he pushed his hand further back, threading his fingers into her hair so he could brush her cheek, and the webbed texture of it, with his thumb.

When that tingling sensation began to gnaw like a festering wound, she reached up with both hands to grab his wrist and pull his hand away from her.

Something is wrong with me.

There had to be.

Because, ever since that day on the hill, surrounded by fresh, wet grass and flying insects, her heart kept twinging. She knew the moment it started, when something inside her seemed to shift.

When this big, goofy, silly Duskwalker had a butterfly land on his deadly claw tip, he'd been so thrilled, so happy, even though he had a bunch of them clinging to his horns and the top of his skull. One had even landed on the tip of his tail and stayed there until he curled it in joy.

It was the most winsome thing she'd ever seen, and the fact he was a monster was why.

There were other reasons why the gnawing in her chest had started, like caring for her wound, or lifting her off the ground so she could pick berries for herself. Or even grabbing her so they could lie in the grass together, something she'd never done before. How could anyone justify a peaceful moment such as that in a world filled with horrible Demons?

But when that butterfly landed on his patient and awaiting claw, the gnawing became impossible to ignore. And it only grew when he continued to be sweet, and caring, and... charming.

Somewhere along the way, she'd stopped wanting this journey to end.

Did they have to go find the Demon King, when they could just do this instead? Simply travel the world and experience all of its hidden beauty... Emerie had only ever been outside of

Zagros Fortress for work, to go on dangerous and scary missions to kill Demons or bandits.

She'd seen hills, meadows, and kaleidoscopes of butterflies. She'd looked up at the stars, not in wonder in the way Ingram had taught her to, but with wishes for the suffering and torment to end.

Not once in her life had she looked at the world through a light, lacey veil, instead keeping up the harsh, cold lens of reality in front of her at all times.

So, all this... going to places she'd been but seeing them differently, all because of him... He was teaching her how to live freely, while she taught him about the world. She wanted to keep doing that.

But their journey had a destination, and she knew Ingram was steadfast in leading them to it.

I don't know what will happen to me at the end of this.

Did death await her? Whether it was at the claws of this Duskwalker or the fangs of a Demon, or the Demon King himself, would she die? Say she didn't. What would she do afterwards? Once Ingram was safe from being hunted, he wanted to find Aleron. Emerie didn't know if she had the heart, or strength, to go on a journey that was based on a lie he'd told himself – a false hope.

She would have to choose to either go with him and pity him – perhaps even watch him go insane in the process – or return to the human world.

There is no real future for me with him.

The big guy didn't even truly understand the concept of what a brother or family was. How could Emerie expect him to feel anything more towards her? Lust, apparently, came easy. But that was a physical reaction that didn't necessarily require an emotional cause.

Yet, the invisible creature nibbling at her heart was cruel and unfair, allowing her to wallow in possibilities that didn't seem realistic.

It's what caused her to smile up at him, despite the bitter feelings that bubbled within. She slapped her hands together to direct his attention to the clapping sound, rather than the falseness of her expression.

"Alright, up we get."

She brought her leg off him and stood. She limped over to the tiny fire she'd made and kicked sand on it, getting rid of its evidence for her own peace of mind. The sight of it, the smell of it, even the sound of it, made her skin crawl. The sun glittered off the quick-moving stream just beyond it, as mini waterfalls and natural dips created a trickling song.

It was a beautiful day, the early autumn still warm.

The weather had been kind to them on their travels, and only one day had there been rain – which wasn't long after they started.

She turned and found the Duskwalker still sitting there. His orbs turned a reddish pink, with his shoulders hunching inwards like he was feeling... shy? Maybe it was uncertain, as he likely knew what she was about to say next, and was planning to rebuff it like he always did.

"Time for you to shoo, Ingram." She waved her hands at him. "You said this would be the last chance I get before we reach the edge of the Veil."

Emerie thought they'd need to go all the way to the west to reach his brothers, but apparently not. He claimed it would be quicker, and faster, to cut through it earlier. She was hesitant, as he said it was through some kind of swamplands.

"I want to stay, Emerie," he pleaded vehemently.

Her lips tightened, and she stomped closer. "We've spoken about this."

She pointed to the forest so he would leave. From a distance, he saw her as small, so towering over him seemed to work much better.

Usually, but not this time.

Instead of backing up, he reached up and slipped his palm on her hip, letting his claws slip underneath her shirt. The somewhat blunted points of them tickled the flesh of her back, making goosebumps rise and prickle over her sides.

Just the simple contact made her knees wobble.

"But I want to see," he beseeched, dragging those delicious but frightening claws forward to ghost them over her hip bone.

With a pant, she quickly gripped the back of his hand before he could lift her shirt any higher.

"No," she croaked, her right knee crumbling when he skated his other hand up the back of it.

She quickly righted herself and stepped back, knowing that his tongue slipping over the top of his beak meant he could scent the light arousal she could already feel.

Her reaction had been instant, and it was no longer surprising.

It wasn't the first time she'd felt desire towards him since she'd last touched him, but she'd never acted on it. She couldn't, and she often tried to pretend that she hadn't grown slick, or that her nipples hadn't pebbled.

His orbs would always flash deep purple in those times, and she would quickly have to distract him.

After last time, she couldn't risk it. Even if she wanted to, she couldn't. Too much was at stake – her life, apparently, being the main thing.

"Why not?" He darted forward and grabbed the backs of her thighs to pull her back to him. He dragged his tongue over the side of her neck, causing a strangled squeal to come from behind her sealed lips. "You have that nice scent. I want to see where it comes from."

Emerie pushed at his head to get away from him, wishing her nipples hadn't tightened at that. He freaking licked her. She wasn't used to him doing that – or opening his beak at all!

And his tongue was so warm... and wet. It was thin, flat, and a dark purple, which was nothing like she'd first expected it to be. When she saw it a few days ago, she never thought it'd feel so nice slipping across her skin.

"Because, Ingram... we can't do this." Her voice sounded embarrassingly breathy, but she managed to get out of his hands and back up out of his reach. Her brows narrowed when he let out a light growl. "Don't you growl at me! I said no!"

"You have not said why," he argued, leaping to his feet. "I want to touch you, Emerie, and you say no. I want to see, and you say no. Yet, you let me hold you, tend to your wound, sleep by you."

Her nose scrunched up as she groaned, and she dug her hand into the side of her hair to scratch her scalp in annoyance. "That's different. I'm happy to do those things with you."

"*Why* is it different?" His left hand fisted briefly before he loosened it. "I want to know what secrets you keep beneath your clothes. I want to give pleasure like you have for me."

She eyed him, noticing his tense muscles, yet the defeated slump of his posture. Her eyes crinkled in a mingle of sadness and concern.

Gripping her left shoulder, she gave him the truth, but only the part that would hurt her, not him.

"I... don't like anyone seeing underneath my clothing, Ingram, especially my torso. My scars are worse there, and I'm self-conscious about them."

He tilted his head like he often did when he didn't understand. "But you are beautiful, Emerie," he stated sincerely.

The laugh she let out was cold; she was beginning to wish she hadn't taught him that word – not when he wielded it like this.

"You can't call something beautiful when you've never seen it, Ingram. You think you're the first guy to want to see under my shirt, only to be horrified afterwards?"

"Then let me see, and I will tell you again." He said it so confidently, so arrogantly, that she wanted to believe him. Yet his orbs slowly began to morph to green.

She'd only seen them turn that colour once, and she wasn't sure what they signified.

Gosh, she felt like she was having an ugly competition with a Duskwalker! Here she was, worried he'd find her repulsive when he had a fucking skull for a face and a purple dick!

But she couldn't help it.

Her chest *burned* with insecurity, smothering her until she was afraid she'd turn to ash. She'd suffered enough fire from her wounds, so why did it have to linger in her heart, and in her skin? For so long, she'd wanted to shed her skin and feel... wanted, attractive, loveable.

Instead, people found her hard to look upon, and that included strangers that tried their absolute best to look at anything other than her damn *face*. And her face had suffered the least. It was marred, it was noticeable, but it wasn't as intense. With the right shadows, she thought maybe people wouldn't notice anything if they didn't look carefully.

Her body she couldn't hide, and any guy that had snuck their hand up her shirt had immediately pulled away from the left side.

"Just... please let me bathe privately," she uttered quietly, gripping at her biceps as her shoulders curled inward.

He turned his head to the side with his left hand clenching into a tight fist once more. "Why can other males see and touch you, but I cannot?" he growled so quietly that it was almost unnerving. His orbs brightened in their green hue. "You allow them to leave their scent on you, but you will not let me do so freely."

Her lips parted in disbelief. He did not just say that to her. She doubted he meant it as though she easily spread her legs for anyone, but that was how she took it. Or rather, how she interpreted it... because she had started to feel that way about herself after Bryce.

Had she given in to sex too easily with him because she hadn't wanted to be alone anymore? For a long time, she'd begun to wonder if Bryce liked her at all, or just that she had a warm hole she'd made available.

Even his parting words to her were 'ugly bitch,' which had been a fatal blow to her already small ego.

"That's not fair," Emerie whispered, feeling like a hypocrite.

"Your scent changes, Emerie. It grows warm and nice, different." Her cheeks heated as a blush spread across them, embarrassed that he could smell when she grew aroused in his presence... *by* his presence. "I don't know why, but it tells me that you are aroused. I feel it in my body. It calls to me, and I want it."

How am I supposed to tell him that I want him to touch me... but can't let him? How was she to do that without hurting his feelings, while knowing her rejections were already doing that?

He's probably terribly confused. Her body was giving him the go ahead, that she wanted him, while her mouth said otherwise. She couldn't imagine how much that would be eating at him.

"I want to touch you, as you touch me. I want to pleasure you like other males have." The green in his orbs flared even brighter. "Why am I not good enough for you?"

He's jealous... that's what that colour means. And she figured the brighter it was, the more it bit at him. *Oh, Ingram.*

If only she could tell him that a guy hadn't made her orgasm in a long time – years, in fact. It was like her pussy had been telling her the truth about Bryce, even if her stupid head and desperate heart wouldn't.

Ingram lifted his hand to wrap it over the side of his beak with his orbs shifting to blue. "Is it because I am Mavka?"

Tears instantly welled in her eyes, for him, for herself. She stepped towards him, reaching out with trembling hands.

"Ingram..." The rest of her response clogged in her throat.

How do I tell him yes and no at the same time?

The closer she got to him, the more she could see the big guy was trembling as well. Confused, upset, unsure. He even darted his arm away from her before she could grasp his hand and offer him comfort.

"I do not have a face like you humans. I have scales whereas you have skin, a tail whereas you have none. Do you hate these things about me?"

"I don't hate them at all," she reassured. "That's not why, Ingram."

"Your people called me a monster, Emerie," he snapped at her, his orbs flashing bright red. "They called me ugly and horrible as they held my heart in their hands. Do you see me as a monster?"

"You're not a monster, Ingram!"

He may be monstrous on the outside, but she'd met humans who were vile and despicable on the *inside.* He may be a monster, but she didn't want him thinking that about himself. She didn't want him to associate that word with himself negatively, when she'd been using it endearingly in her mind.

"Then why am I not good enough to be special to you?!" he roared. "I don't know what I am doing wrong, and you will not tell me so I can fix it."

Despite his sudden burst of aggression, she didn't back away in fright. No, instead desperation and self-loathing set in.

Emerie couldn't take it anymore.

Ingram was so damn sweet and kind that he didn't deserve to feel this way, not when she knew he was more than good enough, and more than she thought she deserved. There were far prettier, smarter, and kinder people out in the world than her, so what right did she have to keep the truth from him?

She darted forward before he could even react and grabbed his wrist. She shoved his hand, palm facing him, upwards in the air between them.

"This is why, Ingram!" He flinched at her shouting, and that only made the fresh tears falling from her drip faster. "Because you have claws!"

He brought his hand closer to his skull, like he wanted to inspect his own claws, then his orbs morphed to a deeper blue. He pushed through her hands so he could cup the side of her face.

"But I have been gentle with you. I have been trying to show you I will not hurt you again."

"How you touch me is *inside*, Ingram, and your fingers are tipped with blades. I am soft and delicate, and if you were to shove these inside me, you would hurt me, no matter how gentle you are."

She bit her lip, unsure if what she said would make matters worse, but she wanted him to know the truth. She didn't want him to think the reasons they couldn't do this was because of *what* or *who* he was. She didn't want him to think he was terrible when she thought he was pretty in an otherworldly way.

"I want you to touch me," she admitted, her brows knitting so tightly it pulled on the webbed scarring on her forehead.

"Can we not touch in other ways?" He slid his hand down so he could cup the side of her neck and brush his thumb up and down between her collar bones. "Every time your scent changes, I have this desire to... lick you."

Just the idea of his tongue on her pussy, her chest, or in her mouth, had her body warming in want.

She shook her head.

"I'm afraid of you," she said, causing his orbs to whiten and for his hand to fling away. She reached for it so she could hold it reassuringly. "If I let you touch me in other ways, or show you what sex is, I'm afraid you'll try to fuck me and split me in half in the process." She knew she was saying words he wouldn't understand, which was the only reason she felt safe to do so. "I'm not just soft, I'm breakable. You don't seem to know your own strength, and even when you hug me, you hold me too tight. You'll be excited, distracted, and you may not realise I am in pain."

He'd already shown her he couldn't control himself when he fucked her tits and came against them. Even though she'd enjoyed it, she'd been afraid when she'd been pinned beneath him. They'd been lucky, and that was only until he stabbed her thighs with his claws.

Since he didn't remove his hand, as though he was frozen as he tried to digest what she was saying, she petted him. From the creases of his palms all the way to his claw tips, she stroked him.

"You cannot prepare me, and I cannot do that on my own. I'm too small, and I would need help." Not that she thought the weapon of destruction he had between his thighs would actually fucking fit. "I want you to touch me, and the more you show me how sweet you are, the more I want you, but you being a big Duskwalker with sharp claws, and me being a small human with no healing capabilities, makes that impossible."

Gosh, she was rambling, but she didn't know if she was getting through to him. It sometimes took a while for Ingram to understand, and she was happy to explain it to him, to be patient with him, but his humanity only seemed to reach so far.

This, however, she *needed* him to understand. She wanted him to know that it wasn't her emotions stopping her, but the dangerous parts of him.

He was big, and scary. He was violent, and rough.

And she *knew* he'd be really upset with himself if he hurt her, and even more so if she bled... and he ate her because of it.

I can't believe I want to fuck something that is always one wrong move away from making me a snack.

"I don't know how to change these things, Emerie," he eventually stated with a whine in his voice. "I don't know how to make myself more... human for you."

Just when she thought her tears were calming, his words made them dot her eyelashes and threaten to fall again.

He wanted to *change* for her. No one had wanted to be 'better' for her, had wanted to fit her rather than try to fix or put up with her.

Yes, his exterior was the problem, but she didn't want it to change. She just didn't want it to be in the way. She liked his beak, especially when he rubbed the smooth side of it against her in affection. She'd liked the way his claws tickled her skin, or how his scales scraped against her.

And his heart... his winsome and tender heart... how could anyone not be attracted to it? He wasn't perfect – sometimes his lack of intelligence could be frustrating – but it was also what made him who he was. A creature that wanted to be kind and gentle, even if he didn't know how.

His tail curling around the side of her ankle or knee as he slept had her stomach quivering in tenderness. Her face would turn red as she bumped against him so he would unconsciously do it.

Even just his cuddles and seeking of platonic affection was more adoration than she'd received in all her life.

Emerie was beginning to pathetically crave it.

"You don't need to be more human. Human men have made me feel horrible. You shouldn't compare yourself to them, okay? I've regretted all of them, even the one you smelled on me back at Zagros Fortress." She tried to give him a smile, even though her lips shook the entire time. "And you shouldn't be envious that they've looked under my shirt when they haven't."

Even though his orbs remained blue, his head jerked at her last statement. "They did not see either?"

"No," she answered. At least... not for many years. Only in the beginning, when she hadn't yet learned it was just best to keep her clothes on. She'd had three partners in her life, both sexual and emotional, and they'd all let her down in some way. "I... don't feel pretty. I haven't for a long time, and it makes me want to hide. Not just from you, but also from myself."

"But you are beautiful, Emerie," he repeated once more with unwavering conviction. "You are colourful and lovely, like a pretty butterfly."

"Okay," she conceded, while licking at the salty tracks of tears that had trailed across her lips. She was unwilling to convince him otherwise, when nothing he said would change how she felt about herself. "Like a pretty butterfly."

With the hand she was still holding, he brought it up, only to hesitate right before her face. He semi-closed his hand and used the back of a knuckle to wipe her cheek as though he wanted to avoid placing his claws against her.

"I did not mean to make you cry."

"It's fine." She tried to laugh. "I'm secretly a big crybaby. I just don't usually let people see that."

"You have cried around me before."

Her smile was weak, but genuine. "Because I trust you."

It was strange that she trusted him with her emotions, when the last person she'd trusted with them was... Gideon. To her, that was more significant than letting any man who played nice freely fuck her.

"You trust me, but are afraid of me?" he grumbled, lifting his head. "I do not understand how this is possible."

"Humans are complex creatures, and how we feel can be singular and opposing to other emotions. It's what makes us... fun, and interesting."

Emerie finally stepped back to put space between them, relieved that he was calm now, even if his orbs hadn't changed from their solemn hue. *I told myself I wouldn't add to his sadness and pain.* And yet, she felt as though she'd done that. It ate at her.

"O-okay," she said, taking in a deep breath so she could shakily sigh it out. "Time for me to wash so we can move on. You said we were only a day from the Veil."

With that, she managed to get him to back up and go into the forest. Emerie quickly moved to kneel at the water's edge, wishing she could jump into it. She couldn't. It was too small, and she was injured.

She didn't feel the need to check over her shoulder when she pulled her pants and shirt off, knowing Ingram wouldn't break his promise and peek like a creepy jerk.

Scooping water into her hands, she washed her legs, trying her hardest to ignore her light skin and the pale scarring. It became harder as she washed between her stomach and side, then just underneath her breasts, where more skin had deformed.

Fresh tears sprung when she scooped water over her right breast, brushing her pink nipple, only for them to fall when she did the same to the other that looked completely different. Her areola was white, the nipple itself pale and smaller. The side of her breast was concaved with scarring, making it no longer appear or feel round and soft.

She hoped her sobbing couldn't be heard by Ingram, but she couldn't help it as she cleaned her shoulder, only to grip her biceps right where her scarring stopped.

Her shoulder and chest were the worst.

They were where she first landed in the burning puddle from the oil lamp. The rest of her had just been the straw and dry grass easily becoming alight around the worst of it, along with her clothes catching fire. Throwing a blanket over her had stopped the flames, but the material had stuck to her melted skin – requiring additional skin to be cut away.

Not wanting to be exposed for much longer, she quickly finished washing. She wished her conversation with Ingram hadn't made her mind linger on these when she usually pretended they didn't exist as she bathed.

However, once she was dressed again, managing to find a clean pair of underwear for underneath her dirty guild clothing, she sat at the shoreline. She brought her knees up, hugged them, and just gave herself a few minutes to let how she felt out.

How is anyone meant to love me like this? She was covered in more wounds, like Demon claws on most of her limbs, sword slashes from bandits, her knees and elbows scraped from countless falls during training.

Emerie was a map of scars, to the extent that not even her hands and feet were spared.

I don't want to let Ingram see what I really look like... What if he hates it? She bit at her bottom lip until she feared it'd bleed. *He called me a pretty butterfly – what if he stopped?* Gosh! She thought one had sprung up in her *chest* when he'd said that, only for it to wither and die inside her.

He's the first 'guy' to compliment me in so long. She squeezed her legs tighter. *What if... what if I only like him because of it?*

Oh god, I'm so pathetic. A quiet sob broke out of her like a whimper. *Do I want someone to love me so badly that I don't care who or what they are? That they've hurt me and tried to eat me?*

Emerie didn't *want* her feelings towards the Duskwalker to be so shallow. She wanted them to be real, rather than a dark twist of perversion because her mind and heart desired to no longer be alone.

Which is why she couldn't trust herself.

I only dated Bryce because... because he was nice to me.

He'd given her attention and had been the one to ask her out. He'd never once complimented her, but she thought his soft touches to the unmarred side of her face were his way of showing it. Yet, he never snaked his hand up her shirt after the first time, never asked her to take it off. It was only ever her freaking pants.

And Jason... She'd been much younger when she'd dated him. Naïve, stupid, and hopeful. Only to find out he took advantage of her because she was lonely, and because she didn't have a womb for him to impregnate.

Not like his wife... one she hadn't known he had until her friends found out about their relationship and told her.

Apparently, many people within the guild had known, but Emerie hadn't. It was why he'd kept their relationship a secret, and made her promise not to tell anyone, not even her friends. He'd just wanted someone to ease his dick while he was away from his wife, and Emerie had been like an injured baby deer, an easy target for a bit of sport hunting.

She'd been used. She hated that she'd been part of such a horrible betrayal to another woman.

But before that, there had been Declan. The first person she'd been in love with and had hoped to marry before that fateful and terrible night.

Right when she needed someone the most, he said he just couldn't do it. That he couldn't handle seeing her wounds, her pain, and that he shouldn't have to suffer anymore. Well... he didn't actually tell *her* that while she'd been bedbound and bandaged in the hospital, instead cowardly telling her friends at the time so they could inform Emerie.

It was no surprise she was the way she was. Her history had shaped her into something broken when it came to love and her body.

The only thing that had saved her was she'd enjoyed being a Demonslayer and did have some really good friends back in Zagros Fortress.

Friends she'd abandoned without saying goodbye to, just so she could do the right thing.

I never thought I'd be in this position. Why did Ingram have to be so benevolent and endearing? *If I hadn't jerked him off... he may not have tried to pursue anything with me.*

That whole incident right after they'd escaped Zagros Fortress was just a blur of panic.

If it had never happened, her romantic feelings may have been more like her affection towards an overgrown dog, rather than a person she wanted to touch her. She assumed it would have been different. Or maybe it wouldn't have. She may have felt her heart and pussy flutter for him regardless, but at least it would have been easier to ignore if he didn't try to make them happen.

If he wasn't seeking... more.

Emerie pushed back the left sleeve of her uniform so she could examine the bracelet at her wrist. This was her one and only precious possession, given to her by her parents and Gideon. She stroked the beads, and the last remaining charm that she hadn't lost – which was a silver disc with a 'G' engraved on it.

I wish Gideon was here. He'd be able to help me. He'd been so good with advice, and always listened when she really needed him to. *He'd tell me to stop being a crybaby.*

He would have teased and poked her into an annoyed rage to quell her sadness. Then, when she was settled, he'd help her to think logically. Right now, she needed that more than ever – someone to be her mind when her heart felt all over the freaking place.

I don't know what I'm doing, or if I can trust how I feel. She let out a shuddering breath, her mind starting to calm and her tears drying. *I don't want my selfishness to hurt him.*

TWENTY-ONE

Sitting on hard dirt, loose rocks, and small sticks with his back towards where the little human bathed, Ingram stared down at his hands. Legs crossed, tail curling around the right side of his body, he let his shoulders slump forward.

He wished he couldn't hear her sniffling. He hadn't meant to make her cry, and he hadn't known a human could *whimper* like that. He wanted to go to her, but the splashing of water informed him he would only make matters worse.

This had started because he wanted to see, so to violate that now... he didn't want to break her trust.

Instead, he inspected the sharp points of his claws.

He'd already blunted them days ago, but they were still so sharp to her. Their crescent-shaped edges underneath were particularly dangerous as well.

Blades on my fingers...

He tightly gripped his left index claw between two fingers and tried to pull it off. His orbs flashed white and a quiet yelp burst from him at the pain. He stopped.

He brought his middle finger to his beak and tried to bite it off, only to yelp once more when a crack appeared, followed by shooting agony down his entire finger.

I cannot remove them. Not without agony. It was like there were little nerves inside them, and his middle one was even producing droplets of purple blood from the tiny split.

Ingram desperately wanted to touch Emerie, but he wanted

to enjoy discovering her. He knew he wouldn't be able to do so if the pain was too distracting.

He wished they would fall off. Why did he have to have such terrible things? Big blades that would hurt this tiny female he craved learning all the secrets of.

What did she mean by touch inside? Like... a wound? That didn't sound pleasurable.

Go away, he growled at them.

He didn't care if they fell off or exploded off the tips of his fingers. He didn't care if that would leave him vulnerable in a fight; he would just use his beak and strength to destroy anything that tried to harm her.

It would be worth it if he could make those soft noises fall from her again, the ones that had his body puffing with the most tingling thrill.

The black, glossy backs of his hard claws glinted in the dappled sunlight that glittered through the tree canopy. The tip of one claw sparkled.

Change. Be human hands. He tried to will it, just like the humanoid transformation of his body.

Nothing happened, and he growled in irritation.

He'd seen some animals' claws could go back and forth. Not humans, but feline creatures. He wanted to do the same. *Go inside!*

Ingram yelped sharply when slamming agony shot up every single one of his fingers. Wincing, he brought them to his chest to shield them while curling his body around them protectively. His sight shifted to white.

Yet, the pain dulled before disappearing completely.

He brought his hands forward, only to tilt his head at them. His claws were gone. Well, not truly, but they had retracted.

Inspecting the change, he noted that the curled tips of his claws were not only sitting flush to the flesh of his fingertips, but were snug against them. He couldn't even separate them.

I did not know I could do this. His tail curled in joy. *I can touch her now.*

Ingram leapt to his feet to show her, but paused after a single step, knowing she'd be upset if he disturbed her. He didn't want her to be mad, not when he'd found a solution.

Can I make them extend? Like changing back into his monstrous form, was it possible to have both?

Rather than go to her, he experimented with them. Willing his claws to extend, they slowly slipped forward and, this time, he experienced no pain. It was just as effortless to retract them, and he thought maybe them slamming back was what hurt him before.

He wondered how much longer it would be before Emerie was finished. She was taking a while, and she hadn't called him over even though he could no longer hear splashing. Her whimpers were still present, but quieter.

I want to go to her, he thought with his sight shifting to blue.

He wanted to comfort her and be the reason she stopped crying. Would showing her he could do this ease her tears? He wanted her to smile at him for it.

"Ingram!" she screamed.

The suddenness of the panicked shriek caused his scales and spikes to lift in dread.

Ingram bolted past the trees to the small clearing where the stream was. Orbs white, he skidded to a halt when he saw her, then froze.

With the sun present, he hadn't thought he needed to worry. He also couldn't scent anything dangerous. No humans, no Demons... at least, he hadn't before he entered the clearing. He'd been distracted while she was alone, unprotected.

And now...

Ingram knew if he charged the strange and unknown Mavka holding the tiny female in their arms, they'd quickly slice her.

They appeared startled, like a deer unsure of what to do now that it'd been caught in its predator's sight. They'd been moments from sprinting off with a struggling Emerie clawing at the ground. Her hands had just broken off a tree root she'd clung to on the other side of the stream when he broke into their line of sight.

The Mavka stood and stepped back at his presence.

With their long, thin, and sharp claws wrapped around Emerie's shoulder and side, his heart nearly stopped beating.

Is... was this how the world saw him? Something to be worried and terrified of when near those who the humans cared about? That seeing their companion in a Duskwalker's long, angular arms – their death likely – struck like a serrated blade of panicked dread in their chest?

He saw a *monster* holding his colourful butterfly.

Her wide, panicked eyes screamed for help. She'd stopped moving, all except her chest expanding and compressing. Did she remember him telling her squirming only excited him?

There was the lightest tangle of fear in the air. It was too distant to make the invisible hands of bloodlust squeeze his mind into a frenzy, but it was there.

His sight darted away from her pale, freckled features, to the smear of mud in the Mavka's nose hole. White orbs stared back at him, as small velvet antlers shadowed their rabbit skull.

The Mavka was so thin around the waist that even Emerie's hips flared wider. It was young, even he knew this. Made even more evident by all the bones that covered its body, from the collar bones to the tops of its long, rabbit-like feet. It stood tall on its toes, and even with the distance between them, he knew it would tower over him.

Lowering himself to a crouch with his hand out, trying to show it he was submitting, all Ingram could do to save Emerie was demand, "Give."

The Mavka clicked and clacked their jaws, chittering as though trying to communicate. He expected bass and depth, and instead a higher tone sparked from them.

"Please tell him to let me go," Emerie softly pleaded.

Ingram's head tilted sharply, and he stepped sideways as he came a little closer. He was able to take in thin ribs, and barely noticeable mounds, but it was the wind blowing towards him that made him realise he could smell *two* feminine scents.

"She," Ingram corrected, as a small amount of awe filled him. His sight turned dark yellow in curiosity. "The Mavka is female."

I have never seen a female Mavka before.

"I don't care what it is!" she cried, only to wince.

His orbs flashed crimson, and a snarl tore through him. There was no blood in the air, but Emerie's features twisted as though she was being crushed.

The female Mavka's orbs mirrored his own, and she parted her fangs to hiss at him. She stepped backwards out of the sun and into the shadows.

White once more filled his sight, and he lowered further with his hand out. "Give."

Her orbs darkened, and her hissing strengthened. She wasn't going to give up Emerie.

"I cannot charge her," he stated aloud, sharing his thoughts with Emerie. "I cannot chase her. She will grow enraged and attack you."

To be honest, he was unsure why the Mavka hadn't made a meal of her already. He was thankful for it, though, as it gave him a *chance* to save her.

"What do I do?" he heard over the growing distance.

The rabbit-skulled Mavka backed up further, putting space between them. Yet Ingram remained where he was.

"Do not smell of fear, and do not allow yourself to come to harm. I will follow your scents from a safe distance."

"It's growing dark, Ingram."

The blade of dread cut deeper. *I know.*

He knew night would fall soon, and they were closer to the Veil. The direction the Mavka was going was towards the canyon, taking Emerie closer towards danger.

Luck had been on their side. Other than their first night together, they hadn't come across any other Demons. They were now closer to the Veil, where it was likely they'd come across one in the next few nights.

But there was nothing he could do.

His instincts told him to be patient. That if he wanted to save her, he had to battle against the desire to chase and fight for his prize, his prey, for *her.* Otherwise, this Mavka would kill her within seconds, or Ingram's own rage would force him against his friend.

She was caught in the middle of two Mavkas, neither who seemed to want to hurt her right now, but absolutely might.

He watched them shrink into the trees before disappearing

out of sight. He waited, even as his flesh tightened in aversion to doing so. He waited, even as the sun began to fade, and the shadows grew longer and crept over him.

His sight never left where he last saw them.

I already lost Aleron... He didn't know, until this very moment, that he was worried about losing his little butterfly as well.

Ohmygod. Ohmygod. Ohmygod! Sitting in darkness, Emerie tried with all her might to remain unafraid and calm her whirling thoughts, but each time the female Duskwalker patted her hair, terror threatened to bubble over.

The strokes were hard. Starting from her brows, the Duskwalker would run her hands back, pulling on Emerie's entire face until her eyelids were stretched up. Then she would roughly stroke over her hair, and each time Emerie worried she'd either pull her hair out, or her claws would slice her.

With long, thin legs trapping her in from the sides, the Duskwalker's torso was hard and lean against her back. At least she was warm, protected from the chill within the dark underground den she'd been dragged to.

Even though she couldn't see in the pitch dark, Emerie still chanced glancing back and up at the rabbit skull she'd earlier seen, and knew it had additional teeth. There were many fangs on the sides, making her buck teeth not as intense – and even they had seemed shorter than normal.

She chittered to Emerie. Her orbs were the only things she could see, and they were bright yellow as she patted Emerie's long orange hair. Her nose hole was filled with mud, but her orbs reflected against her free hand wrapping the end of her snout, as though to block out even more scents.

It was like she knew Emerie would be afraid, and was *trying* not to let the smell of her make her frenzied.

Emerie felt tiny between the towering, angular legs

surrounding her. The Duskwalker's torso wasn't actually very long, most of her height seeming to be in her legs. The more features Emerie took in through touch, the more she realised that she was actually... small.

Her waist was thin, her hips a little wider. There were no true breasts from what she could feel, but there was an impression of a womanly swell beneath her flesh-protruding rib bones.

She seemed pleased to have Emerie in her clutches.

Her eyes darted around the darkness, knowing what surrounded her was lots of dirt and tree roots. When she'd been brought here, there had been just enough light from dusk to show she was being taken into some kind of deep and barely spacious burrow.

The entry was shielded by a large collection of bushes, and the massive tree's roots above them further covered the entrance.

They weren't in the Veil. They were somewhere on the surface world, that's all she knew. The air was stale and cold, but at least the Duskwalker was keeping out the worst of the chill.

Any time Emerie crawled forward to escape, she would clutch her and shove Emerie back against her hard and gangly torso. She wouldn't hiss, but her orbs would flare red and she'd chitter as though she was trying to speak.

Why could she hear a... *caring* inflection? Emerie felt like she was an animal that had been captured, and the Duskwalker was a human trying to soothe her.

The Duskwalker almost tore her hair out and poked her in the eye with a claw as she stroked her head again. Her vision grew murky when she thought the skin of her face was about to rip away from bone at the intense swipe.

She'd noted a carcass of a recently deceased fox near the entrance when she was dragged down here. Its body was intact, likely why it hadn't been eaten, but its neck was obviously broken.

She petted it to death.

Emerie whimpered in uncertainty, and the rabbit Duskwalker tried to say something. Then she smacked her on the top of the head a few times in a different form of pat, and Emerie's neck kinked each time. At this rate, the creature was going to comfort her by petting her to fucking death as well.

Creepy. This is so creepy.

She searched for the entrance, wishing Ingram would hurry up and come save her.

Emerie flinched when the point of a claw came too close to her eye. The suddenness of her jerking caused those blades to slice her face.

With her hand over her rabbit nose, she didn't seem to notice until her next swipe was met with wetness. The Duskwalker froze, brought their hand away to look at it, and Emerie thought she was dead. So dead.

Her fear was palpable, and tears welled. Her trembling worsened until she was nothing but a shivering mess. She didn't even have the mind to crack a joke – which was the most alarming part for her.

I don't want to be eaten. I don't want to die.

The Duskwalker whimpered and covered Emerie's entire face with her large, thin hand. She chittered at her, a frantic edge to her voice.

Emerie stilled when the bleeding wound on her face began to heal as an aqua-coloured magical glow glittered around her. Even the mild throbbing in her right leg from Ingram wounding her dissipated. It was so bright, it illuminated everything within the burrow.

Her hand drifted to her exposed wounds – since she hadn't bandaged them yet – and she watched her scabs growing smaller until she was left with smooth skin. There was no new scar added to her body.

Within seconds, that bright light dimmed and then disappeared completely.

She healed me...? Her eyes widened as disbelief soared through her. *Duskwalkers can fucking heal?!*

If she'd known that, she could have helped Ingram figure out how to do that!

Under this new revelation, Emerie's panicked shivers faded, only for the female Duskwalker to do so instead. Her orbs were bright orange.

She feels bad about hurting me. Her lips tightened. *Why did she take me then?* She tried to think on why it had grown interested in her, why it was doing this.

One minute Emerie had been crying next to the river, the next this Duskwalker had stood over her like a frightening tree sent straight from hell.

Her gaze drifted to where she knew the fox to be, although she couldn't see it in the dark. It had been unharmed, other than its fatal death. It was unlikely it would have crawled into this burrow to be in the Duskwalker's clutches.

Had it been injured? Had it possibly been crying in the forest, as Emerie had been?

She stopped theorising the moment she heard movement outside. The rabbit Duskwalker let out a long and terrifying hiss when someone or some*thing* disturbed the bushes at the entrance.

Emerie's chest tightened. It was either a Demon, or Ingram.

Please be orbs. Please be orbs.

Two purple glows slowly came into view, and Emerie let out the biggest sigh of relief. Only to wince when strong arms tightened around her. The Duskwalker kicked back, trying to escape as she pushed them further into the bottom of the burrow's curved wall.

Loose rocks and dirt clattered under her struggling heels.

"Ingram, wait! She's freaking out."

He paused at the entry, and she only knew that because his orbs had stopped moving. She couldn't see anything else. It was too dark, but they brought her so much comfort, even as they turned white.

The Duskwalker holding her eventually settled, but Emerie could feel her quick breaths and heartbeat against her back. She had tried to squish Emerie between her and the wall, almost... protectively.

Claws glinted for a moment, as though they were shiny and reflecting the two sets of glowing orbs within the burrow. Ingram had reached his hand out.

"Give," he demanded, quietly but sternly.

The Duskwalker hissed in return.

"Give," he snarled, his orbs flashing red for a moment.

She hissed louder and then barked chitters at him. Dirt shifted as Ingram came closer, and her hand came up to cup the side of Emerie's head. She tried to shield her.

"I-I think she's protecting me, Ingram," Emerie explained, *hoping* her wild theory was correct. "She thinks you want to hurt me."

"I would never want to hurt you, Emerie." His orbs turned blue. "She does not have enough humanity to speak. I don't know how to make her let you go."

Emerie turned her gaze up to the Duskwalker, whose orbs were white with fear or worry. She braved reaching up and tentatively touched a warm jawbone.

She flinched, and darted her skull towards Emerie in surprise, yellow forming in her glow instead. Emerie pet her, and each one made the squeezing press of her arms lessen.

"Please let me go," she whispered, unsure if the Duskwalker understood what Emerie was saying.

She incoherently chittered back.

"Please let me go with him." Emerie then stopped petting her so she could reach her hand out to Ingram's awaiting one.

Dirt shifted as Ingram closed the gap. Just when the points of hard but blunted claws scraped against her fingertips, she was yanked away. He let out the tiniest rumble.

"Just wait," Emerie pleaded. "Stay calm. Let her see that you're safe."

Emerie soothed her hand against the Duskwalker's sternum, like she often did for Ingram. When her arms loosened once more, she reached out to him.

"Don't take me, yet. Don't pull me," Emerie told him, when she was able to slip her fingers against the pads of his far larger ones.

The Duskwalker's orbs turned dark yellow at Emerie and Ingram reaching out to each other. She didn't try to yank Emerie away this time, even when Ingram's warm and calloused palm swallowed up her dainty hand.

A link had been created; one that made her heart soar.

For a few minutes, they just held hands as cold silence was shared between all three of them. She adored how safe his big, meaty paw felt, how it eased her fears with its roughness and conflicting strength and gentleness.

"L-let me come to you," she stated, gingerly pushing at the Duskwalker's arms while she leaned towards him. "Let her see I want to go to you."

It happened slowly, but she did eventually release Emerie. Just before she could be collected into Ingram's arms, the Duskwalker grabbed her wrist. Emerie stared back at the blue glow in her orbs.

She doesn't want to let me go. Emerie's eyes crinkled with pity for her.

Still, she gingerly pulled her arm until she was freed and let herself fall into Ingram. He scooped her into his strong arms, and his rapid heartbeat thumped against her when she slipped her arms around his neck.

The Duskwalker chittered and whined, her orbs darting between them as though she was moving her skull from his to Emerie's face. Her cries were heartachingly sad, enough to make Emerie wince for her.

Ingram dragged Emerie across the ground as he backed up, cautiously bringing them out of the burrow. Sticks and leaves scraped against her pants as he exited the shrubs hiding the entryway before he stood. Facing the burrow the entire time, as though he worried the Duskwalker would follow, Ingram moved to create space between them and her.

The sounds of faint whimpers could be heard.

He paused when he bumped into a tree, then waited.

If Ingram was hesitant about any sudden movements, she knew there was truly cause for alarm.

When the female Duskwalker didn't come out, even as moments passed, his arms securely tightened on her. Then, he bolted to the right, darting through the forest to get Emerie away from there as fast and as far as he could.

She squeezed his neck, so thankful she thought her heart was going to explode. She didn't know how else to relieve it, how to thank him, other than wrapping her legs around his waist until all her limbs had ensnared him.

She let his decadent aroma of burnt sugar and hickory bark bleed into her entire being, taking in its richness, the way it tingled her senses. His neck was tight with corded, strong muscles, the scales covering them a soothing texture. Both sensations were so masculine and felt divine.

Even his warmth, heartbeat, and snorted breaths were so greatly appreciated that they were doing funny things to her insides. She knew her fight or flight instincts were on the fritz since her nipples tightened and deliciously scraped against his big chest.

Her own breaths warmed and grew panted, rolling between them as she buried her face against his throat.

He did it. He did it without harming me. She didn't know if he'd be able to pull her out of that creepy hole in the ground, but he'd been so patient. He hadn't used violence, hadn't roared or snarled.

He'd been brave enough to follow her lead, even when she was sure it was against his nature when something had what he wanted.

Emerie tightened her legs around his narrow waist, wondering if his hand placement on her arse was done purposefully. She almost bit her lip and sat into it in welcome.

Right now, she wanted to be as close with him – her saviour – as possible. So much so, it ached her.

He saved me...

TWENTY-TWO

Once he put a great distance between them and the female Mavka and knew they weren't being followed, Ingram placed the human on her feet. Crouching around her, he gave the way they came one last check before turning his skull to her.

Even though he enjoyed her clinging, he *pried* her from his neck so he could examine her. His hands were frantic as he checked her, especially since he could smell hints of drying blood – only light enough to stir hunger but not enough to make him crazed.

"Are you okay, Emerie?" Panicked, he examined her dainty hands and her thin arms, then cupped her pretty face with both his hands. He used the pad of his thumb to wipe and scratch off the tiny pricks of blood he saw, surprised to find no wound.

Her heart was beating just as wildly as his own, yet she was sweeter than usual. Was he going insane with worry that he was imagining her scent deepening and turning tangy?

He drifted his hands down her waist, seeing if she would yelp in pain so he could know to be careful of those places in the future. His assessing touch found her injured thigh, and he paused as he looked down.

"Emerie... your wound? It is gon–"

Before he could finish, Emerie threw herself at him and wrapped her arms around his neck again. "I'm fine, Ingram."

She squeezed him with all her might – which was barely anything to him. Then she drew back, only to dart her head forward and press her lips to the side of his skull. Then she did it again, and again, moving randomly across the bone and the curve of his beak.

His orbs turned white, and he flinched each time, unsure as to why she was attacking him with her lips. *Is this punishment for letting her be taken?* She kept doing it, pecking him with a *mwah* sound each time she made contact.

"Gosh, I'm so freaking happy to see you right now that I just want to kiss your damn face off."

Kisses? Is that what she was doing to him? *These are good things?*

He stopped flinching.

Since she said she was happy, he tried to view them differently to how he would violently peck with his beak. Now that he wasn't fretting about them, nor wanting to escape them, he realised her lips were so soft as they moulded against the hardness of his skull bones.

Because she was doing them so close to his sight, he could see how her lips were curled upwards. She was smiling, and they *did* feel nice. *I like them... these kisses.* The next time she gave him one, his heart clenched in his chest, only to ache and radiate with joy with the rest that followed.

And her scent... He nearly groaned as he sat, unable to handle the surge of her tangy arousal hitting him like a wave.

"You were such a good boy, Ingram," she whispered against him, her voice thick and her breaths airy. "You were so patient and gentle. You even grabbed my bag before coming for me."

Of course he'd grabbed her bag. It'd been sitting on the ground between them when she was taken, and he knew it was important to her survival.

Good boy?

He didn't know why these two words curled his tail with a thrill while piercing his cock with a deep throb. His orbs changed to a darker purple than normal, and he had to grip his seam shut to stop his cock from extruding.

"I'm a good male," he agreed, liking that she saw him as this.

He didn't know why Emerie was acting this way when she'd been afraid inside that female Mavka's burrow. He didn't understand why her scent was growing tangier by the second, but he didn't want his uncontrollable desires to upset her.

She was calm and giving him these *kisses*. He didn't want her to stop. Not when he wanted her to give him more, to lather his entire skull with them.

Emerie paused with her lips near the end of his beak, and her eyes slipped to his orbs. They crinkled with fondness and perhaps... humour?

"Did you like me calling you that?"

Then, she gave him slower, deeper, and wetter kisses up the curve of his beak, while she leaned her body more and more against him.

"Yes," he grated, wrapping one arm around her to bring her even closer, while keeping the other on his seam.

"Your orbs have turned purple." When she was right before his orbs, that were focused and unwilling to move from her face, she nibbled at her bottom lip. Her knee bumped against the back of his knuckles, like she was trying to feel him. "I really want to give you a reward right now for being so good."

I will get a reward for being good? But all he'd done was save her after failing to protect her. When he realised this, he didn't feel as though he deserved one.

"I did not protect you," he rejected, his orbs turning a reddish pink when shame trickled down his spine.

"Because I wanted to be alone. That's not your fault, but mine, and you still came and saved me."

She gave him a lingering kiss on his cheek bone. He was still about to reject her, but her hand started slipping down his chest. It made an obvious path down his abdomen, meaning her destination could only be where his hand was stopping his dick from slipping from him.

She... wants to touch me?

This was the first time Emerie had reached for him like this, had wanted to touch him when his cock wasn't already waiting and achy. Although it throbbed and was stiffening behind his seam, he wasn't desperate.

But he did crave her, and that's what almost broke him when she lowered herself just enough to brush her welcoming palm over the backs of his knuckles. The idea sent a spike of need through his groin. When he wouldn't let his seam go, his tentacles squirmed. Then they swirled around his growing erection in the strangest comforting cuddle.

He felt them tugging down to aid him, to keep him in.

As much as Ingram wanted her hands on him, he wanted something much, *much* more.

He braved releasing his hand from his seam and was thankful he didn't extrude. It allowed him to skate his hand and claws up the front of her hips and under her shirt.

"I want to touch you, Emerie," he pleaded.

If she was offering a reward, and since he was selfish enough to take one, he would prefer this.

She stood and yanked the bottom of her shirt down. The desirous heat in her gaze fizzled into worry. "I told you why you can't."

He brought his hand up between them and demonstrated what he'd learned. His claws slowly retracted, giving him no pain. Her lips parted in surprise, eyes wide and riveted to them.

"I did not know I needed to learn this until you told me *why* I needed to," he explained, wanting her to be more open and honest with him in the future.

Ingram had only gained much humanity recently. He'd also spent all of his life with his kindred, who he had never needed to change or be different for. His kindred was as hard, sharp, and rough as he was; he'd never held someone soft and delicate.

But he was willing to learn, wanted to more than anything if it meant he could be closer with her.

To demonstrate his control, and that she no longer needed to fear him, he ghosted his very fingertips against the ridge of her jaw. Then he danced them down the pulsing jugular of her throat, somewhere so vital and fragile.

Emerie's gaze was locked on his skull, her blue eyes flicking side to side as they bounced between his purple orbs. The hue of them darkened when she didn't stop his fingertips from slipping lower, and lower, until he was at her hand fisting the bottom of her shirt.

Holding in a worried breath that she would reject him still, he dug beneath her hand. She didn't stop tugging her shirt down, but she did allow his fingertips to tenderly brush over her abdomen until he touched her shallow navel. His release of breath was overshadowed by a groan when his palm met her supple flesh.

Textured skin greeted him at her side, but her arm clung to her torso to stop him from reaching up to her left breast. He dipped his hand out and shoved it back underneath, but behind her side, so he could glide his palm across the bare flesh of her back.

Little bumps, like claw slices, marred the mostly smooth skin of her back and shoulder blades. He lowered his other hand so he could grip her thigh from behind and drag it upwards.

The tiniest pant fell from her lips, and her pupils dilated. Her gaze drooped lazily. Her stiff posture eased. Emerie grew relaxed in his embrace, and nothing had felt better.

Although it was obvious she still wasn't going to let him see, she gave him space so he could come forward around her side. Ingram swallowed thickly, in excitement, nervousness, and curiosity.

He'd been dying to know what her breasts truly felt like, and why they were so special she hadn't allowed him to explore before.

He knew they'd be soft from when they'd been pressed against him, but he hadn't known they would be so malleable even with the *slightest* caress. Her right breast moved under his touch.

He grazed something tiny and firm, and he startled from both surprise and her sharp gasp. Worried he'd hurt her, his gaze darted to her features to find they were even more lax than before, and her eyes held no displeasure.

He tentatively grazed it again. She bit her bottom lip as she moaned and lifted her chest into his touch. Her arousal scent deepened, grew fangs, and chomped at his groin.

This, he groaned, pulling her to him so he could slip his face and beak against the crook of her neck. *Touch here. She likes it.* He slipped his entire hand over her little breast – unsure if it was truly small or if he was just big – and made sure his roughness always abraded the sensitive point.

He grabbed her arse just so he could feel its round softness as well. With his legs crossed, he drew her closer as his twitching and jerking cock finally broke free of his seam, reaching to the length of his tentacles trying to hold him safely back.

It was a losing battle, and they gave in easily.

Freed and unbearably hard, his lubricant-covered cock jutted between her knees. Ingram licked across her throat, giving into the deep craving that warped his mind every time her scent even had just a hint of its current deliciousness.

The only thing that saved his exposed cock from stinging was her little gasps and tiny moans making it swell and jerk in time. His excitement kept him slick with fresh lubricant.

At peace with this moment, just finally being able to do this, Ingram would have kept touching her plush breast until the sun rose.

"Ingram," she whispered.

He kneaded her arse as he played with her breast, trying to be even gentler with her supple body. He feared she wanted to take it away from his embrace.

He didn't want to let her go.

"Emerie," he pleaded when she pushed against him.

He was forced to retract his hand from her breast, instead holding her side underneath her shirt – unwilling to truly part from her.

She pulled it out herself, then finally let her shirt go so she could release the ties of her pants. They gaped open. She tugged at one of the bows of her underwear, and it loosened as well.

Ingram had been planning to eventually try to dip his hands against her and discover what lay between her thighs. Was she instead... inviting him there?

Fuck, he thought, his orbs darkening and his cock swelling so hard that a bubble of precum welled at the tip. He was *hoping* she was.

"Be... be really gentle, okay?" she whispered around airy pants, placing his hand between her hips.

She pushed it lower until he slipped underneath her underwear, and something tickled him. Soft hair greeted his fingertips, and he wondered if it matched the bright-orange colour on top of her head.

He didn't get the chance to play there, not when she pushed even lower and confusing wetness greeted him. Her thighs parted, giving him more room... and Ingram wasn't sure what to do with it.

He'd never touched a pussy before.

Uncertainty tightened his flesh at what he felt. It was slick like his cock, but he immediately understood why she'd been hesitant about him touching here before.

It was so soft, so delicate, that he worried about tearing the thin folds he felt. He even worried just the callouses on his thick fingers would scrape her.

Ingram looked away from his hand partially inside her black pants to stare at her face. He watched her reactions to make sure he didn't do anything wrong.

He sunk his hand lower, and a tiny, firm bud moved against his middle finger. Her head jerked back as she let out a sharp gasp, her hips dipping away. Ingram paused.

At his stillness, she tilted her face down and noted the flash of white in his orbs. She let out a quiet giggle.

From outside of her pants, she pushed his hand against her until his forefinger found it again. She ground the firm nub against it.

"It's my clit. It feels good, but really sensitive." She wrapped her arms around his shoulders and buried her head against the side of his neck. "Don't worry. I'll let you know if something hurts."

Did that mean he could be bolder?

Ingram dug into her pants deeper, and Emerie let out a little cry as he petted her *clit*. His cock swelled in reaction to the delicious sound, and he was already desperate to hear her give him another.

With his arm around her waist to hold her against him, he carefully and lightly moved his middle finger against her clit, since having all his fingers against it felt too imposing. As he explored, feeling the folds and lips of her *pussy,* he tried to see what would give him the best reaction. Going side to side seemed to make her tremble, but circles made moans break from her at the same time.

Drool filled his mouth, and he quickly swallowed. *She smells so nice like this.* The more he touched, the stronger her arousal was.

But he remembered she said he was supposed to touch inside somehow. He followed the path of slick and found a little pool. He pressed his finger pad against it, stroking to find... he wasn't quite sure.

However, as he pressed deeper, he expected to find an end. Instead, hot, soft flesh slipped around his finger like it was melting as he pushed. It was only when he was barely first-knuckle deep that he realised he'd found it.

Excitement curled his tail tip, and he pushed a little harder and faster than he meant to, curious to know where she ended. He made her mount his finger, and she tensed and arched as a rasp broke from her lips.

"Ingram," she moaned, her knees buckling inwards as snug plushness clamped his finger.

But now what?

He swirled his finger to explore all her hot textures. The back wall was smooth, the front bumpy and plump, and everything was tight. He wasn't sure where to touch and wiggled when he knew he hadn't reached all of her depths.

He wasn't sure if the trembling from her chest was because of pleasure or laughter, especially since the noise she was producing was stifled by her face buried against his neck. She lowered her hand to cup the back of his own, to keep it still, and moved her hips back and forth.

"Like this," she whispered.

Oh. Embarrassment prickled the back of his neck when his finger moved in and out of her snug channel.

He took over, and she slipped her arm back around him.

As he thrust his finger, Emerie rocked against him, her breaths growing more shallow and shorter each time. He also moved it around, trying to see if there was some kind of... special spot that felt even better for her; like how the head and sacs of his cock were more sensitive than the rest.

"Oh fuck," she bit out when he curled against the front of her inner walls. Her nails dug into the scales on his back, before she clasped two spikes to leverage herself to grind against him. "R-right there."

"Here?" He pressed hard and moved in and out.

Emerie let out a loud cry and clung harder, her lips shaking against his neck. Her entire body tightened and shivered, while her pussy grew slicker.

He groaned at the fresh wave of her arousal scent, and he slipped his free hand under her shirt from behind her so he could deepen the contact between them. She darted her hand to yank her shirt down, but he didn't mind; not when she was too distracted to notice that he'd grasped her left breast so he could... tease it.

It wasn't the same as her right, not as soft and her nipple was smaller, but it still felt wonderful in his rough palm. All that mattered to him was that it belonged to her, and that it could give her pleasure.

"Oh god, oh fuck," she whispered around pants. "I'm so close."

Close to coming? What would it be like when this little female lost her mind to bliss, like she'd done for him with her hands against his big cock?

He needed to know.

He wanted to go faster, to dig harder. He couldn't. His movements were limited by the restriction of her pants.

With a small snarl, he forced himself away from her lovely breast so he could grab the back of her pants. He yanked them down her legs until they were around her ankles, giving him blessed freedom to do what he wanted with this delightful little hole he'd found.

"Hey– Ohhh!" Whatever protest she'd begun morphed into a haunting cry as he speared her with his finger, over and over, not too roughly, but in a swift rhythm.

The plump ridge he'd been playing with swelled before her entire channel tightened. Emerie went to the tips of her toes, as her pussy spasmed and sucked on his finger, liquid squelching inside her.

But it was her scream, her drool-inducing scent, and the way she shook, that informed him she was coming – even if it wasn't like how he did. His cock reacted to it, pulsating until seed bubbled at the eye of his cockhead and dripped down the groove underneath it.

Such a pretty sound, coming from such a delectable female...

Now that he knew how he could pleasure her, and how her sweet pussy could gobble him up, he wanted to give her as much pleasure as he could wring from her.

Which is why, when she collapsed to her knees on top of him, he didn't relent. With soft moans, she lightly bounced as he thrust, like she wasn't quite ready to let go of him either. He cupped the back of her head and gently pulled her back so he could watch her expression.

He would have been upset that she wasn't truly looking upon his raven skull if her eyes didn't look so cloudy with need, in the same way his mind was foggy. He had to fight through it to keep being gentle with his fragile butterfly.

"Cute," he groaned, noticing the pinkness of her face, the wetness of her lips. She looked lost in a way he'd never seen before, and it was completely erotic.

Her pupils were blown, her lashes damp. Her hair was messy and riotous as she bounced, causing his palm against it to make strands loop and tangle.

She must have felt his tentacles tickling her inner thighs because she managed a glance down between them.

His cock was jerking between them. It was drenched in his lubricant with a line of precum filling the groove underneath. He was hard, and each of her reactions to his touch kept him needy, aching, and quite happy about it.

That was until she cupped the head with both hands and squeezed him.

The snarl that cracked out of him was aggressive as pleasure shot all the way down his cock. His tail smacked against the ground as a thrill quaked down his spine.

Ingram yanked her hands away from his cock, worried when her touch almost made him lose the control he had on his claws.

"Don't touch," he growled.

As much as he wanted to achieve his own release, she couldn't give him that right now. He wanted to keep touching her. After rejection after rejection, he was finally getting what he wanted, and he wasn't ready to give it up.

This was better. Her pleasure tickled his mind in a way he could never have imagined. It kept him right on the edge of need and desperation, roiling inside him like a violent battle.

He would cave eventually. He would need her to take him in her blessed hands and soothe him, but not until he knew she had nothing left to give. When she was pushing his hand away, rather than grinding on his thick finger jammed inside her as she was now.

Since she'd knelt on him, he also didn't like how he had less control, having to reach so low between them. He turned her to sit with her back against his front, shifting her a little to the right so she wasn't lying against his cock.

He'd never removed his hand from between her thighs to do this, and he resumed moving it back and forth before she could make any kind of protest. She melted for him, her cute nails trying to cut into the flesh of his thighs. Cute, because there was absolutely no way this female could hurt him.

Now that he'd spun her around, he realised two things.

One was that he had far more freedom with her thighs spread and could touch her chest again. She yanked her shirt down as he snuck his hand underneath it, but she didn't stop him from grasping her right breast to tease the firm but sensitive nipple.

However, secondly, and more importantly, he could *see.*

With his head over her shoulder, he tilted it enough so his beak wasn't impacting the sweet vision of this. Of her and his own dark-grey hand, white bones protruding as he plunged between her creamy thighs.

He lifted his hand and angled his wrist back so he could view what her pussy looked like, finding she was a pale pink. Now that he was looking at her clit and folds, they made more sense to him, and he was able to remove his finger to play with them better. She twitched and bowed when he pressed against her clit, moving it side to side before going in a circle like before.

Her hair is orange there. He liked that it was the same as the luscious strands currently tangled against his chest.

He slipped his finger back inside her hot, damp pussy, watching intently, and a violent shudder rippled through him. She didn't feel as snug as the first time he'd entered her.

She is... stretchy.

He pulled his digit to the side and tried to see if he could fill the new space with a second one. When he realised it was possible, he quickly worked it inside until she'd taken both with a hitch of breath.

She touched the back of his knuckles to feel what he'd done. Considering how snugly she was holding him, how tight she was, he knew she must have deeply felt the intrusion.

He also realised he could dig... deeper like this, and something brushed against the pad of his middle finger. He'd found the end of her pretty little pink pussy, and he was quite pleased with himself about that.

Now he just needed to learn how much of his fingers she could take. He had this desirous craving to shove his entire hand in there.

"Y-your fingers are so big," she said, before letting out a trembling moan. Her legs shook as she grasped the back of his hand.

"Do they feel good?" She was hot and wet, but he'd like her to tell him he was being good. He was trying his hardest.

"Mhm." She nodded and ground against them.

His tail curled in delight, his cock jerking along with it.

"I like touching your little *cunt,*" he rasped, thankful she'd once taught him some of the names he could call it. "It smells so good, and I like that you're all slick for me. That you are letting me see and touch you."

He groaned and rubbed the side of his skull against her temple to show just how much he appreciated it.

His fingers picked up speed again as he covered her, done exploring with his sight when he'd rather just make her come apart for him again. He angled his thrusts towards where he hoped her tender spot was – the one that had made her scream earlier.

Trying anything to get her to let go like before, he cupped

both her breasts at different intervals, unsure of which one felt better for her.

When her nails returned to digging into the scales of his thighs, and she started bucking her hips with constant moans, he went faster. He wasn't willing to go harder, unsure if he could tamp his strength down, which proved even more challenging when she started to wriggle.

One minute it was as though she wanted to escape him, and the pleasure he was trying to bring forth, the next she was panting and helping him work her. She'd squeeze his hand with her thighs, and then open them wide to let him play.

"W-wait," she rasped, her legs knocking inwards. He grabbed one of her knees with his tail to spread her again and stop her from restricting his movements. "Something's–"

"Come, Emerie," he pleaded with deep huffs. "I want to watch this time."

"S-slow dow– Ohhh!"

Her back arched into a tight bow, her lips parted, and her eyes widened – right before they rolled back. Her loud, sultry cry echoed into the forest, while the quiet but distinct squelch of his fingers moving inside her tight pussy was only for them.

Wetness burst from her as she came. Her channel filled with feminine cum and liquid squirted into his hand.

Ingram would have been alarmed by the difference of her coming to the last time, but her squirming in his arms gripped his throat and mind like a set of invisible hands. Every wriggle, every toss of her body – like she was trying to flee – stirred something dark in him.

He held her tighter, held her still, and slammed his fingers faster and harder within her spasming cunt. His little butterfly was fluttering against him, and he wanted her to flutter wildly.

Her legs buckled, kicking and writhing.

"More," he begged with a twisted snarl, his sight darkening until he thought it would fracture. "Keep doing *that*."

Keep coming, keep squirming, keep crying out high-pitched screams. All because of him, for him.

Her pussy clamped his fingers constantly, twitching and surrendering to him. It was so hot, so wet, so fucking perfect that he just needed it to give him... more.

His cock felt like it was moments from exploding, twitching along with her until seed was leaking from him in constant drips. He wished it'd spend and give him release instead of easing the pressure – until she ramped it up again. Even his tentacles were writhing, flinging lubricant and seed they'd incidentally collected on their tips.

Liquid stopped bursting from her, yet she continued to twist and contort. Her features were so furrowed she looked like she was in agony, yet her hard nipples and scent said otherwise. He ignored the anguish on her face, and let her body speak to him.

"Oh god. Fuck, please, Ingram," she cried, until she had to let go of her shirt to still his hand with both of hers. It rode up to her ribs, flashing him her navel and stomach. "Please. No more."

The tiniest growl rumbled in his chest, but he did stop.

He was rewarded by her falling against him languidly, thighs spread. His fingers were still deep within her as her chest rapidly expanded and compressed with fast breaths. She twitched the entire time, the muscles of her biceps, legs, and back spasming. He was a little confused when she clasped his hand between her thighs and ground on his fingers. She bit her lips as a stifled, quiet groan escaped past them.

Once she was no longer moving, sense flittered back to him. Had he gone too hard or rough? He hadn't realised he might have been too aggressive and uncontrolled in his enthusiasm.

"Did I... do good?" he asked, wriggling his two fingers inside her. "My hand and legs are all wet with you now."

She'd come everywhere, and he was pleased that it was marking him. He had the urge to remove his fingers and smear it across his chest.

"That felt amazing," she whispered around pants. "I've never squirted before."

Ah, so that's what it was called.

He would have been upset that she was talking about past experiences with other males, but it was overshadowed by his own self-pride. If he was the first, then he was the only one. By her reaction, he knew she'd adored it.

Ingram lifted his palm so he could look at his fingers buried again. The inside of her felt different than before, rougher and like he was being sucked deeper.

Since he'd loosened her further, he earned himself a surprised gasp when he slipped out a little and then shoved back in with his index finger joining the other two. It was tight, required a bit of pressure, but she'd easily given way – at least against his strength.

"T-too much!"

He didn't think so.

He couldn't scent blood, and she had accepted them. Could he work in another? He was having fun playing with her stretchy hole.

Just as he pulled back a little, she grabbed his hand. "You better *not* be about to shove a fourth in."

"Fine," he bit, pushing back in with just the three. "You are so warm inside here. Soft." He rubbed the back of his thumb against her clit, and she twitched in his arms. "You feel like the inside of my seam."

Well, not currently, as it was all pushed forward to stabilise his throbbing erection. But before, when he was soft and needed a place to be sheltered...

At his thoughts, his head jerked. His sight found his aching cock.

Currently, the nagging, mind-fuzzing desire in it was... comfort. It sought release, yes, but it also sought more wetness, more warmth; a place to shelter him while he blissfully thrust until he could drain his sacs of their seed-swollen pressure.

His sight darted to her cunt. Her warm, sweet, wet cunt fluttering her fragile heartbeat around his fingers.

Desire and need clung to his chest, digging its claws in as realisation dawned.

Ingram groaned as he wriggled his fingers inside her snug channel, realising he'd been playing exactly where he needed to be.

Her thighs clamped his hand once more to still him, her features twitching with a wince.

"Nhn. Sensitive," she whimpered.

"Emerie." He shuddered, removing his fingers and spreading

her lips with two of them. He spread her entrance to peek inside her, to see for himself that she had a place for him. "Inside here. I want to bury my cock inside here."

She immediately stiffened in his arms before rolling to her side so she could partially kneel while facing him.

"No, Ingram. You won't fit."

Sure, he could. She was stretchy, her little pussy showing him it was adaptable to size.

He wrapped his arm around her and drew her closer, almost forcing her legs around his hips. "Please. I will be gentle. I will go... slow." When the heat of her folds pressed against the underside of his throbbing cock, he had to fight with himself not to quickly shove her on it. "I will not hurt you."

Suddenly, her scent became suffocating in the most wonderful way.

He lifted his hand, inspecting where it was covered in both clear liquid and a creamy substance. An overwhelming need to taste it made his mouth flood with drool.

"I'm too swollen and tender for you to even *try* right now. You're too big, too hard, too... excited."

Ingram stopped listening the moment he licked his fingers. He was too busy trying to shove his entire hand into his maw so he could curl his tongue around it and steal every bit of her tangy liquid.

His sight blackened, closing, as he violently shuddered.

Had he known she tasted so good, he would have speared her with his tongue.

He gripped her arse, shoved himself against her, and rocked her as he thrust his hips. "Inside, Emerie." What had she called it, the action? "I want to *fuck*. I want you to shelter me as I come."

Would that ease how violently his seed was ripped from him? It often felt like he was about to release his very soul through his cock. If she comforted him through it with her snug inner walls, would it not feel so damning?

"Ingram," she warned, but the panicked hint in it was what caused his sight to open to the darkest purple he'd ever seen.

She looked pale, nervous... afraid.

He whimpered in need, but released her to dig his extended claws into his thighs to settle himself. He didn't want her to be scared of him, but he was shaking.

"I don't want to hurt you," he rasped. "Please... touch me."

Her eyes crinkled with uncertainty, before her gaze darted to his claws embedded deep into his own flesh.

"I want to. I want to ease you, Ingram." She didn't reach for the agony jutting between them. "But you're too excited right now for us to do it like this."

Was it because of last time? Because he'd flipped her onto her back and thrust against her chest?

He wished this desirous emotion didn't grip him so cruelly. He wanted to be calmer, for it to not eat at him the way it did. Did other Mavka have this problem, or was it only Ingram that suffered so?

He thought she was intending to abandon him in this pathetic state, until she soothed her hand against his sternum.

"Can I try something? Do you trust me?"

"Yes. Anything."

Right now, he'd say or do whatever, so long as she freed him from this.

He almost grabbed her in panic when she lifted off him. Emerie kicked her shoes and pants off, rather than pulling them up, and darted to her bag tightly strapped over his torso. He watched her as she pulled some rope from it.

Then she went behind him. His skull followed her.

"Can I have your arms?"

Although he was uncomfortable with the idea of being bound, Ingram still placed them behind him. She strapped his wrists to their opposing elbows, coiling the enchanted rope around his forearms to lock them together. Unless he wanted to rip his arm from his shoulder, he wouldn't be able to escape.

"Just... listen out for Demons, or that Duskwalker, okay?"

Fuck, he was supposed to *listen* to their surroundings with his body in this state? He could barely register anything past his lust-filled senses, hyper-focussed on her sounds, her scents, the sight of her.

By the time her hands encompassed the head of his cock, he

was so pent up that he whimpered. Even he could tell he was engorged, like every second longer he waited was punishment.

"You, uh, wanted something warm and wet, right?" she purred, her tongue dabbing at the seam of her lips.

With the fact she was kneeling between his now-spread feet, he didn't think it was her pussy she was referring to. Yet, a Mavka could hope.

Beginning to stroke just the first half of him, keeping away from his latching tentacles, Emerie leaned forward. Then she opened her mouth, poked her tongue forward, and ran it from the groove just below his head, all the way up and then back over the top.

His clawed toes curled at the intense sensation of her tongue gliding over him.

"You *licked* me," he grated, letting out an exhale of pent-up breath.

"Mhm." She nodded for emphasis, licking at her lips.

He also noticed that her tongue had collected seed by doing so, and that she willingly drank it down, tasted him.

Emerie did it again, causing the muscles of his stomach to tighten. She squeezed the centre of his cock as she stroked, then she sunk the very tip inside her mouth. It was warm, damp, and her breaths ghosted over him like teasing waves.

His arms tugged, wanting her to go deeper. To sink her mouth down around him until she'd taken all of his throbbing, aching cock inside it – and probably down her throat too.

Had she not tied his arms, he might have pushed at her head to do so.

Instead, he was forced to experience blissful torture as she licked and sucked at him, all the while moving her delicate hands over his hot, hard flesh. Ingram's skull tilted back further and further with each wet caress, his body wanting to rock and thrust.

The only thing stopping him from falling back was his tail propping him up, and the only things preventing him from bouncing forward were his legs, and her between them.

He was stuck, trapped by her.

She even kissed the sides of him, swiping her tongue over

the spikey yet pliable scales that ran down him. Each of her tastebuds teased him, greeted him, and she seemed to have absolutely no qualms about drinking down his lubricant.

Actually, she quietly mumbled, "Your cock tastes really nice. It's sweet and salty." Then she nibbled up to the tip to dab her tongue at the hole where his seed kept bubbling from. "Even your cum is tasty. It's like a diluted version of your scent."

"Emerie," he rasped with a shudder.

She was talking to him about his dick, complimenting it, complimenting *him*. She was swiftly pushing him closer, and the heated delight in her features made her appear giddy over it.

She was fucking killing him.

"So hard," she stated, worshipping his cock with her hands. "Such a pretty colour of violet." She sunk her mouth around the tip again and gave a little moan as she pulled back, like she truly found him delicious. "You've been so good tonight. So gentle. So patient and obedient."

A growl burst from him when his shaft swelled at the word *good.* "Don't stop," he begged, huffing as he turned his head down to watch her.

He was greeted by the vision of this colourful, pretty butterfly using her hands and lips against him. Her blue eyes connecting with his orbs did strange things to his mind, his heart, and his body.

"Did you like finally getting to touch me?" she asked. "Feeling my pussy, my clit, and making me come for you?"

His whine was acute as his sac clenched.

"Faster," he pleaded. "Harder, Emerie."

His groin was in agony, moments from giving him soul-soaring relief. So close to release, he could feel it in his spine. His scales, fur, and spikes lifted and softened with each of his pulsating swells, like ripples and prickles were dancing across him.

She moved her hands faster while squeezing tightly, her mouth licking all over the thicker head. Smacking sounds came from her lips.

Her scent was ripe with desire, like she was enjoying doing this. It only reminded him of what he truly wanted, of what he was missing.

"Can you be a good boy and come for me?"

How could those two words, *good boy,* pierce through the fog, and shove him violently into bliss when everything else had been a crawl? His chest dipped forward as he threw his head back, parted his beak, and roared, seed shooting from him. The corded muscles of his neck strained at the tension that stiffened him. His arms pulled to break free so he could flip her and thrust through his mind-breaking release.

Instead, he was stuck where he sat as she worked her hands over his cock, helping him push liquid up his shaft so he could ease the pressure. Each spurt was spine tingling, each one had his roar dying into groans.

Then he looked down as he jerked and huffed through the last of his pulses, only to find her face stained with ropes of his release. Her lips were open, welcoming the liquid into her mouth and on her tongue. She was flooded with it.

He shuddered at the perverse sight of her playing with his seed like this while heavy white ropes of it released from him. "Emerie," he whimpered.

She'd covered herself in his scent, marking herself with it, and it shot a thrill through every fibre of his being. She even fucking smiled up at him, like she was pleased that she'd showered herself in his essence.

The quake that rippled down him was intense as he grew enraptured by the sight of it.

How was he supposed to calm down after all this?

I want more...

He wanted them to touch each other more. He needed them even closer, until their scents mingled into feral chaos.

Emerie stifled a whimper when two fingers entered her abused pussy from behind. Even though she was swollen, tender, and oversensitive, she made no other sound of protest.

Instead, she just kept her eyes on Ingram's hand stroking his cock while she sat limp and languid on his lap.

She knew he pressed his fingers into her depths because he wanted inside, wanted to feel where he wanted to be, so it could help him fall over the edge. With his quiet groan, the veins on his cock thicken as he swelled.

She would have thought after multiple orgasms, he couldn't produce a large amount of semen. She was wrong, made evident by his current release, as rope after rope shot from him. He shuddered the entire time, squeezing her against him as he removed his fingers before his claws extended and tore at her.

Something had sent the big guy into a lather, and the sun starting to pierce her eyes meant it had gripped him all night.

At least he hadn't tried to squeeze that monster dick of his into her tender pussy, but she had needed to help him for most of the night. Her lips twisted into a smile at the fact he hadn't been alone in that, since he'd utilised his fingers for her pleasure between each of his own.

She'd grown tired halfway through and just let him touch her however he needed while he stroked himself. He didn't seem to care that he was masturbating over her, so long as he wasn't by himself.

He'd said he was content to do it so long as Emerie stayed on his lap – she took that compromise so she could just... rest. The more he came, the less it seemed to mess with his mind. He was more controlled after the third time.

I swear... he's the horniest fucker I've ever met.

She wondered if all his kind were like this, or if Ingram was just... different. She hoped it was just him, otherwise any female they set their horny dicks on might be doomed.

When Ingram was finished doing a good job of covering his own hand and both her knees in Duskwalker jizz, he started softening.

She took the opportunity before it was too late.

"I'm tired," she whined, burying her face into his firm chest. "No more. Put it away."

"I don't know how to make it go away," he admitted, still gripping its drained length.

"Stop touching it!" She would have tried to push it inside him, but the last time she'd attempted that, it had given him an erection again because of her touch.

"But it feels good," he falsely whined, burying his face against the crook of her neck and shoulder, rubbing it back and forth. "And you smell so nice – it keeps making me ache."

She clenched her already closed thighs together like that would help. "Awaaay."

The chuckle that rumbled from him was so carefree and charming, it dissolved any irritation she held.

"Okay, little butterfly. I will try."

He pushed his deflated dick down and his tentacles wrapped around it. Then he pressed both within his seam and held it shut. Just as he let go, a stray tentacle tip flopped out, and he had to grip it closed once more.

"Bloody hell," she cursed. "What an effort to put one's own penis away."

He chuckled once more, and her chest was warmed by it, followed by a tender ache. "It is all your fault. You made me wait so long to touch you."

Her lips pressed tight as her eyes narrowed into a glare. "The fact a Demon didn't stumble upon us so close to the Veil is a miracle."

"Perhaps all your screaming scared them off."

Her jaw dropped, and her face grew blistering hot in embarrassment. "You did not just say that to me!"

This time, he burst into laughter as his orbs morphed to bright yellow. "This is fun."

"What? Teasing me when it was probably all your roars that freaked out the entire forest?!"

She threw her hand behind her to emphasise their unnaturally silent surroundings.

"Yes," he admitted, before leaning back. He cupped her face with his cum-covered hand, which only mixed in with the dry streaks and globs of it already stuck to her. "But I have also never felt... this. I have not felt satisfied in some form, or laughed like this with someone who is not my kindred. Thank you for sharing in my desire."

Her blush turned into a shier one as she averted her gaze nervously under the heavy weight of his yellow orbs, as well as her own emotions.

"Please don't be charming right now," she quietly grumbled. "It just makes me want to..." She eyed his beak, her heart shrivelling a little. "I wish I could kiss you."

"But you did kiss me," he answered, tilting his head as though he was puzzled.

She bit at the corner of her lips and rubbed at her arm. "I mean one we can share."

He pet her lips with his thumb. "I do not have these." He parted them so he could touch the point of his claw to the side of her tongue. "But I can lick you."

That was Ingram, always looking for a solution or compromise to any problem she brought up.

As much as she didn't want to hurt his feelings, she didn't want to lie. "It's not the same."

"Can... we try?" He removed his thumb so he could place the knuckle of his forefinger under her chin. He lifted her face towards him. "I would like to try and share a kiss."

Her lips flattened. She loosened them and nodded, parting them slightly as she tilted her face in nervous welcome.

Ingram was slow as he brought the tip of his beak closer, and then opened it just enough to give her a peek inside.

His purple tongue wasn't wide. It was on the thinner side, and it was pointed to fit the shape of his mouth. It was moist as he slipped it across the seam of her lips, and she flinched at the strangeness of it. She wasn't used to something so long and versatile.

Definitely not a normal kiss.

He slithered it sideways between the small gap of her lips and then past her teeth. Her surprised hum was muffled by his tongue as he brushed it against hers.

Like he could tell she was uncertain, or maybe he was as well, he was slow and gentle. It vividly allowed her to feel him exploring her tongue and greeting each of her tastebuds, as he swiped over and underneath it lightly. It kind of felt... nice.

Growing accustomed to it, she met his tongue a little more

confidently, trying to brush it in return.

Emerie had always adored kissing, but this was very different. It felt odd to have a long, thin, and pointed tongue now trying to twirl around hers. Yet... a swirl of tenderness bloomed behind her sternum when he gave a quiet, satisfied moan. In its wake, shyness warmed her cheeks, ears, and chest.

The more she melted for him, for this dancing kiss, the more she realised it hadn't been the locking of lips she'd been seeking, but that feeling to radiate within her. There was still warmth, still wetness, and his sweet groan became hers to swallow until she gave her own.

Her eyelids grew lazy as she pushed her tongue against his more forcefully – like her flat, short one had any chance of taking control against his long, windy, dexterous one.

"Emerie," he rasped, grabbing her backside to knead it.

When his orbs changed purples, darkening, her eyes snapped open wide. She pulled back, yanking her tongue from him.

"No," he lightly bit out. "More."

Next thing she knew, his tongue was brushing against hers again. He also pressed more into the cavity of her mouth. She greeted it, melting for it once more, until he squeezed one of her arse cheeks in appreciation again while trying to bring her closer.

She pulled back and covered her mouth with the back of a hand. "N-no more," she demanded with panted breaths, realising she'd begun trembling with rekindled desire. "I need rest. I need sleep."

The sun was shining, and she hadn't slept all night. She didn't doubt she looked awful, likely with dark smudges under her eyes.

Ingram licked her palm since it was in the way, making it tickle. "Fine, little butterfly. I will let you rest."

Every time he called her that, Emerie had the urge to squirm in self-consciousness. It was too big of a compliment for her to swallow.

He changed her position by slipping one arm under her knees, while the other supported her back. He also tilted to the side so his tail could slip forward and curl around her waist from between his thighs. He shuffled over to lean back against a tree not too far behind him so she could lie on top of him.

Emerie eyed the shadowy forest. "A-are you sure it's safe for me to fall asleep here, even in the day? Wouldn't it be best to find a sunny clearing?"

She really was alarmed by how close they were to the Veil now.

"Don't worry, Emerie. I will protect you."

He said that, but... "Won't the Demons be able to smell me from a distance?"

She was a piece of bait, just ready to be eaten!

"They will not be able to smell you," he stated. She didn't know how that could be true, and she didn't understand why he'd said it so genially – like he was filled with humour.

"How can you be so sure?"

He finally chuckled, and she still couldn't believe how much she adored the sound of it. "Because, Emerie, you do not smell like a human." He affectionately brushed the smooth curve of his beak underneath her jaw. "If I was not so close to you, I doubt I would be able to smell you past my seed."

Oh. My. God! She covered her face as she whined and buried into the side of his chest. *I'm so covered in Duskwalker cum that not even Demons can smell me.*

I need a bath so badly.

TWENTY-THREE

"Are you sure about this?" Emerie asked, kneeling on Ingram's back while he was in his more monstrous form.

It still wasn't super comfortable, but she was getting used to riding him like this. She'd figured out if she sat just a little further up his back where his bigger spikes were, she could slot her pelvis between them. Honestly, it'd been an accident from when she climbed onto him – she'd been planning to re-adjust like usual, but then discovered she didn't need to.

She trailed her gaze away from the back of his raven skull and small goat horns to look at the descending path he was taking.

Bright sunshine bathed them and the Veil's canyon wall in protective light. The rocky path was wide enough to just fit his massive, hulking body, but it was a steep decline. She had to lean back on straightened arms or she worried she'd roll forward right off him.

"The swamplands are the quickest way." Ingram answered, his voice deeper and more distorted than usual.

The inhuman way his voice reverberated, like it was split into three different levels of bass, used to make her skin crawl. Now, though, it made pleasurable goosebumps prickle all over.

"Yes, you said that," Emerie croaked, her throat thick from the way her body reacted to his voice. "But is it the safest?"

While she waited for his response, she warily eyed the forest creeping closer with every step down Ingram took.

She wasn't sure if it was justified paranoia or not, but she swore she could *feel* a set of red eyes hungrily watching them. She tightened her Demonslayer hood over her head, hoping it was enough to hide she was human. Her uniform was stained in streaks of dirt and dried Duskwalker cum, and at first, she'd been utterly grossed out by having to wear it.

The closer she got to hell on Earth, though, the more thankful she was that it might be hiding her scent. Who cared if it was spunk when it could save her life?

It took her a while to notice that Ingram wasn't answering her.

Her brows drew together and her lips tightened underneath her mask. "Ingram, is it the safest?" she repeated.

"Nowhere is safe," he bit out with a huff, turning his skull so he could look at her from the side. *"The swamplands are one of the most dangerous parts of the Veil."*

Gripping two spikes on the back of his shoulders, she tugged. "Then stop. Let's find another way."

He shook his head. *"We cannot. The creatures that linger in there... they are no ordinary Demons."* He faced his skull forward to watch where he was going. *"However, other Demons are also afraid of them. I don't know if it is safer, Emerie. I know I can fight against one Demon, but I have... I have already learned that I cannot win against a horde of them."* Once more, he glanced at her by flashing the side of his raven skull. Blue orbs, filled with sadness and loss, were bright even in the sunlight. *"I worry that if I take you any other way, we will be overrun, and if I get separated from you, I may not be able to save you."*

"Damnit," she muttered under her breath, palming the side over her mostly covered face. She squeaked when he dipped and she had to right herself. "What are we going to do if we find ourselves in a fight? I don't have any weapons besides my dagger."

She hadn't put her weapons belt back on before the female Duskwalker stole her, and he hadn't thought to pick it up – only her bag.

"Just stay low, stay quiet, and hold on tight. Hopefully we

will not need to fight. The swamp Demons mostly leave us alone. If they try anything, I will run in order to protect you."

She narrowed her eyes into a tight glare, her lips thinning with them. He could avoid the ugly truth, but she needed to be prepared for anything that might come her way.

"Yes, but if a fight does happen, I'll be in the Veil, Ingram. Not only will I be surrounded by Demons, but you might turn on me. I'll be a sitting duck."

"Duck?" he asked, tilting his head in the direction of their path. *"You can change forms? And why would you sit when in danger?"*

"Ughhh!" she groaned, throwing her head back. "It's an expression. It means I'll be defenceless."

"If a fight happens... run north. Find the green or yellow lights, or the salt circle. They are wards belonging to three Mavkas, and the Demons cannot get through them." He halted and tensed beneath her thighs. He didn't face her as he said, *"Just survive until I am* me *again, Emerie. No matter how."*

Until I am me again, her mind repeated, pity aching in her gut.

He knew what could happen, that his mind could switch over into some feral, frenzied state. It hadn't taken long for Ingram to start developing a fear of his enraged self, and she was acutely aware it was because of her presence.

He'd likely once embraced that side of him, so she couldn't imagine how it felt to suddenly be fearful of it.

He doesn't want to hurt me.

And yet, his hands touched the bottom of the canyon and he immediately headed for the shaded and eerie trees of the Veil. The mist cloaking it was thick and white, making it appear like a haunted graveyard. Just staring into it brought on a wave of disquiet that had all the tiny hairs on her body standing on end, alert.

Emerie laid down on her chest to make her and her black uniform blend in with the darkness of his scales.

From above, and standing at the cliff's edge, she'd been able to see out over the Veil. In the short distance, there had been noticeable gaps between the trees where there was space – she assumed they indicated where the swamplands were.

It didn't take them long to reach them, but the ground had been miry under Ingram's steps long before they truly did. No Demons attacked them, and weirdly enough, she found that more disturbing than she should have.

A place even Demons are afraid of.

Rather than letting his hands and feet thwap against the sticky mud, his movements were cautious and quiet as he slipped through mushy grass. He was wisely moving in a swift crawl, assessing each step before he took it. Moss and duckweed on top of the water's surface gave the illusion that it was solid.

At first glance, had she not known any better, she would have thought she was above the surface of the Veil.

Since the canopy of leaves above wasn't thick, dappled, dust-filled light filtered throughout. The area was bright when she expected it to be dark and foreboding. It was serene in its own way, and quiet except for the odd buzzing dragonflies that skated on the cloudy water's unmoving surface.

Due to the cold moisture in the air and condensation from the sun, thick mist blanketed them wherever they went. Ingram, as much as he could, tried to remain in the sun, and she assumed it was for two reasons. First, because it was unlikely the Demons would attack them in it, and secondly because there was less mist to impact his vision.

She eyed the brightly lit, blanketed water they were skulking past. She knew, despite the light and heat, the greenery provided the perfect shade beneath the water's surface. Everything was still.

The loudest thing in the entire area seemed to be them.

Ingram's squelching steps and the tiny plops of mud that dripped from his fingers. The drag of his tail. Her huffing breaths of exertion from having to hold herself down and remain as still and unmoving as stone. Even her hair moving inside her hood was loud and scratchy.

A bird squawking from above made her flinch, and she looked up to find a swamp harrier's yellow eyes on her. It flapped its brown wings, like a threat or a warning, before squawking again. It flew off in the direction they were heading.

Why did it feel like it was following them?

Vultures follow what they think will die so they can scavenge. Emerie shuddered at the thought.

A dragonfly flew close, and she wasn't fond of it either, knowing the tiny fuckers could bite. To be honest, she just wasn't fond of insects in general.

Against her torso and hands, Ingram began producing a rumble that had all her muscles tensing. She bit back her fear and squashed it as much as she could, hoping to keep it out of her scent. Her eyes darted to the same harrier as it landed on a branch, rustling the leaves, and one fell to the swamp water on her left.

Emerie didn't mean to whimper, but when that leaf fell right next to a line of bubbles disturbing the duckweed, it escaped her.

She clenched her eyes shut and buried her face against Ingram's back. *Something is following us in the water.*

It was lucky the ground became solid for a long while, with the water's edge nowhere near them.

Just as they came to another body of water, Ingram's spikes lifted as his growl started back up. He lowered, backed away, and diverted to a new path. Since she hadn't seen any bubbles when they'd been approaching, she didn't know what spooked him.

That was until she looked behind them and gulped when something void-like in appearance had popped half its head above the surface. She'd never seen a crocodile in person – only ever in books – but she knew what she laid her eyes on wasn't... right.

The long scaley snout of its face appeared like a crocodile in shape, but its red eyes and short black hair *didn't*. It also had pointed ears and, when it dived under the water, an odd set of wings on its back was briefly visible.

She clenched her jaw so tight in apprehension that her jaw muscles knotted. Any harder, and she worried she'd crack her teeth.

How much further? she thought, wishing she could ask him.

The quiet was starting to really creep her out after seeing that Demon. It hadn't attacked them, despite obviously sensing and seeing them.

She glanced behind them even though they had long left where she'd seen it. Every part of her was on high alert and she wanted to scratch at her skin to make the raised hairs on her body go down.

Fuck. It feels like there are a million eyes on us.

Was it just the ones belonging to the dragonflies and the harrier that continued to follow, or was it the sinister creatures lying in wait just below the water's surface?

She shuddered as wet vines crawled down her back when Ingram was forced to duck beneath a low-hanging branch. *For the love of everything good in the world, please don't let a snake fall on me.*

They approached a section of dirt that ran between two different waters. One side was blanketed in duckweeds with bubbles right in the middle, the other was muddy and still. Ingram diverted to the mud side on the right to avoid what had made those bubbles.

The hissing roar bellowing from the mud happened at the same time a Demon exploded from it. Emerie squealed as Ingram released a surprised bark.

Mud flung on them in a wave as the Demon with the crocodile head from before flopped with its long fang-filled maw open to latch onto a limb. Ingram reared back and yanked his hand up to his chest just in time to avoid being bitten into. He backed up to the left when he landed.

Emerie knew a trap when she saw one. Since nothing came out of the moss side, it was obvious the Demon had set this one up. It was frightening that it had been *smart* enough to lay out a trap and wait.

Ingram didn't hesitate to sprint forward to escape, forcing Emerie to hold on for dear life. Behind them, a hissing roar followed as the Demon gave chase, sprinting on four short legs. Its long tail swiped right and left, tossing dirty sludge and grass in its wake. Its fluttering wings gave it some speed, but not enough.

It was slow, out of its element on land, and quickly fell behind.

She chanced a glance back. *Shit! That was a close one!*

When Ingram's left arm caved into elbow deep mud, he was quick to free it before he continued on. He was no longer being cautious, and in an environment where the ground was not as it seemed, that was dangerous. He was also being loud, whereas she sensed they needed to be sneaky.

That crocodile Demon had followed them through the water. What else would come and intercept them?

"Slow down," she pleaded, patting the side of his neck to calm him.

"We are almost free," he huffed out, diverting to the right just in time to avoid another Demon, a much smaller one, as it leapt from the water.

Up ahead, the world changed.

Across a sizeable body of still water was plain forest. They'd found the end of the swamp.

However, Ingram skidded to a halt in the middle of a large clearing. She followed his roaming gaze as his beak pointed from the left all the way to the right. They were surrounded by water except for the way they came.

There was swiping movement behind them from something – or many somethings – chasing them on land. Sticks cracked, wetness squelched, and mud plopped.

Oh shit, Emerie mentally screamed before flattening herself to Ingram. He was backing up. She only had enough time to really, *really* make sure she had a good grip before he sprinted as fast and hard as he could.

She'd known what he was going to do the moment she saw the water separating them from freedom. He was going to jump it. She just hoped she didn't break a rib again like back in Zagros Fortress when he'd leapt to the wall to escape.

Holding back her scream, she clung as he leapt.

Seconds in the air felt like agonising minutes.

They'd make it, she knew they'd make it – that didn't stop her from worrying they just *wouldn't*.

Her breath was knocked out of her when they landed, and one side of Ingram's body collapsed against the soft mud and dirt as he slipped. When they stopped slipping, she looked back to find a void-like figure on the land they'd just been standing on, staring at them with narrowed red eyes.

It didn't sink into the water to continue chasing after them. She wondered if that was because of the bright sun bathing them in protective light.

"Are you okay?" he asked, his orbs white as he looked at her from over his shoulder. He rose to all fours.

"I knew I could trust you," she whispered, wishing he could see her thankful smile. "However, we're still a little too close for comfort. Let's g–"

Before she could finish, a Demon shot from the water.

When something massive, dark, and horrifying shielded the very sun that had been protecting them, her heart nearly gave out. Neither one of them had time to avoid the eight long limbs that coiled around Ingram's midsection, effectively trapping her to him.

With a pained hiss, she only had enough room between two tentacles to see the Demon had landed on its side. It flipped onto its stomach, sunk its body into the mud to protect itself from the sun as best it could, then swiftly dragged them into the water.

She managed to gulp a breath before she went under.

The water was so murky that it was impossible to see, but she knew the important features of the Demon that had them trapped. She didn't think anything could be bigger than a Duskwalker, yet this octopus Demon was long, even if its body was thin and nearly human shaped.

Oh, god! I thought octopuses were only possible in saltwater! She'd grown up near the ocean, so she knew plenty about them.

She never would have imagined a Demon could become one. Nor that it could survive in the Veil.

Thankfully, the water wasn't deep. They bounced off the bottom and created a plume of loose, slimy sediment around them.

Emerie wriggled to free herself from between Ingram and the tentacles holding her down, but only gained enough room to yank one arm out. Her heart was pumping so heavily she thought her head was going to pop, anxiety making her lungs even tighter.

Bubbles burst out of Emerie as she screamed. The Demon rotated so it could place its hands on either side of Ingram's back and towered over her with a sickening grin not even an inch from her nose. The gleam in his red eyes told her everything she needed to know.

Considering what it was, and that it had probably been stuck in this swamp, it would have rarely eaten a human once it was fully formed like this. It was delighted it had one now.

Tentacles parted, forcing a gap so it could get her free.

Just as it grabbed for her head, uncaring if its claws tore her open, a dark-grey hand wrapped around its slim forearm. Its red eyes widened before it was yanked downwards and to the side.

A drowned shriek pulsed in the water, and purple blood mixed into it. The tentacles released her, giving her space to kick.

Nothing could have stopped her from getting the fuck out of there.

She looked up, and the reflection of light wasn't too far out of reach. She shot for it, sparing a glance down to where two frightening black creatures fought in a growing cloud of muddy sediment.

Wincing, her lungs feeling as though they were shrivelling without oxygen, she kicked harder. *There, almost there.* Just when she thought she wasn't going to make it, her eyes clenching as though that would help her air last, she broke the water's surface. Her gasp was agony and bliss all rolled into one, but it put her into a coughing fit when she breathed in water through the fabric of her mask.

She yanked it away from her nose and mouth before she waterboarded herself.

Splashing from her left had her frantically swimming to land when the Demon from before, the one that had stared at them from across the water, was slithering her way. It'd decided to brave it now that the octopus Demon was distracted by Ingram.

But panic clutched her like a set of claws when she met land.

Oh no! Fuck! The muddied edge was difficult to climb, like quicksand that swallowed her arms as she tried to crawl out of it. The ledge kept breaking off in thick lumps.

A cry of pain exploded from her when the Demon latched onto her shoulders and dug its claws in. It sliced down her back in deep, long rows, flaying her flesh open. Then it was gone, like it had been ripped from her.

She didn't care to find out if that was true.

Whimpering with pain-filled tears falling, she managed to haul herself onto solid land.

Warm blood mixed with cool water as it sluiced down her back. On her hands and knees, she crawled away from the crumbling ledge and then staggered to her feet so she could figure out where the fuck to go.

She searched, and all she knew for certain was two things: she was lost, and she was *alone*.

TWENTY-FOUR

North. Go north. Emerie looked around, bouncing from foot to foot nervously. The forest was the same, no matter which way she turned. *Which way is fucking north?!*

The ferocious, frenzied snarl from behind her spooked her into turning. Clawing at the mud just like she did to escape the water, a hulking form with red glowing orbs and a white raven skull greeted her.

Fuck. Her friend wasn't home right now, and she doubted she could leave a message on the door he called a brain!

Before she could react, the octopus Demon shot up behind him. With purple blood gushing from its throat and claw marks spanning diagonally across its face, it flipped Ingram backwards into the water.

Screw north. Screw this.

Whether the Demon realised it or not, it'd just saved her from certain death and had given her a small window to flee. It's not like there was anything she could do to help Ingram; she wasn't a fish, and she wasn't strong or fast.

That, however, didn't mean she wasn't worried for him. *Please be okay, please be okay!*

Emerie bolted in the direction she thought they'd been heading the entire time. Her back ached, and it sparked pain all down her legs.

But she could run, she could move, and that's all that mattered.

A roar vibrated through the forest and was so loud she thought the very leaves had trembled in fright. Soon she could hear the double thump of two sets of limbs giving chase, plus the intermittent slap and swish of a thick, long tail.

And, because of it, she knew for certain she was fleeing from a Duskwalker rather than a slithery octopus. *Oh fuck. Here he comes.*

Emerie had to veer to the right when a medium-sized Demon rustled through the forest. She was attracting them with the scent of her blood, but there was little she could do about it. Even if she didn't have them, her pleasant dip in the swamp water would have cleaned her of Ingram's scent anyway.

The cool wind cut through her soaked clothing. She thought it might tear where it stuck to her while she ran as hard as she could, trying to limit her movements. Her hood had partially slipped back just enough to allow some of her long hair to wrap around her neck and face, but she didn't dare swipe it away in case that somehow slowed her.

Just as Ingram was upon her, so was the Demon.

The Duskwalker tackled it, intending to destroy it so he didn't have to share his food, his prey – her.

She thought all hope was lost. It had to be. There was nothing that could save her now.

Something glowing in the distance caught her eye. Was it hope or more disaster? At this point, who cared? It was *something*, so she headed for it.

The closer she got, the more glittering green illuminated the forest from the very ground – like the earth itself was glowing. Even as she freely passed through a transparent green dome with some kind of nautical star pattern on it, she didn't stop.

There was nothing in the world that would have stopped Emerie from running right then. Not her pain, not her panicked and huffing breaths, not the burning muscles in her legs, nor the stitch in her side that told her she couldn't maintain her pace for much longer without collapsing.

She was in the middle of the Veil, surrounded by monsters, and her absolute favourite one was back on her trail. In a few seconds, she was about to be dead.

Ahead of her, the trees opened up. A *house* came into view.

A lovely, freshly made log cabin home sat in the middle of a tiny clearing like a beacon of hope. Then again, she wondered how long it would take for Ingram to break down the very wall like a freaking boulder to smash his way through.

She wasn't going to knock on the door, not when a monster could be inside it. What was the chance a human with the ability to stop a Duskwalker would be living there?

However, as she veered to the left to go around it, movement caught her eye, just as she caught theirs.

A woman, a *human* woman, gasped and dropped a ceramic container. With a shatter, blue paint gushed against the steps she'd been walking down.

Oh dear lord, Emerie had just doomed this woman.

All she could think to scream was... "Run!"

Where? Who fucking knew. Better than dying like a sacrificial lamb.

A bursting snarl behind her was the only warning either of them got before Ingram sprinted into the clearing.

She hooked a sharp left, hoping to lead Ingram away from the woman so she couldn't get caught up in his bloodlust. Her Ghost wouldn't be able to handle the shame if she was the reason this woman died.

"Magnar!" the woman screamed. "Help!"

No! Don't call for help!

A panicked laugh bubbled to her lips when she saw a second Duskwalker heading straight for her from the right just as she was passing the house. A fenced garden came into view. What were the odds she'd head straight towards another Duskwalker when she was trying to flee from one?

Then again... the whole point of coming to the Veil was to find his brothers. She just hadn't thought she'd be a bleeding piece of bait.

Both Duskwalkers leapt for Emerie at the same time.

She closed her eyes, tripped the fuck over from doing so, and landed on her face. She waited for the inevitable. For claws, fangs, and a beak to start chomping and slashing as they fought over her.

When nothing happened, although she heard the evidence of a struggle and the sharp clipping of a beak, she rotated to her arse. Leaning back on her hands, her chest heaving in and out with rapid, sawing breaths, her stark gaze grew riveted to the scene just beyond her parted thighs.

She frantically kicked as she backed up.

Above Ingram, who was clawing at the ground to get to her, the new Duskwalker had him pinned down by laying on him. His fox skull reared back to avoid being bashed by short goat horns. Somehow, he'd managed to thread one of Ingram's arms between them to keep him down, while his knees had found a way to pin his tail and legs.

All that was free was one arm and his head.

She could feel the fox-skulled Duskwalker's white orbs on her before they turned dark yellow in curiosity. However, a sharp backwards head-butt under his bony jaw had his orbs turning white again.

He lifted his skull back, parted his fangs, and let out a bellowing roar. It was loud, long, and unnatural – more like a signal rather than an emotional release.

The woman from before sprinted past them, running to the two Duskwalkers like a fool.

"Stay back!" the Duskwalker yelled, cutting his roar short.

Like she didn't care about the very serious and threatening command, the woman ran to Emerie. All she could digest about her was that she had short black hair that came to her shoulders, tanned skin, a plump, round body, and she was wearing a lavender dress.

Emerie was too freaked out by what was going on to think about anything else, or what to do. How was this woman so calm with two Duskwalkers here? Especially since one of them was in a dangerous mental state and the other one was pinning him down.

The new Duskwalker's antlers were imposing, and they seemed odd coming from his skull. He was also thicker than Ingram in body and had fewer bones protruding from his skin. At least, she assumed so, since he was wearing *pants*. His long and fluffy tail swayed side to side due to Ingram's wiggling.

Suddenly the woman's face was less than a foot from her own.

Comforting brown eyes were filled with worry, as were the crinkled lines of it in her lovely, rounded face. "We need to get you inside. Magnar has called for the others, but we need to get you away from the Duskwalker in case he gets free."

The logic of that only broke through Emerie's shock long enough to give her a reason to rise to her feet. With the woman grabbing her arm to steady her, she led Emerie like she was a horse.

"Delora," the new Duskwalker warned. "We do not know her. She could be dangerous."

"I don't care. We can figure that out later, after you heal her. Right now, she needs to stop bleeding before she bleeds out and we can't find out how or why she got here." Then she pointed to Ingram. "Please be careful."

Magnar... Delora... Emerie's gaze slipped from the woman to the fox-skulled Duskwalker who was battling to keep Ingram down. *They know each other.*

"Oh my god, you know each other!" Emerie shouted as she ripped her arm from the woman.

Delora winced as she fought Emerie's slapping hands to grab ahold of one again. Magnar growled behind them... at Emerie, for some reason.

"Please! I'll explain later." Delora tugged her along to the front of the house where there was a porch. "You're really pale and look like you're seconds from passing out." She gestured to the stairs to make Emerie sit. "Please, stay here. I'll only be a moment."

Was she about to faint? Right now, her adrenaline was so high she thought she could take on a bear if she really wanted to. Yet, when her arse found the steps and she was forced to wait on them, her eyelids began to droop.

She didn't even flinch when cloth was pressed against the multiple claw wounds down her back. Actually, they felt rather numb; *she* felt rather numb.

"I'm guessing you were travelling with that Duskwalker," Delora mumbled behind her. "You couldn't have picked a worse time to come here. The Demons have been running in packs, attacking us any chance they get when we're alone. You should have stayed out of the Veil."

Sight and sounds were growing muffled and dim, so Emerie couldn't distinguish if the woman was being condescending or was just voicing her worries and concerns.

Regardless, Emerie weakly gave a thumbs up to her. "I'll remember that next time I decide to come for a stroll."

Just when her head started to loll in grogginess, movement in her peripheral caught her attention. A fuzzy blob, as tall as he was monstrous, walked towards them on two legs. A whisp of white was fluttering behind him.

Emerie threw her hands up. Or rather, tried to. Instead, her hands only flopped between the gap of her thighs.

"Great! More fucking Duskwalkers, just what I need," Emerie slurred.

That whisp of white turned solid. The only things Emerie could detail through her fuzzy vision and the black swirling dots, was that the person was short, had golden hair, and was wearing some kind of pale-pink outfit.

"Oh, thank goodness," Delora rasped, getting to her feet. "Orpheus, can you please heal her?"

Delora quickly steadied Emerie when she sagged to the side, the back of her hand falling from her lap to thud against the stair she was on. Nausea bubbled as her head swam and spun in circles, causing acidic saliva to flood her mouth.

"Don't look at me!" the new woman yelled. "Heal her before she dies."

With a deep grunt, the Duskwalker placed his massive hand over her drooping head. It kind of felt nice, like it was stabilizing her. She even leaned into its warmth, since she felt like she was freezing into ice.

She closed her eyes. All she could sense now was her light panting breaths. Her ears were simultaneously filled with cotton and yet a thousand birds were chirping inside them – so quiet and yet so loud all at the same time.

Then cold pressure pushed into her, starting from her forehead. Her eyes flung open as her energy was restored, and all the blood she'd lost was returned in one startling and swift wave. Her wounds pulled until she could feel them closing from the edges inward.

When the hand slid away from the hood partially covering her hair, Emerie was left looking up at a towering Duskwalker with a wolf skull for a face and impala antelope horns. Blue orbs stared down at her, and for a moment, she wondered why he was... sad.

It was just one of the many strange things that had snagged her thoughts over the course of the recent events, but it was the one that she lingered on. She couldn't help it, not when he silently towered over her, blocking the sun and making it glow around the back of his white skull like an angelic halo.

It didn't escape her notice that, out of the three Duskwalkers she'd met so far, he seemed to be the bulkiest. He was also the only one fully dressed, wearing a black shirt, pants, and even boots.

He looks like a gentleman. Well, if Duskwalkers could look like one. All he needed was a fancy cane.

Sparkling in the sunlight, two charms dangled from his horns. Blue, black, and purple beads had been threaded three times in that pattern, with silver jingle bells on the ends.

They softly chimed each time he moved his head.

"Orpheus, you better go help Magnar," the blonde woman stated, drawing Emerie's gaze. She was looking over her shoulder towards the snarls and growls that could be heard, and it allowed Emerie to get a good profile view of her full pink lips, small nose, and flawless cheek. "He sounds like he's having a hard time."

She turned to Emerie, and deep-green eyes, like a forest, met her own blue ones. They narrowed disapprovingly, untrusting as those full lips flattened.

The fuck is she looking at me like that for?

"No, Reia. I will stay with you," Orpheus, the wolf-skulled Duskwalker, firmly stated.

She folded her arms across her generous breasts, pushing them up through the low neckline of her pink dress. Her arms were bare, and they revealed pale skin, like she hadn't greeted the sun much in her life. A sword hilt at her side glinted.

"What's more dangerous, an unknown woman or a Duskwalker losing his shit?" Reia bit back.

A soft growl rolled out of him that seemed more from annoyance than anger, and it ended on a defeated huff. He turned and headed towards where Ingram was still pinned down.

Emerie watched him leave, noticing the back of his shirt was wet and sticking to him from the inside, as though his back was bleeding. That was before his upward-curling deer tail fluttered.

She was beginning to get her bearings when quick huffing from her left drew all of their attention.

Just when she thought shit couldn't get any weirder, she watched a woman riding the back of a feline-skulled Duskwalker like he was a damn horse. It was also very similar to how Emerie rode Ingram's back, since he, too, also had spikes running down his spine – although much smaller.

He had backwards-curling ram horns, their tips jutting up past his feline cheekbones. His long, thin black tail flicked to the side as he halted, and the fawny-skinned woman slid off his back in a well-practised move. With the hilt of a short sword strapped to her waist, she marched towards them, and her long, black high ponytail swung behind her.

The woman was dressed differently than the first two.

Instead of wearing a dress, she was clad in a pair of brown leather pants, black boots, and a winter coat made from deer hide. She also had a dagger to go with the sword on her weapons belt.

"Okay. What the hell did I miss?" she barked, while the feline-skulled Duskwalker shifted from his monstrous four-legged form into one that was standing.

A pair of pants pushed up through his short fur until they covered him, seeming to come from beneath his very flesh. He wore no shirt, and she didn't think his pawed feet would have fit inside any pair of shoes known to humankind.

Unlike Ingram, he didn't have as many bones covering his body. His bottom two ribs were missing, like they'd sunken into his flesh, and only his knuckles were visible, rather than the entirety of the backs of his hands.

"Mayumi," he called with a whine, chasing two tiny blob creatures that were moving around his body with his clawed hands. He even lifted one of his arms to reach for his side. "I let you come because you promised you would stay out of danger and with Delora."

Both the tiny blobs let out harrowing shrieks before leaping through the air, only to be caught mid-way by the Duskwalker's swift and swiping hands. It was like he knew it was going to happen and was prepared for it.

That didn't save Emerie from jolting in surprise, especially when it seemed as though they were coming for her.

They kind of look like... little Demons. She wondered if it was the smell of her blood drying against her back that caused them to jump at her.

Since they wouldn't settle, he walked away while shaking his head. It looked like he had his hands full, with both of them squirming to get free. They continued to shriek, even over the distance.

Mayumi's brown eyes found Reia's face, then she lifted her upper lip as though she was sneering. Mayumi poked her thumb back at the feline-skulled Duskwalker, with an expression that screamed 'the audacity of this guy.'

Instead of responding, Reia glared at the black-haired woman, while nodding her chin at Emerie.

Mayumi's eyes crinkled into a narrowed stare, one brow a little higher than the other in puzzlement. "You're a long way from home, Demonslayer."

Emerie raised her arms as she looked down at herself, before swiping her hand over the top of the hood of her uniform. Understanding dawned as she pulled it off.

For whatever reason, these three women were living in the Veil with three Duskwalkers. Since she was wearing a Demonslayer's uniform, they were considering her an enemy of their companions – which, usually, they would be justified in that assumption.

Emerie laughed, and it sounded spiteful and exhausted at the same time.

She was done. The last few weeks had been a lot, and she

was too freaked out about running through the Veil right then to hold back the dam of her emotions.

The fact she hadn't exploded already was a miracle.

"Screw this," she snapped out, before pointing in the direction of Ingram. "I did not travel halfway across the fucking world with that Duskwalker, just to bring him here, only for you all to look at me like I'm the fucking enemy! Do you know what the hell I went through? What I had to do to get us here all by myself? I have almost died so many times I can't even begin to count! He has also attempted to eat me *numerous* times, and I almost drowned today because of a giant Demon octopus. So, no. I don't care who you all are, why you are here, or what your fucking problem is, but you can go and shove it back up your arses because I am *tired*. I am so tired, and hungry, and I just need five minutes to collect myself before you all start questioning me and my motives, like I'm being interrogated. You don't know shit about me or what I've done wrong."

Once she was done venting her frustration, she slapped her face into her hands.

That was probably the worst way to introduce herself, and it was absolutely out of character for her to have an outburst like that, but she really did not give a shit right now.

Everything she said was true, and she could still hear Ingram struggling. All she wanted was to go over to him and make sure he was okay because she sure as hell wasn't. She'd never been more frightened in her life, and most of that was because she feared how he would react when he came to his senses and realised he'd killed her.

Right as they got here. Right when this long journey was supposed to end.

It would have eaten him up inside, and she just knew it.

Maybe it was the strange but heart-warming kiss they'd shared right before they *both* passed out in the forest together. How she'd been able to feel a tangle of... something in it from both of them that probably shouldn't be there.

Or maybe that's what her stupid head and foolish heart wanted.

Regardless, if he felt anything at all towards her, she knew he'd be upset. He'd already lost his 'kindred,' so she didn't know how he'd take to losing a second person – and she'd be the cause of it.

So no, these people could fuck right off if they were going to treat Emerie as enemy number one after everything she and Ingram had been through together. Just for *his* sake.

She would have pleaded that she wanted to go home, but she didn't even have one anymore to wish for.

To her surprise, she heard a giggle.

She looked up to find the blonde, Reia, still had her arms folded, but her gaze was filled with mirth as she stared at Mayumi.

"I like her," Reia stated with a grin.

Mayumi returned her grin. "Straight, direct, and no shits given? Of course you like her."

"Sorry," Delora jumped in. "We probably should have given you some time to take this all in. Orpheus only just healed you, and I can only imagine how hard it was to get here."

Emerie reared her head back and pointed to Delora, who had taken a seat on the step next to her and placed a comforting hand on her shoulder.

"I like her," Emerie admitted. "She's nice."

"We're all nice." Delora laughed as her gaze fell on Mayumi and then Reia. "Well, most of the time. We're all pretty weird about strangers, and you *are* wearing a Demonslayer's uniform."

"You couldn't have gotten changed first?" Mayumi added with a chuckle, as if that was a realistic question. "What sector are you from, anyway?"

Emerie didn't know why that was important. "Eastern."

"Zagros Fortress?" Mayumi said while cupping her chin. "Wren runs a brutal guild. If you're from the eastern sector, there's no surprise you were able to survive. Don't let that go to your head, though. Hawthorne Keep has to deal with Demons from the Veil *and* the mountains."

Her lips parted on a small gasp. "You're a Demonslayer?!" Emerie yelled. "Why the hell were you giving me shit?"

"*Was* a Demonslayer," she corrected while folding her arms.

"I'm Mayumi, and the big guy you saw me riding in on is Faunus."

Faunus was nowhere to be found, like he'd gone into the forest to put as much space between Emerie and himself.

"I'm Delora," the woman, with hair such a dark colour of brown it almost looked black, said with a smile. She raised a hand like a student would when being called on.

"Reia," the pale woman said, nodding her chin upwards in greeting.

"I'm Emerie," she sighed out with her shoulders falling. "And, like I said, I'm hungry. *Please* tell me you have real food."

If she had to eat another berry, she hoped she choked on it.

"Sure, I'll get you some food," Delora said while patting her knee. Finally, some true kindness! She rose to her feet, but instead of running off, she pointed between Mayumi and Reia with her brown eyes narrowing into a fierce glare. It didn't match her sweet face. "You two, behave while I'm gone."

Reia threw her hands up like she was surrendering, while Mayumi lifted her gaze to the sky while whistling like a deviant.

"I mean it!" she yelled. "And while I'm gone, can one of you wash her back so we don't attract a swarm of Demons with her blood. I don't want to have to hear them howling all night." She visibly shuddered. "It's fucking creepy."

Then she was gone, heading to the green painted door behind them to go inside. Emerie still couldn't believe she was sitting on the steps of a log cabin home belonging to a human who lived within the Veil.

I didn't think people could live here.

She wondered if it was the green glittering ward surrounding them like a dome.

"She's scary when she's serious," Mayumi admitted on a laugh.

Emerie turned back to the two women standing before her.

Mayumi pushed back a few of the many black strands that had fallen from her high ponytail, like she had a choppy fringe she'd haphazardly cut with a dagger.

"Here, I'll wash your back," she offered.

She came around, knelt behind her, and wiped at her back.

She occasionally dipped the cloth into a bucket of water Emerie hadn't known was behind her.

"I don't see the point," Reia stated. "Her clothes are soaked with blood. When everything settles down, I'll give you some new clothes to wear. What size shoe are you? If you're a nine, you're out of luck, because that's my size."

"Yeah, and I stole all her sixes," Mayumi mumbled. "And I'm not giving them up to no one."

"I don't care," Emerie stated, puzzled about why the hell they were talking about shoes. Yet, the... normality of it was easing her anxiety, and she wondered if that's why they'd started it. She eventually shrugged and played along. "An eight, I guess."

"Long week?" Mayumi mused behind her, yet her voice was soft in comparison to before.

She let out a deep, exasperated expire. "The longest."

TWENTY-FIVE

Coming out of a bloodlust frenzy could either be startling or bring on a wave of grogginess.

For Ingram, who was terribly injured, his reawakening was slow. An elbow jutting into one of the wounds on his side caused a quiet whine to escape his chest. There was pressure all over him.

His red vision morphed to white from pain and confusion at his surroundings. He also didn't like that there were two Mavka around him, one standing over him imposingly, while the other lay upon him to keep him pinned.

His rapid breaths began calming. He slipped his head one way and then the other across the ground, trying to make sense of his surroundings.

The sun was bright, but it was descending over the horizon – although the forest would make that feel like it was happening sooner than it actually was.

To his right was a fenced garden, and a little behind him was a human dwelling connected to it. To his left were trees that were obviously thinned out by someone cutting them down. The grass beneath him was soft, and the freshly cut swaying stalks tickled the underside of his skull.

Once he observed his environment, it didn't take him long to figure out where he was. The green, glowing dome above filled him with relief at the safety of being in another of his kind's protective ward.

"He appears to have calmed," the fox-skulled Mavka lying on him stated. He gingerly lifted off him, but it was obvious he was ready to shove his weight back down if Ingram suddenly attacked.

"He has," the wolf-skulled Mavka answered with a nod of his head, stepping back to give them room.

"Hurts," Ingram choked out, his voice deeper and distorted due to being in his monstrous form. The release of pressure on his torso allowed him to assess just how heavily wounded he was.

There were many slices down his back, shoulders, and tail, as well as numerous bite marks around his neck. The multi-limbed Demon had been in his element beneath the water, and Ingram was surprised that he'd been able to escape him.

The only thing that had stopped him from drowning was that he was able to hold his breath for many minutes. The water hadn't been too deep, so he'd been able to kick off the bottom and leap out of the lake. Not all the way, though, and the muddy edge had been difficult to climb over.

He remembered little, but enough to give him some orientation of his memories.

Hissing shrieks from under the water, sharp fangs, and a second, smaller Demon that had tried to take his prey.

Prey... Ingram shot to all four limbs, knocking back the fox-skulled Mavka.

"Emerie!" he yelled, searching for the little orange-haired female.

A small distance away, her scent fluttered to him. If his orbs could have turned any whiter, they would have, when he noticed the tangles of blood in it.

He bolted in that direction, only to be slammed to the ground by the wolf-skulled Mavka before he barely made it three metres.

He growled at Ingram when he dug at the dirt to be freed. *Did I hurt her?* He needed to check on Emerie, to make sure she was alive and unharmed.

"Calm, Mavka," the wolf-skulled one snarled.

"Release me," he whined. His groan of effort ended with the

bubbling of a snarl.

Just in front of him were multiple humans, but he could barely see the bright glow of Emerie's hair between their bodies. They were crowding her and weren't giving him a chance to make sure she was okay from a distance.

She was quiet. Why was she quiet?

He didn't care about his wounds, not with the way his heart frantically pounded at him to check on her.

"Our females are there," the wolf Mavka snapped. "There is too strong of a blood scent to allow you near them."

Red filled his vision. He stopped struggling forward and instead wrapped his tail around the Mavka's ankle. He yanked back and to the side, surprising him just enough to pry him off. Before the fox-skulled Mavka could stop him, he slashed his tail to the side, colliding with his calves and knocking him over.

Once more, Ingram bolted forward.

He had no interest in the other females here.

Since they hadn't expected him to suddenly approach, they didn't have time to react.

He pulled one wearing a pink dress to the left and her blonde hair fluttered as she fell. The one wearing brown pants with her long black hair tied back stumbled when he pushed her to the right. The woman wearing a long dress and sitting next to Emerie on a set of steps flinched, gasped, and turned incorporeal like a Ghost when he gave her a fright.

His colourful little butterfly had just been lifting a spoonful of a liquid meal to her pale-pink lips when he got to her.

"Hey!" the blonde one yelled.

She was ignored as he reached down to Emerie, knelt, and placed his hand on her shoulder while the other one cupped the right side of her face.

"Are you okay?" He checked the front of her with his gaze, not seeing any new wounds but smelling the tang of coppery blood on her. His orbs reddened as hunger stirred, but it wasn't enough to make him fall back into a mindless state. It was diluted and stale. *"Why can I smell blood on you, Emerie?"*

The worst of it seemed to be gone, washed away, and he was thankful for that. He could breathe through it, and his worry let him fight past his gut giving empty grumbles.

Before she could even respond, he pulled her into his arms to hold her. Her liquid meal fell from her hands and onto his thigh, but thankfully, it looked as though it was almost finished.

Emerie gasped but gave no protest as he squished her face against his chest. With one arm around the back of her head and the other around her hips, he darted his gaze a full circle around him.

The wolf Mavka's orbs were bright red as he lifted the blonde-haired, pale female from the ground by scooping her into the cradle of his arms.

The fox one had righted the long-haired, thin female, whose fawny colouring had paled at almost falling. However, he was quick to move to the female who was now standing on the steps with space between him and her.

There was the scent of a third Mavka, but Ingram couldn't see or hear him.

"You almost hurt Reia," the wolf Mavka growled. "I told you not to approach!"

Ingram darted his sight to the female named Reia before focussing back on his skull. He snarled and held Emerie tighter when he tried to approach, and the wolf Mavka backed off.

He was injured, stressed, and was surrounded by humans that, with just one claw swipe across their supple skin, could send him back into a rage. They were wise to not touch him or try to pry the female in his arms away.

"I'm fine, Orpheus," Reia weakly laughed. "He just surprised me."

"Speak for yourself," the second female he'd pushed sneered. She pointed to her flat stomach. "Carrying precious cargo here. Last thing I need is to fucking fall over, then Faunus would be furious."

He figured by the scent on her, the Mavka named Faunus was the one who was currently hidden away nearby.

However, that scent did cause his sight to morph to dark yellow in curiosity. It was familiar, and the only one he was truly... comfortable with.

"Kitty?" he asked, tilting his head.

She smelled like the feline-skulled Mavka with curling ram horns.

"Faunus now," she answered, her brown eyes narrowing on him.

He has a new name? To be fair, he hadn't really known what names were until only a few months ago – when he and Aleron had received their own from Merikh.

They all have names. He wanted to learn them all, liking that they had individual identities past their skulls and horn variations. His being the best, obviously, since he was the only one he'd met without fangs, instead having a beak.

"Fox Mavka," Ingram said to gain his attention. *"Your name. What is it?"*

"Magnar," he answered, wrapping a clawed hand over the shoulder of the dark-brown-haired female next to him. "This is Delora."

There was a little flame hovering between his imposing deer antlers. Upon inspection, it looked like it was a flaming woman, who, oddly enough, had the same shape and hair as the female he was touching.

He turned to the wolf Mavka and noticed he also had a flame woman between his backward-spiralling horns. It was the same shape as the female in his arms.

He didn't know what they meant.

"Reia," the little woman said, placing a hand to her chest before doing it to the wolf one. "Orpheus. And the one over there with the frowning face is Mayumi."

He looked back at the tiny woman, since she appeared to be the shortest of the bunch, and saw she had her hands on her hips. She was still annoyed with him, made evident by her furrowing brows.

"Ingram," Emerie whined in his arms, although rather muffled since her face was cushioned against his chest. "Can't breathe!"

He loosened his hold just enough to give her some room and turned his skull down while tilting it so he could see past his beak.

"Sorry, Emerie." He moved his arm from around her

shoulders so he could brush his claws into the side of her hair. *"Are you in pain?"*

"She is fine," Orpheus firmly stated from the side. "I have taken her wounds for her."

"Taken her wounds?" he curiously asked.

"I have healed her, and in doing so, I must bear her wounds for her."

Oh. So that's why he could scent Mavka blood coming from him.

Ingram's sight shifted to a reddish pink as shame nagged at the nape of his neck. *"Did I hurt you?"*

"No, but a Demon did get me pretty good when I was in the water. I think you saved me, though."

"I see," he hummed, before shifting his form into his more humanoid one now that he knew everything was... okay.

He shouldn't need to run anymore and saw no other reason to stay in his four-legged form. She'd never stated it, so it was just an assumption, but he changed for her comfort.

"Your name is Ingram, yes?" Magnar asked. When he nodded, Magnar's skull drifted over the forest behind them. "Where is your twin? The bat-skulled Mavka."

The blue shift of his orbs was so swift and sudden that it cut down his spine like a blade of ice. He didn't know why he averted his gaze down to the pretty female in his arms, but he just couldn't look at anyone else right then.

"He is gone," he stated, his tone so cold with sadness that it burned.

"Gone?" Magnar asked.

"A horde of Demons came," he answered, looking down at icy eyes that crinkled into sorrow – for him. "I could not save him, and the Witch Owl would not let me. She protected me to stop us both from having our skulls destroyed."

When Ingram did look up, he noticed both their orbs had turned the same blue as the one that filled his sight. Even the gazes of the three females around him shone with sorrow and perhaps... sympathy.

The one who looked the most saddened by that knowledge was the one who stood by Magnar.

He didn't understand why any of the humans here, other than Emerie, would feel anything for Aleron's loss. They did not know him, to know the world was less bright and beautiful without him.

"Faunus told me about you two," Mayumi said, right before he felt her delicate and gentle touch on the rounded joint of his shoulder. "I'm sorry. I know you were inseparable, and that you must miss him greatly."

This was the first time Ingram had properly spoken to Orpheus and Magnar, but he and Aleron had spent many days and hours with Faunus. He was their favourite Mavka because he'd always been willing to play with them and teach them new things. He'd always been patient with them and, on the odd occasion, had chosen to rest with his back against the outside of their kindred cuddle.

Faunus had been an outsider to them, but they'd never known that he'd truly... cared. Not enough to detail them to another like this female.

Was this the bond the Witch Owl had tried to explain to him? That, although he did not know them and did not stay by their sides, there was room for fondness between all Mavka because of who and what they were?

It was too much for his mind to take in right now. He had questions, but he didn't know where to start or what they truly were.

"It is why we are here," Ingram said as he slightly lifted Emerie.

He wouldn't say it was fine or brush it off, when his chest always ached at Aleron's disappearance.

"Before we get into that," Mayumi said as she stepped back and removed her unfamiliar touch from him. "I need to go to Faunus. There is too much of Emerie's blood here right now for us to stay, even if we've removed most of it."

"She could probably use an actual bath," Delora added, curling into Magnar's side as she gestured to Emerie with her hand. "And some rest. She looks like she's been running for days."

"We have a spare bed," Reia offered. "However, she'll need

to have a scent-cloaking bath. We don't have a ward at our home, since Orpheus can't place one down for another eight years. The salt circle is being broken a lot these days because of the number of Demons scouting, so we try to avoid bringing more upon us if we can."

"Scent-cloaking bath?" Emerie asked, her brows furrowing.

Reia averted her green eyes as she rubbed at the side of her neck. "One of the Duskwalkers will have to wash you in order to push their magic into your skin and hide that you're a human. But, I'm guessing all of us would be pretty uncomfortable with that. So, if Ingram would be will–"

"No," Emerie quickly cut in. "I... can't do that, sorry."

Reia lowered her hand to shrug with it. "Then you won't be able to stay with us, and no one else's home has a spare bed."

Ingram noticed that Emerie's cheeks reddened as she squirmed slightly in his arms. He knew why she was against this. As much as he would have been delighted to do the spell on her, after learning if he could even do it, he didn't argue with her.

"I can just sleep outside." She gave a grin he knew was false. "I've been roughing and toughing it with Ingram for over two weeks. A few more days won't do me any harm, so long as you give me a blanket. I'm a Demonslayer, so I'm used to sleeping outside in the elements."

"There's no need for that," Mayumi said with a sigh, pushing back a few strands of hair from her face. She clicked her tongue. "We have a ward. Although our home won't fit another Duskwalker, I do have the war tent I stole from Colt's Outpost that we used while we were building. You can stay in there."

It was like they knew Ingram would put up a fight if they tried to separate Emerie from him. Maybe it was the way he was currently holding her, or something they knew that he didn't. Other than Mayumi, who was standing by herself, the other two Mavka were holding their females rather closely.

And they were definitely their females. He could tell by the marking scents that lay upon them.

Emerie's eyes brightened as her lips curled more genuinely. She turned to Mayumi. "Really? I'd appreciate that."

"Yeah, but you'll still need a bath before you come over."

"Okay," Reia started, stealing everyone's attention. "So, I'm guessing the plan is that Emerie will stay here so she can use Delora and Magnar's bath, while we go back to our place to fetch her some clothes and new shoes."

"While you're all doing that, Faunus and I will go back to ours and set up the tent and give you guys time." Mayumi placed her hands on her hips and nodded. "We'll reconvene with you all back here in a few hours. Say... just after the sun finishes setting?"

"Sounds good to me," Delora piped up. "I can cook us all some dinner."

Just as one of Mayumi's feet backed up half a step, Emerie tried to reach out to her.

"Hey," she grumbled, finding anywhere to look that wasn't either a set of orbs or eyes. "I just wanted to say thank you, to all of you. You don't know me, so I really appreciate you all for being so accommodating. It's not often you find such kindness in the world."

"We know that better than most," Delora stated with her already sweet gaze softening.

Reia snorted a laugh. "Ain't that the truth!"

One side of Mayumi's lips pulled up into a slight smile before she placed her hand on the pommel of her sword and turned. She headed off into the forest, and just before she could fade from view between a pair of trees, the feline-skulled Mavka intercepted to join her.

He'd been watching and waiting for her.

"See you in, like... an hour or something?" Reia stated.

Before any of them could respond, Orpheus had spun to take her away. His deer tail flickered in obvious joy at being able to leave, and Ingram watched as he licked her high, arching cheekbone as he walked off with her.

That left them alone with Delora and Magnar.

His orbs returned to their normal purple.

For some reason, that caused Magnar to lift his hand to cover Delora's face, as though to hide it from Ingram's view. His orbs darkened in their green hue, and the tiniest growl echoed through his fangs.

He flinched when Delora smacked him in the stomach with the back of her hand before she said, "I'll give you both some time before you bathe, since it'll be a while before we can change your clothes. I'll bring you more food and some water in the meantime."

"Thanks," Emerie grumbled as they went inside, then she lifted her face to Ingram. She gently brushed her fingertips against the corded muscle of his throat. "Are *you* okay? That octopus Demon sure did a number on you."

"I am fine, Emerie," he reassured as he tightened his arms around her. Somewhere in the murky, fast pace of his memories, he remembered chasing this female through the forest with the vile desire to tear her to shreds. How close he'd come to that... he shuddered at the thought. "You are alive, and that is all that matters."

"Why didn't you tell me there were humans here?" She lightly shook her head with her brows knotting. "It would have been really useful to share that with me. I could have been better prepared."

"I did not know the other females would still be here," he stated honestly.

He finally sat back so he could cross his legs and bring her into his lap. He curled his tail around his body so the tip lay near his feet.

"We thought they would eventually eat these humans." He lifted his raven skull to the green door and then the long, open shelter of the house in front of him. "It has been some time since my kindred and I were on this side of the Veil."

Emerie's pretty lips pursed, and she squinted up at him.

"Fine. You're forgiven, only because you did actually save me today."

TWENTY-SIX

Emerie lurched in the bathtub at the knock on the door, followed by someone asking if they could enter.

"Ah, no! Give me a second," she shouted, holding the wooden tub's edge so she could safely shove to her feet.

Her foot slipped out from under her just as she placed it on the ground. Her squeal was accompanied by her righting herself before she almost went arse over head. The door handle moved as though the person didn't care about her rejection in light of the alarming sound she made.

Emerie grabbed the handle with both hands to stop them. Then she was the one to push it down and poke her head through.

A set of forest-green eyes blinked at her. Reia's pale, yet sharp features were twisted with worry, so Emerie flashed her a grin.

"You're back," she said with a sigh.

"Yeah," she confirmed before shoving a blue gown through the small crack Emerie had made. She was unwilling to allow anyone even a slight chance of seeing anything other than her right shoulder. "Here."

Emerie took the clothing and shut the door.

The towel she used was more like a sheet. *I guess it would be hard to get an actual towel in the Veil.* Regardless, she used it, thankful she had something to wipe herself down with.

As she did, she looked around the dimly lit, narrow room that held little in it. There was a single potted plant in the corner, and a window above the far end of the oval bath that allowed a small view outside.

Once she was dry, she slipped the gown over her head and threaded her arms through the sleeves, relieved to find that they came to her elbows. The rest of it swayed just below her knees.

The quality wasn't amazing, as the material itself was poor, but it was well sewn, thick, and prettier than anything she'd worn since the night of her accident.

All I've worn for the past eight years is hunting gear or my Demonslayer uniforms. I guess I miss dressing more... feminine. It was a sad thought, but one that didn't particularly bother her enough to dwell on.

She opened the door to Reia still standing there. With a bored hint to her eyes, she held a pair of brown slippers in her left hand. Emerie's cheeks heated in embarrassment and then grew hotter when a brush was pushed at her.

"Sorry. I didn't mean to be rude earlier," Emerie grumbled, taking everything from her. She was quick to put the shoes on.

"Huh?" Reia let out a small laugh. "No, you're fine. I wouldn't want a stranger waltzing in on me while I was bathing either. Just heard you scream, so I got worried. I did have to stop this one from running in."

She hiked her thumb behind her, and Ingram's raven skull appeared off to the side of her. His orbs were their usual orchid purple.

Has he been there the whole time?

"He was sitting outside the door and wouldn't let me through at first," Reia continued, then sighed and shook her head. She threw her hands up as she turned to walk down the hallway. "Duskwalkers, so protective for no damn reason!"

She imagined Ingram sitting with his back against the door, barring anyone entry. As much as it would have been unneeded, it still made her feel like fluffy dandelions were sprouting in her chest.

Not long after they'd been alone, Delora had offered for Emerie and Ingram to come inside.

After they made their way in and were standing in the spacious living area, Magnar had explained to both of them how he would need to fill the tub.

When he said he would need to cut his wrist open and place a few drops of his own blood in the tub to form a warm water spell, Ingram had grown... distressed. He'd offered to do it, despite never having done so before.

Having to watch him use his own claw to hurt himself, then grow frustrated when it didn't immediately work, made Emerie feel terrible. Magnar had been telling him not to worry about it just as the spell finally glowed to life.

Purple glittering magic filled the drops of purple blood to turn them clear and then they increased in volume.

Her relief at finally being able to have a proper, private bath overshadowed how disturbing she found the process.

Ingram had come across as uncomfortable and nervous inside their home. He adopted a crouching position, balancing himself on one hand, as though he wanted to appear smaller. He also rarely allowed more than an inch of room between him and Emerie, and often made sure she was between him and Delora.

Honestly, she'd expected Ingram to be his big, imposing self. So, to experience him be so unsure only made her understand that he was not used to any of this.

She doubted he'd ever been inside a home that was furnished, let alone one that not only belonged to a living human, but another of his kind. It seemed like he was worried about breaking things, and his skull was always set on facing either Magnar or Emerie.

His spikes and scales had been raised in alertness; whether that was in fear for Emerie or just uncertainty in general, she wasn't sure. The fact he'd sat outside the bathroom door still didn't answer that question.

Ingram approached her now that Reia was out of the way, just as she pulled the brush through the tangled strands of her hair. Still low, keeping at her eye level, he sniffed at her.

He let out a sneezing huff. "You smell different."

"It's called soap," she happily hummed, feeling clean and fresh for the first time in two weeks.

"I do not like it," he said, causing her to smile.

How did she know he was going to say that?

"You should try it sometime," she teased, not that she thought he smelled bad or anything – quite the opposite in fact. Although, she currently wasn't a big fan of the coppery, odd scent of his blood, like it was stronger than a human's.

The bathroom was on the right of the hallway, so it didn't take her long to lead them to the open living area. She asked if she could take one of the ribbons currently tied to the hairbrush, and when given permission, removed it.

She placed the brush on the massive dining table that sat in the centre of the kitchen on the right.

Emerie didn't like tying her hair back, as it often revealed more of her scarring and the hair loss she had around her left ear. However, she wanted it out of the way and in a style that would prevent it from tangling in the future.

Pushing all of it to the left, she plaited it down one side so it flowed over her shoulder and stopped just past her breasts. At the same time, she tried to ignore the five damn stares that were obviously on her as she took in the house once more.

She'd never been inside a home with ceilings over eight feet in height, but with how tall Magnar's forking antlers made him, it was no guess as to why it was necessary. There was a simple chandelier made of timber, plain but giving plenty of light with its candles.

She drifted her gaze to the right where Delora eventually turned away to work at a cooking hearth, the counter cupboards next to it open and without doors. Directly in front of her was a big fireplace that was lit, giving the area a warm, comforting glow.

There was only one living room chair, but it was plenty big enough to fit a Duskwalker and human on it if they were to sit side by side.

Delora likes to paint, Emerie mused, since every bit of wall had some kind of colourful image or pattern on it.

Well, almost all of them. The one right next to the door on the left was of her, Magnar, and... a tiny Duskwalker? She wasn't sure since it lacked horns, but she guessed it was a white skull on a human-shaped, black blob.

She didn't know they could be small.

Against the large dining table that came to her rib height, there were two chairs that were small in their seating bases, but tall enough to allow a human to reach the table's surface. She figured they were for Delora and Reia, when she was a guest here.

There was a singular bigger one, which she assumed was for Magnar.

However, Reia wasn't sitting on one of two human-sized chairs. She was curled up on Orpheus' lap, who had chosen to sit against the wall next to the door – on the other side of the painting.

Delora gestured to one of the available chairs. "Sit. Food will be ready soon."

She did as she was told, and Ingram was quick to sit by her. She brought up one leg to tuck under her, not wanting it to dangle, but didn't bring the other up since Ingram had curled his tail tip around her ankle. He was being awfully needy, which was making her bashful about his behaviour.

I don't want them getting the wrong idea.

It didn't take a genius to realise Delora and Reia had intimate relationships with their Duskwalkers. She was just going to pretend it didn't make her extremely uncomfortable.

Not because she was against it, but because she worried they thought she had come here with the intention of building a bond with Ingram. She hadn't, and she wasn't so disillusioned to think that just because a human and Duskwalker *could* be together, it meant they *would.*

They came here for a reason, and Emerie was set on helping. She was temporary. Her reasoning was her own, and a big part of that was the idea of being a plaything between two massive Duskwalkers freaked her the fuck out. Ingram was already too much for her to handle at times, and if Aleron had less humanity than him, she just didn't see how she'd survive it.

That's if Ingram was right and he could truly bring him back, which she still didn't think possible.

She fiddled with her fingers as she turned her gaze down to the table's surface. She was at least thankful that Magnar had stopped staring at her in curiosity and turned towards Delora.

Ingram was busy darting his skull between everyone with dark-yellow orbs, whereas Orpheus appeared tense with everyone in the room, especially them. Reia was the only one who truly appeared calm.

The silence was uncomfortable.

The only thing that filled it was the crackling from the fireplace and the hearth, as well as the bubbling and sizzling from whatever Delora was cooking. It smelled wonderful, and her stomach instantly grumbled like a ferocious beast.

"What..." Ingram started, indicating with his claws at the space between his short, upward-jutting horns. "What are the flames between your horns and antlers?"

Emerie's brows instantly furrowed as she bounced her gaze between Orpheus and Magnar. "What flames?" she asked.

"You can't see them?" Reia asked, one of her blonde brows lifting. When Emerie shook her head, she let out a laugh and turned her face towards Delora. "I guess that answers if humans can see them or not."

"I had a feeling they wouldn't be able to," Delora muttered with her back to them, too busy making sure nothing burned. "I can't even see the string bonding you two together, only ours, and only Magnar can touch mine. It's like there are levels to who can see what."

Was Emerie the only one who was sane, or was she missing something here?

When she brought her eyes back to Reia, the woman had a funny look on her face, like a mix of humour and understanding.

"I guess you can't see the soul flames between their horns."

"Soul flames?"

"Yeah." She pushed down on the top of Orpheus' wolf skull as though to have a better look at... nothing. "Duskwalkers are soul eaters. I gave Orpheus mine, and it looks like me but made of flames. However, we figured out that only the bonded pair can see the black strings that tie us together, and other Duskwalkers and Phantoms can only see the flame itself."

"Phantoms?" Emerie rasped out.

As if to demonstrate, Reia turned ghostly in Orpheus' arms and began to hover.

"Oh shit!" Emerie shouted with her posture stiffening. She pointed at her, waving her forefinger up and down. "You're like Lindiwe, the Witch Owl lady!"

Reia turned solid and plopped back into Orpheus' awaiting arms, and he was quick to curl them tight around her with an annoyed huff. He brushed the top of his snout underneath her jaw.

"You've met her?" Reia asked, her features twisting into mild concern.

"Well yeah," Emerie grumbled, averting her eyes to Ingram beside her. "She's the one that told us to come here."

Reia's lips thinned, and she turned her face up to Orpheus. "I don't know if that's a good thing or not."

At Emerie's confused head tilt, Orpheus lifted his snout in her direction. "The Witch Owl is dangerous. She has helped us many times, more so now than ever before, but she never truly explains her reasons. All she says is that she is Mother."

"Yeah, she explained that you're all brothers," Emerie said, rubbing at the side of her neck in uncertainty. "I just promised to help bring Ingram here."

"You have not explained the purpose of these soul flames," Ingram butted in, his orbs an even darker yellow.

"It means that she is my bride," Orpheus gently stated, brushing the backs of his claws against Reia's cheek. "That she is eternally mine, in body, heart, mind, and soul."

"I... see." Ingram hummed, cupping his hand around his beak in deep thought.

However, his tail tip squeezed around her ankle, and her chest tightened so quickly and powerfully that it hurt. She yanked her foot away, causing him to dart his skull in her direction before she tucked it underneath her butt on the chair.

Her reaction hadn't gone unnoticed.

Reia's expression had turned dull but not spiteful, while Orpheus and Magnar tilted their heads. Emerie fought back with a broken and weak smile.

Just at that moment, the front door opened, and a billow of cool air pushed its way inside. Her relief at the distraction from their conversation was immense as Mayumi sauntered inside with a big Duskwalker in tow.

She'd almost forgotten that Faunus had a cat skull with backwards-curling ram horns. He was already in his more humanoid form and wearing a pair of pants.

It surprised Emerie just how different all four Duskwalkers truly were from each other.

Now that Orpheus had rolled his sleeves up, she was able to see the multi-spined, curving fish fins that lay flat against his forearms. They occasionally rose to their full lengths, coinciding with his orb changes. He had an upward-curling deer tail, and seemed to be mainly covered in long wolf fur and short deer fur. His horns were long and twisty as they spiralled back and up behind his wolf skull.

Magnar, on the other hand, was covered in a mixture of fur and long feathers that sprouted all around his neck, shoulders, and back. His tail was long, the tip just brushing against the ground, and appeared to be fluffy like a fox's. His fox skull was the thinnest out of all of theirs, but his antlers made up for that by being the most daunting.

Then there was Faunus, who had short fur all along his body, and little lizard spikes going down his back and forearms. She imagined they no doubt went down the backs of his calves like Ingram's too. His tail was long and thin, with short fur, and it was very animated as it curled around Mayumi's thin waist.

Removing their horns or antlers from the equation, Magnar appeared to be the tallest, with Ingram a close second, then Faunus and Orpheus.

Ingram was the thinnest, and had the most bones on the outside of his body, from what she could tell. Magnar was denser, but not by much. Faunus was thick with muscle, but Orpheus appeared to be the strongest.

They were each so different, even all the way down to what she assumed were their base orb colours.

Ingram's were purple, which she knew for certain. She guessed everyone else's by what she had seen the most from them. Green for Magnar, which often darkened in colour whenever Ingram appeared to be looking in Delora's direction. Orpheus' were blue, and even he occasionally had a green flicker in his orbs.

Faunus had walked in with bright-yellow orbs, and he was quick to dart them around the room as he tucked Mayumi into his side. He was the only one who had a gold-filled crack down the left side of his bony face.

"Did I miss anything important?" Faunus asked, his voice booming through the quiet like a hammer.

When everyone shrugged, he nodded. Then his orbs turned a fierce red as he approached Ingram so swiftly that he barely had time to react.

Before anyone could stop him, he'd shoved his knee into Ingram's chest, knocked him back, and pinned him to the ground with it. Ingram growled beneath him while pushing at the pressure of his leg.

Ingram's orbs mirrored Faunus', and Emerie knew by the coiling of his tail that he was deeply agitated.

Faunus let out a menacing snarl and separated his sharp fangs threateningly.

"Touch my female, or hurt her again, and I won't care that we are brothers." Faunus' thin tail swiped through the air behind him furiously. "This is your only warning."

Emerie was about to get to her feet and do... she didn't know what. She bet she could slam her entire body into his side and not budge him an inch. At least it would have been *something*.

However, she froze when Ingram's head tilted sharply, just as a little blobby creature crawled up and over Faunus' shoulder to sniff down.

"Faunus, you really don't need to do that," Mayumi said with a sigh. She approached to take a second small creature, no bigger than her hands, from somewhere else on his back. "He was just concerned for Emerie. You would have done the same thing."

His head swiftly turned sideways to her. "Yeah, but she's not the one–"

"Don't want to hear it," she cut in, walking over to the wide chair by the fireplace. "You would have done it regardless."

With a growl in her direction, Faunus eventually huffed at her, before looking down to Ingram and giving him a deeper and louder one. He lifted off and approached Mayumi, only to steal the creature from her, pick her up and sit down with her between his thighs. He laid back against the arm of the chair, with only one pawed foot touching the ground.

It was obvious he'd been here often and had no issue making himself comfortable. His position appeared relaxed and lazy, whereas Mayumi was stiff as she glared at him. She didn't move though, seeming to be content right where she was between his thighs.

"You made it just in time for dinner," Delora stated as she began serving up four wooden plates. "How was the trip over?"

"Shit," Faunus bit out, his tail swaying just beneath the underside of the chair, the legs of it high enough to allow Emerie to see the action. "We were attacked by two scouting Demons."

"I can't tell if they're getting more confident or not," Mayumi added. "They're pretty nervous about attacking us though. Probably because I'm a force to be reckoned with."

"That you are." Faunus hummed, reaching forward so he could brush her ponytail forward over her shoulder with his claws.

His arm linking him to her allowed one of the little black creatures to crawl up it and attach itself to her shoulder. As soon as it was on her, it tucked itself into the back of her shirt and formed an unmoving lump between her shoulder blades. The second, however, crawled over both of them like it had bundles of energy, even occasionally sneaking over the backrest of the chair to explore, attempting to get away from them.

Mayumi or Faunus would take turns bringing it back into their cuddle, but they seemed to do so absentmindedly, like they were used to it.

"Do you mind if I ask what those are?" Emerie finally spoke up, unable to bear another second of not knowing.

They weren't truly a black blob, but it wasn't easy to make out their features. They had four short limbs and chubby little bodies, but they looked very soft and squishy. Every time Faunus grabbed the more active one with his massive hand, his fingers dug into it like soft, moist clay. It didn't appear to have a proper face, since it was oval, featureless, and only had a point where it seemed to sniff from.

It had no eyes, not even a concave to highlight the potential for any, and she couldn't see any ears. Its mouth was just a jagged line, and she hadn't realised it had one until it opened its mouth and gave an annoyed whine at not being allowed to explore.

They kind of look like... Demons, she thought, surprised to find any living with the Duskwalkers and their females.

Mayumi's lips twitched into a warm smile as she stared tenderly at Faunus.

"Younglings," Faunus answered. "Or children, I guess you humans would say."

"You're taking care of baby Demons?"

Reia burst out into laughter, and Mayumi was quick to chuckle. Emerie looked around with an embarrassed flush staining her cheeks.

Delora's gaze narrowed disapprovingly with her hands on her hips. "That's not fair. It's not her fault she would think that. I thought that too when I first saw one."

"They're *our* children," Mayumi corrected. "They aren't Demons, but baby Duskwalkers."

Emerie paled as realisation dawned. This time, when she looked around the room, her eyes were wide and her lips were parted.

"You had a baby with him?" she said, her voice squeaky and high pitched.

"Yeah, happens when you let them turn you into Phantoms," Mayumi explained. She turned to Reia. "I'm guessing you've already explained the whole soul eating thing?"

As Reia confirmed, Emerie just sat there trying to process that.

Oh my god. She had a baby with a Duskwalker. She placed her hands on her cheeks while resting her elbows on the table to lean on them. *How is that even possible?* Her eyes darted to the corners of her lids to look at the woman. *Look at her! She's fucking tiny. How did he not break her in half with his cock?!*

Either Ingram just had an unusually large cock for his kind, or something else was at work here.

She was less freaked out by the likelihood that all the women here had been sexually intimate with a Duskwalker, just like her, than she was about this new information. And, by the fact she had a second child who appeared to be hiding and asleep in the back of her shirt, it meant it had happened twice.

Unless... "Twins?" Emerie squeaked out.

"Nope," Mayumi quickly rejected.

"Faunus has a breeding problem," Reia chimed in, her expression mischievous. "Made obvious by the fact they're about to have a third."

"Doooon't say it like that," Mayumi groaned as she let her head fall back with a whine. Her cheeks had even reddened, which came across as odd, since her features previously appeared cold and unfeeling when she was relaxed.

"A third?" Emerie asked, her lips parting once more in shock. "You–you're pregnant?"

No wonder Faunus had been angered by Ingram pushing her!

Faunus let out a shudder as his orbs flickered purple. He appeared to be holding back the emotional change as best he could. He was quick to place his hand upon Mayumi's stomach before sliding it up to her side to grab her and drag her closer.

That, in itself, was enough of an answer.

Delora hid her giggle behind her fist, as Reia laughed – even when Orpheus' orbs changed to a bright green in what Emerie knew was jealousy. Magnar, on the other hand, appeared unphased.

"Listen, when you've faced death like I have, you're pretty excited to create life," Faunus argued in his own defence.

Emerie eyed the golden crack on his skull, and something pinched at her chest. Then something that was said from earlier finally clicked within her mind. It was an answer to a question she'd always wanted to know but hadn't wanted to press with Ingram in case she lost his trust by asking it.

"That's how you die," she rasped, her expression turning meek as if saying she discovered how to kill them out loud could bring her danger. "If your skulls are broken, you don't come back."

"Yes," Magnar and Orpheus confirmed in unison.

"And he has already experienced it," Orpheus continued.

"Which is why he has the gold line in his skull. Mayumi and the spirit of the void brought him back."

"Spirit of the void?" Emerie asked.

Ingram's head perked up at that, his orbs turning bright yellow in joy. "We can use gold to bring another of our kind back?"

Ingram's question overshadowed hers.

For some reason, Mayumi winced. "I don't know. I'm not sure."

"Why not?" Ingram asked, tilting his head as the hue of his orb colour darkened instead.

"Because... it'd happened before a day passed from when I glued his skull back together, and Weldir, or, uh, the spirit of the void, needed to use my soul to help bring him to life."

"Why are you here?" Orpheus asked, cutting to the chase. "Because, if it's to bring back the bat-skulled Mavka, we don't have answers for you. If we did, we would share them."

"Oh," Ingram murmured, his orbs swiftly switching to a deep blue.

He pointed his raven skull towards the timber floor, as if he didn't want to look upon any of them under the weight of his grief and disappointment. Emerie hated that his shoulders and neck sagged in defeat.

"Aleron," Emerie quickly interjected, causing the other Duskwalkers to direct their bony faces to her. She squirmed under the stare of so many orbs and eyes. "Stop calling him the bat-skulled Mavka. His name is Aleron."

Emerie couldn't handle them speaking of him in such a detached way, when it was obvious he meant *so much* to Ingram. She wanted to give him life, and for him to be spoken of warmly, even in his absence – for Ingram's sake.

"We didn't know he had a name also," Orpheus said, and she figured that was his way of apologising. "We thought you named Ingram."

She shook her head. "No. I didn't." Then she leaned on the table more, laying out her hands beseechingly. She knew what she was about to ask was futile, but if Ingram didn't have the humanity to dig deeper and could only take things at face value, then she would be the one who would try. "Are you sure there is no other way?"

"We believe Faunus is a special circumstance," Mayumi stated, drawing her gaze. "And a lot of dumb luck, on my part."

"I will find another way to bring Aleron back," Ingram said, making Emerie wince at his determination. "But the Witch Owl directed us here for a reason." He finally lifted his head towards Magnar, and then Orpheus, as he said, "I want to destroy the Demon King."

A heavy, still silence blanketed them.

So heavy, in fact, that it made Delora pause just as she was placing a plate in front of Emerie. A sliced piece of carrot rolled off and landed on the table, and she quickly set it down before any more could follow it.

Ingram's skull darted around as his orbs whitened, likely unsure as to why he caused everyone to suddenly freeze.

Emerie connected eyes with Mayumi, who was directly across from her. She watched as the shock that had settled onto her features turned into determination, then she quickly looked down. She placed her hands against her stomach before her nose crinkled tightly.

"Oh, for fuck's sake. Come on!" Mayumi yelled, causing the baby Duskwalker who had been trying to escape to shuffle back to Faunus. "Finally someone wants to kill that bastard, and it has to be right as I'm bloody pregnant?!"

Faunus released a quiet growl up at her. "You think I would have let you face Jabez regardless, little hunter?"

"Well, you can't go!" she shouted back, pointing her index finger not even a centimetre from his feline snout. "I lost you once, and I'm not losing your big furry ass a second time."

"I'll go," Reia chimed in, and although her voice held a hint of excitement, her features said otherwise. Her brows were furrowed with concern, then her lips pursed – as if she was already trying to formulate a plan.

"No, Reia," Orpheus firmly stated. "We have spoken about this. None of us will face the Demon King."

"Yeah, none of *you* can," she argued, gesturing to the three Duskwalkers.

"None of you can come back," Delora muttered, so quietly it was like she didn't want to be heard. She rubbed at her left biceps. "But we can."

"No, Delora," Magnar growled as he stormed to her and wrapped his arms around her soft belly to grab the crook of where her arse met her thigh. "You cannot do this."

Delora turned incorporeal in his arms to escape, floating away as he gave chase. Her sweet features suddenly became sharp, and she glared the tall Duskwalker down. She turned solid, letting her feet thud against the ground, before pointing up at him.

"Yes, I can. You can't come back, Magnar, but *we* can," she repeated. "Even if we aren't successful, we will live to try again. You Duskwalkers, on the other hand, have a glaring vulnerability."

Reia attempted to push her way out of Orpheus' arms, only to be slammed back against his torso repeatedly. She eventually let out the cutest version of a human growl and turned ghostly as well to escape her latched-on Duskwalker. She walked over to the table and slammed her hand against it.

"We've all been wanting this from the moment he began specifically targeting us." She lifted her chin up at Orpheus, who rose to his feet and came over to stare down at her with reddened orbs. "Delora's right, and we all know it. Only us brides can take this risk without the chance of permanently *losing* anyone."

"You and Delora cannot do this alone," Orpheus argued. "You may be good with your sword, but he is an Elf! You have not fought against him. My skull may be breakable, but it takes force." He reached out to cup the side of her face, being careful of his sharp claws against her skin. "You, my little doe... I can shatter your entire body with barely the slightest touch. One hit, and he will kill you."

"And I'll come right back here, to you!" Reia shouted. "You said you wanted to start our own family, but I can't and will not do that when there are thousands of Demons out there threatening us and our children. I'm tired of waiting now, Orpheus. I'm ready to take that step with you, but I never will if he is out there, taunting us."

For a woman who, seconds ago, had appeared fierce, she
suddenly looked pale and afraid. Ingram's orbs reddened with
hunger, but he quickly covered his nose holes and turned his
beak away from her.

Orpheus curled his arms around her and gently pulled her
against his chest. His red orbs turned blue, but darker and deeper
than normal.

"I know, Reia. I want this too, but the thought of you coming
to harm again fills me with agony. I would rather have my skull
crushed than know you are there, alone and unprotected."

Emerie realised what she and Ingram were asking was... too
much. Even if they hadn't said it, each woman in this room had
fear in their eyes.

"They wouldn't be alone," Mayumi pushed, her eyes bowing
into a glare that held no animosity for anyone here. "If we wait
until I give birth, which is only in a few weeks, I can go with
them." She held her hand up before anyone could speak over the
top of her. "That gives me more time to train everyone. I may be
small, but I was one of the best Demonslayers in my sector."
Then she gestured her hand towards Emerie and Ingram. "We
would also have them. They both seem to have a death wish, so
if we have at least one Duskwalker on our side who can take on
Jabez, everyone else just needs to keep a horde of Demons from
him."

"We will go with you," Faunus declared, finally sitting up. It
seemed he could no longer lazily lie about while his woman was
considering going on such a dangerous mission. "If you think
we wouldn't follow our brides into a battle, then you are sorely
mistaken, Mayumi."

"And what about them, Faunus?" She picked up the child,
who was actively moving between them, and shoved them in his
bony face. "One of us would have to stay behind regardless. And
I'll be damned if you go and get yourself fucking killed, take me
with you to the grave, and leave them to fend in this world by
themselves. You wanted children so much, then you must bear
the weight of having them, even if that means you let me go to
fight a battle that involves *all* of us – without you."

The growl that rumbled from Faunus was as terrifying as

thunder – loud, and a hellish warning of the brewing chaos. Mayumi raised a brow and shoved their child in his face again, their little limbs flapping about but seemingly unbothered.

He huffed, pushed her away from him, and sat up properly to place both feet on the ground. He shoved his skull into his hands with his claws digging into the back of it.

"You know I'm ri–"

He cut Mayumi off by roaring, yet his orbs were white and the big guy was... trembling? Mayumi, taken aback, flinched and smoothed her features.

Emerie bit at her bottom lip in distress.

This was... unbearable to watch.

All of them arguing between each other, and revealing just how deeply they cared for their partners, was harrowing. Emerie was getting a vivid peek into their hearts and bonds, and she felt terrible that she and Ingram were the cause of their current grief.

"Yes, you're right. I get it," he eventually muttered, before placing his skull back in his hands. "But just the idea of you coming to harm, like Orpheus said, fills me with agony. We are meant to protect you, not the other way around."

"This is your way of protecting us," Delora softly said. "Sometimes we have to make painful sacrifices for the ones we love. Sometimes we have to give someone else something precious while we take on the fight and burden." She leaned into Magnar's side as she brought his arm around her herself. She turned her head up to his fox skull. "I've already done it once, for Fyodor. I want to do it for all of us, but as well as for them again because I've been terrified of Fyodor being out there in the world by themself."

"Fyodor?" Emerie asked.

Delora turned a pained smile to her. "Magnar and I have our own child, but they're fully grown and didn't want to stay with us."

Emerie's gaze flittered to the painting next to the door, and she realised it was a family portrait of all of them from when it was little and bearing a small skull. She couldn't make out what kind.

"Little raven," Magnar groaned, turning her so he could cup

her cheeks with both hands. "You are too sweet. The other brides, they are strong and fierce. You are not."

"You're right, I'm not very strong, or even fast, but I can be brave when I really need to be." Delora let out a laugh. "Mayumi said I'm a natural with a bow, and I can take down Demons from a vantage point if I can get to one. I don't need to survive, but just buy everyone time like I did for you when protecting Fyodor. I'll probably be the first one back here, I know that, but if I can help at all, I want to." Then she reached up with a gentle touch to make Magnar dip his snout so she could nuzzle it. "But you will have to stay here, Magnar, or accept that you coming along could mean that I don't get to come back because you'll be gone as well. Plus... I really want to show that asshole that I can look at him without trembling in fear, like he promised me."

Magnar pulled her off her feet as a whine escaped his chest. "I don't know how to convince you otherwise."

He held Delora like she was the most precious and delicate thing in the world, and she embraced him as though he wasn't a terrifying monster.

"So, is it settled?" Reia asked.

"No. I will not allow it," Orpheus growled. "I have spent all my life waiting for you. I told myself when I finally found my bride, I would not let her come to harm, and yet I have already had you *die* and wither into ash in my arms."

"I will go without you, Orpheus. You can either give me your blessing, or I'll borrow some of Mayumi's enchanted rope and tie you to the bed and leave."

"You forget." He pointed a claw at her face threateningly, but it felt empty of actual potential for harm. His tone was dark and menacing as he said, "It's a four-day walk just to his castle for a Mavka. You will return to me by the end of the first day, my little doe."

Reia shrugged her right shoulder. "I'm sure we can figure something out. I will go, Orpheus, without you. Accept it."

With a ferocious snarl and his orbs flaring red again, Orpheus turned and stormed away to leave. Emerie didn't know if anyone else noticed it, but just as he was shoving himself through the threshold, his orbs morphed to a stark white before he slammed the door behind him.

Reia's lips were tight, and now that he was gone, tears filled her eyes. She looked extremely hurt, and perhaps even a little betrayed by his leaving. She took a single step forward to chase after him, only to stop and clench her hands into fists at her sides.

"Give him some time, Reia," Delora soothed, as Magnar put her down.

"I know why he's against it," she said after releasing her clenched jaw. "I know it's because he's tired of seeing pain and death come to the humans he's kept, but our future is stuck in this fucked-up limbo, and I already can't take it. He's too afraid to try in case something permanent happens to me, but he asked for my soul *knowing* I can't sit still with the Demons around us." Then she slowly spun to them with her arm crossed over her stomach, as though it was tied into knots. "He's also never just... left like that."

All Emerie could do was sit in silence, and she was thankful Ingram had chosen to do the same.

What could she say?

She never could have imagined this was just as important to them as it was for Ingram. Not because they wanted to make a better world, but because they wanted to make a safer one for themselves.

This had obviously been a discussion they'd all tentatively had before, but they'd never had a Duskwalker offer their life up like this. Emerie knew she was irrelevant in the equation. She was a measly human, and likely wouldn't be anything more than a piece of bait.

Of course she hoped she would live, but the chances looked slim. Not enough to deter her, but enough that she knew she had to be smart in order to survive.

Weirdly though, as much as that should terrify her... it didn't.

Maybe if she had thought it was futile, she would have clung desperately to life and figured out a different way to save her own skin. A better, easier path. But, as she looked around the room and took everyone in, while they seemed to have forgotten completely about her presence, something blossomed in her chest.

They were strangers to her, yet the love they held for each other was so beautiful, adoring, and... pure, that she wanted – all the way down to her own flame soul – to preserve it.

The feeling deepened when Delora brought Reia in for a comforting hug. It was obvious the blonde-haired woman was trying her hardest to fight back tears – Delora already sprouting many. Even Magnar had come forward to wrap his arm around his bride's side, while placing his large hand on Reia's slim shoulder.

He cared for her, was comforting her, even though she wasn't his female.

Mayumi was kneeling on the lounge now with her arms wrapped around Faunus' shoulders from behind, with her face buried into the side of his neck. He still had his feline skull in his hands, like he couldn't bear to lift it under the weight of the truth that had just been placed on him. He knew he needed to stay behind for their children and let Mayumi face this battle without him.

Not even Emerie could see another way out of this, and it didn't even seem as though it would work. This would be an attempt, nothing more.

If they succeeded, they succeeded, but they were all so desperate for a solution that everyone was willing to try *something*. Even if that something meant pain for the ones they loved dearly, and for themselves.

TWENTY-SEVEN

Lying on their sides, Ingram held Emerie in his arms while a multitude of questions bombarded his mind.

After Orpheus' abrupt exit, Mayumi had suggested they leave the conversation for the time being and return to their home once all the females were finished eating. Emerie and Ingram had followed.

He now understood why they were afraid.

Even in their travel between the homes, there was a torrent of Demons waiting. Both he and Faunus had needed to sprint at their fastest speeds in their monstrous forms, just to avoid being harmed. They had been carrying humans, and the Demons had sought to attack and separate them.

Mayumi, who could escape by turning into a Ghost, faced little issue with this. Emerie, on the other hand... Faunus and Mayumi had taken a place at their side to help protect the vulnerable female.

Then, when they arrived, Faunus shifted back to his more humanoid form, and picked up Mayumi in his arms. He nodded his skull towards a tent some distance away from their home. Mayumi wanted to personally show them inside, but Faunus had stolen his bride away with orbs still blue like he couldn't shake his sadness and fear.

After Emerie changed into something called a *sleep gown*, kicking him out in the process, she'd laid down. Ingram had been quick to curl around her small form as she huddled on a sleeping bag and pillow, and had a blanket around her. She'd put up no fight, and instead curled into him.

He liked that she was small.

Her knees were able to lock in against his groin and abdomen, while his own sheltered her from beneath. With her head on his elbow, her arms cupped between them, she blinked her orange lashes with alertness.

"I feel really bad for upsetting them all," Emerie grumbled before her bottom lip pouted forward.

Since she'd untied her hair so she could comfortably sleep, he was given the freedom to brush his claws through the long, silky strands.

He looked around as he answered her, noting the lack of furniture other than their sleeping arrangements and a tree stump Emerie had already begun using as a table.

"Why?" he asked. "These are their own choices."

He was thankful she was lying on his elbow so he could easily see her features pucker up at him.

"Not really. None of the Duskwalkers are happy about the girls going to battle without them, and Reia is threatening to take Orpheus' choice away." The corners of her eyes crinkled. "I think I feel bad for her the most. You can tell she really wants his blessing, but she also wants to do this for them, for all of them."

"I could smell their fear," he admitted.

It was strange, though. Yes, all the females' fear had made his gut churn with hunger, but it was the other Mavka's fear that overshadowed it. Their fear did not make him hunger, twisting his stomach instead.

He continued to brush Emerie's hair, finding the action soothing.

"But the females are right. This will make the world safer for all of them. I will be by their side."

"So will I, but that doesn't really make a difference. I don't really have anything left to lose in my life, but they do."

Her words pinched at his chest, and he lifted his skull so he could use his beak to hide his orb change. He hoped the blue glow of them wasn't visible against the tent's rough floor or walls.

I... do not want her to come to harm. Somewhere along the way, he'd begun to care for Emerie. He hadn't thought it would be possible for him to truly care for anyone besides his kindred.

I also do not want the other Mavka and their brides to come to harm. Their bonds seemed just as deep as the one he'd shared with Aleron, but totally different.

Perhaps it was because his heart was born already full of Aleron that he'd never needed anyone else. He didn't know if he was allowed to have a deep bond with someone outside of his kindred.

I only have one heart.

And each beat of it told him to avenge his kindred. Each beat told him to do whatever it took to bring him back to life. Each beat bled agony into his veins, and all his mind could think to fix it was to kill Jabez, the Demon King, and then find a way to be sheltered within his Aleron's strong, fluffy, encompassing wings.

Yet... an invisible force bit at him constantly. With sharp fangs, it threatened him from the inside to keep this pretty little butterfly safe and protected, or it would eat him alive.

He didn't know what that meant, or why.

"I do not want you to come," Ingram finally admitted. "You should stay here, where it is safe, until I return."

A soft, warm, and delicate hand wrapped around his beak and tugged his skull down. Her glare was fierce, and adorable.

"Don't even think about it. If you go, I go, that's our deal. I didn't come all the way to the Veil just to sit around twiddling my thumbs. You want to avenge Aleron, and I want to avenge Gideon. You don't get to take that choice away from me."

"But you are not a Phantom," he quietly argued. "You don't come back if you die."

Emerie shrugged. "No, but I am the only human here that knows you. I may be the only one who can direct you to the Demon King if you go into a bloodlust, Ingram. You're doing this for Aleron, so don't worry about me. I'll figure out a way to survive, just like I figured out a way to get us here safe-*ish*."

Ingram wanted to argue with her but fell silent.

I want Aleron back more than anything... or anyone? Did he want his kindred back more than he wanted to keep Emerie alive?

His sight turning a darker blue made him unsure, especially when he didn't know how to answer that question.

But my heart is already full of Aleron. Both cannot fit in it... can they?

Emerie stared down at the little baby Duskwalker who was sitting on top of the table, sniffing up at her with the oval point of their face. Thicker than the rest of it, two slitted nose holes opened and closed as they huffed.

Mayumi had already explained that everyone preferred to call baby Duskwalkers *they* or *them*, since they didn't have a gender when they were born. Apparently the first human they ate would dictate their sex, so until then, they were considered androgynous.

They had no distinguishable features, lacked eyes, had jagged lines for sharp teeth and lips, and were such a dark grey that they almost appeared black. They were baby-shaped, and yet their softness made them sag into blobby creatures as if they didn't have any bones or organs.

A clean slate of nothingness.

How the hell can you look so cute and yet so creepy at the same damn time?

Part of her wanted to push them away, another wanted to curl them into her arms and sing them a lullaby.

Mayumi and Faunus' home was large, spacious, and had not a single other room or wall besides the outside ones. Everything had been placed into one open area, as if neither truly wanted nor needed privacy from each other.

A thick, dense mat had been rolled up and placed against the wall to make room on the floor, and she assumed that was their bed. It was close to the fireplace on the far-right wall, which was farthest from the front door she was currently facing. There was a back door that led straight into a garden, and to the left of it was the kitchen with open cabinets.

Emerie was seated at a large table that appeared to be able to fit the height of a Duskwalker, with a chair to match. There were two other smaller chairs, and she'd seen outside that a third was being made – one for each of the brides, she figured.

Two were filled currently, as Reia sat quietly across from her with Orpheus nowhere to be seen.

There was a *massive* bag chair, likely filled with wool, which Faunus was already sitting in and watching Mayumi from. It didn't escape her notice that it was far from the fireplace, whereas a smaller version was much closer.

His feet were against the floor, his knees bent, with his arms slightly flopping to the sides. She could tell, if he chose to, he could have curled up and lain completely within it.

There wasn't much else in the house in terms of furniture or decorations, but there was an impressive collection of weapons piled up to one side. A few had been fixed to the wooden walls by hooks and could easily be taken down.

The house was tall enough, she thought even Magnar's imposing antlers wouldn't come close to scraping the flat ceiling. In one corner of it there was a hatch with an attached ladder that led to an attic space.

The baby Duskwalker in front of her bawked up at her, and Emerie reached forward hesitantly to pat it.

"I wouldn't get any closer if I were you," Mayumi said as she moved around a small kitchen.

Emerie backed up and turned her face to the woman. "Why?"

Mayumi climbed down from a step stool after reaching for something from a top shelf. It was obvious it'd been made for Faunus' height.

"Because," Mayumi said, glancing back at her, "that one bites."

That made Emerie stiffen.

With another bawk, the little Duskwalker opened their gaping maw on a yawn. Their purple tongue swiped across their entire face, and it oddly reminded her of a gecko licking its eye.

"We've taken to naming them what they're like," Faunus stated from his bag chair. His tail tapped and curled against the ground lazily, even when he moved to stroke his hand down the one lying on his sternum. "That one's Bitey, this one is Sleepy."

Her features crinkled into a frown. "You're not going to give them proper names?"

Faunus shrugged as he let out the weirdest, snapping meow, and Bitey squealed as they bolted for him. They were surprisingly spritely and speedy.

"I was called Kitty for a long time until Mayumi gave me a new name. I was called something else by my mother, but I don't remember it, and I don't care to. They will also forget, so what's the point when I would rather meet them and learn their proper names after they have found them?"

Emerie guessed that was one way to look at it.

Her gaze drifted to Ingram sitting on the floor by her, and he was staring at the babies across the room with dark-yellow orbs of curiosity. He'd tried to figure out a way to sit comfortably on the chair at the dining table but had been unsuccessful due to the thick, wide base of his tail.

Apparently, it was also the reason they hadn't shoved a pair of pants at him, since it would just get in the way.

Once he turned his curious gaze to Emerie, she averted her eyes as quickly as possible. *Don't get any ideas, Duskwalker.* To avoid him, she chose to look at Reia, who was just staring at the table with a heart-wrenching, despondent gaze.

She seemed lost, which was so different to the overconfident woman she'd met yesterday. By the dark and noticeable smudges under her eyes in comparison to her general paleness, it didn't seem like she'd slept well.

She's really upset that Orpheus didn't return last night.

She'd stayed at Delora and Magnar's home in order to give Orpheus space. She'd come here this morning, since Emerie and Ingram were already imposing on Mayumi and Faunus.

"I know I said it when you waltzed in here, but I'll say it again." Mayumi regarded her morose friend shrewdly as she laid down a berry porridge in front of each of them. "You look like shit, Reia. Go home."

"I can't do that," Reia said while shaking her head. She reached for her spoon to play with her food, rather than eat it.

"I'm sure Orpheus would prefer you near," Mayumi rebutted while climbing onto the big chair that was obviously made for Faunus. "Out of all the Duskwalkers, he's the most... clingy."

"I know," she mumbled, plopping porridge into her bowl. "Which is why, if he wanted me with him right now, he would have collected me from Delora's. I *really* miss him, but I'm worried if I go home, he'll just want more space and go off by himself into the Veil. I don't want him to endanger himself."

Emerie's eyes crinkled in sympathy for her, yet she found Reia's care for Orpheus sweet. She was willing to put herself through a tough situation and be away from him, just to make sure he remained safe.

Mayumi's lips tightened, but she didn't argue back.

Like he didn't care for the conversation, Ingram reached up to steal Emerie's bowl before she could dig into it. He pressed the tip of his claw into her food and stole a piece of fruit with the very point.

"What is this called?" he asked, eyeing the red berry he'd taken. He sniffed at the freshly cut open half.

Emerie took her bowl back and then placed it as far from him as she could. Porridge was one of her favourite breakfasts, and she'd be damned if she let this Duskwalker play with it.

"It's a strawberry," Reia muttered, as if she was used to having to answer random questions.

"A strawberry. I see..." He placed his other hand over his beak in thought, before gesturing it towards Emerie. "This smells like you, along with something else, but I am not sure what. A flower of some kind. It is nice to have a name for it."

"I smell like strawberries and a flower?"

"Delora has a bunch of flowers at her place," Mayumi said around a mouthful of food, chewing obnoxiously. "Maybe go through her garden and see if you can find it."

Emerie just looked at her, bewildered, unsure of why she was encouraging this weird conversation. Noticing this, Mayumi's eyes crinkled with humour.

Faunus lifted his head to look at them. "I don't smell

strawberries from her, but I do smell a hint of primrose." He plopped his head back down. "Mayumi smells better. Like pumpkin and sleep."

"How can a person smell like sleep?" Ingram asked with his head tilting.

"I don't know the name of the second half of her scent, but I can only explain how it makes me feel. One day, I will find what else she smells like." He hunkered down further into his cushioning seat. "Until then... I will continue to rest peacefully with it."

Emerie shook her head, obviously puzzled, which caught Reia's attention. "Just ignore it," Reia murmured. "It's a thing they all have. Magnar says I smell like sticks and thorns, but Orpheus says I smell like roses and elderberries. They're scent orientated creatures, and we just let them muse over it, so long as it makes them happy."

"Might be because they're born with their noses and ears first," Mayumi chimed in.

A short pause of silence fell over them. The women ate, while Faunus rested back with his children, and Ingram remained fascinated by the strawberry. He even began picking the seeds from the outside of it in curiosity.

Reia was the one to break the quiet. "Hey. So, I was thinking," she said lowly. "If we're going to go after Jabez, Emerie is going to be in some real big danger."

"Yeah, I was thinking about that too," Mayumi muttered back.

Reia's green eyes connected with Emerie's. "I'm going to give you my diadem. It's enchanted to protect the wearer from smaller and most medium-sized Demons touching them. Big ones will still be able to grab you, but none of them, no matter how strong, can touch the diadem itself. Not even Jabez."

Reia wasn't wearing it now, so Emerie didn't know what she was speaking of, but she'd take anything if it allowed her to breathe another day.

"That's a good idea. There's no point in any of us wearing it when we can just turn into a Phantom to protect ourselves." Mayumi then nodded in the direction of her weapons. "You're welcome to take whatever weapon suits you best. I went back to Hawthorne Keep and stole a bunch since I know all the secret tunnels and can just move through doors and shit. I have everything from spears, bows, swords, to whips."

"You still need to figure out how to keep that teleporting bastard still," Faunus growled out. "Otherwise, you won't be able to touch him since he'll just disappear from your hands."

"Not really," Reia answered slowly, while drifting her tired gaze to him. "Delora said that when she grabbed his hair, she teleported with him."

Mayumi's brows furrowed. "What do you mean?"

Reia rubbed at her neck. "I didn't really get a good chance to watch Orpheus fight Jabez, but I knew he couldn't keep his claws in him. When I brought this up to Delora, she mentioned when she clung to his hair, instead of disappearing from her, she disappeared with him."

"Could that be an Elf-related thing?" Mayumi pondered out loud. "Like... maybe a magical weakness?"

"Who knows?" Reia answered, lifting a hand to shrug. "Better than nothing, right? If it's true, then Delora handed us a way to trap him or stop him from getting away, and I know for sure if we cut off his head, he'll die."

Emerie stayed quiet and soaked in all the information. She'd never met the Demon King, only read of him, so she had nothing to add. She also wasn't sure if what she'd read could even be accurate, since some of it was contradictory.

"He seemed cocky when I met him," Mayumi said with a light chuckle. "Never know, maybe Jabez will like the idea of a bunch of women throwing themselves at him."

Reia snorted a laugh, her lips curling into a weak smile for the first time since she'd arrived. It died the moment the front door opened with a *bang*.

Everyone startled, with both Reia and Emerie gasping in surprise. Reia turned to look behind her, just as Orpheus shoved himself through the doorway.

Even though his skull was expressionless, his orbs were a swallowing, deep colour of blue, and his body language screamed he was unsettled. The fins on his arms were raised, and the ones along his back were lifting his shirt to the point Emerie thought they were moments from tearing it apart.

He approached Reia and slammed a hand onto the table, his claws gouging into it, while gently curling his other around the back of her neck.

"No one will be going to fight the Demon King unless we can be assured it will be successful," he wheezed out, as if his very words filled him with pain and sorrow. "If you wish to leave me by myself and go fight, then you will only do so once. You will only allow yourself to be harmed *once*. I will not be able to handle a second time." Then he lifted his wolf skull to point in the direction of everyone else. "Am I understood? If she goes, and he is not defeated, and you all threaten this a second time, I will take us both from the Veil and not return."

"Orpheus," Reia rasped, turning on her seat to kneel on it.

She didn't try to assuage his fears. Instead, she looked relieved to see him, as if that's all that mattered to her, his presence.

Just as she was reaching up to slip her arms around his neck and embrace him, he let out an acute whine. Scooping her into his arms like he was frantic to hold her, he squeezed her tightly against his chest while shaking. With her legs wrapped around his large torso, Reia buried her face into the fur of his neck and clutched the back of his shirt with tight fists.

He was already moving to the exit before anyone could say anything more. He didn't even bother to close the door behind him.

"It'll be a while before we see those two again," Mayumi uttered with a sigh, shaking her head. "He's a bit of a sad guy and likes to be alone with her. It'll be days before Reia will be able to shake him out of this, if at all. He could decide to be overly protective and possessive of her until we leave."

"You all care about each other a lot," Emerie stated, giving a weak smile. "It's really sweet."

"We try." Mayumi returned her smile with an even weaker one before moving to the door to close it. "Reia tries to hide it, but Orpheus is the only person she really trusts. He's her only family, so she wants to protect him as much as she can. That's what all of us brides want to do, protect the ones we care about."

"I agree with him," Faunus said, rising to his pawed feet and walking over to Mayumi. He buried his feline skull into the side of her neck. "Only once. If we must suffer our females leaving, it should be with the knowledge we will not have to do so again."

Emerie glanced down at Ingram to find the strawberry had fallen from his claw and splattered against the ground. He stared at Faunus, before turning his raven skull to her.

After the conversation they'd shared last night, where it seemed he wanted to keep Emerie safe and leave her behind, she wondered if he agreed with both Orpheus and Faunus. Was he willing to be patient... for her?

Emerie hoped she meant that much to him.

I guess we better figure out a foolproof plan then, otherwise no one is going.

TWENTY-EIGHT

With the sound of wooden swords clacking before him, Ingram was seated with his legs bent – not quite crossed, but also not straight. Since Faunus was seated with his legs crossed, the back of Ingram's tail was pressed between the gap of Faunus' knees and the ground.

Together, they watched Emerie and Mayumi 'training.'

Ingram wasn't sure if the feline-skulled Mavka was aware he'd slyly sought the comfort of physical touch, since Emerie was currently unavailable to do so.

The sky was cloudy, giving them no warmth but plenty of light. There was a small breeze, and every day he noticed the temperature dropping just a little. Perhaps that was a good thing today, since sweat had already beaded on Emerie's forehead from battling Mayumi.

Both females had started this hours ago, under Mayumi's request. Apparently, she wanted to see how good Emerie was. Once she stated his pretty butterfly obviously had 'skills,' as she put it, she then wanted to train with her to keep her own body sharp.

Faunus had brought up some concerns, since Mayumi was carrying a youngling, but she'd brushed him off.

Ingram couldn't help bringing his sight to her stomach. He was curious about the whole thing, especially about how Faunus had managed to put a youngling inside her. He planned to ask Emerie for further information about it later, realising now her previous explanation was... vague and only partially informative.

All he knew was that Mayumi smelt heavily of Faunus' marking scent – as though it was fresh. It made him want to be anywhere but near her, as though it would be an offense to the feline-skulled Mavka.

He'd felt the same way about the other females as well.

He brought his sight to Emerie, just as she ducked underneath Mayumi's wooden sword and tried to counterattack – only to fail, as she did every time. Mayumi was too quick for Emerie, and it was obvious who the more advanced opponent was.

His vision threatened to turn blue.

She no longer smells of me. Well, that wasn't true. She had his body scent from sleeping in his arms, but she no longer had his sexual marking on her.

The bulk of it had disappeared after she'd fallen in the swamp water, and the final remnants were washed away during her bath.

It bothered him that it was gone, and that she was surrounded by other males of his kind without it. Now that he'd covered her in it, he had this deep, nagging desire to make sure it stained her. He didn't know why, and he also didn't *fucking* care to learn its meaning – he just wanted to fix it so that it didn't pester him and leave him tight in the chest.

His sight morphed to a bright green as he mulled it over, unsure of how to instigate this with her.

Ever since they'd arrived, Ingram had barely left her side. He was uncomfortable being within the homes of marked females, like he was imposing on their territory and the safety of their nests. It worsened with the tiny one before him, who had an additional scent on her that shouted at his mind that she was utterly fragile and required protection.

The problem was... *Why do I feel like Emerie is avoiding me?*

They'd been here a day, and already her attention was anywhere else but on him. She also often drew away from his touch during certain conversations, like yanking her ankle from the comforting hold he had on her. Now that his essence was bereft of her touch, he was pathetically seeking it from the male next to him.

She'd slept in his arms last night, but there had been this blanket barrier between them. The only reason he hadn't ripped it from her was because she'd looked at peace within its wrappings.

All he'd felt was a warm, living lump.

His tail tip curled in apprehension, just as movement to his right stole his attention from the two females training.

When he looked down at Faunus' knee, Bitey, one of his younglings, was standing upon it with their sightless face pointed up at him. Ingram tilted his head, and his hand twitched.

A baby Mavka... is this what I looked like when I was small?

His sight drifted to the second one, who wasn't as quick and was even smaller as though they were younger. They were currently walking over Faunus' skull, only to slide down his horn and hold onto the curve of it. His large, clawed hand was underneath them, ready to catch in case they fell.

"If you don't mind being bitten, go for it," Faunus calmly stated while keeping his sight riveted on his bride. It was as if he worried the moment he looked away, she'd come to harm. "I can tell you want to."

Ingram's hand twitched again before he reached it out. He waited for the baby Mavka to climb onto his palm, but the creature couldn't see he'd presented it.

He didn't want to just grab it. *What if I hurt it?*

"Don't worry, you can't harm them. They are indestructible like this, and your claws will just sink through them. I wouldn't have offered otherwise."

Ingram and his kindred had never realised that Faunus spoke so well. He *almost* sounded human – at least, he did to Ingram. For the longest time, they'd thought they had the same level of humanity as the rest of their kind, but the more he tried to speak with his fellow Mavka, the more he realised his intelligence was... lacking in comparison.

He was unsure if he was upset by this or not. *So long as it does not bother her...* He was growing self-conscious about it, only because he didn't want Emerie to see him differently.

With Faunus' reassurance, he grabbed the tiny creature by the back and lifted them off. They squealed as their arms and legs flapped beneath them until Ingram brought them into the safe cradle of his other hand.

The baby Mavka immediately bit into his palm and then retched at the purple blood in their mouth. Faunus let out a chuckle, whereas Ingram had to resist every urge to fling the creature halfway across the protection ward in revulsion. For a creature without teeth, that *hurt.*

"I did not know we could create our own," Ingram mused, bringing them nearer to his beak so he could inspect them up close. They bit his thumb and retched again before trying to climb over and around his hand and fingers.

They were a tiny thing, barely bigger than his palm.

"Neither did I until I saw Delora and Magnar's youngling," Faunus admitted. He caught the one hanging from his horn and placed them against his chest to let them crawl on him. "Something awoke within me at seeing them. I hadn't known we could create life."

Ingram was thankful they had stopped biting him and instead walked on him while sniffing at his scales. It gave him the freedom to look upon Faunus, and the soul with its arms crossed over its chest and knees tucked underneath them as though it was kneeling.

"So eating a soul is how we bond with our brides? How do we obtain them to do so?"

Faunus' head cocked, as if he wanted to turn his skull to Ingram. After many moments, he did eventually pull away from Mayumi to look upon him.

"You have to ask for it – that's all I will tell you. It is best you don't know more, otherwise you could make a mistake." Faunus was quick to grab his youngling as they jumped from Ingram, so they could go after their female creator. "Are you asking because you wish to bond with Emerie?"

Ingram hadn't expected that question, and he turned his sight on the pretty female with her hair twisted into a singular big braid going down her shoulder. She squeaked as she went to the tips of her toes with her arms rotating in circles like it was the answer to not falling.

It didn't matter – she fell to her arse. He almost chuckled.

That was cute.

Do I want to make Emerie my bride? He knew he desired some form of connection with her, but he didn't know what having a bride entailed.

But what about my bond with my kindred?

Aleron was important to him, but he was beginning to realise Emerie was as well.

He liked the bright, shiny colour of her hair, and how it seemed to glow in any light. Her eyes were an icy blue, but they made him feel... calm when he looked into them. Now that he knew he could slip his tongue between her pale-pink lips, and have them kiss his skull all over, he'd grown fascinated and enthralled by them.

He adored her face and wished it was directed at him at all times so he could view it at his leisure. His appreciation for her body grew every time he was permitted to touch it in some form, and the absence of it left him feeling cold and barren inside.

And her strawberry, and possibly primrose scent – since he was hoping what Faunus called it was correct – sang to him in a way he never thought possible.

Even though it worried him constantly, he also appreciated that she was short, small, and delicate. She was something he could protect, rather than just being a horrifying monster. Yet, she had this softness to her he'd never experienced with Aleron, where he wanted to grip and hold and touch until his mind fell into bliss.

He wanted his marking on her because he didn't want anyone else to have her. He wanted to smear her in his possessiveness and smother her until everyone within a wide radius of her knew she was *his*.

"You did not answer me," Faunus pushed, bringing his sight back to him.

"I don't know what I am feeling, or what I want. All I know for certain is that I want Aleron back," he admitted.

Faunus' orbs flickered blue, before he drifted his skull in the direction of his bride.

"Well... when you look at her, has your sight ever turned pink, and you got a fuzzy feeling in your heart?"

Ingram tilted his head. "No. I have only experienced this with Aleron."

Perhaps not the fuzzy feeling in his heart, as he'd definitely experienced this with Emerie, but his sight had never turned pink because of her. Then again, it had never turned dark purple for Aleron either, and he was still learning much about the world and his orb changes.

Faunus lifted his hand to wrap it over his snout and fangs in thought. "Your scent is not all over her, so I doubt you have fucked... You have not connected with her properly, so maybe this is the issue."

"She will not let me," Ingram grumbled, feeling a pout in his mind. "She is wary of me, of this. I think it is because I have already hurt her with my claws." The shameful reminder threatened to make his sight shift to a reddish pink. "Can you teach me how to heal, like how Orpheus did for her?"

Faunus lowered his hand so he could place it around Bitey, who was trying to escape from his lap. "Almost all of our magic requires some sort of bargain. The bargain for this is that you must bear her wounds instead. That is all, just will for that trade."

"That does not sound too difficult." He lifted his sight towards the two females, watching as Emerie crinkled her nose up all cute as she swung. Her braid whipped behind her and tapped against her blue dress. "I wish I had known that sooner."

"It's no wonder she fears pain," Faunus muttered quietly, mirroring the direction Ingram was looking. "I have felt that too. Felt flames eating at me. It's... one of the most unpleasant things for anyone to suffer."

The feline Mavka's words only brought attention to the gold-filled crack keeping his skull together.

"Did the Demonslayers do this to you?"

"Demonslayers?" Faunus reared his head back and then let out a quiet but dark chuckle. "As if humans would be able to trap our kind."

Reddish pink flooded his vision, and he was tempted to cross his arms defensively. He almost moved his tail away from him in petty annoyance.

"No, it was Jabez," Faunus continued. "He was trying to figure out how to destroy us, so he did numerous things to see which one would work in killing me. Set me alight, drowned me, buried me, opened up my chest so he could show me my own beating heart. As much as it pains me, Mayumi wishes to avenge all I have suffered at the hands of the Demon King, since I cannot do it without leaving our younglings on their own."

Faunus' honesty was as mind-opening as it was saddening. Ingram was sure the Mavka saw himself as weak, just as he had when he'd been trapped at the mountain fortress.

The fact he'd shared that with Ingram was the only reason he spilled his own vulnerable truth. It also helped that Faunus was the only Mavka he was truly comfortable with.

"Demonslayers managed to trap me," Ingram admitted, lifting his sight back to Emerie to drink in her colourful beauty, letting her soothe him even from a distance. "They also showed me my heart. It is strange, but I feel as though it has not healed properly ever since." It was like they put it back with a shard of Emerie's essence lodged into it. "She saved me."

Even though the Witch Owl had been there and helped, Ingram believed Emerie would have saved him all by herself had she not.

"Ah, so that's why she's here," Faunus commented. "I wondered how you found yourself stuck with a Demonslayer. It seems much has happened along the way from there to here. Did you ask her to join you?"

"No. She offered to help me," Ingram admitted while shaking his head, causing bones to rattle in him. One of Faunus' younglings reared their head up at the noise. "But yes, much has happened, and I find myself wanting to touch her more and more. I have shown her I can be gentle, and I have learned much, like how to sheath my claws and walk like her. I don't know how else to change her mind when she is so uncertain about me."

Faunus let out a deep chuckle as his orbs turned bright yellow. "Sorry, but I cannot help you. Mayumi didn't just fall into my lap, she crawled into it. I had no idea how to instigate this with her, and without her doing so, I think I would still be hiding in the trees surrounding her family cottage."

"That is... creepy," Ingram stated. Only because Emerie had told him the same thing when he wanted to watch her from the bushes while she bathed.

Faunus burst into a fit of laughter as his naturally yellow orbs brightened. "Perhaps it was, but I was doing it to protect her. As I always have."

"And just what are you laughing at?" Mayumi said with a grin, strutting over before placing her hands on her hips just in front of Faunus' crossed knees.

"I was just explaining the first time we officially met," Faunus answered with his orbs an even brighter hue of yellow.

Emerie, huffing wildly with her face pink from exertion, came up beside the smaller female.

"Yeah, you have to say 'officially met' because you tried to eat me the first time."

With a playful growl, Faunus dragged Mayumi into his lap, forcing their younglings to make way. They were unbothered and immediately crawled all over her as though they'd missed her presence. Bitey even began rubbing their oval face against her abdomen fast and frantically, as though to smother themself in her scent.

"You forget I saved your life. What child walks into the forest at night in the middle of winter?"

"An awesomely brave one?" she snapped back with a single arm lifted into a shrug. "I was just too cute, and you couldn't *bear* to let me freeze to death."

Ingram ignored them and looked up at Emerie, finding she was watching the family of Mavka and their Phantom female interact. His skull jerked at her crinkled expression, unsure as to why he thought there was a small hint of... hurt in it.

Is it because I have not pulled her into my lap as well?

Yet, when he tried to do so, reaching out to her thighs, she resisted. Instead, she sat on the ground with her back against the inside of his knee. Even though it was exactly how they'd sat in the grassy meadow on top of a hill, it felt... detached in comparison to the couple beside him.

Her lips were flat and hard, while she had her hands on her upright, bent knees. When he called her name, she didn't respond.

"Emerie?" he repeated, grabbing her thick braid to slip it through his palm.

"Hm?" she replied, lifting her freckled and scarred face to him. She gave him a smile, but he instantly knew it was fake. "Have fun with your *brother*?"

No. His conversations with Faunus were as confusing as they were enlightening.

But he did wonder why she'd used the word brother to reference the feline Mavka. She'd been saying it a lot, as if she wanted him to understand this bond deeper, when it only drew a blankness in his mind. That blankness was growing smaller the more he was around them, but it would take time for his mind to piece together something so obviously complex.

"You are very good with a wooden sword," Ingram complimented, hoping to distract her – especially since she seemed to squirm every time he did.

He very much liked it when she did.

"Pfft." Emerie rolled her eyes. "She kicked my arse every single time. I'm going to end up with so many bruises, and she'll barely have one."

"You got me really good on the arm though," Mayumi mused. "You're better than Reia, and that girl can give me a run for my money some days." She tilted her head back to shine a grin at Emerie. "Difference is, she has absolutely no concept of fear. I could tell you were worried about hurting me the entire time. Reia would still size me up as a challenge and try to best me."

"Which is why you aren't allowed to train with her anymore until this one is out," Faunus said with the lightest growl, palming her stomach.

Mayumi just rolled her brown eyes before giving Emerie a wink. Emerie smiled, until Mayumi lifted her head to face Faunus, then it instantly died. Her features turned dark, dreary.

Is something wrong with her?

She didn't seem truly harmed, but it was like she was in... pain.

She even cringed when Mayumi lifted one of her younglings

into the air with both hands while giggling. She then snuggled her nose against theirs, and their pliable claws bent backwards as they happily grabbed at her cheeks.

Since her face had gone pale, Ingram drew the glossy curve of his claw against Emerie's cheek. "Is something wrong?"

"Huh?" she rasped, directing her face to his swiftly like he'd snapped her out of her thoughts. "Oh, nothing. I think I'm just hungry." Then she gave a light laugh. "Training can do that to a person. I used to eat like a horse after training sessions at the guild."

Why did he feel like that was a... lie? Or, at least, a half-truth.

Emerie was trying her absolute hardest to remain all smiles and light-hearted... she really was. Or, at least, tried to hide her internal struggles as best she could from everyone.

That seemed fucking impossible with the Duskwalker that rarely took his orbs off her. He was getting worse about it too, like he could tell something was off about her. She wondered how much longer she could brush him off without imploding.

With the way she was feeling, she knew she was a hair trigger away from exploding the next time he softly and quietly asked if she was okay.

I don't want to tell him why I'm upset. It was no one's fault but her own, even though it was the situation that was causing it. *Gosh, I feel so damn petty.*

And the longer she sat in the home of this charming little family, the more a hook sunk deeper and deeper into her chest. Would it rip her open, or wait to rise to the surface?

She felt like she and Ingram were imposing on Mayumi and Faunus in their home, but they had nowhere else to go other than the tent they'd been loaned. However, Mayumi was offering to cook Emerie dinner, and she hadn't wanted to deny her hospitality and come across as rude.

Emerie had spent almost every moment with Mayumi today.

Yes, part of it was to avoid Ingram, since he seemed content next to Faunus, following him around wherever he went because he wouldn't come near Mayumi if he didn't have to. Another was because the woman just seemed happy to have a fellow Demonslayer around.

They'd spoken about their different lives in their sectors, reminisced on stories that were similar. Mayumi had spoken of her father and how she'd joined the guild to follow in his footsteps.

Emerie had eventually found it hard to share after that.

They had walked down the same kind of path, but one fateful decision meant they were worlds apart. Would always be worlds apart. Emerie had somewhat regretted her choice for the longest time, but this was the first instance it threatened to suffocate her.

Even if they hadn't spoken about it, Emerie was sure Mayumi was aware of it.

The woman seemed too calculating and had an awfully keen eye. There were times Mayumi's features would tighten, and she'd go silent, or redirect the conversation or what was happening in an attempt to help.

It didn't.

Not when Emerie gave her a reassuring and appreciative smile, thankful she wasn't airing out the problem.

It didn't stop Ingram, though.

Whenever he wasn't facing Emerie expectantly, he was staring at one of the baby Duskwalkers with his head tilting and twitching. If his tail was around her wrist or ankle, it'd curl tighter. That, or she'd feel him tense. He would also do it whenever the other couple were sweet to each other, and his orbs would change to a bright green.

He was jealous.

No matter what he wanted, he'd never get what they had from Emerie. If he tried to push it on her, she knew she would break and that wasn't fair on him. Her past choices shouldn't impact him, or his life, and it just made her acutely aware that she needed to draw a line in the sand between them.

No, not just a line, an entire field.

It'd been less than two days since they'd arrived in the Veil,

382 OPAL REYNE

and already she was antsy about going after the Demon King and ending all this. Either she would die, or they would be successful, and she'd ask to be dropped off at the nearest village or town.

They were her plans... even if it wasn't what her heart was telling her she wanted.

Ingram tightened his tail on her again, and she looked up from the table towards Mayumi in the kitchen. Her pulse raced with urgency. *When will dinner be ready?*

The quicker it was over, the quicker she could go hide.

If she fell asleep before Ingram could even enter the tent, maybe she could avoid him touching her intimately. She wouldn't deny him the comfort he sought by lying down next to her to relieve the wallowing loneliness that obviously ate him up inside. It was also why she hadn't kicked his tail away when she desperately wanted to for her own self-preservation. And because she secretly knew, deep down inside, she pathetically craved it too.

She knew she liked Ingram on a level that no human probably should. Which was becoming easier to deal with now that she understood she wasn't alone in developing feelings for a Duskwalker. Hard not to when she'd met three other women who had fallen for their own.

She wasn't the only one that craved touching them, learning them, pleasuring them, just so they could do so in return. Just the thought had her nipples pebbling for it against her will, despite her despondent emotions.

However, if Ingram wanted a life like theirs, she just wasn't the human for him then.

She was sure he could find a new one, a better one. One that wasn't broken in more ways than she could count. He could use all that she'd taught him to not make mistakes and frighten them, not that Emerie minded any of the times he'd accidentally hurt her or frightened her.

At least she was setting him up for a brighter future, she hoped. *Just one I probably won't be a part of.*

Gosh, why did that make her want to tear up?

"Emerie, if you are cold, I can warm you," Ingram offered

when he noticed her shiver. He placed his big hand over her left thigh.

For some reason, her scars were more sensitive, and she was more self-conscious of them than ever before.

"No, I'm okay," she assured.

She wasn't shivering because she was cold. She was trembling because her mind wouldn't shut the fuck up and she wished it would stop pestering her. She wanted to enjoy her time in this warm house, filled with lovely people.

Stop pressuring me, she silently begged at him.

He didn't mean to. He was just showing he cared, but right now, she felt like an imposter. She was worried she was going to hurt him, whether it be now or in the future, and the guilt of it was already making her skin itch.

Then, to make matters worse, Faunus approached Mayumi from behind while she was stirring something in a frypan. He licked the side of her neck while asking her what she was making, not that he was going to eat it, and placed his hand on her shoulder to bring her closer.

One of their children crawled off her and onto his hand.

At first, when Emerie had met Mayumi and her family, she had thought she was a cold mother to them. She hadn't held them, and only let them walk over her when Faunus was nearby.

It was only partway through today, after she and Emerie had spoken and grown a little closer, that Mayumi's affection with them changed. She held them, spoke to them even though they would never be able to understand, and even openly snuggled with them.

It was totally different to the already hard and abrasive personality Emerie could see she had.

It eventually dawned on her that Mayumi had been distant with them due to Ingram and Emerie's presence, keeping her precious children with the parent that could protect them best: Faunus. Before today, they'd still been strangers. They had been threats to their family.

She'd given up her precious time with them for their safety.

Emerie watched as Faunus moved away from Mayumi. He only made it about three steps before her head perked up.

"Hey!" she whined. "Give them back!"

The chuckle that rumbled out of Faunus was dark, mischievous, and evil as he bolted with the child he'd stolen. Mayumi chased him with a spoon dripping with yellow, oily sauce.

"You've had them for most of the day," she continued.

Emerie didn't catch Faunus' chuckling response; it was dim and inaudible to her ears.

I can't do this anymore today. Faunus obviously wanted to be himself with his bride and family, teasing and picking on her every chance he got if he wasn't lazing around somewhere.

It was killing her.

As quietly as she could, hoping not to be noticed, Emerie slipped off the chair. She threw her hand out to Ingram when he went to rise.

"Please, *please,* just stay there. I just need some air."

"Emerie," he rasped, his skull following her direction as she headed for the exit. She couldn't bear looking at him to see if his orbs had changed colour.

She didn't know if anyone else noticed she'd left, but she really hoped they didn't. She needed air. She needed a few minutes of clean, fresh air that wasn't stifled by their happiness, love, and affection.

Just five minutes to be in the cold, by herself, like she'd been for most of her damn life.

Instead of heading to the tent, something that didn't *belong* to her, she walked just beyond the open clearing and to the fringe of forest. She sat next to a tree. With her arms wrapped around the tops of her knees, she just breathed and tried to push out all the horrible, terrible emotions she didn't want inside her.

She felt petty, spiteful, and jealous all wrapped up into one aching being, and more than anything, she wanted to shed those sentiments. She hated that she felt this way; they didn't deserve it.

When tears began to well in her eyes, she glared at herself while thinking, *Stop it. Stop it. Stop it!* With a shaking hand, she wiped at her cheek with the heel of her palm.

A twig cracking from the direction of the house made anger

flare in her chest.

"Ingram, I said to sta–" Her words died when she saw a woman with long black hair approaching her. "Oh. Um." She wiped at her cheeks to remove the few tears that had fallen, ashamed of them, before giving her a smile. "Hey, Mayumi. You didn't have to come out."

"Sorry," Mayumi muttered. "I know it must be hard–"

Emerie's features twisted into a cringe. "Please stop. I don't want you to feel bad for something that has nothing to do with you. I am happy for you and your family."

"I know." She bent down and placed her hand on Emerie's shoulder. "But that still doesn't stop how it must make you feel. I understand, but Faunus doesn't, so he isn't being very considerate of you."

Emerie was quick to slap her hand away and rise to her feet.

"I don't want anyone changing their fucking lives for me or being considerate. The fact you feel like you have to come out here and apologise to me makes me feel worse, like I'm a damn villain for feeling this way. So please, just leave me alone."

Mayumi sighed as she slid a hand over the top of her hair, before brushing it down the long length of her ponytail.

"I didn't tell you how I was discharged from the guild."

"Let me guess," Emerie sneered. "They found out you lied about going through with it."

"Yeah, pretty much." She rubbed at her cheek. "Like I told you, my father was a really high-ranking Elder. He was able to have it fabricated that I'd done it, but I got caught out on a mission. I chose to do that, knowing I could not only be discharged but imprisoned because I didn't want to have my future taken away from me. I wanted the choice."

Emerie wished her voice didn't sound so angry and shaken, when she said, "Well, I made *a* choice, and now I have to live with it."

She clenched and unclenched her hands, hoping to squeeze the defensive stiffness out. It was futile, and it only made her realise just how clammy her hands were from anxiety.

"What I'm trying to say is that I get it," Mayumi offered. "I get why you're upset, and I wanted you to know that you are welcome to be within my home and just be how you feel. You don't have to hide it. I can't change my life, and you can't change how you feel, but there is no point in you trying to exclude yourself from us when all it will do is make you feel more alone."

"You don't get it, okay?" Emerie gritted her teeth to keep her eyes from tearing – she refused to cry in front of someone she barely knew. "It's not just you, or your family, or the fact I chose to have my uterus removed so I could climb higher through the guild. I chose to go through with the hysterectomy because I had a goal, and because I doubted I'd live long enough or even find someone to make a family with."

Mayumi folded her arms with her feet parted in an offensive stance Emerie had seen far too often in life. Guarded. "Then explain it to me so I understand?"

Emerie couldn't help averting her gaze, wanting to look anywhere but at the same woman who suddenly felt three times her size. How could someone tower over her from so many inches below?

"I don't want to," she grumbled.

If she let it all out, said it all, Emerie wondered how she was supposed to stuff it all back inside and hide it. She wondered how she was supposed to ignore it.

Mayumi snorted a laugh. "Coward."

"Excuse me?" Emerie gasped, turning to her.

"I'm not the kind of person to be gentle with another. I have a very low tolerance for human beings in general, which is why I'm with a Duskwalker in the first place. So, Emerie, I'm not going to hold back the truth from you, just as I wouldn't for anyone else." Then she raised her arm to shrug, her chin lifting. "You're so afraid of your own damn feelings that you can't even talk about them. If that isn't cowardice, then I don't know what is."

Emerie knew what she was doing. She'd asked nicely, and Emerie had rejected it. Now, Mayumi was trying a different tactic to get her to open up, and to her dismay, it worked.

And by the fact that the woman's cool expression never changed, she expected the outburst before it even began.

"Fine? You want to know the damn truth?" Emerie bit out. "Yes, I'm jealous of you and your family because I'm infertile and can't have my own. Do I want you to stop being yourself? No, not at all. However, it does hurt, and it just makes me regret what I did, even if it is what brought me here today."

She took in a deep breath, and let the rest freely flow.

"All I wanted was five damn minutes to take a fucking breath. That's all I wanted. To collect myself and be alone so I could piece together my thoughts. Yet, whenever I try to do so, Ingram follows me, or you do. I feel suffocated."

Then, tears did well, and no amount of teeth gritting or willpower seemed to stop them.

A dam of them, and rambling words, had broken.

"And he keeps looking at me expectantly, and I want him to stop because I can't do any of this for him. I like him, Mayumi. I can already feel it growing inside me, but I'm not going to be his bride. I'm worried me being here with him is going to make him start wanting that from me, and I'm scared of how that's going to make me feel. I'm scared of hurting his feelings, or that he'll find a way to convince me otherwise because he's so sweet and caring and it just makes me want to give him the world. But, if he wants his own kids, then he needs to go find someone else and stop wrapping his damn tail around my ankle like he doesn't want to let me go."

"You could talk to him about it," Mayumi cut in. "Faunus has the desire to make life, but Magnar is less inclined to do so after having one."

"I don't want to explain it to him," Emerie admitted. "I'm not sure if you've noticed or not, but Faunus and Ingram aren't on the same humanity scale. Half of what I explain to him slips through the cracks, and I have to say it in different ways for him to get the basics. This is a really sore and tender spot for me, and I just don't know how I'm going to do that without bursting into tears. He seems to think that if he wills things, it will come true. I've already tried to explain to him that Aleron can't be magically resurrected to life, but he won't accept it. If he manages to convince me to be his bride, and he pushes the desire for kids onto me, when nothing he does will change it, I think he'll crumble me from the inside. I can't be his bride if he wants it, because it'll mean I'm not good enough, will never be good enough, and he will eventually regret tying himself to me."

Mayumi's mouth pulled to one side in uncertainty, as her features softened for Emerie. "Do... you want me and Faunus to try talking to him about it?"

"Oh god, fuck no," Emerie groaned while covering her face. "I know it's really selfish of me, but I... I don't want him to change because of this. I feel like he is smothering me in his affection, and yet I crave it so damn much that I wish he would pull me into his arms and squeeze me until I disappear into dust. What if you tell him and he comes to resent me? I already feel like an outsider, and I just... I don't think I could bear a second of being here if he wasn't there to make it... better."

She pulled her hands from her face so she could look down at them beseechingly.

"I don't think I could handle it if he suddenly started to ignore me. Just thinking of it hurts. I think I'd run off into the Veil to escape and hope I didn't die along the way."

Somehow, Mayumi's silence and lack of comforting reach was... soothing. It was exactly what she needed right now. Someone to just shut up and listen as she vented, someone to not pull her in for a sympathetic hug and coddle her like she was a child.

She had big girl problems. They weren't easily solved or fixed with words or actions. They didn't just disappear.

They were real, and valid, and unchangeable.

All that could be dealt with was how Emerie reacted to them, and how she outwardly showed herself. She couldn't suddenly grow a second womb, but she'd always been hoping that someone would love her.

Not because they had to, regardless of it, but because she meant so much to them that it didn't matter at all. She wondered if that love would be even more pure because it was utterly about her and them, with no expectations of adding to it.

Even if she made this choice, she knew in her heart she deserved unconditional love untainted by guilt just as much as anyone else.

She was just waiting for someone to give it to her.

She wanted it to be Ingram. She was too afraid of learning the ugly truth, and would rather live in a fantasy just a little while longer.

There's a chance I could die when we fight against the Demon King. Is... is it wrong of me to want to hide it in case I do?

There was no promise of more, from either of them. If Ingram decided he wanted to ask her for her soul, she would tell him the truth because he needed to know. That it was the reason she couldn't just come out and give it to him.

How he reacted would tell her what to do. What he said afterwards would either make her steadfast on her current path, or she would give in and just be his.

She hoped if that day ever came, that he would take her heart and her soul at the same time, and she would welcome it fully.

If he never did, never wanted to bond with her, then it was never a problem in the first place. She would have just been anxious and worried for no reason.

Considering how much he wanted Aleron back, and didn't seem to care too much that Emerie could be sacrificed along the way, she had a feeling she knew where his priorities lay.

And it wasn't Emerie.

What's the point in telling him if it doesn't matter anyway?

"My god, I'm complicated," Emerie tried to laugh, cringing at her hands before looking up to Mayumi.

Her lips thinned in returned humour, but quickly faded. "You're insecure."

"Oof," Emerie huffed. "That's not nice."

"Is it not true?" Mayumi answered, roaming her eyes down Emerie before coming back up. "If it helps, I have plenty of fatal flaws. I'm just lucky Faunus is foolishly attached to me for some reason. Honestly thought I'd die alone if it wasn't for him."

"Now you don't get to die at all."

Mayumi's lips twisted. "Don't remind me," she grumbled while slapping her face into her hands. "Did you know I've only been with him for like nine months? Sorry to touch on a sore subject, but we're already on our third child. At this rate, I'll be the sole reason the world is overrun by hundreds of Duskwalkers. Humankind will go extinct before we know it."

After venting and finally having a moment to collect her frantic mind, the subject didn't feel so constricting.

She gave a weak but genuine laugh.

That was until she registered something very important. "Nine months?!"

Laughter burst from Mayumi, and it crinkled the corners of her eyes.

"Took you long enough. Yeah, gestation time for baby Duskwalkers is a month. They don't really have organs or any bones, so there isn't much to make. The whole thing was weird for me when I first travelled here for everyone's help, and I was about to burst when we got here. We'd only been travelling for three weeks." Mirth filled her brown eyes as she looked off into the distance. "You should have seen it. I gave Faunus hell, and my allergies were so freaking bad that I told him to just put me out of my misery. I'm surprised he didn't regret it so much that he never wanted to go through it again."

"You seem fine now," Emerie stated, still reeling about the whole month thing. *A month?!*

"It gets easier after the first. Apparently, we have to adjust to having the whole 'darkness inside us' thing." Mayumi then stepped forward but didn't touch her as she tilted her head. "Feeling more at ease now?"

"Yeah, I guess," Emerie grumbled, rubbing at the side of her neck before wiping her damn face again, this time to remove her drying tears. "Could you do me a favour? Can you not tell anyone else about this? My face already makes people treat me like there's an elephant in the room, and I don't need that to be worsened."

"There's nothing wrong with your face." Mayumi sighed as she stepped back. "I've seen plenty worse at Hawthorne Keep, and I doubt Delora or Reia would treat you any different because of it. But yeah, sure, fine. I won't tell anyone what we spoke about tonight." Then she pursed her lips. "Except for Faunus. When he gets curious about something, he won't let it lie. He'll hound me until I give in."

Emerie chuckled. "Fine. I like him, by the way. He's pretty funny."

"Yeah, he's great." Then Mayumi shuffled one of her feet backwards. "Do you want to come inside for dinner, or would you rather go to the tent? I have some board games we can play if you don't feel like being alone. If not, I'm sure we can figure out a way to keep Ingram from you for a little longer so you can rest. I'll be surprised if he and Faunus aren't already playing catch with Sleepy. They really like being thrown around."

At Emerie's 'what the fuck' face, Mayumi's lips quirked in humour. Puffing out a breath, she answered the petite ex-Demonslayer. "It's fine. I don't really want to come inside, but you don't have to keep Ingram. He gives pretty good hugs."

Right now, more than anything, she wanted the big, sweet, clingy Duskwalker making her feel better, even if he didn't know why.

There's also something I need to talk to him about, even if I don't want to.

She needed to tell him something that had been like a pit of acid in her heart and chest since the very first night she met him, when he was bound and strapped to that table board in the dungeon. Something she'd been putting off until they made it here.

Emerie didn't think she could wait any longer with her guilt over it. It was a wall between them, one she had erected until she could speak of it. One that wouldn't let her get closer to him in fear.

One she needed gone before she could let him touch her again.

I just hope... he doesn't hate me for it.

TWENTY-NINE

Escaping Mayumi and Faunus had been harder than Ingram thought it would be.

The moment the female marched inside, without Emerie behind her, he'd tried to leave. Mayumi had told him to wait until dinner was ready so he could give it to Emerie, explaining humans needed to be kept fed in order to be happy.

So, with irritation, he'd plopped his backside on the ground and waited.

Once he had a plate of various items he couldn't name, even if his life depended on it, he walked it outside in the dark of night. She hadn't been in the open, and her scent was strongest on the other side of the ward where the tent was.

"Emerie?" he softly called as he approached, having learnt he needed to 'knock.' He wasn't sure how he was supposed to knock on cloth material, though, so this was the best he could think of.

Outside the tent flap, he poked his claw through, just as she answered. He peeked inside before entering, finding she was seated under the blanket as if she'd been laying down. She was already in a white sleep gown.

She did not wait for me. He was a little hurt by that, and his orbs shifted to blue.

"Took you long enough," she croaked, her eyes groggy. "I was just about to lie down."

Just like that, she'd eased his hurt.

Ingram knelt in front of her and handed her the plate of food. "Mayumi told me to make sure you ate."

"I'm not really hungry," she answered, before placing it on the ground as far away as she could reach.

Then she straightened, and Ingram drifted his sight over her.

Her face looked drawn, with puffy cheeks and nose. She was even a little pink with the evidence of tears, and he couldn't stop himself from reaching out to her. He cupped the side of her head so he could stroke her cheek.

"What is wrong, Emerie?" he asked, even though she hadn't responded any other time he'd posed this question to her today.

They were alone now, so he was hoping she would finally speak about it. *She does not like to share with people she does not trust.*

She dipped her head. "I don't really want to talk about it. I am sad, but it hurts to talk about it, and I don't know where to start."

Ingram slipped his hand down so he could place the flat edge of his claw under her chin to lift her face back up. "I don't like that you do not want to talk to me. I want to know all your secrets, Emerie."

His head reared back in surprise when she rotated to her knees and rose up with her arms reaching towards his chest. "Can you hold me instead?"

She is reaching for me. And her eyes were warm as they looked upon him like he was the safest creature in the world. How could he deny her, or his own desire to keep her close?

She didn't flinch when he bent forward and slipped his palm and forearm under her arse so he could lift her all the way up until she was able to bury her face into the side of his firm neck. Still seated on both his knees, his thighs slightly parted, he held her tightly. He gripped the underside of her thigh with her soft backside safely perched on his forearm, while the other hand slipped across her back so he could hold her biceps.

Emerie wrapped her arms over his shoulders while the heels of her feet pressed against his back. He was thankful his narrow and lean waist fit between the space of her thighs, although he was acutely aware his wide hips wouldn't be gifted such a treat.

She was warm, soft, and light in his strong arms.

He curled his tail around his legs and knees so he could sit back comfortably. She didn't start crying, which is what he'd been expecting from the last time she'd needed a hug, but she did go all lax and languid in his arms.

"Ingram," she started. Her lips brushed against the sensitive scales on his neck, sending a thrill through him all the way down to his tail tip. "If I told you I did something bad, and that I regret it, would you believe me?"

"Yes," he easily stated, tempted to start petting her long, silky hair.

Was she going to share more secrets with him? Maybe not the ones that had made her cry, but deep ones nonetheless? He was ecstatic about this.

Plus, what could this pretty female have done that was so terrible that she needed to be shy about it with him? He was a Mavka. He was sure he'd done plenty of worse things.

"Would you forgive me?" she whispered.

Ingram cocked his head, a little confused by that. The thrill that had torn through him was quickly replaced with a trickle of uncertainty.

"Emerie?" he asked, trying to pull back, but was unable to when she clung tighter with all her limbs. He worried about breaking her, so he didn't force it.

"How much do you remember of the night you were captured by the guild?"

His tail curled when a bad feeling lifted the spikes down his back and limbs. "My memories are foggy when I am enraged. I only ever remember fragments."

"Do you remember someone standing on you and tying your beak shut?" she asked with her voice shaking. "And that same person connecting a rope from your neck to your tail so you couldn't use it properly?"

Ingram tried to think back, but that night was a colliding mess of too many scents, too many people, and far too much hurt to truly remember.

"I remember feeling these things happening," he admitted solemnly, his orbs turning blue at the memories. "But no, I do not know who did this."

"If that one person didn't shut your beak, Ingram, or still your tail, it's true someone else may have. However, that isn't certain. There were only five whip bearers, and two had already died by that point. You may have killed everyone and gotten away. You may not have suffered all the pain you went through."

"I do not like this conversation, Emerie," Ingram whimpered. "Why are you telling me this?"

He'd been trying to push any lingering thoughts about his time at the Demonslayer stronghold as far down and deep within his memories as he could. He didn't want to resurface them, didn't want to dwell on all the pain he'd suffered because of them. Explaining it lightly to Faunus had been hard enough, but Emerie was diving down to the very bottom of the abyss where it all started.

He was not thankful for it, even though it brought her to him, because his pain had not started that night. It had been the byproduct of his insanity and stupidity from Aleron disappearing.

He'd made a terrible mistake. Now, he could no longer sleep without this tiny, feeble female protecting him from his nightmares by being up against him in some form.

So why was she trying to pry open his wounds and dig at them like she didn't care for his pain?

He saw no point to this.

She clung tighter, like she was trying to crush him, as she whispered, "It was me. I'm so sorry, Ingram, but it was me who captured you."

For a moment, he thought his spirit had left him.

His reaction was slow at first, as the warm flow of betrayal began to bubble beneath the surface of his hard exterior.

Then, all he could feel, all he could sense, was rage flooding him. His body tightened. He didn't even realise he'd begun growling until the strength of it forced his beak to separate.

All this time, the person who had inevitably put him in that dungeon and was the cause of all the torture he'd faced... who he'd been protecting, and touching, and wanted to connect with... was his precious, colourful, *lying* butterfly?

She let out a sharp hitch of breath as he squeezed. The urge to squeeze harder until she was crushed made his flesh tight with the desire to maim. Her soft skin was currently safe from his fingers digging in hard to her thigh and biceps, but soon enough his claws would begin to shred. Already, he smelt pinpricks of copper in her scent as the tips dug deeper and deeper, penetrating through her thick dress until they met yielding skin.

His sight was so red it threatened to spill from his orbs like blood drops.

She didn't ask or plead for him to stop, but he wasn't quite sure what he was doing as he registered the lash of betrayal across his entire being.

He didn't know what to do with it.

He'd trusted her, which hadn't been an easy feat to begin with, but it had been strong, and, up until this point, unbending. It also didn't disappear suddenly, and only became confusing and painful.

"I promise I didn't know what they were going to do to you," she wheezed out through the crush of her chest. "Otherwise, I never would have agreed to help. I couldn't bear to watch it, and I've felt so guilty from the moment Wren shoved me into that room to watch. It's why I freed you, Ingram."

It's why I freed you.

With short, sharp breaths, his grip loosened when he realised he needed to think on this before he succumbed to his first instinct to maim. To hurt her as he'd been hurt. To slice open her little stomach and show Emerie her own heart before it eventually ceased beating before her very eyes.

Or before he ate her.

He softened his crush. *She saved me.* And her promise had not gone unheard. She'd taught him the weight of that word, and he'd adhered to it each time he uttered it. He *wanted* to believe it was true, and that she hadn't knowingly bound him in a state of suffering.

She saved me. And, since then, had been by his side.

Ingram knew his mind was flawed, knew there were blank spaces where thoughts should be. Yet Emerie's patience with him was almost unflappable. He'd hurt her, had tried to eat her and kill her – although he hadn't meant to do any of these things – and she still desired to be in his arms right now.

Arms that, just seconds ago, were intending to squeeze her until she popped.

"Why are you only telling me now?" he grated, his voice dark, hoarse, and vibrating with malice.

Why now? Why tonight?

She'd had weeks to do so. To explain the truth and let him make an informed decision about her. He'd been choosing to trust and care for someone who may not have truly deserved any form of kindness from him.

"I'm sorry I didn't tell you sooner," she whispered around huffing breaths, catching them now that he'd ceased crushing her to death. "I didn't know how you'd react, but I had to get you here. I was worried you'd venture through the Veil, or get lost and distracted along the way. I wanted to make up for everything, but I always knew that when I got you here safely, I would tell you. I just... couldn't leave you by yourself."

By myself. If I kill her, I will be alone.

Not truly, he was discovering, since he had the other Mavka who seemed to have welcomed him within their group.

He couldn't dismiss what she said, though. Ingram was easily distracted, and he was also impatient for the death of the Demon King and Aleron's return. Keeping her safe, and following her, was likely the only reason he hadn't gotten frustrated and just sprinted on all fours to Magnar's ward.

He whimpered, wanting to put space between them, but just couldn't seem to bear the loss of her warmth – even despite everything he'd just learned.

I... don't want to let go.

"Why... everything else?" he asked.

Why had she touched him and let him touch in return? All the times he'd held her, slept by her, and spent fond memories with her, like experiencing a moment of peace in a meadow filled with butterflies. Did she truly care for him, or was it a farce to keep him placid until now?

Fuck. He didn't want any of it to have come from a place of deceit.

Ingram had enjoyed all of their time together, even if much of their journey had been confusing. Learning of her, slowly having her open up to him, had been a gruelling wait, but worth it.

Like she understood what he meant, what he'd been trying to ask despite his unclear and pained thoughts muddling him, she let out a contented sigh.

"Because you are just so sweet, it makes me want to give you the world." She stroked her soft hand against the back of his hard skull. "But I can't do that. All I can do is help you kill the Demon King and give as much of myself as I can until then."

Is that why she had instigated this hug?

She'd chosen to be within his arms, completely and utterly trapped to him, when she had known he may not react well. He'd been moments from hurting her, and she'd still trustingly clung to him and told him the truth.

Emerie had placed herself in a vulnerable position.

Did she want to show me she cares in case her words were not enough? That's all he could think. *She asked me to forgive her before she even began speaking. Told me she regretted it.*

All of this was enough to stroke the worst of his shaken mind into calming. She had shown him the ultimate trust. It was enough to stir him into just embracing the feel of her while he tried to decide if he could forgive her, or even trust her anymore.

He stared at the dirtied cream tent wall as he took in the essence of Emerie.

Her heartbeat fluttering against his chest like it wanted to battle against his much bigger one. Her warm, shuddering breaths waving over the corded muscle of his throat. Her soft body moulding against his much bigger, harder, and imposing one.

Her hair didn't glow in the dark, but it was a shaded red in a way that wasn't angry like his orbs, yet stirred passion. It was silky as it crawled over the back of his arm and spilled her scent into him.

Her strawberry-and-primrose aroma was so luscious and mind-numbing that it pushed away any trepidation he'd been feeling.

"I'm really sorry," she whispered languidly. "I never meant to hurt you, and that was even before I learned how wonderful you were."

She did not do it out of callousness or hate towards me. Perhaps to a Duskwalker, a monster, but not the *Ingram* she had come to discover. The one that wanted to cling to her as much as she was currently. The one that wanted to touch, and taste, and experience her, as she had with him.

She made a mistake. That was what he wanted to believe.

He had made plenty of them.

He'd almost made another. *I was about to destroy her.*

"It... is okay, pretty butterfly," he grated with a voice laden with so much emotion, it was thick and heavy.

He squeezed her once more, but in an entirely different way. In a protective, safe, and adoring cuddle, rather than a violent, aggressive crush.

He heard her wince as much as he felt it. She even whimpered.

She is hurt. His orbs morphed to orange as he bumped the side of his skull against the back of her head to nuzzle her.

Trade. I want to trade with her. He wanted to take her wounds and heal her.

Perhaps because of how deeply he desired this, the purple glittering glow of his magic was instant. It didn't take long for the transfer to happen.

Immediately he felt tenderness around his ribs, like they had almost been snapped moments ago. There were also two massive palm-sized areas on his biceps and thigh that ached, with ten deeper presses to account for his own finger pads digging in.

"You didn't have to do that," she said, although he noted the sigh of relief that exhaled from her.

Her breathing returned to normal, no longer shuddering even though he hadn't loosened his gentler hold. She also didn't feel as weak.

For a long while, they just held each other in a comforting embrace. It carried no resentment from his side.

He was deciding to let what happened remain where it should

have all along: in the past. He appreciated learning the truth of it, only because he hoped it helped to alleviate her own misgivings.

If it had been a barrier between them, then he wanted it gone.

He nuzzled the back of her hair again. "I am sorry for hurting you."

Ingram then slipped his palm up from her biceps so he could place it against the side of her neck, wanting to feel her pulsing jugular. A place so vulnerable and soft, and proof of life.

"Thank you for forgiving me," she said against his neck, her legs securing themselves around his waist even more. He smelt the tiniest speck of salt. "I was really scared that you would hate me once I told you. That you wouldn't want to hold me anymore."

He wished he could squeeze her even tighter to show her that he was content with where she currently rested against his chest. Her weight was light in his arms, and the silhouette of her petite body moulded perfectly against his own.

But, if he squeezed her much more than this, he would only hurt her as he'd been doing before.

Ingram wasn't strong with words. He wasn't good at articulating them into what he truly desired. How else could he convey to her that his feelings had not been diminished, but rather... strengthened?

If his words couldn't be used, was touch his only option? He was beginning to worry that it wasn't a good way to show his affection. Pleasure between them had started with a lack of emotional connection; its only meaning was to gain release for self-satisfaction.

He was unsure if this was how Emerie still saw his approach to it, when, somewhere along the way, his mind had begun to hunger for her pleasure rather than his own. The first time he'd released against her chest, something visceral had shifted within. It was when his mind, heart, and body started truly being... possessive of hers.

But it was before that when something had started to change. As she slowly opened up to him, and showed him more kindness and understanding than he'd ever received except from his kindred, he'd wanted to learn her. To discover Emerie and see if they could connect on a level that took them from being two beings, into one.

To fill those voids that had been left within him by Aleron's disappearance.

He had not originally been seeking this from her, or anyone. It was only when she showed him herself that he'd begun experiencing these unfamiliar and unknown wants and cravings.

And he wanted more, simply because she had been so against it in the beginning. He'd started hoping that her acceptance of his touch meant she felt something for him. Trust, companionship, safety. If her feelings meant touch was an intimate and heart-connecting thing, if he continued to show his affection this way, and she welcomed it, would that bring them closer?

I wish I knew the answers.

His cock wasn't even hard or stirring. His desire to feel her was stemming from somewhere else – like his heart.

Then Emerie did something that had his chest radiating with tenderness, and gave him the path he'd been seeking with his thoughts.

Even with his silence and lack of answer, she pressed her lips against the side of his neck. His scales lifted in a rippling wave out from that spot. It was subtle, but he experienced it all over.

Placing his hand firmly around the back of her neck with his fingers dipping into her hair, he gently pulled her back. The moment her pretty blue eyes were able to connect with his sight, he parted his beak slightly and licked across her lips.

She let out the tiniest gasp and Ingram retracted his tongue.

Did he do the wrong thing?

As much as he hated to admit it, he'd never truly needed to instigate something like this without words. His orbs threatened to shift to a reddish pink as a shyness made him pull his head back.

"Wait, no," she rasped, yanking on his neck to bring him closer. "A-again."

She was looking up at him so expectantly that when he drew his tongue across a second time, he tried to dip the tip inside her parted lips. He was unable to.

Emerie had tilted her head, slid her tongue forward with her mouth opening more, and licked him back. She was more forceful, rougher than him, and she let out a deep, satisfied exhale the entire time.

A groan bubbled in the back of his throat as his scales puffed.

He licked her again, only for her to lick back, and there was something about the way her tastebuds rippled against his own that had him losing his mind. There was texture, sweetness, warmth, and wetness. He was sharing his taste as she shared her own.

His orbs morphed to a darker purple than normal.

I really like these kisses.

The mildness of his tongue's pressure evolved into a steady battle with hers, pressing harder and harder as she greeted each sweep. Her tongue was flat, short, and much wider than the tip of his own pointed one.

But that was only the tip, and the more she played with him, the further his beak parted to let more of his lengthy one through.

The moment the centre of his tongue, which was thicker than hers but not yet wider, obtained just a small gap between her parted lips, teeth, and her pesky lick, he pushed the rest through. The tip accidentally licked across her cheek before it flicked in from the corner of her lip.

She tensed, but then moaned as he swept his tongue across the top of hers. Within seconds, he'd filled the cavity of her mouth. They continued to dance, his tongue dominating as it swirled back and forth, his own saliva flooding her mouth, which he drank back as hers mingled with it.

Their combined drool dripped from the corner of her lips.

Ingram got lost in just the feeling and taste of her. The way she was seated on his forearm with his fingers digging into her soft thigh, her hair tangling around his other hand, had his other senses disappearing for a moment. Her eyes closed, and his sight did as well.

Which is why, when she wriggled against him, the warm apex between her thighs grinding against his hard chest, he only just noticed her scent had changed. The moment he registered how heavy and laden with arousal it was, his slowly stiffening cock clenched, swelled and engorged, and broke from his seam.

"Fuck," he groaned, violently shuddering against her. "Emerie."

She couldn't speak with his tongue partially folded and completely filling her mouth, but she did moan around it.

He didn't want to put her down, didn't want to separate their tongues, didn't want her legs to unwind from around his narrow waist, but he *needed* to touch her.

Sheathing his claws, he shuffled his arms around until he dipped under the skirt of her dress while his left hand was gripping the crook of her thigh and arse. He was thankful she was supporting herself along with him by her heels digging into his back and her arms around his neck.

His other hand cupped the hot slit of her cunt entirely over her underwear, and the next time she tried to grind on him, her clit squished against the tips of his fingers. Like she'd been seeking something to press it against, her breath hitched, and she shivered in his embrace.

There was no rejection. She didn't flinch or pull away from his touch.

His tongue slowed when hers did, as he pet the little hard bud nestled between her folds. Her head tilted back, so Ingram lowered her just enough that he could follow her mouth. Her eyes peeked open, but her features were languid as he moved his fingers back and forth while she moved her hips to control the pressure.

They were working in tandem, and he was able to watch as Emerie's eyelids flickered with pleasure. He listened as she moaned, as her breaths shook. He felt her slowing as her legs twitched and her nails began to dig.

What had started as dry material turned damp against his fingertips. The tanginess of her scent wrapped around the inside of his skull like a set of blissful, coaxing hands.

Just as her tongue stopped greeting his, he was forced to let her mouth go as her head dipped to the side, then all the way back. He drew the long length of his tongue against the exposed column of her throat, just as she let out a quiet, but spine-tingling cry.

Her eyes closed and clenched, while her lips, wet and swollen, remained parted. Her features were twisted as though she was in agony, and yet she kept grinding, kept waving her body back and forth against him.

"Are you coming?" he rasped, unable to tell with his hand on the outside of her like this. It looked like she was, and it was... beautiful.

Her head bobbed slightly, and he groaned.

Within seconds, he moved his fingers from her needy clit, dug them into the side of her underwear, and slammed two inside her. She gasped at the sudden intrusion, but Ingram found what he'd been seeking.

Her inner walls were quivering, twitching, and pulsating, and he'd wanted to feel them. Wanted to touch her orgasm and experience it. She was so hot, tight, and so fucking wet that it was like an endless pool.

He wanted to prolong it, to keep her here in this blissful state.

He moved his fingers in and out, unsure of how to touch her from behind like this. All he knew was that she drenched them, moaned around them. That she enjoyed them so much, she was quick to spasm around them again and let out another delirious cry.

And every sound she made, every twitch that danced across her body, every bit of her in this moment, had his cock swelling in waves. His cock was slick, and already a bubble of seed had formed at the tip.

He didn't even need her touch for her to stroke him. She was doing it to his mind, his senses, and his entire essence ached for more.

Ingram laid her down gently against the thin bedding on the floor of the tent.

She tried to stay latched to him, so he licked at her lips to distract and ease her. He removed his fingers and pushed her thighs apart, forcing them off him so he could bring his arm between them. Any worry or trepidation in her features was lost when she suddenly arched with her body twisting as he shoved his fingers back inside her.

Kneeling over her on a straightened arm, he watched her squirm as he pumped his hand between her thighs. Her orange hair spilled against the brown bedding moved side to side like a bendy river. Her chin lifted, exposing the precious column of her throat, and revealed just how fast her delicate pulse was going.

"That's a good little butterfly," he grated around panted, scent-tasting breaths, as he leaned down to lick across her neck. "Flutter for me."

His other hand roamed under her dress so he could palm her thigh, her hip bone, her side. When he made contact with her right breast, giving the hard and firm bud a flick, she let out a sharp cry.

Ingram moved lower and slipped his tongue across the part of her chest that was exposed, letting it dip into the valley between her breasts that was hidden away by her dress. Despite material being in the way, he went lower and swirled it over and around her left breast. He continued to tease it when she clung to his entire skull and one of her hands fisted one of his horns.

He wet her dress with his copious amount of drool, and it revealed pale pinkness behind it right where her hard nipple was. He hadn't known if it had a colour or not, but it was a similar, yet lighter, shade to the flesh his fingers were delving inside of.

He hated that he couldn't see properly.

He wanted her fully unclothed and bared to him. He wanted to see all of her, and touch without a barrier keeping him from her.

Leaning back to stare down at her, one nipple barely visible through her dress while the impression of his hand played with the other, he considered it. He considered ripping this vile piece of clothing off her until he had exposed her to his sight and touch.

It would be so easy. With just a small amount of pressure from his claws, he could slice it open.

With the way she was moaning, her cunt clamping around his fingers like she was close to spilling again, he doubted she would have noticed what he'd done until it was too late.

But he didn't.

He wanted her trust. He wanted her to enjoy this without the taint of betrayal. He wanted her to think of him as good, and gentle, and patient, so that she would widen her thighs around his hips and let him sink his deeply aching cock into her hot, snug pussy.

Ingram was becoming crazed for it, his orbs such a dark purple that the only bright thing in his vision was her.

He darted his sight down, his beak pressing against his chest, so he could watch his fingers touching. He saw nothing but glossy orange curls, her white underwear hiding everything else from him.

With an annoyed growl, he tore that strip of cloth from her body. She'd already done it for him, seeming to have no issue keeping his sight from here. His growl faded until it was a pleased rumble as he viewed her.

His dark-grey fingers were stark against her slick pink flesh, her entrance stretching around them as he moved them back and forth.

Fuck. So pretty. His cock jerked, and a drop of seed fell down between them and splattered against her inner thigh. Her lips were puffy, swollen, and yet her folds were spread like the wings of the very creature he named her after.

She looked just as delicate and fragile.

Her core was soft, plump, and dripping. It cuddled his fingers with heat and rippling texture, and her arousal smelt so fucking good it was muddling his mind.

He wanted to taste it, fuck it, nuzzle his whole body and face against it.

The arch of her foot knocked against the side of his throbbing cock, kicking a thrill through his entire being. He was so aroused, just that simple, accidental touch blasted him with need.

He slipped his fingers from her and drew away from her breast so he could lean over her on straightened arms. Ingram shuddered, resisting the urge to wedge himself against her little hole until he'd breeched it.

Gentle, he reminded himself. He needed to. He needed to remember that she was afraid of him, that he'd already shown her he couldn't control himself. He'd been too rough, too excited in the past. *Don't hurt her.*

"I-Ingram?" she panted, closing her creamy thighs while staring at his cock hovering above her. She'd bitten her lip, but her eyes were stark and nervous.

Still, he grabbed her knee and shoved it down, stopping her from escaping. Her look had told him all it needed to.

She wasn't ready, and he was beginning to worry that she never would be.

But right now, he had a dozen wants, and he was going to give in to one of them. He just hoped she was willing to welcome it because he thought he'd drown in his own drool if she didn't.

He leant back, wiped her slick over his chest to mark himself in her scent, then grabbed both her thighs. She struggled against him, then gasped in surprise when he pushed her across the bedding.

He bent over her, keeping her knees parted for himself, and kept his sight on her expression as he lowered his head. His tongue slipped out and over the curve of his beak as he drew closer.

When she bit her lip and didn't even try to stop him, her eyes glued to his skull and orbs, he slipped his long tongue out as far as he could. It dipped into her damp folds, and he softly abraded her sensitive clit with his tastebuds as it slipped down the slit of her pussy. Her taste tingled his tongue and made his scales, spikes, and flesh react instantly. Every inhuman part of him puffed and trembled – even his tail curled.

Her moan and his groan mixed into the air to become one quiet song.

Fuck. He wished he had another form of praise he could utter, but it would do for now. *She tastes so good. So sweet and pleasant.*

He dipped his body, leaned on his elbows and knees, and pushed all of what could extend past the tip of his beak inside her pussy. She coated all of him in her decadent taste, and he couldn't stop from twisting his tongue as he pushed it back and forth, desperately hoping she'd give him more.

Emerie threw her arm over her face as her back bowed. The other one shot down so she could palm the curve of his beak, gripping it so she could hold on as her hips tilted back and forth.

And, little by little, her dress rode up until her little shallow navel was exposed. He'd never seen the dipping plane of her stomach before, and the fact she was so lost to her pleasure because of his tongue, had him falling deeper into his own.

Giving was just as exciting as receiving, but that may have been because he was stealing her sweet nectar in return.

His tongue wiggled inside her, discovering and licking every part. When she didn't come for him like he wanted, just squirmed and bucked with high-pitched but quiet cries, he slipped two fingers between the inner walls of her deliciously soft pussy and the underside of his thin tongue.

He took up more room, wanting her to feel his long and dexterous tongue more firmly against the places he'd already discovered were more tender.

"Ohhh, *god*," she moaned, her thighs spreading as her feet lifted off the ground. She gave in when he twisted his hand so his knuckles were facing downward, and he added a third finger. "Ingram!"

The snarl that came from him was one of utter satisfaction.

Her stretched cunt not only clamped his fingers and tongue as she came, but sucked on them like she wanted to swallow him deeper into her depths. Ingram stole every little drop, greedy and hungry for it, wetting his dry throat with her tangy taste.

The sight of her coming from him like this was beautiful. She fluttered like he wanted her to, her hair moving in rivers as she tossed her head. One moment her thighs and calves tried to squish his beak and skull, the next they parted as her back arched in waves.

So pretty. So arousing. So perfect.

And when she was done crying out for him, he slipped his fingers from her and took back his tongue. He gently buried his beak into her instead, so he could carry her scent on it permanently, and he could breathe her in for as long as it lingered. He even wiggled his head subtly.

He'd almost, *almost*, messed up when he pulled it out and had been about to lick it off so he could taste just another drop more.

She was so languid and dizzy from her own pleasure that, when he grabbed her knees and yanked her closer, she didn't do anything but lay there. Her head lolled to the side, her eyes barely open, and her lips stayed parted on shaking huffs.

That was until he ground the head of his cock up through her pretty pink folds and all the way down him. She moaned, as did he, while he stared at her exposed abdomen.

When he'd tugged her closer, the weight of her on her dress had gotten it caught. It was crumpled just underneath her breasts, so close to giving him the naughty peek at her chest he was craving.

Emerie looked down and pushed against his stomach when his tentacles circled around her thighs.

He grabbed both her hands and wrapped them around the head of his cock to help stroke him, as well as show her what he was intending. He kept his left palm around both of hers and fucked his cock into their tangled hands. The underside of his erection stroked where he desperately wanted to sink inside of, and he let the wetness, softness, and heat of her pussy soothe him.

If this was all he could take right now, then he would take it. His cock was hard, and it throbbed with such a profound ache after tasting, teasing, and watching her, he knew he was about to lose his mind.

Already his embedded seed sacs clenched hard, threatening to make him spill. He was close from his own excitement pushing him along without assistance.

With his free hand, he dipped it underneath her dress to hold her left breast. He didn't know if he was playing with it right, if it felt good for her, but it was divine in his palm. So soft and jiggly as he bounced her with his hips. So much fun to play with.

Ingram's head tilted back all the way until he was looking up at the tent's ceiling.

"Emerie," he groaned, his hips twitching as he thrust. He could feel her clit moving back and forth inside his groove, and he never thought something so small could feel so wonderful.

The fact that she seemed to like it there, her wicked mouth letting out sharp, hitching sounds, made it all the better.

His panted, Emerie-slick-stained breaths grew sharper, more frantic. *I want inside her. I want to feel her around me as I come.* It would feel amazing – he just knew it. So warm and blissful as she held him within her.

Like every time he was about to spend, agony and ecstasy clutched at his groin like two sets of claws. He thrust harder, faster, pitifully seeking its soul-stealing, mind-shattering end.

It was like his first rope of seed crawled up his cock rather than shooting out like the rest that followed.

So close. Why did it have to feel like forever? *Please... I need release.* He didn't know who he was begging; he didn't care so long as they saved him. *Hurts so badly.*

She whispered little moans for him, like his thrusting against her clit felt as good for her as it did for him.

Her soft palms trapped between his big fist felt divine around the head and rim of his cock. He squeezed tighter, needing more pressure even as he worried about crushing her delicate fingers. Even more so when he let out a roaring groan as his body finally gave in to his feverish movements.

With shorter, twitching, wet pumps, he came into both their hands. Ingram shuddered, his sight going dark, as he let euphoria take hold and set his spirit alight.

His beak parted further and further, and he trembled with each hard spurt. He only looked down when the worst of them had eased the pressure and tension within him.

He found Emerie with her eyes wide and glued to their hands as he drained hot liquid into them. By the end, he'd drenched them both, and his thrusting had created the tiniest gap for a single burst to shoot up her torso.

When he was done, his vision pulsing from his satisfaction, he released his fist.

With her lips parted, she gaped at her seed-soaked hands. The liquid webbed as it clung to itself, to her, to his fist and cock.

In a visceral, feral need, he pushed her hands against her own stomach until he'd marked her with his fluids all the way to her crumpled dress sitting just underneath her mounds.

Then he removed his hand from her breast, pressed it against the ground near her shoulder, and leaned over her. With his seed-covered hand, he cupped the side of her face and drew a wet line across her pale-pink lips.

"Did I hurt you?" he grated, his voice hoarse and croaked.

"No."

He dipped his thumb inside her mouth so he could coat her tongue with his taste. She flinched at first, but then sucked on it, claw and all, and a jolting thrill shot through him.

"Good," he answered, hoping that meant next time she would welcome him inside her.

For now... he just wanted to play with his seed and spread it all over her. Mark her, as the other Mavka had marked their females. To keep them away, to keep everything away, or it would face the wrath of his claws.

"W-what are you doing?" she whispered when he palmed down her stomach and collected more of his scent.

"I don't understand why, but it makes me uncomfortable that you are near other males." He sheathed his claws again, slipped his fingertips over her clit and then pressed two seed-drenched fingers inside her.

I like this. I want to put it everywhere, cover her from head to toe in my seed.

"Nhn," she groaned and twisted away, her legs closing. "Sensitive."

He'd done what he wanted. Made her taste him and pushed some inside her. So he removed them.

His head tilted when he noticed something he never had before. *She... has a second hole?* If he'd known she had a second place to pleasure, he would have teased it earlier.

He didn't know why she had two pussies, or why this one looked different. Still, he dropped his wet fingers down to it, wanting to fill it with seed too. Since he'd been able to see it was tight and small, he only pushed one finger inside.

Emerie squeaked and tensed, and the stretchy ring – that felt very different to her pussy – clamped tight around his middle knuckle. Her knees shot up to her chest, and she grabbed his wrist.

"Ingram," she rasped, the docile, lazy-lidded gaze she'd been wearing now bright and alert.

"No?" he asked, not understanding the problem. He'd been allowed to touch everywhere else.

Her mouth, her pussy, her breasts, even her legs and arms. There was not a place on her body Ingram hadn't touched at some point, except for here – apparently.

"I did not know you had another place I could touch."

Her lips had flattened disapprovingly, but then relaxed at his words. He didn't move his finger, unsure if he could go deeper or should pull away. The longer it was there, the less it clamped and eventually softened.

"Y-you should give someone warning before you slip a finger in their ass," she grumbled, as she pushed his hand away.

"*Oh.*" He bent forward so he could scoop her into his arms as he laid down. His orbs turned a reddish pink. "I am sorry," he apologised, nuzzling the side of his beak against her sweat-dotted temple.

Well... at least she didn't say it *wasn't* a place he could touch. He just needed to give warning?

"I'm only letting you get away with that because you didn't know," she said before she relaxed and snuggled into him.

I will play there next time, Ingram thought with a contented hum.

Just more of Emerie for him to discover.

THIRTY

Bringing the aromatic, hot tea to her lips, Emerie took a light sip from the ceramic cup. The hints of mint, ginger, and honey sang against her pallet. The fact she was drinking this in the Veil was as weird as it was to be casually sitting in a log cabin home surrounded by two Duskwalkers and another human.

She eyed Delora from across the table, who was letting Magnar bump his fox skull against her cheek and even fondly bumped back with her hand on his long jaw. The affection was one of deep love, and the more time Emerie spent with them, the less it ate at her. Delora was happy, and after hearing how terrible the woman's story was before she met Magnar, it was hard to feel any jealousy or envy.

She was literally thrown into the Veil to die for murdering her cheating ex-husband. And Delora had been so depressed that she wanted to stop existing, only to fall from the canyon ledge to land on top of Magnar and tie herself to him instead.

Emerie had learned of this by asking how the woman came to be here.

"Fyodor really frightened me at first," Delora admitted while averting her caring brown eyes to the tea in her hands. "They bit me and chased me around while letting out this shrill noise. I was just so afraid of the pain, and my own child eating me, that I couldn't help it." Then, the corner of her lips twitched like she wanted to smile. "Magnar showed me that if I stopped being scared, they just wanted to be with me, like how you saw with

Mayumi. They just wanted to cling to me because they were anxious about the outside world since they couldn't see or navigate it well and they knew I was safe. I made a lot of mistakes."

As if he could tell his bride needed comforting, Magnar wrapped his hand around the crook of her shoulder and neck, while his long, fluffy tail moved to cuddle around her waist.

"*We* made a lot of mistakes, my pretty raven," Magnar reassured.

"Yeah, I guess that's true," she responded with a small smile.

Just as Delora lifted her eyes away from her tea to Emerie, a massive sneeze made their gazes duck to the left, where Ingram was sitting by the fire. They laughed as they watched him shiver.

Ingram had a cold, and wasn't taking well to having a fever, sniffly nose, and body aches. Well, in truth, Emerie was the one who had been sick when she woke up this morning. It may have had to do with the fact she'd cried, was worn out emotionally, then had a pretty intense intimacy session, in which Ingram covered her in his seed and let it go cold and then dry.

She'd woken up ill, since a human could only take so much.

Although she explained she'd be fine in a couple of days, Ingram had wanted to heal her of her illness. He'd been odd about it, as if he thought she would suddenly pass out and die. So, he was now sick in her stead – at least until tomorrow morning and his own healing capabilities took over.

Her lips curled, and she had to stifle her giggle.

He was cranky and didn't want to be anywhere but near the fire – even at the cost of losing his ever-constant touch against her. It was kind of adorable to think of a big, scary, tall Duskwalker being frazzled by a wittle itty bitty *cold*.

Ingram spun his head around to look at her, his orbs flaring red as he growled because she'd laughed at him. She quickly lifted her gaze up to the ceiling and almost whistled.

He didn't like being made fun of while sick.

She dropped her stare to Delora.

"It's nice that you found happiness here," Emerie said, while offering a sincere smile. "All of you seemed to have."

Delora shrugged. "We do what we can. Life isn't perfect

here. I can't just walk outside and go to the markets, and a lot of what we have is self-made. We all work together and each of our gardens have different foods and vegetables so we can trade."

"We Mavka help to cut down trees and build. I am not the best at it," Magnar said while scratching at the side of his snout bashfully. "But Orpheus has taught me much."

"It's just... it was better when we could move freely between all our houses. Now, with the Demons scouting and lurking around our homes, waiting for us to slip in our defences or catch us while we move in between, it's becoming more dangerous by the day."

"Yeah. I was pretty nervous coming here today," Emerie mumbled as she rubbed her neck.

However, nothing would have stopped Emerie from visiting Delora. After so many days of being with Mayumi, she felt like she was imposing on their family too much. She wanted to give them a break, so she came here for the day.

Visiting Reia wasn't possible for now, as Mayumi had suggested leaving her and Orpheus alone until he willingly brought her around again.

"It just makes me worried for Fyodor," Delora said as she bit her lip, her eyes quickly welling with tears. "It's really hard not knowing if our child is out there alive or not. They are alone, and I had no idea that if they fully grew, they would want to leave."

"It was an accident, Delora," Magnar argued. "Orpheus and Reia didn't know bringing the deer here would make them form their antlers. They remained small when they obtained their rabbit skull. No one knew what would happen."

"I know," she eventually sighed. "I just can't help but constantly worry. I think about them all the time."

Look at the way he reassures her. He's so kind to her, even when she's beating herself up. She couldn't help warmly smiling towards Magnar. *All the Duskwalkers are really sweet to their brides.*

Because she was just admiring them, it took Emerie a few moments for what they'd said to truly register. Her brows eventually drew together tightly.

"Did... did you say a rabbit skull and antlers?" Emerie asked shyly.

"Yeah," Delora answered, turning her exasperated gaze from Magnar to her. "The Duskwalkers become what they eat. Fyodor ate a rabbit skull first, and then a deer head. After that, they suddenly became a full-sized Duskwalker. They even obtained their orbs."

"She," Ingram randomly threw in while staring at the flames, his skull tilted. He spun his head back around and found all their eyes on him. "The Mavka you speak of. Not they, she."

Delora's lips parted as she pressed her hand against the table to stand. "What are you saying, Ingram?"

"I... I think we met Fyodor," Emerie chimed in, causing Delora's bewildered expression and Magnar's dark-yellow orbs to spin to her instead. Talk about awkward. She rubbed at her arm. "We came across a female Duskwalker with a rabbit skull and antlers on our way here. She didn't have a lot of humanity, so it was hard to speak with her, but Ingram said she was definitely a female."

"When?" Delora excitedly exclaimed, standing fully. "Where did you see them... her?"

"A day from the Veil, just south from here. I think she made herself a burrow on the surface."

"Oh my god, Magnar," Delora cried, as she threw her arms around his waist. "Fyodor is alive, and she's a *girl*."

For a few moments, there were tears and some sobbing from Delora as she hugged the tall Duskwalker. He'd wrapped his arms around her shoulders and placed the cheek of his skull against the top of her head.

Emerie didn't know what to do.

Should we leave? This felt like a pretty special moment for them. Once more, she and Ingram were imposing on another family.

Situations like the ones she was currently facing didn't happen in the guild. Couples were formed, but none ever had children due to women requiring surgery that stopped them from menstruating once a month.

The only time someone would see a family member was

when a male Demonslayer was visiting his family in a town or village – and most of the time it was an accidental family they made. Horny men doing silly things while out on missions.

Emerie fidgeted in her seat, then rose to head in the direction of Ingram, when he sneezed again. Fucking hell, it was like an explosion every time.

"No, wait. Please," Delora pleaded as she put her hand out to Emerie. "I'm sorry. You don't have to go on account of us."

"It's fine," Emerie said with a weak, reassuring smile. "I'm sure this is something you both want to digest alone."

"No, really," the woman pushed. "I was just overwhelmed. You don't know what a relief it is to learn that she's safe, but it's fine. I would prefer you stayed. I would like to make you some lunch as a way to show my appreciation."

Emerie would have fought her, not requiring such gratitude when her meeting with Fyodor had been accidental, but she couldn't refuse. Not with the way Delora's face had gone all cute and pink from her tears, and the grateful woman now faced her with a big smile, as if Emerie had just offered her the entire world.

"I guess I *am* kind of hungry," she grumbled with a blush.

She was starving, actually.

"I'll go to the garden then. Mayumi brought me some bread the other day, so I can make you a sandwich."

A sandwich in the Veil? So weird.

"I'll come with," Emerie offered, putting her hand out to Ingram, who looked as though he was about to spring to his feet and follow. "Stay. I'll only be a few minutes."

Emerie had ulterior motives for going outside, and she needed the guys away from them in order to do it.

With a huff, Ingram parked his tail back on the ground.

Just as she and Delora were leaving, Magnar walked over and sat next to him. Her features crinkled in humour when Magnar attempted to roughly and crudely pat him on his raven skull and was almost pecked for it.

The door shut with a bang that made Emerie wince. Delora gave a small laugh and showed her the way. They walked right off the porch, and already a small fence on the side of the house came into view.

"What do you feel like? I can make you a spiced potato, lettuce, and tomato sandwich," Delora said as she walked into the garden, looking around at what she had available. "We don't have any meat at the moment for me to offer you."

Emerie just paused at the open section of the fencing, her lips parting in surprise. "Delora... did you paint that?" she asked, her voice filled with awe.

Against the outside wall was a painting that consisted of a waterfall and forest in the background, with a rainbow. In the middle was a beautiful unicorn standing in a meadow.

If Emerie was honest, it was a little girly for her taste, but it had been painted so well that it was hard not to appreciate it. The artist had a skilled hand and had obviously been filled with passion when they'd painted it.

Delora's cheeks reddened, and she nibbled her lips bashfully. "Yeah. It's one of the first things I painted while I was here. It was really cathartic to draw and paint something I think my inner child wanted." Then, as if it was important to make the distinction, or perhaps she just wanted to divert her attention, she pointed to a stick figure with blue blobs for eyes. "Reia painted that. It's Orpheus."

Emerie snorted out a laugh. *It doesn't look like him at all.*

Delora returned her humour with her own giggle. "So... food?"

"Yes, but" – Emerie entered the garden and grabbed Delora by the shoulders – "I really need your help with something. It's really important, and I don't know who to ask. I was worried if I asked Mayumi, she would make fun of me."

"Oh no," Delora gasped, her eyes going wide. Concern immediately filled her features, her heart soft and tender. "What is it, Emerie? I'm not sure if I can do much, but I'll try."

This poor, *unsuspecting* woman.

Emerie cringed. Perhaps she was taking advantage of the fact she could tell Delora was overly kind, and perhaps the most trustworthy. She seemed susceptible, whereas Mayumi had a hard personality.

Right now, Emerie needed someone who wouldn't make her

feel embarrassed, even if they both were awkward about it.

"How..." Oh gods, was she really about to ask this from someone she barely knew? "How... does it *fit*?"

It took the woman a few seconds to register what Emerie was trying to ask. When it did, her whole face went blistering red, her ears included.

"Ah, um... ha," Delora stuttered, then opened and shut her mouth several times.

Emerie's cheeks were hot with her own blush, but she persevered through her bashfulness.

"Please," Emerie begged. "Because either all the other Duskwalkers have tiny dicks and Ingram is just well endowed, or something is happening here."

"Emerie!" Delora squealed. "Magnar does *not* have a tiny..." She squeaked at what she was about to say and covered her shaking lips with her hands.

"I know I'm asking you a really personal question, but I'm *dying* here. I really want to fuck Ingram, but the size of his dick really freaks me out. I think I might be able to fit its girth, but it's the *length,* Delora. The length."

The more she spoke, the more she wanted to expire. Delora looked like she was moments from fainting. She was surprised both their hair wasn't producing steam or smoke from how hot and uncomfortable they were.

Emerie bowed her head and bent forward while still gripping the woman's shoulders. "I'm worried if we attempt it he's going to pulverise me trying to get it all in. I really don't want my metaphorical tombstone to say: 'Death by dick.' Help a horny woman out. Please. He's really rough and doesn't quite know how to control himself."

Someone had to give her the answer because if Mayumi, who was the smallest out of them all, could take Faunus, and produce three freaking kids, then there was something she didn't know. And she needed to know *now*.

Last night, she'd been so tempted to just let Ingram have her.

She wanted it so badly, but she also didn't want it to be the last thing she ever did. She had plans, goals, and had made a promise to Ingram to help kill the Demon King. Emerie couldn't just toss everything to the wind for this.

But every time that sweet Duskwalker touched her, she could feel her resolve crumbling.

At some point, Emerie was going to part her thighs for his gigantic, tentacled purple cock and say 'come hither' while crooking her finger. If she could do that without any trepidation, that would be just fan-fucking-tastic.

She dug her nails into Delora's shoulders, tempted to get on her knees to plead.

"There's a spell," Delora quickly uttered.

She darted her head up, although didn't unfold herself from her sagging bow. "A spell?"

Delora squirmed, her hands clenching into tight fists. "Yeah. I-I can only tell you what happened for us because I don't know about the others. When he, uh..." She covered her face to hide it, practically slapping herself. She shook her head. "I can't believe I'm telling someone this. When he put it in the first time, he shoved his claws into me and then my body just... made way for it. It's like he magically rearranged my insides to fit it."

Emerie's features paled, and she straightened. "Didn't you give Magnar your soul really early, and it took away his hunger?"

Delora was finally able to step back to put space between them. "Yes."

"Well, shit," Emerie groaned as she palmed her forehead. "We can't do that. Ingram can be really sensitive to blood, so if he puts his claws in me, it won't be death by dick, but he'll try to eat me instead."

She could picture being pinned underneath him by his cock, with nowhere to go, as he bit her head off. Emerie wouldn't even have a fighting chance.

"The more humanity they have, the better they are at suppressing their hunger and urges," Delora mumbled as she gave Emerie her side. "I think that's why Reia and Mayumi survived it. Magnar was around Ingram's level when I met him, so I don't think I would have survived it had we tried then without me giving him my soul first."

Emerie cringed so hard that her squinted eyelids almost

blocked her vision. At least now she knew there *was* a way for her and Ingram to join their bodies like this, but now she had a new problem!

At her twisted face, Delora's own morphed into one that was apologetic. "I'm really sorry. I wish I had more answers for... you." Just as she was speaking, she leant to the side with her eyes widening and her lips parting.

She'd looked off into the forest.

Emerie looked over her shoulder and narrowed her eyes at the person approaching. Then she gasped, turned, and faced the woman wearing a cloak of white feathers.

Bare-footed, her white dress caught fractures of sunlight as she strode silently towards them.

"Lindiwe," Emerie rasped. She walked out of the garden to greet the woman. "I was wondering when or if you would show up."

She nodded her head to Delora after pushing back her hood, and her loose corkscrew curls fell freely around her face. Her rich-brown hair looked shiny and glossy in the sun before she dipped into the shade of the house with them.

She brought her sharp gaze to Emerie. "I was unsure if you would survive, but it appears luck was on your side."

"I'm a firm believer that you have to make your own luck," Emerie argued. "I survived because of my own cunning."

Surprisingly, Lindiwe's features softened and her full lips curled upwards. "That's one way to think of it."

Delora grabbed Emerie's forearm and tugged her back slightly. She stepped forward to be partially in front of her, as though she wanted to protect Emerie.

"What are you doing here?" There was no accusation in Delora's tone, but it was obvious she was unsettled by the Witch Owl's appearance.

"Can a mother not visit her children?" the woman mused.

"Yes, but every time you come here, there's either danger or someone needs help," Delora answered.

Lindiwe sighed, her expression falling into one that was dull. "I think it is best if we have this discussion with everyone present." She diverted to the right without anyone's direction and headed towards the porch. "Magnar can call for everyone."

"Hey!" Delora exclaimed, running after her with Emerie in tow. "You can't just go inside my home."

The feather-covered woman glanced over her shoulder. "I go where I am needed, and right now, I am needed here."

For some reason, she kept her gaze locked with Emerie's for a lot longer than was normal, or comfortable.

A sense of foreboding washed over her.

She mentally threw her hands up. *Great. There go my plans of figuring out how D plus V equals a great time.*

Simply because all the other Mavka had drawn their females into their laps and arms, Ingram made Emerie join him on the floor by dragging her onto his thighs. She didn't make any complaints, but her cheeks did pinken a little.

He liked it when her lightly tanned skin did this. It made her multiple brown freckles more prominent. He also liked that she warmed the front of him, while the fire from behind kept the worst of his fever chills from striking him.

He wasn't bothered by the Witch Owl's appearance. However, there was a staleness in the air, like the other Mavka and their brides were worried. He didn't see any reason for them to be wary of her; she had played with him and his kindred plenty of times, and had tried to protect them.

It was unfortunate she had not been able to save Aleron as she had with him. Even though that betrayal still lingered like he'd eaten a thorny bush, the time since then had worn him down. Being around Emerie had taught him much, and he'd begun to... accept why she'd done it, even if it had hurt him deeply.

Ingram watched her closely, noticing how she was tense with her arms loosely folded across her chest. Her stance, although confident, was also defensive as she blocked the hallway in front of him and across the table.

That may be due to the many stares upon her, most of them mistrusting.

Faunus was seated on the long chair to his right by the fire with Mayumi and his younglings on his lap. Magnar was sitting on the big dining chair with Delora curled up in his arms, and her hand was tightly clasping his loose shirt.

Orpheus had taken himself and Reia to the furthest wall, which just so happened to be next to the door. It was like he wanted to be close to the exit so he could sprint off with the blonde-haired, pale female who was sitting on his crossed legs. He had huffed with red orbs when he'd entered, and had been carting Reia around in his arms.

He didn't wish to let go of her, and she seemed content to stay with him.

Ingram had pressed the right side of his back against the rest of the rustic lounge Faunus was half-laying back on, with Emerie's butt on the ground between his crossed legs. She was stiff as she pressed against him. She was the only female that didn't appear natural, and no amount of hair patting had calmed her into relaxing for him.

He would have been disheartened about that if he wasn't too busy trying to breathe through his blocked face. Had he'd known that having the illness called a *cold* would make him feel stuffy and drained, he may not have traded his own health for Emerie's wellbeing.

At least he didn't feel the urge to *sneeze* right now, but his throat was scratchy.

"I am assuming you are all aware by now of why Ingram has come to you," Lindiwe began, her dark-brown eyes roaming over them all. "What is your current plan?"

"Nothing," Orpheus growled from the right. "The females have offered to go while we stay behind, and I will not allow Reia to come to harm like this."

"That's not what you promised," Reia uttered up to him, her green eyes squinting into a glare. "You said if we can come up with a plan that we think will be successful, then you would allow it."

His growl cut off into a huff as he darted his head away from her and everyone else. His hands tightened on her, like he feared she'd suddenly disappear if he didn't hold her. The blonde turned her face to them all and gave a wincing apology.

"Ingram will come with us," Mayumi stated. "As well as Emerie. But we have to wait until I'm no longer pregnant." She gestured to Magnar and his bride. "Delora will take a bow and defend us from somewhere above if she can. We can float in our Phantom forms, so fuck it, she can just stand on a chandelier or something."

He didn't know why that made all four females giggle.

"Reia, Emerie, and I will take to the ground and fight with swords. We just need to grab Jabez's hair to teleport with him, and if we attack him as one unit, someone might get the advantage enough to slit his throat. I may even be able to drive a dagger up through the back of his skull." Mayumi turned her gaze down to Ingram, as he twisted his head back and up to look at her. "That's, of course, if Ingram can't rip his head off his shoulders himself. We will have a Duskwalker, but with how volatile their kind can be, we can't rely on him. I'm actually thinking he'd be more useful mindlessly slaughtering Jabez's army as they're trying to get to us."

"None of this is certain," Orpheus snapped out. "You will all be picked off, one by one. The Demons are faster, stronger, and there is a chance Ingram will turn on you."

"Yeah, but Ingram will also redirect to whatever is attacking him," Emerie butted in. "He may turn on us, but he's easily distracted. No offense."

She patted his chest in apology, and he tilted his head at her for it. What she said was true, so there was no need for her to do this.

"I can make him chase me instead," Delora offered. "If I shot him with an arrow, I might be able to grab his attention and fly away long enough for a Demon to take it."

That, he didn't like, simply because he didn't actually want to be hurt. He knew arrows could be *mean* little weapons.

"All of you are willing to come forward and help?" Lindiwe asked as she bounced her stare between each of the females in the room. She kept it on Delora the longest, but then ended it on

Emerie. "Even knowing that you may be harmed, eaten, and killed?"

"Yes," was their collective answer.

"My sons have all chosen such brave women," she complimented firmly, as she dug inside her feathered cloak. On her side was a bag strapped to her waist that Emerie was only able to peek at from her cloak hem shifting back. "Then I bring you our possible solution."

She took out a small stone no bigger than a thumbnail and revealed it as it lay flat on her palm. It was blue, at first glance, but it pulsated with a golden yellow, as though it was filled with magic.

"This... this is our answer."

"What is it?" Reia asked, her brows furrowing deeply.

"Weldir, the spirit of the void, has informed me it is some kind of sun stone."

"Sun stone?" Delora asked, her full lips pursing. "Where did it come from?"

"It looks like the diadem I used to wear, the one that protected me from Demons. If you've had something like this all along, why didn't you bring it to us sooner?" Reia bit out. "We could have ended this months ago!"

The Witch Owl cast her a hardened stare and closed her fist around it. "Because I only just obtained it."

"Where did you obtain it from?" Orpheus asked, his tone sharp.

Lindiwe's features fell as she opened her palm just enough so she could look down at it. "I... found it in Merikh's cave after he disappeared. I can't even see him with my viewing magic, but when I went to his home to investigate, I found this."

"It has a similar magic scent to Raewyn," Ingram happily chimed in, wanting to be part of the conversation.

When all eyes darted to him, he stiffened uncomfortably. Most of their expressions appeared confused about who that was, so he explained.

"We were chasing the Witch Owl and found ourselves within Merikh's ward. There was a female there with grey-brown skin, white hair, and long, pointed ears."

"Pointed... like an Elf's?" Reia asked, dipping her head to the side and letting her hair curtain down.

"Yes, exactly," he confirmed. "Merikh was keeping her there."

"What was Merikh doing with an Elf?" Faunus asked, and Ingram only just noticed he was sitting upright. "He won't talk to me, but he'll fucking keep an Elf?"

"Who... is Merikh?" Magnar asked, his head tilting.

"The bear-skulled Mavka," both Orpheus and Faunus said at the same time.

"I have never seen this Mavka," Magnar grumbled, scratching a claw against the side of his fox snout.

"You wouldn't," Faunus stated. "He doesn't like other Mavka. I'm surprised he didn't kill you two," he continued as he pointed at Ingram's raven skull.

"He has. Many times," Ingram rebuffed, although not permanently, since Merikh never crushed their skulls. Merikh always won. "But he always let us rest under his ward."

"The point is..." Lindiwe cut in while shaking her head. "Merikh is gone, and so is the Elf. I think they went to the Elven realm, but I cannot see where he is. However, they left this behind, and it could be what saves us all."

"How will a stone help us?" Emerie asked. "I know Demons can't withstand the sunlight, but that doesn't look very useful."

"To be honest, none of us can wield its magic, not even me," Lindiwe admitted. "Weldir is able to, but he doesn't have a physical form in this world. However... we can break it, and it will be like a mini explosion that consists of sunlight."

"Even Jabez is not immune to the sun," Mayumi added while cupping her jaw in thought. "When I met him, I watched it burn him. This could definitely work."

"Brilliant!" Reia squealed as she bounced to her feet, only to be dragged back into Orpheus' lap with a quiet growl. "We can smash it against the ground in Jabez's castle and fucking blow the place up! We'll kill him and any Demons within his radius."

"Exactly," the Witch Owl said, as she drifted her gaze to Reia. Lindiwe didn't smile – she didn't even look pleased. Ingram didn't know why, but he thought there was a tiredness to the dark creases under her eyes. "Whether Merikh meant to or not, he has handed us the answer. Now it's up to us to do the rest."

"You'll be joining us?" Mayumi asked.

"Yes, I will go with you. This is too important to do by yourselves, and I can wield Weldir's magic and protect you all for as long as I can." Then she looked off to the side, out the window above the kitchen. "It would not be fair of me to ask you all to do this by yourselves."

"So, you'll need all of us," Emerie stated. "If Reia is still willing to give me the diadem, that will stop the weaker Demons from touching me, and I'm wicked good with a whip. Plus, if we managed to coil a rope around the Demon King's hair and attach it to something, maybe we can stop him from teleporting away from the blast?"

"I knew I liked you," Reia said with a wide grin on her face. "It'll be like an anchor, keeping the bastard from running away like a coward."

"No need to start calling me a genius, but you're welcome to if you really want to," Emerie teased, bashfully flapping her hand up and down.

Ingram didn't know what her hand flapping meant, but he was tempted to mirror her. He was learning all sorts of new ways to be playful.

"You're all just lucky I stole a bunch of weapons," Mayumi basically cackled.

"And that I figured out Jabez's weakness," Delora said with a smile. "I can't wait to look that jerk in the eyes. I'm hoping I can get a good punch in."

"Delora," Magnar gasped, and the female grew flustered at herself. "You are to stay away from him."

With her eyes firmly on Emerie's, the Witch Owl said, "You are all important in this, and each of you has unwittingly brought in key elements to this. Reia's diadem, Delora's information, Mayumi's weapons, and this, Raewyn's stone."

"I guess I brought Ingram," Emerie joked while poking her thumb at him.

This did not humour the Witch Owl. Instead, her gaze bored

into Emerie, and there was something... haunted about it.

Ingram's skull jerked, and he tightened his arms protectively around his pretty little butterfly. Something cold and dark wrapped around his chest like a flowing, constrictive cloth.

Why is she looking at Emerie like that?

THIRTY-ONE

As gingerly as she could, Emerie removed the heavy Duskwalker's arm from on top of her, and it fell limply between them. Then she carefully wiggled the rest of her from his embrace.

Once she was on her knees, she hovered her hands out, *willing* with all her might for him to stay asleep.

He still wasn't well, which was working to her advantage right now. He was out like a blown-out lamp, and she almost fist bumped the air.

Yes! She got to her feet and tiptoed out of the tent. *Now I can pee without him trying to freaking follow!*

She didn't even bother to poke her head out of the entry flap. Emerie got her butt out of there and put as much space between her and it as fast as she could.

To her left, she noticed there was light coming from Faunus and Mayumi's home. It was past the middle of the night, the waxing moon bright above.

She figured Mayumi just couldn't shake the backwards sleep cycle Demonslayers lived by. They were almost nocturnal. Emerie, however, had always been an early-morning riser.

Emerie found a spot, did her business in the forest, and made her way back to the tent. Just before she could reach it, a thump sounded behind her.

As a gasp of surprise escaped her, a human hand slapped across her mouth. She fought while turning in their arms, only to find herself staring into a dark-brown pair of eyes framed by long, delicate lashes.

"Lindi–" Before she could finish, the woman slapped her hand over Emerie's mouth again.

She placed her index finger to her own lips, indicating for Emerie to be quiet as she slipped her gaze to the tent. *She doesn't want to wake Ingram.*

Perhaps the wise thing would have been to shout and wake him, but she was too curious about why Lindiwe wanted her alone. Emerie flicked her gaze up to Mayumi's brightly lit home but couldn't see movement at the window like she had before.

"Follow," Lindiwe whispered so quietly she was barely heard.

She hesitated. Yet, against her better judgement, Emerie did.

Lindiwe's white cloak was easy to spot in the darkness, picking up just enough moonlight to reflect it. The quills of feathers glinted. Her bare feet were much quieter than Emerie's, and she walked almost silently as she took them both into the forest and far from view.

At the border of Faunus' glittering yellow dome, she gestured to a large tree stump big enough to seat both of them. In doing so, she showed that their conversation would not only be long, but probably deep.

Emerie didn't take it.

"I can't be long," she explained. "Ingram will eventually wake up and come looking for me."

"Which is why it is best if you do as you're told, so we can end this quicker."

Rolling her eyes and folding her arms in annoyance, she plopped her backside on the stump. She shifted over when Lindiwe took a seat next to her, which was surprising, but she appreciated she was not going to be stood over like a mother giving a lecture.

Then, for a short while, with their sides in the direction of Mayumi's home and Emerie's temporary tent, they said nothing.

It was quiet, and being so close to the rest of the Veil was creepy. Mist surrounded them like a light, wet blanket. No crickets chirped; no bugs buzzed in the background. It sounded empty of life, which made it all the more... eerie.

The tiny hairs on her arms lifted in aversion and apprehension. She rubbed at her biceps as if that would help soothe them.

There were no Demons lurking just outside the ward, but Emerie was sure her scent would bring them eventually. At least, she assumed so, even though she could smell an odd, but really sweet smell coming from Lindiwe.

"My children don't trust me," the woman started, her tone solemn and holding a note of... pain. "It has been difficult all these years to watch them grow without me, to watch as I give them their skulls and horns, only for them to forget who I am and all I have done for them."

Lindiwe lowered her face, staring down at where she picked at the edges of her long nails. Her dejected voice continued, her posture weakening by the second.

"Merikh has been the hardest. I have made many mistakes as a mother, but there is only so much I can do. It does not excuse it, I know, but much is out of my control, and I am learning along the way with them. I wish to protect them, but I'm unsure of how to do that when they do not trust me. How can I protect them when they will not even allow me to get near?"

Why is she telling me this?

"Ingram seems to trust you," Emerie offered, nibbling at the corner of her lips.

"Ingram and Aleron were different. They were the most playful of my children, and it was easier to insert myself into their existence as they bounced off each other's joy." She lifted her face enough to glance at Emerie next to her. "It is one of the reasons why Aleron's death has weighed heavily on me. I tried to save him, but it was impossible. I had to retreat before I was killed."

"But can't you come back to life?" Emerie asked. "If you cared about them so much, why run away when they needed you the most?"

Lindiwe reached into her cloak and around herself. When her hand came back around, she was holding a baby Duskwalker across her forearm. They clung on for a moment before she placed them into her lap and comfortingly covered their back with her palm.

This one had a tiny skull, but Emerie couldn't make out what kind in the darkness. Still, they looked small, and still so fragile.

"Oh," Emerie rasped. "I see. You couldn't because you didn't want to leave your baby by themself."

"Exactly. I carry two, and have been since Orpheus and Reia bonded. This one has a skull, whereas the other does not. I... have been keeping them small on purpose after I realised Jabez was making moves and had truly started to target all Mavka. I decided it was easier to protect them if they stayed attached to me."

"But it means you can't truly help the grown ones when in a fight."

"Yes, this is the problem I face. I can only do so much, and I can only be in one place at a time. I had to make a choice between Aleron and Ingram that night. I could not get to Aleron, not without possibly dying or having one of these two harmed in my attempts. I saved the son I could, while I was forced to watch the other die before my very eyes."

She lowered her head to face the little Duskwalker on her lap. Her eyes didn't well with tears, but Emerie thought she could hear them in her voice.

"It's not fair for a mother to outlive her children. It is not how it is supposed to be. Then the others blame me for my failure, although I could do nothing to prevent it. Aleron is not the first to die, but my serpent child was the one who taught me that destroying their skulls is *how* I will see them all perish if I do not protect them."

Emerie clasped her hands and looked out into the forest, wishing it didn't look even more dreary than it did a few minutes ago.

"Why are you telling me all this?" She whispered the question, unsure of why Lindiwe was pushing this burden onto her.

Emerie's heart ached for the woman, unable to imagine all the sorrow, grief, and suffering she'd gone through. It was obvious she cared about her children very deeply, more than they seemed to realise.

Even though she was a Phantom, she was still human. Just one that could possibly be centuries old.

"I want to give this to you," Lindiwe said, offering the sun stone.

Emerie glanced down at it, while jerking back. "Why? Wouldn't it be better for you to keep it, or to give it to one of the others? I'm not a Phantom, and to be honest, I don't think I'm going to live very long in this fight."

"Because, Emerie, you are the only one who can use it."

She forced it into Emerie's hand, and she stared down at it. The golden-yellow glow faintly pulsated within the blue stone.

"What do you mean, I am the only one who can use it? I don't have any magic."

"This stone is... volatile. When I gave it to Weldir, he activated it, and I was instantly in pain. It was like my Phantom spirit was trying to separate from my human body. He deactivated it when he felt my soul rippling, like it was trying to break apart."

Emerie's lips parted, and she gawked at the tiny stone in her palm. It was barely bigger than the fingernail of her thumb.

"The rest of the souls in Tenebris were unaffected, only mine. I remember this sound, and it was like a ringing I felt all the way through me. Even Weldir was affected, but it was his Elven heritage that kept him from withering."

"I would say we should give it to Ingram, but I don't think he'll be in the right frame of mind to be useful," Emerie tried to laugh out.

Lindiwe's sharp, tight features sliced at her humour.

"If it affected Weldir and me, then I don't think a Mavka will survive its blast, as they are part spirit, part human. It is likely the same thing that happened to me will happen to them. I don't think it's the light that affected me like it would Demons, but the sound, the frequency of it, separates a Phantom soul from their physical form. For a Mavka... that could mean death. They have nowhere to resurrect to, as they have no anchor to return to like their brides."

"Are... are you saying we have to leave Ingram behind?"

"Yes. I also don't think the stone wielder will survive, no matter who or what they are. It produces a lot of heat and radiation. It is like you are holding a droplet of the sun in your hand, and shattering it will release an immense amount of power. We will still need the others' help, but that is only so they can clear a path for us to reach the Demon King."

Emerie tightened her hand around the stone until it was secure in her fist. Her eyes welled with tears that were both sad and fearful as she glared at the nothingness before her.

She knew what this meant.

"You know..." she weakly started, her voice trembling as salty liquid obscured her vision. "I was kind of hoping there was a way I would somehow live through this."

"I am... sorry," Lindiwe softly stated. "If I could do this, I would, and I cannot bear to hurt my mated children. I cannot rip their brides from them, not when they are finally experiencing happiness."

"So, basically, what will happen is" – Emerie licked at her lips as tears began to slip across the seam of them – "you will protect me until I make it to Jabez, knowing the others will eventually be killed and returned to their Duskwalkers, but you hope they will help us reach him."

"Yes."

"Then..." Emerie let out a sob as she covered her eyes with her other hand. She persevered through her emotions to explain what Lindiwe's plan was, to show she completely understood it. "Then once they are gone, you will leave me by myself with Jabez, so I can kill us both with this stone."

"I know I am asking a lot from you. That you have no real reason to make this sacrifice."

"But you need a human." Emerie quietly cried as she voiced her realisation. "You need someone who is not a bride, otherwise it will emotionally destroy their bonded Duskwalker if one of them dies permanently."

"That is my fear, yes. I'm also worried that the soul rippling and breaking apart may, by proxy, kill one of my children in the process. Both Mavka and Phantom become intertwined on a spiritual level, their souls eternally linked. If one permanently dies..."

"The other could follow. I get it." Emerie lowered her hand so she could wipe at her tear-stained cheeks. "Wh-what would you have done if I had given Ingram my soul?"

"Waited until another human came along. I would have searched for someone willing to do this for us."

She slapped her face into her hands again and shook her head. "You and I both know no human would have done this. We consider them monsters. No one would make this sacrifice for them."

The silence that followed Emerie's words was choking.

"I know," Lindiwe eventually admitted. "When you offered to travel with Ingram, I wasn't sure what I was hoping for. I want him to find a bride, but... I also want to save my children. Orpheus, Magnar, and especially Faunus now – they are all at risk. Every time they travel between each other's homes, they risk the potential of being overrun. Weldir can obtain a new mate, unlike our children. If I did not have these two little ones to protect, I would have made the sacrifice."

"Is this why you didn't come here straight away?" Emerie asked with her voice cracking. "You let me stay here, let me fall in love with everyone, so I would be more sympathetic to your cause."

When she glanced at Lindiwe, she averted her gaze.

She didn't deny it.

"I know this is cruel. I know it is unfair. I know I should not be asking this of anyone, but I cannot find another solution. For over three hundred years, I have been searching for a way to destroy Jabez. That man has killed me, over and over and *over* again, for the past three centuries. This stone..." She gestured to it in Emerie's closed fist. "This is the only time I have had an answer, and if I were not backed into a corner, I would not be asking this of you. Aleron's death... I cannot bear it again. I cannot see another one of them die. My heart will not survive it."

When Emerie finally looked at Lindiwe again, a single tear had managed to escape from her left eye. It was obvious by her shaking she was fighting to hold them back.

The woman was just as distraught as Emerie, but was better at controlling it, hiding it.

"You do not have to do this," she offered.

"I do," Emerie croaked. "I know I do. No one else is going to."

God. Fuck. Shit. She didn't know what curse word would make her feel better, what would stop her from trembling. *Bitch?*

A deep, yet feminine voice behind them had them both startling. "Then you better fucking hope we can figure out how to do this without Ingram tagging along."

There stood Mayumi, her hands on her small hips, looking down at them with a disapproving glare. Emerie immediately rose to her feet and backed up.

"How long have you been standing there?" Emerie squeaked, placing her fist over her chest to calm her unsteady pulse.

"Long enough for her to know I've been here the whole time," Mayumi said, pointing to Lindiwe. "So, this is your fucking plan, Witch Owl? Has no one considered how this will make Ingram feel?"

"Of course I have," Lindiwe snapped back, before biting her plump bottom lip and lowering her head. "As long as my children are all safe, I don't care if everyone... *hates* me by the end of this. I will wear it, as I have with Merikh."

"Have you truly thought on this, though? Because, to me, they are bonded except in freaking soul. Hasn't he already lost his twin? Now you want to throw her out of his life as well."

"I have no other option."

"I never said I would give Ingram my soul," Emerie muttered, although she *had* been considering it.

How could she not? She wanted what everyone else had here. She wanted to be loved and adored, and Ingram often made her feel that way. She was also completely and utterly fond of him.

After watching everyone else be happy together...

She would have followed him wherever he wanted to go, even if it was on a wild and foolish goose chase to bring back Aleron. She'd kind of just been waiting to see if their bodies could be compatible.

It's why she'd asked Delora earlier in the day how his dick

was supposed to fit and not pulverise her to death.

"I know there's no other option," Mayumi said in a sharp and brutal tone. "It's why I'm not stopping this. However, I just wanted you both to take into consideration how much this will hurt Ingram."

"Please stop," Emerie said as she turned around when the tears came back, hotter and more despairing than ever. "I know, okay?! I know. But at this rate, it won't just be his twin that has died, it'll be all of you. He... he can find someone else. There's plenty of people in the world."

"I like you, Emerie," Mayumi said with a sigh. "And the only reason I'm not stopping you is because I have a family to think about. Call it selfish, but something in your brain changes when you're a parent. You will throw yourself and anyone else between your kids and the enemy. It's probably the only reason *she* is asking you."

"Then why the fuck are you shouting at me for?" Emerie snapped back.

She wasn't really shouting, but her tone was harsh and painful against the fragile emotional exterior she had right now.

"I don't know," she grumbled back. "Maybe because I think this is fucked up and I wish we didn't have to do this? I'm angry because we shouldn't even be in this shitty situation in the first place."

Emerie spun around and narrowed her stare at Mayumi. "Then can we think of a solution for keeping Ingram away so I can do this utterly fucked thing?"

"Faunus will help," Mayumi stated. She threw her hand up when it was obvious Lindiwe was about to protest. "He will. I'll be honest with you. None of the Duskwalkers care about anyone more than their brides. Each of them would throw each other under the carriage if it meant protecting them. Orpheus may be the most selfish and protective, but Faunus is cunning. He will find a way to get the other three to leave, Ingram included."

Rubbing at her arm, Emerie turned her face away. "Sorry, Mayumi, but I don't think I can wait."

She lowered her hand and stomped forward a step. "What do you mean?"

"I can't wait for you. I know the longer I'm here, the more I'll cave. I'll either back out, or if Ingram asks me for my soul, I'll give it to him in a heartbeat."

As long as he was okay with Emerie not being able to give him children... of course.

"You're kidding me," the woman almost growled. "Are you really telling me I have to stay behind?" When Emerie winced, she threw her hands up. "Why now? Why when I'm pregnant? I could wring Faunus' neck so hard right now."

"I'm sorry, Mayumi," Emerie muttered with her shoulders falling.

"We can do this without you," Lindiwe stated. "Reia and Delora would be enough of a diversion to keep the worst of the Demons away with Weldir's magic protecting us."

"Do you want to know what I've been dying to ask since I met his stupid chalky face?" Mayumi sneered with spite. "Why the fuck isn't he doing anything to help?"

"Because he is unable to. In order to just have a *visible* form in this world, he must consume a soul totally, destroying it in the process. It weakens him every time afterwards. He also cannot touch anything here, so he cannot even hold the stone unless he is in Tenebris."

"Well, isn't that just convenient?" Mayumi bit back. "I was wondering why the deadbeat hadn't been helping more."

Lindiwe's glare turned so sharp, it was like she wanted to stick daggers into the short woman. "You think this doesn't pain him? He watches over all of them, and it eats at him that he cannot help. I am both of us in this world, and it's his magic I use in order to protect everyone. That is how he contributes, because it is the only way he can. Even though it weakens him for me to do so, to the point that sometimes he is forced to sleep to conserve his energy while I drain him more and more. He is at risk of death every time I do so, which will endanger not just us, but the Elves he has sworn to protect."

Mayumi rolled her eyes and walked to Emerie. "Say I believe you, he or you better figure out how everyone is supposed to make it to the Demon King's castle within the span of a day, otherwise none of this will work."

"Like I said yesterday, I have a way."

"Which is?"

"A portal."

That quietened Mayumi. She placed her hand on Emerie's shoulder, before yanking her in for a hug. Emerie froze, not expecting something like this from the usually hard woman.

"I'm sorry you're being asked to do this, but if it works, there's nothing in the world I could say or do that would show my appreciation." She tightened her arms around Emerie's waist while she plopped her chin on her shoulder. It spurred her into returning it. "I don't even like hugging people, so this is the best I can do."

"Neither do I," Emerie admitted.

"Then why the hell did I start this for?"

She didn't know how it was possible right now, but Emerie weakly laughed. She pulled away, and Mayumi let her go.

"It'll take time for me to round up the others and for us to make a plan to get rid of the boys. I'll let Faunus in on it, and we'll go from there."

Emerie gave a nod, her throat too thick with emotion to speak. Her shoulders fell, and she looked at Lindiwe, who appeared guarded, when only a few moments ago she had been vulnerable and soft.

She averted her gaze to the eerie forest before drifting it up to the moon.

Part of her wanted to back out of this more than anything.

Emerie wished she and Ingram had never come here to begin with. They could have journeyed anywhere they wanted to go, and she would have fallen more and more in love with him until her soul jumped out from wherever it came from for him to take.

Maybe he would have accepted that she could never give him what Mayumi could for Faunus. He didn't seem to mind her scars, and over time, she'd begun to feel more at ease about them around him. He'd provided her solace in times when she really needed it, when no human had been able to do that for her. Even though he'd almost eaten her multiple times, his arms still felt safe and protective, and she'd started seeing him as a shield from the horribleness of the world, as well as her own mind.

And he was *trying.*

Ingram tried his hardest to be gentle, when everything about his exterior was monstrous and frightful. His raven skull, short goat horns, his scales, spikes, and long, thick tail. His claws were deadly, and yet he'd managed to dance them across her skin with such a lightness it stimulated her into gulping at the air with need.

Sometimes, he was frightening in the most titillating way. His growl unexpectedly had her thoughts clouding.

In the back of her mind, and in a corner of her heart, she was hoping Ingram would find a way to stop her before she did this.

If I'm going to die... would it be selfish of me to ask for one real night with Ingram? A parting gift for her, not just from him, but from the world, and a way to teach him something for when he, undoubtedly, found the bride he was meant to have.

The one that wasn't her.

Sadness washed over, so heavy and cold it threatened to drown her. She wished her eyes didn't bubble with tears again, but she couldn't suppress the ache in her chest no matter how much she tried.

It wasn't fair. None of this was.

I want to be with him.

THIRTY-TWO

Emerie had decided if today was truly going to be her last day on Earth, then she would shamelessly milk it for all it had to give. Other than having a bath at Delora's because, well, she wanted to go out clean, she spent the rest of the time doing what she wanted.

Which just so happened to be spending almost every single second of the rest of it with Ingram.

With them secluded in their tent, she'd attempted to teach him how to play one of the board games Mayumi owned. That had gone poorly, as nothing, not even checkers, seemed to really stick in his mind, since they all required forethought and cunning. It did allow her a bunch of giggles, though, especially when he picked up a disk-shaped piece with his claws, and it flicked out between them like a projectile – straight into her forehead.

Her giggles had erupted into full-blown laughter when he'd grown overly apologetic.

At least scissors, paper, rock was simple enough and based purely on luck. He chuckled each time he won, and him covering her hand when he picked paper seemed to make his chuckle deepen each time.

She even taught him how to count to a hundred, although he often got muddled on the bigger numbers. He was quick to learn. She found it endearing when he started tapping at her freckles, like he wanted to count them all.

Since she'd been teaching Magnar how to read, Delora had lent Emerie a fairytale book Reia had given her.

Teaching Ingram how to read was too big of a task for just one day, although she did start with the alphabet so he could attempt to read along. He did occasionally tap a claw at the page at certain words she repeated regularly.

He'd grown giddy whenever he was correct, scooping his arms around her from behind in innocent joy.

Really, she'd just wanted an excuse to stay curled up in his lap, even until the sun went down and she was forced to light an oil lamp. Emerie wasn't fond of anything with fire, but she'd grown comfortable with lamps, candles, and campfires over the years.

This was the first time she'd truly been enthralled by one. Once she'd gone through every story, she laid the book down to stare at its flickering flame.

It was a quiet flame as it burned its wick, but the smell of it brought back terrible memories.

Fire, whether she wanted to truly accept it or not, had brought her to this moment. *I wouldn't have joined the Demonslayers if Gideon was still alive.* She would never be thankful for it – no person should have suffered what she did that horrible night – but if it didn't happen, she wouldn't have ever met Ingram.

Just another reason to regret it, and although the pain in her chest wasn't physical, it corroded like acid.

She never would have been faced with knowing tomorrow could be her last.

She wished it didn't have to be.

Does it have to be? Emerie thought when Ingram stroked his claws through her freshly washed and silky hair. *Lindiwe said she would try and find another human if I don't want to. Or, if I bond with Ingram.*

But did he want that with Emerie?

It was possible, considering his obvious attachment to her. *He hasn't asked me, though.*

It was likely he'd thought about it, considering the three other couples around him. He'd had ample opportunity to ask Emerie for her soul, yet he'd chosen... not to.

She wanted to ask him about it, but she also didn't. She didn't want to know the truth if it was terrible, and she didn't want this day, her final day, to either end in a fight with him, or her in tears.

So, could she find out the truth without having to directly ask it? Because, if she was being honest with herself, the real reason she was doing this was for Ingram. Yes, Delora, Reia, and Mayumi were part of her desire to do this, to help them and be a reason their love continued.

Yet, as selfish as it was, she didn't think she would have done this just for them.

Her reasonings weren't so noble.

She'd started this journey for him. She was intending to end it for him as well.

And also for Gideon and her parents. To finally have revenge for the loss of their lives – and how much it had affected her own.

However, her heart was at war with itself.

Half said to go to protect everyone, and the other half told her to give Ingram a chance to change her mind.

"Ingram," Emerie whispered, as she kept her stare fixed on the tiny flame, letting it entrance her.

The length of his beak was plopped on top of her head, and she wasn't sure what he was thinking about or even looking towards. At least his strong arms around her felt warm and comforting, and his tail wrapped around her knee was kind of endearing. She needed this hug.

"How much do you want Aleron back?"

His tail tightened on her. "More than anything."

"And you want to make the world safer for him before that, right?"

"Yes," he answered firmly. "I want to bring Aleron back into a world where I will not lose him again."

Emerie took in a deep, strengthening breath. "Would... you do anything to make that happen?"

"Absolutely. Even if it means my own life."

Okay... that isn't a good sign.

She swallowed thickly, then lowered her voice even further.

"Would you sacrifice anyone and everyone for that?"

"Yes," he grated, squeezing her waist. She was just about to drop her head when he added, "Except you."

"Pardon?" she rasped, glancing up and twisting to look over her shoulder.

"I... do not want to lose you. I do not want you to come with us, Emerie," he admitted. "The other females... they can come back, you cannot. I want you to stay where it is safe." Then he looked down at her with his orchid-coloured orbs and dipped his knuckles into her hair so he could brush it forward with his claws. "I want you to wait for me."

This should have elated her. This should have been enough for her to sit her arse down and stay here until he came back.

But that was the problem: until *he* came back.

If he didn't want to perish alongside Jabez, Ingram needed to stay behind. There was no way in the world he would be able to control his thoughts and run from the blast. Hell, he was likely to run headfirst into the big shiny ball of whatever the hell was going to come from the stone once it shattered.

"I feel like it is selfish of me," Ingram weirdly confessed. "I do not understand what I feel or why, but I feel it in here."

He placed a claw tip to her chest, right where her heart was. Well, where it would have been if he didn't place it against the wrong side.

But... his orbs have never turned pink like the other Duskwalkers' do when they look at their brides. And it wasn't hard to guess what the colour signified.

Whatever Ingram felt, it obviously wasn't love.

She'd been hoping he would eventually shine that bright flamingo pink at her. He never had.

Maybe he didn't have enough humanity to understand what the emotion meant, or how to feel it. He could have lost all capabilities to do so when Aleron disappeared.

Who knew? Not Emerie, that was for sure.

She was aware her next question was unfair on him, but she asked it anyway. She needed to assuage her own thoughts and feelings, so she could make up her mind with unwavering conviction.

"If you had to choose between us, Ingram, could only choose one of us, would it be me or Aleron?"

His orbs flashed white, before darkening into a blue. "Neither."

"Say you had to–"

"Neither, Emerie." His tone sharpened. "I am not me without Aleron, but I also don't want to be without you. I cannot choose."

Emerie gave him a weak smile, as she lifted up and turned around to slip her arms around his thick and muscled neck. "Okay, Ingram."

She hid her pain behind the hug, burying her face against his scales.

If he could not pick, and he could not be the one to take on the Demon King, then it had to be Emerie. He'd already said he wanted his twin back more than anything, would sacrifice anything and anyone – except her.

Unfortunately, if she decided to stay here, she would be in the way of that. What if he learned of it and ended up resenting her?

He could find another human to be his bride, but no one could replace his twin. Whatever he felt for her, he would get over it. It would wane over time. Just as Orpheus had eventually gotten over all the offerings that had been given to him before Reia.

Someone would replace her.

Someone beautiful, and perfect, and not missing chunks from them. Hopefully by that stage, Ingram would have gained more humanity and taken everything he'd learned from her and applied it to them.

If she could help him in that way, it would be worth it.

Emerie stifled her sadness and sorrow and gave herself a relieved smile. She had her answer, and she could now move ahead, steadfast in her decision. It made knowing what would happen tomorrow... easier.

She adoringly petted the back of his smooth, white skull. *Still, this day is for me.*

Even if it was selfish and self-absorbed, she would do what she wanted, and no one could tell her otherwise. No one had the right to, not with the sacrifices she was about to make.

And today wasn't over yet.

THIRTY-THREE

Emerie brushed her lips over the soft scales of Ingram's neck, then drew back from their hug to slowly traverse them up to the corner of his jaw. Her lips curled slightly when his body puffed in reaction to the lightness of her mouth.

She continued her caresses over the side of his beak, seeing if she could get him to open it.

Instigating a passionate kiss with someone who didn't have lips was a challenge. She couldn't just hungrily lock their mouths together.

He gave her room to do as she pleased, even as she trailed to the very tip. Then she pecked it. Still, he didn't open up for her. Instead, he cupped the back of her head and drifted his own back.

"What is wrong, Emerie?" he asked, his orbs morphing to blue. "You have not been yourself today."

"Nothing is wrong," she lied, and even *she* thought her tone was convincing. Having a steady resolve could do that to a person.

He bumped the side of his beak against her temple. "As much as I have enjoyed it, you do not usually... cling to me like today."

She returned his nuzzle with more flutters of her mouth. "I just wanted to spend time with you."

"You have not been the same since meeting with the Witch Owl. She looked at you strangely yesterday."

Emerie knew he meant when they had been at Delora and

Magnar's home, as he was not aware of her midnight chat with the woman. She was sure Mayumi had told everyone else today while Emerie was with him.

She leaned back in the security of his arms, folded her own across her chest, and pouted. "Do you want to kiss or not?"

He quickly closed the space between them to lash at her lips with his long tongue. "Always I want to kiss," he grated.

"Good boy," she praised, as she drew her tongue up his when he licked her a second time. His hands gripped harder.

She unfurled her arms and cupped the corners of his jaw to keep herself steady. Rather than fighting his tongue, she welcomed it into the crevice of her mouth, and moaned at the indulgent taste of burnt sugar and hickory bark.

It was intoxicating, making her mouth water.

Balancing her knees on his thighs, she lifted up slightly to meet him. She let him play with her tongue, her teeth, the bumpy roof of her mouth. His body was against her, and she pushed any thoughts of worry, any fears, to the back of her mind so she could focus on just this moment with him.

She took in the feeling of his hard body and strong, yet overly lean muscles. One of her hands trailed down his chest so she could feel his scales and the bones protruding outside of his flesh.

Emerie eased herself into desire, letting out a shaken exhale when her nipples stiffened against her day dress. With her eyelids low and heavy, she witnessed when his glowing orbs shifted into a different purple – one that mirrored the depths of her own want.

One of his hands slyly drifted to her arse. The claws of it dug through the material, poking tiny holes into it, as he kneaded her round cheeks.

Just as he leaned forward to bury more of his tongue past her teeth, feeding her the thicker part of it, Emerie made him jerk and flinch. She sucked on his tongue, drawing it in herself, and drank him down.

He shuddered out a fierce groan.

His palm slipped from her arse so he could dip it underneath the skirt of her dress. Returning to it, he paused when he felt bare skin instead of the barrier of underwear.

Oh yeah, Emerie had planned this *entire* day – especially how it would end.

She gripped the bottom seam of her dress and drew it up until she'd hooked it on the webbing of skin between his thumb and forefinger. Then, she pushed his hand up her hip, her side, forcing him to glide a sinful path up her body, and he happily complied. His rough, calloused palm simultaneously abraded and tickled her skin, sending shivers of goosebumps across her body.

He petted her right breast when he got to it, giving it a rough squeeze.

A slick hardness poked against her navel before it rubbed a trail up her abdomen. Firm, wriggling tentacles tickled her inner thighs once his cock was fully engorged and past his seam.

"You always smell so nice like this," he rasped, flicking her nipple as he moved his palm up and down. She moaned and squeezed his hand against her. "It makes me want to lick every inch of you."

He pulled away from their unique kiss so he could lick across her jaw. Before he could get any more ideas, she pushed his hand higher up until it was caressing her throat. Then further still, until she was able to duck underneath the neckline.

His hand fell away, as did both her own, when her dress slipped off her arms and cascaded behind her. Although her skin was flushed with desire, her cheeks pinkened further, as she shyly peeked up at him through her long lashes.

Ingram paused, then his head reared back slowly and tilted so he could see.

This was the first time Emerie had been fully unclothed in front of someone since the night she'd lost everything. She'd always been too afraid her partner would grow... uncomfortable. She'd been worried their attraction to her would dissipate or they would act differently in the moment and steal all the sensuality from it.

She didn't feel any of that with Ingram.

There had never been any judgement from him, nor any human biases of beauty. At every turn, he'd made her feel bewitching, like she'd put him under some kind of lust-filled spell. He touched at her scars as though they were like any part of her: not too much to bring attention to them in an attempt to reassure her, or too little and make her feel as though he was avoiding them.

He reminded her they were there, that they were a part of her, but his touch and gaze had always made her feel like it was because it was just her. He accepted them like he'd accepted her freckles or her orange hair – not something less or more, but something simply there.

Her bashful, self-aware gaze was akin to what any woman would feel when being exposed to their partner for the first time. Somehow it heated her skin in the most delicious and lascivious way.

She panted through lips that were tender and tingling from his tongue petting back and forth between them. Her nipples stiffened further at his stare on them, and her pussy pulsed more arousal slick from her centre, that crawl of liquid slipping along her folds.

His cock resting against her abdomen jerked and tapped her when he suddenly swelled. The subtle yet visceral reaction from him had her licking at her lips to re-wet them.

A shiver tore through her when he raked a claw up her side until he found her bare chest. He teased her left nipple before drifting to the side where the tightness of her scarring was. Most of it was numb, but the spots that were sensitive caused her to rasp out hitching breaths.

He brought his other hand up to cup her other breast, and the softness of it moulded straight into his palm like a contained drop of water.

"Pretty female," he panted out as he circled a claw tip around her right nipple, following the bumps of her areola, while flicking his thumb over the smaller one. "Such a lovely colour."

He drifted his right hand down her body, teasing it along his path. Her side, her abdomen, the orange hair on her pubic mound. Emerie gasped and shot up higher when he sheathed his claws of that hand without her knowing, and shoved two fingers inside her.

Then he lifted her, braced her back with his arm so her spine would bow, and gave her a heavy lick across her sternum. Her head fell back, and the tips of her hair danced at the top of her arse. She cuddled his skull as best as she could, eventually grabbing ahold of his short goat horns when he dabbed over both her nipples.

His fingers inside her were slow, and she was so turned on that the glide of them was easy. She wantonly ground onto them to get them deeper.

"More, Ingram," she pleaded around airy pants. When his fingers only picked up speed, her vision split and her insides clenched. *Feels so good,* she thought, but she still shook her head. "I-I want you to stretch me. Fill me up with your fingers."

He let out a heated huff through his opened beak, and the wave of it tickled across her damp chest. His hand shot down to grab her arse in a firm squeeze, holding her still as he fed her a third, thick digit.

She tightened around it, but he'd already done this to her multiple times. Emerie easily loosened up.

Just a little more.

His long, thin tongue swirled around each nipple at different intervals. How could such a lengthy, drooling limb feel this wonderful against them? The sensation was so strange, especially when he managed to wrap around one totally and even give it a pinch.

His cock slipped back and forth against her waving abdomen as she undulated. His lubricant smeared her, and she wanted nothing more than to grip him and pleasure him in return.

She couldn't, not yet. She didn't want Ingram ticking over to his own need too soon.

"C-can you spread your fingers?"

She let out a squeaking moan when he did it, and the stretch of all three had her wincing. She stilled his hand before trying to push it away, just as she pulled his head back from her chest.

Okay, I... I think I'm ready now.

"You did not come, Emerie," he quietly stated, his voice low and hoarse. He closed his fingers, pressed them deep, and wiggled them.

She clamped them as she let out a shaken moan. *Oh fuck.* She was tempted to let him continue until he'd forced an orgasm from her. Still, she halted his hand, not wanting her energy to wane just yet.

Her eyelids were heavy as she took in his raven skull.

She dabbed her tongue at the seam of her lips. "Can I tie you up?"

His head cocked. "But I want to touch you." He removed his fingers from her pussy so he could circle them around her clit. "Was I not making you feel good?"

"It was amazing," she purred reassuringly, brushing her hands up his beak. "But I want to give now. I *promise* you won't regret it."

Like a carnal, wild male, he smeared her arousal across his chest to cover himself in it. He nodded, and that trust from him meant so much to her.

She quickly hopped off him.

With rope already prepared and close by, she coiled his forearms together with his wrists locked to his opposing elbows. Then she made him wiggle until his back was resting against the stump they'd been using as a makeshift table.

She slotted a pillow in between to make sure he'd be comfortable.

It was strange, but the fact that a massive, towering monster was bound for *her* had her pulse racing. He'd allowed himself to be put into a vulnerable position, trustingly, and she would be able to do what she pleased. Pleasure him how she wanted to, tease him, even leave him to suffer aching with his cock and giving nothing.

He absolutely wasn't helpless, and she knew that, but it was still titillating.

With the way he was seated, his chest bowed forward, making the large cavity of it seem even bigger. The white bones of his rib cage almost glistened in the low light, and the scales around it had a black-and-blue oil-slick reflection.

With his dark purple orbs focused on her, she crawled between Ingram's spread legs, being careful of his tail between them, and his cock jerked. Her mouth watered at the delicious feast of the creature bound before her, and she greeted the tapered ends of his tentacles enthusiastically.

Keeping high on her knees, she gripped the base of his cock and let his tentacles wrap around her forearms. At the same time, she leant forward and swiped her tongue over the blunt head, stealing a voluminous drop of seed before covering what she could completely.

The tremor that ripped through him had his head tilting back and the softer inside of his tail coming up to rub against her folds momentarily. The softest moan rippled out of his chest.

She liked when his noises were soft. They were so cute and light it made her eager for more.

"Such a good boy," she purred against the tip of his cock. "Letting me tie you up to do what I want with you."

"Fuck, Emerie," he choked out, as his head dipped to the side.

She circled her tongue around the flared rim, feeling his textured spiking scales that puffed at every touch. Stealing sweet lubricant from him, she sucked it straight off the surface of his cock. He was so hard and hot against her mouth and hands, and visibly pulsating.

She nibbled gently at one of the raised dark veins on him.

"You really like me calling you that, huh?" she murmured.

"Yes," he admitted.

She drew her lips down one side until his tentacles were caressing her cheek, while her right hand stroked upwards to pet the head in a circle. Everything she did, no matter how small or subtle, had more pearly seed rising to the tip of his shaft. She licked and stole that too, enjoying the heady hint of burnt sugar and hickory bark that burst across her tongue.

"Do you like my mouth and hands on you?" Instead of responding, his beak parted as he let out a deep huff. "Do you want me to keep going until you come in my mouth?"

Her lips curled devilishly against the side of him, then she gave the head and rim little nibbles.

"Nhn. Yes. I want you to drink from me." He snapped his head forward. "I want to see your face messy with it again."

"You do?" she purred before pulling away.

Emerie kissed and nipped her way up him, and even licked the protruding bone of his hip, his sternum, knowing he could feel them. She even gave his nipple a flick, which caused him to violently twitch, as she crawled onto him and placed her knees on his thighs before going to his hips. She forced him to let her under his beak, so she could nip at his neck.

She palmed the broad and blunt head of his cock, only to grab him just under the rim to keep him steady. "What if that's not what I want?"

"Then what ar–" Before he could finish, he choked out a groan when she positioned the tip against her entrance and backed onto it. "Inside you?" He let out a deep expire.

"Mhm. I want to feel you inside me," she whispered against his neck.

"More," he encouraged as she wedged the very tip inside by moving in circles to ease herself over him. *"You're so soft."*

She hadn't even gotten the entire head in yet, and he was already losing it. Ingram rocked his hips as if he wanted to help, to make her pussy swallow him faster, to reach deeper.

He seemed desperate after she made him wait so long.

Her brows knitted tightly, and she placed her forehead against the crook of his neck and shoulder for leverage. It wasn't easy balancing herself on him like this, high up on his torso. Gravity wasn't helping with how thick he was, nevermind the awkwardness of their positions.

Had his hands been free, she knew he would have tried to ease her down – and possibly ripped her in the process by accident. He wasn't very patient, and she may have let him with how much she wanted him right now.

Wincing as she stretched over the head, she bounced to add pressure to her weight baring down. His lubricant aided them, and she was utterly thankful for it.

Then the head popped past her entrance. Her bounce shoved her down at least an inch as well.

With a wince and a pained gasp tearing through her like a blade, her nails dug into his chest. She couldn't hold it.

"So tight," he groaned. When she lunged forward off him to flee, he let out the smallest whine. "Down, Emerie. I want more.

I want inside your little pussy."

He brushed the side of his skull against her sweat-slicked forehead, his chest heaving with excited breaths. It almost felt like he was silently pleading for her to mount him.

"I will," she rasped out. "You're just... big, Ingram. I need to adjust."

But she would. Because no matter what happened tonight, she was getting that big fucking Duskwalker cock in her, whatever it took. It might be slow and painful at first, but she was going to ride him, and she was not stopping until she did. She wanted to be so full and messy with his cum that it was dripping down her legs.

She was also intending for it to feel good for both of them. His arms were tied for that reason, to force patience on him.

Now that she'd given her body a breather, she nudged the warm, slick, already seed-drenched head against her entrance once more. She bit her lip hard as she pushed herself down. The head popped through faster, and although it was chunky and felt like it was trying to split her in two, it wasn't so painful that she needed to run away.

Ingram let out a contented growl and continued to brush his skull against her to encourage her. His hips rocked, desperate to move her on him but unable to.

Emerie wiggled her hips side to side as she shoved further down, slowly gaining more and more inches. He was so thick that the pressure was immense, and she knew she was stretched to her absolute limit.

She'd always been small, had always struggled a little at first when taking even a human. Now, she was sinking around a monster dick, and it was a challenge.

She was also really turned on and wanted this more than anything. She wanted *him* more than she had ever wanted anyone.

Everything was moist, and his heat was soothing. The burning stretch was also accompanied by him pushing against all of her most tender places in such a deep and unfamiliar way. Everywhere inside her received attention, and his little spiking scales scraped her G-spot and had her panting and trying to swallow more.

He bottomed out, and she squirmed to make absolutely sure he had utterly filled her to her limit. Even her clit felt tight, as if the tension and pressure radiated beyond her insides. For a little while, she rested and waited for herself to soften.

I can feel his heartbeat, she thought dazedly, tenderness radiating in her chest. Then she giggled as the very tips of his tentacles swayed under her thighs. *That tickles.*

At least they told her she'd taken him halfway, which is more than she thought she would be able to.

He's finally inside me. Gosh, she'd wanted this for days – since back in the forest. A part of her couldn't believe they were finally doing this, that she had a Duskwalker's cock wedged as deep as it could go inside her.

His chest released tiny whines, and she leaned back just enough so she could face him.

"Are you okay?" she asked, pressing her lips and face against the side of his hard beak.

"More," he pleaded, causing her to laugh weakly.

Of course he wanted more. How many times had he demanded or pleaded for it now?

"I can't give you more." She rotated side to side to show him he had nowhere else to go. "But I can move for you."

She slid up about a quarter of the way, then pushed back down. His moan was instant, and he let them out frequently as she moved on him.

"I adore the way you sound," she whispered against his cool bone. "It's so faint and soft."

"You're so warm inside," he rasped, as more whines echoed from him. "Tight and hot. How can you feel so good?"

His deep voice washed over her like a wave, and she moaned as she quickened her pace. She wanted him to keep talking and knew anything he said right now was going to make her deliciously burn hotter, more feverish with need.

"Yeah? You like the way I feel around you?" she purred, her lips parting on a moan at the way his cock stroked her insides and her nipples scraped against his scales.

"Feels even better than I thought. I never imagined..." His

groan was bubbly and broken. "Deeper, Emerie. I want to feel you completely."

He tilted his head back the faster she stroked him with the walls of her pussy, and his hips tried to thrust harder. He jiggled side to side as if he was trying to free his arms. The more he spoke, the harder he pulled.

"So close. You're so close to taking all of me," he rasped, his voice laden with need. "I want us to be one, for your cunt to consume all of me. My tentacles *ache* to hold you, little butterfly. Please let me."

Feeling terrible for him, seeing how much he craved it, she tried to fuck his cock for him faster. She put her entire body into it to give him some form of comfort. She even fluttered kisses against his neck and petted his chest, moaning as pleasure swelled where they were joined.

Her body had finally adjusted, and she was able to be freer in her movements. Yet, nothing seemed to settle him, and the more she teased him, the more restless he became.

Despite how close her own orgasm was, her brows furrowed deeply at the distressing noises he made.

"D-do you want me to stop?" she asked, slowing down when she grew worried.

"No!" he bit out. He nudged her cheek with his own as his hips continued to roll, to get her to go faster. His body quaked as he yanked his arms to the sides to try and snap the rope. When he couldn't get free, he grated, "Release me, Emerie."

She paused and pushed back against his chest so she could look at him properly, worried about how much he was beginning to fret. This was supposed to be enjoyable for both of them. He'd been so excited at first, so she didn't understand why he was fighting it now. He wasn't going soft, so she didn't think she was hurting him.

The moment she stopped moving, everything got... worse. It was like her slipping up and down his cock had been the only thing keeping him *sane*.

His orbs flared bright red, and he released a deep, reverberating growl. "Release me!"

"Holy shit," she rasped, hopping off his cock.

Ingram fell to the side, and all he did was try to get his arms free. He produced horrible whimpers mixed with snarls as he clawed at his own biceps to get free. His cock wasn't going down, remaining a stiff, bobbing rod as he wriggled.

Oh shit. Oh shit. She bounced from foot to foot as she panicked. *What the fuck do I do?!*

Letting him free right now did not seem like a wise decision at all! But... *I can't leave him like this.*

Clenching her eyes shut, she made her decision. She sprang into action when his movements became more jarring as he moved to his knees and chest.

Despite her better judgement, despite knowing shit was about to get real and very scary for her, she grabbed her obsidian knife from her bag. She freed him.

She bolted for her dress so she could... she didn't know. Run? Not be naked when she screamed for help?

She didn't even make it that far.

Her ankle was grabbed, and she was flipped to her back. He swiftly dragged her across the strewn bedding on the tent floor until her knees were pressing against his hips. His cock slipped over her from pussy to abdomen.

"Got you, butterfly," he snarled, pulling his hips back.

His orbs were red, but the jutting erection he was about to press to her said his mind was focused purely on her and her pussy.

"W-wait," she begged, crossing her ankles under his dick so that if he thrust forward, even if he did enter her, he wouldn't get far.

"Inside, Emerie," he whimpered, halting – and quaking as if that was the very last thing he wanted to do. "I want back inside you. You were so perfect."

She stared at his dick, and what had her moaning just seconds ago suddenly terrified her. "You'll hurt me if you try to go deeper."

"Trust me." He shoved his hand under the back of her head to support it in a claw-filled cradle. He gripped her thigh to spread her, then palmed up to her chest to pet her breasts, grinding the length of his cock against her clit. "I promise I will not hurt you inside."

She looked up and found his orbs had cooled to the desirous purple she preferred. He was promising, but did he understand what that truly entailed? Even now, she could feel the danger behind his trembling restraint.

Oh, fuck it. Hopefully the spell Delora told her about worked, and Ingram didn't go crazy from the blood involved. *Please work.*

"Okay," she conceded. "I don't want to fight it anymore." She unlocked her ankles and slipped them around his hips to give him room. "Just be careful."

"Gentle." He rasped the confirmation, as he deliciously slipped his claws down her sternum to tickle a path to her abdomen.

Unlike her weaker human strength, Ingram was able to wedge the head at her entrance and penetrate her with little effort. Her body was forced to make way once more until he bottomed out.

She didn't know what made her gasp and bow her back so deeply she worried her spine would snap: him beginning to push beyond the natural boundary of her body, or the fact he'd shoved his claws into her stomach right before he started to.

Cold magic burst between them in a flurry of purple glitters and dancing streams of light.

"Oh!" she moaned, just as her toes curled, her feet pointed, and her back arched in blissful anguish.

With her bright-orange hair spilled out across the messed-up bedding, Ingram's claws stuck up through the strands like a crown as he cradled her head. He supported it, even when it tipped back as he, in one solid, firm, and steady thrust, mounted her until he bottomed out.

Then he gave a deeply satisfied growl as he struck her flesh with his claws and shoved even further.

He watched her gaping expression, her icy-blue eyes dilating into saucers when her eyelids flashed open. Magic radiated between them, and the glitters of it made her appear even more entrancing and mesmerising than before.

It added to her colourful essence.

It was difficult to drink in her features when his legs quaked, his tail twisting and thumping in reaction to her sweet little cunt rippling along the length of him. It sucked him as he dug deeper and deeper.

The further he went, feeling her body making way for him with a snug, squeezing pressure at the tip of his cock, the more his aggression and anxiety from earlier were pushed from him. Instead, they were replaced with utter exhilaration.

He didn't even know when Emerie had slapped her hands over his beak to cover his nose holes with her palms, but he barely noticed them over the intensity of their bodies joining.

When she'd been riding him, all he'd been able to think about was them becoming one. A physical bond so deep it transcended their flesh and moulded them into a single being. To connect until they were linked, and his tentacles had her in their grasp to secure it.

It'd nagged at him, ate at him with sharp fangs, shaking and tossing its head. He'd needed her to accept all of him until she greedily took every bit he had to give.

His claws and fingertips had ached, and all he'd been able to register was that he needed and craved them puncturing. Not in a way that was violent, but in a way that had his heart swelling with tenderness.

So, when he was seated all the way inside her and his tentacles could cuddle her within their depths, something within his mind and heart shifted.

When he slipped his claws from her, he enacted two spells. One that was conscious as he healed her to reduce her mind-numbing blood scent, and a second that was subconscious.

In that moment, buried within the nurturing warmth of her damp core, all he wanted was to completely and utterly protect her.

His sight closed just as a purple dome formed above them,

and the blood scent in the air reduced significantly – as if it was the sacrifice required.

For most of his life, he'd rarely used magic; he'd never needed it... until her. Now, it was as though he'd been holding onto it just so he could lavish every drop of it on her.

He lifted her just high enough so he could grip her plump arse, and ground in harder just to make sure she'd taken every bit of him. Then, with him nestled in the cradle of her thighs and leaning on his elbows, Emerie completely sprawled in his arms, he lay there.

He didn't need nor want to move. His cock was unbelievably hard, but her tender, snuggling core melted away any unbearable ache in it. She was warm and wet; it was absolute perfection.

The fact he could feel her fragile heartbeat softly fluttering not just against his chest but also around his cock meant he could stay there forever.

"Ingram...?" she croaked, only to pause when he slipped his pinkie claw into her mouth to quieten her.

Her uttering his name had his cock engorging with blood and seed. He was in a strange limbo, unsure if he was able to come after just one thrust or not.

He felt as though he was a single movement away from shattering into her. How could she feel this wonderful, this serene and mystical at the same time? It was like he'd been waiting his whole damn life for this moment with her.

"Please," she pleaded, her voice so soft and heated. She wiggled her hips back and forth under the tight press of him crushing her. "I'm so close. Please fuck me."

"Nghn, *fuck*," he groaned, his cock jerking in reaction to her begging for him to thrust.

The moment he pulled back and her body clung to him, desperately trying not to let him go, Ingram was lost – tangled in her trance. All his senses fizzled out, except for everything involving her.

The feel of her in his arms, her sweet cunt, her breaths against his chest. Her strawberry-and-primrose scent twisted into the naughtiest, most wicked aroma. Her little sounds.

He thrust back in when he was only halfway out, needing

back within her warmth. His sight darkened completely as he began to tense, his body shaking wildly.

"Oh, gods." She braved letting go of his beak to dig her little nails into his sides.

With his second thrust, she weakly bit into his chest. His head lay upon the ground as euphoria took hold, too heavy for him to hold up under the onslaught of sensation.

So good. His slow movements hid just how much he was losing his mind inside her. *She feels so amazing.* His head slid back and forth along the ground as his beak parted on laden breaths. *I'm going to...*

By the third pump, he was letting out a choking moan as hot liquid bliss broke from him and filled her channel. His body took over as he came, twitching violently as he began to pound harder, his hips waving as he ground into her. There had been no agony, no slow crawl of seed. Like his body had been purely seeking the inside of her pussy, he was rewarded with just mindless pleasure.

Dizziness overtook him as he drowned in bliss.

"Oh my god, I can feel you coming!"

She squirmed beneath him as he drained his seed until it overflowed and squirted out of her. And as he continued to move, a loud cry sung out as she stiffened and milked him for the last of it.

His knees buckled inwards, and a whine ripped from him.

His claws sliced through soft skin at the intensity of her coming, while his cock swelled and pulsated, so sensitive now. He healed her, and whatever crimson bled from her added to the longevity of the dome around them.

Right now, he was hers. All he wanted was to protect while being allowed to stay within the sheath of her body as it sucked, quivered, and spasmed around him. Then, when he'd ceased twitching inside her, he sagged against her as aftershocks blasted him.

She didn't give him a moment of peace.

Emerie wiggled her hips beneath him, trying to move his softening cock in and out of her pussy herself. She barely had any room, and yet her greedy need gave her strength.

Each tiny stroke around him had him seeing fucking *stars*.

"Please don't stop," she demanded in a hoarse, cracking voice. "I need more of you, Ingram."

His narrow waist gave her room to dig at his back, while she kissed, licked, and even chomped at his chest. A vortex of heated aggression swirling behind his sternum caused his orbs to go from purple to bright red when she squirmed harder, faster, *desperately*. She fluttered like a little piece of prey trying to flee, when what she wanted was to escape her desire.

The more she kicked, the more she tried to pleasure herself with his rehardening cock, the more the gentleness within him was snuffed out.

She was tempting him on a level she did *not* understand.

"Fuck me. Please." Now she was the one to beg and plead for it, completely flipping their dynamic. Like a needy, aching little thing, she scratched at him for more. "I need you so much right now."

From the very first time he'd had his fingers inside her, and knew his cock was supposed to nestle within her, he'd been craving this. For days, he'd ached, and even longer still, despite not having the knowledge to know *what* he'd been longing for.

The fact she was now pleading for it after denying him so fervently, twisting and contorting around his dick as she did, snapped his control in half.

Ingram leaned back, grabbed the back of her left knee, and pushed it until it was next to her breast and almost touching the ground, forcing her hips to tilt upwards. His other hand shot down around her throat so he could keep her still in the most vulnerable place possible. He leant completely on his knees and his knuckles with his arm straight, snarling as he started slamming into her.

Not once in the change of position did she show an ounce of fear. He rewarded her with speed, with him giving her everything he possibly could.

Her arms fell back above her head, and her face relaxed until it grew completely dazed.

Seed clung between their hips as he thrust, and he felt it sticking between the undersides of her thighs and the tops of his own. Her cute, soft breasts bounced and jiggled, and they were a tantalising show.

As he drew his sight down, her stomach, which now had a small roll from her curled position, jiggled as well, as did her thighs when he slammed against them.

He became enraptured with where they were joined.

The orange curls on her pubic mound were glistening with his seed. Puffy pink folds were spread around his plunging purple cock, and watching them shift around with either his forward or backward motion was erotic.

She was already filled with his seed, marked from within as well as what had dripped from her. *That* was immensely satisfying.

His tentacles around her hips and thighs kept trying to pull her towards him, but his hands firmly around her pretty little throat and knee allowed him to pull back until they almost unlatched. He didn't squeeze her neck, he barely had any pressure there, but it was a cage of claws designed to quell his predatory need to dominate.

There was something about the way he was holding her, about having her trapped underneath him like this, being fucked with every bit of his might, that excited the wildest part of him. All the slowness and gentleness he tried to give her, *always*, became irrelevant and non-existent. He was exactly where he wanted to be, getting what he'd hungered for, and his docile, pretty butterfly was fluttering lewdly in welcome.

Her eyes rolled back as her delicate lashes flickered, and she let out the loveliest cry. With his speed, all he could feel was her squeezing him so tightly it was like she wanted to crush him into dust.

But it was her body giving him bursts of tangy liquid as she orgasmed that had him drooling. Had him breaking under whatever power she had over him. Had him just as lost for her as she appeared to be, while bouncing beneath him.

Ingram had no idea how long he pounded into her, unwilling to change their position when it excited him on such a visceral level. All he knew was that she enjoyed it, coming for him repeatedly.

Like before, his seed shot from him suddenly and with little warning. The bottom of his spine tingled as his embedded seed sacs clenched, and with a shaken, quiet groan, he watched himself flood her with just a single pump of his cock. The rest squelched and bubbled out of her as a pearlescent liquid that dripped in every direction.

His thrusts slowed until he was just rocking himself through his release in subtle but body-aching movements. Unfathomable pleasure tingled his flesh, bones, and scales all the way from the crown of his raven skull to the pointed tip of his lizard tail.

When he was done, he sat back and released her throat and the back of her knee, letting his claws dance over her skin. Deep huffs exploded from him as he gazed down at her.

She looks even more beautiful like this. Messy from their intimacy, lazy with sated desire, bare naked for him. She didn't even fully close her thighs, letting him view how he was still all the way deep inside her pink, overfilled pussy.

Without a care in the world, her eyes focused just enough to view the dome over them. She reached out to it above her with such a blissfully groggy expression, and it nibbled at his heart in the most wonderous way.

She tried to touch it with her fingertips but missed completely. She reached out to his skull instead when her hands rotated towards him, with her well-pleasured gaze flittering to him.

"So pretty," she rasped at him.

Something about her right then stroked the very essence of his being. Whether it was her covered in seed, or tenderly reaching for him, every piece of the scene before him was magnificent.

She is... mine, he thought, as he placed his skull into her welcoming hands with his orbs closing.

THIRTY-FOUR

Having a Duskwalker around that could heal her at any given moment was both a blessing... and a curse.

A blessing because, as she sat on top of him and moved her hips like a wave to stir his cock in her, there was no tenderness or soreness where they were firmly joined. Although her pussy was swollen from their current bout of sex, and she'd long ago started to go numb from overuse, she could still keep going. Keep moving as he grasped her hips in his big hands and helped to shunt her down on his unbelievable girth.

Her muscles weren't stiff, and the only part of her that was truly tired was her mind.

This was also her curse, since the sun had long ago risen, and she still had Ingram's cock inside her.

She didn't care.

Her nipples were hard and aching for attention, which he happily gave. Her core was wet, desperately clinging for more of this Duskwalker and refusing to give him up. Her brain was dizzy, hazy, and so saturated with unbridled lust, she knew at some point it'd broken.

She'd had small naps throughout the night, mostly from passing out after coming. Sometimes he joined her, but most of the time he was the reason she'd wake needy and aroused.

It was as though he was trying to squeeze a lifetime's worth of fucking all into one night and make up for all he'd lost.

Emerie was doing the same, for an entirely different reason.

She could rest later... when she did so eternally.

Right now, all she wanted was this, was him, was *more*.

She let her muddled stare fall from the tented ceiling down to him, her head resting on one shoulder as she ground his cock inside her. Purple orbs glowing in a raven skull tipped up to her, giving away that he'd been staring at where her body had just finished milking him.

His rough palms came up to her breasts so he could flick her nipples, and she winced and tensed up at how sensitive they'd become.

She'd forgotten why she needed sleep – what was supposed to be happening today, and why.

She'd spent the last eight years of her life bored with sex because her heart had desired feeling full, while her mind had wanted her partner to make her feel beautiful. This was the first time she'd truly given herself over to someone, and Ingram deserved every bit of her lust-addled want since he'd been the one to bring her to such a happily messy state.

She was... *free*.

Free from her thoughts, the pain of her past, of her unknown future. So free, in fact, that something warm and radiating often wanted to float out from between her breasts.

When a bright yellowy-orange glow had emerged from her chest when he'd been taking her from behind at some point throughout the night, she learned what it was. Seeing her own soul cupped inside her hands was... enlightening, but she never let it fully float from her.

She always pushed it back in before he could see it.

It was her secret.

One that had her heart feeling as though it was brimming with love and adoration, but overflowing with sadness. Sadness she never had time to truly register with Ingram pounding away at it and pushing her to further heights.

She let out a near-silent moan, her voice too tired and overused to truly muster anything more than a whisper of sound.

Her obsessed partner, on the other hand, was full of them. It was his noises she truly wanted to hear. The lewd sounds of their bodies joining, the wet squelching, and the pwap of their hips and thighs, were just an added bonus.

Even his growl, which he released while pointing his beak towards the tent flap, had her nibbling on her bottom lip. She would have been concerned by the ominous noise if he hadn't emitted so many pleasure-filled ones throughout the night.

She reached her hands out to him, and he gave her exactly what she wanted. He placed his palms against them so she could use them as leverage, unable to link their fingers with their size difference, but she did dip her fingertips between the gaps of a few of his own.

His growl deepened, his orbs flaring bright red when grass rustled outside the tent.

"Emerie?" Mayumi called, a mild hint of concern in her tone.

Emerie's only response of life was her eyelids fluttering as Ingram's cock kept stroking the nestling flesh of her most tender spot.

"Leave us," Ingram snarled with a ferociousness she only ever heard when he was in his monstrous form.

Perhaps she should have blushed or stopped moving. Instead, she moved faster at the booming depth of his voice. She bit her lip, finding it kind of sexy. Then again, she foolishly thought everything about him was sexy right now.

"Are we doing this today, or not?" Mayumi asked. Emerie could almost picture her hands on her hips with a sharp glare in her brown eyes. "I need to know if I should round up the others."

Whether she realised what was going on, or she just simply didn't care, it was obvious Mayumi wasn't leaving without an answer.

The moment Emerie turned her face towards the tent flap to respond, Ingram gripped her cheeks with one hand to force her eyes on him. Then he rolled them until she was on her back, making sure her gaze stayed on him the entire time.

His orbs flared a dark green in the empty, dark eyeholes of his raven skull, and she shivered at the possessiveness of them. "Only look at me, little butterfly," he whispered menacingly.

As if he went unheard, Mayumi exclaimed, "Fucking hell. Is she even alive in there?"

Ingram yanked himself from her, causing her to gasp, then

he stood. His cock dripped with excess lubricant, remnants of his prior releases, and probably her last orgasm. Just as he was stomping to the exit, Emerie rolled over with her hand out.

"Your dick!" she shouted, only for it to come out as a pathetic, broken croak. "Hide your dick!"

He must have heard whatever garble truly came from her because he yanked the flap open while keeping his groin covered.

"Fuck. Off. Little female," he snapped out, lowering his head at her.

Emerie met Mayumi's concerned eyes. She should have been horrified she was caught bare-arse naked on her stomach, and had obviously been this Duskwalker's plaything for the last few hours, but she absolutely *wasn't*.

Honestly, the worst part about this whole situation was that her interruption meant Ingram had let all this fucking sun in. It was too bright, and her eyes squinted in dry pain. She wanted the dimness back, where the only light she could truly make out was his glowing orbs.

Mayumi's features crinkled into humour, and... pride? Yes, she seemed pleased that Emerie was a sexually satisfied heap still laying upon the floor. Emerie's lips parted as she gave her a mischievous, toothy grin in return.

Mayumi threw her hands up at the Duskwalker towering threateningly over her. "Fair enough. Sorry for interrupting." She winked at Emerie. "Enjoy."

Then she turned and left.

Tomorrow then. She'd gained a day.

And, when Ingram spun around, his erection bobbing as he came back over, the sense of urgency she'd been experiencing before dwindled. *More time with him.* She had more time to enjoy every piece of Ingram.

His knees heavily thudded against the ground as he knelt behind her. She didn't move, letting him put her into whatever position he wanted her in.

He just lifted her hips in a way that had him sliding in to the base in one go, like he couldn't wait another second to be inside her. Her thighs pressed together at the sudden intrusion and being filled again, her knees firmly on the ground but her feet kicking up between his legs.

He did pause, though, and lean around her on straightened arms. Brushing the curve of his beak against the back of her ear, he licked down the side of her neck. She glanced back to find his red orbs had turned yellow for a moment in joy, before they morphed back to the purple she'd been looking into all night.

"Emerie," he started, before leaning back once more. He grabbed her arse cheeks and spread them with harsh kneads. "I want to try in here."

One hand fell away so he could collect some of his own lubricant, then his middle finger slipped base-knuckle deep into the tight ring of her arse. Her feet kicked up again as her spine dipped into a bow and flattened her chest against the ground.

She made no other sign of complaint.

It didn't hurt, and all she experienced was additional fullness. It wasn't the first time a finger or two, or even a tentacle, had found its way there – especially after the first few times he'd warned her. She'd gotten used to it, and long ago realised Ingram just wanted to touch her everywhere he could.

By the fact he began thrusting, she knew it excited him.

His tail wasn't very flexible, but he still managed to dip it between their knees. Just as he added a second lubricant-covered finger inside the tight ring, his cock picked up speed within her pussy. The softer underside of his tail came up to pet her clit.

She moaned around all of it, her vision splitting.

I promised myself I'd give him everything. What was a little more?

Plus, she was aware the human ass could take a much bigger and deeper pounding than a pussy – except maybe one a Duskwalker had changed for himself.

"Okay, but this will be the last time we have sex for a while," she rasped with heated pants. If he wanted more after this, then his dick would need to be *clean.* "Just be slow."

As long as he was slow, it should be okay. Honestly, if she hadn't been able to get his cock in her pussy, she'd been considering anal as a way to just have him inside her somehow. Thankfully that hadn't been needed, but it was an option she'd already been considering.

He also seemed to have better control over his urges after so many hours and releases – although he was still unrelenting.

Ingram pulled both his fingers and cock from her, and her toes curled when he ground the entire length of it between her cheeks. He covered her in slick, making everything deliciously wet.

When he nudged the tip against her softened hole, she gripped the bedding beneath her. "A-and can you be ready to heal me?" she pleaded. He didn't have an ass, so it shouldn't hurt him... right? "Please be gentle."

"Slow, heal, gentle," he repeated, as his rough and calloused hand stroked over her arse to the middle of her back to hold her.

The tip wasn't too bad, but when he started to slowly push over the rest of his broad and flared head, she winced and tightened up. He paused, and she knew by the rattling of dry bones he'd tipped his head.

She took in a deep breath and forced her body to relax, before pushing on it herself. "It's okay."

She made sure to keep her face hidden from him, so he couldn't see her reaction. As he continued to penetrate her, she felt the burn of the stretch and how it trickled an uncomfortable shiver up her spine. She hated how wrong that shiver felt, but it was quick to dissipate.

Although there was pain, it was easier than when she'd tried to force her pussy around him.

"Fuck. Tight," he bit out. "Why is it so tight?"

A sharp gasp blasted out of her when the head popped through. He groaned and stopped, his fingertips digging into her back. She moaned against the bedding as her fists tightened on it.

His huffs were deep, shaken, and loud as he shuddered, his hands quaking where they gripped. Another shiver crept up her spine.

Yet, he started pulling back as he stated, "You are not enjoying this."

She darted her hand back to grab his wrist. "Wait," she gulped out. "It's okay, Ingram. It just... hurts at first, like when you were first inside my pussy."

She turned her head against the ground so he could see the reassuring smile she gave him. She *wanted* to do this for him.

"But I want to make you feel good." He tickled her spine as he leaned over her until he was forced to put his weight on a straightened arm. "You came from me touching it earlier."

Emerie blushed at that. She actually thought the surprise of him doing it made her clamp up just as the head of his cock pounded directly against her G-spot, which had thrown her over the edge.

"It will once I adjust," she answered hopefully, finding his desire to pleasure her and willingness to stop all the sweeter. It just made her want to do it more. "The hardest part is over."

The wider head of his cock was in, and now all she needed was to take the length. She'd also relaxed during their conversation and didn't find it too unbearable.

That was until he started feeding her more.

Uncomfortable shivers ghosted up her spine in waves, and her arms and legs prickled with goosebumps because of them. When he tried to pump his way deeper, she had to ask him to stop. It only made it worse, as each new depth made her skin crawl.

She found it easier when it was just one solid thrust, especially since his cock was so big in comparison to her tiny human size. He was also reaching further than any human dick could, and she felt things moving around inside her that probably... shouldn't.

Still, her ass made way for him, and she breathed a sigh of relief when he was seated so deep his tentacles were snuggly wrapped around the creases of her thighs. Her shivers dissipated completely, and soon warmth and a deep heartbeat that didn't belong to her radiated within.

To try and ease herself further, she glided her hand down her abdomen. She halted along the way when she noticed a bulge pressing from within because of how deeply her back was arched. It took her a moment to realise it was the head of his cock and a few inches, and she almost chuckled at how... weird it was.

She moved down to her clit to pet it, but Ingram quickly took over when he realised what she was doing.

A soft but muffled moan hummed from behind her lips. The longer he touched her, his fingers so careful, and now, after learning her, expertly pressing against the sensitive bundle of nerves, the more she relaxed.

He slipped his tongue from between her shoulder blades, over the crook of her neck, then swirled it against the shell of her ear. Her breath hitched and she pushed back on him.

When his fingers moved side to side, her hips started dipping up and down. She needed movement, as her pussy clamped around nothing – although it didn't feel empty. Her channel was getting wonderful pressure, just from somewhere else.

Her knees knocked inwards at the jolts of pleasure that came from her clit and she bucked against his fingers harder. She shoved her hands between her chest and the ground so she could grasp her breasts and pinch at her nipples.

Desire flared, rekindled by both of them touching at the places she needed the most.

"I like how greedy your body is, no matter where I touch." His growly voice echoed over her. "More, Emerie."

It was only then that she registered she had been fucking his cock with her ass with her subtle rocking. With her lips parted from heated pants, she shoved her herself halfway off his girth. She let out a moan when she shunted back, and the head gouged through her body and straight against the channel of her pussy.

By the third time she did it, letting out little noises and letting him know she enjoyed it – despite that lingering pain and uncomfortableness she doubted would truly fade – Ingram leaned back. With his hands on her hips, he took over for her.

He was slow at first, but he drew all the way back until she flinched when the flared rim of his cockhead popped out. It popped back in when he surged forward. Why did it feel like he was... feeling her? Exploring her hole with his cock rather than truly fucking it?

"It is so different," he rasped. "It's still soft and warm, but smoother. You don't feel so tight like inside your little cunt, except for here." His thumb touched at where they were joined.

"Here feels like you are trying to crush me and squeeze my seed from me at the same time." His hips picked up speed, and she turned her head back to see his had tipped until his beak was pointed to the ceiling. "It's like you are cuddling my cock with your body."

And the airy groan he released revealed just how amazing that felt for him. The looser she became, the better it felt.

She bit at her bottom lip as her arousal flush deepened and took hold. She slipped her hand down and petted her clit exactly how she liked it, and a moan burst from her. She felt him stroking her pussy through her ass, and she dipped her hips back and forth until she was in a position where he was hitting against where she needed him to.

She started helping him, rocking back and forth on her knees so she could reach bliss and melt.

I'm going to... I'm about to–

Her eyes crossed and her toes curled. "Nhnn. Coming," she choked out.

The cry that escaped her was so loud she feared all of the Veil heard it. Her entire body tensed up, and her pussy flooded with her own orgasm. It dripped down her clit and to her fingers, giving her more wetness so she could be rougher, more frantic with it as she came.

If he groaned, she couldn't hear it. All she knew was that his hips had slowed and started twitching like crazy in reaction to her milking him like this. His claws shot out to slice her from the intensity, but she was quickly healed.

Emerie was – as she decided to think of it – adoringly scarred by his claws.

When she came down from her tower of bliss, Ingram's hips were faster than ever. She was dizzy from crying out and not breathing, her body hot and sweating from clamping up. Her mind frayed at the edges in lustful delirium.

Since she'd gone so lax that he was forced to hold her up or she'd slip forward and away, he wrapped his arm around her waist and yanked her to his chest. He then tipped them until they were lying on their sides.

He wrapped his arm around her from underneath and cupped

her pussy, letting his thrusting bounce her and stroke her clit against his hand. The other arm had threaded behind her knee to keep her spread with the crook of his elbow, while his hand gripped her jaw and supported her head with his fingers.

He tipped his head back in ecstasy, his beak slightly parted to let out deep and shallow pants.

Then he just tightly held her in his big, comforting, and trapping embrace as he pounded into her. With her back firmly pressed against his stomach, the changed angle of their hips spelled her doom. Emerie clawed at his forearms as she let out cry after cry.

It was too much. This should *not* feel so amazing.

His big cock was thrusting forward, straight into the front of her abdomen and all along her pussy. Why did it feel even more intense coming from her ass?

"Sing for me, little butterfly," Ingram groaned as he tipped a claw into her mouth to push her jaw down. "Just like that. Be louder. Show me how much you like my cock inside you like this."

Ingram didn't talk much during sex, like he wasn't able to collect his thoughts well. Yet, when he did, he always had Emerie liquefying into a horny little puddle of sexual obsession.

"Come for me again," he demanded, as he pushed down and shoved two fingers inside her sopping pussy.

She immediately clenched around them, spasming so she could greedily suck them in further.

Her lungs gave out and stopped working. Every muscle in her body clamped up, stiffening and contorting to the point of threatening to snap her. Yet, his cock didn't stop working her, didn't stop pounding into her with hard, deep, and fast slams, even as she tightened and tightened.

She thought her heart might have stopped as she orgasmed. Her legs kicked, her nails dug, and lightning strikes flashed across her tightly shut eyes. Liquid burst from her, and his fingers moving inside her pussy aided her to make sure she came *hard*.

His cock swelled, his tentacles bruised her, and he lifted her knee higher as he let out a roaring groan. As he pumped, flooding heat spurted inside her ass as he came within it. The fact she could feel it spreading and filling her like this had her trembling, even as she went lax and came down from her orgasm.

Surprisingly, none of his seed escaped her.

When his own tension bled out of him, Emerie didn't know whose heart was beating harder or faster. His was loud against her ear as she pressed it against his chest, and she dozily closed her eyes again.

I like listening to his heart. She'd done it many times over the last night and morning. *It sounds so big, like it has enough room for me in it.*

She hoped that was true, even if it was pointless.

Call it selfish, but she wanted a piece of her to permanently remain inside him. Whether or not he understood love, or if her own was unrequited, she wanted him to think of her fondly in the future.

She nuzzled against his chest, and his arms squeezed her affectionately.

"Did you like that?" she asked, her lips curling with humour, already figuring by the load of semen inside her that he did.

He gave a small quake. "Yes. But I think I like your pussy more," he said, dipping his fingers in and out of it twice. "It *hurt* when you came. You squeezed me too tightly, and it felt like you were about to rip my cock off. I just liked knowing you did. You smell nice when you come, and your lost little cries feel good."

Emerie let out a "pfft" before she giggled. *Gosh, why was that so adorable?*

"I *am* small compared to you." Then she wiggled her hips, since she could feel him softening. "Okay, time for you to come out."

She was surprised by how much she missed his warmth as he drew his hips back and pulled away. She knelt up, thankful nothing spilled out, and looked at his dick. Weirdly, it was... clean of anything unseemly. It was also lacking in lubricant, although still moist, so she figured her tight ring had removed most of it upon his withdrawal.

She felt way too wet with his liquid... everywhere.

Still, Emerie searched for a cloth and turned to him with it in her hand. He was already upright on his knees, and she waved the cloth at him.

"Okay. Time to clean you."

"Why?" he asked, tilting his head.

"Because... I don't know... your dick is dirty now? My ass is not the most hygienic place to be," she said while trying to laugh off the awkwardness of saying that. "If I'm being honest, I really want to lie down and nap with you. However, if you want to play with me again later, I need to clean you, because *that*" – she pointed to his cock – "is not going back inside my pussy without me doing so. Also, I'm sure you don't want your dick going back in your seam like this."

Before he could stop her, she wrapped her hand holding the cloth around his flopping shaft and began to wipe him. She was unsure if this would truly be an adequate way to remove anything unsanitary. *Should I get some water?*

The more she did it, however, the more something became apparent.

As she stroked, fresh lubricant seeped from his flesh like he had glands all along it. No matter how much she removed, making sure to get into the crevice of his groove, each of his spiking soft scales, and the rim of his cock, more came to the surface.

"Oh wow," she exclaimed. "I just realised... your lubricant cleans you."

It stopped anything from sticking to his cock, including her cum and his seed. *No wonder he has no issues with it going back inside him.*

"Emerie..." he grated as he patted her head to turn it upwards. His orbs were white, and the way his body was puffed alarmed her. "That hurts."

"Oh, I'm sorry," she apologised, seeing his cock was drying and turning pruney in certain places because of her cleaning him.

Since she was satisfied nothing bad was on him, she threw the cloth as far away from them as possible and gripped him with both hands. She stroked him until he was saturated once more.

She smiled up at him. "Better?"

"Don't stop?" he asked almost sheepishly. He even scratched at the side of his beak, pretending to be bashful!

Gosh! He was like a sexual deviant with a cock that just didn't. Seem. To empty.

Emerie rolled her eyes. "No more sex." Instead, she laid back against the bedding and opened her arms out to him. "I would like to cuddle while I sleep. And you are going to promise me that you'll actually let me this time."

He let himself fall until he was above her on straightened arms, then licked across her lips. "I promise."

Then he scooped her into his arms, and rolled to the ground until he was on his side. However, he gripped the back of her thigh to spread her, and not only slotted his knee between her legs, but sheathed his cock inside her pussy.

She gave a surprised, raspy moan at the easy glide and how quickly he fully mounted her.

"H-hey!" she shouted.

"You said no more sex," he grumbled as he gripped her arse and turned slightly so the knee between her thighs had created a little pocket for the leg she was lying on to fit through. "But I would like to rest with us as one."

With her head cushioned by his biceps, he switched hands, holding her arse and the crook of her thigh to keep her leg comfortably up. Then he wrapped his other arm around her so she was securely and warmly trapped within his embrace.

"I promised I would let you sleep," he reminded her. "So nurse and cuddle me as you do."

Emerie puffed her cheeks out as she pouted, then released them with a huff before tucking herself against his chest. It was a contrast of hardness from his exposed ribs, and plushness from the muscles around them.

"You're lucky you're cute," she mumbled in mock annoyance.

She passed out as soon as her eyes closed, but her contentment radiated within her dreams.

THIRTY-FIVE

Standing on the tips of her toes, Emerie was thankful Ingram lowered his raven skull so she could wrap her arms around his neck. She hugged him with all her might as she buried her face against him, taking in the roughness of his scales, the warmth and strength of him, and his wonderful scent of burnt sugar and hickory bark.

She fully took him in... for the last time.

"I don't want to go." Ingram grumbled his protest, as he had many times this morning. He wrapped his arm around her waist and dipped forward even more.

"Everyone needs food," she murmured against him. "It's better and safer for everyone if more of you go to hunt."

"I still think bringing the Mavka who cannot control his hunger is a poor decision," Orpheus stated as he hugged Reia in his arms, who was embracing him just as tightly as he was her. "But she is right. Travelling through the Veil will be safer with all three of us. The Demons are less likely to attack."

"Will you be okay by yourself, Delora?" Magnar asked as he stroked the back of her dark-brown hair.

"I won't be alone," she laughed in response – although Emerie could hear the nervous tremble in her tone. "I'll be with everyone else." Magnar let out a disappointed huff, his head turning away, until she added, "But I will miss you."

His long, fluffy fox tail wagged behind him at that.

"The quicker you leave, the quicker you can come back,"

Faunus stated with his hand gripping the side of Mayumi's waist. One of their children crawled sporadically between them. "Hopefully you return before night falls."

Emerie finally let Ingram go, and she gave him a warm smile.

He cupped the side of her face and brushed the back of his glossy claw underneath one of her tearing eyes. "Why are you crying, little butterfly?"

"Because goodbyes are hard?" she laughed off, before gesturing to Reia, but more importantly, Delora. "See, even she's crying."

And thank fucking goodness for that, otherwise Emerie's pain would look out of place. Reia's expression was warm, lacking in tears, but Emerie had already discovered she had a strong personality. She tried to keep her more extreme emotions inside when she could.

That's how she usually was, or rather, had been before she met Ingram. Who knew it would be a monster that would bring her out of her shell?

"Then don't say goodbye? I can stay."

Emerie groaned as she dipped her head back. He was really making this hard.

She placed her hands on either side of his beak and shook his head around. His chuckle was deep and playful, and it lifted her spirits slightly. She gave the end a kiss.

"Here, I have a gift for you." She tipped his head down until she could reach one of his short, upward-jutting goat horns. "It's the bracelet my parents and Gideon gave to me for my eighteenth birthday."

Although only one charm out of three remained, consisting of a silver disc with the letter G engraved into it, every one of the colourful gem beads was intact. When she realised it wouldn't fit, she took off the ribbon keeping her braid together and used it to link one side of the brown leather twine to the other. She tied it as securely as possible to him, making sure it sat in the recess where his horn and skull met so it couldn't slide off.

He looked a little funny with a floppy red bow hanging down the side of his skull, but she also liked it. It was obvious against the stark whiteness of his bony head.

Hopefully the next human you meet sees it and realises... *someone loved you.* Her jaw clenched at the pain her thoughts brought. *And gives you a chance because of it.*

"Why are you giving me this?" Ingram asked as he tentatively touched the triple-knotted bow.

She grinned. "Consider it a good luck charm."

"We'll need it," Orpheus stated solemnly.

"I have a horn charm like you now," Ingram said, his orbs turning bright yellow while his tail tip curled.

"Mine's better," Orpheus huffed.

Ingram growled at him just as Reia tapped him on the stomach. "Be nice, Orpheus!"

"I *am* being nice." Orpheus turned his head away and folded his arms, his bell charms jingling under the momentum. "I was just being truthful." Then he reached up and flicked one with a claw, his own orbs turning bright pink. "But I know it feels nice to receive a gift like this."

"You should have painted my face before we left, Delora," Magnar whined as his orbs turned bright green in jealousy.

"Sorry." She laughed at his unexpected sulking. "I'll paint it when you get back. How about that?"

His tail wagged once more. He was easy to placate, and Delora knew just how to make him happy.

The discussion as to why Faunus was staying behind was brought up again by a jealous Ingram. Someone had to protect the women in case of Demons, and no one was willing to take his pregnant bride from him when it was obvious he'd maul them all for it.

Then, with much reluctance, Orpheus, Magnar, and Ingram left – all three of them unaware of the true reasoning as to why.

Reia, Delora, and Emerie shared a look between them. They all feared their partners' eventual reactions when they discovered what had happened, but it was Emerie who the others' gazes lingered on. She wouldn't be here to make the knowledge of it better for her leaving Duskwalker.

She averted her gaze when Mayumi and Faunus moved closer and fixed their sights on her as well. "I better get changed," she said to escape.

With a heavy heart, Emerie went to her tent while pulling her hair free to redo it after she ripped some cloth to create a makeshift, crude bow. She removed the blue dress she'd been given and instead donned her Demonslayer uniform. Reia had repaired all the holes in it by patching it with brown material.

The soles of her shoes were worn, but that made them more flexible. Hopefully there weren't any sharp rocks within Jabez's castle.

She also fixed the silver diadem tiara to her hair so the blue teardrop would sit in the middle of her forehead. The gem was cold, and it tapped against her skin as she ducked under the tent flap to leave.

Faunus approached from their home with his arms full of weapons, and they both arrived to where the other women waited at the same time.

A sword for Reia, a bow and full quiver for Delora, and a whip and sword for Emerie.

She turned to Mayumi.

"I wanted to thank you for all your hospitality over the last few days. I know it's a lot for you to stay behind, but I really don't think I could have survived staying here any longer with this decision."

"It's fine," Mayumi answered with a deflated tone. She scratched at the side of her hair tied back tightly before humour twitched at the corner of her lip. "I doubt after yesterday, you would have lasted much longer. I bet I have to disinfect my tent. How's your ass? I saw you limping around when you jumped out to pee."

By the simple fact that Mayumi was trying to hold back laughter, Emeric knew she'd said that simply to rile her up. Whether it was because she liked to tease her friends, or she was trying to lift the sorrow clouding Emerie's gaze, she didn't know.

Still, she couldn't help blushing in embarrassment all the way to her ears. As she fidgeted and brought her eyes to Reia and Delora, she wanted to expire right there and then.

"Oh my god! I was only joking, but you did, didn't you?"

Mayumi bellowed with a laugh, bright humour alight in her eyes. "You took it up the ass!"

Emerie jumped forward and covered her mouth. "Oh my gosh, shut up!"

Delora gave a horrified gasp as Reia's already pale complexion whitened further.

"What the fuck? You can do that?!" Reia screeched. She patted at her face like she wanted to bring warmth back into it. "How... what..."

Faunus' chuckle was telling as he folded his arms.

"You didn't!" Reia gawked at Mayumi before turning to Delora with a flummoxed stare. "Don't tell me..."

"Gosh, no!" Delora squealed while flinching, as if she'd just been slapped. "I would never." The poor woman's face turned just as red as Emerie's felt. "Although... Magnar *has* tried. I'm surprised you haven't."

"Why the hell would I have tried?! I was a virgin when I met Orpheus!"

Emerie winced. *Ouch.* She didn't think she could have taken Ingram if he had been her first.

"He's just so curious about everything," Delora grumbled defensively as she rubbed at her arm.

"Can this awkward conversation *end?*" Emerie squeaked. She turned to Mayumi, utterly mortified. "Why did you even do this?"

Mayumi's features suddenly went harsh. "Because all of you needed to elevate your anxieties and fears. Now you have to prepare for what's to come, and I can't be there to help you all through that. Emerie, you are the most skilled fighter here, and the one we're truly relying on."

That sobered them all swiftly, but Mayumi had succeeded in her scheme. Although her heart hurt, it was a little lighter. Everyone else also didn't look so... depressed.

A human-sized white owl descended from the sky in a flap of feathers, startling them all. Emerie sucked in a breath, hoping the *mother* of Duskwalkers didn't just hear all that!

As soon as she landed, Lindiwe transformed into a human. Her hood slid back as a yellow beak receded, then disappeared altogether, revealing the sharp features of her face. Her dark-brown eyes were steely with determination, but not unfeeling towards their plight.

"Are we ready?" Lindiwe asked, brushing at her white dress to push it into place.

All three of them nodded.

Mayumi didn't come in for a hug, but she did reach her fist out. Emerie stared at it, before hesitantly knocking her own fist against it, unsure if that was what she'd been seeking. With dark-yellow orbs of curiosity, Faunus did the same thing, to which Emerie knocked her knuckles against his far larger ones.

I just gave a fist bump to a Duskwalker. She never thought she'd do that.

"Okay, let's go," Emerie commanded with a nod.

Lindiwe turned incorporeal, and muttered, "Weldir, we're ready." When she became solid once more, and noticed their gazes, she awkwardly looked away while shrugging her shoulders. "I can't do portal magic."

Everyone stepped forward, except for Emerie. She peered around at them, a little lost as to why they'd closed in on a certain spot.

"It's a soul," Lindiwe explained. "You can't see it, as you are only a part of life and not death like everyone else. Weldir has sent it here and intends to rip it in two and use its life force to create a rift to Jabez's castle."

"Uh huh," Emerie said with a nod and bewildered, wide eyes. "Thought he couldn't use magic on Earth?"

Lindiwe sighed. "He can touch souls here. This one is linked to him, so he is able to manipulate it from Tenebris."

Emerie winced when a hot white light tore downwards through the air like a lightning strike. It pulled open at the same time, like a wide tear that had chalky black dust floating around the outside.

Lindiwe gestured to it, and said, "Now, we must walk through, but we must do so together. Once someone steps across, it will open the other side and give away our element of surprise if we delay."

Emerie's mouth went dry, and she wiped her hands on the

material of her pants. *So, this is it?* She'd step through that portal and leave her life, and Ingram, and everything else behind?

She looked over her shoulder in the direction he'd gone, wishing he'd come back and stop her. Of course he didn't, but just picturing him made tears well in her eyes.

I'm scared.

I don't want to do this.

Her jaw clenched until she thought she'd shatter her teeth. Her hands trembled, while her chest ached so terribly she wondered when someone had pushed a searing blade into it.

I want to be with him. This isn't fair.

"Emerie," Delora gently called.

"Yeah?" she croaked, turning her head forward to find all eyes on her.

"Are you sure you want to do this?" Reia asked, her lips tight and flat with worry.

"No," she half-laughed, half-cried.

"Then–"

Before Reia could say anything that could possibly change her mind, Emerie cut her off. "I'm doing this to help all of you, but I'm also doing this for him. He wants Aleron back, and a safer world for him." She stepped towards the white rift that looked frighteningly empty and cold. "If he wanted me to stay, he would have asked me to be his bride yesterday."

With everything that had been shared between them, all the intimacy and touch, if he wanted her to be his bride, he would have made her his.

"Did you ask him about it?" Delora's features twisted in sympathy. "If you gave him more time..."

"I didn't need to," she responded, giving her a dull look. "Plus, the whole point of doing this today was to *not* give him time."

"What if he loves you, Emerie?" Delora pushed.

"He doesn't," Emerie stated firmly.

Why the hell is everyone trying to make me change my mind at the last freaking second? She clenched her hands into tight, shaking fists. Why were they trying to make this harder for her? This was already painful enough without them throwing more baggage on her.

"You don't know that," Reia argued, scratching at the side of her head. "I already told you of our story, and how Orpheus was... He was devastated the first time I died. Neither one of us knew if I would actually come back, if it was too late. If Ingram loves you as much as Orpheus did me back then... he may not get over it."

Everything Mayumi had done to settle Emerie's tears was made pointless by Delora and Reia.

"He doesn't, okay?!" Emerie exclaimed while swiftly darting her face from them, her eyes shut tight and her teeth clenched. "I've been watching all of you, and it doesn't take a genius to realise what colour their orbs turn when they feel love."

"Emerie." Mayumi said her name firmly, attempting to cut in and stop her spiralling emotions.

"I have spent almost every minute of every day with him for the past three weeks and not once have his orbs turned pink because of me."

Somehow, Emerie had managed to stem the worst of her tears so that the remnants of them only dotted her eyelashes. She opened her eyes and gave them a weak and beseeching grin that likely just revealed her anguish more than anything. She hoped it was enough to make them leave her alone.

"But they have because of Aleron," she continued. "No matter what he does feel for me, his kindred is the most important thing to him. I am replaceable. He is not. He will get over it, and I will have died knowing I did what was best for him, what will protect him."

She knew Ingram felt something deep for her: tenderness, fondness, trust, and absolutely lust. He cared about Emerie and had made it obviously apparent. Anyone would be an idiot to deny that.

But it wasn't enough, and she wasn't going to give him time to figure it out or fall any deeper.

Not if she wanted to help him in the long run.

She wanted him to be happy, and to have the future he wanted.

He'd spoken many times about wanting to be back in

Aleron's wings. That had always been his true desire; it was why she'd come here in the first damn place.

And when faced with a choice between someone who was alive and who wasn't, he'd chosen neither. She'd been sitting right in front of him, with a beating heart and working lungs, and he couldn't choose between her and someone who no longer existed.

His love for his twin was too strong to allow Emerie in. Their bond transcended time, space, and existence.

My life has always been meaningless... She'd spent most of it mourning for herself. *At least it will now have a meaningful end.*

Although the last few weeks had been filled with pain, fear, and uncertainty, it'd also been the most fun, exciting, and sensual experience of her life. For a little while yesterday, she'd been truly... happy.

She'd found that contentment within the arms of a monster, after being thoroughly fucked by him. She'd even pretended their cuddle had radiated with love from both sides, rather than just her own.

That was more than she'd ever hoped for in her life, and she'd take that gift to the afterlife. She could tell Gideon all about it.

So, with a sniffle and renewed courage, she looked at Lindiwe. Her expression was one of sympathy, but Emerie gave the woman a thumbs up.

"Now, let's go kill the king of Demons."

Lindiwe grabbed her arm, giving her a stern, disapproving look when she tried to step through the portal. The woman took the lead, going first rather than Emerie – the human with the least protection.

With a heavy silence, everyone else followed swiftly.

THIRTY-SIX

Ingram stood in the sun at the edge of the Veil's forest, staring into its mist and foreboding shade with a sense of... disquiet.

Something didn't feel right.

Perhaps it was the ribbon bow he could feel flapping lightly against the side of his skull, or the sorrowful glint in Emerie's icy-blue eyes when she'd given it to him, but dread nagged at the nape of his neck.

A soft gust of wind blew leaves resting around his feet towards the shade. The area was quiet. The world was at peace.

She was safe within Faunus' yellow ward. She wasn't alone; she had people to protect her.

So why did he feel like it was a mistake leaving her?

He wanted the elation he'd experienced just this very morning to return. He'd finally connected with Emerie and formed a physical bond with her, then thoroughly affirmed it over the course of the past day and a half.

Just the thought of it should make him shudder with satisfaction.

Instead, he was left cold as he searched for any sign of Faunus' ward from a distance. It was too far and there was too much dense forest between them.

A large warm hand cupped the rounded joint of his shoulder. He glanced at it, the white protruding bones of the knuckles stark against dark-grey flesh, before he looked upon its owner.

"You will get used to the feeling," Orpheus said, before

removing his comforting touch. "It feels wrong to leave them, but it's what we must do in order to provide for them."

I am not alone in this feeling? He wanted that to ease him.

It didn't.

"Come, we must move on. The sun is on our side."

Orpheus turned, and Ingram looked towards Magnar. He nodded his fox skull in encouragement, and Ingram reluctantly followed.

At least this would teach him how to hunt for Emerie, rather than to slaughter in a mindless craze. It was the only reason he'd agreed to this.

Orpheus took the lead, and Ingram inspected the clothing he wore to hide his unique Mavka traits. Magnar too, wore pants and a shirt, but he'd chosen to forgo shoes.

Ingram was the only one naked, and he thought they both looked rather... ridiculous.

It also meant when he'd shifted from his monstrous form to his more humanoid one, he hadn't needed to wait additionally for clothing to form. He'd been comfortably standing long before both of them when they'd reached the edge of the Veil's forest.

All three had sprinted on all fours. Despite being followed and chased by Demons, none were foolish enough to attack. It'd taken them barely an hour to make it to relative safety.

They walked within the very slip of sun that touched the ground right next to the Veil's cliff wall until Orpheus started them up an incline. It was steep, but wide enough that two humans could walk side by side; a Mavka just fit.

Just as the surface's edge became visible, Magnar, who had been walking between him and Orpheus, dropped back. He glided his claws against the wall to keep himself from walking off the edge of their path, as he turned his head to the side to look at Ingram.

His green orbs morphed to dark yellow within in his bony eye sockets.

"Are you going to ask Emerie for her soul?" Magnar enquired, tipping his head. His antlers blocked the sun and caused streaks of shade to branch over the white of his skull.

Ingram looked at the horizon as he climbed.

"No," he answered plainly.

Magnar, growing more interested in the conversation, turned his head around completely to face Ingram while he walked. "Why not?"

He was beginning to wonder why not as well.

Whenever he tried to think too deeply on the subject, a blankness muddled his thoughts. Between that nothingness, other thoughts trickled in, sharing with him the limited information he'd retained.

"Because I cannot."

"Why not?" Magnar pressed, just as their path tipped and their feet met the surface's edge.

"I am not allowed to," he uttered quietly, unsure of how to answer.

Orpheus turned and halted them.

"If you give her time, she may change her mind." He cupped the side of his long wolf snout. "It's difficult for a human to accept Mavka. Most of them think of us as monsters, but Reia and Delora bonded with us of their own will. Emerie seems... warm towards you. You already have her scent on you."

"You can ask her again later, when she has grown comfortable with you," Magnar added.

Ingram's head jerked. "I have not asked her."

He wasn't sure why they'd assumed he had.

Now, Orpheus' orbs turned dark yellow in curiosity, mirroring Magnar's.

"Why are you both looking at me like that?"

Orpheus stepped forward and dipped his head. "You said you weren't allowed, so I thought that was because she has rejected you. Why is it you think you cannot?"

Ingram scratched at the back of his neck, then rubbed the side of it when his orbs turned a reddish pink. Slowly, he drew his foreclaw to his chest.

"I only have one heart," he grumbled, tapping just next to his sternum. "It already belongs to Aleron."

Magnar and Orpheus' snouts darted towards each other, and they twisted their heads in opposite directions.

"I am already bonded in spirit," Ingram continued when it appeared as though they were confused.

"Do you not love Emerie?" Magnar asked. "You are even clingier with her than Orpheus is with Reia. I thought that meant..."

"She is my female," Orpheus softly growled. "I will hold her as much as she allows." He snorted out a wild huff before bringing his skull back to Ingram. "But I'm also curious. Other than the fact you don't have her soul, together you act like Mavka and bride."

"I love Aleron," Ingram stated. "He is my kindred, my... *twin.*"

"I don't understand," Magnar grumbled, tapping a claw to the side of his bony fox snout.

Orpheus cupped the end of his own, looking over at the vast distance of the Veil.

Their silence as they pondered on what Ingram said weighed on him. Was he just not making sense or was something wrong with his thoughts?

The reddish pink in his vision deepened.

"I guess the better question would be, do you *want* Emerie as your bride?" Orpheus asked.

"Well... yes," he answered, his vision swiftly turning blue. "But as I said, I cannot."

"I see..." Orpheus hummed, tapping his claw on top of his snout as he continued to hold the end. "I think you are mistaken, Ingram. You are allowed to love more than one person. A bond with Emerie would not interfere with the one you have for the bat–... with Aleron."

Ingram's head tilted sharply at that. "It would not?"

"Oh! Now I get it. Orpheus is right," Magnar exclaimed, before letting out a deep chuckle. "There are different kinds of bonds and love. For instance, I love Delora. She is my female and bride, but I also hold a place within me for Fyodor, our youngling. You do not need two hearts, just enough room for both. Or more, if you so choose it." Then Magnar grumbled and tossed his head side to side as he bashfully said, "Orpheus, although quite prickly at times, is important to me. He is my...

friend as much as my brother. He helped me with Delora and many other things. There is a place for him and Reia within my heart as well."

Orpheus turned his head away as his orbs shifted to a reddish pink. "Reia should not be in your heart at all," he grumbled awkwardly. "But thank you."

Magnar chuckled again and stepped away from Orpheus' side while gesturing to him, as if to say, 'See?'

"I can have both?" Ingram asked.

"Yes," Orpheus confirmed.

Why did learning this make his chest swell with emotion?

Perhaps he should have spent more time with the other Mavka, rather than being constantly at Emerie's side. He hadn't been particularly interested in learning about them other than what he accidentally observed while sitting in their presence.

He hadn't even realised this entire conversation was one big question he'd needed to ask.

He knew what he knew, and hadn't seen a need to have someone explain it to him. His separation anxiety was a big cause of his apprehension and was stunting his potential learning; it was also another reason why him being here with these two Mavka was making him restless.

I can have both...

He had not known that.

He'd known he could share a bond with both, but he hadn't realised it could be on such a deeply ingrained level: kindred and kindred, Mavka and bride. Aleron and Ingram were one being, so it hadn't made sense to him to allow Emerie to mesh her essence with his until they were also one.

I can have both, he repeated to himself, turning away as he scratched at the side of his beak almost bashfully.

The sharp blade that had been the piece of Emerie lodged within his chest, like it had been trying to force its way into his bond with Aleron, began to melt like hot iron. It dripped inside, sinking within the limited well of his heart.

The longer he allowed it to seep in, the more it mixed – and grew.

A warm, fuzzy, fluffy feeling tingled his chest, and he

slapped his hand over the tip of his beak when it made him want to giggle in reaction. It was almost... ticklish.

Bright pink bled into the edges of his vision, slowly creeping forward like the shift, too, was shy in this realisation. However, the moment it fully encompassed his sight, the emotion it belonged to blossomed like a bud that had just been waiting for him to allow it to fully flower.

It had been there for a while, patiently waiting.

Before he knew it, the love he shared for Aleron was doubled, and half was given to someone else. Not a drop of difference in measurement, but the adoration he felt was... different. The two sides were not at war with each other; there was no competition.

I love Emerie...

Holding the end of his beak, Ingram clawed at his chest when it felt too full, too fluffy and light. His affection for Emerie was so strong he feared the molten ore of it would burn him from the inside, and yet it was so wholesome he hoped it did.

Orpheus and Magnar both flinched when he turned suddenly.

He made it about two steps towards the decline that would lead him back to the Veil, to Emerie, when Orpheus snatched his horn.

"Where are you going?" Orpheus shouted in disbelief, yanking and turning him back around.

Or rather, just his head, as his legs fought to get away.

"I must go back," Ingram rushed out. "If I had known all this, I would have asked for Emerie's soul sooner."

He would have done it the day of the fucking meadow!

The sensation in his chest... the first warm droplet of it started that day. Had he not been so unaware and ignorant, had his mind not been obsessed with Aleron, he would have realised he wanted her to be eternally his.

His little butterfly, in his mind, had been claimed by him that day. He'd just been trying to claim her in every other way possible since then, unwittingly seeking to fill the void of longing.

"You will have to wait," Orpheus snapped out. "We must hunt. Bring your human food, take care of her needs, then ask."

Ingram let out a whining groan. *I don't want to wait!*
He'd already waited too long.

THIRTY-SEVEN

Having at least half a dozen non-glowing red eyes upon her was... creepy. Especially when every single one of them had homed in on Emerie specifically, as if they could smell she was the true human within their troupe.

With Reia, Delora, and Lindiwe covering her from all three sides, and just her front free, her gaze flittered across those she could see. The Demons had created a circle around them to stop them from escaping, but their curious yet nasty gazes were predatory.

Every member of her group wore weapons, and they had come here of their own volition. The Demons were wondering why. Or perhaps they were waiting for their King to show up before they attacked. Whether it was by their scents or sounds, something about their group brought the small horde of Demons to them.

"Throw a shield up or something to stop them from coming," Emerie suggested frantically, darting her gaze between the three doorways they were slowly piling in from. Two on either side of the throne room, and the main double doors behind them.

"I can't. We must wait for the Demon King," Lindiwe quietly bit back. "He won't be able to teleport in or out once I place it down. Not even a Phantom can escape it."

Won't be able to teleport in or out... Emerie swallowed thickly.

It was a trap, not only for him, but for them. There would be nowhere to run or hide.

One by one, more Demons came and joined the others to stare at them.

The air was thick and stale with tension, combined with a foulness that only permeated from Demons. Like tree rot and the sweetness that came from a decaying corpse. It wasn't too bad, as if the smell had diluted over time with their growth – since she could tell most of these were medium and larger Demons – but it was still enough to singe her nostrils.

There were a few candles lit on a mostly darkened chandelier above. Spiders had made their cobweb homes on its inverted golden arches, but it did look as though someone attempted to half-heartedly maintain it.

The floor was clean except for right in the corners where the wall met the flagstones. A red carpet, worn down and faded in a wide strip down the middle, ran from the heavy timber double doors all the way up the podium steps and underneath the throne. The chair itself was made of varnished timber and adorned with red cushions. It was the only real furniture in the room, and the only thing well maintained.

The clear glass arching window behind it was... eerie. Although it was the middle of the day, black and purple swirling magic stopped any light from shining through. It made everything dim and ominous.

They'd only been here for a few minutes, and already Emerie wanted to run for the hills. The passage of time was drawn out, like the sand in an hourglass had slowed to a trickle in this agonising wait.

It allowed her to take in the whisper of her companions' breaths, each one of them shallow and filled with anxiety. Her heartbeat was a pounding drum in her ears, so loud she worried its secretive pulsing was heard by all. Even her hair trailing down her shoulder was scratchy and distinct.

Most of the Demons had turned into grinning statues made of mixed flesh. Patchy sections that, instead of skin, looked like the night sky, threatening to twinkle with stars throughout the human brown, fawny, and white skin. They almost appeared to have vitiligo, which was separated by the human-like parts of them and the obviously inhuman animal parts.

Most had tails of some form, yet only a few had snouts and muzzles. Some had horns and fur. All had claws.

Emerie avoided looking at the two with wings, but her curious gaze had checked to make sure they weren't the ones who had tried to steal her. To make sure they weren't the ones who had ruined her life and killed Gideon.

They weren't.

There were a few on all fours who strutted between their brethren, never taking their fierce red eyes off them. They snickered and whooped like wild dogs or hissed like feral cats. They wanted to lunge, they wanted to attack, they wanted to... eat.

One almost poked itself in the eye when it licked across its muzzle while giving a disgusting slurp.

She took in a deep breath when she *swore* there was an echo of one or two stomachs gurgling.

Wrong. All of this was *wrong*.

She should not be here. No human should be here.

Emerie had gone to the Veil, the most dangerous place in Austrális, and decided to go... fuck it! Why not toss herself into the very middle of the cesspool of *death*?!

Fright had completely dried her tears. Yes, she thought of Ingram – it was the only thing stopping her from screaming and bolting. Her determination to know he would be safe, and that she could, *somehow,* be a step towards him and his kindred reuniting, was the only thing keeping her feet firmly placed where they were.

She was choosing to believe in his dream, even if it made no sense. Even if it was pointless.

It was what he wanted.

With an arrow nocked but not foolishly pointing at an enemy, Delora's quiet voice trembled through the silence. "W-why are they just standing there?"

"Because they are not mindless Demons," Lindiwe answered, her head lowering so she could glare. "These are his guards. They will wait for his command."

The Demons within the room either snickered or remained

silent but oppressing.

"Where the fuck is he?" Reia snapped out as she rotated back and forth on the balls of her feet, pointing her sword at multiple monsters.

"He's either taunting us" – Lindiwe stepped closer to Emerie – "or waiting for more Demons to arrive."

"Well, fuck that," Reia muttered under her breath before stepping forward. "Knock knock, you fucking bastard!"

The laughter that reverberated against the walls echoed throughout the room, diabolical and sinister. It was soft and sane, which made it all the more bone-chilling.

Emerie only had enough time to turn her head and gasp as the Demon King appeared and picked Reia up by the throat. Then he was gone, taking her to the podium where his throne was.

Lindiwe threw her hand against the ground and the doors sealed shut with a thunderous bang, causing Emerie to jump in surprise. Black glittering sand blocked any more enemies from entering the room.

"Reia!" Delora screamed, lifting her bow and arrow in their direction.

"I have a fucking bone to pick with you," Jabez snarled, rotating the hand not around her throat like a wave until his claws were facing upwards towards Reia's abdomen.

She kicked at first, one of her hands grabbing at the clawed one he had wrapped tightly around her throat. In the next moment, she turned incorporeal, eyes narrowed and a sneer marring her features.

She flittered back as she hovered in her ghostly form.

His shark-toothed grin brightened at the woman, as if he knew she'd escape him all along.

Emerie took in his side profile and tried not to gawk at the oddity of him.

His skin was dark brown but made utterly inhuman by the grey undertone to it that only became obvious when shaded from the candles above. His ears were long, pointed, and appeared Elvish, whereas the black horns curling up and back over his head were Demonic. He was tall, perhaps not taller than a

Duskwalker, but he still towered over Reia's tiny form.

Although he wore long, genie-like dark pants that had a layer of loose material draping over them like a skirt, he was shirtless. It revealed he had strong but lean muscles, as well as void-like, thick black streaks – that almost appeared like claw marks – over his sides, neck, shoulders, and down his biceps.

Red eyes flicked to Lindiwe, and his long white hair, coming to the base of his spine, flowed in a glossy straight curtain when he turned.

His lips were full, his nose straight and thin, and his cheekbones were high, framed by a sharp jaw. His large, grinning mouth widened even further to reveal more sharp fangs. He had a chomp that would be devastating.

His features were handsome, despite the strangeness that came from the Elvish and Demon mix of him.

A multitude of jewellery glinted from him in the form of gold bands. Three pliable ones hung around his neck, whereas the other seven were hard. Two dug into the meaty flesh of his left biceps, versus only one on his right. Four more were in pairs around his ankles, and they jingled when he moved.

His black, curling claws, that also tipped his bare feet, glinted as he cupped the side of his own face and drew his claws down his jaw. His grin gentled into mocking humour at Lindiwe.

"This is your plan?" He laughed. "Three Phantoms and a human? The least you could have done was to give me the pleasure of killing one of your Mavka."

His gaze diverted to Reia as she floated through the Demons to return to them.

"It seems pointless to bring three reincarnating Phantoms to a battle they'll lose. They will return to their Mavka only to dwell with the loss and the pain they suffered beforehand." His grin twisted back into snide humour. "I'm guessing they don't even know their females are here."

"You underestimate our determination," Lindiwe stated darkly when Reia turned solid at their sides.

"My head, is it?" Jabez asked rhetorically as he swiped his claws across his own throat. "Have to get to it first. You haven't been successful the many other times you've tried."

"I could just put a sword through your heart like I did to Katerina," Reia mused. The Demon King's expression morphed into a dead stare. "I'll make you pay for everything you put Orpheus through. Should have killed me when you had the chance, Jabez."

"No. It's much more fun to see you pitifully fight first. It's entertaining, just as it was entertaining when you crumbled to ash in Orpheus' arms and I watched him *cry*."

Emerie could almost taste the hateful tension between Jabez and Reia. The fight between them was personal and bitter.

Emerie couldn't help it. She tucked her hand into the pocket of her borrowed weapons belt and clenched it around the sun stone.

They had one shot at this. If Emerie failed... if she died, they'd have to find someone else willing to make this sacrifice.

That wasn't what had her feeling like the entire world rested on her shoulders. *What if I mess up?* What if she shattered the stone at the wrong time and Jabez got away?

They didn't have a second one. This was it. What was currently nestled in her sweaty palm was their only hope.

To Emerie's left, the tension of string and wood pulling against each other creaked. An arrow was purposefully loosed, and it sailed through the air with a whistle.

He ducked to the side, his hair fluttering as he caught the arrow aimed for his forehead. He stared at it, inspecting the sharp point of the arrowhead before bringing his gaze to Delora.

"You talk too much," Delora announced, her usually sweet voice hard as she confidently stomped one foot forward. "I would like to go home."

They all wanted to go home.

"You," Jabez chuckled. "I remember you being quite... tasty when–"

"Yes, yes, when you ate me alive," she bravely cut in, making him scowl. "I remember, and I'm still here. I'm not cowering like you said I would."

This was personal for Delora as well, and Emerie dearly hoped she didn't disappoint them all. Every second longer weighed on her fear of failing.

"Enough of this," Reia shouted, as she stepped forward and sliced her blade through the air.

The surprised silence was swiftly interrupted by the wet plop of a Demon's severed head falling to the ground.

She backed up when its body fell on top of it.

Nothing happened. No one leapt forward to defend or fight. The tension vibrated to a new height as malice bled from the Demons.

Emerie's wide gaze trailed from the corpse to Jabez. Although prideful, his expression darkened at his obedient servants.

"Go," he whispered.

When the remaining Demons all leapt at the same time, a squeal erupted from Emerie, and she ducked down, holding her sword up. A wave of them rained down with their thick, meaty bodies from all around.

She hadn't expected them to all come at once and to jump like that!

Reia and Delora both turned incorporeal to evade them, while the Witch Owl stood above Emerie with her hands up. A small chalky black dome formed above and held back the Demons trying to smother them.

Emerie stared up at her as Lindiwe connected their gazes.

"I have you," Lindiwe whispered. "Move, fight. I will be at your side as much as I can."

With a nod, Lindiwe threw her arms back, and the shield expanded, tossing all the Demons away. Renewed confidence burst within her chest, and Emerie rushed forward with her sword raised.

Reia was gone, already in the middle of a small group of Demons. She evaded swipes and attacks by turning incorporeal, and would become solid only when she knew her attacks would deliver debilitating blows.

As they all moved, strange chalky tentacles would shoot up from the ground, curling their limbs around Demons to toss them. Those Demons were quick to get to their feet or paws and relaunch their attacks.

Delora had taken to standing on top of the stone doorway, but she couldn't shoot with the wall behind her. Instead, she jumped off it and unleashed arrows as she fell, only to turn ghostly before she landed in the sea of writhing bodies desperate to catch her.

Emerie's main focus was reaching the Demon King. She fought Demons along the way to the podium, with Lindiwe placing small oval shields up when she needed to protect her. They moved at a snail's pace, having to divert and back up when charged.

The monsters that towered over her with sharp claws and fangs were the hardest to fight. It wasn't natural to slash upwards, and her sword would lodge into their arms and sides rather than cleanly slicing. She almost lost her sword when it got jammed in between the ribs of a Demon and they pulled her with them when they yelped and jumped backwards.

Thankfully, they separated, and the motion of her bouncing back accidentally sliced the face of a medium-sized creature sneaking up on her right on all fours. It grabbed her sword with its fangs and tossed its head around to get her to let go.

Lindiwe came up beside her and drove a dagger downward through the top of its skull, effectively piercing its brain and rendering it immobile.

Holy shit, that was close, Emerie thought, thankful for Lindiwe's interference.

She watched its eyes drift in two different directions as consciousness drained from it. Purple blood bubbled up from its fatal wound when Lindiwe yanked her blade free, and the Demon thudded chest down against the ground.

By the time Emerie turned back to look at the podium, her heart stung on each beat, utterly filled with fear and anxiety. Her chest ached, her lungs working too hard and fast. Her lips dried more and more with each ragged breath, and already she felt parched.

Her muddled, bouncing gaze searched for Jabez near his throne.

He was gone.

A high-pitched, pained shriek behind her had her spinning.

Lindiwe had been lifted off her feet, clutched in Jabez's fist by her long, curly brown hair. Before she could turn incorporeal to escape, lowering her chin to protect her neck when she was pulled, he ripped his claws across her face.

He laughed when her ghostly body flittered through his fingers.

Lindiwe covered her cheek with her hand and then turned to face Emerie, like Jabez was insignificant. Emerie had just raised her sword up to block, as a set of claws came down while she'd been looking away. The Demon roared as his fingers were chopped off, and Lindiwe pulled Emerie's shoulder to put her behind her.

She stabbed her dagger into the white human flesh of a medium-sized Demon's chest while it was distracted and sliced upwards. Emerie spun on the spot with her sword raised, ready to defend Lindiwe while she finished carving it up.

Once more, the Demon King disappeared from view.

He materialised at the podium for just a second to assess his next placement.

In front of Emerie, Delora floated in the air as she tried to evade the two flying Demons – one with bat wings, the other with feathers. Emerie shuddered, but turned her focus away when she looked relatively okay.

She wished she hadn't.

She wouldn't have witnessed Jabez standing behind Reia, who had been lifted off the ground by the claws he'd stabbed into the back of her skull. The stain of red flowed down the blonde strands like a macabre river. Her lips were parted like she'd gasped, and she was forced to look up at Jabez, who had bent over her from behind with a twisted sneer.

Her legs weren't still, but they didn't kick; they twitched, like her pierced brain was sending strange signals to them.

Her sword clattered to the ground when her body went limp. Demons sliced her arms and legs into ribbons with their claws as they dragged her corpse off Jabez's fingers. They began to devour her, along with the three Demons she had managed to kill by herself.

Like he was unbothered by the fact he was in the middle of a battle, surrounded by the carnage his servants created, he licked her blood and whatever brain matter had clung to his fingers.

Reia, Emerie thought with a sob. She'd barely made it a few minutes; an obvious target for Jabez.

She had to look away from the Demons mauling her corpse and bringing bits of her to their mouths. Bile rose in her throat, and she threatened to dry retch when the smacking of lips, slurping, and hungry snarls flooded her ears.

Delora descended to the ground only two metres in front of Emerie.

The yellow skirt of her dress was in tatters, but she appeared fine. Then she let out a cry and cupped her ribs from the force of a Demon shoving her down and landing overtop of her.

Emerie charged.

There was no battle cry from her as she jumped and came down on the small, bat-winged Demon's back. With her arms above her, both hands gripping the handle of her sword, she shoved it through its chest from behind. When she steadied her hand against its back to support herself from its thrashing, her palm print slowly began to singe and burn into its rough flesh.

Surprised, Emerie pulled her hand back. *The diadem?* Although she said it would only work against some medium and smaller Demons, no wonder Reia had given it to her.

Emerie didn't have time to linger on it.

Whatever the Demon had been able to do to Delora was forgotten. The enraged creature roared and swiped its arm back, throwing Emerie across the stone floor. Within seconds, Lindiwe was bent above her on her bare feet, a single hand extended.

A shield formed, just as the Demon lunged.

When it landed on the shield, Lindiwe was quick to react. She opened up a hole in it so her hand could fit, grasped it by its foot, then glanced at Emerie.

She nodded and moved into a crouch.

When Lindiwe released the rest of the dome, Emerie grunted as she shoved her sword through its throat. Lindiwe kicked the pommel, and the blade rotated, slicing through its neck and partially beheading it.

Emerie stumbled back in surprise, not expecting Lindiwe to

pull such an insane, badass move.

"Watch out!" Delora squealed, unleashing an arrow right for Emerie.

She turned and watched Jabez dematerialise just as he'd been reaching out to grab her. She startled and nearly tripped over her own feet.

She'd almost been fucking grabbed!

Delora flittered to them and turned solid. Lindiwe threw a shield over them so they could take a breather, and Emerie assessed their opponents.

The feather-winged Demon landed right in front of her with a double *thwap* of its pawed feet. Terror and painful memories bubbled hot inside her consciousness like acid, threatening to corrode the remnants of clear-headedness she'd somehow been pulling out of her arse for this fight.

Emerie pushed herself between the two women waiting near her and turned to give the winged Demon her back. Someone else could deal with it because she sure as shit could not.

However, other than it, only two more Demons remained besides Jabez. Four enemies in total, not bad.

Reia had managed to take out quite a few on her own, and many were littered with Delora's arrows. Emerie was sure those black magical tentacles aiding them had crushed one or two as well. She and Lindiwe hadn't been so successful, considering Emerie couldn't just turn intangible within the blink of an eye, but every monster they killed had helped.

"What are we going to do?" Emerie asked. "Reia, she... Won't the guys come now?"

"Every Phantom's return time is different," Lindiwe explained. "It could be a few minutes, or an hour. It won't matter anyway. It'll take them a day to get here in their monstrous forms. This will be over long before that."

Guilt squeezed Emerie's heart, and she wished the reminder of Ingram hadn't been pushed into her thoughts. *This will be over soon...* Her life was about to be over, and she worried how Ingram would react to that.

She clenched her eyes and shook her head. *No. I'm replaceable,* she reminded herself, hoping, *pleading* that was true.

"I-I need to collect my arrows," Delora muttered through heavy pants of exertion. "I'm almost out."

"We need to focus on Jabez," Lindiwe demanded. "The barrier... It won't last much longer. Weldir's magic is waning. We're running out of time."

Even now, Emerie could see it pulsating and growing smaller before it suddenly expanded – only to shrink again. Weldir must be helping from wherever he was, pushing more magic into it sporadically as it continued to weaken.

"I thought he was powerful," Emerie accused, panic threatening to settle in completely.

Honestly, watching Jabez disappear and reappear out of nowhere was frightening her. How was she supposed to get him before he teleported?

And the fact he could just slyly come up behind her had her spine tingling with awareness of how... vulnerable it was.

At any given moment, she could end up like Reia and everything would be lost.

"He is, but it's limited," Lindiwe quickly defended. "Everything I do drains him."

"Fuck it then," Emerie rasped. "Guess we better hurry up."

"Delora, keep the Demons from interfering with us."

She nodded, shoulder-length hair waving around her sombre face. "Got it."

Their backs bumped up against each other's in encouragement before they lunged forward. Lindiwe and Emerie ran for Jabez standing on the steps of the throne's podium, while Delora ran in the only direction there wasn't a Demon so she could grab what arrows she could.

The ones she picked up would be blunt, but the force of her shots should still penetrate. Not as deeply, but hopefully enough.

"He'll focus on me," Lindiwe said under her breath, glancing at Emerie from the corner of her eye.

That was all Emerie needed to know.

They separated, going around him to split his focus. Just as she foresaw, Jabez turned to Lindiwe.

At the top of the stairs, Emerie fought against a medium-sized Demon that looked like it had been grotesquely mashed between a lizard and a human. It wasn't very tall, but it was thin and fast. It was completely human in form besides its tail, with pale patchy skin, but it was covered in scales and spikes.

It kind of reminded her of Ingram, just ugly and without a raven skull.

Delora perched herself on top of the throne's backrest and kept the other Demons at bay. They were one person down; it would have been a lot easier with Reia here.

Behind her, Emerie heard the clatter of a fight. Slaps, snarls, and gasps echoed, and the only time she saw anything was from her peripheral.

At one point, Lindiwe had taken to hovering in the air while solid, like her cloak was giving her the ability to float for a few seconds. Jabez would materialise in front of her, allowing himself to fall as he tried to grasp her before she turned incorporeal.

The Demon grabbed Emerie's arm to protect itself when she attempted to cut it across the face, causing her to wince when its claws began to cut into her arm. It was too big and strong, and the diadem did little to protect her skin this time. However, it yowled in pain when it tried to grab her head, yanking its hand away from directly touching the diadem.

With the help of Delora, who shot the lizard Demon in the eye, Emerie was able to slice across its neck.

Then Delora moved, going to the rest of the throne room littered with Demon corpses. She took the attention of the two remaining monsters who still breathed, and the winged one took flight to stop her from shooting from the air.

This was Emerie's chance.

Jabez obviously didn't see her as a threat.

Why would she be? She was human. She was the weakest one out of all of them.

That was his mistake.

Emerie uncoiled her whip from her weapons belt, along with the enchanted rope that already had a securing loop ready. She held it by the knot while threading her hand through the hole, and waited while keeping her senses open for the last two monsters in case they approached.

Lindiwe pushed him closer and closer to Emerie. Then she flung herself at him and clamped her arms and legs around his torso, trapping his arms to his sides. Black sand wrapped around his body like tentacles, trapping him further.

Emerie leapt forward and grabbed a chunk of his long hair before he could dematerialise. She squeaked when everything went black, like she'd closed her eyes despite them being open. Then she was shoved back into light, and the dimness of the room was suddenly too bright.

Overcome with dizziness, Emerie was disorientated and couldn't work out where she'd ended up. She felt like she'd drank an entire bottle of booze and had woken up with a killer hangover, and her head lolled when it felt like the room was spinning.

Humans were *not* meant to teleport. She grimaced.

None of this was enough to stop her from shoving her hand fisting Jabez's hair downwards as she pushed the rope up.

"The fuck?" he spat, as he spun in a circle and Emerie followed.

He lost interest the moment Lindiwe dropped from the air above him.

She had just enough time to secure the rope by tying his hair into a knot before he teleported away. The rope was short, with only two metres of leeway, but she secured the loop on the other end around her wrist.

Their original plan had been to anchor him to something, but Emerie had other ideas once she saw Lindiwe's barrier. A link was created between them, one that would stop him from materialising behind her. Wherever he went, Emerie would go too.

When Emerie teleported back into the room, her spinning sight searched for the woman with a bow and arrow.

Now Delora just needs to...

She winced when she saw her body lying on the ground, while the winged Demon, the only one remaining, held her decapitated head by her shoulder-length hair. When it started withering away into ash, it tossed it like it'd lost interest before stalking towards them.

Despite how much it would have hurt, Delora was gone, and that was what she needed.

"Emerie," Lindiwe called, and she spun to her.

Jabez had her by the throat until she became intangible and floated back. He gave a menacing snarl.

"I grow tired of this. Two are dead, Witch Owl. All that is left is you and this human."

Lindiwe and Emerie shared a look, and a thousand silent words were spoken. *Thank you. I'm sorry.* These were the two sentences that were the loudest from Lindiwe.

Emerie gave her a weak smile.

Lindiwe floated up and up, and Jabez watched her with shoulders heaving from heavy breaths until she disappeared through the ceiling. The barrier flickered, allowing her out before reforming to keep everyone inside. However, it'd grown much smaller during the fight.

Hopefully it was enough to keep them all contained within its slowly shrinking trap.

Jabez turned to Emerie, and he burst into a fit of laughter.

"She fucking abandoned you." He pointed a claw at her while covering his stomach. "I bet that betrayal cuts deep, human. I always knew she was a self-centred vermin at the core of her righteousness."

To be honest, at first, Emerie had thought the Witch Owl's request was self-serving. But the longer she dwelled on it over the course of the past few days, the more it settled in that Lindiwe was... desperate. She knew what she was doing was wrong, but she was a mother who just wanted to protect her children – even if it meant hurting one in order to save them all.

Not just them, but her grandchildren as well. Those who were small, sightless, and vulnerable.

I hope... she finally gets a chance to be with them properly. Without any more fear for them, without any more painful sacrifices.

Digging into her pocket, Emerie pulled the sun stone out and kept it hidden in her fist. With her right hand, she slipped her obsidian dagger from its halter and charged. She'd dropped her whip when she'd threaded the rope through his hair, realising it had been useless to bring it.

Jabez chuckled low and deep as he stepped back with each of her slashes to dodge. He didn't attack, and she instantly saw the game he was playing.

"You smell like the raven-skulled Mavka," he commented as he dodged her strikes. "How is he after my minions killed his brother?"

"Be better when you're dead," she answered, trying to keep him close.

She eyed the barrier, deciding to let it get smaller before she made her final move. She didn't know how big the blast would be.

I need to give Lindiwe time to escape.

The area felt cold now that it was just the three of them. The winged Demon had halted to watch, letting its master have his fun with the puny human plaything before them. The quietness was unnerving, and her hot, airy breaths echoing through it were... harrowing.

He teleported when she came too close to slicing his face, and she went with him.

Jabez jerked in surprise when she appeared right in front of him; he'd likely been expecting her to be on the other side of the podium still. Her momentum wasn't lost. She swung her arm outward across her body and slashed his face apart from cheek to nose.

He hissed and stumbled back. When she got too close, he kicked her in the stomach, sending her flying. With a surprised yell, he went with her when the rope connecting them yanked his hair.

She almost lost the stone while airborne, but managed to tighten her grip on it as she hit the ground.

Come on. Take the bait, Emerie thought as she staggered to her feet.

Her prayers were answered. Jabez grabbed their link and yanked her off the ground again when he pulled her closer with his inhuman strength. Her throat landed directly in his clawed hand, and he tightened it on her.

He snarled down at her with red eyes full of hate and spite.

"So, they know, do they?" He reached back and swiped his long strands in front of him to inspect the rope knotted in his hair. He bounced it in his hand. "Elves... such a stupid weakness."

Now that she was close, and the barrier was small and hopefully still enough, she raised her fist. The winged Demon was forced to shuffle forward when it was pushed by Lindiwe's dome.

She should be far enough away, right?

Jabez's gaze lifted to her closed fist in curiosity, his twisted expression falling.

Her heart clenched in fear, in sadness, in hopelessness. The anguish of it was unbearable as she trembled in the Demon King's grip.

"Bye, Ingram," Emerie whispered, as tears welled even though a smile curled her shaking lips.

She threw the stone against the ground between them, and the shatter of it was lost to the blinding white light that exploded and pierced... everything.

The last thing she felt was Jabez shove her between him and that light. The last thing she heard was a boom and a high-pitched ringing that felt like it vibrated and disintegrated her bones. Heat blasted her from within as well as all around.

The millisecond of her remaining consciousness beyond the impact didn't even have a chance to think anything other than, for the first time in her life, she was terrified of the light.

THIRTY-EIGHT

With an annoyed huff, Ingram turned to Orpheus and Magnar instead of going down the decline leading to the Veil's forest.

He couldn't fault them on their desire to hunt. He, too, wanted to care for Emerie in this way.

But now that he knew he could love both Emerie and Aleron indiscriminately and in different ways, he wanted to link them. He'd spent the last two days burying his cock in her any way he could, secretly hoping their essences would just... combine.

That, somehow, the universe would tether them together without his knowledge. On a physical level, they had been one, so why could it not seep beneath their skin?

Obviously, that'd been unsuccessful.

But he'd been craving it, while unwittingly suppressing his affection for the pretty female in worry he'd be betraying Aleron somehow.

When I return... I will ask. As soon as he did, in fact.

He was impatient, as always.

He could almost picture it.

Orpheus and Magnar would be with him, likely everyone else also, but Ingram wouldn't care about their presence. He'd just pick up the little female, embrace her in his arms, and ask her to be his bride.

Whether or not he was just being foolishly disillusioned, all he imagined was her smiling face kissing the side of his bony face as she said yes.

Just the mere thought had his sight glowing bright pink again. Even his tail tip curled in delight.

His feet itched with urgency, and he nodded to them both.

Okay, let them hunt and return as quickly as possible.

Magnar and Orpheus stepped to the side, creating a small gap, and faced the direction they'd been originally heading. Both froze, just as a little Ghost had her back turned and looked as though she was tiptoeing in an attempt to sneak away.

Orpheus cocked his head. "Reia...?"

The Ghost halted and straightened as though someone had shoved a board up her dress. It was hard to tell who it truly was, being see-through and cloudy white from head to feet.

She turned solid, and blonde hair fluttered as she spun around with her arms out in greeting.

"Orpheus," she exclaimed, with an awkward cringe. "Fancy meeting you here."

"Reia!" he yelled, closing the small space between them so swiftly she let out an oomph of surprise when he impacted against her. He crouched as he wrapped his arm around her midsection and pushed her hair back like he was checking for some kind of non-existent wound. "What are you doing here, Reia? Why did you die?"

"A-about that," she stuttered as she looked in every direction except them. Her green eyes were filled with a deeply troubling emotion.

The growl that rumbled from Orpheus was low and thunderous as his orbs turned red. "What did you do?" It was as if he knew she'd gotten herself killed. "You were supposed to stay within Faunus' ward. Why did you leave it?"

"What if I didn't leave it?" she grumbled defensively with a pout. "You're jumping straight to conclusions. We totally could have been attacked."

"You were attacked?!" All three Mavka roared.

Magnar and Ingram darted their heads towards the Veil, white bursting into their orbs. *Emerie!* His heart had only ever constricted this tightly once in his life – when he'd seen part of Aleron's skull in a Demon's clawed hand.

"Eep!" Reia put her hands out with a cringe marring her

features. "No, no, no! I left the ward. Shit, fuck. What a way to put my foot in my mouth."

Before anything more could be said, another Ghost wavered and warped as she materialised by Magnar's side. She lay asleep, curled up on her side with her knees tucked up.

Ingram was the first to notice her, but the moment she stirred even a little, Magnar darted his head in her direction.

"Delora!" He knelt down around her and desperately tried to pick up her intangible form.

Delora suddenly sat up when his yelling shoved her into alertness. "Magnar," she cried as she turned physical and flung herself at him.

She sobbed into Magnar's neck after she hooked her arms around it, and Ingram was forced to cover his nose holes when the scent of fear rolled off her in violent waves.

Iciness trickled through his veins and into his chest as his sight shifted between the two Mavka and their females, then to the Veil. His hands clenched and unclenched.

Two brides had been returned to their partners...

Before he could think or ask anything, a bright-yellow ball of exploding light erupted in the distance. The *boom* that followed was distant but distinct enough to draw all their gazes to it.

It came from the far horizon, and the trees of the Veil danced in a singular, powerful wave that rippled outwards in all directions. Ingram was forced to throw his arm up when that wave hit them, and an intense gust of wind and dust blasted over them. He'd almost been shoved off his feet and stumbled to right himself.

But it was the sound of it that made him whimper.

His bones vibrated, his entire body shook, and for a moment, he thought he saw a spectral, ghostly arm trying to leave his own – as if his physical self and spiritual self were trying to separate. Weirdly enough, it was purple and matched the colour of his normal sight.

It was only for a second, just long enough for that wind to cut through him, but it was as bizarre as it was... worrying.

Then it was quiet and peaceful once more – except for the

screech of birds rushing away.

The sun was warm, the air fresh despite their proximity to the Veil. Even the mists, one black and one white, had dissipated momentarily, making the Veil less oppressing.

All Ingram could think was... something was wrong.

This had never happened before. Other than the sun, nothing had ever been a bright-yellow light – especially not in a dark place like the Veil.

He stepped back as he returned his sight to the females who had... died to come here. Worse still, they were looking in the direction the blast had come from.

Delora had her mouth covered to stifle her sob, and her eyes crinkled tightly, as though she was in utter agony. Reia, on the other hand, was biting her lips so hard they'd disappeared within her mouth, as tears easily bubbled and then fell.

"Where is Emerie?" Ingram asked, taking another step back so he could head towards the declining path they'd take to get to the surface world.

Both females turned their gazes to him.

Their sorrowful expressions *deepened.* And, in doing so, his orbs whitened impossibly further.

"I'm so sorry, Ingram," Reia sobbed through trembling lips.

His scales and spikes lifted as dread puffed him. *No.*

He refused to accept her apology, refused to require one.

Before anyone could stop him, he turned and shifted into his monstrous form. On all fours, he sprinted down the decline.

"Ingram!" Magnar roared.

He knew why he was being called. He knew why they held fear for his sake.

He didn't care.

He didn't care if it was too dangerous for him to venture into the Veil by himself. He had to return to Faunus' ward, to Emerie.

He needed to make sure his little butterfly was safely where he left her.

Have to go back. Have to go to her.

His chest was tight with anxiety, and every quadruple stomp of his limbs only made it twinge and sting further. It forked agonising pain all throughout his torso.

The speed with which he ran was harder and faster than he'd ever achieved. Any Demon that did attempt to intersect him was lost the moment he spotted their scents within the dense forest. He easily evaded them.

By the halfway point, his beak had parted so he could frantically huff around agonising breaths. His muscles burned from the exertion as he sprinted, yet the returning foreboding white mist cooled his skull.

Having to dodge tree after tree only slowed him down. He wished he could borrow his kindred's wings for just a moment so he could fly over the Veil.

He worried any second that delayed him would mean he was too late. He couldn't be too late. He refused.

She will be there. She had to be there.

Ingram could not lose another person he cared for.

His heart could not be filled with two people who had left him.

He first passed a green glow that came from a distance within the Veil. Then a yellow glow glittered between the trees before him, and his legs and arms found a way to double their speed. Less than an hour had passed, the distance long, and each second of it had been... terrifying.

The unknown of this terrified him.

As soon as he broke into the narrow clearing that separated Faunus and Mayumi's home from the tent they'd placed down for him and Emerie, he skidded to a halt. His claws tore up the earth, leaving behind gouging marks.

Faunus and his female were waiting for him, as if they'd known all along he would come. The fact there was no orange hair brightly glowing in the sunshine alongside them sent another chill of dread down his spine.

His spikes lifted threateningly. *"Where is she?"* he snarled, but it was so mangled with a whine that it came out twisted and even hurt to produce.

Mayumi clung to their younglings tighter. Faunus stepped in front of her with his arm out protectively, his orbs white with worry in Ingram's direction.

"She's gone," Mayumi stated softly, like she didn't want to

utter those two words.

A wheeze echoed out of him, and he stepped to the side. *"Where did she go?"*

Her features, which had been saddened, instead twisted into a guilty cringe. "Emerie, Reia, Delora, and the Witch Owl left to face the Demon King."

Ingram lifted his skull towards the middle of the Veil. He didn't think it was possible, but his heart hollowed out even more.

"Then I will go to his castle."

Why did she go there without me? He'd meant to go with them. He was meant to be the one to fight the Demon King, to get revenge for Aleron and make the world safer.

It was *his* fight, not hers.

He'd been hoping to figure out how to make her stay behind so she would be safe from harm. Convincing her had been a battle his lack of humanity hadn't been successful in winning. She was too... smart for him, easily redirecting his thoughts.

Usually, it was to soothe him when he was feeling despondent or angered.

It didn't help that he didn't always understand.

"It's too late," Faunus stated, voice low. "We all saw and felt the explosion."

Ingram wasn't listening, at least not properly. He was too busy skulking away from them to go in the direction of Jabez's castle, backing up to put space between them.

"Stop, Ingram," Mayumi exclaimed. "She won't be there."

"Then I will go find her!"

"She's not *gone* from here – she's *dead*," Faunus beseeched, his voice cracking in sorrow on the end.

"No," Ingram choked out, his sight shifting to blue. He reared back on his hind legs so he could cover his skull with his hands, his claws and fingertips pressing down hard. His body quaked at the loss and grief that bled into his veins like venom. *"You were supposed to protect her. She was supposed to be safe here."* The gaps between his fingers turned red as his sight changed into one filled with fury. ***"I left because you all promised she would be here when I returned!"***

So *this* is what happened when a promise was broken. This was how damaging and betraying it could feel.

Faunus' orbs shifted to bright orange in guilt.

"She sacrificed herself to protect us all," Faunus stated, as he curled his arm backwards and around Mayumi to pull her flush against him. "She was the only one who could do it."

"I would have done it!" Ingram roared. *"I did not mind if I died so long as the Demon King did as well. I would have just gone to the afterworld to be with Aleron!"* Once more, he wheezed as blue flickered in his reddened sight momentarily. *"Emerie... she... I did not want her to* die *for* me.*"*

At first, he had not cared. He would have killed her himself if it were the answer to his problems.

But now? After everything they'd shared?

He couldn't think of anything worse.

"You wouldn't have been able to stay conscious!" Faunus yelled. "You would have fallen into your bloodlust and hunger. You were too unpredictable, too unreliable. You wouldn't have even remembered the task bestowed upon you."

It was true. What the feline-skulled Mavka said couldn't be argued with, but...

Not her. It should not have been her.

Ingram looked down at his claws, but the shaking of his hands made him feel dizzy. He retched when it felt like his heart was trying to crawl up from his throat so he could vomit it. He dug at his chest, right over it, unsure if it was to keep it from violently exploding from him, or to rip it out himself.

I cannot do this, he internally whined. *I cannot lose another I care for.*

Aleron's loss had been devastating to his psyche. The only reason he'd survived it was because he believed there was a way to bring him back. Mavka were a part of life and death, this he'd always known; he'd been told it dozens of moons ago.

His revenge had given him meaning and direction since Aleron was no longer there to lead him, as Ingram led him in return.

Then Emerie had come along and begun to... distract his thoughts. The pain from his kindred's loss had been waning, and each time she melted some of the frozen ball inside him, she slowly replaced it with herself.

He didn't think she would have fully removed it from him, that icy chill, but she'd started *shielding* him from it. Through her warmth, her touch, or just simply her embrace, she'd given him something else to dwell on: her.

Even if he hadn't truly understood that he loved her, it had still been there, just waiting for him to accept what he thought he couldn't have. He'd been obsessed with that little female, every fibre of his being frantic to be up against her until she'd totally and irrevocably stained him.

Ingram wasn't too late in figuring out his feelings. He wasn't devastated and only valuing what was already lost.

No. It had already been there. Whether it was before or after today's realisation that he wanted her as his bride more than anything in *this* world, learning of her death would have devastated him either way.

As it did now.

I cannot do this. The anger and betrayal towards Mayumi and Faunus – who obviously knew what was happening, and had let it happen – deflated out of him. Dark blue flooded his orbs, before the bottoms of them cracked and produced cold, ethereal tears in his wobbling sight.

As much as he wanted to attack them, the chilling shiver that assaulted his spine ate away at the flames of his rage. His pain was too heavy this time, engulfing him in hopelessness.

"Aleron... Emerie," he whimpered, reaching up once more to his skull to hold it. *"Why did you leave me here by myself?"*

Was he cursed? Was he not supposed to keep hold of anyone in this world? If so, why the fuck was he trying to stay in it?

Other than trying to bring Aleron back, and he had no idea how to even begin that journey, there was nowhere else for him to go.

He had no home, no path, no *revenge*. It had been taken from him by the female he'd just lost... and needed just as much as he needed his kindred.

There was no point in being here when they were *there*.

His floating tears tickled his fingers and palms as he started to dig his fingertips and claws into his skull. With heavy, agonised breaths, he pressed harder and harder until there was pressure all around.

He shook and shuddered in repulsion at what he was trying to do, and his neck dipped instead of giving way. His scales and spikes puffed, while tangled growls and whines echoed from him.

I do not want to be here if neither of them are.

"Fuck!" Faunus bit out, before his paw steps could be heard sprinting closer. "He's trying to break his skull!"

Just when Ingram felt his rigid skull starting to bend in multiple places as it creaked, one of his arms was ripped back.

He immediately roared and turned to the Mavka, his orbs bleeding red droplets. He'd been so close! Just a little more, and he would have gone to where they were, to the afterworld.

Ingram saw nothing, and felt nothing. His mind was completely disconnected from his body as he attacked in a blind rage.

Faunus gave a high-pitched, ear-splitting yelp. The scent of blood that was not his own penetrated his nose holes. He tasted blood, and it was foul to him. It should not be on his tongue, yet he didn't stop his attack.

He knew at some point the feline-skulled Mavka got out from underneath him, then a split second later, he was tackled to his front, a writhing mess of limbs capturing him.

Ingram grabbed ahold of something hard – a skull, perhaps – and it gave resistance against his strength. He tried to crush it, ignoring the claws that dug at his throat, the pain of it lost to the wounds of his soul.

Someone grabbed his horn and yanked him back.

His spine slammed against the ground, just as cool tendrils wrapped around him from tail to throat. Ingram bucked and writhed to be free of his bindings, releasing roars as he arched his back.

At the same time, he bashed the back of his skull against the ground, wishing the soft grass and dirt would shatter him. He wiggled, squirmed, and twisted with all his might to be free.

Voices argued around him, but nothing was distinguishable

to him. All he saw was red. All he heard was his own rage. All he felt was tormenting misery.

A hand was foolish enough to try to soothe him by petting his skull, but it did not smell like strawberries and primroses. It made his hackles rise with the *wrongness* of it touching him. He pecked it.

He'd take being back at the Demonslayer stronghold over this. If they pulled his heart from him enough times, would it stop *aching* the way it did? Would the physical wounds be easier to bear than the ones he could not touch or soothe?

Mindless, wild insanity sunk its fangs into him, and he yearned to be completely consumed.

For once... he didn't want to bite back.

THIRTY-NINE

Ingram had no memory of the events that led to his head being removed. It was likely done in order to reset his mental state and bring him back from his deranged and violent outburst.

His body had grown back like thick, muddy black sand, his limbs soft and heavy like they were still just globs. Even before he had fully formed, the same cold tendrils as before wrapped around his body and pinned him against the ground by his front.

He was still in his monstrous form.

Before he even opened his sight, the trickling droplets of ethereal tears floated around the bone of his skull. The deep blue glow of his vision was dazed, more because he just didn't want to think...

My heart hurts.

He wished the removal of his head made him forget why he was in pain.

He wanted it to go away, to leave him alone.

Then the remnants of strawberries and primroses fluttered in his senses, and he searched for the source. The tip of his beak caught on loose material, and he dragged it closer across the ground.

He didn't know if the blue dress, empty of Emerie, amplified or alleviated the throbbing behind his sternum. But it was her scent, and he wanted to lay his head on it so that no one could take it from him.

He wanted it to somehow envelop him once more.

Closing his murky sight, like his orbs were empty of the vortex of liquid fire they consisted of, he wrestled with his bindings once more. Why did everyone want to trap him?

The only times he'd ever enjoyed it was when Emerie did so. She always brought him pleasure when she did, and he'd begun to see the bindings as... sensual. He wanted to think of them positively.

"I need to talk to you, so stop fighting and rest," a deep, feminine voice uttered quietly. "I brought you her dress because I knew it would help."

He peeked open his sight once more, and the Witch Owl's white cloak was bright enough to shine through his dim vision.

The snarl that tore out of him was weak at first, but it strengthened with every second she knelt before him.

"You." His orbs flared crimson, and once more it looked like human blood floated around his skull. *"You took her there, didn't you? This is all your fault."* Her hands reached out to him, and the bark that came from him was aggressive and beastly. ***"Don't touch me! Do not touch me ever again."***

"Ingram," she whispered, retracting her hands from the air.

"You keep taking everything away from me," he whined, and once more, his orbs drowned in the colour of sadness.

"I just need you to stay calm so we can talk."

Ingram tossed his head to the side to show her he didn't want to talk to her. Emerie's dress twisted beneath his beak, cushioning him against the hardness of the ground.

Looking to the side, he spotted a small and pale woman with blonde hair making her way to them, followed by the wolf-skulled, impala-horned Mavka.

"We saw his body grow back, so we thought we could come over," Reia said as she placed her hand on Lindiwe's shoulder, forcing the woman to be her leaning pole while she sat. "How's he doing?"

"Did you know?" Ingram asked as he turned his head to Orpheus.

"No," Orpheus stated, his tone unnerving as he crouched behind Reia. "And I still am not pleased."

Reia tenderly covered the back of Orpheus' hand with her

own when he grasped her side, and gave his wolf skull a small, apologetic cringe.

"You understand how I feel, yes? You have lost many humans." When Orpheus confirmed, he asked, *"Break my skull. Let me leave here. I cannot take it."*

"Ingram," both Reia and Lindiwe cried out.

Orpheus leaned around Reia as though he'd planned to do as he pleaded, and Ingram lifted his beak up to reach out.

Reia grabbed his wrist and yanked him back. "No, Orpheus!"

"Why not? It is what he wants." He brushed his claws into Reia's long blonde hair. "It... is what I would have wanted if you disappeared. If I hadn't tried to mindlessly search for you that night, this is what I would have done."

With her eyes wide, baulking at the thought, Reia rasped, "Just... no."

"You will cease this talk of ending," the Witch Owl demanded, her eyes narrowing on Ingram. "Don't make what Emerie did pointless. She did this for you, to make sure you were safe."

"She should not have done this at all!" he shouted, causing the two females to flinch.

Ingram attempted to push his arms out from his body, wrestling the dark chalky tentacles of magic that had wrapped around him. He was tired of lying here trapped and helpless. He was tired of this conversation.

He was just... tired of everything.

"Wait," Lindiwe demanded when his orbs flared red as he fought.

"Release me! Let me go!" He bucked and flailed.

"I'm trying to tell–" He snapped his beak at her to shut her up. "Do you want to revive Emerie or not?!"

He paused, and his heartbeat thundered within his massive chest cavity. *Is... is she saying there is a way for me to bring her back?*

"Revive her?" Reia asked with her lips flattening in a confused pout. Her eyes then widened, and she rose to her feet so she could stand over the Witch Owl. "If there was a chance to revive her this entire time, why didn't you say anything?!"

Reia's shout was loud, and her pale face reddened in irritation. "Emerie went to Jabez's castle knowing she was going to die, and you said nothing even though we could all see how much she didn't want to! Why didn't you–"

"Because I was not going to give a promise I couldn't keep," Lindiwe snapped back while facing up at her. "I had no idea if her soul would survive the blast, and even if it did, Ingram had to make this decision just as much as her." She lowered her gaze to Ingram. "But I did not need to ask him; I can see how much her absence is paining him. However, there are questions I must ask first, things I must explain, and he needs to be *calm* for them."

Hope swirled in his chest like a gust of wind.

He nudged his head at her across the ground. *"Calm. I can be calm."* He would be if it meant he could go find Emerie.

"Now... do you mind?" Lindiwe asked, gesturing her hand towards Ingram. "I would prefer some privacy."

The laughter that burst out of Reia was hollow and mocking. "Fuck yeah, I mind. To be honest, I don't particularly trust you. I'd like to be here for him, and I know Orpheus does too."

Orpheus nodded in agreement, making his bells to jingle.

"He is my *son*," Lindiwe bit out defensively.

"He is my brother," Orpheus snapped back. "And she is my bride. We will stay. He is 'a few sandwiches shy of a picnic,' as Reia likes to tease Magnar. I can understand his thoughts better than anyone and help explain if need be."

Lindiwe turned to Ingram and placed her hands on her knees. She was assessing him, and although he didn't have a face to reveal how much he preferred their presence than to be alone with her, she seemed to be able to read him.

"Fine," she eventually sighed out. "First, I must explain that it is dangerous. I have spoken to Weldir, and he has told me that you will have only a day to convince her to become your bride, or... he will consume you."

"Okay," Ingram stated, not caring at all.

He would do anything and risk anything to cease the cold throbbing ache in his chest, and to stop the ethereal blue tears that continued to drip from his broken orbs.

"Why would he consume him?" Reia asked.

Lindiwe's cheek twitched with annoyance. "Because Tenebris is within his stomach. It is a part of him as much as it is detached. He is a soul eater, and he will begin digesting you the moment you enter. It is no different to a human eating food, although a human would not survive the threshold and would be consumed instantly. A Mavka, however, has a day of freedom."

"You've done this before," Orpheus commented.

"Merikh," Lindiwe grumbled. "He has ventured there in curiosity, only to leave when the process began."

"Is that all? If so, I would like to go now." And because it always made Emerie more susceptible to his plight, he added, *"Please."*

"I must make sure you understand what you are asking of her," Lindiwe said, as her shoulders fell. "Emerie is... different from the others. I know what the Demonslayers do to their women. I know what they take."

"I do not understand."

Lindiwe gestured her arm towards the house across the narrow clearing. "You will not be able to have what Faunus and Mayumi do. Emerie is infertile, so she cannot give you younglings."

He tilted his head. *"Why not? If she is wounded, I can heal her. We can find a way and–"*

"No, Ingram." Lindiwe's tone was firm. "There is no healing this; it was too long ago. If this is something you seek, then find a different human."

"Hey!" Reia exclaimed. "That's not fair. You're making it out as if there's something wrong with her."

"No, I am making sure he understands. I tried to explain this to Merikh, but he didn't want to listen to me and went off to make his own uninformed choices."

When Reia opened her mouth to argue, Lindiwe threw her hand up. Her features twisted up into severe rage.

"I will not have my sons *torment* women for desires that *cannot* be achieved!" she roared. "They cannot always wish things and have them magically change! I have already asked Weldir if we can heal her soul of this, and he cannot. Emerie is wonderful, and she is perfect exactly how she is, but Ingram must make this decision knowing that she cannot do this for him, so that he doesn't hurt her in the future. So he doesn't accidentally make her feel as though she isn't enough." She brought her gaze back to Ingram's orbs and bore it into him. "Emerie is who she is, and she will be exactly as you last saw her – with the addition of a few new claw marks. So, knowing all this, do you still wish to make her your bride?"

"I can have Emerie back?" he asked.

"Yes," she bit out.

"And... she will not leave me again?"

Her features softened, and the corners of her lips curled knowingly, as if she could already tell what he desired. "Only for a day, but that is as long as you will be forced to miss her. She will come back to you, no matter how far you are from each other."

Ingram's tail tip curled in hopeful delight. "Then yes, this is all I care about."

He just wanted her, his pretty little butterfly.

She was all he needed to be at ease in this world.

FORTY

Ingram didn't care to look back at Faunus, Orpheus, or their brides, and for some reason, Magnar and Delora were nowhere in sight. His vision was focused on the tear of white light before him that had formed after Weldir, the spirit of the void, had torn apart a soul.

Apparently, the Witch Owl could be called to his dominion by nothing but his thoughts, as they were connected, but Ingram needed a portal.

Although he was part of life and death, he couldn't pass through spaces and existences freely. Assistance was required, and Weldir was willing to sacrifice his own strength to do so for Ingram's sake.

Without hesitation about the unknown that lay before him, he entered it.

What lay on the other side was... nothingness.

Yet, the blackness wasn't frightening, or sinister, or even cold. It just was, as if nothing existed here, not even light.

In its own way, it was... comforting. It felt safe.

Darkness stretched across the vast horizons that were unseen. There were no edges, no lines telling him which way was up or down. Even though there was no ground, he was still able to step forward on all fours, as though he was walking across something solid, but invisible.

Strangely, the Witch Owl appeared to be walking on a higher, non-existent level. It made her short height tower next to him.

Her hair delicately floated around her head, and her loose corkscrew curls waved back and forth with each of her movements. The barn owl feathers attached to her cloak also raised as the seams of it opened.

Two creatures lifted away from her. It was hard to see them with the darkness, and it was only possible due to the fact that their skin was not true black, but a dark grey. Only one had a small skull, but he didn't have enough time to see what kind.

The two baby Mavka kicked and swiped at the air as they were both sucked in a certain direction.

A figure materialized, one Ingram had never seen before.

Much of his chalky and black glittering form was missing. Half of his face was visible, starting from one twisty horn sitting just above his temple to the opposing jaw. The shoulder on that side was gone, as was most of his chest, stomach, and the opposing leg other than the foot. He was also missing a knee, along with his right arm except for his hand.

Hands reached out and took hold of the baby Mavka so he could cradle them across his forearms, and they instantly turned into transparent white versions of themselves upon touch. The only part of him that never disappeared was the arm holding the two younglings, who lay upon it as though peacefully asleep.

He was tall, perhaps even more so than any Mavka Ingram had ever met, and he was lean, with only the smallest amount of muscle.

Parts of his body slowly withered from him like ash, while others formed like mist and cloud. The outline shape of his essence constantly changed, but he always appeared... half created, or less so – never more.

Once he had contained the younglings on one arm, he reached his hand out to Lindiwe.

His voice was echoey, soft, and so distant it was like he was speaking from another realm entirely. "Hello, my little owlet."

She hesitated, but then drifted towards him.

Her hand reached out to his, but she only went through it, as though she couldn't touch him. That was, until she turned incorporeal like a Ghost, and contact was made possible.

The spirit of the void dragged her closer, and she floated

gracefully. He didn't bring her into his side, nor hold her affectionately as she turned to face Ingram.

"You have come a long way," Weldir stated, attempting to turn his chalky face to him. It disappeared entirely within the motion, and only the upper half of his face coalesce to reveal two horns, similar to Aleron's thick, backward twisting spirals.

"Where is Emerie?" Ingram asked, searching for her in the vast amount of darkness.

"She is neither here nor there," he cryptically answered. "She is with us, but is not."

The soft growl that bubbled from Ingram was muffled by the thick air around him... or lack thereof? He wasn't very adept at understanding what most people said, so it wasn't wise to speak with him in riddles.

Weldir let out a small chuckle.

"She is within me, little one," Weldir stated. "Currently, where you stand is in my consciousness. This is the only safe entry point in which we may speak."

Little one? Ingram had never been called small.

"Then how do I enter you?" Ingram asked, eyeing him for a way inside his body.

That didn't seem possible. Weldir may be large, but not enough to fit Ingram within him, or even Emerie.

"She is in my stomach, or rather, the path to Tenebris is through it." He waved his hand to the side, as if gesturing to something. "It is part of me, while also being separate. I am a soul eater. That was my purpose when born, since I formed with a realm within me."

Ingram sat back on his hind legs and gripped his skull in confusion. None of this made sense, and the blank spaces within his mind gave no insight.

"Emerie is in Tenebris," Lindiwe further explained, her voice echoey but not as much as Weldir's.

"Then bring her here," Ingram whined, releasing his skull so he could hold his hands out beseechingly.

"He cannot do that," Lindiwe stated. "When he takes a soul from there, it is at random."

"Why?"

"Can you reach into your own stomach and know for certain what you have taken?" Weldir asked. "Would you know what corner of your stomach you have placed something? Once a soul is eaten, it is lost to the thousands of others that have been placed there."

"Tenebris is huge, Ingram. It is vast," explained the Witch Owl.

"Then why eat her at all?" Ingram asked. *"Why did you not bring her to me when she... died?"*

"When my magic on Earth shrouds a soul, it cleanses and brings it here. I have no idea whom they belonged to while I eat them, and I have eaten many others in the time since then. She was lost amongst them."

"Then how did you know that her soul survived at all to be eaten?"

"Because I was there," Lindiwe said, her ghostly features crinkling. "When Emerie shattered the sun stone, I was close enough to watch Jabez's castle crumble around itself, and her soul floated through it, unharmed. However, the force had pushed me so far back that by the time I was about to collect it so I could keep it safe, Weldir's shroud took it. It is unconscious and indiscriminate."

"And it touches this entire world, not just the lands you roam. Emerie's soul was not the only one that was taken at that time, so I cannot even track which soul was hers or where I placed her in Tenebris once I consumed her."

"Entire world? But I have been to every edge and your magic is only present in the Veil."

Weldir's entire face disappeared as he chuckled, instead coalescing to his chest to show it twitching.

"There are many lands on Earth across the oceans, and many forests where I dwell."

Ingram was surprised to learn Earth was bigger than what he could touch or see.

"I am just thankful her soul survived the impact. The sun stone affected Phantoms, but after watching what happened, we believe the reason for that is because we are completely attached to our physical selves through our anchors. The sound it produced touched everything, and it passed through the bonds we share as a vibration that wanted to destroy everything it travelled across. Emerie, on the other hand, had been so close to the centre point that either the initial blast moved through her so suddenly her soul didn't have time to crumble, or, once her physical self was destroyed, her essence was spared of any damage. If we take your soul from you, you will die. If a Phantom's soul is taken from their anchor, we fear it will tear both of them apart."

All Ingram cared about from this knowledge was that Emerie had survived. The rest was irrelevant to him.

And he was growing impatient to have her within his grasp again.

He also didn't want to hear about her end. He didn't want to know if she had been alone, frightened, or in pain. He just wanted to think that she'd blinked out of existence, and that he must go save her.

Her soul was his to revive, and he would make sure nothing happened to it, or her, ever again.

"That's why it had to be her, or rather, a human," Lindiwe continued. "I would have done it if it weren't for your young siblings."

"No, you would not have," Weldir unnervingly snarled, just as the bottom half of his face formed, and snapped shark-like, razor fangs in her direction.

The sound that the spirit of the void produced was so utterly inhuman that it wasn't even bestial or animalistic. It rumbled like thunder underneath water, as though it hadn't come from something living but from existence itself.

Even though Ingram stood upon nothingness, the world around him shook like an earthquake had trembled.

Lindiwe's back stiffened, and she averted her gaze to the side.

A touchy subject had been brought up between the two, and it left tension radiating within the darkness. It was almost like Weldir's irritation was tangible enough to change the air here and charge it with lightning; perhaps all of his emotions were.

They were in his consciousness, after all.

He handed the two younglings to Lindiwe. She tucked them back underneath her cloak to hide them with her gaze still averted.

Then he grew his form until he had taken on the size of a giant, with Ingram being no bigger than one of his chalky fingers. The air became stuffy with the annoyed menace that rolled off him now that he was bigger.

Ingram's head tilted upwards to his towering form, since he and Lindiwe were floating near the centre of his sternum. He didn't back away, even when his massive hand crept towards him.

"Let us go find your human," Weldir said.

The pressure that gripped him was gentle enough to not squeeze or crush, but he was uncomfortable being picked up as though he was a tiny animal. Inadvertently, his legs and arms kicked to be free.

He froze up when Weldir parted his fangs as his maw opened. Horrified, he looked past sharp teeth to the back of his throat and saw nothingness.

Then he was tossed inside.

It was cold and tight when he was swallowed, but he experienced nothing else. He attempted to claw into the walls of his throat, or whatever passageway he was sinking inside of, but he was unable to get purchase.

Then, before he knew it, he was spat out from somewhere and began to fall as a white world filled with mist opened up. He spun and flipped through the air, and a roar he was unable to hold back escaped him.

The longer he dropped, the more he could see land coming towards him.

There was no cold cut of wind, and the ground was strange, appearing almost reflective, like the top of a lake's surface. In the distance, there were ghostly trees that were see-through and didn't seem tangible. That was all he could make out as he fretted, unsure if landing would be painful.

At the last second, Ingram turned right side up and gently landed on all fours.

The first thing he did was spin in a circle to assess his

surroundings. Thick mist shielded his sight completely, making everything beyond a few metres indistinguishable, even with his hyper-sensitive vision.

He could just make out transparent tree trunks and branches, and the mist moved all throughout them.

He didn't know if he'd turned back around or not, losing his orientation within seconds, but darkness snagged in his peripheral. He faced Weldir, who had materialised in his proximity.

"You can enter your own stomach?" Ingram asked.

"Like I said, Tenebris is part of me, while also being separate. I can access any part of my body as a physical manifestation of my consciousness."

Physical manifestation? Ingram reached out to see if he could touch him, but his hand merely passed through his form.

"You cannot touch me, as you are not dead. You will also be unable to interact with or touch anything within Tenebris." Weldir then shoved his intangible hand into Ingram's torso and pulled a multi-coloured piece of string from him. "We must not waste any time. You will begin to notice me consuming your physical form, and once I do, you will be unable to leave here. You will have died and passed over."

The multicoloured strings separated like someone unravelling twisted twine. A small number of the threads shot towards the sky and their ends disappeared through the mist, whereas many more branched outward around him throughout Tenebris.

Most within Tenebris were white, except for four different strings.

One was twisted with a purple and pink glow, another with purple and orange, and one that was purple and black. The final one was purple and rainbow, and it linked between Ingram and Weldir's chests.

"What are they?" Ingram asked, tilting his head at them.

"I guess you can call them strings of fate," Weldir explained as he followed the one that was purple and black. "The white ones are all the humans you have consumed and brought to me. Three of them are your familial bonds. The one we are following is the bride you have chosen and have connected with physically."

Ingram inspected the black-and-purple string leading their path. *"It will take me to Emerie?"*

"Yes. It is why I had to come with you. It is the only way we will be able to find her, as I am not connected to her on any level."

His blue vision lightened from its depressive colour. His Emerie was at the end of this line.

Within the span of a heartbeat, Ingram was sprinting.

Along the way, he noticed multiple things. Firstly, there were no scents here. He could not smell the trees, the ground, the mist, or even Weldir.

Secondly, between the spaces of nothing, there were hundreds, if not thousands, of Ghosts that interacted with each other. They didn't seem to notice Ingram passing literally through them, as he refused to deviate his path for them.

Their sounds were soft and inaudible with the speed in which he ran past.

Although he was curious about them, about Tenebris itself, he only had one objective. Nothing would stray him from it; it was all that mattered.

The third thing he noticed was, the longer he was with Weldir, who kept up with his speed with ease, the more his chalky outlines grew smaller. Less of him was noticeable, as if he was losing the capability to remain seen.

And lastly, he'd noted that the purple and pink string was moving as if the person on the other side was in motion as well. The one with orange in it had long since moved to be behind him.

A strange form, entirely pink, dived at them from above.

Ingram had planned to just avoid it and keep going forward, but Weldir chuckled and halted. He stopped as well, unwilling to part with his guide, and spun around.

He witnessed the moment Weldir opened his arms out in welcome, and an entirely pink creature with large wings tackled him, as though he was touchable to them. Their body didn't appear as cloudy as a Ghost, having more of a spectral glossy sheen to their transparentness.

"Was wondering how long it would take for you to find us," Weldir mused, rising to his feet by floating.

The pink spectre spread their wings out behind them as far as they could reach and lowered themselves. They were about to pounce on him once more, as though Weldir had inadvertently gotten himself caught in some kind of play. The creature had pink tail feathers that spread out in warning as they lowered their chest in preparation.

Ingram's sight flared red in annoyance at the interruption. He wanted to keep moving.

He wanted to find...

His thoughts trailed off, and his irritation fled out of him so fast that it turned the glow of his vision a dark yellow.

He tentatively stepped forward, his head lowering in uncertainty. *"Ale...ron?"*

The spectre twisted their neck to dart their head over their shoulder, and a bat skull, with twisting, backward facing goat horns, locked on him.

"Ingram!" his kindred exclaimed, spinning his body around to face the direction of his head.

"Aleron!" Ingram shouted, his vision bursting into a brighter, cheerful hue.

At the same time, they sprinted for each other on all fours. Aleron jumped, using his wings to give him height, and dived to tackle Ingram. He'd never done that before, had never utilised his wings in such a way.

Ingram did not fucking care. Not one bit.

With his arms wide open, Ingram reared back on his hind legs to catch his kindred as the ache of his loss dissipated... only to come back as a sharp sting when they passed through each other.

Ingram stared down at his claws before he fell to his hands. *I... could not grab him.*

They turned to each other, both reaching out a hand to try to touch their palms together, only for Ingram to feel nothingness.

Not the comforting familiar balm of Aleron's flesh, not the pressure of his strength. He couldn't even smell him. He looked so different to what he remembered. It was his kindred's distinct shape, but completely lacking in anything physical – like his black feathers and fur, or even the whiteness of his skull.

"Neither of you exist on the same plane as each other," Weldir explained, when it was obvious both of them were confused as to why they couldn't touch.

"Then how come you both are able to touch, but I cannot?" Ingram asked, while refusing to remove his gaze from his kindred in case he disappeared. *"Are you not alive?"*

"I am absolutely alive," Weldir mused. "But I lack a physical form. I can only interact with the world as a spirit, and therefore can only interact with those who are truly dead."

Is that why he and Lindiwe were unable to touch until she turned into a Phantom? he wondered.

Regardless, his curiosities unravelled as he and Aleron stared at each other.

"You look strange, Ingram," Aleron stated as he tilted his head. *"Like a purple Ghost."*

He let out a half-hearted chuckle as his orbs turned blue once more. *"You look like a pink one."*

"Does that mean the prominent colour of our orbs is actually the colour of our souls?" Aleron asked Weldir.

"Yes. You will see each other from the other side as your souls." Weldir came closer to stand beside them. "You are unable to see what I have truly made of this world, Ingram. It is very beautiful."

"It looks like Earth," Aleron explained. *"But... brighter. There are no Demons. The humans cannot see me unless I touch them, but there is another Mavka here. He is shy, though. He does not wish to play."*

Ingram could feel his ethereal tears trickling faster and faster as droplets hovered around his skull. He reached his hand out past his kindred's, moving through it, so he could brush his hand through his torso.

"I have missed you, Aleron," he said with a whimper.

His kindred's form did not change colour, but Ingram could see his own ethereal tears glittering around his pink, spectral skull.

"I have missed you, Ingram," he answered quietly, lowering his bat skull until his flat snout was facing downward. *"It is... lonely here. I do not like being without you. It feels wrong."*

"We are one."

"Yes, we are." Aleron rubbed at his sternum as he looked up and away. Then he bounced back and spread his wings. *"I have learnt to fly now though, since I consumed a few souls I should not have."*

Aleron was trying to distract him. It wasn't working.

Nothing could erase how he felt, although being able to see and speak with his kindred did bring him a small amount of tainted joy.

Weldir crossed his arms, and one disappeared despite the other remaining in that position. "Yes, you should not have."

He bashfully scratched a claw at the side of his bony bat snout. *"It gifted me some humanity, but it, uh, gave me the human's memories. Weldir struggled to remove them from me. It was very disorientating."*

"I thought we could not eat more than one soul," Ingram commented.

"It is like eating flesh here," Weldir answered plainly.

"I see."

Just as Ingram lifted his hand to cup the side of his beak in thought, the glow of purple halted him. He stared down at his claws and the tips of his fingers, that had turned spectral like Aleron's entire form, except purple.

Then he darted his head around to check his body, finding the same thing was happening to his toes and the tip of his tail.

Weldir must have noticed where his attention had focused on because he commanded, "We must move on. The process has begun."

He clenched his fists before he leaned forward to walk on all fours. Following Weldir's lead once more, it was slower.

As much as he wanted to sprint headlong towards Emerie, he was unwilling to separate from Aleron. He even tried to curl his tail over the top of his long feathered one, only to pass through him.

A part of him considered... staying here.

Emerie and Aleron were both here. The two people he wanted most in all the worlds were in the same place.

"Why can I not stay here?" Ingram asked Weldir's back.

"If that is what you choose, then so be it," Weldir responded. "However, you will not be able to bond with Emerie, and she will... forget you if you part from her for too long here. I will only be able to save the most recent memories gained here between memory sleeps. Only Mavka remain fully conscious."

Oh, he internally muttered.

Emerie had once asked him to choose.

At the time, he'd said he was unable to choose between her and Aleron. Was he... going to have to?

He peeked at his kindred beside him.

Who do I want more?

He tossed his head to shake it, snorting out a huff. *An impossible choice.*

His heart was evenly split between them.

"If you want my advice," Weldir lowly muttered, "choose the human. You cannot take back your life if you choose to leave it behind, and you will learn that not being with her is painful – especially since she will be in your grasp, but utterly unobtainable. However, and I do really mean this, don't tell her if you plan to stay if she rejects you. That is not fair to her."

It isn't? He didn't understand why.

"You are here for a female?" Aleron asked with his head tilted. *"A bride?"*

"Yes," he rasped.

Aleron jumped in front of him to bounce around. *"This is fantastic! We have a bride!"*

A random and completely surprising growl burst from him. *"I have a bride,"* Ingram snapped at him. *"Find your own."*

Aleron paused and tilted his head. *"We cannot share?"*

"No. She is mine. Obtain your own."

Guilt tingled the nape of his neck, but he couldn't contain the way fury choked him at the thought of Aleron touching Emerie the way he had. Inside, on such a deep and profoundly intimate level. Her smells, her sounds, the very temperature of her skin... all of these were his to experience.

He didn't wish to share that with Aleron.

"You cannot share a bride," Weldir chimed in. "Either one of you would be left out of the bond, or you would split the soul in half and destroy it while trying to share it."

"Then..." Aleron lifted his head to the spirit of the void, in a way that was slow and unsure. *"How do I obtain one?"*

"Here? Impossible," Weldir said, turning the fragments of his face that were visible towards his kindred. "However, I am hoping that not all is lost for you."

"What do you mean?"

"I don't have an answer for you right now, but I do suggest you begin interacting with the humans that are here. Perhaps your bride is already among them." Humour lifted into his tone as he mused, "You may yet steal another soul from me."

Weldir's open-ended and cryptic answer shoved both of them into silence as they pondered it.

Had Ingram been right all along?

Is there... a chance for Aleron's return?

FORTY-ONE

When Ingram first came to the end of the tether, he'd been confused that it was connected to the back of someone who was obviously not Emerie.

The ghostly figure had been masculine by what he could tell of their height, physique, and stance. Even their hair was short and somewhat spiking around their head.

However, it was the high-pitched giggle beyond them that, while distant, was familiar.

The fucking male had been standing in the way!

The tether had been going through his form to reach her.

Hope had warmed his sternum as he stepped to the side, only for it to... wane.

This wasn't Emerie. At least, not the female he knew.

And the most heartbreaking part of it was that she stepped away from the spirit she'd been speaking to, started walking as they followed, and passed through him as though he wasn't there. Even though he felt nothing, a cold shiver still crawled through him when she evaporated into his body, only to turn solid behind him.

She didn't look entirely the same, yet he knew her voice, the shape of her face, her height and figure.

It was just... altered.

He couldn't help following her, creeping beside her while wishing his hand constantly reaching out to her would make contact. That she would turn to him and smile in greeting. That she would... see him.

Her peel of laughter as she held a basket of food, speaking with her companion, only echoed a yawning loneliness within him. How could she appear so... happy here without him? So carefree, as though he hadn't mattered at all.

Her smile was bright, her expression cheerful.

How was he supposed to disturb her eternal rest, if it was apparently so pleasant without his presence?

"Why is her face different?" Ingram asked, noting that it looked younger, livelier, and unmarred by her burns. *"The Witch Owl told me she would be as I last saw her."*

Was he disappointed she looked different? A little, only because he struggled to register her as the female he'd chosen, the one he'd fallen in love with.

He'd adored every part of her, from her freckles, her scars, and even the sorrow in her sometimes haunted, far-away stare.

"What you see here is a memory," Weldir explained, causing Ingram to stray from viewing Emerie to give him his full attention. He was headless, making it impossible to see his expression. "I bring the souls here and link them to their strongest bonds, allowing them to play out their fondest memories together. It brings them peace, and it stops them from... *screaming.*"

Weldir shuddered so violently that his entire essence dispersed. It coalesced into random parts of him swiftly, leaving him like a silk cloth, twirling and floating to reveal different parts of his body and limbs. It was less than before, thinner and becoming harder to see.

Learning this lessened the burning betrayal that had started to singe him. It wasn't that she did not care for him, she was just lost in her own past   one which he hadn't been a part of yet.

Ingram swiped his hand through her spirit once more. *"If I cannot speak with her, how am I to ask her to be my bride?"*

"Here, I can help!" Aleron exclaimed, bouncing forward with his hand out.

"I wouldn't do that," Weldir stated, but it was too late.

Ingram paused to watch as his kindred placed his large hand over her entire head from the side. Emerie paused her walking next to the stranger, freezing up completely like she was waking up to reality. Then she turned, looked up at Aleron towering over her with his menacing, clawed hand out, and let out a horrible shriek.

She yanked her companion forward, who slammed into Aleron's chest, and also seemed to awaken from a trance. The human male gave a roar and practically fell backwards on top of Emerie, who had tripped over her own feet.

For a split second, both had been utterly naked until clothing wrapped around their bodies out of thin air with a puff of smoke. Emerie's features returned to the ones he knew, her scar lifting to the surface like growing ash.

Aleron yelped in surprise and backed up while lowering himself to the ground.

"What the fuck is that?!" the male shouted, while pointing at Aleron's bony face.

None of the other spirits nearby noticed anything happening, despite the commotion. They even walked through Emerie and her panicked companion crumbled against the ground.

She stared at Aleron, her chest heaving up and down, before it began to eventually settle. She blinked, looked up, down, and then around. Her gaze fell on Weldir, and her eyes widened in disbelief.

"Where am I?" she asked before bringing her stare back to Aleron. It was like she hadn't seen Ingram at all. "You're... you're a Duskwalker." She groaned while gripping her forehead. "One minute I was at the castle, then I was talking to..."

Her features stilled, and she darted her head to the right while leaning back. Then the brightest smile he'd ever seen upon her face shined from her as she squealed and threw herself at the human male.

"Gideon!" she shouted, wrapping her arms around his neck as she tackled him to the ground. She stopped caring about Aleron's presence, or even Weldir's, as she began to joyfully weep. "Oh my god, Gideon. I never thought I'd see you again."

"What are you doing?" Gideon asked, one of his arms coming around her waist as he picked them both up off the ground. "The hell you clinging to me for when there's a

Duskwalker there? We need to run."

Emerie laughed through her tears. "Because you can't die twice, and running from a Duskwalker is *stupid*," she giggled as she held onto him and stopped whatever attempts he tried at getting them to run.

"Die twice?" His fear dropped away, replaced by a moment of speechlessness before he continued. "That night... the Demon."

"Yes. You died."

"How long ago?"

"Eight years," she answered.

His features grew even more bewildered as he turned a wide stare to the ground in thought. He even loosened his hold on her.

As much as he wanted to give her this reunion, Ingram selfishly wanted his own.

"Emerie?" Ingram softly called as he sidestepped to the left so he could, hopefully, come into view. He held his breath, wondering if she would even be able to see him or sense his presence at all.

Gideon snapped his face in Ingram's direction and squeezed Emerie as he backed away. Emerie's face pulled away from Gideon's neck with her lips parting on a gasp, her eyes widening. She darted that shocked expression to Ingram, and the moment her gaze connected with his own, his worries waned.

"Ingram!" she squealed, even *louder* than she had for Gideon. She even shoved the man to the ground to get him off her so she could fling herself with arms open at Ingram.

"Wait," he rasped, backing up a step.

She jumped, flew through his intangible form, and fell flat on her face. He jumped to the side with his arms up, oddly worried about crushing her ghostly essence.

"Ow! Why did that *huuuurt?*" she whined from where she landed. Weldir laughed at her and had Ingram growling in his direction menacingly, then he brought himself closer to her crumpled form while she was rising to her hands and feet. "Why didn't you catch me?"

The fact she had so trustingly pounced on Ingram made him chuckle warmly at her. *Silly butterfly.* She had been so excited to see him that she'd acted on instinct.

"I am not truly here," Ingram stated as he lifted his hand under her jaw, hovering it there even though he couldn't truly tilt her face up to his own.

Her lips tightened as she fully took him in. "Is that why you look like a big purple Ghost?"

Once more, Ingram was the one to laugh. *"You are the one who is a Ghost, Emerie."*

Like he couldn't help himself, too curious to care this was an important moment for Ingram, Aleron shoved his face less than a foot from hers.

"This is the female you have chosen?" he asked, tilting his head left and right, before poking her in the forehead. *"Her hair is so... red. Are you sure you want a red one?"*

That answered the question on whether or not Aleron could truly see Emerie.

"Her hair is orange and yes, she is perfect." Ingram tried to push him away from crowding them, only to accidentally shove his entire arm through his bat skull. He drew it back with an annoyed rumble.

Emerie blinked at Aleron, her lips closing and opening. She peeked at Ingram.

"Is that Aleron?" she whispered, which made it almost impossible to hear her since she was already so quiet.

Heart-aching joy flittered through him.

Emerie and Aleron are meeting. His kindred and his chosen female were looking upon each other. And even though they were on the same plane and he wasn't, it still satisfied a strange part of him he didn't know existed.

One day, they would be bonded in different threads, and he hoped they shared one, even if it wasn't the same as the one he and Emerie had.

"Yes, this is my kindred," Ingram grated, craving to brush his claws through her hair and touch Aleron's wing at the same time.

She opened her mouth as if she wanted to say something, then closed it. The curiosity in her expression faded into something sad and unsure.

"Why are you here, Ingram?" she asked, and he wished he

wasn't able to see the tears springing in her eyes – especially since he couldn't even see the icy blue of her irises. "I'm really sorry I didn't tell you what was happening. You must be so upset with me, but I-I did it to protect you. Why are you here in the afterlife then? You're not supposed to be here."

He was unable to stop her from rising to her feet and turning her back to him, her hands coming up to grip her biceps.

"You weren't supposed to follow after me. I did it to keep you alive." She covered her face and shook her head in her hands. "Don't tell me I did it for no reason."

For a moment, he'd grown disheartened that she didn't want to see him or have him chase after her, but it wasn't hard to figure out what was truly upsetting her.

"I am still alive, Emerie." For now, but his body had been eaten all the way to the tops of his limbs. He was just a floating torso, and he was aware he did not have much longer. *"I did not come here to die."*

From what he'd been told and what he could tell... Tenebris was just another form of life for Mavka. One where he would not be able to obtain a bride, which he didn't want if he could not have Emerie.

He may change his mind on the answer he'd give her, depending on if she rejected him or not. He just... wouldn't tell her that, as Weldir told him not to. He'd like to be with Aleron if he could not have Emerie.

The two creatures currently before him were the only ones that mattered to him. Everyone else could fade from existence for all he cared.

"Then why?" she asked, turning to him.

Ingram came closer and sat on his hind legs around her, wanting to crowd her even if he couldn't hold her. Her adopted brother, Gideon, was off to the side, utterly bewildered and unsure of what to do.

It looked like he wanted to approach. When he tried, Aleron quickly interfered by slotting himself between them, and softly growled down at him. Ingram could tell his feathers had puffed in aggravation, warning the male human back.

His kindred had already grown protective of Ingram's chosen

female. The fact he had so swiftly, simply because of Ingram's want of her, made tenderness wash through him.

Ingram cupped the side of her intangible face and hovered his palm there, giving himself the satisfaction of seeing his hand on her even if he could not feel it.

He swallowed thickly to remove the stuck emotions in his throat.

"I want you to be my bride," he told her, tension he didn't realise he'd been holding finally easing out of him.

"But I can't," she cried, her expression twisting horribly with anguish. "I'm not alive anymore, Ingram."

Ingram lifted his skull towards Weldir, who did nothing but watch. He wanted his help to explain this as clearly as possible to her, but didn't seem to realise that's what he'd been silently asking.

Guess he had to do this on his own.

"Your soul survived, Emerie. They did not know if it would, but it means I can bring you back."

Once more, he looked up at Weldir to twist his head at him. That was correct, right?

He received no answer.

"Y-you can?" she asked, her voice breaking an octave.

"Yes." He completely gave up on Weldir's assistance and just focused on the ghostly female before him. *"Your soul is mine to revive, little butterfly."*

"I know why me," Emerie rasped, averting her gaze to the side as she bit at her bottom lip. "But there are other humans, Ingram. Ones that aren't scarred, or a little broken inside... or missing pieces. This seems like a lot of effort just for me."

"I don't want another human," he warmly argued. *"You are perfect, just as you are. You are colourful and patient with me, and your kindness touches me here."* He pointed to his chest, just where she once told him that someone special would touch him. *"And you are so brave, even when you smell of fear. No other human could compare to you."*

Like she wanted to make humour of the situation to deflect her own emotions, or the fact his compliments had made her squirm like they often did, she grumbled something that had him chuckling.

"You just like how I make your dick feel." She pouted.

"That too." Spirit of the void help him – although he was being *very* unhelpful right now – he absolutely liked the way she made his dick feel. Having more, an eternity worth of pleasure, was hard to give up.

But he would give it up if it was not shared with her.

"Emerie," he started, about to tell her the depth of his adoration for her, and how he realised it even before the blast that had stolen her from him happened.

She cut him off.

"I need to tell you something," she whispered, gripping at her elbow. "I-I made some choices, ones I regret but can't take back. It means I can't give you what Mayumi has for Faunus. I can't give–"

Her expression morphed into one that stung behind his sternum. One of regret, of pain and tears, of loss and grief.

"I'm really sorry," she said as she covered her face so she could sob into her hands. "If I knew... If I knew I would meet you one day, I wouldn't have done it. I wouldn't have let them take this away from me. I can't be your bride if you want children, Ingram. I-I can't do that to you, or me. So, p-please, if that is something you want, go back."

Ingram now understood why the Witch Owl had been so adamant in explaining this to him.

If he'd tried to convince Emerie otherwise, or say that he was sure they could find a way to change it, he would have irrevocably hurt her in this moment.

He would have lost her, forever.

"I know," Ingram stated softly, wishing he could lower her hands to see her.

"P-pardon?" she rasped.

"I already know, Emerie. And I do not care." She slid her hands down just enough to peek at him over her fingertips. He sat back slightly to give her room and let her fully see him. *"The idea of having younglings... yes, I wanted them, but only with you. If you cannot have them, then I don't want them at all."*

"Ingram," she whined, as if his honesty had been painful to

hear.

"I don't want another human, Emerie. I cannot picture a future in that world without you. Now that I know this about you, I do not see younglings and desire them. I only want you and your warmth, your scent, and your presence. You are all that I need."

"W-what about Aleron?" Emerie asked, glancing over her shoulder at him.

"I need him as well, but it is different. He is here, and he cannot come with me. But you can, and that is all I crave right now."

She turned back to him, and her expression no longer appeared distraught, but rather... shy. His sight turned bright pink as he looked upon her, and it ignited heat within his chest. Ingram hoped his next words made her smile.

"I am sorry I did not realise it before you tried to take yourself away from me, but I love you, Emerie. We are connected, but I would like to make us one. I would like for you to be my bride, so I can show you that love in all the forms I can."

Her bottom lip trembled as both twitched and curled upwards at the edges.

"I-I really wish I could hug you right now," she said with her voice shaking. "But I love you too, Ingram. I've known that for a while."

She did? He gave an annoyed huff. *"Then why did you not tell me?"*

Even though he asked this, a thrill shot through him at her saying she loved him in return. His tail tip curled so tightly in delight it coiled halfway up its length, and his spikes tremored. The pink in his vision brightened around the edges until all he could see was her.

"I didn't know if you really understood it or felt that way towards me." She lowered her gaze to avoid his. "Your orbs never turned pink for me."

"They are pink now," he assured, looking at her ghostly form with tendrils of pink in it from his own vision.

"They are?" She reached up around the side of his empty eye

sockets like she wanted to touch them. "I want to see them. You're just... purple."

"They are. So, my little butterfly, will you let me revive you so I can make you my bride?"

"I would like that more than anything." However, she looked over her shoulder once more. "But... can we stay here for a little longer? I want to be with Gideon while I can."

Ingram looked down at his purple, spectral claws, then his arms and legs that were entirely transparent. He faced his beak towards Weldir.

"You have time," he answered. "I will let you all speak privately. Just have Aleron call for me when you are ready." Then, right before he left, he stated, "Also, make sure to have Aleron touch them within an hour, otherwise they'll slip back into their memories and forget."

Yellow lifted into his orbs, and he let his gaze land on the male staring at Emerie with wide and concerned eyes.

I would like to meet the person who is special to her, just as she met mine.

With her body facing Gideon, Emerie shyly glanced over his shoulder towards Ingram, who looked like a purple Ghost version of himself, and his twin, Aleron.

Actually... she tried not to look at Aleron and his wings – they creeped her the fuck out.

They were massive, obviously spanning metres, and black with hints of dark blue shining through them. He had a long train of feathers for a tail, and walked on his hands and three-toed bird feet.

It looked like Ingram had eaten the head of a raven, and Aleron had eaten its body.

She wondered if the short fur that sprouted sporadically all over Ingram belonged to a fruit bat, since Aleron had the skull head of one. Aleron also seemed to have a small amount of lizard scales on the softer parts of his body, like his stomach, inner elbows, and the backs of his knees and hands.

The rest of him, however, was very fluffy with long fur.

They've shared everything they have ever eaten. She could tell just by looking at them, while picturing what she remembered of Ingram in his non-ghostly form.

The twins were talking to each other, and she thought it was sweet that Aleron's orbs were pink. Or were they always that colour?

"Are you sure about this?" Gideon asked her, his voice kind but rough, just like it'd always been.

She couldn't help the way her cheeks heated as she gave him a bashful smile. "Yes. Absolutely. I'm sure about this."

His light-green eyes were bowed with uncertainty, and with an affection only a brother could shine at her. Although she could barely feel it, a light gust of wind made his short caramel-brown hair shift.

He had a small dark shadow of a beard. He usually liked to keep it shaved, preferring to be well-presented in a time where hygiene and cleanliness were difficult to achieve.

Gosh, he looks exactly as I remember.

He still looked twenty-three, only four and a half years older than what she'd been.

His shoulders were still bulky from working the forest as a tree cutter, his arms flexing with lean muscle. His legs, however, were strong from bracing his weight while tossing an axe around, and his stomach was flat, his shoulders broad.

Gideon had always had a handsome face.

His jaw was wide, his cheeks high, his nose wide but nicely pointed. Even his bushier brows were neat, but sharp. Yet, the rest of him, like his full mouth, his eyes, and chin, was softer.

Emerie had been one of the many people who had found him attractive.

He drifted his wary expression to the side where the two Duskwalkers were. One of his gold earrings glinted in the bright sunshine that came from goodness knew where in this afterlife.

Ghosts walked through them, one or two she knew, most she didn't. They were on the outskirts of her old town of Fishket or, rather, a falsified and created version of it. Brown brick houses behind Gideon were familiar, as was the sandy path they were standing on.

She didn't know what she'd been doing before she'd woken up to find Aleron's claws just in front of her face, but it must have been walking with Gideon. She vaguely remembered holding a basket of fruit and vegetables before she'd flung it somewhere and it disappeared.

However, instead of there being wooden stakes behind her like a wall, it was a field. Long grass, vibrant and green, swayed with the light wind that constantly swirled. The sun was perfect – not too hot, not too cool, and didn't sting her eyes.

Ghostly birds chirped in the distance, and she could hear the pleasant rush of moving water. She thought it may be a waterfall.

Tenebris was... peaceful.

There was a serenity to it, especially knowing that she could stand in the vast openness behind her, even in the night, and a Demon wouldn't come to tear her to pieces.

This is what Earth should have been like, not the nightmare it'd turned into.

She guessed this was Weldir's version of heaven. She was surprised it looked like this.

"A Duskwalker, huh?" Gideon muttered as he rubbed at the side of his neck. "Never picked you for doing something out of the general norm."

Emerie couldn't help the pitying smile that tightened her lips.

"A lot has happened to me since you died," she admitted.

His own lips tightened but curled downward. He cupped the left side of her face and brushed his thumb over her scars. "Did this happen that night?"

She tried to keep her voice from shaking. "Yeah."

"Guess you owe me one."

Her head reared back as her brows knitted tightly. "Excuse me?"

"You know... for saving your life and all."

"You practically ruined it!" She tried to give her voice a shouting inflection, while keeping it quiet, tempted to start bashing on his chest.

Gideon rolled his green eyes. "That's what you get for arguing with me." Her lips parted in disbelief, but he chuckled, wrapped the bulk of his arm around her head, and yanked her in for a forced hug. "How were mum and dad afterwards?"

She buried her head further against his shoulder. "They died the same night. My oil lamp, it... set everything on fire."

He squeezed her. "I'm sorry. I can't imagine what you've been through. To lose all of us and your face all in the same night."

"You just couldn't let me be eaten, could you? You just had to be a big hero and save my stupid ass," she grumbled with a pout, for some reason not feeling an urge to cry when she would have while speaking to anyone else about it.

Maybe it was the familiar comforting warmth of Gideon, or his soothing brotherly voice, but she felt... relieved. Calm.

He was gone, and she was only talking to his spirit, but he wasn't suffering or in pain. He wasn't in some dark place, scared and alone.

She wished she could smell him; it would have been comforting. Especially since the world here smelt odd, wrong, false even.

He squeezed even tighter. "I'm sorry for leaving you by yourself. Your family welcomed me into their arms when my own died, and I had people to lean on through it. You had no one." He pulled back to look at her. "Did you at least find some happiness in your life?"

"No, not really," she answered honestly, averting her gaze to the side. "I joined the eastern sector of the Demonslayers."

His head shot back in surprise. "What the shit? You became a Demonslayer?" He let out a deep laugh. "Emerie... you'd get scared when there was a rodent in our house. How the hell did you manage to become a Demonslayer?"

She stepped away and threw her hands up. "I don't know, okay?! I wasn't a very good one, if I'm being honest with you. The only thing I had going for me was my smarts."

"Pfft! You? Smart?!" His laughter got louder. "You're the biggest goofball I know. You're the kind of person who couldn't even be bothered to attend school because it was boring."

"Well, that changes when your brother decides to fuck off to the afterlife."

He sobered from his humour. "I always pictured you running off into the sunset with some man, not going to the Demonslayer guild." His sight drifted to the Duskwalkers. "Is that how you met him?"

"Yeah. I freed him because I couldn't handle what they were doing to him."

Gideon's eyelids crinkled knowingly. "Of course you freed him. Still as soft-hearted as ever."

Emerie turned her shoulders inward in bashful awkwardness. "Do... you want to meet him?"

She'd asked Ingram to give her a few moments with Gideon so she could reassure him and have some free, non-Duskwalker-weirdness time with him.

"Absolutely, I do." He lifted his chin and firmed his expression. Then he tossed her a smile while bending his arm in the air. He patted his flexed biceps. "Have to give him the ol' 'hurt my sister and I'll break your legs' chat."

"Gideon... I'm not sure how to tell you this, but... he'd destroy you." She patted his shoulder and gave him a sympathetic look. "You just aren't strong enough, no matter how much you think so."

"Fuck, that was rude," he exclaimed.

They both burst into a quiet fit of laughter.

As she laughed, feeling lighter than she had in a long time, she swept her gaze over to Ingram and Aleron. Their backs were semi-turned to them, and it appeared as though they were having a very important and hushed conversation.

"I just have to know one thing before I meet him," Gideon started, his voice warm but also serious. "Is he nice to you? Does he make you feel... safe?"

"Of course he does," Emerie defensively muttered, her attention lost to Ingram and Aleron.

Well, it was lost in trying to figure out the hand gestures Ingram was making. Especially since Aleron had cupped his hand over his fanged mouth in thought. He was nodding, as though he was listening very intently while Ingram explained something.

"I'm just making sure, considering he's a monster. It's hard to accept."

"He's not a monster..." Emerie trailed off, and her eyes widened.

Her heart almost leapt to her throat, just as her face heated in deep-seated embarrassment.

"Ingram, no!" she squealed, running towards him.

Both Aleron and Ingram turned their skulls towards her, just as Ingram put his forefinger through a ring he'd made with his other hand.

Oh shit, he was explaining to Aleron what sex was!

She shouldn't have left him alone. Now he was telling his twin about his – *their* – sex life!

"What is the matter, Emerie?" Ingram asked, tilting his head without removing his finger from the circle, like he saw nothing wrong with what he'd been doing.

Even though Aleron was right next to him, she waved her hands through Ingram's ghostly ones, wishing to flap it away. He remained, unfortunately, until he turned around to face her.

"Don-don't just tell people stuff like that about us."

"Why not?"

"Yes, why not?" Aleron asked, tilting his head in the opposite direction to Ingram. *"He has been teaching me all about these things I did not know. He said you feel very nice inside. I wonder if, when I also obtain a bride, I can use my d–"*

"Anywaaaay!" Emerie squealed, since Gideon had come up behind her.

She was sure if she had been alive and her breaths didn't feel... pointless, she would have expired or fainted from embarrassment.

"What's wrong?" Gideon asked, placing his hand on her shoulder since she'd suddenly run off.

"Nothing. Don't worry about it." She pointed at Ingram. "Don't tell people that stuff. It's private."

Even though he was just purple, she figured his orbs had changed to another colour since he huffed and tossed his head around while folding his arms across his chest. He was obviously pouting.

Gideon shook his head in bewilderment at her, whereas Aleron's orbs had turned dark yellow.

"Ingram," she gently called to get his attention, as she waved her hand to the side. "This is Gideon, my brother."

Gideon put his hand out with it flat and on its side. "Nice to meet you, I guess."

Ingram's beak pointed downwards at his hand before mimicking him. He did not attempt to clasp it, just mirrored him.

"What is the point of this?" Ingram asked. *"Is this a human greeting?"*

Gideon gave an awkward chuckle. "Yeah, it is, but it was kind of pointless for me to do it with you, since you're a Ghost and I can't touch you."

"Can I try?" Aleron asked, shoving his hand out like everyone else.

Gideon cast Emerie an uncertain glance. She just shrugged in answer.

Gideon hesitantly grabbed Aleron's large and imposing clawed hand, although rather awkwardly due to their size difference. He clasped as best he could as he shook it.

"I'm Gideon."

"I'm Aleron," he answered, copying him, and shook back far too hard.

Gideon went headfirst to the ground when Aleron tugged his arm downwards, not knowing to control his strength. His orbs turned white, and he threw his hands into the air frantically.

"I am sorry. I did not mean to make you fall."

"Fuckin' hell," Gideon grumbled against the grass. "That was one hell of a handshake."

A small giggle escaped her.

Just as Gideon was rising to his hands and knees, Aleron grabbed the man by the waist. He lifted him off the ground completely until his arms and legs were flailing, then plonked him on his feet.

Gideon stumbled back a step as though he was disorientated. He cast Emerie another uncertain glance, only to scowl when it was obvious she was resisting the urge to laugh more.

"You get used to it," Emerie reassured.

"I doubt that," he answered, brushing at his pants like they were covered in dirt, when they absolutely weren't. "So... Ingram, was it?"

"Yes," he confirmed, as he skulked his way closer to Emerie.

She stepped away from them, certain that Gideon would do a good job of making conversation, so she could go to Aleron. He twisted his bat skull at her as she approached him while he stood on all fours.

"Hello, Aleron. Ingram has told me a lot about you."

"He has told me much of you."

Oh gods, that sounded ominous in the most perverted way possible. Heat flared in her cheeks once more.

Still, she slowly, as though not to startle him, leaned forward. She wrapped her arms around his thick neck and openly buried her face into the fluffy, furry side of it. She also did it to hide from the sight of his wings right before her – she really didn't like them and was thankful he hadn't spread them while being in her presence.

Aleron stiffened, likely unsure of what to do or what was happening.

But that was okay; she just wanted to hug him.

"He misses you very much," she softly stated. "I'll try to take care of him for you."

Within an instant, all his tension deflated out of him in a single false breath. He loosely wrapped an arm around her waist.

"I miss him, too. I will try to find a way back to him."

Tenderness flooded her chest for Aleron. He seemed kind and gentle, just like Ingram.

I really hope that's true.

She squeezed him tighter with all her might, hoping he could feel the strength of emotions she was trying to convey.

"We'll be waiting for you."

FORTY-TWO

Standing in his more humanoid form, Ingram stared down at Aleron on all fours. Aleron tipped his snout down to his feet before trailing it back up to his short, upward-jutting goat horns.

Before he left his kindred, he wanted to teach him and show him as much as he could. Hopefully it would help him in the future.

It would have helped Ingram had he known about all his abilities. His body, how to sheath his claws, that he could mimic the way humans walked.

I don't want to leave him, Ingram thought with his sight turning blue. Yet, he faced Emerie instead, who was standing right next to his kindred. *But I must.*

Finally, Ingram dipped his head towards Weldir.

"We are ready," he stated, lifting his claws towards Emerie, wishing she could take his hand.

Even though she couldn't, she still played pretend with him and hovered her palm above his own. She came to his side.

"Good, because you are almost out of time," Weldir stated, what remained of his face dropping to the last, palm-sized amount of flesh remaining right where Ingram's sternum was.

"Actually, I do have one question for you," Emerie stated, turning to Weldir. "Did I do it? Did I destroy the Demon King?"

Weldir was silent for a moment, and the hand that was visible tightened. "I am not sure."

Emerie's brows furrowed deeply. "What do you mean you're

not sure?"

"I can no longer sense his magic, nor have I seen him among the rubble of his castle from my viewing discs, but my mist has not touched his soul." He waved his hand through the air, his claws pointed upwards. "It may have been destroyed since it belonged to a half-Demon, but an Elf's soul is blue. If I had touched it, I would have noticed immediately when I tried to eat it. But yes, for now, we believe he was destroyed. That is all we can hope for."

"I guess that's better than nothing. I'll be really angry if he survived after that, though."

"So will we." A small chuckle left him. "Now, this will not hurt."

That was the only warning he gave as he shoved his hand into Emerie's spirit. Thankfully she'd already said her goodbyes to Aleron and Gideon because, once he yanked his hand out, she disappeared in a puff of smoke.

Instead, a small, white flame became visible in Weldir's tight fist. Ingram couldn't see the body of her soul, but he knew it was there.

Ingram held his hand out for it, but the part of Weldir's face that showed his lips smirked.

"Not quite yet," he stated. "First, you must leave the way you came in."

"I don't understand."

Weldir disappeared in a mist of glittering black sand with that smirk still in place.

Was he supposed to walk back? He inspected his chest. *I will not make it.* There was only a little of him left, and it had taken a long time to get here. He also didn't know the way.

He stepped back from Aleron and Emerie's brother, only to flip upside down like someone had grabbed his feet and tail. He began lifting off into the sky.

At first, he panicked, but that was short-lived. He'd fallen from the sky, was that what Weldir meant by him needing to leave the way he came?

He looked down to find Aleron before he was too far through the mist.

He expected to find his kindred staring up at him. Instead, Aleron had pointed his skull towards Gideon, and even flared his wings slightly at the male as he dipped his chest low.

Ingram knew his kindred well enough to recognise his most curious stance. He'd made a friend here.

So, Ingram looked up to see where he was going. Before long, darkness surrounded him.

Then it was tight and cold again.

He felt the urge to yell when he was spat out of Weldir's mouth, but that was only for the few seconds he was flying. He landed into the cushion of his gigantic hand, and was carefully placed on his feet before him, once more, standing on nothingness.

He was back to being his full Mavka self, grey skin, black scales and all.

Weldir shrunk his form until he was the same height as when he first met him.

A white and fluttering cloak caught in his peripheral. In her Phantom form, the Witch Owl lay on her side, curled up into a ball in the air. One baby Mavka had chosen to curl against her stomach between her knees and elbows, while the other lay sprawled on top of her side.

She seemed at peace while she slept. Vulnerable and not so... unnerving. She looked fragile, like the human she once was.

Weldir approached her, his form only visible by a foot, a hand, and half his face – including a horn. His chalky outline was disappearing, and there was little left of him.

He gingerly placed the only hand visible under her face. "Owlet, we have returned."

Rather than flicking open in sudden alertness like he expected, she opened her eyes dozily, as if she felt safe in the environment in which she had been resting. It didn't take her long to fully open her eyes.

When she did, she stood, brought her younglings back inside her cloak, and faced Ingram. For the first time, she appeared soft and meek as she rubbed the heel of her palm against her cheek.

"Emerie?" she asked.

"She is here." Weldir brought a chalky hand forward and

Emerie's soul formed.

"Why is it white?" she asked.

Ingram had been wondering that too.

"It is currently a soul belonging to someone who is not alive. Once I bond it with Ingram, it will return to its normal colouring."

Weldir approached, and Ingram met him in the middle, excited to bond with Emerie and have her returned to him.

Like he had before, he held his hand out for her soul.

He was able to see it now, as Weldir held his palm flat and it floated above it.

Her posture was straight with her legs closed, and one hand covered her left shoulder, while the other held her right hip. Her long hair floated above her like she'd been dropped into water.

Ingram could see where her many scars were, not just her burns but also claw marks. They appeared darker than the rest of her brightly glowing flame soul.

It looks like her, he thought with his orbs turning bright pink.

Weldir glanced down to Ingram's reaching hand, and tsked.

"Today, little one, you will not be the soul eater you were meant to be." When Ingram tilted his head at him, he sighed. "Your female is dead, and her soul can no longer be touched by any living Mavka. In order to make her your bride, I will have to attach the bonding threads myself."

He floated so he could be just above Ingram's skull, and he felt the tiniest bits of movement around his horns.

"Did she gift you this horn ornament?" Weldir muttered. "I hope if I ever have a physical form, that Lindiwe will do the same. I would like to be adorned with affection."

Before Ingram knew it, Weldir backed up.

He didn't feel different, other than in his gut, which had stopped gurgling. That was not something he had ever experienced – silence and lack of motion from his stomach.

Wanting to know if he could touch it now, Ingram reached between his horns. Warmth tingled his fingertips as he caressed it, and he kept his gaze on Weldir and Lindiwe to make sure he wasn't doing something he shouldn't.

Neither stopped him as he pulled Emerie's soul from

between his horns so that he could hold it in his palm. Bright yellow filled the edges of his vision as he inspected her yellowy-orange flame.

It was floating above his palm, asleep and with its arms resting in the air near its hair – like the few times she'd splayed across the ground after they were intimate, relaxed and sated. One leg was bent, while the other was straight. The position warmed Ingram. Even though it was naked and bared, showing little white flame markings where her scars were, it looked as though it felt safe and free now that it belonged to him.

It was slow to wake, but it eventually moved its arms and legs as it settled to stand upon his palm. Blue little dots opened upon its face as it tilted it up towards him.

Just as it was reaching its arms up to his skull, as though it wanted to embrace him, Weldir cut into his long-awaited moment.

"It's time for you to leave and be with your bride," he stated, just as a second white soul formed.

It hovered before him, before he stabbed the claws of both hands into its centre and tore it apart. A white rift formed like a tear in space.

Ingram didn't even spare them a glance, nor did he waste any time so he could truly have his female back. Perhaps he should have thanked them, but they were the reason he had to go to them to obtain her soul in the first place.

Ingram merely placed her soul back where it belonged, right between his horns, and entered the portal.

Bright sunlight enveloped him as he stepped into a small clearing within the Veil. It was so small that only a sliver of a sunbeam was offered as protection, with a radius of no more than a foot on either side of him.

He was surprised that Weldir hadn't created a portal leading back to Faunus' ward, or anywhere protected belonging to the other Mavka. He imagined he had a reason for that, as it had already been made obvious the spirit of the void didn't do things without one.

He'd chosen Ingram's location on purpose.

At least he couldn't hear or smell any Demons nearby.

So, he knelt within the sun, and he waited for his little butterfly. He would remain here until she appeared to him, no matter how long it took.

The sun continued to rise above him, moving along the path of the beam and never truly shortening or lengthening it. Although he continued to breathe as normal, his lungs were tight from his impatience as if he'd held his breaths. Despite his steadiness, he was restless.

Then, she appeared.

Transparent, ghostly white, and peacefully sleeping.

It didn't take her long to twitch and open her eyes, only to lift her arm to uselessly block out the sun as she sat up to one side. She paused, then lowered it to inspect her Phantom hand.

He didn't move, his impatience gusting out of him at just being able to see her. Just one more step, just one more thing needed to be done, and she would be in his arms again.

"Ing–" she started as she went to search. She didn't need to turn her head far. "Ingram," she sighed out.

His tail tapped against the ground once, and he reached his clawed hand out to her. She reached her own out, hesitating halfway, so she could will a solid form like all the other brides had done in front of her.

As soon as the lightly tanned, freckled flesh of her hand formed, it was within his own larger one. The change started from her extremities and quickly spread over her like a wave. Once it was complete, Ingram didn't delay.

He pulled her to him, wrapped his arms around her torso, and lifted her until she was forced to lock her legs around his narrow waist. With one of his hands spanning her hip and thigh, and the other supporting between her shoulder blades and the back of her neck, he rubbed the side of his skull against her temple.

"Emerie," he grated.

Her warmth spread across his chest and heated him from the outside in. Her strawberry-and-primrose scent swelled in his lungs, so pretty and alluring it quelled any remaining anguish that had befallen him in her absence. Even just her tiny breaths tickling across the scales of his neck, or her chest waving with his, brought him so much contentment he held her tighter.

His hand dipped around the side of her neck from behind so he could place the pads of his fingers against her fragile and precious jugular. He felt it pulsing, letting him know she was truly alive within his embrace.

The edges of his vision swirled into bright pink, just as the bottoms of his orbs broke and little droplets floated around his skull.

I revived her, and now I will cherish her.

"T-too tight," she squeaked.

He compressed her just a little more, before loosening his hold.

With his hand supporting her arse and the rest of his arm locking her to him, he dug the claws of his free hand into her hair when he cupped the side of her face. He didn't realise he'd been trembling until he tried to stroke her freckled, smooth cheek with his thumb.

Her blue eyes dilated and flicked between his bright-pink orbs, as her expression twisted into a mingle of joy and sadness all rolled into one at seeing them.

She reached up to hold one side of his jaw, like she wanted to hold him still. The openness of just a simple, subtle gesture of her delicate, soft palm, was enough to quench every bit of longing he'd had for her.

"So beautiful," he firmly stated, before pressing the crown of his bony forehead against hers. "You are mine now, my little bride." He trailed the tip of his claw behind the shell of her ear, enjoying that she shivered in reaction for him. "And you will not spend a moment apart from me. I have already proven that I will travel across existences to obtain you, rescue you, and keep you, and not even the afterworld can hide you from me. You are *mine.*"

"Thank you for coming to get me, Ingram," she whispered with her eyes closed and twisting her head side to side so that the tip of her nose would brush the base of his beak. "Thank you for wanting to."

He pulled back so he could look upon her fully. Even though she had taken this leap with him, he didn't understand why she still had fears.

"Why would I not want to, Emerie?" he asked, simply so he could get to the root of her insecurities and pluck them from her.

"I'm not perfect," she muttered while turning her gaze away, only for him to direct her back to him. "I'm a flawed person."

She was perfect to him, and he would spend their entire lives together showing her this.

However, he decided to come at this from a different way, trying to use a piece of Emerie against herself by deflecting. To be cunning in the way she often was.

"I am also flawed," he said, tipping his head. "So let us be flawed together."

When she nibbled at her lips as though unconvinced, he had an urge to lean forward and lick across them to still her.

"You are *tender* towards me, Emerie. You are stern when you need to be, and correct me when I need it, but you still give me the freedom to make up my own mind about the world and the decisions I have made. You aided me through a time in which I was very lost and confused, and helped me to see the world in a warm and colourful way again, when all I saw was blue and red, when all I felt were the emotions that go with them. You have shown me so much and have been patient and forgiving." Then Ingram drew his claw from the back of her ear, down the side of her neck, so he could graze it down her chest. "And you are beautiful and sensual in ways that I had never imagined possible."

To finish off his words, he circled his claw around her exposed, scar-marred nipple. She shivered for him, and it hardened from his caress.

She gasped, covering her chest as she shot her gaze around them. "Holy shit, I didn't realise I was fucking naked!" Since she'd accidentally squished his hand against her bare breast, he gave it a knead before sliding his palm to her back. "Where are we?"

"We are in the Veil," he answered, noticing that they were still in the safety of the sun by her orange hair glowing. It appeared silkier than ever. "But you will always be safe with me now," he reassured, since she had a light fear scent.

It didn't stir hunger in him like it had once before, only worry for her comfort. *She no longer needs to fear me.* And he no longer needed to fear *himself.*

"I guess that's true," she grumbled, before lifting her arms to look at herself. She blushed, as she had the entire night, day, and then the following night she had been bared to him. "Why am I naked though? Is it because the blast destroyed my clothes?"

"You are asking the wrong person, little butterfly," he said with a chuckle.

For once, she reminded him of Aleron from when they would both, foolishly, ask each other questions about the situation they had both been a part of. He found it quite humorous coming from her.

Instead of trailing just one finger over her, Ingram tickled all the claws of his free hand from the soft curves of her arse, all the way up the indents of her spine. She twitched and shivered while letting out a cute, raspy moan.

Even though her scent had turned tangy with light arousal just from the simple touch, Ingram felt no desire to have her mount him other than a singular throb behind his seam.

All he sought in that moment was her embrace. Her warmth, her scent, the soft outline of her body. Just Emerie and her essence up against his own.

He wanted to view her at his leisure so he could take in her supple skin, and the little dark-brown freckles that were scattered across it. The many white scars of claws that she had bravely survived, which allowed her to be in this moment with him. The burn scars that ran down the left side of her, that didn't make her more or less, but were just part of what made Emerie, Emerie.

He touched every inch of her, satisfying his craving to brush either his claws, the pads of fingers, the backs of his knuckles, or his palms over her softness, her silkiness, and know that it all belonged to him. Just as every one of his scales belonged to her and would always welcome her gentle caress – or the scrape of her nails in their moments of sexual intimacy.

Even the tips of her hair were played with as he twirled his fingers around the ends to tangle himself in their trappings. All the while, her icy-blue eyes stayed on him, and he would occasionally peer into them so he could lose himself in their mesmerising depths.

His heart was overfilled with adoration for the female who was letting him touch how he wanted to, how he needed to.

She wasn't shying away like she once had when unclothed, instead allowing him to drink his fill of her with his greedy gaze. She had no qualms about being exposed to him, although it was obvious she didn't want the world to see.

He was the only one special enough to her.

Like he couldn't help himself, he circled his claw around her nipple once more, just because he wanted to see it stiffen in reaction to him and his touch. So sensitive, and all his.

Her scent had long ago flooded with deep arousal that had flushed her chest and cheeks. Every second that he didn't place his hands directly against her pleasure spots, the more she fluttered for him.

Twitching, she gave pants and sharp breaths – even when he only grazed innocent places like the back of her calf or thigh. He liked that he could elicit such a carnal and passionate reaction with just the barest of teases.

"Why are you still crying, Ingram?" she asked. He paused as he darted his sight to her face. "Especially when your orbs are pink."

"Because I am... happy you are here when I thought I had lost you. I am overcome by my love for you right now."

"I love you, too." Her own eyes prickled with tears, and she cupped the underside of his jaw with both hands. "You are very pretty like this."

If he had feathers, she would have ruffled them completely. Her compliments always made his chest feel light and fluffy.

The colour brightened in intensity. "I always thought I was pretty," he playfully grumbled. "I am the only Mavka with a beak."

Her smile grew. She cupped the underside of his beak and bent closer. "Kiss?" she asked with such an airy and heated voice.

It stroked him on a deep level, like she was trying to brush against his soul with just a single word.

Yes, he wanted to kiss. He always wanted to, now that he knew how good it felt, and how much it spread tenderness throughout his heart, thawing it completely for a time.

A pant fell from him and parted his beak, as he held the side of her face and licked across her tongue when she shot it out for him. The moment their tastebuds tickled across each other's, he sought to fill her mouth completely.

She wouldn't let him – at least, not without a fight.

It was her way of playing with him, of making the kiss equal before he always won. Each lick had him holding her tighter and tighter like he wanted to sink her inside his torso.

"I never thought I would get to kiss you again," he almost groaned, just as he sunk his tongue inside the warm, damp sweetness of her mouth. "Or hold you, touch you."

Her eyes crinkled in anguish, but it was quickly replaced as he pushed more inside, dominating her mouth and her thoughts. She moaned, before swelling a panted, lost breath around it. Then, she tossed her head to the side and buried it against his neck.

"W-why aren't you touching me?" she softly whined, and her hardened nipples grazed over the scales on his chest, making them puff. She started rubbing them against him now that they were sharper for her.

She ground her clit against his abdomen, as she had been for quite some time. Other than sweeping her hands over his chest, shoulders, back, and neck, touching him everywhere she could, there was no other way for her to tease him.

He was holding her in the air, safely up against him.

"My pussy aches. I know you can smell how turned on I am." She brushed little kisses against his neck. "Please. I can't take much more."

"I want to touch you," he answered. "And be one with you."

Ingram had just wanted to worship his bride first.

To hold her in an adoring embrace.

However, the fact she was trying to instigate further intimacy all on her own, made his scales and spikes lift all over his body. His cock gave a deep, groin-piercing throb, and his sight finally flickered from pink to deep purple.

His love, and his desire for her, battled in his vision.

When his tentacles shifted to circle his engorging cock to keep him inside, purple won out.

She kept grinding on him as she whispered, "I was so scared that I wouldn't see you again, that I wouldn't be able to be with you. I... need to feel that this is real, that I'm really here with you."

He drifted his hand down her body and gave her arse a rough knead and grab. Then he dipped between her pretty thighs as he sheathed his claws.

He'd been intending to slip between the lips of her folds so he could pet her clit, but when just the pad of his middle finger touched her, it was instantly saturated.

The pool of her arousal had overfilled, flooded her slit, and then more. Ingram groaned as he buried two fingers straight into her hot, swollen core, just so he could feel how drenched she was.

"Fuck, Emerie," he bit out, removing his fingers so he could feel that not even the air could touch his flesh through her sticky, slick moisture. "Your little cunt is so wet for me."

He slipped his fingers back inside and moved them back and forth for her. He was slow, playing with her slick by splitting his fingers or wiggling them to show her just how wet she was for *him*. She bucked against them, and her head lolled against his shoulder as she moaned.

"Inside me," she panted. "I want you inside me so badly."

With a quiet, pleased growl, Ingram lowered her until she was seated on his bent thighs. He was still kneeling within the small patch of warm sun.

"My *bride* wants my cock inside her, even though we are in the Veil?" he asked, making sure she understood what she was requesting.

He slipped his fingers from her so he could grasp her thighs and spread her around his hips. He couldn't see well, not with their position and his beak in the way, but he could just glimpse her cute pink clit through the valley of her breasts.

Emerie had a dazed look in her icy eyes. She turned them down so she could pet at the seam hiding his dick away. It twitched and trembled under her naughty caresses, and each one had his cock rapidly hardening.

His claws shot out from him as he shuddered, almost extruding hard and fast into her awaiting hand. It was nearly impossible to hold himself back, as an unbearable pressure-laden throb pounded inside his groin.

He winced when it became too much.

"You will protect me." She bit at her lip, like she couldn't wait to see and touch his pulsating, purple cock. "O-or you could just make another protective dome around us."

Her level of trust, in the most dangerous place in the world, felled him.

He cut his claws into her arse, causing her to gasp in surprise from the pain before he removed their tips. He willed for her protection, to keep her completely and utterly safe so he could desperately bury his cock inside the deep well of her waiting core.

Ingram had only meant to make the small dome form.

Instead, a purple, multi-pointed star shot out from under his knees, and cut through the grass and forest as it grew and reached a far distance. Within seconds, a massive, glittering ward formed as a dome around them and the *entire* area.

Her lips parted as she gazed above them once he healed her of her wounds, or maybe she didn't realise he had over her shock.

He didn't care about it.

All he knew was that she was completely protected under his magic now, and once more her lips had called to him.

Ingram gripped her jaw so he could tilt her head back, and unnaturally curved his spine so he could bring the tip of his beak closer. Without warning, he sunk his tongue into her awaiting mouth, and shoved her pussy against his hips until she was seated over his seam.

He stopped holding back by forcing his tentacles to release him. Impatient to feel her, his cock shot from him as a single deep, full thrust straight inside her dripping cunt.

Emerie let out a sharp cry, just as he answered her with a deep and low groan.

He knew he had stretched her, but she had taken him easily enough. Her body had already been claimed by him, moulded by his, and was utterly perfect in its snugness.

Connected. They were one, on all levels.

My bride. Something he had not wanted, but now utterly needed.

With impatient movements, she wiggled against him, and even used her shins to try and move him. Desperate and moaning for more, her pretty breasts swirled as she gyrated.

He drew back from her mouth so he could lock her knees over his elbows and wrap his hands around her waist. Emerie gripped his shoulders tightly as he started slowly bouncing her on his cock, working her to bring them both pleasure.

He intently watched her features daze and become completely lost, and all he could do was pant at her to show her the same. He was so heated, feeling and watching her moving around him, that he was seconds from crawling out of his own scaled flesh.

She was so light to him, easy to move, and she let him dictate the strength, the speed, and how far she moved up and down the length of his cock. Ingram swelled, releasing bubbles of precum inside her tight channel, while her entrance began to leak with his lubricant.

But there was one thing bothering him, even as she wonderfully clung: the sun had moved behind him.

He didn't like that now he'd lowered her, he was a looming shadow over her fragile and delicate body. That he was shading the beauty of her.

Perhaps it was the nag of the past, being called a monster, but he didn't want any part of him to feel foreboding or scary when it came to her – not even his own shadow.

Her beauty deserved the light.

With his cock nestled within the warm cuddle of her pussy, he leaned forward until his biceps touched the ground, and rolled so she was above him. He had to wiggle back into the sun a little, but he was rather pleased with himself once he did.

Especially since he flattened his clawed feet against the ground, lifted his backside, held her by her hips, and pumped into her from below. Emerie threw her head back as she arched, letting the sun wash over and warm her from behind.

Her shadow was cast over him instead, but she was so small it barely reached his skull.

Ingram finally let the fever of his desires fully take hold. His hips picked up speed, wanting to see this female break apart. He wanted her to reach the tip of her pleasure so she could scream for him and let all the Veil know she was completely and utterly his now.

That he had saved her, and nothing could take her from him again.

She is mine. His orbs flared dark green for just a moment as the aggressive swell of his emotions gripped him, possessive and covetous. *My bride to take, to cherish.*

Her breasts jiggled and bounced with each of his long and measured thrusts, as did her thighs when his hips impacted them. Her fingers touched against his pelvis whenever he was seated deep, and then slipped away to wait for his return whenever he drew back.

And Ingram drew back far, bringing his cock almost all the way out of her so he could see the flared rim pop out as much as he felt it. He became enrapt with where they were joined, at where his thick, long cock kept disappearing into. Purple, veiny, with soft scaley spikes being tickled by her rippling insides, he watched himself take his female.

His tentacles didn't stand a chance at clinging to her, but they constantly caressed her flesh.

"Oh god, yes. Take me." Her pussy clamped and spasmed around him, and his cock's lubricant was slicker than ever as it mingled with hers. "Faster, Ingram. Fuck me faster, I'm so close."

Part of him wished she hadn't begged him for more, not when it was obvious she was about to lose herself around him.

The base of his spine tingled, and he flinched when his seed sacs clenched unbearably hard. He growled, and pumped his hips as fast as he could for her, only for his mind to blank out in bliss with only a few short strokes.

His emotions, his own need for her, twisted his mind and

body into an ache. His thrusts became erratic, his pumps hard. His tentacles latched and clung, forcing him to only pull back so far or he worried he'd tear her soft skin.

Her scream was unusually loud, her cute little lungs giving him a wild and carnal song, just as she milked him for his seed. His own orgasm slashed at his groin like a menacing beast, clawing at him with a swift, unpredictable swipe.

He couldn't take the intensity of movement while she orgasmed around him.

He shoved her down as he pushed in hard, his tentacles locking around her as he quaked, back arched. With his head tilted back all the way, his body was suspended in soul-crushing pleasure.

His lust-filled sight darkened under the power of it, of her body spasming around him while he flooded it.

Oh, fuck. His claws sliced into her until blood welled, but he couldn't stop crushing her with his hands. Couldn't stop gripping her for dear life, like it was the answer to keeping his heart beating when it felt as though it was about to give out. *Oh, fuuuck.*

Perhaps it was all the emotions that had led to them joining, or the fact he could *feel* the connection of her as his bride, but something had stroked his mind and body on a deep, visceral level. He released so hard he thought his soul was about to leave him.

For a long while, Ingram held the position even once he'd drained himself inside her, his body jolting with aftershocks. Her heartbeat fluttered around him, so soft, and gentle, and intimate around his hardened centre.

It was only when she palmed up his stomach, as though to *lovingly* soothe him, that he finally touched the ground again. His feet came out from under him, and he collapsed as he laid down. Tilting his skull to face her, he found her eyes were warm and tender as they watched him.

"Emerie," he rasped out, cupping the side of her neck so he could rub his thumb across her smooth and freckled cheek.

She welcomed his palm by leaning into it and holding the back of it to keep it to her. Her fingers petted the exposed bones.

He thought she would be docile with him. He was wrong.

She touched her toes to the ground, lifted up and off his cock, and leaned back to sit on the length of it. Despite its softening state, his waning erection jerked at watching her stretched pussy leaking with his seed.

Then, she rubbed her clit against it as she bit into the side of his palm.

"You're not done yet, are you?" she teased, her lips curling into a smirk. "You're usually not after one time."

Ingram chuckled, surprised to see she still had so much energy. Perhaps she was well rested after being in the afterworld.

He slipped his blood-stained thumb against her lips, content that the smell and sight of it didn't stir hunger in his stomach, but in other more titillating places. He liked that he was further marking her. "What is a person called when they are addicted to sex?" he asked.

Her brows twitched, unsure of where he was going with this.

"I guess a nymphomaniac, or nymph for short?"

He drew his claw down her chin, her neck, so he could tickle it between her perky breasts. "Are you a *nymph*, my little butterfly bride?"

The last time they'd been intimate, Emerie had barely rested as he took her, repeatedly, for almost two days. Although she'd grown tired, she'd asked for more, just as she had now. Considering how much she'd rejected him in the beginning, had been bashful and shy, he never would have guessed she could be this way.

He was *very* delighted to learn of this development.

"Says the purple-eyed Duskwalker." She giggled as she slipped the soft and luscious lips of her pussy over the groove underneath his semi-hard cock. "But no, not usually. I guess... I've just always wanted someone to make me feel loved, and that I was beautiful, inside and out. That I'm good enough, just as I am." Even though she was saying things that should have been sad, she cast him a tender smile. "You make me feel all those things, and it just makes me want to ride you until my eyes cross and I become so dizzy that I can't think about anything else but you. It makes me want to be as close to you as I can be.

You mean so much to me, and I want to show you however I can."

How was it possible for his heart and cock to throb at the same time?

He didn't know if he just wanted to bring her back into his arms for a cuddle, or fuck her until her expression went silly again. If he wasn't a towering Duskwalker, and she wasn't a small human, he would have done both.

Although, he did, absolutely, try.

With the sun on his back and Emerie below him, he was exactly where he wanted to be when he buried his cock inside her.

She is perfect. She was the bride Ingram needed.

EPILOGUE

Emerie had already been on high alert when she'd seen the wanted poster pinned to the notice board just within Greenshire's gates. Seeing a sketch of her own face with a reward prize had been unsettling. The title 'deserter' had been scribed, with the Demonslayer emblem pressed onto the very top in ink.

She was a criminal. A wanted woman.

Eh, she thought with a shrug.

There was only one person who currently wanted to capture her, and he had elongated, scale-covered arms. He was the only one who could have her.

She didn't really care if humankind was turning their backs on her. She had already turned hers to them, quite happily, if she were honest.

She loved people, so it wasn't in hate or spite towards humans, but more because she loved someone, or rather, some*thing* else so much more. She was willing to give up normality for him.

That didn't mean when a guard holding a spear pointed his big finger at her, she didn't gasp and tightly hold the bag of supplies she had... stolen. What? She didn't have any money! Kind of hard to have a dime when she had returned from the dead with nothing, not even a pair of underwear.

"You there! Halt!" The guard yelled, as his companion turned around in surprise.

The second guard looked at her quizzically for a moment before he registered who she was. He bolted for her, which caused the first to run for her as well.

Emerie let out a high-pitched squeal, hiked up the skirt of her dress, turned, and legged it. No way in hell was she going to be captured.

Holding her bag of supplies to her chest, trying to make sure nothing fell from it, she turned down a path between two houses. Since they jumped into it, she just kept running. Then Emerie turned left, and then right, before going straight.

She knocked into a few people, having to cartwheel her arms so she didn't trip and fall over with them, but she kept going.

When she was close to the edge of the town, she checked over her shoulder to make sure they couldn't see. Then she turned incorporeal and drifted through the town's protective wooden walls.

She became physical once more.

Running in the direction of the gate, so she could go to the hill beyond it, she glanced to a dark figure who stood on all fours at the top of it. He was mostly hidden by the long, swaying stalks of grass, and perhaps, to an unknowing eye, would be invisible.

Someone must have noticed her pass the open gates because two guards started to chase her from a fair distance away. They should have given up, considering she was leagues ahead of them.

"We need to go!" she shouted just as she came upon Ingram.

"Why?" he asked, shaking his head as he turned his raven skull towards the guards. His orbs flared red. *"I can just kill them."*

"I'd rather you didn't," she countered, as she grabbed the horn that still had the ornament she'd give him in preparation to leap.

He lowered himself just as she jumped to his back. A makeshift saddle, a special one just for him and his spikes, cushioned her.

She liked how it disappeared whenever he shifted into his more humanoid form. It was a neat trick.

"Go, Ingram! Before they see you."

Hopefully with the distance, they just thought he was a horse or something. It was doubtful the guild would have shared that she hadn't only deserted them but released a Duskwalker. They wouldn't want to share their failure.

They were secretive for a reason.

Ingram, with an annoyed huff, galloped at his top speed. Within seconds, the town with a cornfield beside it disappeared from view. In minutes, he'd crossed over a wide and vast meadow, then up a sharp hill.

He veered to the left at the top and bolted along it before going right.

She knew the path he was taking, as they had taken it twice in the past. A little over a month ago, and then recently.

Looking at the back of his white skull and jutting goat horns, the smile that curled her lips was simply because where he was taking them was... sweet, and also adorable.

"Here is perfect," she stated, patting his neck when he'd begun slowing down on his own.

He turned his head to the side, and bright yellow glowed from his orbs.

Emerie kicked her leg over and slid down the side of him, straight onto the soft, short grass. Butterflies had already lifted off in a small kaleidoscope, even before she laid back with a cheerful giggle.

One that only got louder when he fell to his front, with his skull plopping sideways across her abdomen.

"Well, that was fun," she laughed.

"That is the second time you have been chased from a town, Emerie," he grumbled, even though his orbs remained bright yellow.

"Guess it makes life interesting for us," she answered, turning her face up to the bright sunlight. "It's not like it matters. Even if they capture me, I'll just hover my Phantom butt out of there when no one is looking."

He twisted his head to look at her better, another annoyed huff bursting from him. "Yes, but it means you will be away from me for longer."

Her lips pursed. "Another hour won't hurt. I need supplies.

Clean clothes, fire starting tools, fresh food."

"But you do not need to eat."

"But it *feels* good," she argued playfully.

That was enough to win, and he crawled up until he was beside her. He pulled her into his side so she was cuddling him and looked up at the sky along with her.

She took in the clouds, thankful they weren't shielding the sun. A flock of birds passed overhead, likely migrating for food or to breed since winter was almost upon them.

After a while, she softened her tone, and asked, "You like this hill, don't you? You keep bringing us back here."

"I... do," he admitted.

"Why?" she asked, laying her face in the direction of his bony one.

His orbs flared bright pink, as his hand tightened on her hip. "Because it is where I first started truly loving you." And just like that, he made her fall even deeper for him. Then, he grabbed her bag to shake it. "Did you obtain another dress I will tear off you?"

Her lips pursed at that. "I did. Two, actually. But try not to rip them. It's such a waste."

"But it is fun," he stated, and his quiet chuckle told her he was just trying to tease her.

Ingram was turning out to be rather... playful. He could turn anything into a game and then that game into something perverted.

Like tag.

If Ingram ran, he'd find a spot to hide and tackle her since there was no way she'd be able to keep up with him. If she ran, using her Phantom form to get away and hide her scent, he'd tackle her when she was physical.

Both times ended in her being tackled in his four-legged form, and being thoroughly taken by his cock while he was more monstrous.

She embraced it all, especially since it seemed to be healing him of Aleron's loss.

They were both better after seeing their loved ones again in Tenebris. Although she knew she'd never see Gideon unless she truly died again, it was nice to know he was in a place where he wasn't alone, scared, or confused. He was resting in peace, with his happiest memories.

Ingram was under the belief that, although there was nothing he could do to bring back his kindred, Aleron would find a way to return to him.

Emerie didn't know if that was true, but she fed his hope. Who knew? Maybe he was right. He'd been able to do the impossible and go to the afterlife and come back.

He'd even brought her with him.

In the meantime, Emerie knew one thing for certain.

Ingram needed someone to give him purpose, to guide him where to go, even if it was truly nowhere. He needed someone to make him feel like he wasn't alone by pressing up against their body as much as he could.

He didn't want to remain within the permanent ward he'd accidentally put down, even though it bordered the other Duskwalkers' territories. It was right up against both Magnar's and Faunus' wards – and smaller since it'd tried to form over them and failed. Their wards were there first.

It's sad he doesn't want to stay with his brothers. He was used to freedom, to roaming the world as he pleased, and tying him down to one location kind of freaked him out.

He wasn't ready to settle.

But that's okay. Emerie didn't mind. She would love to get to know the other couples she'd met and become part of their little community. She'd adored Reia, Delora, and Mayumi, and could see them truly becoming friends she could count on for anything, but they had time.

An eternity of it, so long as nothing bad happened.

For now, we'll just go anywhere we want on a whim.

The direction she pointed, would be their heading.

But we'll visit often, she thought with a smile, burying her face into the side of Ingram's chest. She caressed the rib bones protruding from the outside of his body. *And one day, we'll build our own home and fill it with everything we've found along the way.*

Until then, they would be two lost souls who were wandering

the world, but were loved and constantly intertwined.
    Free, and without responsibility.
    That sounded perfect.

Also by Opal Reyne

DUSKWALKER BRIDES
A Soul to Keep
A Soul to Heal
A Soul to Touch
A Soul to Guide
A Soul to Revive
A Soul to Steal *(TBA 2024)*
(More titles coming soon)

WITCH BOUND
The WitchSlayer
The ShadowHunter
(More titles coming soon)

Completed Series

A PIRATE ROMANCE DUOLOGY
Sea of Roses
Storms of Paine

~~THE ADEUS CHRONICLES~~
This series has been **unpublished** as of
20th of June 2022

If you would like to keep up to date with all the novels I will be publishing in the future, please follow me on my social media platforms.

Website:
https://www.opalreyne.com
Facebook Page:
https://www.facebook.com/OpalReyne
Facebook Group:
https://www.facebook.com/groups/opals.nawty.book.realm
Instagram:
https://www.instagram.com/opalreyne
Twitter:
https://www.twitter.com/opalreyne
Patreon:
https://www.patreon.com/OpalReyne
Discord:
https://discord.gg/opalites
TikTok:
@OpalReyneAuthor